DAWN of the VAMPIRE

REVIVED

William Hill

Otter Creek Press, Middleburg, FL

William Hill/Otter Creek Press
Otter Creek Press, Inc.
Middleburg, FL
otterpress@aol.com; www.otterpress.com

Publisher's Note: This is a work of fiction. All the characters, organizations, and events portrayed in this novel are either products of the author's imagination or are used fictitiously.

Dawn of the Vampire: Revived/ William Hill. – 2nd ed.
ISBN 978-1-890611-56-9 soft cover

Book Layout © 2016 BookDesignTemplates.com
Cover Art by David Loew and William Hill

Originally published as Dawn of the Vampire by Pinnacle Books: January 1991

Books by William Hill

Dawn of the Vampire
Vampire's Kiss
California Ghosting
The Vampire Hunters
The Vampire Hunters Stalked
Vegas Vampires

Wizard Sword
Dragon Pawns
Impatient Fire
The Magic Bicycle
Chasing Time
Prey of the Spirit Bear

Acknowledgements

I appreciate the wonderful Bristolians and Tri Cities denizens who embraced the original work of fiction, and my friends from there, you know who you are, for tolerating me as I write with them in mind as inspiration. Bristol is the friendliest place I have ever lived. Thank you, Benny, for introducing me to Dave. I revised Dawn of the Vampire, partly in memory of Woody Fleenor, a TN/VA school librarian. Woody loved DOTV and would be thrilled to know that I reworked the story and used the correct names of places. I am grateful, now, for my parents who dragged me to Bristol after they moved there in 1977, and over the years have supported my other novels and creative endeavors. DOTV would be less readable, less polished, and might not have happened without Kat, my delightful and tech-savvy wife who typeset and edited the second edition. So yes, if you can read this, thank a teacher.

California
Ghosting

A sense of impending doom washed over Troy. He felt like he was too deep down under water as he watched bubbles rise past his mask. He wanted to follow them and swim to sunshine for fresh air. Why was he scuba diving? How had he gotten here? He didn't remember getting on a boat or gearing up. He didn't remember anything before now.

He had pulled a lot of crazy stunts over the years, and he had been adept at compartmentalizing his fear . . . until now. When Troy saw the sunken mansion emerge from the shadowy depths, panic surged through his body. He wanted to scream and bolt.

Troy fought his emotions and physical response, breathing through the distress and keeping his teeth firmly clamped on his regulator. He wouldn't let fear kill him. Besides, he had already died and lived to tell the tale.

After a few deep breaths of bottled air, he relaxed. He adjusted his mask, blowing bubbles through it to clear it. Even so, he had difficulty believing his eyes. The creepy, two-story building of river stone and timber appeared almost untouched by sixty years of submersion. The copper roof remained untarnished, and the rocks were unnaturally clean. Where was the slimy green of algae? The mansion defied time and the power of water. The wood panels, framing, doors and shutters appeared free of rot and unnaturally preserved. A heavy accumulation of sediment had settled underneath the first floor's shuttered windows, giving him the impression that the building was squatting.

Troy worried he might be suffering from nitrogen narcosis. He checked his gauge, finding he was one hundred feet below the surface. It was possible to have issues below forty feet, although he had never been narked before. He wanted to swim up twenty feet to see if that change improved his thinking, but his partner swam deeper. Raquel kicked powerfully toward the mansion, heading for an open window. Its shutters waved invitingly.

Troy was forced to follow, although he wanted to ascend not descend. Dive buddies were meant to stay together, at least within sight of each other. Safety was the priority when diving. So many things could go wrong.

His sense of impending doom grew as Raquel reached the chimney and crawled down to the copper roof. Troy pursued, closing, but she always seemed to be just beyond reach. The water felt colder, and he thought the chill radiated from the metal panels. He blinked. When did Raquel turn blond? She dove over the edge of the roof and vanished from sight. Troy really felt confused. Had he mistaken Ava for Raquel? He had no sense of when or where.

Grabbing the copper gutter, Troy pulled himself over the edge and downward. He followed Raquel, her hair dark again, her ponytail trailing her. He couldn't catch her before she accepted the silent invitation and swam inside the mansion.

Troy reached the window. He recoiled as a burst of light blinded him. Darkness recaptured the room, even as his vision swam with red spots. Blinking to clear his sight, he pointed his flashlight ahead and entered the second story of the mansion. He flinched and clenched his teeth against the cold. The temperature plunged, stabbing him with invisible icicles.

Several boards in the floor were warped, having escaped their nails. Over time, the wall paper had fallen loose and shredded. Small carp and gray catfish swam among the papery tendrils. The fish darted for safety when a big shadow swam into their midst.

Large, shiny white teeth appeared from the darkness. Behind the double row of daggers an amorphous shape swayed closer. Sharp teeth formed a vanguard for the grinning gar. The monstrous fish was longer than Troy was tall and twice as weighty. The beast's tail flicked lazily, easily moving its bulk through the water. Flailing and kicking, Troy swam backward out the open window. He pressed himself tightly against the shutter and waited for the monster to pass. His pounding heart seemed to count down his last moments.

He struggled to be alert and opened his eyes to light. He breathed stale indoor air, but it was better than drowning. It was far from his first nightmare with Raquel, but the setting was different, underwater in South Holston Lake. He hadn't been there in years, and he had never gone scuba diving in its green waters.

Where was he now?

Troy looked around the interior of the commercial jet. The flight attendants served drinks from a cart. The passengers read or used laptops, tablets and phones. No one appeared nervous. Some slept.

Still exhausted, Troy hoped for more a pleasant dream and fell back asleep.

When he reached the door and pulled, it fell off its hinges and startled Troy. To avoid the door, he slammed into the wall where his tank wedged and stuck. He struggled to get free, but the wood stubbornly held him. He focused on his breathing and slowed his heart, so he could think. He needed leverage.

He pressed the bottom of his fins against the wall and shoved. The wood protested as he twisted his tank and wrenched free. He followed the weird light down the hallway. The glow ebbed around a corner where the passage widened.

The radiance vanished. The darkness clenched around him. Only his lights kept it at bay. Troy could feel Raquel in trouble. He surged ahead, pushing through the slimy tendrils of old tapestries and clinging, rotten rugs.

The sudden, loud squealing and creaking of the house caused him to stop and cover his ears. The grating noise overwhelmed and disoriented him for a moment. The whole place shuddered as if a wave struck the building. The water sloshed back and forth, shaking Troy.

What the hell was that?

His headlamp died. The darkness swallowed him. His glow stick's illumination seemed pitiful, but its dim light gave him hope. His heart skipped a beat then rampaged as his breathing rushed. He fumbled for his extra flashlight and felt the empty loop on his belt. Damn! When had it fallen off? He removed another chemical stick from his bag and cracked it, adding more feeble light to push back the intense darkness.

Dizziness assailed him. The disorientation was so powerful that Troy was confused about which way was up. The room spun. He closed his eyes and clenched his jaw to keep from vomiting.

Troy awakened briefly, fighting out of the dream. He heard the captain over the intercom telling them they should touch-down in ten minutes. Troy couldn't escape the nightmare. It dragged him back down.

He pushed open the left door. It swung easily, ushering him inward. A green light washed over him. The glow made Raquel look sickly. She was engrossed in her search of a huge, mahogany desk with numerous sliding shelves and drawers. What appeared to be a half-dozen shrouded, high-backed chairs encircled the desk. She drew open a compartment then knelt, disappearing from his view behind the mammoth desk. Its black leather chair reminded him of a throne.

Raquel's air bubbles drifted up and bounced along the ceiling, looking for a way to escape to the surface. Troy wanted to leave, too. He had the absurd thought that the mansion had swallowed them.

What was this place?

Nearly empty bookshelves covered three of the walls. Most of the paper had dissolved, leaving the books' leather carcasses behind to soften into clumps. One bookcase behind the desk remained full of bloated tomes crammed on its shelves. The other wall possessed a portrait of a handsome but grim-looking man, palely complexioned with dark hair. He wore a haughty expression to go along with glaring eyes that blazed.

Raquel standing up caught Troy's attention. He swam toward her and passed one of the shrouded pieces of furniture, causing the cloth to slip away, revealing a grinning skull and skeleton. Its teeth were large and reminded him of a feline's incisors. Startled, Troy flailed backward, bumping into a chair. Its shroud slid free to reveal a second set of bare bones facing the desk. This skeleton's fangs were even larger.

The water pressure seemed to increase. His sense of impending doom heightened.

A sudden movement to his left caught his eye. He swung his flashlight, capturing the falling object in the beam. He watched in amazement as the man's portrait slowly slid down the wall. The bottom of the frame hit the waist-high lentil. The portrait seemed to pause for a timeless moment, allowing the man in the portrait to wink before its top tilted forward, and the painting tumbled downward.

Troy heard harsh laughter. It was followed by a disembodied voice. "I live and, ah, breathe again. Soon I shall feed. Viktor Von Damme is free! Oh, this body is young, vital and will suit. Its flesh is as clay to me."

Shaking his head, Troy figured the painting winking and the voice inside his skull was due to nitrogen narcosis. Any other possibility was unimaginable. This was proof it was long past time to leave. He hated this place, and it hated him. He wanted out, now!

When he frantically tried to open the door, the knob turned, but the door refused to budge. It was locked. How could that be? He turned the knob to unlock it. Troy heard the bolt click, but when he again tried to open the door, it acted glued to the frame.

He felt a tug, almost dislodging his regulator. When he inhaled, he gagged on water. He couldn't breathe, drowning. He sensed death looming over him and turned to face blazing red eyes bright with murder.

Troy coughed, shuddered and then bounced. A second bumping jarred him awake. Troy glanced around. The passengers seemed pleased, chatting, unbuckling early, and preparing to deplane. Nothing was wrong, even if his heart was bounding like each breath was a matter of life or death.

He sat back and willed himself to relax, letting others hurry out. Everything was fine. Situation normal. Wow. What a nightmare. He rubbed his neck. Usually his vivid nightmares were flashbacks about the mountain shaking apart and snow chasing him while he plunged down the steeps on a pair of metal boards bound to his boots.

Most of his nightmares involved Raquel Sterling. She had pushed him over the edge in life and in bad dreams, but they had never gone diving.

It seemed to Troy that if he was going to have nightmares, he should be having them about suffering a heart attack at 15,000 feet like Miles and Wilson. Just yesterday, he had witnessed their collapses within minutes of each other.

He shivered. The nightmare had felt too real. He knew what death felt like: the creeping cold, the finality, the loss of connection to your body, and the door opening to the vast ethereal unknown. Time had no meaning. He didn't believe in the supernatural or such phenomenon, but he knew now from his experience that there was more to life and death than the eyes could see. He knew he had yet to come to grips with the broader universe that he had discovered.

Troy figured he was pining for his hometown of Bristol. Today, his blood brothers were meeting there for their ten-year reunion. Led by John, the eight of them planned to dive the underwater ruins of Wreythville. Now that Troy was more awake, he figured his nightmare might have taken place near Cemetery Ridge.

He would love to go back home, but his medical bills and assignment in Alaska had prevented it. Wilson's death, Troy's mentor, had changed everything, and ended the shoot and Troy's job early. That didn't matter. Wilson had suffered an

M.I. while helping carry Miles who they had just resuscitated from a heart attack. Two heart failures within minutes of each other. What were the odds?

Death seemed to be shadowing Troy. Was it trying to reclaim him? And yet, Troy felt that he had been sent back to life for a reason. He would keep looking for his purpose.

Out the window, Troy recognized the Seattle-Tacoma airport. He saw the ground crew unload his skis and snow gear bag. He noticed Wilson's equipment and grew melancholy. He wouldn't need his worldly goods anymore. Now Troy had several days of down time before he had to fly out on his next assignment.

While deplaning, he checked his phone. Dillon had left a voicemail. "Hey there, Troy, I hope you're doing great, getting where you're going safely. Anyway, the rest of us are here for the reunion, except for John. It seems that he and his sweetheart, Sherry, have gone missing with one of Marader's boats. Call me when you can."

He returned the call. Neither John nor Dillon answered. Troy grew frustrated. What could he do? Besides, this could be a prank to convince him to fly back to the reunion. His blood brothers had done worse.

Another incoming phone call made the decision for him. It seemed fate wanted him to go home to Bristol. What trouble had his blood brothers stirred up this time?

Two: Cemetery Ridge

The dream of a kiss from the Dark Lady vanished as Dillon awakened underwater and drowning. He closed his mouth and opened his eyes. Where was he? Was this still South Holston Lake?

He was disoriented and struggling as he felt something holding him down by the throat. Red eyes, large and commanding, stared down and demanded he surrender and die. Dillon fought back, trying to strike whatever held him. He felt no contact, but the pressure on his throat released him.

He swam toward the light. The darkness around him faded as he neared the surface. With a gasp, he popped up like a cork into the fresh air. He inhaled a deep, humid breath tasting of campfire smoke.

After wiping the water from his eyes, Dillon looked around. He glanced at the red inflatable raft floating on the water. He shook his head in disbelief, having freaked out to near drowning. That, he admitted to himself, had been one hell of a dream.

He stared longingly at an empty stretch of beach and wondered if the Dark Lady of the Lake would be out strolling tonight? He yearned to see her again. Although her name implied she was a brunette, the Dark Lady was a gorgeous blond, more stunning, charming and graceful than the legendary Marilyn Monroe. Thinking about the encounter with her made his heart quicken. He had become obsessed, as had any man who had seen her. Dillon had experienced more than his share of ladies in an attempt to find someone to help him forget her and failed. No one compared. He had seen her twice. Could lightning strike thrice?

Unlikely, he figured, as he was skiing with loud and fast company.

"Hey, Dillon, did you hurt yourself?" Knives yelled.

Dillon treaded water in a circle, turning to face Bug Island. On the shore, Dr. Stephen "Knives" Curran stood tall, tanned, and athletic with a Frisbee in hand. As a surgeon, Knives possessed deft fingers, but all that brain power was turning his skull into a solar panel. Along with dark glasses, his receding hairline made him look older and too wise for twenty-eight.

"I surprised myself, forgot where I was and panicked for a moment, but I'm okay now," Dillon replied. He spat out pink lake water. He checked his mouth, having bitten his tongue.

"I thought I was going to have to jump in and rescue you," Knives replied.

Behind him, his partner in Frisbee tossing laughed

uproariously. Dillon didn't find it that funny, but Spider cracked up. Frank "Spider" Adder had been named such because of his long, slender arms and legs. Umber skin, fuzzy sideburns, and teeth compared to fangs reinforced the pseudonym. The gangly architect wore tie-die to show off his earth child side.

Those on the boats working on the surprise didn't spare them a glance. Someone turned up the music. "Waiting for the sun. Waiting for the sun," Jim Morrison intoned. The Door's song was heavy with drums and an impatient guitar.

The blood brothers were waiting for the sun to set. Dillon and a half dozen of his best friends had set up camp for their ten-year reunion without inviting the rest of the class. He and his blood brothers had no class, they had joked among themselves. It was fabulous to be home again and among friends in God's Country. Dillon wished Troy hadn't had to work and miss out on all the fun, but he had medical bills to pay off. Dillon worried about the near-death survivor, the new all-work-and-no-play Troy. At least he wasn't flying down cliffs for Go Pro.

And where was John? He was supposed to be here and dive with them tomorrow morning. The lower water would allow them easier diving access to Wreythville. Tom had mentioned that John and a sizzle-lean babe had rented a boat around 0900. The couple had planned to dive and reconnoiter Cemetery Ridge, but there was no one there, on that barren hunk of rock, or here. John might have rethought bringing Sherry along, or they could have fought, suffering a lover's spat. At least he could have sent a text, Dillon mused.

Did the lack of communication mean anything? He pushed away his great Aunt Jada's voice and a memory. He didn't believe in psychics. Troy wasn't here, and they wouldn't find death on the lake.

Dillon decided to seize the moment and enjoy life, what was, instead of what he wished for. He grabbed the raft and swam back to Bug Island. On their first camping trip, now more than a dozen years ago, they had awakened to a beetle infestation, forcing them to evacuate.

His feet found ground, and he waded to shore. The drought had a stranglehold on the Appalachians and the lake, leaving the island larger than ever. In the brittle dryness, the air felt charged. Dillon sensed something wrong, but he couldn't put a finger on it.

He breathed deeply and savored the beauty of the lake swathed in twilight. A cloud from their cook fire clung to Bug Island like a patch of Smoky Mountain fog. The wind remained calm, and South Holston lied placidly as if it were resting for nightfall. The lake's mirror-like surface glowed bright pink as it reflected the clouds building to the southwest. To the east, the near full moon peeked over the darkly forested mountains.

Perfect conditions, Dillon thought. Tom would hate this, and then he would love it, as he hated being ignored and appreciated a good pranking.

Dillon saw only two boats, Knives' Stingray and Tom Marader's Mastercraft which he had dubbed Maverick. Using PVC pipe and bungee cords, J-Man was mounting temporary spotlights all along Mav. He took off his orange Tennessee Volunteer cap and set it aside. An Alabama grad should know better than letting a UT engineer work on his boat, Dillon mused. Unbeknownst to Tom, J-Man was setting up a few surprises. A second engineer, Father Dennis, helped J-Man arrange Go Pro cameras on the ski and board rack arcing over the craft so they would catch the event on video.

The day had passed, and the sky was nearly dark, making it show time. The blood brothers had talked about doing this when they were younger but had never gotten around to it. The fact it was illegal might have deterred them, but they were ready for any emergency, or so they hoped.

Dillon didn't see Jambo, but he heard loud snoring. Jamie boy could really sleep and audibly sawed logs like a black coffee-powered lumberjack.

While Jambo slept, Tom seemed to vibrate with kinetic

energy even as he sat. God's gift to women, blond and bronzed Tom Marader was sprawled in a beach chair. He drank a Heineken and cooled his heels in the water while he impatiently waited for J-Man to finish working his magic on the red and gold Mastercraft. He gave Tom the thumbs up and then smiled at Dillon.

It was a go to gig their buddy.

"Let's get this party cruising!" Tom shouted. He let loose a wolf howl as he leapt from his chair. He whipped off his red Roll Tide cap and shook it in the air. He wore a huge used car salesman smile, cracking his sunburned face. His blue eyes sparked with inebriated delight when he broke out in maniacal laughter.

Jambo snoozed on, but the rest of them gathered, making six. Dillon would have preferred a lucky seven. No, he wasn't superstitious. *Where are you, John?*

"Are y'all ready to light up the night?" Denny Rentzel asked. He greeted Dillon with a perfect smile. The tall, big-boned and sandy-haired engineer worked for the family construction company as well as the church. He was blessed with an open, bluff face with a heroic, lantern-jaw begging for a Batman mask. He had a knack for construction and destruction. Somehow, he always looked innocent no matter what he had blown up or razed. After some troubles in college, he had turned his life around and found God, recently becoming a priest. Dillon still tried to wrap his thoughts around that. Father Dennis loved youth ministering, claiming it was akin to hanging out with his blood brothers sans alcohol.

"Go ahead, Jay. You can drive. After all, you're the professional pilot," Tom said.

J-Man raised both palms to the sky, settled into the pilot's chair and said, "Awesome. The lake gods have once again smiled upon me. Besides, someone has to be there to pick up the pieces when Marader goes splat."

"That's what I'm here for," Knives said.

"Doesn't this risky business go against your Hippocratic

oath?" Spider asked.

"The eradication of disease and the end of human suffering is the primary goal of any physician," Knives replied. His broad smile created pronounced cheekbones before his face turned serious. "And Tommy is about as disease ridden as they come. Think of all the human suffering, especially by females, that would be prevented if he was laid up and put on antibiotics."

"Oh, I just like being laid. Up, down or sideways doesn't matter," Tom laughed.

"I packed my first aid kit, just in case you hit a large turtle, a swimming bear, or the carcass of one of those mythical ten-foot catfish," Knives said.

"No worries. I just patrolled the area an hour ago. I didn't see any driftwood, and the only boat out is the Bassmaster's. Pat's fishing off the ridge. There's no wind and little current, so, God-willing, it should be perfect," Denny said.

J-Man's phone beeped. He checked it and announced, "That figures. I told you if we went skiing we'd bring rain. There's a thunderstorm warning. It goes into effect in thirty minutes."

"Rain is coming? I won't believe it until I see it," Spider said.

"Thunderstorms mean lightning," Knives pointed out.

"Well, we better get our butts in gear and this show on the lake," Tom said. He sprang into his boat. He stared down at them from atop the sun deck while he fiddled with the blinking light on his ski vest. The orange beacon pulsed like a rapid heartbeat. "What's taking you guys so long? If we hear thunder, we jet to the marina. So far, all I see is clouds to the southwest. Come on! Time's wastin'!"

Dillon grabbed his gear, binoculars, a camera, a towel, and a flashlight before he joined the boarding party. He was the last man on Maverick, so he shoved off shore and hopped onto the bow. His push sent the spotlight-bristling Mastercraft away from land into deeper water. J-Man turned on the fan to vent and flipped the switch for the regulation night lights. Red and green radiance spilled out across the water's surface and illuminated excited faces.

"Here we go," J-Man announced. He set the throttle lever to choke and turned the ignition key. With a powerful roar, the inboard motor fired up, drowning out all sound. He throttled back and put the gear in reverse. The motor responded with a muffled growl. Once the boat was away from shore, J-Man checked the depth, spun the wheel and turned Maverick around to face open water.

"Let's rock and roll!" Tom yelled over the motor.

"Ah, a symphony of light," J-Man said as he flicked a switch. On the bow, four LED-clusters snapped to brilliance. The other lights followed, along the sides and stern to beam out over the water, turning it silvery. On the island, the illumination seemed to change night to day.

Dillon thought he heard Jambo yell. "Turn that out!"

"Did you hear something? I guess not. Light, sound," J-Man said. There was a loud hum. Moments later, music blared from the black plastic bagged speakers strapped to the sun platform, adding to the sound coming from the speakers in the ski rack above them. ZZ Top's classic Texas rock filled the air. "And of course, speed."

J-Man shoved the gear shift all the way forward. The boat leapt ahead, its bow springing high before it flattened and planed out. Dillon moved up front into the bow seat. He absorbed the music, the sensation of flying across the water, and the thrill of the wind whipping about him. The boat lights cut a swath through the growing darkness. The brilliance turned the lake's surface into a mirror, a stretch of calm, molten silver stretching ahead of them.

Dillon could see at least five hundred feet in every direction. He was impressed with J-Man's work and the visibility. The glow touched Cliff Island, a gigantic fin of rock to the southwest. Dillon stayed alert, his attention dancing along the edge of the forward lights. Being able to see would cut down the odds of the boat hitting something.

"Excellent job, J-Man," Dillon said.

The burly pilot beamed, oozing satisfaction. The test run completed, he geared back and slowed the boat.

"Sounds kick ass! Where's the rope? I'm ready. I'm ready. I'm ready. This is gonna be so, so, so much fun. I feel invincible," Tom howled.

J-Man cut the motor, making the music seem louder. He turned it down as Robert Plant with Led Zeppelin sang, "In My Dying Time". It seemed appropriate. Knives took the handle of the rope and threw it into the water, letting the rope trail out behind them.

"Jay, you are truly the Man. The lighting is superb. I'm ready to record," Denny said. He held up the remote to the mounted cameras. With a strap, he placed another on his head, arranging the Go Pro.

Tom ran a gloved hand through his unnaturally thick hair as he hesitated. Knives smiled and assisted his friend by pushing Tom over the edge and into the water. Dillon handed Knives a single board, a yellow, KOBE slalom ski. He slid it out to their blood brother.

"I'll get you back, buddy boy," Tom called. He grabbed the ski and pushed it under water to wiggle his feet into the boots.

"Actions speak louder than words. You said you were in a hurry, but you just stood there, waiting to be struck by courage or lightning. Out of the kindness of my heart, I solved your problem for you," Knives replied.

"I'm ready. Are you ready?" Denny called to Tommy.

J-Man started the engine. He put it in gear, a touch faster than idling to pull the rope taut.

"I was born ready! Crank and pull," Tom yelled.

J-Man gave it full throttle. The motor growled, roared, and then Maverick surged forward. Hauled behind the boat, Tom rose majestically like a divine being from the white foam. He looked confident on one ski, taking time to adjust his trunks, goggles, gloves, and the harness of lights. They blinked orange and yellow like a hazard warning beacon.

J-Man eased back on the lever and turned up the music, AC/DC's "Hell's Bells", before steering them south. As night deepened, only a few lights at the marinas provided a hint that shore existed. It felt like they were cruising through their own world.

Dillon felt Maverick accelerate. The boat's motor's whine heightened, blending with the music. For a brief moment, the boat dragged a bit, and then J-Man adjusted the trim. The Mastercraft now sliced smoothly through the water.

Tom skied expertly, his rooster tail bright white in the light. When he whipped out from the foamy wake, he carved dark streaks in the silvery surface. He pulled back hard and cut fast, nearly dipping his elbow in the water before flying back across the low wake.

"In front of a camera, he's a daredevil," Knives mused.

Dillon looked ahead. He could see the dark mound of Cemetery Ridge ahead.

"Marader skis through a cemetery. How macabre," Spider said.

"Is it time to unleash the surprise?" J-Man asked him. Denny rubbed his square jaw and shared a conspiratorial look with Knives.

"Hey, what are the PVC pipes for?" Spider asked. He pointed to three tubes painted silver to match the rack's chrome. The port side had a matching set. Tom had been Inebriated and in a rush, so he hadn't noticed the new additions to his boat among all the lights.

"Most definitely, it's time," Denny said. He reached into the starboard storage area, drew out a tube with legs and set up a mortar on a tripod. Knives seemed to miraculously find a second one on the port side and readied the pyrotechnics launch tube. Dillon appreciated the safety glasses shared with all by Denny. Spider was laughing so hard he was having trouble donning his pair.

Denny leaned close to Dillon and said, "I didn't tell anyone, except Knives, but I got a special permit for this, calling it an advertising video shoot."

"Good idea, on both counts. Do you think he'll see this coming?" Dillon asked.

"Never. He's too busy concentrating on kickin' butt and looking smooth. He can use it in advertising," Knives said. He reached underneath the dash to retrieve three fire extinguishers. He handed one each to Spider and Dillon.

"Show time," J-Man said. He threw a switch under the dash.

Hissing and whistling, a horde of pyrotechnics repeatedly fired from the racks. A dozen missiles followed by twenty screamers streaked into the sky. The first fusillade erupted into large weeping willows. The next group exploded into stars with loud reports booming like thunder. Tommy watched slack-jawed and wide-eyed as he skied in an evasive pattern. The busy bees and the loco locus whirled and spun, a few flying off target. Once glanced off the shoulder of Tommy's vest. He flipped them the bird, shaking his middle finger until he had to duck below a sparkling red brocade of sparks. A wild missile skipped off the water. He cut in time to dodge. It detonated behind him, backlighting him in a dazzling white glow. If someone read Tommy's lips it would hurt his advertising.

A towel on fire caught Dillon's attention. He unleashed the fire extinguisher. It blew the towel up into the wind where it whipped by him as it flew out of the boat to land in the water. Giving it a look, Tommy skied around the smoking towel.

Spider was laughing so hard he had curled up into a ball.

"You're no help," Dillon chastised him.

Tom fully got into the show, bobbing and weaving, leaving him less of a sitting duck. Knives and Denny fired off the mortars. With booms and whooshes that shook the air and the boat, the shells blasted upward, tumbling in the night. They burst into Saturn like planets, their rings spreading out, nearly reaching the water's surface.

"Cemetery Ridge dead ahead," J-Man said.

Curious, Dillon turned. The flares' light turned the water's surface a scarlet red. The barren knob of the exposed ridge stood like a giant tombstone. Dillon shook off that thought as J-Man steered Maverick starboard, staying away from the shallows and the underwater graveyard.

Dillon blinked. He thought he saw a large dark shape floating in the water. It seemed to slowly shift and roll. He yelled to catch J-Man's attention and snagged Spider's.

"Log! Over there!" Spider yelled and gestured at the bobbing mass. The headlights struck an edge, geometric in shape like a box or crate.

J-Man peered over the windshield, drew back on the throttle and steered around the obstacle. The boat veered as it cut starboard, throwing everyone to port. Dillon clung tightly to the bow railing to keep from tumbling. Spider lost his balance and crashed to the floor. J-Man righted the boat, drew back on the throttle, slowing a little.

Regaining his balance, Dillon peered over the bow. He saw another boxy floater and pointed.

"What is this, a minefield? We were just here. There was nothing like this. Jay, I hate to say it, but you should stop," Denny said. He continued to record.

"Could it have floated up?" Dillon wondered.

Spider climbed off the floor. He touched his forehead. "Wonderful, I'm bleeding."

"Tommy doesn't like your Jedi driving. He's flipping you off," Knives said.

"Flipping us off," J-Man replied. He pointed. "Another one. Hang on!" He steered hard to port. Everyone held fast, so nobody was slung across the boat.

Dillon glanced back. Tom slalomed like a pro, deftly handling it with style.

"Those things look like crates," Dillon said.

"Or caskets," Denny said, frowning.

"Marader wants to go faster. He's crazy. Thinks he's invincible," Spider said.

Tom swung out to the left. J-Man drew back on the throttle,

slowing to twenty. Tom grew agitated. He continued jerking his thumb in the air, wanting to go faster. Just as he flipped them another bird, his eyes enlarged to the size of golf balls, and he ejected out of his ski. Arms spread wide, he yelled as he tumbled head over heels. He somersaulted several times before catching a shoulder, auguring, and burying himself. Water sprayed far and wide.

"I pray he's all right," Father Dennis said.

J-Man piloted the boat in a slow circle to return to the spot of the crash. They located Tommy by the blinking lights on his chest and his thrashing making white water.

"Help," he yelled. Blood covered his face and stained his hair red.

"What's he doing?" J-Man asked as he slowed more and steered closer. He put the gear in neutral and drifted in.

"Oh no, he's going into convulsions," Knives said. He buckled his life jacket and prepared to jump to the rescue. It wouldn't be the first time he had to haul Tom out of the drink, or out of a drink. Knives dove into the water, swimming to Tommy.

"Hey, man, it's all right. It's me, Stephen. The doctor is in the water," Knives said. He reached out to Tommy to calm him.

"There's something else in the water with them," Dillon said. It looked man-sized to him, but most of it was under water. It seemed to grab for Tommy. The hairs stood up on the back of Dillon's neck as his imagination ran wild. Could it be John?

Tommy's flailing hand hit Knives in the face. He reeled back. "Stop fighting me. I'm trying to help," Knives said. He took a foot in the jaw and went slack.

Dillon jumped into the water, swimming to Knives. He caught him before he rolled face down into the water. Dillon shook the doctor. "Hey, buddy. Are you okay?"

"Uh. I think so," Knives groaned. His lower lip was already swollen.

"Grab onto this," Denny said. He tossed the floatable cushion to Tommy. He grabbed it and held onto it like a lifesaver. Using it as a kickboard, he swam toward the boat. For the first time, he noticed Knives and Dillon.

"Hey, guys, what are you doing here?" Tom asked.

"Trying to help you," Knives growled. His lower lip bled.

J-Man eased the Mastercraft closer.

Their swimming caused the figure to roll over. Dillon saw a ghostly white face with dark, bushy eyebrows and a goatee. By the gasps, he wasn't the only one to see it. The party was over. The atmosphere seemed dangerous now, and their moods turned deadly serious. Several of them were familiar with death and dying.

"Knives, there's a body floating near you," Dillon said.

Spewing profanity, Tommy reached the back of the boat. Spider helped him climb onto the teakwood flats of the swim platform. Tommy collapsed against the stern and rested. Despite the warmth of the night, his body shook. "Did I hit swimmer? Kill somebody?" he asked. Many of them were sympathetic having been on the Tennessee High swim team.

J-Man grabbed a polearm. He snagged the body's clothes and helped guide it closer. Knives climbed up onto the swim platform. Spider handed him medical gloves. After slipping them on, Knives reached down and checked the man. His fingers shifted around as the body rolled, finding open wounds, two ugly slashes across the dead man's jugular.

"Relax, Tommy, he's been dead a while. He's been murdered," Knives told them.

Oh, crap, Dillon thought. Aunt Jada was right. Did that mean Troy was on the way?

"Oh, dear Lord," Father Dennis began and uttered a prayer.

"We can't leave it here," J-Man said.

"You're not putting him in my boat," Tom snapped.

"Not in your boat, on the ski platform. We can transport the corpse to land and leave it on Cemetery Ridge. I wouldn't move a body, except it's floating, and it might be hit again."

"I wouldn't want someone to leave my corpse as a hazard," Denny said.

"All right, I get it. I feel the same way. Make it snappy," Tommy said.

Dillon and Knives stood on the ski platform. When they grabbed the back of the floater's shirt, it rolled him over. They gasped in shock, recognizing the man.

Dillon felt punched. They had gone to high school with Pat Ackles. He had never cared for skiing or tubing, preferring to fish. And oh how he could catch fish, a near master. Now it had come full circle, of a sort, back to the water as he had been feeding the fish by the looks of his skin. What a horrible thought. What a waste of a life, but then, Dillon always thought that when he saw someone die young. Somehow, Spider and Troy had both come back. I didn't appear that Pat would be a returnee.

"I recognize the scar on his cheek and those crazy eyebrows," Knives said, his voice catching. He was the most accustomed to encountering death. Dillon knew he thought of the human body as a machine, but it was different when you knew the person.

"Oh, man, the Bassmaster has gone to the great fishing lake in the sky," Spider bemoaned.

"His throat has been slit," Knives said.

"I saw him about an hour ago. We waved and bellowed a hello," J-Man said.

"He's already bled out. An autopsy will tell us more," Knives said.

Dillon tried to call the county sheriff and 911, but his phone couldn't find service. Everyone tried to call. Nobody could get a connection. It made Dillon think of someone cutting the phone lines. Murdered people, even when there was little to no blood, always made him nervous and heightened his senses. Paranoia isn't paranoia if they are really out to get you. He had learned to trust those journalistic instincts. Aunt Jada had told him he would find death on this reunion with his buddies. He hadn't listened to his creepy great aunt, the psychic and matchmaker.

Looking at Pat, Dillon felt a need for justice. The slash in the body's neck was clean, likely done with a sharp knife.

Father Dennis led a prayer, and they lowered their heads and joined him. He finished to the distant roll of thunder. With Pat's body secured to the stern platform, J-Man eased the ski boat ahead at a wakeless speed toward Cemetery Ridge. Nobody felt like celebrating anymore, but they were all glad to be alive, especially Tom who was drinking Jagermeister from the bottle. Going to the graveyard seemed sadly and morbidly appropriate under the circumstances.

The boat's headlights illuminated a blue bass boat with silver flames and a prominent, black Evinrude outboard. The Bassmaster, as it was christened, sat anchored in the shallows off shore. He heard music, Jimmy Buffet, still playing. Two fishing poles had baited hooks. Everything looked like Pat had just wandered off for a minute.

Is that how it happened in life? Normal one minute, dead the next? Dillon wondered. Pat had been their age, only twenty-eight.

When they drew broadside, Dillon boarded the other boat. He felt uneasy even without seeing any other signs of trouble. The tension and humidity made him break sweat. Dillon donned gloves, trying to limit compromising the crime scene, if it was one.

A rumble of thunder caught his attention. Dark clouds rolled low over the dam, coming their direction. Forking chains of lightning crawled between the misty masses of the thunderstorm. In the flashes, it appeared to be raining. Streaky purple tendrils of precipitations brushed the surrounding foothills. The trees and vegetation needed it, but now was not the best time. Rain would destroy evidence.

Dillon opened the glove box and found Pat's driver's license in a wallet and a set of car keys. The wallet still had money and credit cards in it. Dillon discovered no blood, no signs of a struggle, and no dropped knife. Caught fish still swam in the live well. They needed fresh water, or they would die in an hour. Pat had been murdered recently. But where? There was no blood here. Had he been killed on the island?

After more thunder, J-Man spoke up. "Hey there, Dillon pick up the pace."

Nobody wanted to be on the water if lightning struck.

Dillon returned to the Mastercraft and shoved off. J-Man guided them to the gravelly, red-mud shore of Cemetery Ridge. A huge chunk of gray driftwood was the only distinctive feature among three low mounds. A lightning flash washed out the sky and over the ground. They all saw the pits near the piles of upturned lake bottom. Scattered about were rags and what looked like an old leather shoe.

"I've been in Haiti. I know bad juju when I feel it. It killed me," Spider began. He grimaced as he wiped the heavy perspiration off his face with his shirt. He sounded seriously frightened.

"Your point?" J-Man asked. He ran a fidgety hand across his beard stubble.

"This place has God-damned bad juju. That's my point, fool!" Spider snapped.

"Drop it, guys. Do you think Pat was involved in sacrilegious grave robbing?" Father Dennis asked. "I was out a week ago, and this wasn't above water."

"Hurry up and get that body off my boat. I'm not staying on this island a minute longer than I have to," Tommy said.

"How about we put Pat on his boat and tow it?" J-Man asked.

Dillon and Denny performed a quick sweep of the island while J-Man returned to the Bassmaster to rig up a towline. Dillon took photos of the different shoe treads and bare feet in the mud, especially those near the water-logged leather shoe. Using his flashlight, he could read the faded golden words Made in Italy. Gucci. One pile of rags was a tattered dress with pearls across the bodice. He put them in a net bag.

He couldn't escape the feeling of being watched. Several times, Dillon found himself glancing up, hoping to see the Dark Lady strolling along the shores of the island. Had anyone ever seen her in a swim suit? He wondered. Was that her scent on the air? No, his mind was playing tricks on him.

"Come look at this pine box," Father Dennis said. He held out his crucifix and spoke a prayer. The coffin appeared to have been opened with a hand axe. The interior had been scored with long grooves. Dillon shivered. To him, it looked too much like someone had been buried alive and tried to escape. It was empty except for a metal spike, like that used in railroad tracks. Neither of them found any bloodstains, but somebody had left a shovel at one of the three recently excavated pits. Dillon had counted more coffins than graves. What did that mean?

An angry and long roll of thunder rumbled across the lake to put an end to their investigation. Scattered rain drops pelted Dillon. He decided to take the shovel, and have it checked for fingerprints.

While they pulled away towing the boat, lightning cavorted in the sky behind them. Spider spotted a red piece of fabric floating nearby. They were concerned about the storm, but they couldn't resist, knowing the debris would be gone soon, so they paused to retrieve it.

Using a polearm, Dillon lifted the soggy flag out of the water, laying it on the stern sun platform. The red dive flag had a single, white diagonal line from two corners through its center. Had it been John's? Now Dillon was more worried than ever.

Southwest of the dam, a trident of iridescent lightning struck the ground. The dazzling fulgence blinded them. The sharp crack knifed across the water, assaulting them. The air quaked.

When Dillon's blindness finally passed, he thought he saw smoke to the south. With a sinking feeling, he wondered if the flickering of light was flames. He had learned more than he had wanted to know about wildfires while going to school out west. Dillon prayed it wasn't so, but the forests were dry, kindling ready to be torched.

"I believe that is our heavenly last call to go now," Father Dennis said.

The music, beer and fireworks were forgotten, the celebratory mood long gone. The dark, bumpy ride left them with questions, worries and a dead body. There might be more, Dillon feared. He believed this reunion had turned into a story. He would have preferred to have encountered the Dark Lady.

Dillon looked at the storm coming from the direction of the dam. Ill weather and times were here, literally and physically. A friend was dead, and a blood brother was missing. He had to call Troy. He would want to know.

Three: Cemetery Ridge Encounter

Through predawn light and fog, Dillon rode the Sea-Doo across the lake. The water's surface was smooth; the reflections making it appear that the mists engulfed him. He certainly felt foggy about why Pat had been murdered. He had been a good man and deserved better. As an investigative reporter, Dillon refused to tolerate a murderer on his home town lake, unless it was the Dark Lady's killer looks breaking hearts.

Before he had moved away, he had gathered stories and conducted research on the Dark Lady. There were no stories about her being seen by day. After all, she was the Dark Lady, not the Dawn Lady. She had first been reported in the forties, strolling along the river's banks, and although she had changed her hair, her allure and legend remained. Some witnesses had reported her as a redhead. Everyone agreed on her eyes, her captivating beauty, and her compelling voice. She was likely a mystery he would never solve. He hoped the discovery of Pat's murderer would be less elusive.

A rogue wind kicked up, carrying spray. The chilly dampness goose-bumped his bare legs and tickled his face, making his eyes water. The PWC was a red and white two-seater, a combination of a jet boat and a water motorcycle with Maraders Marina plastered on both sides. Tom had been kind enough to let him use it. Why not? Tom was always going on about friends with utility.

Dillon needed goggles. He could barely see where he was going. Fortunately, he had been blest to grow up near South Holston Lake and had enjoyed nearly two decades of summers here. He knew it better than the back of his hands, and yet, he had never seen the water level this low. Dozens of sandbars, small islands, and rocks protruded above the surface. In 1990, the Tennessee Valley Authority had reduced the water to make improvements to the dam, but nowhere near this low. Cemetery Ridge, usually part of the lake bed, waited ahead somewhere.

He felt a gust of headwind on his face. There, he saw the ridge through the thinning fog. The tip of the island cleaved upward from the lake like the horn of a mighty leviathan. It seemed as though it had just risen as oncoming waves rocked the Sea-Doo. The watercraft cut and bounced through them, carrying Dillon nearer. The high hill of shale and limestone appeared above water for the first time since the reservoir had been filled back in late 1950. The rocky knob stood as tall as a monument, a massive headstone above a red-clay beach with fresh dug plots. Last night, Father Dennis had blest this place, but it still felt cursed to Dillon.

The winds abruptly died. The waves died, eerie in the way they laid flat like they had been beaten down. Dillon accelerated the craft when he reached the shallows, slowing to idle into shore. He planned to research the island and dive the shallows. He beached the PWC, uncased his camera, and began to explore and take photos.

While afoot, he kicked up a piece of jewelry. The brooch seemed to shed the mud, allowing thirteen red rubies to gleam in the wan light. The arrangement created a smile, or a red crescent moon set in tarnished silver. With polishing, the brooch would be stunning. For now, it would be kept as evidence. Such jewels and riches, like buried treasure, could be motivation for Pat's murder.

He had seen this symbol before. He couldn't recall just where, though.

Ouch! Dillon jumped as he felt a spiking pain in his left foot.

He hopped about, having stepped on something sharp. He stood on one leg and examined the sole of this foot. It had been pierced and bled, but he couldn't find the instrument of his spindling. The pressure could have driven it into the mud. Cussing loudly, he limped back to the Sea-Doo and bandaged his perforated and bleeding foot. He was surprised to feel a little woozy. Usually the sight of blood left him unfazed. He wondered if he would need a tetanus booster.

He checked his watch. Burt would likely be tardy, but Dillon had a few hours before he had to pick up Troy at the airport. Dillon shivered. Aunt Jada was right again, first about finding death on the lake, and now about Troy's arrival. She had also predicted that Dillon would meet the love of his life. He gave no credence to psychic prognosticators. Too bad she couldn't have foreseen who would do the killing or who would die. That would have been helpful.

Dillon avidly anticipated seeing Troy. It had been too long. He prayed his best friend didn't encounter Raquel Sterling. Troy had already survived the Silver Queen, his own death and a broken body to walk among the living. Aunt Jada had called him one of the Heavensent.

While taking a selfie with his waterproof camera, Dillon heard the smooth purr of a boat approaching. It sounded alien among the drone of gnat clouds and the occasional splash of a jumping fish. Burt might be timely after all. Would wonders never cease? Dillon turned to see a gleaming, classic wooden boat approach out of the mists.

Fishing gear and equipment surrounded the elderly couple in the boat, the multiple poles making the classy craft look prickly. "Hullo! We're a mite confused, young man," the old gentleman called as he waved to Dillon. "We got turned around in the fog. Would you direct us to the American Legion Memorial Bridge?"

"The 421? Yes, sir. It's to the north and a little east," Dillon said. He limped toward their boat. His stomach roiled, and he felt queasy. A hint of vertigo struck him with an odd surge of adrenaline to fight or flee.

"Thanks. I think I can find my way," the man said with a smile. He had perfect teeth and large eyes. He removed a compass from his pocket, noted its orientation, and nodded.

"Thank you, honey, we sure appreciate it," the elderly woman said. Her pink cap rested askew on her salt-and-peppered curls. She might be a senior citizen, but her eyes were amazingly gorgeous, the black of night glinting with shooting stars. She must have been a beauty back in the day. She smiled at him and seemed decades younger.

He blinked. How odd. He would swear he had seen these eyes before. "Have we met?"

"I don't believe so. Who can we think for getting us going in the right direction?" she asked.

"Dillon. Dillon Urich."

"Ah, you're that handsome reporter, who was born and raised here in these parts, aren't you?" she asked. Something about her voice changed, silken and seductive.

"I will own up to that," Dillon said. He flushed as a strong desire surged through him. What was this? She was more than twice his age, and yet, his body reacted as if it were sensing a female in heat.

The old guy put the engine in reverse, and it died. He shifted into neutral and tried several times to start it, but while the motor coughed, it refused to turn over.

"Maybe you blew a fuse," Dillon said

"I imagine I did that a long time ago," the man said sourly.

Dillon laughed. "Ah, electricity and water, sometimes they don't mix. The lake patrol will be coming by soon, but I'll be glad to see what I can do," Dillon offered, despite suddenly wanting to run. A sense of escalating danger tried to overwhelm him. He shook himself. He helped people in trouble because often he found himself in wild, remote, and dangerous places, and more than once he had needed aid.

"That would be very kind of you, Mr. Urich."

"Please, call me Dillon," he replied. He waded out and pulled the boat onto the beach to steady it where it would be easier to access the motor.

The lady's smile was broad and thankful. Where did he know her from?

"Are you feeling well?" the lady asked. "You don't, do you? I can see if in your eyes. You look drawn and pale."

How could she know? Well, he was sweating profusely. "I am a little dizzy," Dillon said. For balance, he hung onto the boat.

"He's dying," the old man said.

"What?" Dillon asked. His knees threatened to give away. His thoughts swam in circles. "Did you say dying?"

"I'm sad to tell you that you have been poised with an old but potent paralytic meant to immobilize the Day Walkers. You will not survive it."

Dillon's knees buckled. He held fast to the boat to keep upright. He looked up, seeking a hand and found those incredible eyes. A bonfire burned in the lady's intense, dark eyes. He knew those eyes! No, it couldn't be, he must be addled.

"Yes, we meet again under dire circumstances. My name is Elke. I wonder if I should save you since it appears fate had thrust you into our dark affairs. You desired to meet me again, and so it is," Elke said, her voice compelling.

He couldn't listen to anything else, even as his heart failed. Elke! What a beautiful name. "Elke? You saved me from the wild dogs?" he asked in disbelief. He knew those eyes. He recognized her presence. Elke was the Dark Lady. "A dream come true," he whispered. Oh, God, had Aunt Jada been right again? She hadn't mentioned that meeting his true love would be the death of him.

"The curse of Von Damme will take another," the old man said sadly.

"This should have never happened. Now we will all suffer the consequences," she said.

Dillon didn't understand. She would be the last thing he would ever see, not exactly what he had been hoping for, but it was his dying wish. He lost his grip, slipping into the water.

The Dark Lady grabbed him by the wrists. With a firm grip, she easily held him.

"Let him go," the old man said.

"Relax, this is in your best interest," Elke said. She dragged Dillon into the wooden boat and into a seat like he was a baby. He shook and shuddered, unable to control his limbs. She kissed his forehead, his cheek, his lips, and his neck, sending fiery chills through him before an intense pain drove needles into his body, mind and spirit.

Four: Home Welcomes

"Sir? Are you all right?"

Troy jolted awake, shuddering in the seat of a commercial jet. Gently shoulder-shaking him was a redhead flight attendant.

"Thank you for waking me up," Troy said, trying to shake off the nightmare. It had been a doozy. He hadn't had it before. Why did he keep having bad dreams about a wonderful lake? Had he really dreamed of being Dillon? Troy felt a vague unrest when he thought of his best friend's obsession--the Dark Lady.

Right now, the jet seemed too confining, so Troy peered out the oval window. He studied the rounded, mountainous land of hardwoods and deciduous trees where he had been born, raised and learned to play in the Great Outdoors. The Appalachians were stunted compared to where he had been since, but for the east coast, they were tall, a welcomed escape from the long summers' heat. Humidity still reigned, though, creating the smoke-like haze, the signature of the Smoky Mountains.

Now he recalled that he rode an Express Jet flight to the Tri Cities Regional Airport in Blountsville, Tennessee. It served northeast Tennessee, the Sullivan County area, and southwest Virginia's Washington County.

Far below were two concrete landing strips leading to a midsized, two-story terminal and a sprawl of metal aviation buildings and hangars covering over a thousand acres. East of the airport, rounded Boone Lake glimmered like quicksilver. Boone was small compared to South Holston to the northeast and at the edge of his vision.

As the plane banked around for a landing, Troy got a better view toward Holston Dam and the same named reservoir, where a friend had been found dead and a blood brother was missing. Smoke billowed from the Cherokee National Forest near there, rising into a smeary, sickly yellow and gray cloud.

His home town woods were burning.

He hoped it wasn't an omen.

From the moment Troy left the plane, he felt followed. He glanced back over his shoulder, but no one in the jetway seemed to be watching him. Mirrors and reflective glass offered many opportunities to check about him, but he saw nobody he knew. Only ghosts, he thought and shivered. He smelled chocolate and peppermint, much like the candy Wilson had munched non-stop.

Troy looked around. It had been close to three years since he had been in the Tri Cities. He wondered if the place had changed. The airport was the same with everything a regional airport needed: the video arcade, insurance booth, post office, news stand, gift shop, Tailwinds Restaurant, three airlines, and four rental car agencies. Comparing it to the multiple terminals, concrete ramps, tram railways, and on-site hotels of DFW, SeaTac or even modest Reno-Tahoe made him smile. Times were blessedly simpler here in the Appalachians.

Already perspiring after a few steps, Troy felt followed and watched when he exited the security zone. Dillon was nowhere to be seen. Troy started to wonder if something had happened to the man. Dillon was investigative by nature, known to stir the pot or poke the bees' nest.

Troy also wondered if he had been duped, moments away from being pranked. And yet, he had checked the news. Pat Ackles was dead. Perhaps John wasn't missing. It wouldn't be the first time his friends had pulled a stunt to get him to come back, or get him back, or simply get him.

The sense of being observed grew stronger. He paused to check in a window to see if he had a shadow.

He was startled by his reflection. Was that him? He looked like crap warmed over. His dark, wavy hair was unkempt, even his eyebrows had gone wild. He had deep shadows around his bloodshot, blue eyes and bags underneath them. Beard stubble made him appear rough around the edges. Years ago when he had walked through the airport, people had recognized him. Now he looked like he could be forty-something. Those bizarre nightmares and changing time zones had mucked up his sleep and body clock, leaving him feeling muddled.

At the luggage carousel, he grabbed his bag. He had shipped his ski equipment and winter gear directly home outside of Tahoe City, while he had traveled from frozen water to warm water, the great white north to the steamy south. He wiped sweat from his brow. He had not missed the humidity.

He paused at a colorful and picturesque display of the Tri Cities—modern Kingsport, Johnson City with East Tennessee State University, and Bristol, the Birthplace of Country Music. The town had partnered with the Smithsonian to house a museum about the Carter sessions and the rhythm and roots of country music, now that the home sat in Nashville. Photos of northeast Tennessee showed the dazzling fall foliage, crowd-packed Bristol Speedway, the green hills and water of South Holston Reservoir, the First Baptist Church under the downtown arch, the glass-walled downtown library and Bristol Caverns. His parents had loved this area, too.

A tribute to hometown heroes displayed statues of Tennessee Ernie Ford and Raquel Sterling racing on skis to one of her Olympic medals. This confirmed the presence of ghosts. After earning silvers in the Combined, Super G, and GS, the Silver Goddess won gold in the downhill. He was glad she had been successful, sorry she was injured, and wondered if he would have enjoyed the ride.

Strong, slim hands covered his eyes and surprised him. A feminine body, a luscious combination of supple and firm, pressed against Troy's back. He froze even as his pulse bolted like a race horse, and his body stirred despite his fatigue. He knew this touch and recognized Raquel's zesty and physical presence.

Her lips touching his ear, she whispered, "You look fit and ready to play." That single sentence said a lot. A rush flowed through him as though he were free falling.

Troy slowly turned around, conflicted, wanting to run and wanting to seize her and kiss her. Her arms remained loosely on his waist. He met large, dark eyes smoldering with a fierce joy, a silvery sparkle that he had once loved as much as being alive. His body still reacted to her as if he were an addict. He took a deep breath and wished he hadn't, catching her scent, a hint of vanilla and cinnamon, sweet and spicy.

Nine years had only made Raquel Sterling more desirable, if that could even be. A raven-haired knockout, she was an unusual combination of brains, beauty and physical grace—model looks with an athletic physique and sports skills to match. She looked a touch Brazilian, tan enough to be returning from Virginia Beach or the Caribbean. Before she had won, some had mocked her as the Raquel Welch of skiing.

"Troy, it's fabulous to see you," Raquel gushed, her words

flavored by a hint of sultry, East Tennessee drawl. An impish smile graced her features, accentuating high cheekbones. The sun cast purple highlights through her wavy hair as it flowed over her shoulders. In private he had referred to her as the Amazonian princess or simply Wonder Woman. Well, she had left him wondering.

She wore flattering blue jeans and a rainforest green blouse underneath a white waist jacket, a contrast to her wealth of dark hair. Long legged and clad in knee high boots, she coolly studied him.

"Raquel. Wow, what a surprise. You look . . . divine," he managed, shocked.

"How are you? I look divine? You're the miracle. What's it been? Nine years?"

Nine years since June 2nd when he had packed up and left to head west. How was he? "I feel lucky, even blest, considering. Funny, here I am standing next to your statue, and a moment later, here you are."

"Were you standing here . . . wishfully thinking?" Raquel asked. She sounded hopeful. Troy figured his imagination was messing with him.

How should he answer that? His hands almost didn't obey him, but he took her hands in his and moved them away from his body. Electricity seemed to dance up his arms. Troy really didn't know what to say to his high school and college love. At one time he couldn't breathe without thinking about Raquel Sterling.

"Yes. Yes, I was," he mused. What an opportunity.

"Oh?" she asked. He had piqued her curiosity.

He decided to be kind. This was a new life, right? "I was wishing that I could ski like the woman in the photo because she really knows how to fly down a mountain."

Raquel laughed delightedly.

A touch of euphoria washed over him. Troy felt he was fighting a losing, uphill battle. The ground was slipping away under his feet as swiftly as an avalanche. "But then, I know something other wishful guys have yet to learn from reading Homer and Greek mythology," he said and paused thoughtfully. She arched an inquisitive eyebrow for him to continue. "It's unwise for mere mortals to get involved with a goddess."

"Don't believe all you read. No goddess would have my right knee. Surgery only does so much, right? Then it's divine intervention," she said. Like he was a wild animal, she gently reached out and cupped his chin, slowly turning his face from side to side. "Besides, no one has ever flown down a mountain like you. Ask anyone about Bane's Downhill Race Against Death."

It was the sort of notoriety he had not been seeking, dying while trying to escape a rockslide and avalanche caused by an earthquake in Chile. Many people still thought he was dead, as his death was more spectacular than his fight back to life. That had been a grind, an inch forward, a half back. "Two minutes of my fifteen minutes of fame."

"Ha. Speaking of flying . . . I heard you were a natural in those wingsuits soaring through slot canyons in Utah. That sounds wild and risky. What's that like? Hmm?"

"A lot like flying when you're disembodied, after you're dead," he said, startling her. He got that kind of reaction when he referenced dying, a reason he rarely spoke of it. He had stopped flying because he had kept dreaming about dying in a fiery crash in the woods, which had nothing to do with the red slickrock desert of Utah.

"By the way, my compliments to the plastic surgeons. If I didn't know, I would think the changes due to years, instead of mileage, or should I say changes in elevation," she said, scrutinizing him. That piercing gaze had haunted him. "And your body looks well-conditioned."

"They left medical tattoos all over the rest of me."

"All of you? That would be a sight, wouldn't it?" she asked, teasing him.

He flushed like a teen. Where the hell was Dillon? Likely,

laughing his butt off. Is this why he had felt watched and experienced goose-bumps?

"I notice you haven't posted a recent photo on your site or any social media. You should when you catch up on sleep, let all your fans see you. But . . . ah, your eyes. They're not right. Damn, I knew I should've flown to see you in the hospital. You almost died," she said.

Troy smiled wanly. "I did die, Raquel. They revived me on the slopes and then a second time in ER." That made three times he had died, he thought, but he kept that snarky comment to himself. He tried to gather the emotion and compartmentalize it, as he did before a particularly tricky or dangerous ride, climb or jump. He was calmer before his first base jump than now. "I just didn't stay dead. I have been told I am stubborn."

"I am glad you were. If you'd like to talk about it, walk and chat like back in the day, I'm ready and willing to listen," she said.

He managed to release her hands. It was a start. "Raquel, forgive me. I'm not at my best. Yesterday, I was in Alaska, this morning I'm here. I'm jet-lagged, fuzzy-headed and not thinking straight."

"Were you skiing in Alaska?" she asked, unable to hide her envy. After all, it was summer in the northern hemisphere.

"Yes, I was lucky enough to ski under the northern lights, but mostly I was taking photos and writing and snow-shoeing to take photos," he said, then he mentioned Miles' heart attack and Wilson's passing. Troy wished he had done more. "I went from the wilds and death to life and civilization at the speed of the jet stream."

"I'm sorry for your loss. Ends can come abruptly. Sometimes second chances never come along. Sometimes, though, they do," she said. Her dark eyes sparkled, and she seemed radiant, like seeing him was the best thing that had happened in a long time. "I love your photos, especially the landscapes. I have Garmisch at sunset with the rainbow cloud on my living room wall. Others I use to decorate my stores. Listen, I have a copy of *Outside: The Extreme Skiing Championships.* I want you to sign it. Will you come by the main store and let the ladies swoon, or do I have to hunt you down?"

Troy was surprised that she had kept a copy, so he said nothing.

"Hunt you down, then. You know, I could give you a lift to your destination."

She had given him a boost, but letting Raquel take him for a ride was inviting disaster. Repeating an action and expecting different results was one of the definitions of insanity. "The search for John starts at Maraders Marina." He got the reaction he expected, tensing and flushing, but she kept her composure, though her eyes brimmed with fury. Troy let go a breath and explained what little he knew about John's disappearance and Pat's death.

"That's so sad. Pat was a great guy and family man. I'll have to call Peggy." After a pause, a breath, and what seemed like a lack of confidence that he found disarming and charming, Raquel said, "Troy, have lunch with me. You should talk to someone about what happened on the mountain. Facing our mortality, even our athletic decline, can be disturbing. At least it was for me. Is for me. Can we talk, like we once did?" she asked.

Her bold honesty disconcerted him. Blessedly, Raquel's phone rang.

"Sorry. It's the county sheriff's department. I hope none of my staff is in trouble. Please don't run off. I know that cornered look. It's not like I'm introducing you to my mom for the first time."

Troy took this moment to step away from Raquel and breathe. That helped his brain work as a mere two feet lessened some of the intense sexual attraction. He breathed to help him tuck it away where he could deal with it later, go bike or swim it off. He should have stepped back sooner, but he had been caught off guard. Where was Dillon? When Troy tried phoning him again, he was interrupted by a calming touch on his arm.

"Hey, Troy. Are you calling Dillon? I hope you have better luck than I did," the bespectacled, redhead asked. Gorgeous, she was gray eyed and freckled with wind-blown, red-gold hair cascading over her shoulders. Svelte in the way of dancer with legs other women wished for and men longed to caress, she stood poised atop anklet boots, bringing her almost eye to eye with him. Her tawny skin, sunny hair and wide smile were radiant. She made a simple black, slit-skirt and half-jacket over a red shirt patterned with dark lightning look classy and fashionable. But then, this woman would look good in baggy rain gear. Her sensuous lips matched her outfit, black and red, and drew too much of his attention.

"Yes, I am. He's supposed to be picking me up. Do you know where he is?" Troy asked. Who was she? Dillon's girlfriend? He hadn't mentioned her, and he always waxed poetically about his squeeze, currently named Gina. Then again, sometimes, he went through relationships so swiftly Troy couldn't keep up. Add to that, Dillon had friendly ex-girlfriends still living in the Tri-Cities.

"No, and that worries me. It's not like him to no call and no show."

"Not at all," Troy agreed. Who was this?

"Troy, I'm glad you're here. You look so much better than the last time I saw you," she said. The young woman threw herself into his arms to kiss him on the cheek, shocking them both with a jolt of static electricity. She yelped as she rocked back to stand with one hand on her lips and the other on her slim hip. Behind emerald-framed glasses, speculation filled her smiling eyes. "That was electric."

He felt he should readily recognize this foxy lady. Who was she? When had she last seen him?

"I didn't think you were coming to the reunion," she said.

"My last job in Alaska ended early and the work I had in

Chile was canceled. The heliport was overrun by rebels."

"Sounds like a place to avoid. Well, I'm glad you're here since I am starting to wonder if Dillon's in trouble."

Troy had experienced the same thought. "Trouble and Dillon? What makes you think that?"

"Besides T being his middle initial? He asked me to bring him information and old news stories on the building of Holston Dam."

Troy had heard her say that before, T being his middle initial. His sluggish mind couldn't pull it together.

"You . . . you don't recognize me, do you, Troy?" she asked. Disappointment was heavy in her voice. "Well, to be fair, the last time you saw me my hair was blond with blue tips and before that pink. That was my wild fashion phase. I've calmed down considerably. I'm getting old. Spinster age soon."

Pink hair? Who in the area would greet him with a hug and a kiss? He wracked his already whacked brain. There was familiarity here, but they had never dated. He was certain he would remember her, that smile, those eyes, and those long dancer legs. He frowned. Legs. He knew those gray eyes flecked with gold and green. They changed in the light. When she removed her glasses, it struck him.

"Silke?" he asked.

Silke beamed, her smile healing some of his jet lag. "Ah, be still my beating heart. You haven't forgotten me."

Dillon's little sister! Troy was rocked and shocked. Not only had she matured magnificently, she had blossomed into a graceful, beauty queen who healed the mind and body. He had worked diligently to forget about her, but his body and mind recalled her well, and pleasingly so, and he smiled. The spectacles nicely added the impression of maturity.

"Now I know why Dillon is so stupid and homely. You possess all the smart and good-lookin' genes."

"Thank you, kindly. He has the smooth-talkin' genes."

"The last time I saw you were at Squaw Valley. You were skiing better than Dillon and driving all the guys crazy."

"Was I? All the guys? Truly?" she asked. Her eyes twinkled and laughed at him. She was almost as big a flirt as her brother.

Troy nodded. "Your glasses confused me, and well, I would expect to see you with a beau on your arm."

She grimaced. "Oh, please. I just moved back here to escape one. I almost had to shoot him. I called the cops instead. Enough about me. Are you well?"

Shoot him? Troy wondered. "I'm okay after hours of being cooped up sitting on planes, yes," he replied. She was a breath of fresh air and sunshine.

"You look tired and your aura is out of balance with dark spots around your knee and neck," she mused.

"My aura?" he asked. He heard Raquel hang up.

"Troy, I have to go. Oh, hello, Ms. Silke," Raquel said, noticing her. Both ladies smiled what seemed to be in a friendly manner, but he felt as if he stood below an air conditioning vent. He had seen Raquel turn into the Ice Queen but never Silke. What had he stepped into? The two exchanged stiff greetings and banal pleasantries. "I heard you had moved back to town. The boys at the store say you're working downtown."

"At the State Street Fitness and Spa, teaching yoga and fitness classes. I also teach a healthy eating cooking class and do PT work."

"PT work, you say? You look fit, like you're in training," Raquel said.

"My roommate says you can't catch a Ferrari with a VW bug, but you already know this," Silke said.

Raquel's smile tightened. "Speaking of which, Troy, I hate to rush off, but the sheriff wants rescue divers out at the lake, so I need to call my crew. Think about doing a promo for your sponsors at my stores. Here's my card. See you soon." She leaned close, lightly kissing him.

His lips felt pleasantly singed, and his body reacted like he'd been shot up with morphine, washing all pains away. Kissed by two beautiful women. He must be dreaming. If so, why did he feel a sense of storm about to strike? "Rescue drivers at Holston?" he asked.

"Remember to come by the store. Call me if you're curious or brave," Raquel said.

"Be safe," Troy replied. He turned away, so he wouldn't have to watch her stride off. He was the only one. Everybody else noticed her pass by. Several people stopped her for autographs, and that's when her chauffeur bodyguard, a tough-looking blond named Carter, closed in to accompany and protect her.

What was he doing? Troy asked himself. He intended to pitch the card, but he found himself stuffing it in his pocket. To say he was confused and of two minds was an understatement.

Hands on her hips, Silke glared at him. She looked enchanting even when angry. He had known the Urich family so long he had seen her throw some classic tantrums. She had been hell in high heels as a teen, although she had usually been sweet to him while being mean and sometimes even nasty to Dillon. That was a benefit of not being related.

"Troy, I can't believe you're going to have dinner with the Silver Goddess," Silke growled. She almost called her something less pleasant. "What would Gina say?"

Gina? He hoped his website hadn't been hacked with news of a phantom romance.

"Believe me, you can do better than Raquel."

Troy chuckled. He never imagined Silke being bothered by Raquel trashing his heart, but then, he could see Dillon grinding an ax about her to his sister. Silke had probably gotten sick of hearing it. "Next time, don't hold back what you think, okay? Let me know how you truly feel. First though, who is this Gina you refer to?"

Silke appeared flustered. "What? She's your girlfriend, isn't she? Dillon said . . ."

His best friend had been lying. Why? "Silke. Virginia is Dillon's current sweetheart, not mine. I am footloose and fancy free."

"Gina is his girl?" she asked. He nodded. She blushed, embarrassed and stammered an apology. "I'm sorry. He's never mentioned dating her, or much of anybody else for that matter."

Troy covered his disbelief with a cough and hoped he managed a bland expression. Dillon hadn't been as gregarious or wild as Marader, but he had been very active. Often, Dillon had hoped aloud that Silke didn't share his lustful genes.

"Dillon says he never meets anyone interesting. No one can compare to the Dark Lady," she said loftily.

They shared a laugh. Troy knew the tall tale of Dillon meeting the Dark Lady of the Lake. Once, she had saved Dillon's life from rabid pit bulls. He said she looked like an athletic Marilyn Monroe.

"Do you think he's been lying to me?" Silke asked.

"It does sound like he's been disingenuous," Troy said. He knew better than to get between angry siblings. She would only be enraged when she learned the truth, and Dillon should be there for her wrath. "Tell me, why the glasses? Everyone in your family has great eyes. Dillon is always bragging about your keen sense of vision."

"You're right. My eyes are fine. I wear them to be taken more seriously. My eyes tell me you're out of whack. Not just your knee. And, as much as I hate to admit it, she was right about your eyes. And . . . how's your neck?"

"Tweaked courtesy of the airline seats and a fall."

"I can fix that."

"The thought of getting fixed sounds uncomfortable."

Silke chuckled then grew serious. "It does, doesn't it? Say, do you ever feel like you're being watched?" she asked.

He nodded. "Now that you mentioned it, yes. Ever since I got on the plane in Anchorage I feel like I'm caught in an intrigue that I'm unaware of."

"I thought it was only me. I think I'm paranoid after my stalker experience."

"Understandable," Troy said. He could understand why guys would watch her. "Anyone in particular?" he asked and studied the people in the airport. No surprise that several men of varying ages gave Silke either appraising, admiring or covert looks. Nobody appeared any more suspicious than anyone else, whether it be the guy in the cowboy hat, the yokel in the Duck Dynasty cap, the dude in the bowler, or the man leaning on a cane. Women noticed Silke, too. He knew they often dressed to impress each other. A young girl grinned at her, and Silke grinned and waved back. A boy pointed her out to his mother and asked if she was a princess.

"I'm off work today. So how about I chauffeur you around? We're both looking for Dillon. I'm armed so I don't mind driving you to see Tommy. You can read the articles I printed off for Dillon. What do you say?"

Troy thought about it for a moment. He could call a buddy for a ride and wait, or he could be driven around by his best friend's gorgeous sister. Could this be the set up? One of his good friends, a blood brother, had sent her so that Dillon would see them together and blow a fuse, or worse, the whole fuse box could go up in flames.

It was a no brainer, even with the danger of a broken nose. "Sure. I appreciate it. You're fabulous company when you aren't accusing me of cheating on a non-existent girlfriend," he said.

As soon as he set foot outside, beyond the airport doors, Troy expected to be pranked. Silke must have sensed it, because she asked if he were well.

"Yes, I'm outside in the sun. That always revives me," he replied.

When nothing odd happened, he began to grow worried. "I thought there was a practical joke in progress. Who told you I would be here?"

"Dillon when we talked last. Do you think I'm in on it?"

"No," Troy said. She might unwittingly get him in hot water when Dillon saw them together. What might have happened to

Dillon? Old girlfriend? Troy wondered as they entered the crosswalk. The feeling of being tailed and observed remained. When had he developed paranoia?

"It could be something to do with last night. He called me about ten, told me about what had happened at the lake, bless Pat's soul, and John's too, wherever he is. Dillon asked me to look up some information on the Net, like I said, about the building of the dam and such. Based on the last text at 5:14 this morning, I thought that I would find him here meeting you," she said.

"Is he still out at the lake camping?"

"Out at the lake, yes. Camping. No. A storm washed out the boys. When he called last night, he was at Maraders Marina on one of the houseboats. God's Gift to Women might know where Dillon is. I haven't called Tommy yet, and I rather not deal with him on my own. I might shoot him," Silke said.

Again, Troy could relate. Not all blood brothers got along. It had been easier to work things out when they were younger.

"Aunt Jada warned Dillon about going camping, and she's often right. I do know Dillon planned to go back out to Cemetery Ridge with a deputy. Am I rambling on? Sorry, I'm concerned," Silke said. At a topless, tan Land Rover, she stopped, jangled her keys and unlocked the driver's door.

"I recognize this car! I'm amazed it survived Dillon's high school years. If it could talk, I think he would still be grounded."

Silke pealed with laughter. "I'm glad it can't. I drove it for four years of high school, too. Troy, you're walking crooked like a dog."

"Thank you for that comparison. At least think of me as a Labrador or a retriever," he replied sourly. On the other hand, they were often petted and rubbed upon.

"Well, you have a hitch in yer giddy-up. How's that analogy?"

"A horse comparison. Great. Plow horse or race stallion, glue material or pampered stud?" he mused.

Silke rolled her eyes. "Ha. Seriously, though. Will you let me help you? I think I can . . . adjust your neck here and now," she said. He could use an adjustment, so he agreed. With a satisfied smile, she glided behind him, gently running her fingers along his neck, shoulders and down his bony spine. "Relax. I said, relax," she whispered in his ear. His body finally responded, melting around her fingers while they dug in and pushed on tense muscles. He hadn't realized he had been so tightly wired.

His neck finally responded with more than pops and creaks. Something shifted, realigning, and he hurt for a brief, dizzying moment, then he felt relief as muscles, ligaments, and tendons found their proper placement. He stretched and walked around the Land Rover. "Wow. Amazing. Thanks. You have magic hands."

"You're welcome. I'm pleased to hear all my education, practice, and diligence pays off. I think you could use more work, but I would need to get you on a massage table."

The visual mental image Troy had seemed inappropriate for his best friend's sister. Some guy would be very lucky one day. There was no doubt Troy had been away from feminine company too long. Now he remembered why he didn't come back here. Raquel and Silke were both trouble of the sweetest kind, big air with a flat landing.

"Mine's stored at my mother's. I'm using one that was already at the spa," she continued. That broke the image of Silke on a massage table. "I've only been back a couple of weeks. I'll try Dillon again then Mom."

While she made her calls, he phoned Jambo, Marader, J-Man, and Knives. Getting their voice mails, Troy left messages. He kept alert while he called, looking for anyone who might be a stalker or one of his friends recording him for the pranking. The bowler-wearing guy was taking photos of everything like it was his first time here. Two ETSU students recorded their every move, posing and mugging for the camera. They could even be watching by drones, he mused.

"Last night Dillon sounded scared, and I can't remember the last time something frightened him. Uh, excuse me. The phone, maybe it's, no, it's not Dillon." She answered and greeted Aunt Jada. While they chatted, Silke started the Land Rover and let the engine idle to warm up.

Troy pushed in the old cigarette lighter, then he rolled down the window. When the lighter popped out, he took Raquel's card and ignited it. "It had her private number on it. I couldn't just throw it in the trash," Troy said. He held it out the window and let it burn to a plain white corner.

"Do you feel better?" Silke asked. Her eyes searched his.

Troy shrugged and mused. "Up in flames? Or down in flames?"

"I hope you don't mind a brief stop along the way. Aunt Jada's all worked up in a tizzy over something," Silke said. She shifted into reverse and backed out of the parking space.

"Fine by me. What are you doing here? Last I heard, you had graduated and were working out west in a clinic near San Francisco."

She drove fast while she chatted. "Until a month ago, I was working in a pain clinic. We explored anything that might help a patient cope. As you know, pain is often more than just physical. When drugs, surgery, or physical therapy don't work, we finally look at alternative methods of easing the suffering; tenser units, biofeedback, yoga, relaxation, and creative visualization and meditation. I've even seen laugh and scream therapy work. Just recently we've begun to study Non-Contact Therapeutic Touch. One of the doctors is investigating healing by laying on of hands and manipulating etheric body energy."

"Whatever you did worked on me. California sounds like the perfect place to study all of that. And it must have agreed with you. You look radiant."

"Thank you, kindly, sir. California did work, for a while. Then, there was the stalker. Here, I don't feel alone with family close by."

"I don't recall Dillon mentioning Aunt Jada."

"She's really a great aunt. I had lunch with her yesterday, and she morbidly told me that she doesn't think she has long to live. She suffers from a little dementia, so she might think you're Dillon or the guy reading the electric meter. Sit back and relax. You're not flying in a wingsuit. Speaking of which, did you really fly with one of those . . . bat suits?" she asked.

He nodded. "Yes, I played at being bats. Better than squirrelly," he said, referring to another name for it.

"You are crazy. I'd only do something like that in desperation."

"I have a guardian angel."

"You need a team but not for today, okay? Relax, cool your jets, and we'll be in Bluff City in about fifteen minutes."

"I'm still waiting on viable jetpacks. Wingsuits only let you glide," he replied.

"Does your hair always have to be on fire?" she asked while she turned right onto Interstate 81. As they headed northeasterly, she unleashed her lead foot. The Land Rover roared and lunged to accelerate.

"I thought you said I wouldn't need my guardian angels? Fast cars, machines, have never really been my thing," Troy said. He glanced back, noting the cars and trucks to see later if anyone was following Silke.

"Looking for tails? Any black SUVs?" she teased. He shook his head no. "Then they're probably not after the articles that Dillon asked for, are they?" She read his quizzical expression and continued. "The material is in the door pocket."

Troy found and opened a manila envelope. He skimmed the articles. Most were printed from the Net. What did this have to do with the building of Holston Dam, Holston Valley, moonshine and the Dark Lady? And how long had Dillon been researching them?

Five: The Seer and Dam History

Drab green, the woods, faded and strained by the drought, undulated away from the highway into the surrounding hills. Off to the right, Troy saw too many dead and brown trees in Steel Creek Park. He had never seen the forest like this, dry and withering. Usually it was vibrantly green and lush. Once, his mother had claimed that if you napped in one place too long you would mold.

They passed Celebration Church, then the Johnson and Gunnings Cemeteries. Why so many cemeteries? He hadn't really noticed before. Perhaps he had grown sensitive, noticing the plots instead of the buildings. By the wealth of religious structures, one would know without being told that this area was part of the Bible Belt.

Likely, it would take more than prayer to bring rain and find Dillon. What was he into? Troy hoped the file of material would help.

He skimmed it, newspaper articles mostly, and some sections from books, personal accounts from the forties and fifties. He knew some of the history from a research paper he'd written his junior year about the lake and South Holston Dam. The plans had been approved in 1941, like many things, after a disaster— a huge flood of the Tennessee River watershed wiped out Kingsport and Bluff City. The old ads for employment seemed simple, the hourly pay a pittance compared to today's princely sums. The dam was intended to be part of a system of dams to prevent flooding and generate hydroelectric power. Work started in 1942 but was delayed until 1947 due to World War II and later, funding. Amidst controversy, work was completed in late 1950. Shortly thereafter, November 20, the lake level began to rise.

Similar to creating Shenandoah National Park, relocating people had been a challenge. Census taking had underreported locals, many of them corn and tobacco farmers and drive-by-night moonshiners, the forerunners to the NASCAR circuit.

Some 522 people had been moved from farms and a tiny town, some 300 graves from burial sites and cemeteries. Disappearances and deaths, wild dog attacks, and hauntingly seductive appearances by the Dark Lady were described in personal accounts. Dillon had requested a great deal of material about the mysterious woman of the lake shores, describing her as a gorgeous raven-haired beauty. Troy was surprised by the number of encounters with feral dogs roaming in packs. An editorial claimed they were guard dogs, four-footed sentinels of the Dark Lady.

He paused, looking up as the Land Rover drove by the Bluff City town limit sign on 394. Silke noticed. "Find anything interesting?" she asked.

"Only for a history buff. If something is here, it eludes my tired brain."

"So. How is the traveling life?"

"Like anything, it has its pros and cons. It can be a grind. I like writing and recording, but I miss the rush of doing."

"Like I said, does your hair have to be on fire all the time?"

"No, not any more. Dying has given me second thoughts, so I'm working on a career change. I know, it makes me sound like I'm getting old, but most sports are for young studs. Guys and gals your age."

"My age? I am only four years younger than you, Mr. Bane. We have a lot of great years left, I would say. As far as a career change, Aunt Jada might be able to offer some helpful advice."

"You said your aunt warned Dillon not to go to the reunion? Why?"

"She saw death, literally not figurative, and now Pat Ackles is dead. John Traylor is missing, so is his girlfriend, and my brother. Aunt Jada said you would be coming to Bristol, even when Dillon told me you said no, and here you are."

"I can't say I put much stock in psychics."

"Fine. But many do believe in the supernatural. That's why the news that graves have been unearthed on Cemetery Ridge has spread like wildfire online. The locals are spooked. A

Bristol Herald Courier editorial claims there weren't supposed to be any graves where they were found. No record of them exists."

"I thought by law that the TVA would have relocated all the coffins in the graveyard before flooding the valley."

"The TVA must have missed a few. No doubt it will be investigated. They already have their hands full with dam maintenance and repair. There's been some coverage recently, because of a series of accidents similar enough to back in the day to put them behind schedule. I saw online that some workers quit this morning when they heard about the graves. I guess flash flooding from that sudden storm did some damage, too," Silke said.

"Tell me a little more about your aunt."

"My great aunt is a psychic and fortune teller going on eighty-six. She is where Dillon and I get our keen sense of intuition. I can see etheric bodies, so I have sense of what's ailing someone, such as your knee."

Troy had always been extremely skeptical of psychics. They took advantage of people who wanted to believe in the paranormal and hopes of a better future. The future was what you made it.

"My aunt is amazing. She reads tarot cards, auras, palms, and horoscopes. Of course, her neighbors think she's a kook. They call her 'the Babbler'. I know the local children make fun of her . . . or avoid her when she is out walking. In the early forties, her father, a doctor, disappeared while administering to workers on the South Holston Dam project. If you go back and check the records, quite a few people died or disappeared while employed by the TVA. My aunt tried to warn people that there was evil preying on the workers, an evil that killed her father, but no one believed her."

"That was the forties. Women's opinions were held in far less esteem."

"I'm glad I wasn't born back then," she sniffed. "After the dam was built, the deaths and disappearances stopped. The locals shunned her, so she withdrew from the world. Unless someone comes to see her, she remains reclusive. They still do to this day, professing her to be a matchmaker. Personally, I think she's a wonderful lady."

"I'm surprised to find you're interested in the occult."

"It's not the occult. And I'm not much different than you. I've read your book, *Mind Over Gravity*. Look, you're proof of it. Even dying didn't keep you down."

"I'll use that as a subtle title."

"Ha. We are both interested in the mental, emotional, and spiritual side of the body as well as the physical. You studied kinesiology and psychology in sports because the intangibles, like desire and gut feelings often make the difference between winning and losing. I study the mind. At the pain clinic, I've seen people make themselves sick, as well as healthy. Those events have kept my mind open to mental and psychic abilities. My aunt seems to have them. I think I do, too. I knew the instant Dillon found Pat, because I got really queasy. I asked him about it, and the time matches. Did you sense he was in trouble? Am I rambling? Sorry."

"No worries."

"Aunt Jada uses tools, like star charts, numerology, her cards, and crystals," she said and noted Troy's reaction. "Please. Humor me. She's old but a dear. You look skeptical. Or, do you think I'm kidnapping you?"

"The thought had crossed my mind. One time, when I came back, the guys pretended everyone was in the hospital."

A sign said turn back, you missed the Backyard Terrors Dinosaur Park and Funhouse. The road gradually narrowed, becoming shoulderless. The edge immediately dropped off steeply into the thick woods. He hadn't seen a house for a while.

She steered left, turning the Land Rover into a driveway nearly hidden by overgrown foliage. Leaves raked the sides of the car and smacked the top of the windshield. The property needed a mowing, trimming and weed-whacking.

Silke parked in a circular, gravel driveway in front of a two-story brick home with white trim snuggled among a copse of deciduous trees. Under the front porch, the stout oak door held a stained-glass cross. A ramp appeared recently built to aid the handicapped. The Star of David hung in the panoramic front picture window.

When Troy climbed out of the car, he felt scrutinized. It reminded him of standing before a crowd, perhaps invisible because of the weather and unheard due to the roaring in his ears, but he could sense they were there, watching him.

He noticed the circular driveway was a star pentagram made from a mixture of gray and white gravel. He started taking photos of them and of Silke. She was incredibly photogenic.

The sense of being observed heightened. He saw movement out of the corner of his eye, glimpsing an animal. He was sure he spotted a pale, bushy tail before the beast disappeared into the bushes. He thought it looked like a wolf, but he assumed it was a dog, perhaps a wolfhound or husky.

"This place was her father's in the late thirties. It has a maid's quarters over the three-car garage. There are some truly spectacular gardens and fountains out back, even a creek. Once there was a stable."

"I wonder why Dillon never mentioned this place."

"Aunt Jada scared him, always predicting the future. She knew y'all would become blood brothers," Silke said. She grabbed her purse and took his hand to lead him to the front door. He let her sunny enthusiasm carry him along.

"Does she own a dog?" Troy asked.

"Yes, a chocolate lab with a red tinged coat named Ginger. There are also coyotes around and sometimes black bears. They're more scared of us and will run, unless you're carrying out the trash, then they might ambush you," she laughed.

Along the front walkway they passed more religious symbols, much of it lawn ornaments and statuary, cherubs—angels, and holy warriors, held or perched on crosses.

Different kinds and colors of rocks formed shapes. He recognized the Masons' symbol, and Yin and Yang. Rose bushes and rose vines were everywhere, another sacred symbol. Crosses had been engraved in the steps.

"Faith keeps her alive," she said and stopped suddenly. Troy bumped into her, nudging her purse. It felt heavy, like a gun bag.

"Are you packing?" he asked.

"I have a C&C permit. Like I told you, I've had issues with stalkers. Knowing Tae Kwon Do and Jujitsu isn't enough. What? You look surprised."

"I just don't think of you as a gun toting mama," Troy said.

"You weren't there to kick him in the balls, so I had to do it," she replied in a voice that would pause anyone thinking of stealing a kiss.

"I hope it wasn't a match Aunt Jada suggested," Troy said.

Silke smiled grimly. "No. She warned me about him, so I wasn't caught unaware. C'mon, let's go in. Remember, she might think we're somebody else," Silke said. She knocked, waited a moment, then she pushed the door open, calling Aunt Jada's name. Strong aromas wafted out, tempting him, a mixture of cornbread and garlic.

Troy felt as if he were entering another world; time had stopped within the house decades ago. Everything was an antique and had the musty smell of years despite the savory aromas. Even the pictures were yellowed. A mirror etched with a unicorn and a waterfall hung on the wall opposite the door. On a table below it, candles flickered on each side of the statuette of the Virgin Mary. Numerous votives and tapers burned throughout the room, giving it a golden glow.

"I can see why Dillon might have been a little spooked by this place. I feel like I've stepped into a colorized episode of *The Twilight Zone.*"

The furniture looked stiff, elegant, and uncomfortable. The space between his shoulder blades itched, and the hair on the nape of his neck stood under observation.

"Silke, this place looks like something out of an occult film."

She laughed and hugged his arm, breaking the spell of the room. "Forty years ago, people thought my great aunt was a witch. Blessedly, burning people at the stake was illegal."

"Well, I guess everyone has a weird relative or two. I have a great uncle who was a moonshiner."

"Don't we all? Let's look in the solarium. I hope she's all right. Aunt Jada? Sister Elva?" Silke called more loudly. She swiftly swept through the parlor into a doorway of light.

The sense of being watched grew stronger. Troy felt another presence, then he heard movement behind him. He caught the blur of something large and dark barreling toward him. He was almost blindsided, barely able to brace himself. "Silke, look out!"

The beast slammed into Troy, driving him back. He used one hand to protect his face, and the other to fend off a large, reddish retriever. She was gray-muzzled, likely having licked away all the color with her flailing tongue. Her tail battered him as well.

"Ginger really likes you. Usually, she's skittish around visitors."

He grappled with the dog, finally getting her to put all four paws on the floor. Her tongue flicked out rapidly, giving him unwanted kisses.

Silke continued into the solarium. "Aunt . . . Oh, here she is. Troy, she isn't moving! She's just staring ahead!"

Ginger and Troy followed Silke. When he entered the solarium, his senses were assaulted. All the drapes and curtains were wide open, letting in the day light. It refracted brightly through crystals which cast dazzling beams of light. Brilliant colors cavorted about the room. Troy spotted amethysts, rose quartz, and various stones with green hues. Every tabletop, every surface, housed a crystal. A rosewood statute of Buddha sat in the far corner. Plants hung from the ceiling, and vines crawled along the walls.

Among it all, an elderly, red-haired woman, her curls as light as fire, sat at a table. Colorful placards of aces, wands, cups, rods and celestial figures had been arranged in a pattern, five like a wheel and four in a vertical line to the right. The Lucile Ball lookalike faced them, her eyes open but vacant.

"Did she have a stroke?" Troy asked.

Silke rushed to her side and knelt. "Aunt Jada! Can you hear me? It's me, Silke. How can I help?"

The old woman's lips moved, but no sound escaped. She shook, and her blazing red hair thrashed in all directions. A wealth of glittering jewelry swung from her ears and flashed from around her neck as she seemed to suffer a seizure.

"Aunt Jada, are you all right?" Silke asked.

The elderly woman attempted to gather her wits. As if to communicate by sign language, her hands fluttered in front of her, causing her bracelets to rattle. "Oh Silke, I'm so glad you're here! I saw a dead man walking in my garden."

"What? Aunt Jada, did you say you saw a dead man?" Silke asked.

"Yes, dear, I did, just a little while ago. He was walking in the garden, well actually, beyond the garden wall in the wild section since the garden itself is warded and thereby protected. He gave me a warning, though. You don't believe me, do you child?" the elderly redhead asked with a sad smile. "No one else believes me, but I was so certain y'all would. I always felt we were kindred souls. And now you think I'm a senile, old fool, but not Ginger, she sees him. That's why she's all riled up," she said and patted the dog on the head. Ginger settled a bit, sitting but squirming.

"No, it's not that. You were staring off into space. I was afraid you'd had a seizure or a stroke. Are you well? Do you know where you are?" Silke asked. She had relaxed her hands no longer in fists.

"Yes, on the cusp of death. I stared it in the face. It's so close, I can feel its breath on my cheek," Aunt Jada said as she picked up a hand fan. She waved it, trying to cool herself. "Oh, who is this with you? Is this your husband? Oh, my! You two will have beautiful and brilliant children."

Speechless, Troy managed to smile and raise his eyebrows in a question. Silke shrugged while she mouthed a silent apology, then she leaned close to her aunt. "No, Aunt Jada. I'm not married. I'm not even dating anyone. This is Dillon's childhood friend, Troy Bane, and a dear friend of mine, too. Dillon didn't show at the airport, leaving Troy without a ride, so I offered him a lift. My brother isn't answering his phone, which isn't like him. We're both worried, because he's so good about keeping in touch, and he hasn't called his office either."

"Oh, I see! Yes, I do. I told you the Prince of Cups was coming to town. I'm glad you're here in the flesh, young man. Dillon needs someone bold and courageous and a little bit crazy to help him. When I drew you, the Prince of Wands and Cups were stuck together, probably with honey."

Troy looked to Silke for an explanation, but she flushed and broke eye contact. He felt left behind and clueless, as if he were late to a weird murder mystery. He kept thinking he saw movement with his peripheral vision, but he had yet to figure out what it was. When he turned toward it, he saw nothing odd. It annoyed him.

"Do you have birds?" he asked.

"No, but I do have ghosts. That's probably what you're seeing." Aunt Jada chuckled. "No worries. They're friendly. See, honey. I'm fine. I had a shock, I must admit. It certainly was somethin' seein' Zane out back before the sunrise. He told me that those of the damned have risen. I should leave as even the day light would no longer stop those of the damned."

"Why would Zane come see you?" Silke asked.

"Oh, we were engaged before he disappeared in 1948," she replied casually, sounding as if he had only been gone a month or so. "He is part of whatever mysterious was going on when the dam was being built and my father was murdered." She paled when she glanced at the tarot cards spread in a cross on the table. Troy understood none of the symbolism, seeing figures and swords, along with one gushing cup. "There will be many deaths, I am so very sad to say. It started yesterday and grew worse last night." She studied their faces, her gaze now clear. Her eyes blazed with a religious zeal, then, she sighed loudly and slumped. "My memory is going, but I still envision clearly. Sometimes, though, I can't hold onto what I saw. I'm sad to say that the older one gets, the more one's credibility is questioned."

"Sometimes we doubt the senses, not the mind or honesty of the person. People make mistakes," Troy told her.

"I did not mistake seeing Zane Aldridge in the garden. Did I tell y'all that we were engaged when he went to work for the TVA, building the South Holston Dam, in 1947? He was nineteen and I was seventeen. Seventeen wasn't so young then, though I was nowhere near a spinster! This morning, just before dawn, when Zane called out to me, he looked just as young as he did back then. Handsome he was like this strapping young man you brought with you, Silke. Your husband looks like a fit one and an outdoor lover. I can see the sun in your eyes, the wind in your hair, the wolf in your face, and the shadow of death around you. Are you Heavensent, a returnee?"

Troy nodded. "I died in an avalanche. I was in the wrong place during an earthquake," he replied.

"And you've only died once?" she asked.

A timer went off, ringing.

"Would y'all like some homemade cornbread?" Aunt Jada asked.

"I would love some," he said over his growling stomach. He wasn't sure how to answer her question.

"I'll get it," Silke said. She hurried off to the kitchen, glad to get away. Troy knew the feeling. He could see why Dillon would stay away.

"Hmm. Mr. Heavensent, please open the door and let in the ghost y'all brought with you. He can't enter without my permission, and he would like to thank you, but you've been ignoring him," Aunt Jada said.

"What? Who?"

"Wilson something. Bam? He's at the door," she said. Ginger strolled over to sit by the front door. Her tail wagged, and she lightly barked.

"Barr? Wilson Barr? He died on the trip," Troy said. How had she known? It would have been on the Net, he realized, even if it didn't make the local news. He hadn't seen a computer, though.

"Open the door and let him have his say, or he'll keep following y'all around. He really does appreciate the fifteen minutes of breathing for him and pushing on his chest," she continued.

It had taken that long for the paramedic to reach them. Troy had been exhausted and a failure. To humor her, Troy opened the front door. A pleasant wind, somehow cool with the crisp scent of the high mountains and a touch of chocolate and peppermint, breezed around him. It swirled for what seemed half a minute or so, then it was gone. Wilson had constantly been snacking on chocolate-covered peppermint Altoids.

"Farewell, Wilson," Troy said. He wasn't sure what he believed about ghosts, but he felt better than before. The scent and winter chill departed, while the humidity and heat returned. He closed the door, glad he had opened it.

"So how long have y'all been hitched?" Aunt Jada asked.

Troy frowned. "Hitched isn't a word I would use even if I was married. Silke and I are friends. I've known her most of my life."

"Hmm. What day is it?" Aunt Jada asked.

"Sunday morning. August . . ."

"Ah ha! That explains it! Dear boy, I am a seer, fortune teller extraordinaire, matchmaker, and a bit of the walking dead, as I can no longer see myself beyond this week. You know, y'all make a lovely couple. Honey, would you take out the chocolate chip cookies?" she called to the kitchen. "I don't know where Sister Elva went. Is it Friday? Doesn't matter. You can take them with you, Honey. Boys of any age like chocolate chip cookies."

"That's true," he said. It didn't take a psychic to know that.

"Ah, you think that's common knowledge. Well, I bake when I'm nervous or have to say farewell. May I read your palms?"

Troy nodded, holding in a sigh. She looked at both hands then examined and traced the lines of his right palm.

"Ah, I haven't seen your kind in a while, a free spirit."

Troy smiled. He had been called that before. Free and crazy. "Yes, been a long time since I met an astral traveler," she said, then she tsked disapprovingly. "Your hands are dry. You should take better care of them for the woman in your life," she said, then she cleared her throat. "Ahem. Women in your life."

"I don't have any women in my life," Troy replied.

"So you say, so you say. Only the Good Lord knows how long we have here on planet Earth. Hmm. What kind of scandal do we have here? Oh, that's right. It's Sunday. The cusp of death warps my vision. Well, you're right. You are still single. Yes, I see. Here, you are at a third fork in the trail of your journey. At the second, you died when the world fell on you, now to be reborn as a phoenix."

He did feel transformed, though, he thought he lacked an inner fire.

"See this split here? Things are changing. This is a time of great mental, emotional, physical and even spiritual challenges. It often happens around twenty-eight when the planet Saturn returns to the same point as when you were born. Challenging is a nicer word than turmoil, isn't it? If you survive the week, you will live a very long life," Aunt Jada said and smiled pleasantly. In a sudden switch of moods and appearance, her head rolled back, along with her eyes, and her voice changed. "Troy Bane, y'all must help Dillon, no matter the odds, no matter how odd, y'all must help him stop the flood of blood."

"I will. That's why I'm here, to find Dillon," Troy said. Flood of blood? He reminded himself to roll with it. She wouldn't remember his visit tomorrow. He felt something slide across his back, tickling his spine. He glanced back and saw nothing. Ghosts? He should be concerned with the living not the dead.

"Help Dillon. There is more than just the dead or the living. There is between. Blood is far thicker than water, and love is stronger than hate," Aunt Jada said. She shook herself, like the start of a seizure, and then she sat straight and smiled, her eyes aglow. "Troy, you have known Silke a long time, yes?"

These switches in moods and topic were throwing him off balance. He figured he should just nod and improvise. "Yes, since she was a toddler and brat until about high school. I went off to college, so I haven't seen her in years, even though it doesn't seem that long," Troy admitted.

"She made your heart jump, didn't she? And you smiled, much as you are smiling now just thinking of her," Aunt Jada said.

"She is a ray of sunshine. I'm sure I wasn't the only one."

"She is that. I'm glad you see that clearly. Well, life is full of complications and decisions." Aunt Jada stiffened. Her eyes rolled back, again and then her face muscles slackened. "Beware the woman with dark eyes, black as opals. She means you ill," she said, then she blinked rapidly, as if she were just awakening. "I see your confusion. Why is that? What are you waiting for? What has happened to bold men? Kiss her soon or lose her forever."

"Kiss who?" Troy asked.

"The love of your life. If you believe nothing else I say, believe you this. Kiss her soon or lose her forever. You never know when that kiss may be your last. Your lady love could brush your lips farewell, off to work, never to be seen alive again, dead to this world," Aunt Jada said wistfully, her voice turning bitter, too. He could see her thinking of Zane all those years ago. He realized she had never forgotten him, never moved on. Was he that way, too? "Troy, help Dillon and stop the bloodbath to come."

Confusion overwhelmed Troy. One minute she seemed sane, the next she came across as suffering dementia, jumping from kissing to floods of blood and blood baths.

"What about a bath?" Silke returned. "What? Why are you looking at me like that, Troy? Oh, that's right. You're hungry," she said and handed him a plate with two wedges of buttered cornbread and four, hot chocolate chips cookies.

"Now, listen while y'all eat. As I said, Zane Aldridge stopped by to warn me. I know I stood there with my mouth gaping like a fool when he said that the damned are loose, and that many will suffer. I refuse to leave. It's already too late for me. He looked like he hadn't aged a day, but he was so pale. His eyes were red like a fiery sunset. He wanted to approach, but he couldn't. I wouldn't invite him in. I knew better. He is one of the damned. Ah, now you are truly looking at me like I have lost my marbles."

Silke kept silent. Troy reminded himself Aunt Jada was in her eighties. He knew the brain could play tricks on anyone and did more with seniors. He could see Silke suffering with her aunt.

Troy looked around on the ground. "Lost your marbles. What color are they? Should I be careful of stepping on any? My balance isn't what it used to be."

Aunt Jada bellowed a hearty laugh. "Oh, Silke, I'm so glad y'all here and that you brought your husband. Y'all will need any and all the help you can get."

A door slammed open, followed by a harsh voice. "Jada, you must have been dreaming or seeing things, you old fool! There was no sign of anyone. No foot prints. Nothing crushed underfoot in the garden. I've checked everywhere! Wasted twenty minutes on a wild goose chase!" a stern woman said as she entered through the back door to the garden. Her gruff voice matched her severe appearance.

"Come in, sister. Silke finally brought her husband home

for us to meet," Aunt Jada said.

The thin woman was one of the harshest-looking people Troy had ever seen. Her salt and peppery hair was severely pulled back from a widow's peak, revealing a high forehead and deep-set, beady eyes. Wrinkles etched her face, giving the impression of ancient parchment, and her sharp nose twitched as if smelling something foul. She was dressed entirely in black. "Good morning, Silke. When did you get married?"

"Hi, Sister Elva. Aunt Jada is confused. I'm still unattached. This is my friend, Troy Bane. He's come back home looking for a mutual friend gone missing at the lake."

"Hello, nice to meet you," Troy said.

Sister Elva's eyes dismissed him as she focused on Silke. "A good morning for delusions, that's what it is! Silke, as you can see, your aunt has worked herself into a tizzy. She is having difficulty discerning now from then. Well, she's had enough excitement for one day."

"Please don't talk about me like I'm not here," Aunt Jada said.

"She asked me to leave! To move away to someplace safe! Ha! Why wouldn't I be safe here?" Sister Elva asked them.

"I warned you. Nightwalkers hunt again," Aunt Jada announced. She toyed with a pendant, a rose-colored orb with a silver snake wrapped around it. "Sister, would you bring us some more tea? It will help ease the shock of the news."

Taking Ginger with her, the witchy woman departed, scowling all the while.

"Bless her soul. She has kept me safe and well for a long time. Troy, what do you know of South Holston Dam?"

Troy summarized what he knew for her about the TVA project. He recalled some from his high school paper and more from the set of articles Silke had printed for Dillon.

"Well, it's a pleasure to chat with a young man who has some knowledge of history. There were deaths during the construction, but the biggest mystery was the number of disappearances. People would walk off the job and never be seen again."

"And you think you know why?" Troy asked. The topic had been one of his favorite assignments. Doing physical research had been fun.

"Back in the 1920s and 1930s, the area had a nightwalker problem. Many were moonshiners or white lightning runners. It was a reason they were so hard to catch. None of them feared death. History reads that disease was the problem in this region, but the pox was the parasitic nightwalkers. Well, God just about finished them with the flood of 1940."

She paused as Sister Elva brought a silver platter with a teapot and teacups. Silke poured them all cups of green tea. A sip seemed to ground Troy, and the house seemed less surrealistic.

"Moving water and sunlight are two natural banes of nightwalkers. They like the Smoky Mountains because of the remote peaks, thick woods, and fog which lengthens the nights for them. I believe they didn't want the dam built because it would flood their lairs. And, I believe they tried many ways to stop it, including murder and buying influence, but it only ended up delaying the dam."

Troy didn't believe in mythical bloodsuckers, just the backstabbing type, and cling-ons.

"Usually, by the time you discover proof of nightwalkers, what y'all call vampires, the coyote is already in the henhouse," Aunt Jada said. She removed two necklaces from her blouse pocket. "Take these, they will protect y'all. I purchased them in Egypt then had them blest by the holy men that I encountered during my two years of traveling."

Silke accepted the crystal ankhs and kissed them. She put one around her neck and the second over Troy's head, letting it settle on his chest. It felt warm and almost seemed to throb with a pulse. He remembered reading that ankhs were symbols of life.

"You think Dillon stumbled onto this secret?" Silke asked.

"I do. I think it found him. Darkness has returned to walk in the light," she said. Her eyes rolled back, and her face went slack. "Did I tell y'all that I saw it today in Zane Aldridge?"

"Aunt Jada, please. Focus on Dillon. Where is he?"

Aunt Jada closed her eyes. "I looked. I read. Red lights, like burning eyes, dance around him. And . . . and a blond woman, too beautiful and ethereal to be wholly flesh and blood. She and the earth hold him captive. Above, there are thousands of trees. Trees upon trees and rocks piled upon rocks and water should be everywhere but is not. He is lodged near the brown cemetery," she stopped and shook. Aunt Jada's attention returned to this time and place. She yawned broadly. "Whew, I don't know why I'm so tired this morning. It could be time for my nap, and I have kept y'all long enough. Y'all must find Dillon and soon. Farewell, Silke. It was a pleasure. Young love makes me yearn to be in love again."

Silke didn't bother denying her words or trying to correct her. Troy understood. It would be pointless. "Good day, Auntie."

"Troy, remember what I told you. Stay by Dillon no matter the odds, no matter how odd, love is stronger than hate, blood than water," Aunt Jada said.

Six: A Good Place to Live . . .and Die

Behind the wheel of Land Rover, Silke was contemplative as she drove back northerly on 390 between the rows of trees on the Bluff City Highway. Troy studied his smartphone's map. The best route to the lake followed 394, named Sweet Knobs Trail, until the blacktop merged into 34, Highway 421, and the Carl Moore Parkway, named after a local man who had the idea to build the speedway, now a jewel of the NASCAR circuit.

Troy was relieved to get out of Aunt Jada's musty house into the fresh air and away from her predictions. He and Silke married. If he survived the next week, he would live a long life. What was there to survive?

"I'm sorry about that," Silke finally said. Sadness seemed to age her, giving him a glimpse into the future. She would be gorgeous for a long time. Some guy would be lucky. Troy noticed that she was holding back tears. He reached over and took her hand.

"So how long have you been pretending to be married? Hmm?" he asked, gently joking. "I was afraid I would have to make up an excuse, so she wouldn't think I was a cheapskate and didn't buy you a ring. Is that why she gave us matching ankhs?"

She chuckled. "Oh, Troy, I needed a laugh. I'm glad you understand. She really does mean well. I know you don't believe her, but I have an open mind. Dillon found death on the lake at the reunion, much as she said he would."

Silke drove past the turn off on 394 and turned on 11E.

"You're not taking me to visit another character in the family, are you?"

"No. My office is off 6th Street on the first floor of the State Street Fitness and Spa. It's an upscale gym. I keep an overnight bag there. This way we won't have to stop by the house."

"Aren't PTs usually near hospitals and doctor's offices?" Troy asked. Unfortunately, he was over-experienced with PTs. He referred to them as Pain Therapists, since they worked him through pain to regain what he had lost.

"That's true. But where I am, I get ballet dancers and actors from the Paramount Centre for Performing Arts and Theatre Bristol, weight-lifters and body-builders from the gym, as well as the normal clients who don't have to drive across town to see a PT. Plus, I can walk out the door and teach classes."

Silke left 11E and turned the Land Rover onto the Bluff City Highway. It would take them to Edgemont Ave, MLK Blvd and into downtown to the state line and State Street. Troy saw numerous signs advertising the August and September concert series. Jambo had always loved this area's music. He often announced that he lived here for the friendly people, the music, the natural beauty, and the beautiful women, if not exactly in that order. Another sign proclaimed a Full Moon Jam Concert this Friday.

An even bigger sign displayed the date for this weekend's NASCAR race at Bristol International Speedway and events at Thunder Valley. In just a few days, the population would swell from forty thousand to two hundred thousand. It was fabulous for the local economy, but he would be glad to be out at the lake and miss most of the crowds.

"Troy, you kept looking around Aunt Jada's house. Did you see any of the ghosts?" she asked with a small, secretive smile.

He told her about his fellow photographer dying of a heart attack while hiking at high altitude. He hesitated then mentioned the wind he let in at Aunt Jada's and about the fragrance of the mountains and chocolate peppermint.

"Curious things happen at my great aunt's. I've read articles about people who have survived a near death experience and return with a broader view of reality. I talked to Spider just last week about it. He half-jokes he sees dead people," Silke said.

Troy frowned. Spider was an odd bird. His broader view of reality could come from Carlos Castaneda and peyote buttons. And yet, Spider volunteered and served other people by working with Habitat for Humanity and building projects in the Caribbean. He had been very sick in Haiti, dead until revived. He had walked among the world as a ghost for a while, he believed. They should talk; see if they had any similar experiences.

"I'm more afraid of being incapacitated than dying."

She glanced over, her brow furrowed.

"I sometimes wonder if I was told to do something upon my return, and I can't remember what. It bothers me. I probably should just accept it, but . . . do you think we can talk about something else?"

"How about coming back to the living?"

"One minute, I'm at peace, then bam, the world slams back into you full of pain and sensations. It hurt to blink, to breathe, to think," he said, letting out a long slow breath. "I wouldn't even be here without angels. Honestly, Silke, I would prefer to dwell on the present. I can breathe without pain. Eat. Hike. Ski. Get paid to take photos in beautiful places. Living the dream, as they say. You said you'd been back a month?" he prompted.

"Yes. I left California immediately after the legal proceedings. I had to keep Dillon from coming out, and well, that might have gotten ugly. Wow. I never knew he was so protective," Silke said.

Troy had difficulty keeping a straight face. Silke had no idea. He noticed the sign to Bristol Caverns and tried not to think of he and Raquel there in the dark with a power outage. This is why he didn't come back. He and Raquel had been all over, so everywhere reminded him of her.

"You said Dillon was dating Gina. What about Rebecca? I think before Gina you were dating Rebecca or Tracey," Silke said. She rattled off a bunch of names. Troy recognized most of them and nodded. Had she really not known? This was not the change of subject he had been seeking.

He decided to counter. "Dillon didn't mention any names, but he said you were dating somebody new every month. Something about kissing frogs to find your prince."

"Oh, you know Dillon. He loves to embellish, But, yes, I had some wild days, I must admit, until my twentieth birthday when I wised up," she said. He thought she winced at a memory. "I couldn't get a date around here, so when I moved out to California, I found guys' attention refreshing, even intoxicating. I learned quickly to be more discerning."

"Oh, the hunt for the One," he said.

Silke punched him in the shoulder. Troy could have told her that she couldn't get a date because Dillon had threatened everyone, especially his blood brothers. They had been warned of the consequences of revealing that secret. He suspected she would be furious when she found out.

As she drove past Anderson Park, Silke pointed out the sculpture, the *Bear in a Tree* and *Tractor Fin*, part of the Art in Public places. She took State Street to 6th, so she could show him the *Earth Dancer* near the Blowfish Emporium art gallery.

Silke pulled the Land Rover into a parking lot near the gym. The brick building had a storefront facade with lots of windows to watch those working out. It looked quiet this morning, being Sunday.

As they left the car, Silke turned and asked, "Troy, would you do me a favor?"

"Sure," he said, curious. When she hesitated, he wondered if he should have asked what she wanted first.

"Uh, I know you already pretended to be my husband without any warning, that was so kind of you, so would you mind terribly taking a demotion and acting like my boyfriend for twenty minutes?" she asked, and then added quickly. "Just long enough to convince the guys at the gym that I'm happily unavailable, dating you long distance. Please?"

It seemed ludicrous to him that she needed a pretend beau. "I don't know. It might sully your reputation since mine is obviously that of a scoundrel and philanderer."

She frowned. Her fists went to her hips. He was certain her ex-boyfriends had seen this expression and stance before. She was gorgeous when impassioned.

"Okay, fine, my resistance wilts before your charm, brains, and beauty."

"Smile and act like you are thrilled to be in my company," she suggested and beamed.

"I think I can manage that without straining my acting skills," he said. It seemed appropriate that they were near the performing arts part of town.

On the walk from parking, she possessed his arm, and they strolled together, close, like lovers. She pointed out one of the locations for the Hungry Caterpillar Hunt, telling him she had gone on it with the gym's owner's wife and their daughter. Being Sunday morning in the Bible Belt, the workout facility was quiet except for a few body builders and the place's staff. On the way to her office, Silke introduced him. He shook hands and watched as guys' hearts and hopes sank. He could see the envy. Now he knew why she felt watched. Little did they know, they had a better chance of romancing Silke than he did. They hadn't met Dillon. He probably wouldn't appreciate Troy pretending to be her beau. *Where are you buddy?*

Her office was a nice space, two rooms, one for admin and waiting and another with rehab equipment and a table for treatment. He loved the decor, surprised and pleased to see a half dozen of his photographs on the walls, dramatic in the front office and peaceful in the back room.

"Sterling Sports isn't the only place to find your work on the walls. I get comments about them all the time. Now they can put a face to the name."

"Silke, I'm glad you're here," a buff young stud groaned. The bodybuilder limped, bent over like an old man, to her doorway. "I threw out my back."

"Come on in, Matthew. I'll have you fixed in a jiffy or two. Is that all right . . . sweetie?" Silke asked Troy. Her voice promised things unlikely to happen.

"Sure, honey. I'll walk around outside," he replied with a smile. He wondered if anything had changed downtown in a couple of years. He didn't find out, as his stroll was preempted by a big guy in purple shorts and a green shirt, reminding Troy of a mini Hulk.

"You Silke's boyfriend?" Mini Hulk asked.

When Troy introduced himself, Mini Hulk shook his hand and then threatened him. "She's a wonderful gal. If you're toying with her affections, there will be consequences, you hear me? A bunch of guys would like to be in your place, so don't screw her over, or else."

"Dexter, sweetie, I see you met Silke's beau, Troy Bane. Hello, young man, I'm Mrs. Fleenor, co-owner of this place," the woman said from behind her curls. The wealth of hair was salt and peppered, but the petite lady smiled, walked, talked and gestured with the brisk, bouncy energy of a cardio workout. Dexter expressed one more menacing glare then departed. Troy wanted to get outside, but Mrs. Fleenor cornered and besieged him with questions about his relationship with Silke. Troy didn't really concoct a story, mentioning they had known each other for a decade and had been attracted to each other for years. Her wise gray eyes studied him, searching for falsehoods.

"Hey, Brew, about time. You're late. What kept you, man? Too much fun at the lake yesterday?" a young man asked. Troy turned. "Oh, hey. Sorry, man. My bad."

Mrs. Fleenor shook her head. "Josh, you should be wearing your glasses. This here is Troy Bane, Silke's boyfriend."

"She has a boyfriend? Aw, what a shame for the rest of us. Nice to meet you. She's a great lady. Seriously, though, you and my friend Brew look so much alike. You're taller, come to think of it."

"Don't listen to Josh. Dave is a goof off. He's lucky I keep him on here. If I didn't know his mother . . ."

Having heard it before, Josh grumbled and stomped off.

"Now, I'm not usually one to give warnings," she began.

Troy braced himself. When it came to Silke, warnings seemed plentiful.

"But Mr. Bane, you better be wonderful to that young lady or your name will be Mudd. She's somethin' special, she is, yes, sir, and she's sweet on you. Mercy my, I've never seen her glow like today. Never," Mrs. Fleenor said.

"She is special. I am a lucky guy," Troy said. He hadn't considered the trouble it might cause by pretending to be her man.

"Keep reminding yourself of that, and you'll do fine," Mrs. Fleenor said.

Troy peered out through the front window and noticed the guy in the bowler. He had found a bench within sight of the gym's door. He seemed to be texting or searching on his smartphone. He glanced up infrequently to make sure nobody left.

So intent was Troy that he didn't notice Silke sidling up to him. She took his arm, and it seemed natural to put his arm around her. She smooched his cheek.

"I'm surprised you didn't tell us Troy was coming to town," Mrs. Fleenor said.

"I didn't know. He surprised me," Silke crooned. She looked at Troy with adoring eyes, playing her part well. He almost believed.

"Pardon me, but are you by any chance the Troy Bane? The extreme skier world champion?" a young man asked. Troy turned to the skinny, sleepy-eyed dude with orange hair wearing a t-shirt reading: READ IT. SHRED IT.

"In the flesh and standing, I'm pleased to say. And you are?" Troy asked a little warily. Was he going get threatened again?

"Martin. I love your style, all out, death-defying dude. Do you do autographs? Group selfie? Maybe even Sharpie-sign my bicep?" Martin asked.

As always, Troy refused to sign body parts. Silke took their photo but declined to pose with them despite Martin's flattery. Troy was amused by his enthusiasm. Mrs. Fleenor rolled her eyes and chortled.

"When I heard the news, I told everybody you weren't really dead," Martin gushed. He wore a self-satisfied smile. He didn't seem to notice Troy's bewilderment. "Yeah, man, heroes always have to face death, and the legendary ones come back from the dead, bringing back some new insight or way of thinking. Plus, the heroes usually have babes like your honey to inspire them to live again."

Silke's smile lit up the room. "Martin, are you for real?"

"I've seen interviews with Lucas and read Joseph Campbell, including *Hero of a Thousand Faces*. Listen, I know my heroes. Truly epic heroes throw themselves off cliffs, defy gravity, help people, and come back from the dead, even if only figuratively and allegorically. Or is that metaphorically. I get confused between those," Martin said.

"Amazing," Silke said then turned to Troy. "Heavensent

and epic are you?"

"You bet! His race versus death, the earthquake avalanche broke YouTube viewing records. Who could resist? That part where you swerved, leapt off that overhanging cliff, plunged down three hundred feet and glanced off an ice cornice to redirect your fall. Wow. Awed," Martin said and bowed.

Troy had watched it once and never again. He didn't need to as he flashed back too often. "I keep asking myself, what am I going to do for an encore?" Troy joked.

"What a question! Have you tried wingsuits? I would love to give it a whirl, over water, of course, when I take a header," Martin asked.

Troy nodded. Silke interrupted. "Martin, do you love to ski, too?"

"I'm a knuckledragger and proud of it. I love jumping off, dropping in, and defying gravity. Plus, there's more babes on boards than chicks on sticks. I'll bet you ski, since you two are together," Martin said.

Now he seemed much more normal to Troy. He chatted a while longer and promised to post their photo on his site, if Martin sent him video of himself riding.

"Hey, I heard you're going out to the lake. Be careful out there. The Dark Lady is on the loose. I saw her last week. Second time. These simpletons don't believe me. Anyway, she only comes out at dark. She isn't dark. She's a to-die for white blond with big dark eyes and Angelina Jolie maxi lips, almost as beautiful as Silke. Almost," Martin said and winked.

Silke chuckled. "It's been a pleasure, all, but we have places to go and people to find and my time with Troy is limited. Nice to meet you, Martin. 'Bye everybody."

On their way out, Silke stopped out front, making Troy pause. "Be convincing," she whispered and slid her arms around his neck, drawing him down to passionately kiss him.

The shock passed almost immediately, pushed aside by a pleasant heat, and he returned her false ardor, except, his wasn't pretend. She tasted succulent, and he wanted to savor her. His body recalled kissing her before, having forgotten the beating shortly thereafter, and reacted as if it had been starving for a sweet treat. He was lightheaded and momentarily oblivious to everything else, including he was supposed to be acting. For those timeless moments, his worldly cares and concerns faded away.

"Get a room," Josh joked lightly as he ambled by.

That brought Troy back to reality. He relaxed his grip, although he didn't want to let go.

Silke slowly drew back, beaming. "Um. I missed you, too," she breathed. She appeared flushed, combing her fingers through her hair. He wondered if her pulse was racing, too. She seized his arm and strolled off, guiding him down the sidewalk. "That was convincing."

He needed time to recover from the pleasant moment of vertigo. He almost expected Dillon to show up and punch him. For the moment, Dillon could stay absent a little longer. "I apologize, I got carried away. Uh, where are we going now?"

"Back to the . . . oh, silly me. The other direction. Thanks, Troy, that kiss should buy me some time." she said, turning him around and laughing as they took the direct route to the parking lot. The stroll had turned into a brisk stride.

Ahead, he spotted the source of feeling spied upon. Camera in hand, the man in the bowler stood coolly while they approached him. The black SUV sat parked nearby. Troy couldn't see if anyone sat in the vehicle. He decided on the direct approach. The man smiled a ticket scalper's grin. "Can I help you, Troy Bane?"

Troy was surprised at being recognized, but this guy seemed confrontational, not a fan. "Yes, you can," Troy replied coolly.

"Why are you following us? Is this about Dillon?" Silke snapped. She stepped forward, aggressive.

"Us? Dillon who? And who are you, lady? Someone saucy, I hope, with a scandalous background," the man crooned. He smugly ignored her and turned to Troy. "Bane, I read you died."

"God sent me back. He gave me carte blanche to hunt down and embarrass nosey gossip reporters. Your name was?" Troy said.

"Uh, the name's Deng, Jimmy Deng. I'm a photo journalist," he stammered. He reached into his pocket, and Troy, already feeling paranoid, prepared to defend himself. Deng grinned again, removed a cigarette pack, shook one free, and lit it with flare as though he were being auditioned for a modern The Fonz. "I freelance. I've been doing research on the Silver Goddess. The most gorgeous woman to ever rip snow and walk the planet."

"Raquel Sterling," Silke growled.

Troy thought she might punch Deng.

"You're following me because of her?" Troy asked. Deng nodded.

"Did you take photos of us?" Silke asked.

"Yes, at the airport, I saw her kiss Troy and whisper in his ear. Now you're kissing him. Lucky him and I hope, newsworthy. Hey, Troy, weren't you and Raquel a couple a long time ago before she left you in ruins like all the others? Any chance of a reunion?"

"I want those photos deleted," Silke snarled. Before Deng could blink, she swiftly seized his right arm in a painful hold. Howling, he dropped his cigarette and slipped to one knee.

"I didn't give you permission, and I've had issues with stalkers, Mr. Deng. You either erase it right now, or I sprain some fingers while Troy calls the sheriff," Silke said. Her eyes had a dangerous slant to them.

"You can't do this!" Deng cried, even as he handed over his camera.

She checked it, deleting photos. For good measure, she removed the memory stick, too, then she returned the camera.

"Who do you think you are?" Deng asked.

"No one of consequence," Silke said. She handed the camera back to Deng. Troy captured a photo of the expression on his face. The sheriff might want it.

Looking stricken and worried about Silke's state of mind, Deng retreated toward his big car. "You haven't heard the last of this."

"No one of consequence. *The Princess Bride?*" Troy asked as they both settled into the car seat and buckled up. Silke nodded, and they shared a laugh.

She steered them over to State Street, the main street and state lines of Tennessee and Virginia, so he would feel at home, or so she claimed. They cruised by King Clothiers, White Dog Paper Company, Mountain Empire Comics, and Mccraken Antiques, as well as the renovated Paramount Theatre, and Theatre Bristol, the latter State Street mainstays. Their marquees announced live performances of *Cats* and *Love Bites.*

She drove toward the huge, white and red brick First Baptist Church, past the landmark train depot, across the tracks and under the huge metal sign proclaiming: Bristol TN/VA, A GOOD PLACE TO LIVE. Was she reminding him of what he already knew?

She followed Pennsylvania to Maple to Virginia Street, and it eventually turned into State Route 34 and Highway 421. The road was four lanes wide here but would get narrower and curvy soon enough. The terrain around the lake meandered up, down and around.

"Again, thanks for being my beau."

"You've made a good impression on folks here in a short amount of time. People care about you and don't want to see you hurt. That Mini Hulk, Dexter, and Mrs. Fleenor told me I had better treat you well or else. It sounded ominous," he said.

Silke laughed. "Dexter is a pussycat, but, do you want to know that Mr. Fleenor is president of the local gun and shooting chapter? I hear he's an expert marksman and hunter. He thinks of me as the daughter he never had."

"That's great. Now I have a target on my back," Troy said.

"I will appreciate the peace. You don't make me seem a liar about my quest for The One, as you put it. So what are you looking for?" Silke asked.

"The reason I'm still alive," Troy replied. He turned to stare out the window because if he looked over at Silke, his imagination would flirt with the impossible.

He prayed for strength and guidance as they passed church after church, with signs leading to gatherings of Southern Baptists, Lutherans, Catholics, and Mormon and Jewish temples. Though the latter was empty, the other lots were full this morning.

Often, cemeteries were part of the yard, standing stone after headstone after tombstone. He had almost been there. He couldn't help but wonder, though, if he had used up his share of miracles. Well, if one could gather prayer power, this seemed a likely place.

He would need tolerance and patience to survive Maraders Marina. The search for the missing liar and philanderer, Dillon, would start there. Troy was a little worried what they might uncover.

Seven: Blood Brothers

Fading light greeted Troy when he woke up. He felt like he was floating, and he laughed when he realized he was resting peacefully on an inflatable raft bobbing on a lake. Wherever he was, it smelled delicious. The savory aroma of cooking meat hung over the water almost as thick as the Smoky Mountain fog. It must be late in the day, as the sun's rays angled low over the treetops of the forested peaks surrounding the lake. A stone splashed next to him, skipping past him and startling him alert.

"Get up! Dinner is ready!" John called. His jar-headed friend paused before tossing another stone. A long time ago, he had been a pro-pitching prospect, even throwing a summer for the Bristol Pirates. An excellent butterflier, he had been an

Olympic swimming hopeful. None of it would pan out, but John was part fish, so he signed up with the Coast Guard as a rescue diver.

Troy rolled off the raft into the water and waded ashore. He stopped, shocked when he saw his eight friends. They looked as young and hairy as they had a decade ago and relaxed around a campfire with game meat on a spit. Venison sizzled, and the flames flared and danced under dripping fat. The fire light warmed the faces of his friends. They were a mixture of personalities, from outdoorsy and athletic to geeky and techno.

His vision was fuzzy, and his balance was off. Was he inebriated?

No, not drunk, Troy realized. A memory from the past when he was younger.

How would it twist this memory of them celebrating Jambo's sixteenth birthday by hunting and feasting? He knew how it ended in the real world.

With blood.

The last to turn sixteen, Jamie Boy was already taller than any of them, as well as prone to nap attacks. Even now, his face covered by a curly mop of hair, Jambo's fuzzy chin sat on the chest of his East Tennessee State shirt, which he would attend one day. He would claim leading yells and lifting girls wore him out. Today, rising before dawn to go bow hunting had left him exhausted. One day he would be renowned for his restoration of classic cars at his own auto body shop, ETC, East Tennessee Classics.

"Tasty," Dillon said, licking his lips. Besides being Troy's best friend, Dillon would become an investigative journalist for CBS out of Dallas. A strapping figure, he also loved sports and the outdoors, making the hunk a good fit for Texas.

Troy would never be able to thank him enough for the gift of a kidney. His own had quit working at thirteen, and Dillon had been a match, going under the knife for him. When Troy had gone west for college and skiing bigger mountains, Dillon had come along, too. He possessed a devil-may-care smile and adventuresome air. Because he was as eye-catching as his sister, people were compelled to chat with him. They certainly didn't want to fight with him. At sixteen, he earned his black belt. He would go on to earn college scholarships in Karate and Tae Kwon Do. Careers and travel finally separated the inseparable duo.

Dillon grinned. "Jambo sure excels at sports with patience, like fishing and deer hunting."

"Oh, he was patient all right. He fell asleep and woke up with the buck standing almost on top of him," Jay chortled. J-Man, they called him, because Jay was The Man Who Could Fix Anything with duct tape and bailing wire. He was built like a bespectacled bear with furry limbs and a curly beard. J-Man had skinned the buck and prepped it for dinner, like the Boy Scouts of yore, or so he had proclaimed. The Eagle Scout was destined to pilot helicopters and own his company, Beck N Call.

"I'm surprised he didn't scare it off. Oh, that's right he doesn't move that fast," Marader said. Dashing and studly, if you asked him, Tom Marader poked J-Man in the shoulder with a comb, and then the cocky SOB ran it through his platinum blond hair. It looked that way from too much time in the pool, swimming, life guarding, and scamming babes. He had a few manly scars from the fights that followed. Marader adjusted his Crimson Tide hat and paused to swig from a plastic cup of moonshine, and then he grinned like the cat that just ate Tweety Bird.

"Even a blind squirrel finds an acorn now and then," Spider said. Troy's moody buddy wore tie-die. As the unofficial keeper of the flames, he sat with his long limbs folded next to the fire he occasionally poked with a stick. Below a Beatles' style-haircut, his sunken eyes were in shadow, and his expression was distant with one eyebrow always cocked like Mr. Spock contemplating a conundrum. Likely, though, Spider was pondering the philosophies of life in the small inferno.

Was God in the fire? Destructive and yet, bringing heat and life? Spider would become an architect, builder, and avid, global-trotting supporter of Habitat for Humanity. Almost dying had made Spider more introspective. Troy could relate. With teeth sharp like a vampire, he looked up at Troy and grinned as if Spider knew that Troy was thinking about death.

Blond, big-boned and lantern-jawed, Dennis Rentzel breathed on his glasses, then he rubbed them on his gray Wash U t-shirt before putting the shades back on. His future was so bright as an engineer that he had to wear sunglasses. They might be *The Matrix* issue specs for all Troy knew. Denny's father was in construction, while the son was into destruction. He liked to blow things up, whether it be demolition or special effects. Denny would earn engineering, plus, later, a surprising degree in Divinity studies from local, prestigious King College. Two months ago, Denny had been ordained, a far cry from his challenging years of excessive boozing. Fortunately, he had found a wonderful woman named Hope to go along with his faith. Still, Father Dennis sounded strange when directed toward Denny.

"Anybody care for fish?" wild-haired Knives asked. His slim friend wouldn't have that hair in ten years, but he would be just as lean and toned, still swimming and skiing. He often caught and cleaned the fish on their outings. He was an expert with all kinds of blades, including tossing and juggling them. Dillon's most cerebral of friends wanted to continue the legacy of his father and grandfather to become a doctor. A graduate of UVA's med school, he was in surgical residency at Bristol Memorial and working part time for the county coroner's office.

This moment of dual knowledge was unsettling. But then, dreaming rarely made sense. Troy tried to wake up, but he found it changed nothing. He trudged in the sandy footsteps of the past.

"It doesn't get much better than this! Oops!" John pronounced as he rose to his feet and stumbled. His can of beer foamed and ran over, dripping to the ground. "Being outdoors in a beautiful place, good food, a blazing fire, beer . . . and fantastic friends."

"A toast, I propose a toast," Knives called out. Everyone turned to him. "To the best of friends. May we all stay that way."

To a man, all nine of them vigorously raised whatever they were drinking, slinging moonshine, beer, Coca-Cola and root beer every which way. It rained down upon them in celebration. They had hunted, fished, and played together for years. They hoped it would never end.

But it would end. Everyone would graduate in the spring, except Jambo, and go their separate ways to different universities. Some would stay local. Most stayed in the south. Denny had attended college in the Midwest while Troy and Dillon had gone west. Everything had changed over the next year or so. Troy tried to savor this moment with friends who were better, of course, than the brothers he never had.

Belches and sighs were numerous before Spider spoke again. He had a crazed look in his dark, sunken eyes. Troy wouldn't be surprised if he had been eating morning glory seeds and tripping. "I say we do more than toast our friendship. We must bind ourselves closer together."

"Such as?" J-Man asked suspiciously.

"We're like brothers, right?" Spider asked. He eyed them all, causing them to study each other.

Over the years, they had helped each other out of difficult jams, physical, mental and surprisingly, emotional. Spider had lost his father. Jambo's brother had died in a work accident. All of them lost a friend in a stupid drinking and driving car wreck, likely saving some of them from drinking and driving and dying. Thanks, Robby, might you rest in peace.

Spider held up a knife, one he had borrowed from Knives. The blade was the color of bronze. The edges glinted in the flickering light. With a great show, he lightly ran it across the palm of his left hand. A thin line of blood welled. His face was serious when he said, "We should be blood brothers. Blood is thicker than water, beer and moonshine, more precious than money. We should confirm our friendship as the natives of this land once did."

"I'm not that drunk," Marader said.

Spider offered the knife to J-Man. Without hesitation, he nicked his left hand, the thin line barely drawing blood along his palm. He gave the blade to Troy who gave him a dubious look.

"Don't you want to be my brother?" J-Man asked.

"I'm not sure I want to share blood with everyone," Troy replied, pointedly staring at Marader.

"You're just jealous! With my blood, you'll be virile and in demand," Marader crowed.

For a moment, Troy thought about stabbing Marader, but this was before Raquel had come between them, and the blade seemed to move of its own accord, nicking and drawing blood from the meaty part of his own hand. "Happy? I need a chaser now."

Troy passed the knife to Marader who grinned as he joined in the bloodletting, then he gave the blade back to its owner. With a comment on sanitation and blood borne diseases, Knives grazed himself. He presented the handle to Denny. The ritual continued on to John and Jambo who both only grunted for a comment.

Dillon was last. He caught his breath as the warm blade bit. Crimson seeped from the wound into his palm. They shuffled around in a circle. The blood of friends blended as they clasped hands and pressed palms.

"Live long and prosper," Denny proposed. They lifted their drinks. Smeared blood marked their fingers and then oozed down their arms.

"Friends until death," Dillon suggested.

"And beyond! Jinx!" Spider and Troy added.

"Now that we're brothers, I want to talk about something, brother to brother," Dillon said.

"It's about eating your spray cheese, isn't it?" Marader asked.

Troy looked up expectantly. What his friend said next was mildly surprising. Even so, Troy never expected it to cause him any personal problems.

Dillon held up the knife for emphasis. It caught the fire light and winked, signaling it was ready to draw blood. "There will be no incest."

Marader chuckled. "You're not only not my type, you're the wrong gender, dude."

"But Silke isn't," J-Man said, realizing what Dillon meant.

"Exactly. Keep your hands, your lips, your thoughts, especially your imaginations off Silke," Dillon said.

"She's thirteen," Denny said.

"Soon enough, she'll be fifteen or sixteen."

"And she is going to be so hot. Those legs!" Marader said.

"Exactly. Touch her, eyeball her, even flirt with her, and I will rip off your balls," Dillon grinned. He was the only one smiling. "I'm serious. You start looking at her or getting ideas, I'll give you a first warning courtesy of a black eye, then a second by breaking your nose, because you probably doubt my seriousness and resolve. How's that? Welcome to the family. Cheers."

Troy opened his eyes. Well, Dillon was right. Along with intelligent, caring, and charismatic, Silke was an alluring beauty. What would Dillon think about them kissing? If Troy believed in omens, which he didn't, he would believe the dream was telling him not to find Dillon. Ridiculous. Last time Troy had kissed Silke, Dillon had only given him a black eye.

He knew they were close to the lake when they passed the 421 Area Emergency Service. He hoped they would never need it.

"A penny for your thoughts."

"I was recalling the day we became blood brothers," Troy said.

"You've been good for one another, especially those who stayed locally. You know Tommy remodeled, right?" Silke said.

Troy nodded. "Yes, but no details."

"Troy, are you all right?"

He nodded, though it wasn't true.

"I wanted to make sure you weren't practicing your moody boyfriend act. Tell me about your latest trip."

He smiled and recounted his recent job in Alaska, of flying by helicopter, snow-shoeing, riding a dog sled, skiing and taking photos. How they had trekked and skied under the midnight sun, including a night when the Northern Lights were active. He promised to show her the photos later.

Several miles rolled by and soon a sign proclaimed MARADERS Marina 1 MI. The last road before the bridge was Knob Park Road. Back in the day, Troy and his friends had launched the boat north of here at Observation Park on Knob Road, what they called Ob Knob in Virginia. They would warm up the boat and their bodies by cruising down the serpentine channel and under this bridge en route to the largest open basin of the reservoir.

When they reached the 421 Warren Continuous Truss Bridge, the vista widened, and he could see far from above South Holston Lake. Patches of fog still lingered, but the smoke wasn't blowing their direction, so Troy could see the green water spread out on both sides of the bridge and sprawl to the southwest. He was shocked, despite his nightmares, by the amount of faded red, rocky shore. It might be a hundred feet below the normal water line.

Shortly after the end of the bridge, Silke turned the car left at a large Maraders sign and then quickly took a right down a wide gravel road. A series of six signs read: Thanks for your patience. Due to construction. Only boats, gas, bait & restrooms open. Sorry for the inconvenience. It will be worth it! Cheers!

The uneven gravel led through the woods and patchy fog

on the way to the water. Dark green one-ton trucks and equipment from Rentzel Construction sat silent and unmanned, lining both sides of the road. Pallets of boards and other building supplies were stacked, taking up much of the parking lot, except for a landing pad marked off for helicopters.

"Wow, he has his own helipad," Troy said, impressed.

Sitting along the shore was a two-story, white-washed and green-trimmed wood building with a slanted roof, second floor balcony and deck around the ground floor. The shore side housed a general store and chandlery. According to signs, a bar and restaurant sat with a view on the lakeside. To the left of it all, a long ramp followed a concrete driveway down toward the water's edge and then along the shoreline to four covered, floating boat slips. Troy estimated 120 berths, and most were in use.

"Dad's old truck is still here, so Dillon didn't drive off," Silke said, pointing to a nicked and dinged up white Ford pickup. Troy remembered when it was brand spanking new. She parked next to it, and they climbed out to inspect the truck. Wet camping gear had been tossed in the bed.

A big, red Dodge Ram truck with white flames and Maraders Marina painted on the side was parked near the walkway. Next to it, Troy recognized Spider's green 70's VW camper van.

Troy followed Silke down the swaying ramp. They headed for the waterside, passing bait tanks outside the store. The paint on the building looked fresh. Green outdoor carpet had been laid down. A few oily trash barrels were set against the building, but otherwise, everything had been upgraded or vastly improved since Troy had been here three years ago when most of the blood brothers had celebrated turning twenty-five.

They moved along the side of the building, heading toward the lakeside deck. Music could be heard coming from an upstairs window. Moans and grunts mingled with the song.

Silke closed her eyes and blushed.

"He isn't answering his phone because he's screwing around," Troy said.

"Literally. Shall we surprise him?" Silke asked.

"Why not? We want him to be his normal, excitable self. I have an idea that'll have an immediate impact," Troy said.

When Troy turned the corner, he almost fell over a sunbather wearing earbuds and little else. To maintain his balance, Troy grabbed the side of the lounger. The sudden jarring startled the ravishing, wavy-haired Latina, and she dropped her cigarette. She was voluptuous and toned, hot and gleaming. She wore strips of fabric, a jaguar-patterned thong and skimpy, matching top. Troy felt her heat and a nearly overwhelming desire that struck like a wave. He felt like a seventeen-year-old again, off balance from Raquel's touch and Silke's pretend kiss. He barely compartmentalized the sudden tidal wave and almost laughed aloud at the book next to her, *Women are From Venus, Men Are from Mars.*

"Sorry about that. I usually look before I leap," he said. The Latina watched him warily as he retreated. She wore earbuds, so she hadn't heard his footsteps.

"She looks eighteen," Silke hissed quietly.

"She reminds me of you back in the day when you wore that burgundy bikini your senior year. Guys used to ask me all the time if you were my girl," Troy replied.

"You remember that swimsuit?" she asked. She appeared surprised and amused.

When he had told guys no, they called him a fool. Ah what was the saying, fools go where angels fear to tread? "You bet. I have a photo with you, Dillion and I standing together on the back of the boat. Your hair was bright blue. You said it was the most fun you'd ever had in an afternoon."

She nodded, a wistful look in her eyes.

The sunbather removed her earbuds and tied up her bikini top. "Hi there. I'm Desiree, and I'm twenty-one, legal to drink, thank you. How can I help you?" she asked. She retrieved her cigarette, then she lithely stood and stretched.

"We're friends of Tommy's, but we're looking for Dillon Urich, who was here yesterday," Troy said.

"Dillon? Hmm," Desiree said. She studied Troy as she dragged on the cigarette with a sensual flair. She offered a small smile as she peeked over her sunglasses. Her eyes were dark with flashes of green and looked young though not innocent. He felt her visually take stock of him. Silke moved protectively closer to him.

"Dillon's my brother," Silke said.

"A very handsome guy and charming, too. A big time flirt. I see the resemblance. He was here with all the other grads for the reunion, but I haven't seen him today," Desiree said. "Have we met? Wait, I know now. On the bar wall."

"A wanted poster? Or for a good time call?" Silke asked tartly.

Desiree smiled winningly, a cheerleader's victory smile. "Good time call, I'm sure. You're the extremist, the outdoor guy who skis, climbs, jumps and shoots video. Hmm. Troy Bane, you look fabulous considering Tommy said you almost died."

"I died," Troy said and paused. "Now I've returned to haunt him."

Desiree rocked with laughter. "Oh, you sound like fun, and you look scrumptious."

Troy must have blushed. He was unaccustomed to so much female attention.

"How cute. Like I said, I'm Desiree Sanchez. I work the summers for Tommy when I'm not attending VT where I'm a biology major. Funny, I'm looking for a man, too. If I help you, will you help me?" she asked.

"So, you don't know anything about Dillon?" Silke persisted.

"A little. Long before I slipped out of bed, Dillon took a Sea-Doo. He hasn't come back yet. As far as I know, his truck is still out there."

"Is Tommy here?" Silke asked.

"Since you're friends of Tommy's, you know he'll be busy for a while," Desiree said. She jerked a thumb toward the second floor. The grunting and moaning grew louder. "I just work here, I don't get involved with the boss. Wolves are not my type."

From upstairs, a squeal was followed by a devious laugh. A repeated thudding sound followed, the upper walls of the place shaking.

"It's why I wear earbuds."

"And not much else, apparently," Silke said cattily.

"You would look good in it, too. You can borrow it when you're serious about fishing," Desiree replied.

"Anyone else around?" Troy asked.

"Spider's off in the woods meditating and realigning himself with God and Nature," she said and yawned. "The Doc, sleepy James, and Father Dennis went to church."

"Mind if we play a trick on Tommy?" Troy asked.

Desiree debated. "I heard you guys pranked each other. Will you post it on YouTube?" she asked. He nodded and explained. "I'm in."

Troy lifted the barrel and carried it out to the edge of the platform. "Look for something to fan the smoke," Troy said. Silke found a large piece of cardboard. "Perfect."

Desiree returned with an extinguisher and a pack of matches. Silke found a hose and stood ready at the spigot in case of emergency. Troy struck a match and dropped it into the barrel. The rags and newspaper immediately caught and birthed flames. They roared but died down quickly, leaving black smoke to twist upward. Troy fanned the cloud to help it rise.

"Why do you provoke him?" Silke asked.

Troy got his Go Pro video camera out and recorded the dark cloud thickening and crawling over the lip of the balcony. "Blood brothers remember?" he replied. He watched his handiwork. "Besides, he'd rather be given grief than ignored."

"I hope I don't get fired for this," Desiree commented. She stood back, worrying her lower lip, all while she held her phone ready to capture a video of the moment.

The balcony was almost obscured by the oily cloud.

"What if he comes down swinging?" Silke asked.

"I'll take the heat and cool him down," Troy said. At the outside faucet, he turned on the water, filling the hose, and readied the sprayer head to put out a flare up.

Eight: Chopper Ride

The response took less than a minute. The balcony stopped shaking, and the moans halted. Troy heard Marader. "Do you smell something?"

Two voices responded no.

He and Silke exchanged glances. Two girls? Silke rolled her eyes.

"Hey, Desiree!" Marader yelled from upstairs.

Troy shook his head, reminding her to stay quiet. She replied with a sweet, flirtatious smile.

"Desiree? Desiree! Oh shit! Something's on fire!"

"You might want to look away to spare your eyes the trauma of seeing Tommy Boy au natural," Troy said.

Scrambling sounds came from upstairs. Heavy footsteps ran across the ceiling then thundered down the stairs. Nude, sweaty, and carrying a fire extinguisher, Marader burst out the store door. It smacked loud against the wall. He stopped immediately when he saw them standing casually on the dock. Silke had her back turned.

"Thank you, Troy. I would've needed therapy for years," Silke said.

The look of intense concern faded from Marader's expression. Troy tossed him a towel, hitting him in the face. Marader wrapped it around his waist, creating a towel kilt. "You shitheads!" He held himself ready, hands balled into fists, a moment from fighting. A wild look shone in his eyes, a reckless gleam.

Troy wondered if he had miscalculated. Oh well, perhaps this was a long time in coming. A fight might clear the air. Too bad he felt like crap right now. He readied the hose to start with shock and then fight with awe.

Marader stepped forward, fist raised, drawing back, then he broke into a perfect smile and boomed out laughter. "Yeah! I should've guessed I had visiting pyromaniacs. Troy, damn good to see you again. And Silke, you're looking saucy, especially your backside. You must do Pilates. I love a woman who likes ropes."

Her back still turned, Silke crossed her arms. "Tom, so sorry to interrupt, but we knew only something serious could bring you downstairs. Where's my brother?"

"You interrupted me for that? Your brother? But come think of it, that's a damned good question that deserves a damned good answer. Yeah, where is your brother? He borrowed one of my Sea-Doos early this morning and hasn't come back. I guess I should be worried, but he's a big boy and an investigative reporter. He probably found something and is engrossed. Notice the big word there."

"A second question is where are your shorts?" Silke asked.

"Funny. Put out the fire and come on in for a beer. Desiree, would you get these two a brew while I get sartorially attired?"

"Sure. Anything to speed up that process."

Marader looked at Troy. "I don't know what's wrong with that girl. She could have me in a heartbeat. I don't know why I even keep her around." Still ranting, he returned inside.

Troy hosed down the fire and doused the flames. He was glad they hadn't argued with fists.

Beaming, Marader returned with a woman under each arm. They appeared to be in their late teens and voluptuous, wearing short-shorts and tank tops from Virginia Tech. The busty, young woman with long, straight white blond hair nudged Marader. "Troy Bane and Silke Urich meet the sisters of the staff. This is Heidi, and this is Sandy," he said as he hugged the curly-haired blond with doe eyes.

"Some things never change," Troy said.

Marader smiled broadly and strutted over to Troy. They shook hands, Marader squeezing, Troy smiling. "Why would I want them to? Ya know, I've really missed you, Troy. That barrel fire was cute. Takes me back to the fire at your house. Ha!"

"Thanks. Most of my practical jokes involve snow."

"Yeah, how's the body?"

"I can do everything I did before, I just suffer a little more and longer for it," Troy replied wryly.

"Good. Chicks love it that I know a guy in films. I still show them at night during the summer. People know I'm different, but they love me! So, guys, what's up?! Is it party take 2?"

"If you mean search party, yes," Troy replied.

"What's up? You mean besides a murder, a floating body, desecrated graves, driftwood made from coffins, and three missing people? Two of them your friends?" Silke asked, her expression incredulous, hands on hips.

"Yeah, besides all that. I noticed you didn't ask me how I'm feeling. I did launch off a coffin."

"You sounded healthy a few minutes ago."

"Sexual healing. You should try it. Good for anger management, and whatever else ails you!"

Silke closed her eyes. "What about my brother? When did you last see him?"

"He slept here last night, a bunch of us did, after we escaped from Bug Island between storm fronts. Doesn't rain for a month, then it soaks us long enough to rain on our parade, then like a tease, it stops."

"Focus. Dillon?"

"His note said he was going to Cemetery Ridge to meet Deputy Burt at sunrise. He scribbled 5:30 next to his name."

"He was supposed to pick me up at the airport, and he didn't. You know he's a stickler about those things," Troy said.

"Yeah, appointments and schedules. I assume you called

him, or you wouldn't be hassling me."

"He isn't answering his phone," Troy said.

"Lucky you. I rather have Silke pick me up anyway," Marader laughed maniacally.

"Not even in your dreams," she replied.

"What about John?" Troy asked.

"Yesterday, we looked for him and his squeeze—Sherry, who had thighs that probably broke him in half, lucky guy— and cruised around skiing while searching for my boat. We never found any sign of him, her or it, except for the dive flag off Cemetery Ridge. I even have my boats rigged with GPS locators to reduce insurance costs, and nothing shows up. We had planned to go diving today, but well, our normal plans were scuttled. Dillon does seem to be gone a long time. Cell reception has sucked the last few days. J-Man said a tree hit a tower. Took it out. Let's try a landline."

Using the store phone, Silke tried Dillon's number. When all she received was his voice mail box, Marader stepped in and called Deputy Burt Glazier. They chatted briefly. "Burt's at Cemetery Ridge, where divers are searching, but there's no sign of Dillon. He was a no show this morning," Marader told them.

"I want to rent a boat," Silke said.

"I have serious doubts about loaning another one of my watercrafts to another Urich," Marader mused aloud. Silke pouted, and he forestalled her protest. "Look at it from my point of view. I've lost two assets in two days to two friends who didn't return them."

"And how is this my fault? They are your blood brothers and males."

"Tell you what. I'll think about it. Try calling the other marinas first," Marader said.

They all took a number and called a marina. Silke phoned Lakeview, the closest to Cemetery Ridge, while Marader called the Laurel Marina and Yacht Club to the southwest. Troy checked with the Friendship Marina to the southeast, experiencing the same results as the others. Three strikes, and they were out of southern marinas. It seemed unlikely Dillon would be to the north, but Silke called Painter Creek. Troy reached Sportsman Marina, but like everybody else, nobody had seen Dillon or the Sea-Doo.

"Now can I rent a boat to go hunting then diving? If I don't find anything, I want to dive Cemetery Ridge before the lake's clarity worsens from the runoff," she said.

Marader made a show of grumbling and pondering her request. "You have a dive cert?"

"Yes, I've been off the coasts of California and Hawaii."

"Lucky you. You can't see shit here compared to Pacific waters. You know, I think it's a bad idea to let a hot-tempered and impatient, even if foxy, lady out with one of my boats. Encouraging you to dive sounds even riskier. You shouldn't be diving when you're upset, you know that, right? With that in mind, I could relax you, and you could change my mind," Marader asked smugly.

With a huff, Silke stormed outside. The slamming door rocked the place. Marader definitely enjoyed it. "Hate is just a step away from love," he grinned.

Thankfully, they were interrupted by the sound of a helicopter. The whup-whupping grew louder as the whirlybird neared. The cove enhanced the sound, amplifying it.

"J-Man. I'll bet he's here to search for my missing assets. He's such a Boy Scout."

"Eagle Scout," Troy said.

"Yeah, that's right. I love the guy," Marader said. He and Jay Beck had been close friends since second grade, even rooming in college before Marader transferred to Alabama.

Troy hurried around the building, heading for the helipad. When they had been talking on the lakeside, the structure had protected him from the sound and wind. Both buffeted him now, but he enjoyed watching J-Man land the J-copter. He operated it for his company, Beck N Call, Aerial Services. A big part of his business was spraying foliage killer along the phone and power lines through the mountains in the areas too difficult or expensive for manpower to clear. He had also been known to dust crops and transport organs for emergency transplants to the local Tri Cities hospitals.

Depending on its payload, the UT orange, Bell helicopter could carry four. The chopper looked a little odd, racks underneath holding tanks, tubes and sprayers. J-Man waved briefly then guided the J-copter to settle perfectly in the center of the bullseye of the landing pad. The whirlybird's blades immediately began to slow, and shortly, J-Man removed his headphones, adjusted his aviator Ray Bans, and climbed out to amble their way. The big man was part bear, thick-necked and round-faced, hairy with a beard shadow and thick brows below a Tennessee Vols hat.

"Well, you finally made it. Damn good to see you, Troy," J-Man said as he approached, meaty hand outstretched.

"It's good to be here, except for the circumstances. I'm surprised you're not fighting the wildfire."

"They're still assessing the situation. They would call me if they needed extra equipment. Silke, young lady, you're lookin' seriously hot. You'll only give Marader ideas."

"He already had those ideas. It's one of the reasons I carry a sidearm."

"Point made. I'm hoping I can find his boats and that will lead us to John and your brother," J-Man said.

"Now you're talking. Can I come along for the ride?"

"Of course. Troy?" J-Man asked.

"Count me in. I enjoy choppers," Troy said. They had used them in *Powder Drop* to plunge into soft snow when the helicopter couldn't land anywhere near. Could he do that now? Or would he be scared, thinking of dying?

"Hey, Tommy Boy, are you joining our aerial search for your missing water craft?" J-Man yelled.

"I am not riding in the same helicopter with him. What? He won't let me rent a boat to look for Dillon," Silke replied to his look.

"I'll strap him underneath, so he can get a better look, how's that?" J-Man asked.

Marader sauntered over to meet his friend. They high-fived then fist bumped. "You have three pairs of eyes. Isn't that good enough?"

"Fine. Be that way. I think you'd make a sexy hood ornament, but we don't need you. I have cameras set up along the front and sides, so there. Come along, kids. Silke, pretty girls ride up front."

"Hey, Silke. If you three find something, we'll take a boat out and look at it," Marader said.

Troy strolled around the helicopter, checking out its undercarriage and racks. J-Man had attached Go Pro cameras pointing left, right and ahead to capture images of whatever ground and water they passed over.

Troy swung open the door for Silke, getting a beaming smile in thanks. He made sure her armed purse was in, then he closed her door and opened the rear one to climb into the back, taking a seat and shutting the door. He slipped on a headset to protect his ears.

J-Man flipped several switches and waited for the rotors to build up speed. The whirling winds whipped up as the blades spun faster, their moan turning into a mechanical whine. J-Man took the joystick in hand, maneuvered the pedals, and the chopper gradually elevated to two hundred feet. Silke screamed with delight.

Going south away from the metal bridge and the highway, J-Man flew lower and steered them above the shockingly wide stretch of red dirt and shale composing the eastern shore. It seemed twice as wide as Troy had ever seen it. It made him think someone had pulled the plug under the lake and let it drain too long.

The Holston Mountains ran north and south, and the same named forest densely blanketed it. The tree-thick slopes were tinged hazy blue, adding to the woods unhealthy appearance. Branches with wilting leaves drooped, browned as if they had been toasted. Swaths of craggy, dead gray snags seemed to plead to the sky for rain. Looking much greener than the foliage, the lake sprawled southwesterly for a half dozen miles. It appeared to end with a towering wall of yellow-brown smoke.

Dillon, where in the blue blazes are you? Troy wondered. And what had happened to sleepy Bristol? He accepted a pair of binoculars from Silke and started scanning the lake's surface and shoreline.

"All right, here we go, Air Jay. Troy, man, I wish you had been here to see Tommy Boy, in the glow of the fireworks, fly off a coffin in his best Superman imitation. We have it recorded, but to see it live gives you the impression God has a sense of humor, morbid at times, even dark, but a sense of humor," J-Man said.

The copter turned east up an inlet, starting with a stretch of small coves into the Cherokee National Forest. The pontoon boaters leaving the Friendship Marina waved and raised cans of Budweiser in their direction.

They flew on to Lynn Lick Creek where an angler wrestled with his fishing pole, bent nearly in half and forcing him to shuffle around. His buddy was recording it, probably hoping something funny or stupid happened.

Troy could see over the trees and sloping terrain to the nearly dry gulch of one of the Underwood Creek branches as it twisted its way back from the body of the lake. With the low water, the coves were much shorter, so it didn't take long to visually search them before returning to the main channel. The shoreline zigzagged for a mile or so before reaching the mouth of three inlets, including the beginning of the Underwood branches. All Troy spotted was a deflated riding tube. Silke pointed out a lost blue and white IGLOO cooler bobbing all alone.

Suddenly, the helicopter sputtered and dipped ten feet, taking Troy's stomach with it. The bottom simply fell out. His knees jumped up and one almost hit him in the chin. He grabbed hold, but the fall ended.

The props continued to spin. The helicopter flew along, the sputtering just a blip in the moment.

"Jay, what's the deal?" Silke asked.

"It's no big deal," J-Man began.

The sputter and drop, along with gasps, happened a second time. Silke added a short scream while the J-copter dipped a few feet.

"Jay!"

J-Man growled. "No worries. I thought I had that fixed when I cleaned the fuel injectors. It ran fine on the way over. It's not really a problem. It's just annoying."

Silke's expression was dubious. Troy felt the same.

"Scout's honor," J-Man said.

Below them, Camp Tom Howard appeared busy with floating tubers, swimmers, and canoe paddlers. Marader had worked at the place after their junior year. This was the third closest place to Cemetery Ridge, the second was next, Little Oak Camp, where Troy had met Raquel. They had spent weeks cross training by running, swimming, kayaking, hiking and grappling with each other. He felt something digging into his leg, so he checked his pocket, finding a Sterling Sports business card with Raquel's cell phone number. Ha, she knew him well enough to stash a second reminder on him.

"Are you all right?" J-Man asked him.

"I was wondering if I could waterski behind this," he mused.

"I don't know. Never tried, but I don't see why not. Is that how you plan to kill yourself this time?"

"Oh, you know, live fast, die hard," Troy said. His words seemed to trouble Silke.

"Well, you succeeded, so now you can stop," J-Man said. Troy started to retort, found the comment poignant and thought on it. Could that be what was different since he had come back? He hadn't been sure, but he felt changed. His perceptions and perspective were certainly altered, perhaps enhanced or more discerning.

A swirling gust shoved the helicopter sideways. The chopper rocked. J-Man flew with the blustery wind, using it to swing into Roaring Fork Creek Cove. Troy was accustomed to micro-bursts of powerfully moving mountain winds at even higher elevations, but Silke white-knuckle clutched onto the seat and an overhead handrail.

"Wow. We have thermals and winds even at this distance," J-Man said.

"Big fires can create their own weather system," Troy said. Many of the pilots who flew for ski tours in the winter also flew for the Forest Service during fire season.

Shaking his head, J-Man piloted them over the twisty passages. They were all short and abrupt, unlike what Troy remembered, ending in muddy gullies with thready creeks that disappeared uphill into draws and washes among the hardwoods and scattered pines. Fork Island, the hunk of land that usually forced you left or right, no longer stood alone, stretching into a peninsula. He could recall spring boating, when the water was high, and skiing completely around the somewhat circular, earthy hump with its bushy top.

Just to the south of where Roaring Fork Creek Cove usually ended and to the west of Riddle Creek, the massive plumb of smoke dominated the sky. The wildfire was a monster.

At the base of the surging cloud of ash, flames devoured the woods. With his binoculars, Troy could see trees crowning, the fire leaping from top to top and spreading swiftly, driven by western gales. He watched a tree erupt like it had been struck by a missile, burning pieces of it shattering in all directions. Those fragments spread the fire faster. Troy prayed Dillon was nowhere close.

In the distance, a larger helicopter with a cable attached to a huge bucket dripping water maneuvered in close to the edge of the wildfire and dumped its load. Where the water struck a great cloud of white steam billowed upward. The chopper turned and flew to Boone Lake, closer to the fire to the southwest.

"It looks dangerous," J-Man said. He reversed direction, leaving Roaring Fork. Out at the main body of the lake, he set the helicopter to hover, letting them take it all in. The dam seemed straight to the west. It didn't look like much from here, a rock wall of perhaps seventy feet. He knew the other side was a set of boulder-stacked terraces, some two hundred and eighty-five feet tall and sixteen hundred feet wide, the largest of its kind on this side of the country. Northward, Cliff Island poked up like a flooded national monument. Nearby he could see four boats around a horn of rock that he had never seen before—Cemetery Ridge.

Would it look like the one in his dream? He shivered.

The last cove, the most southern called Riddle Creek, was the longest finger of water and often the calmest, protected from south and west winds. Two boats could easily pass each other by, perhaps three, even now. It looked more rock lined and less tree lined. Back then, they frequently started at one end, skied it, then stopped, letting the water's surface settle and smooth while they switched skiers or boarders. He recalled Knives skiing so close to land he plucked leaves off an oak tree hanging over the lake.

On the way back into the cove, they reached the Bent Branch overflow spillway. The massive concrete chute in the earthen ridge loomed far above the water level, designed for when the reservoir could hold no more, diverting it down a ravine away from the population and downstream. It wouldn't be needed any time soon. He thought it all looked depressing, his childhood playground gone hellishly wrong.

He spotted something red and focused on it. Just a seat cushion, he figured, but it wasn't a throwable. It was larger, curved along one side of its triangle shape but angular along the other two. He had seen its like before. It was a bow cushion from a boat. He pointed it out to the others, and J-Man piloted them closer.

Suddenly, Troy felt lightheaded. It took a moment for him

to realize they were soaring, the helicopter rising at a dizzying speed. The trees were far below, where Troy had left his stomach behind. He had to swallow to get his heart out of his throat. The lake seemed twice as far away. A moment later, when Troy got his bearings, he realized they were closer to the wildfire's incendiary cloud.

"Cloud suck," J-Man complained, fighting with the joystick. The helicopter kept rising and drawing nearer the smoky plume. Troy could see pieces of ash floating on the super-heated air. Sparks and embers flared or burned out, carried by the swirling winds.

The thermal changed again. The helicopter dropped abruptly, plummeting for the lake, windshield first. Silke screamed. They stared at green water spreading out wide, rushing closer. J-Man cursed as he tried to work his flying magic on the stick and foot pedals.

It wasn't going to be in time. Troy braced for impact.

Flying backwards, they skimmed across the water. The undercarriage of nozzles, tubes and racks submerged, spraying water up and all around them. For a moment, Troy feared they would augur, pitch, and wreck. The spinning rotors caused the water to chop. It splashed up across the windows.

They hit something solid. The helicopter shook as metal crunched underneath his feet, and then they bounced airborne. J-Man used the momentum to pilot them higher, still moving backwards away from the wildfire and its harrowing winds.

"What the hell was that? I don't see anything, but we hit a rock or something," J-Man said.

"Nice Jedi flying," Troy said. He checked on Silke who had paled. "Breathe," he told her. She nodded.

"Hang on, I'm going back."

"What? Are you insane?" Silke asked.

Troy and J-Man shared a look. Did that require an answer? They didn't think they were insane, but others might believe it.

"Your point?" J-Man asked.

"Men," Silke groaned.

"Women. You asked to come along, you know," J-Man said. He steered them lower until they were twenty feet above the water and close to shore. The rotors-driven winds chopped the surface and created waves that seemed to slap around an underwater point or what could be a rock. Troy thought he saw a flash of white, so he took a closer look using the binoculars.

"It could be the bow of a boat. I think I see a light on the port side," Silke said.

Troy thought she was right. Sometimes it was visible, sometimes it wasn't. He wanted to be sure. The drop was short. "Do you have a rope ladder?" Troy asked.

"Are you planning on climbing down? Come to think of it, you could check the damage. We're going to have to land sometime, and it would be nice to know the condition of our landing rails," J-Man said.

"Well, I was planning on jumping into the lake, but looking at the landing gear sounds like a good idea," Troy said.

"You were going to jump? Oh, of course you were," Silke asked. Her smile belied the tone in her voice.

"It's only ten feet," J-Man said. He piloted to within about fifteen feet above the surface. The rotors' wind ruffled the water.

"Do you ever think doing this kind of thing might be the reason you died?" Silke asked.

"That's a rhetorical question, isn't it?" Troy asked. He thought she might be frustrated with him. Likely, she had already overdosed on male energy.

"I have a life preserver. You can toss it down first," J-Man suggested.

"I like the way you're prepared," Silke said.

"I have a reputation to uphold. And if you survive enough things going wrong, you know what to do next time. I have a vest, too. Take it along. If you find something, I'll drop a buoy."

"Troy, really. You don't have to leap out of a helicopter to impress me," Silke said.

"I know it's too late for that. Besides, I'm not going to leap. I'm going on an inspection," Troy said. He removed his shirt and shoes, then he opened the back door.

Silke gasped.

"Nice scars. You just wanted to show them off and that you're ripped," J-Man said. He piloted away from the shore, hovering over deeper water in the middle of the cove.

"That's me, the exhibitionist. According to Dillon, I'm leaping my way monthly from one woman to the next. When I find him, he has some explaining to do," Troy said as he fed out the rope ladder.

"You are a laugh a minute. Have you seen anyone since Ava?" J-Man asked.

"Who is Ava?" Silke asked.

Troy pretended not to hear. After the rope ladder unfurled, he hung onto it for balance and support. He stepped out onto the landing rail. It felt solid, but the strut was bent, and the runner was now angled, no longer flat. He climbed down another rung to check the undercarriage of sprayers. The tank had a crack in it, and a section of pipe was broken, missing a sprayer head. The rail on the other side bent upward pressed against the hull. It was going to be an interesting landing.

"Yeah, there's some damage. Both runners are bent, so the copter won't rest evenly on the pad. The chemical sprayer tank is cracked, and some of the pipes are broken, but I don't think they'll get in the way. I'm going to see if the rail supports my weight."

"Have a safe splash down," J-Man said.

Troy grabbed a rail with his hands then swung his feet free. If there was a problem with the landing gear he wanted to know now, instead of crashing at the helipad. The metal groaned, then the runner fell loose from under the helicopter.

"See ya!" Troy yelled. He hung onto the vest by the straps

as he splashed down and sank below the surface.

For most of his life, he had been swimming or diving in this water, sometimes every day during summer, so he never expected to freak out.

The cold and the weight struck him, pressing down, the reverse of what he should feel in a splash down. It seemed darker and deeper than he could have reached while coasting from the short drop.

He didn't recall hitting his head, but it spun, and he feared he was a moment from drowning in icy water. His throat burned. The water didn't smell right, didn't taste right, coppery as if he had bitten his lip and bled. Worse, there was the tang of mold, gagging him. He felt the heaviness of a tank on his back and the rubber of the regulator between his teeth. What? He was diving? He saw predatory eyes, burning like flames, stark red and yellow, boring into his brain.

"Damme lives."

Troy recalled the voice. How could he forget it? Like taking a knife and scrapping it across the gravel and flesh of a road rash.

"You die so I live."

Harsh pains, the jabbing of needles in his neck, caused Troy to jerk and cough. He sucked in water and thrashed. With a great downward thrust, he pulled and kicked himself to the surface to gasp in air, oh sweet air.

He spat water, shook himself, and wiped his eyes clear. What was that all about? After that, he felt nauseous. He would have thought he had arisen from the depths instead of dropping several feet into the lake. The water felt wrong, heavier and thicker.

"Troy, are you all right?" Silke yelled.

Up above, poised at the open door, her hair falling about her, Silke looked concerned and ready to leap in after him. Wow. How long had he been down?

"I'm okay. There is something here," Troy said. He smiled and waved, seeing the relief on her face. He showed her the tip of a white and red-striped boat. The bow was only inches under the surface. He swam around, taking a mental note of its registration number.

It was Marader's missing boat.

"Here!" Silke yelled. She dropped down a ball buoy, rope, and clip.

He secured it to the port rails near the bow, then he climbed the swaying rope ladder to the open door. Silke helped him inside. "You scared us."

Troy's look was skeptical when he glanced at J-Man. "Sorry about that. The numbers are a match. That is the boat John rented from Marader. Feel like some snorkeling?" Troy asked them.

"Sure. But first, let's see if we can land safely."

"Yeah, about that," Troy said. He gave a comprehensive description of the damage to the bottom of the J-copter.

"I thought as much. I can tell by the way she's flying she's not handling quite right. Let's talk evacuation plans," J-Man said.

"Are you going to have to ditch it?" Silke asked.

"No worries, but it's always better to talk contingencies before things go wrong," he said as the engine sputtered. The helicopter dropped. "Damn."

Nine: Lake Search

Five minutes later, the last minute growing tense, the J-copter hovered above the helipad behind Maraders Marina. Silke looked worried, teeth gently tapping on her lower lip. "Now what?" she asked.

"Don't worry. You can off load down the ladder, then I can land. This way there's less weight," J-Man said.

"I don't weigh much," Silke said, not sounding keen on the idea of climbing down the ladder. She crossed her arms in anger and resistance.

"No. You're perfect the way you are. Even so, any weight is

more than I need. This way, if things go south, only the captain goes down with the ship. I'll hover a few feet off the ground. *No problema,*" J-Man said.

Silke seized Troy's hand, clenching it in a death grip.

J-Man simply smiled. He brought them in slowly, descending a foot at time, then inches, leaving them about two feet from the runners to the ground.

Troy descended first so he could hold the ladder steady for Silke. She let go and dropped the last few inches. He caught her. Somehow, she kept ending up in his arms. They backed away together to watch.

J-Man appeared supremely confident. With a feathery touch, he guided the helicopter lower until it was merely eight inches off the ground. It looked good, until the engine sputtered and suddenly the props slowed. The dead whirlybird dropped.

The fall was short, less than a foot, but the copter sounded like it crashed.

The damaged runner crumpled. The unbroken one buckled, and the weight of the craft squashed the sprayer tanks. With a muffled whump, it sounded like the life and air went out of the copter. Everything else underneath it was crushed, unless it was sent flying. Debris shot out, whistling past Troy and Silke who had dropped to the gravel parking lot.

He watched as the helicopter rocked. For a moment, Troy feared it might tumble and roll, but it finally settled cock-eyed on the landing pad.

J-Man climbed out. He looked nonplussed, despite the sound of applause. Spider walked from the woods, performing a golf clap. J-Man glared until the tanned, lanky blood brother stopped, and then the pilot focused on Troy and Silke. "That didn't go quite as planned, but you know what they say. Any landing you can walk away from is a good landing. I swear I had that fixed. You two all right?" he asked.

"No offense, but I don't think I'll be flying Air J, again, any time soon. Do y'all always have this much fun?" Silke said.

Troy helped her stand where she dusted off her clothes. She walked a little unsteadily to the Land Rover, so Troy held onto her arm until she leaned against the vehicle. She shook herself and stretched. "No wonder Dillon didn't want me to come along. I wonder what he kept from our momma?"

"Stuff the Land Rover doesn't know," Troy chuckled. He retrieved his swimsuit from his luggage. He thought Silke would grab a bag and go inside to change, but she didn't, startling him instead by stripping on the spot.

"I'll be ready to go in a moment," Silke said. She removed her jacket, putting it on a hanger, then she unzipped her skirt, taking it off to reveal she was already wearing her swim suit. The red and black lightning fabric hugged her svelte body, making her look long and lean as well as fit. She removed her heels and put on sandals.

"What?" she asked.

Troy blinked. He realized he must have been staring. Fortunately, he was saved from stammering by company.

"Wow! Now that was quite a show. Usually you have to pay a cover charge or at least buy dinner," came a deep voice. Troy recognized the East Tennessee drawl faster than Silke.

She whirled to face Jambo and his toothy, sheepish grin. He stood there with a fishing pole, tackle box and a smoking cigar in his large hands. Jambo was easily six foot four and once weighed over two hundred and fifty pounds due to rigorous weight training. Since Troy had seen him last, his soft-spoken blood brother had slimmed down. Without his curly, shoulder-length hair and earring, it almost didn't look like the same man. Married life had changed him. He looked good for it.

"I came out to see if J-Man crashed, again, and I find that it was actually Troy's jaw hitting the ground so hard it shook," Jambo laughed. He grabbed Troy and hugged him before he could retort. "It's great to see you back, Troy, even if you look like crap warmed over."

"Thanks, good to see you and be here. I knew Silke was being too kind to me," Troy said. He and the youngest blood brother had always been closer than Jambo's own brothers who he had fought with constantly. Despite this, Jamie Boy was always smiling. They used to joke he even slept with a smile on his face.

"You certainly took your sweet time coming out to see if Jay was okay," Silke said.

"I didn't hear any screaming or explosions," Jambo replied with a shrug.

"Let's tell Tommy the news so we can go investigate the sunken boat," Silke said. She threw them a smile and hurried off.

A fast saunter counted as Jambo hurrying. Troy explained while Jambo grabbed his rifle from his shiny, newly restored, black Jeep Commando. The yellow and black license plate had the Batman symbol on it.

"Is there something going on between you and Silke? You're wearing her favor," Jambo said. He plucked a ruddy, golden hair, taking his time in drawing the long lock off Troy as it clung to him.

"She seems more eager to shoot males than kiss one," Troy said. He thought of the pretend couple kiss that had felt very real. Likely, he was reading into it when it meant nothing. "Are you offering to protect me from Dillon?"

Jambo laughed so loud he scared the gulls, sending them flying. "Sorry, I have my wife to think about, and my life insurance isn't paid in full," he finally said as they ambled down the gangway.

Ahead, around the corner of the building, Troy heard Marader whistle. "Whoa, baby! Silke. Is that you? Even with those damned big glasses you look like you could work in a strip club."

"I'm not Silke. I'm her evil twin, PMS. I plan to commandeer your boat and find a crew to rescue her brother."

"She does have a gun in her purse," Troy said as he came around the corner. Marader's eyes widened.

"It wouldn't be the first time a woman shot him. I packed

my rifle," Jambo said. He hefted it. "Mutiny at Maraders Marina rolls right off the tongue. Make sure you have the camera rolling for the documentary, Troy."

"Count me in," Spider Adder said. He sat in a chair in the shadows, eyes closed. He might have been asleep, meditating or astral traveling with the spirit of Timothy Leary. Spider stood up, tall, skinny and shirtless, as tanned and dark as most Haitians, a place he often visited to volunteer a helping hand. His legs and arms were long and spindly, much like the Daddy Long Legs which had led to his nickname. Besides, he didn't look like a Frank. Spider bowed to Troy. "Well met, Troy. And Silke, always a pleasure. It's been a day of unexpected meetings. You two and that guy in the woods taking photographs of Heidi, Sandi and Desiree."

Silke flinched, thinking stalker. She wrung her hands. "Oh, no."

"Describe him," Troy asked.

Spider described Deng, the bowler-wearing Paparazzi.

Deng had lied. What if he wasn't really Paparazzi? Troy could see that thought flash through Silke's eyes.

"I'm ready for a boat ride," Silke said.

"Yeah, if Marader crashes, we're closer to the water," Troy said.

Tommy Boy showed off his 24 ft. Mastercraft, named Maverick, and all its gear. It was very similar to one that Marader had often fantasized about back in high school. It could easily hold eight, had a kick-ass sound system with speakers everywhere, including on the board rack arcing over the top of the boat from port to starboard. Like ammo rounds, it was loaded with skis and boards. The prop was set in the middle of the hull, and he could control the size of the wake or flatten it. Dive gear had already been stowed away and scuba tanks tied down.

"As you can see, we expected to dive today. Last night, there were PVC pipes stashed about. I made J-Man take it all down. It was the coolest thing I've ever done on skis," Marader

said.

"You're welcome," J-Man said. He started untying the lines.

"But the scorch marks suck."

"Quit whining. I'll buy you a new cushion. It was worth it," J-Man said. He exuded a satisfied air.

"Don't do that yet. We're not done screwing up his boat," Spider said. Marader glared at him, but Spider was unfazed.

"I thought you would have to fix your helicopter," Troy said.

J-Man shrugged. "It will be easier with help. I called my team. They should be here in about an hour. Until then, I want to see what you found," he replied.

Troy climbed in and offered Silke a hand, taking a seat next to him on the back bench. Jambo, Spider and sexy Desiree rounded out the crew. J-Man shoved off as Marader took the captain's chair and the helm.

"Another picture-perfect day on South Holston Lake. Start with rain and fog, then go to hazy, blue skies, fresh air, and smooth water," Marader cooed.

"And no smoke. The winds aren't carrying it this way, but that's to change tomorrow," Spider pointed out.

"That's all I need for business, a drought, then a wildfire. What next? A plague?"

"And now the sheriff's boat is probably dragging Cemetery Ridge," Desiree said.

"You need to let up on the radio scanner, babe."

"I told you, I want to be forensic scientist or a crime scene investigator," Desiree said. She winked at Troy. "Even a medical examiner like *Bones*."

"Then it's good you're coming along with us. Man, it's sad, the lake," Marader moaned. He gestured all around. "If this keeps up, we'll be down to creeks and puddles. Then old headstones will be sticking up out of South Holston. Man, oh, man, do I ever feel cursed. Business blows because of the low water. It's why I decided to have some reconstruction done. And now floating coffins and open graves. Who's going to want to boat around that?"

"You never know. It might be good for business. The Goth crowd likes haunted boat tours," Spider snickered.

Marader shook his head and turned back to Troy. "Not everyone is as interested in macabre as you, Spider. Hey, Troy, would you like to ski while there's still water? We'll get there about the same time. Look at that surface. It's flat."

True, Holston's waters had that molten glass look. But, the last person to ski hit a body, and now there were three people missing. Plus, Silke said that Dillon noticed the number of open graves and coffins didn't match. There could be more floaters. And yet, the smoothness of the water tempted Troy. He thought of what Aunt Jada had mentioned about never knowing when a kiss might be your last, or anything else, for that matter. He was on bonus time. "Yes, I would. Thanks."

"Vest up, then," Marader said. He turned on the music, AC/DC, as they cruised to the inlet's entrance and No Wake buoys.

"Hey, hotshot. Do you need someone to rub sunblock into your back?" Desiree asked Troy.

"Not yet, thanks," Troy said. He pulled on the ski life vest.

As soon as they passed the green and red buoys, Marader gave the engine full throttle. Maverick smoothly planed out to speed across the placid water. The engine grew quiet and began to purr. Marader drove with his feet as he applied suntan lotion to his burnished flesh.

"Hey, I could use some help here," he said.

"You're on your own, Boss," Desiree said. She and Silke laughed hysterically together.

"This could be why we usually made our outings a guy thing."

From on the water level, the Cherokee National Forest looked even drier, the shore line wider, and the lake lower. The tree line was so far up it would be a hike to shade. Shadows only reached the water early or late in the day. Much of the ground cover and bushes were sunburnt and suffering as if they had endured triple digit heat. Just looking at it made Troy thirsty. Here, closer than when they were in the helicopter, South Holston felt intimately parched.

They cruised under the 421 Bridge. Cars passed overhead, rumbling and zooming. Maverick's engine echo sounded more metallic. In less than a minute, they were in, then out of the shadow and back into the sun.

Troy noticed that Marader kept the boat in the center of the lake. Shortly, they passed through a cluster of buoys, protruding rocks and small humps. He had never seen the Rock Garden so low. They had bent a prop or two over the years and learned to repair them to keep from being grounded. Raquel and their lake days together came to mind, and he pushed it aside.

"When I was lying in the hospital bed, I used to dream of skimming across water like this." He left out that an angel of sunshine would drive the boat. He had started dreaming of her during that time and still did, which was preferred to his current nightmares.

In the water, Troy felt more at home as he should. He had spent much of the year performing rehab in a pool. When it was hot in Bristol, as youths, they had spent all day at the lake or swimming hole. He continued to feel that something wasn't quite right about the water. It seemed heavy, even viscous when he swam, but it appeared to dribble, drip and run as normal. He slid his right foot into the front boot of the ski and his left into the back, then he tightened them. When he reached for the rope, he heard Marader start up the motor. He eased the boat forward until the handle floated to Troy. He set his ski against the resistance and yelled.

"Pull!"

Troy went from a gentle drag and a little drifting to a sudden yank. Ready, he drove his legs down, pushing the ski with his feet, fighting the water, forcing it to lift the ski, and the next moment, he rose from under the lake to skimming across the surface.

Skiing here flooded him with memories. Swimming. Tubing and taking turns trying to knock each other off. The time Marader flew when the tube exploded. Jumping off Cliff Island. Parasailing and looking down on it all. Duo skiing. Raquel showing them all how to get up on one ski, embarrassing the boys with her slaloming prowess.

He realized he was rhythmically cutting back and forth behind the boat. Instead of tired, he felt enlivened. Looking around, they had traveled farther than he expected. They turned into a shallow bay along west shore, and where it should be empty, a craggy knoll stood at the rear of the deserted bay. Cemetery Ridge was barren unlike most of the other islands. Boats were beached on or anchored near the hunk of rock.

Marader steered him toward the gathering. When they were close, Troy gave the cut-it sign, slashing a finger across his neck, and then he let go, sinking into the water. He was braced for a vision or any strangeness, but nothing happened. The water felt invigorating.

"You looked great, but if you're having breathing issues, I know CPR," Desiree said, boldly.

"Thanks, but I'm already dizzy, and you'd make Tommy Boy jealous," Troy told her. She pealed with laughter.

"Are you sure you're all right?" Silke asked.

"The run was a euphoric high, thanks, Tommy."

"Ah, you're just old, tired and out of shape," Marader joked.

"Speaking of out of shape, isn't that Deputy Burt Glazier?" Spider asked.

Two boats, both crafts marked Sullivan County Sheriff, were beached on the shore. A red and white dive flag bobbed atop the water. Everyone else must be diving, leaving Burt alone.

"Hey, Marader, when are you going to do some real work, pal?" the deputy called over to them. "Hey, Troy, I didn't know you were in town. I was given faulty intelligence. Welcome back."

"Hi Burt. It's good to be back among friends. It seems sort of surreal."

"I live here, and it's been unreal. Do you ever remember being able to hang clothes out to dry? Silke, girl, where's your brother? He was supposed to meet me this morning."

"I'm afraid he's missing. He left Marader's dock before sunrise on a Sea-Doo and hasn't been heard of since."

"Yeah, did you find an abandoned one? Or my boat, the one John rented?" Marader asked.

"No but one of our boats has been cruising along the shoreline, searching every acre of the seven thousand five hundred and eighty that we have, along with our friends in Washington County and their territory, for your lost boat and John and Sherry. So far nothing. We didn't find anything on the island, either, including a lack of headstones or markers. The storm rains washed away the footprints and anything else. If Dillon hadn't sent me photos of how it looked before the downpour, we would have no idea, thinking them natural pits. Normally I would bitch about y'all contaminating a crime scene, but, there wouldn't have been a scene without y'all."

"You're welcome, buddy boy. Did you find anything out about the shovel?" Marader asked.

"It was Pat's. By the dirt under his nails, we know he went digging, though forensics found a second pair of prints. They are trying to identify them. We found five spots. Three above the waterline. They're now filled up with rainwater, and two in the shallows."

"No more bodies?" Marader asked.

"Like I said, a whole lot of nothing, including reasons or motives."

"Maybe Dillon discovered something and that's why he's missing," J-Man said.

"Could be. But let's not jump to conclusions."

"It's not like the Dark Lady took him," Spider joked.

Once they passed the Bent Branch Spillway, Silke spotted a

black bear swimming across, so Marader slowed down. Minutes later, they encountered the ball buoy they had left as a marker. Marader idled into shore near the sunken boat, and shortly, Troy, Marader and Silke, all equipped with snorkels, dive masks, and neoprene gloves, slipped into the lake. Spider and Desiree put on vests and jumped in to cool off. Jambo saw a loose cushion and swam after it, leaving J-Man in charge of the boat.

"Be careful, you might stumble over a body," Marader joked.

Troy swam and dove around the white and red speed boat. The hull appeared sound and undamaged, meaning it hadn't sunk from a leak. It hadn't burned, either. Checking the registration numbers, Marader confirmed it was the boat he had rented to John and Sherry. Silke discovered the plug was gone. Had it been intentionally sunk?

Numerous dives told them very little. The keys were still in it. Troy used them to open the glove box, finding both John's and Sherry's wallets, naval tags, IDs, car keys, and a fancy box with an engagement ring. The smart phone was water-logged and didn't work, but J-Man thought he might be able to pull information off the memory card, if it hadn't been fried.

What disturbed them was discovering missing air tanks, two of the four, and all the fins, snorkels and masks. Where had they been left? Had they fallen out? Could there have been a dive accident? Had someone stolen the boat when it seemed abandoned? If so, why not steal the wallets, smart phones, and diamond ring?

Maverick was already loaded with dive gear, so Marader and Troy hooked regulators and gauges onto the two tanks. They should register fifteen hundred pounds Per Square Inch. One contained two hundred PSI and the other four hundred. It seemed likely John, bigger and with larger lungs, had used one while Sherry had used the one left with more air. They had returned after one dive. Where were the second tanks?

"Could the missing tanks be in Wreythville?" Spider

wondered aloud what many were thinking.

At Cemetery Ridge, Deputy Burt stood in the same place, smoking a cigarette, but now he wasn't alone. Several divers had returned from their explorations. Two men were in the boat with a driver, while two others sat on the back platform, removing their masks and tanks. One was Raquel, looking like a dark-haired and wet Bengal tiger. She waved, and Troy returned it.

"You are hopelessly outmatched," J-Man said.

"I'm here to find John and now Dillon," Troy replied.

"Keep telling yourself that, and you might believe it. Somebody once told me to face my fears," J-Man said.

"Well, we weren't talking about women, were we?" Troy said, and J-Man chuckled. His friend had just given him advice that Troy had once given him. J-Man had conquered a fear of heights to fly by repeatedly parachuting. Troy hoped he didn't look as pained or panicked as J-Man had on his second jump. He had claimed it was scarier because he knew what it was like, and yet the experience gave him enough courage to try again. Was that applicable in this case?

"Is that Raquel Sterling? She has dated some incredibly hot guys," Desiree said.

"And some not so hot," J-Man said.

"Screw you," Marader said.

"She dated Tommy? Her taste isn't as refined as I would have guessed," Desiree mused.

"Screw you, too, babe. Hey, Burt! Let's pow-wow!" Marader yelled ahead. From across the water, he informed Deputy Burt of what they had found. He wanted the memory card and anything else they had, so J-Man handed it over to the proper authorities. Deputy Burt wanted the tanks, too. J-Man even gave him the GPS location, although they had left a dive flag there.

"Did you guys and gal find anything new?" Deputy Burt turned and asked the divers.

The tallest guy in the boat shook his head. He reminded Troy a little of the actor, Chris Evans, a Captain America type. "Not a thing. We dove to 60 feet. I was surprised by the clarity, especially after the rain. I expect it to change with the increased run off."

"Did you see the town?" Troy asked.

"No, we didn't go that far," he replied.

"We found another iron stake. It must be recent because there's no rust on it," Raquel said and held it up. It looked like something driven into railroad ties. Troy recalled seeing them in his nightmare.

"We found three so far. Just another piece of the mystery puzzle. I talked to the TVA muckety mucks about the graves. This section isn't on their maps. It's beyond the cemetery they relocated. They tell me that their old photos show no sign of headstones," Deputy Burt said.

"Anything interesting about the coffins? The one we examined seemed to have been clawed from the inside, like there was a bear or tiger buried alive," Spider said.

"They all looked like that, which, not surprisingly, leads to some wild speculations. They'll run some DNA tests to see if they find anything. I expect the TVA to do some of their own diving, so this place might get crowded soon. We've already had several reporters out here earlier this morning, including Rae Kirkland, but no new news is boring, so they recorded what they wanted and went back to the office."

"I can't believe I haven't been interviewed, especially by Rae. I wonder what I did to upset her." Marader mused aloud.

Deputy Burt reacted with mock disgust. "Whatever it was, you didn't make her top ten most eligible local bachelors. Listen, we're giving out limited information about what's going on. The same will be true of finding your missing boat. We're headed to it next. If we can, we'll raise it. If not, I'll have somebody out here tomorrow."

"So, you haven't found any loose tanks or dive equipment?" Troy said.

"I found a lost piece of jewelry. It might be from the missing woman," Raquel replied.

"What is it?" Silke asked.

"A diamond earring," Raquel said.

"May I see it, please?" Silke said, sounding pained. Her expression was worried. "I lost one of the pair given to me by my dad, God bless his soul, for graduation, so I gave the other one to Dillon."

"He wore an earring? Really?" Deputy Burt and Marader asked at the same time. "Jinx."

"What's wrong with that?" Jambo asked. He currently wasn't wearing one.

"It was his California thing. So, may I see it? It should have a silver sun behind it," Silke said.

Deputy Burt removed a white handkerchief from his pocket, then he unfolded it, revealing the sparkling diamond. Silke gasped. It looked like a shining star, the gemstone glistening and shining off the silvery rays of the backing.

"That's it!" Silke said.

"It doesn't mean he went diving here," Marader said.

"But you said he came prepared. So, can we still dive, or is it a crime scene?" Silke asked.

Deputy Burt pondered it. "Diving is fine. Stay off the island."

"Where's the crime scene tape?" Marader asked.

"Are you always this funny? If you find something, let me know ASAP."

Troy and Silke swapped cell phone numbers with Deputy Burt, then he wished them good luck and safety. Raquel winked and waved farewell. When Marader blew her a kiss, she flipped him the reverse bird, wishing him lack of sexual relationships.

"Ah, ten years gone, and she still misses me," Marader said.

There was a time when Troy would have punched him. He found himself still very close to there, and that bothered him.

"Tommy, is that the sign of another satisfied customer?"

Desiree asked.

"All right! Who's going diving?" Marader asked, ignoring her.

"I wouldn't miss it! A better question is, who isn't going?" J-Man asked.

"I'll man the boat," Jambo offered. Some things never changed.

"The one separated from the group is always the next to disappear. Are you wearing a red *Star Trek* shirt?" J-Man asked.

On other occasions, it would have been funnier, but they were about to dive to an underwater town one hundred feet down in limited visibility to look for bodies. It was a dangerous choice but necessary. Troy had to know if either of his missing blood brothers had drowned down there.

Ten: Divers Down

Troy had been snorkeling and tank diving for *Outside Magazine* in April off the Florida Keys, so he felt familiar with the gear. He cracked open the airflow to his tank, blew through the regulator to clear it, and checked to make sure he could breathe easily. He lifted and slipped into his BC, an inflatable vest and harness for a single tank of 1500 PSI. That should give him about twenty minutes of bottom time at this altitude of 1600 and one hundred feet deep. He donned a weight belt, twenty pounds worth, and slipped on his mask and snorkel, positioning them atop his head. He finished by rigging up his waterproof-cased Go Pro camera in his chest harness.

"Are you comfortable with this?" Troy asked Silke. He assisted her while she adjusted her BC and tank and buckled up. She had slipped into a blue shorty wetsuit.

"Do you mean am I ready if we find Dillon's body?" she asked. Her lower lip quivered. "I would rather know. I can't help but feel that his vanishing isn't an accident."

"Geronimo!" Spider dropped backwards into the water.

The splash brought them back to their surroundings.

Silke smiled wryly. "I'll try to tap into some of his enthusiasm."

"Yee-haw!" Marader yelled and leapt out. He frog kicked into the water, spraying everyone and soaking Desiree.

"You did that on purpose!" she cried. Marader swam out of the way so she couldn't land on him when she jumped into the lake.

"Let's go find the truth," Silke said.

They put on their masks, stuck the regulators in their mouths and twisted to land on their tanks, their backs striking the surface. Because of the shallowness, the water here was lukewarm. With his weights on, Troy sank, and since all seemed to be going well, no visions so far, he let himself drift to the bottom. At a little over ten feet, the water tasted normal, and the visibility was relatively clear for about thirty feet where it merged into green murk.

With a little scouting, they found the rounding of the ridge before it plunged steeply to the bottom of South Holston Lake. Along the way, they discovered two empty graves that seemed unremarkable. They skirted the ridge, following its shallower descent. They started losing light, color, and visibility.

Desiree and Marader led the way past the trash at the thermocline and onto sixty feet where the visibility was okay to twenty feet. They swam over a line of old, green stones that could have once been part of a wall. Downslope some hundred feet, but only about twenty feet more in depth, the ridge ended in a cliff, leaving them level with the top of a bell tower.

The structure was missing both its steeple and bell. Algae created a green skin over the rock walls of the tower. The chapel, abandoned and forgotten, sat half-buried in the sediment. Marader swam over to peer inside the shaft of the tower. He turned his light on it then swam within. Desiree waited at the top, shining her light down and watching her buddy.

Troy felt uncomfortable. The water seemed thick and

almost sticky, forcing him to move slower and with more effort. Silke tugged at his shoulder and pointed ahead, the way he felt he needed to go. For a moment, Troy could clearly see an old mansion of river stone with a green roof, twin-chimneys and shuttered windows. He trained his camera on it. The building crouched in the mud, the front doors partly buried while the shuttered windows remained unobstructed. In the headlamps, the wood seemed to gleam and glimmer, winking at him.

Suddenly, it was so clear he could have been floating only a few feet away. An ornate knocker of a wolf and lintel work of crescents decorated the front doors. The green of the water abruptly thickened. Troy hadn't moved at all, but the building seemed to drift away, becoming swallowed by the shadowy depths.

Troy gave Silke a quizzical look. Had he seen a mirage of sorts? The building hadn't looked water-logged or sodden, barely touched by decades of being submerged. Silke pointed toward the place, wanting to go there. He gestured toward Desiree. Swimming back, he let her know by writing 2 big house 2 N on an underwater tablet.

He would swear the water thickened as they neared the mansion. Its shadows were darker and denser and drew themselves tighter around the building. The water temperature cooled as if they had found a cold spring.

Silke headed for the second story where a shutter appeared to have been recently opened. While Troy snapped the glow sticks on his belt to activate them, she used her camera to take digital photos. Symbols had been roughly carved into the wood of the shutters, framing, trim and second story wall. After the first flash of camera light, the lines seemed to wiggle and jiggle like plaid on a TV screen, making Troy's head spin.

He glanced away. He had an unpleasant familiar feeling about this, and yet, he didn't see any choice but to go inside. Deja vu washed over him, knowing he had been here before, and yet, knowing he had never set foot or fin here. He waved to J-Man then, when he had his attention, pointed inside. His friend nodded and gave the thumbs up sign.

Together, Troy and Silke drew the shutters wide open to completely expose the window. The shutters looked fine from the outside, but on the inside they had been chopped by an ax. Had someone been trapped here when the valley had been flooded?

He checked his watch, marking half past and setting a timer for twenty minutes. Silke activated her glow sticks, twin bars of greenish light, and then she pulled on the frame to draw herself inside what might have once been a bedroom. Troy tailed her, bristling at the sudden, intensely cold water bringing on a headache.

Silke seemed just as confused by the abrupt polar plunge in temperature, but she narrowed her eyes and grimaced around her regulator. Determined to continue, she swam deeper inside. Troy noticed her glow sticks were dimmer, and the beam of their headlights seemed murky, almost as if it were shining through swirling smoke.

More lights brightened the gloomy room as Marader started to follow them. When he felt the cold, he swiftly reversed direction, grabbing the frame to haul himself back outside. Troy knew he hated cold water. Desiree peeked in but didn't follow.

The hall seemed alive and animated. Having escaped their rusted nails, the warped floorboards shifted underneath like wooden fronds. His headlamp's beam reflected off an old, wavy mirror, like that of a circus, to illuminate a walk-in closet full of old lace clothing, still intact, ready to fall off the hangers. An uncomfortable looking chair seemed plumply bloated next to a chest of drawers. A sodden mattress and a clump of bedding sat pierced by rusted metal springs.

No John. No Sherry. Just an empty bedroom.

Then why did he feel observed? He had hunted and knew how the predator felt. What about the prey? Pressed for time, short on life, fatigued, and squeezed in an uncomfortable, hostile environment of darkness and close spaces with each breath a chance at death. Is that how prey felt? He mustered his courage.

A movement made him glance back at the bed through the bubbles. He spotted a flash of white amidst the bedding and swam over, taking a closer look. Something was pressed into the mattress creating a small body-sized indentation.

He reached out, starting to touch it, and then changed his mind and readied his exploration stick. He pushed the bedding aside, scaring a catfish and startling Troy. The fish's departure left the hump exposed as a human skeleton. He gasped, almost choking. How had this person died? A rusted spring spiraled up through its ribcage. Another would have pierced its pelvis. The bones seemed unnaturally picked clean, gleaming white. Despite its dark, dead eye sockets, the skull seemed to be grinning at him.

Troy thought he could hear it giggle. "I couldn't get out, and now, neither can you. We're trapped. You're going to die, decay and return to the water. Me? I'm not worried. I'm already dead."

What was it doing here? Seeing the skeleton stirred up third thoughts of doubt. He had already had seconds. The bones proved his worries and doubts, even fears, were well founded.

He turned to Silke to see her reaction, but she was gone. No Dillon in sight, so she swam on. It was a good strategy with time preciously short. She knew better than to get separated, though. Troy had a disorienting moment of deja vu. Why? He hadn't been here before, or had he? The dream with Raquel rushing ahead. He had seen himself as John. Did Sherry have dark hair? Was this what happened to them? Could it be happening again now?

Near the doorway, Troy noticed the recent hole in the wall. Had John made it? Troy thought he saw something dart in the hallway, a streaking fish, then it was gone. The prickling feeling, more like the tips of an ice pick, gigged him all over.

The flitting of light in the corner of his eyes reminded him a little of Aunt Jada's place. How comfortable it seemed compared to here.

Troy caught up with Silke as she opened a door and peeked into a room. Strips of wallpaper now drifted horizontally. The fish hiding here fled, sending the paper streamers swirling. It looked like the arms of several giant origami octopi filled the place.

When Silke turned the handle of the third door, nothing happened. She tried again then shrugged. Locked.

They were turning to leave when metal shrieked, and the door slowly fell off its hinges, away and open. Troy thought it was strange. Was the place coming apart? Could it collapse? Was it his imagination or were things aging, worsening slowly before his eyes, more rust, more algae and rot?

Kicking slowly, Silke swam inside. Wanting to be thorough, he supposed. She returned shaking her head. He was all right with finding no more skeletons, no dead bodies and leaving none behind.

They maneuvered through a thick patch of slimy, clinging paper. He was feeling a little claustrophobic, but he sensed something, an inkling of a blood brother, maybe, drawing him on. Relief flooded over him as they drifted together at the edge of a great room with a banister stairway. It curved down to the first floor to the large front doors. Above hung an elegant chandelier of sparkling crystal. The glass turned the beams of their headlamps into a disco display, light spearing through the murk to speckle lazy fish and glitter on the gray walls, shuttered windows and domed ceiling.

This place, although Troy knew he had never, ever been here, gave him a stronger sense of deja vu. The bitterly cold temps, the tang of rotting and the taste of blood. He had experienced this before, in a nightmare where he had been surrounded by darkness, riveted by hungry, red eyes, and seared by the pain in his neck. He found himself rubbing it, long past ready to get out of here.

Silke descended, heading downstairs. He followed her fins, his attention grabbed by something near the double doors, the ones that led to a study. He remembered them from the dream. The right door was ajar. From the other, a gleam winked from its lock.

During their descent to the first floor, Troy spotted something dark hanging from a rope tied to the banister. He blinked, startled, not believing his eyes. He tried to hold his light steady on the hanged man, his clothes that of a servant, the fabric still intact, jacket, pants, and all. Only his flesh had disintegrated, leaving clean white bones, a mocking grin and the blank eyes of the abyss. For a moment, he could imagine white flesh covering the gaunt man, desiccated of vitality before taking his own life.

The ghostly servant's cracked lips moved. "I didn't get out alive, and neither will you. Kill yourself! There was no light, here, except what you brought with you. It will die soon, too."

Troy wondered if any of that would show up on his camera. He made sure to keep his hands out of the way to give a clear view of the skeleton. It blocked a hallway deeper into the mansion. Did that mean something? He noticed the man's right pants' pocket was torn, and then he forced himself to look away from the macabre and study his surroundings. He turned slowly so the camera would catch it all.

The mud was thick around the front doors where the lake bed had seeped through. He noticed that all the windows could be shuttered from the inside as well as the outside. The inside shutters were open, while the outside remained closed. They were damaged on the interior facade, hacked and chopped, cuts covering them. It sure looked like someone had desperately tried to escape this place.

He tapped Silke on the shoulder and showed her his watch. They had ten minutes left without having to perform a decompression stop, though they were going deeper, down to 125 feet. She nodded, understanding. She pointed toward the ajar double doors. Covered in sediment, twin statues of ferocious wolves crouched as stone guardians on each side of the doors. Troy felt scrutinized while he approached, causing the hair to bristle on his arms and the back of his neck.

The left front door shook. Troy was startled, backing up, at first thinking the wall might be collapsing. A second blow drove the door off its hinges and inwards to a play of bright lights.

Wearing a satisfied smile, J-Man swam in. Spider peeked in high while Desiree swam in low under him and into the grand entrance hall. Marader, looking cold, and Spider acting wary, were the only ones showing good common sense. They remained outside.

J-Man ignited a red fusee, dispelling the nearby darkness and weakening the gloom. The bloody red glow was harsh and garish but better than the unknown. J-Man frowned, fired up a second fire stick, giving it to Troy, and then the big man swam up to the chandelier and used a zip tie to secure the flare. The brightness transformed the room as the shadows skittered away to hide, leaving the place exposed.

Troy waited for the chandelier to fall, but it held, so far. He was amazed by the beauty of the grand room. Much of the entry had been dark marble. Black stone columns held up a grand balcony. Below it there was a hallway and doors to other rooms. Tall empty frames of gold-gilt decorated the forlorn walls. J-Man stopped, shocked, seeing the hanging skeletal body.

Silke showed them a knife, pointing to the floor near the door where she had found it. The initials JT were engraved in the hilt. John Traylor. Dammit, Troy had known it. His hopes sank. His blood brother had been here in this mansion of cold death. And yet, that didn't mean John had died here. Troy accepted the knife handle from Silke and swam over to his friends. Marader seemed fine, but Spider was apprehensive, breathing rapidly, his eyes wide and darting. His left hand had a white-knuckled grip on his crucifix necklace.

Troy glanced over his shoulder to see Silke swim to the

double doors. When he turned to join her, Spider seized Troy and tried to stop him. He whirled angrily, and Spider looked concerned, his eyes large. His friend shook his head then wrote on the pad, bad voodoo vibe. When Troy looked back, Silke, J-Man and Desiree had pushed the doors open wide into the dark maw. For a moment, Troy saw only a black hole, untouched by the light of the flare. The darkness seemed to stretch on forever.

Silke swam into it. The abyss devoured her.

Troy was startled. Wait, it wasn't completely dark. He could spot the pale glow of Silke, her headlight wan but her glow stick bright. The headlamps and flashlights were weak against the darkness, barely able to illuminate the chamber. J-Man entered with his flare held high, burning back the gloom and throwing shadows.

Troy stopped in the doorway, staring past the others at the strange, grisly scene. A grand desk of maple and a throne-like chair were surrounded by a half-dozen skeletons in formal wear, sitting in chairs. Their skulls shone so brightly white they appeared recently bleached. Around them, the sediment had been disturbed.

What the hell had happened here?

Nothing had touched them since their skin had been nibbled or diffused away, becoming part of the water. He started to gag. He might be tasting six decomposed bodies. He pushed that thought away before he vomited, focusing on something else, anything else. J-Man studied the nearest body while Silke's light swept the room, searching for her brother. Desiree broke the circle, heading toward the desk.

A cold current slithered and wound past Troy like an invisible snake. He peered inside, still trying to wrap his thoughts around the bizarre scene. The room appeared normal, the walls were lined with bookshelves, some waterlogged books remaining in places. Most had disintegrated, ending up in the water or on the floor as sediment.

Troy didn't want to go inside, but he couldn't resist. John or Dillon seemed close at hand. Troy prayed he was wrong.

When he pushed his way past the door, it rebounded. Fins swung out at him. Troy thrashed backwards, surprised by the movement, unnerved by the attack. A memory from a nightmare rushed over him, struggling under water, gasping, unable to breathe, then sharp pains in his neck. Just as swiftly, it was gone, leaving him with tears and the echoes of agony. He had died before, and that had felt like being on the cusp.

He blinked, trying to clear his vision. Get a grip.

The attack had been only in his paranoid mind. John's body hung limp, hooked by its tank harness on the back of the door. Troy gulped several recovery breaths even as sadness overwhelmed him.

John's eyes were still wide open. His translucent and puffy face stared at him, seeing eternity. He appeared to have drowned. Troy said a prayer for John Traylor, his beloved friend and blood brother, even as he wondered what had happened to the naval diver.

A savage hopelessness pressed down on Troy as if he were suddenly a thousand feet down. He had lost a friend and blood brother. He wanted to scream, the moment crushing him, but then Troy noticed what seemed like too many hoses, short ones. John's air hoses had been cut.

Troy saw a red haze of fury. Murdered! Why?

The sadness and depression were melted by his rage. Although Troy had been across the country, he felt like he had failed John. Troy didn't know if being in Bristol a day earlier would have made a difference, but he would never know. He should have been here!

Had something similar happened to Dillon? Was he here, too?

A sudden movement to his left caught his eye. He swung his flashlight towards it, capturing the falling frame in the beam. He watched in amazement as the portrait seemed to ooze down the wall. The painting struck the waist-high wall trim, then the top tilted forward, and it tumbled. Troy made sure he had this on camera.

This had happened in his nightmare! Oh, God, had he seen John being murdered? Felt John being murdered?

This time, Troy let the frame hit the ground, but he couldn't resist picking it up. The man in the portrait smiled cruelly and winked, then he burst out in silent laughter that never reached his dark, flat eyes. The color faded, and the canvas crumbled before Troy's eyes, leaving him with an empty frame.

Nitrogen narcosis. Troy figured he was going crazy. Or this place drove him crazy. Did it cause Sherry to cut John's air hose?

That's when he noticed the four puncture wounds along John's neck. They could be anything, but the fanged bite of a snake leapt to the forefront of his mind.

No one else had noticed Troy finding John's body. J-Man was studying the bookcases, taking out a book and flipping it open. Surprisingly enough, it didn't fall apart. Desiree was opening drawers in the imposing desk.

Silke had discovered something in the mud. She lifted up an untarnished silver jewelry box, and then she hastily dropped it.

It fell, trailing blood.

Troy felt the water quake.

It seemed to shove him a foot sideways, and for a moment, he was disoriented. Like a dusty cloud underwater, silt drifted down from the ceiling. He was ready to get the hell out of Wreythville.

He touched Silke, startling her. She relaxed a little when she saw him, but her eyes strayed past and spotted John. She reeled, shocked by the staring corpse. Troy removed John's mask so she could see it wasn't Dillon. Silke settled when she realized the truth.

Troy wanted to get everybody's attention. Sound traveled well under water, so he used the butt of his knife to knock on

John's air tank, creating a clanking noise that caused J-Man and Desiree to look up. J-Man stuffed a couple of books in a net sack and fin-kicked over.

By the light of J-Man's flare, Troy spotted a sparkling in the mud below where John had been hanging. He poked it with his stick and discovered a gold and obsidian cufflink. It looked valuable. He put it in the zipper pocket of his BC.

J-Man left the flare standing in the sediment and forced both library doors wide open. Jewelry box tucked in a net sack, Silke joined them. J-Man helped Troy maneuver John's body into the front hall where lights were darting around. Troy adjusted John's body aside to see ahead.

Spider and Marader scuffled and wrestled. Great gouts of bubbles erupted from Spider's regulator. Panicked, he shoved his way past Marader, clawing through the water and scrambling outside to escape the mansion. Marader glanced at them, shrugged, and swam in pursuit.

J-Man looked over his shoulder. Troy knew what he wanted. Desiree shouldn't be left alone. Troy turned around, swimming back into the bitterly cold study. Despite shivering, Desiree seemed obsessed, continuing her ransacking of the desk's drawers. Tapping on his own tank failed to draw her attention, so Troy finned his way to her. He touched her shoulder, and she whirled, a flashing red knife in hand, barely missing him.

Her dark eyes flared with angry fireworks, and her beautiful face was flushed and marred by fury. He thought she was going to stab him, but then she smiled, as if she had been simply spooked.

In truth, he didn't blame her. It was an understatement to say the mansion was eerie and creepy when you were swimming with skeletons. She showed him her finds: a gold money clip with the initials VVD, a gold stick pin, and a silver, wickedly sharp-looking envelope opener. Troy jerked a thumb over his shoulder. She understood but left reluctantly.

J-Man had inflated John's BC, making him buoyant. Troy

helped float and maneuver the body outside where the water warmed considerably. Radiant beams of light sparkled like ethereal columns supporting a green canopy in the lake above him.

They hadn't finished searching the place, but Troy was short on bottom time and long ready to escape the mansion. With any luck, Dillon would be found alive ashore, and Troy wouldn't need to come back to this underwater hell.

As a group, they waited for a minute to decompress at thirty feet. Troy could tell when they noticed John's cut hoses. Only Silke touched his neck around the puncture wounds. She exchanged worried looks with Troy.

What had happened down there? Murder? An accident? Troy looked at John's hoses, and they were cleanly severed. The neck wounds might be unrelated, but he figured an autopsy would tell them something.

This was not the welcome home Troy had expected. He had never imagined that the last time he had seen John, about a year ago in Florida, would be the final time together. Their phone chat before Troy had flown to Alaska had been their last laughs together. Troy had learned life could be short.

When they floated along with their bubbles again, pushing through the thermocline, Troy could see the bottom of the boat. He fully appreciated coming up into the light and balmy water. Jambo had moved the boat, likely to pick up Marader and Spider. Troy hoped they were well.

He had already lost a blood brother. John had died in darkness, now they were returning him to the light.

Eleven: Impromptu Wake

Breaking the surface brought instant relief. The sunshine warmed Troy's face. He smiled and squinted, seeking faces. Spider looked exhausted. With a towel wrapped around him, he sat on the ski deck slumped against the stern of the boat. Marader paced back and forth on the sun platform. He shivered and pulled a towel tighter around him, trying to warm up. He appeared blue, both physically and emotionally. Jambo called Deputy Burt, and they were told to wait there.

They couldn't leave a friend's remains in the water, so they rested John across the ski deck. J-Man took photos and messaged them to Knives. They all knew there would be an investigation.

Knives replied, texting, "After last time, stashed body bag in bow." Jambo found it, and they carefully bagged their deceased brother.

"An accident seems unlikely," Troy said.

Spider kept repeating something almost under his breath. "I knew it. I knew it. So many bad things happened there. I felt . . . . I never want to go back, again. Never. I thought Haiti was bad, but this . . . the depravations and death. The pain. Horrible," Spider bemoaned. He laid down, covered his eyes, and tried to forget.

"Troy, what do you think? Is Dillon still down there?" Silke asked, dreading his answer.

Troy didn't know what he felt. Besides tired, he felt overwhelmed by the strangeness of it all. "Right now, to be honest, I'm trying to process it all. I don't trust my instincts."

"I'm sorry. He was your dear friend. I was selfish, just thinking about my brother," Silke said. She covered her face with her hands.

Troy hugged her. He sensed they all needed a kind and caring touch.

Troy found the first aid kit and bandaged Silke's wounded hand. Her lips looked a little blue, so he draped her in a towel and rubbed her arms and back. She rewarded him with a dazzling smile that improved his grim mood. Nothing, John had once said, made you feel instantly better than a pretty girl smiling at you.

That bittersweet thought brought a wan smile to Troy's lips, then it faded, remembering that Pat and John had been murdered. Troy could barely wrap his mind around it. They would get answers. Troy wasn't leaving until he knew the truth.

Troy pushed through the veil of sleep, now hearing a babble of voices. Some of the words sounded low, secretive and sinister, saying elusive words he couldn't quite grasp. Above them, he could hear Silke on the phone, talking with her mom, and somebody else speaking German. Oh, that was the babble. Below it all was a low, angry drone, reminding him of upset hornets. He hoped they hadn't floated near a nest or a swarm.

He realized he was no longer cold, finally, and too warm. He opened his eyes to find he had only napped for about twenty minutes. His friends were dry, sun blocked, and sitting in the shade of the canopy examining the treasure from the underwater mansion.

Spider paused in his muttering German to flip through the book, the pages resembling flimsy plastic. "I think this might be made of vellum. You know, sheep skin."

"Can you tell who it was written by?" J-Man asked.

"Yes. Viktor Von Damme, a tobacco magnet and moonshiner. That was his place outside of Wreythville."

In Troy's bizarre nightmare, Von Damme had claimed to be free. How could he have known that name? Could he have researched it back in the day while working on his paper?

Troy blinked, uncertain he was awake, because the book seemed to be smoking. A black mist wafted up in coils, making Troy think of cobras swaying. Some stretched almost two feet long before they diffused into the humid air. Was he really seeing this? Nobody else noticed.

"How interesting. Can you tell anything about him or the place?" Silke asked as she put away her phone.

"I haven't read enough yet. My German is rusty," Spider said.

"I wonder if this is anything special, or if it's just pretty," Desiree said. She held the golden stick pin up to the sunlight. It glinted magically, as if it might hold a secret or a power, and smoldered, the air about it wavering from heat. "What do you think, boss? Boss?"

Absorbed in his own world, Marader fingered the jewelry box. He caressed it and turned the silver box over, exploring all the sides and the bottom. The shadows seemed deep and sharp. The strange markings and decorations flashed hypnotically in the sunlight.

Troy had to look away. The thing made him nauseous just looking at it.

Not Marader. He was captivated, sweating and focused, excited by what might be inside. "I've been messing with it for ten minutes. I can't get the lid to open. I think the sediment cemented it. A knife might damage it, so," Marader said. He took the envelope opener and pried the lid loose. It popped open with a sigh. The angry buzzing grew louder.

"Empty," he said, disappointed. He used a glow stick to poke around the bottom and inside walls looking for false compartments.

"Nothing but it's a great looking piece. Do you think it's an antique worth big bucks? Ouch!" he yelped and pulled one hand back. His fingers oozed blood from what looked to be paper cuts. He offered the box to Silke who turned it down. Although it cut him, he still held onto it.

"Why would a jewelry box have sharp edges?" Silke asked.

Troy agreed with her. He didn't know what he saw around the objects, why they smoldered, wavered, and hummed, and why nobody else noticed it, but he wanted no part of them.

Without the Search and Rescue crew, Deputy Burt and two deputies cruised up in the lake patrol boat. Burt unzipped the bag to peek at John's corpse then declared this would be a homicide investigation. He would need to interview them all, and he did so in excruciating detail. Thankfully, the two deputies also asked questions, otherwise the verbal grilling would have taken all day. Scowling, they transferred the body onto their boat. Their departure waves rocked Maverick.

Troy felt like a suspect, and he hadn't even been in town. He kept turning over in his mind what he had seen. Why would somebody murder John? Where was Sherry? Where was Dillon?

He wasn't the only one frustrated by the murder and mysteries as Marader and Silke pitched fits on the way back.

"Can you believe it?! Burt told us not to leave town!" Marader yelled.

"I have no plans to leave town until I know what happened to Dillon and John," Troy said. His voice wavered. Damn, he was going to miss his friend. Frustration, fury and sadness threatened to overwhelm him. He had to hold it together and find Dillon.

Silke's lips were compressed tight. Lord, she was gorgeous when she was angry, spirited some might say. "I can't believe he told us not to dive again. That it's a crime scene and closed to us. What if Dillon is down there, too?!" Silke snapped.

"If he's found by professional divers, he will be dead, too," J-Man said. He was only telling her what they already knew, but it sounded so final and heart-breaking.

Troy reached out and took Silke's uninjured hand. She squeezed it hard, and he could tell she was holding back tears. "Until we know the truth, keep hoping. Don't let Burt upset you," Troy said.

"Guys, give him a break. Burt was just doing his job. He wants the professionals to do the diving in the morning," Jambo said.

"No, we were doing his job," Marader retorted. "He was off drinking coffee and eating donuts. Yes, I noticed he had little sprinkles on his shirt. I notice these things."

"Women and food," Jambo said.

Troy didn't like it either, but he understood. The professionals were trained and tested to be certified. If anything, Troy and his friends were certified crazy.

Marader let Troy drive since he seemed to have his hands full fondling the jewelry box. Troy loved cruising on the lake, but he found the amount of attention Tommy Boy bestowed upon the box to be strange. Troy thought he could see a silver gleam in Marader's eye. He usually loathed to give up the wheel unless he was skiing, wake boarding, or grappling with a bodacious beauty. Did the jewelry box qualify?

As they neared the dock entrance, an aromatic cloud of smoke greeted them. The wonderful scent of steaks, salmon, mushrooms and onions drifted out from the restaurant's outdoor lakeside grill. Marader had made phone calls during their questioning and interviews, telling Knives and Denny about John's death. They had arrived first and were ready to throw an impromptu wake.

Simply breathing made Troy hungry, and he felt a little guilty about it. He had survived that horrible house. Its gloom, skeletons, and death made him long to eat, drink and bask in the sun. He didn't know if he could manage merry.

A slender and bespectacled Dr. Stephen Curran, topped with a fieldworker's straw hat, paced the dock while he cane pole fished. When he saw them, he stopped to help tie up the lines. Troy was always glad to see the most pragmatic and level-headed of his blood brothers. Knives' tank top proclaimed: If you can't ski with the Big Dogz— Stay on the dock! He gave Troy a hand out of the boat, and they bear hugged.

"Good to see you. A day late is better than not at all," Knives said, then he shoved Troy backward. Having suspected as much, Troy dragged his buddy into the lake with him. It seemed to be something that swimmers relished, pushing each other off the edge and into the pool, lake or any nearby body of water.

He and Knives enjoyed a good dunking and a better laugh. The moment reminded Troy to mourn but also be joyfully alive.

"Was that your prescription for shock?" Troy said.

"If it worked, sure. John would have done it, but he isn't here, so I did the honor. John would want us to eat, drink, and shoot off fireworks to celebrate his life, so I came prepared. I assume the county has his body?" Knives asked.

"Burt and his boat crew took possession out at Cemetery Ridge. We had to wait on that and answer a zillion questions," Marader bemoaned. He reached down and hauled Knives up onto the dock.

"I'll see it tomorrow then. The county coroner is a good man. He knows what he's doing."

"I don't understand why someone would cut John's hose. Why kill him?" Troy asked as he climbed the ladder. He explained about finding John's lost knife, currently held in evidence since it might have been used in the murder.

"It's so sad. Tragic, actually. He survives all those naval missions and dies having fun here. No sign of his girlfriend, Sherry?"

Troy explained what they had found at the boat and in the mansion. How there was more to explore, since they had run out of air and time.

"What happened to Spider?" Knives asked. They watched him walk woodenly over to the bar door and stumble inside.

"Spider had some issues."

"He hasn't been the same since he almost died."

"I can relate," Troy replied.

"I'll bet you can," Knives said, studying him critically. "You had some very good surgeons. Mind if I poke?" The doctor felt along his spine and along his ribs, where he had broken seven. Silke stood and watched like she was at her husband's medical appointment.

"Collapsed the lung?" Knives asked. Troy nodded. "How's the knee?"

"Imperfect."

Knives studied his face. "The cosmetic surgeon was excellent. I wish I could do work this neat."

"He's just as ugly as he used to be," Marader said.

"That he is, but he looks like himself, doesn't he?" Knives asked.

Marader shrugged. "They could have improved his mug a lot."

"Where's Denny?" Troy asked, feeling at home now.

"I think in the houseboat, seeing if Dillon left any clues. That's where he slept last night," Knives said. "Sandy, Heidi and I are sharing duties until J-Man can look over the fixings and deem them fit for consumption," Knives replied.

"First, I need some beer to cry in," J-Man replied.

Silke wanted to search where her brother had been staying, too, so Marader pointed to a nice, single story, Sailabration house boat. It was blue and white, shiny and looked relatively new. The forty-footer had decks forward and stern, a slide, a grill, and deck chairs.

Denny wasn't there. Back in the bar, Troy found him involved in an intense conversation with Spider. Troy hadn't seen Denny in three years, but it seemed longer. His big-boned friend tried to crush him in a hug. It was difficult to imagine that his friend had recently been ordained after completing post graduate work at King College. Long and winding road? Or long strange trip? Troy mused. Denny smiled, showing dimples and extending his big jaw. Marader used to tease him about a heroic parody called The Chin.

Father Dennis finally let go and stepped back to adjust his glasses. "Man, it's fantastic to see you. You should come back more often. Wait, I know, the mountains aren't big enough."

"True, but my friends are here, and need me, I think, so here I am," Troy replied.

"Great. Lucky us. Thank you, Heavenly Father."

"I'll take any blessing. Congrats on being ordained. I am sure John was proud for you, too. Now you're a blessedly busy and respected business man."

"Instead of a pyrotechnics maniac," Spider chuckled.

"Thank you, Troy. I have come a long way. I give thanks every day that I have no reason to preside over your funeral. Sadly, I will conduct John's. I suspect his spirit is near, although we can't see him."

"I pray when I find Dillon he's alive and kicking," Troy said.

"Amen. While you're here, where are you staying?"

"I thought with Dillon. Now I don't know. How about up on your houseboat's roof under the stars?" Troy asked.

"It's yours and a closet to store your stuff. Expect company," Denny said. Troy raised his eyebrows.

"Walt should be here some time before midnight."

It had been a long time since Troy had seen Walt Copper, a self-proclaimed techie and guitarist. Troy returned to the Land Rover to grab his bags, finding Silke getting her gear. This time, she didn't tempt him. She carried her overnight pack to the house boat, where, she informed him, she would be spending the night in what had been Dillon's room.

After removing dry clothes from his carryon suitcase, Troy slipped out of his wet swimsuit into a dry one and a white Snowbird Ski Resort t-shirt and flip flops. It was going to be plenty warm tonight, a sweltering, sultry southern night.

Marader had opened the doors to the bar. He held a pool cue in one arm and Heidi in the other. They played against Denny and Jambo. Marader kept the jewelry box near and fiddled with it often, more than he handled Heidi which was very odd.

The pool table sat near the center of the room with a stained-glass lamp hanging above. To the right of the table was a couch and end table where Denny and Spider sat, continuing their discussion about the underwater mansion, ghosts, and good and evil. Troy thought about adding his dollars' worth, but Marader dragged him away to show off his remodeled bachelor pad.

Marader guided Troy upstairs where Tommy lived in a three-bedroom suite. For whatever reason, he brought the jewelry box with him, tucked under his arm. The stairs led to the living room with a couch, love seat and lounger around a coffee table facing a large HD TV screen.

"Hey, I notice you're hairier. What's up?" Troy asked.

"Yeah, thanks to a hair weave and Rogaine. Now I am hairy

everywhere. That's better than claiming my bald spot is a solar panel for a sex machine, even if it is true. So what do you think?" Marader asked.

The place also held two cabinets, one for wine and another for guns, mostly rifles. The walls were covered with photos of the lake, water skiers, and several generations of waterskis, including a pair of wooden Connellys. Troy found some group shots of the blood brothers over the years, about age eight and up. In one group shot, Silke kissed him on the cheek. Straight ahead, double doors led outside to the balcony overlooking the lake. To the left, there was a bathroom between the master and two tiny guest bedrooms. To the right was a small, pale yellow kitchenette with a refrigerator, appliances and a narrow three-person breakfast table.

"Nice. You seem to be doing very well for yourself," Troy said. Marader had a good business sense, networking skills and a talent for talking women out of their clothes.

"Thanks. This summer has been kind of a downer with the lake being so low, even if the weather's been good for being on it. I know it doesn't look like it, but because I'm here along the bridge, people still come to the restaurant and bar, especially when I have live music. I started that last year. Todd Young has a band, The Coveralls. They can cover any song. Get it? Anyway, they'll play at John's wake. So what are you doing, Troy? Any lovely women in your life? If not, you can prowl the wake. Honestly, you look damned good for someone who died."

"Thanks to the doctors," Troy replied. He mentioned months of surgery followed by rehab. Now he was shooting video instead of being the subject.

"Awful to find out we're mortal, isn't it?" Marader said. "Life can change quickly. It doesn't seem like it's been ten years since high school. Enjoy what you can when you can. Speaking of enjoying, what is going on between you and Legs? At first I thought it was my imagination, but she's got her eye on you, Troy, and her hands, too. She is hotter than ever. Too bad she's Dillon's sister. I remember getting punched just for thinking of hitting on her," Marader said.

"She was seventeen, and you were twenty-two."

"As Jay would say, what's your point?"

"Can we talk about finding Dillon? He's still missing and obviously in trouble," Troy said.

"Seriously, guy, enjoy the moment, because Silke is definitely hitting on you. I know the signs. She was dressed to impress, and with that body, she's been working out. She knows you like fit babes. Of course, who doesn't? The question is, is she worth a beating? Because, honestly, I don't think Dillon would kill you. You're too close. He might kill me, so I have to give it some serious thought, for a few seconds anyway!"

Marader knew about flirting. If he hadn't written the book, he had authored chapters and provided research. Silke had been very friendly. Troy figured she had been commiserating, but some of her catty comments about Raquel made more sense in that light. She had claimed Troy could do better. How? Dating her? He had always thought she would make some guy lucky.

"You're clueless, either focused on finding Dillon or well, still interested in someone else. Are you still pining for Raquel?" Marader laughed. "Oh, I can tell I should stop there. Listen, you already died once. Now stop and smell the roses, buddy. We could both be like John tomorrow. Death and taxes, right? Do everybody a favor and take Silke's mind off Dillon and diving tonight."

"Marader . . ."

"Listen, if you're not interested in her, like I said, I am. She's obviously looking for a guy."

Troy had heard her say otherwise.

"I'll give you a week or until you find Dillon, whichever is less, to figure it out. If you haven't done something besides hold hands and shoulder hug, I'm going to roll the dice. My advice . . ."

"Oh no," Troy said.

Marader was interrupted by a cat jumping onto his shoulder. The small lioness regained her balance and rubbed her head under his jaw. "Aw, this is Tawny, my cat. She's a great mouser. Speaking of pussycats, we were talking about Silke. Just tell her that you think she's incredible, smart, charming, sexy, you know, whatever is true, and that you've had the hots for her for years, I know I have, but Dillon threatened you. When she melts, take her to bed. Wear her out, then, in the morning, you can talk to Burt. I mean, who's he going to have dive the crime scene? Just volunteer to go along, as a guide, now that you've been there."

That last part made surprising sense. But, Marader with Silke? Troy needed to get that visual out of his head before he vomited. She would likely shoot Tommy Boy. He led them back downstairs.

"It bothers the hell out of me that John is dead, and Dillon is missing. What if someone is killing off blood brothers? We could be next," Marader said. Seeing everyone, the cat bolted. "She's skittish."

"What deep dark secret are you hiding?" Troy asked.

"How about my membership in a secret organization of werewolves. That's really why I'm hairy," Marader replied.

Silke sidled over to meet them, bringing a topic change.

"Hey, Silke. I was telling Troy it's great to see him alive," Marader said.

"I was kissed by an angel on my deathbed in Florida," Troy replied.

"Lucky you," Marader said.

Silke appeared a little caught off guard, like she couldn't believe her ears. Well, Troy had told her that he didn't believe in the supernatural. "An angel on your death bed? Really? Interesting. I would like to hear more," Silke said, smiling.

"Sure. You can join us, if it's okay with Spider, when I talk to him about our out-of-body experiences. See if there's any similarity," Troy said.

"Your angel might have brought you back, but she didn't get you straightened out. You're not standing or moving quite right. Your knee and low back need adjusting," Silke said.

"And you're the person to straighten me out?"

"If your energy is better, you might find Dillon more easily. I calculated that if we drink one glass of something alcoholic in John's honor, we would be all right to dive in a couple of hours."

"You have your heart set on breaking the law with a night dive?" Troy asked. She nodded. Troy didn't think he could dissuade her, despite what Marader said. "All right. I'll go with you. I doubt Spider or Marader will, but some of the others might."

"Let's see what Knives says," she said, strolling over to him. "Oh Stephen . . ."

Knives was smiling. "J-Man told me you're searching for Dillon, thinking that something nefarious has happened to him. So, what's up? I just saw him last night. Lord, what a strange night."

"Well, he didn't show at the airport," Troy began. He tersely summarized the dive and the strange, cold and creepy underwater mansion.

"Sounds interesting."

"In the sense that a tornado or earthquake at night is interesting," Troy replied.

"And cold! Did he tell you it's freeze your nuts off cold?" Marader yelled out.

"Tomorrow it will be a crime scene, and we won't be able to dive it to look for Dillon or Sherry. Are you interested in going with us tonight?" Silke said.

"A night dive? Cool. Count me in," Knives said.

"I'd go back. Who knows what we might find?" Desiree said as she passed by.

Silke didn't seem to like her, but Troy figured they could use everybody to cover more rooms. "I'll bet Denny will go with us," Silke said.

"I don't think it's a good idea, but I'd go," J-Man said. "But first dinner. The food is hot and ready. For your pleasure, tonight's dinner movie is a double feature. Last night's footage of Marader skiing Cemetery Ridge, and today's dive of Wreythville."

Almost everyone headed for the serving table. Knives waited, sensing more. "Go on. There's something else isn't there?" Troy hesitated. "Hey, I'm your family doctor, if you can't tell me, who can you tell?"

Troy nodded. Spider stopped to listen. "I've been having strange dreams, both while awake and asleep."

"Could be stress."

"I dreamt of being in that study, of John dying, though I didn't know that's what was going on, yesterday while sleeping on the plane flying into Seattle. I thought it was me in the dream. This morning, I had one of Dillon being kidnapped."

"By who?"

"A man and a woman. They . . . they didn't look dangerous. I was surprised. I don't really remember faces, mostly, I recall red iris eyes, kindly faces, and big hats. I know. I'm a lot of help. Spider, have you had anything like it?" Troy said.

Spider shook his head. "No weird dreams, but I see dead people. Haunts mostly, some wandering ghosts, which I didn't see before I witnessed the other side. It has taken . . . some adjusting to it. At first, I thought I was just seeing things out of the corner of my eyes. Then, I visited Gettysburg. I no longer doubted what I saw. People can doubt. I understand. I can't show proof, and I don't want to interact with them like a medium, you know, hang up a shingle, Frank Adder, Psychic Medium." He laughed, sounding slightly mad, only slightly though. "Don't look at me like that, Denny. There are helpful ghosts in the Bible."

"That is true. Are you sure you're not seeing angels?"

Spider nodded. "Angels don't scream, right?"

"They will to exhort you to do the right thing," Denny replied.

"Not angels then. They wouldn't be yelling at me to kill myself. Troy, listen, do you remember when I called you in the hospital and said you came to visit me?" Spider asked.

Troy nodded. It had been an odd conversation. Spider swore Troy's spirit had come into his house and chatted for a while. Spider had been contemplating taking his life. Concerned, Spider had phoned him, worried Troy might have died. They talked about dying back then but living with it had obviously changed their perceptions. Had he been in denial? Troy wondered. Aunt Jada had mentioned him astral traveling, too. How could he be doing this unconsciously?

He mentally stepped back and looked at himself. He wouldn't have considered this two years ago. He had given it little credence just a few days ago. This morning he had scoffed at such thoughts.

"Well, maybe you're doing it while you sleep and going to visit friends. Then you would know things about them you wouldn't know otherwise, such as the secret of Marader's new seductive hairiness," Spider chuckled, then snorted, amusing himself.

"Visiting them?" Troy asked.

"Astral travel. I've read about it. Since you died, you know that you can escape your physical form and return," Spider said.

"I'm no psychic voyeur, but sometimes I wonder if I am lucid dreaming," Troy said.

"Gentlemen, I've seen and experienced many inexplicable things in the hospital and the operating room, so I'm open-minded about life, death, and spirits, but I still prefer the scientific method. Proof. We know John's been murdered. If his ghost wants to help, great. But don't count on it, okay? Do y'all think Dillon was murdered, too?" Knives asked.

"I think the answer to whatever is going on is related to Von Damme's mansion of death," Troy said.

"Catchy title," Spider said.

"John went there, and he's dead. His girlfriend is missing.

Their boat sank. Dillon was thinking of going there, and he's missing. God, I sound like Marader. Hit me please, knock me to my senses."

Gently slapping Troy, Silke took him up on his request. She grinned and said, "I've been wanting to knock some sense into you."

"Von Damme's place, that's where you found the jewelry box Tommy keeps fondling?" Knives asked.

"Yep. Ask to see it, then tell him you want to borrow it for a few days. See what happens," Troy said.

"I'll do it," Knives said and smirked.

"Folks, the food is gonna get cold. Come and get it," J-Man called out.

Spider laid a hand on Troy's shoulder. "Troy, we died and came back. We are Heavensent. We aren't like other people. Our altered consciousness has changed our minds and vision. We see things that are there that we couldn't see before. That is what I was trying to tell the right Reverend Dennis, here. He was disturbed by what I see."

"What did you see?" Troy asked.

"I told you. Haunts. They resonate with the pain of their horrible deaths, lives stolen too young. Darkness lived there. It still lives there. Don't go back. You're a sunshine kind of guy," Spider said.

"Did you see Dillon?" Denny asked.

"No, but it was crowded with spirits. I was claustrophobic. I had to get out."

Troy understood. "When you look at the artifacts from there: the jewelry box, stick pin and the books, do you see anything odd?" he asked.

Spider shook his head. "What do you see?"

"Black smoke or a haze about them," Troy said.

"I don't see that, but I do feel something strange about the book. It . . . it writhes in my grasp sometimes. I thought I was imagining it, or that the paper was drying out. Even so, I think I'll keep reading, in case its helpful, but I'll do it while basking in the sunlight. Troy, you may not have noticed, but Silke has you wrapped around her finger."

Troy blinked. Did she?

"Please, don't go back down below. You know that place is a killer. Others have died there. It will kill you, too, as it murdered John. Directly? Indirectly? It doesn't matter. It is a deadly place heavy with the weight and stench of evil," Spider said.

Troy remembered feeling the same, a hand around his throat. Pressure and a mood of grim hopelessness. What was he going to say to Silke? That he was too frightened to dive? That Dillon was dead if he was down there, dead tonight and dead in the morning. He would have to find a better way to say it.

After Father Dennis said a blessing over the food, J-Man hooked the camera into the bar's giant HD TV. While they ate, Troy and Silke watched the video recording of Marader skiing with the fireworks blasting all around, some obviously too close for comfort. Of course, he offered to show off his scars. J-Man replayed his accident several times, in slow motion.

"Jay, that's Pat he's landing on," Denny said.

"Point made. Sorry," J-Man replied.

The gravity of the situation returned when those in the boat and watching the recording realized Pat's body had sent Marader cartwheeling. After Father Dennis shared some words of wisdom and comfort, they shared moments of silence for Pat and John.

The recording of the Cemetery Ridge was little help in solving the mystery. Pat had apparently dug up the coffins, but why? And why were they clawed and scratched on the inside? Had a wild animal been trapped or transported inside? It reminded Troy of the shutters inside the damned mansion.

He thought he saw a shoe near one of the pits. "Is that clothing?" Troy asked.

"Yeah. Made by Gucci. We found it and some jewelry. It's all evidence so Burt confiscated it," Denny said.

"Well, we have treasure from it that wasn't confiscated as evidence. Maybe it will give us a clue. Tomorrow, I'll make some calls, do some research," Marader said. He held up the jewelry box like a hard-earned prize possession.

"Wow. That's somethin'. Let me see it," Knives said. He held out his hands, wiggling his fingers.

"Be careful. It has sharp edges and corners," Marader said. He hesitated.

"It cut me," Silke said.

"I guarantee you that I am experienced with and licensed to handle sharp objects," Knives said.

"Sharp jewelry?" Marader asked. He sighed and placed the box in Knives' hands, but Tommy wouldn't let go. He was sweating like an addict about to go cold turkey.

"Is it sticky, too? Covered in glue?"

"Funny. Ha. Ha. It's worth a lot of money, buddy."

"You think I'd steal from you?" Knives asked. Marader hesitated. "The only thing I've ever stolen from you was Pop Tarts because it always pissed you off. Can you say the same?"

Of course, Marader couldn't. There was a time when Tommy Boy was always hungry. There were two types of food: his food and his food on your plate. If he wasn't eating, he was sleeping.

Marader grudgingly released the jewelry box. His skin seemed to cling for a moment, and then Knives carefully lifted the treasure to scrutinize it. "These look like blood stains. Let me see your hands," Knives said.

Marader held out his hands palm up. They looked like he had been handling thorn bushes.

"Now I'm going to have to get some antiseptic," Knives said. He walked away with the jewelry box.

Marader followed closely, complaining. "Hey, careful carrying that around. I might be able to retire if it's an antique."

"What if I tossed it into the lake?" Knives asked. He feinted a throw.

Marader almost leapt out of his skin, falling for the fake. "Nice. Don't even joke about it," he growled.

"I think you're obsessed," Knives said. He carried a first aid kit out from the bathroom and started cleaning his blood brother's wounds.

"Can you perform an exorcism?" Spider asked Denny.

Father Dennis rolled his eyes to the heavens and crossed himself. "I would have to look into that, but I doubt it. They require the Church to sanction it."

"What might the consequences be?" J-Man asked. While the letter opener and jewelry made the rounds, Troy slipped outside for a breath of fresh air. He smelled acrid, wildfire smoke and wondered if the winds might be changing.

Silke followed him out into the night air. Her golden hair gleamed with an ethereal light, and her gray eyes were bright, making it difficult to look anywhere else. Her tanned skin seemed luminous, and her sun dress shimmered silvery as though her beauty might be a vision. He knew better. Her beauty went beyond skin deep.

"Are you all right? You bolted out of there," she asked. She glanced into his eyes, then down, before her attention lingered on him.

"The jewelry box makes me uncomfortable," Troy said.

Silke touched her bandage. "It makes my cut throb."

"I'm sorry you got hurt," he said. He gently took her hand to examine it without thinking about asking. She didn't flinch. "Sorry. I'll be gentle. Does it need stitches?"

"No. I'm okay. I should have worn gloves. I will next time. On that subject, Knives, Denny, and J-Man said they would do a night dive to search for Dillon. I think Father Dennis wants to see for himself and maybe cleanse the place. Desiree volunteered, too."

Troy wondered if this was wise. Going back there wouldn't save Dillon. If he was there, he would be there in the morning. Was it worth the danger tonight? He heard Marader's voice, suggesting Troy keep Silke distracted and entertained through the night.

"Troy, I can't thank you enough for what you've done today. You've been friendly, helpful, spontaneous, and had to improv a few times."

She was concerned, caring, and beautiful. For a moment, he seriously contemplated following Marader's advice. If he kept looking at Silke, he might kiss her. Was there lipstick that sparkled in moonlight? "I can't say I have much experience as a boyfriend. I tried to mimic that lovestruck, dazed look Jambo used to get," he chuckled.

"I didn't know you were such a fine actor. Am I wrong, or did you smile more when we were younger?"

Her words set Troy thinking. Silke remembered who he had been, a guy living with his hair on fire and a chip in his heart. When it came down to it, she really didn't know him now, and he didn't know her. Each knew who the other had been back in the day, so to speak, before she went to college, and before he had died on the mountain.

"Ah, now I made you think of something sad. I'm sorry."

He shook his head. "I'm just weary."

"If you're that tired, you shouldn't go diving," Silke said. She sighed, paused, then finally forged ahead. "And if my brother is down there, he's already dead. Murdered or otherwise. We'll only be finding his body. I hope it isn't so but that's the reality, if he's still down there."

She looked in need of a hug. Troy felt he needed one. She started to cry when he gently took her in his arms. It felt natural. He wouldn't lie to her about the future being all right. Though now, with Silke nestled in his arms, he expected Dillon to show up. She turned her face up to his. "If he's there, he's dead. He wouldn't want you to get hurt or killed looking for him when it's already too late. He would rather you take a calculated risk, right?" she asked. It was true. He nodded. "And if he isn't there, then it would be sad if someone was injured during a futile search because I made a rash decision."

Her words caused Troy to pause. He was about to make a

hasty emotional choice. Silke looked and felt so kissable. Like an omen, the crunching sound of metal and breaking plastic filled the night. The dock shuddered, breaking the tension of the moment and alarming Troy.

"That sounded like car meets tree," Troy said.

Twelve: Wrecked

Nobody inside seemed to notice the crunching metal sound over the raucous music. When the eight-ball game continued, the balls clacking together, Troy and Silke decided to investigate. At the Land Rover, he grabbed a flashlight. Silke strolled, armed with her purse, a flashlight, a gun and an adventurous smile. Still uneasy from John's murder, Troy took the tire iron.

"What do you think it was?" Silke asked.

"I would say alien space craft, but a drone crash seems more likely," Troy said.

"Someone watching us?" Silke asked.

"I'm sorry. I was joking, trying to lighten the mood. I think it was a car crash, though I guess a drone could have hit a tree."

They hiked up the gravel drive, leaving the parking lot. Nothing had driven this way. There was no dust or smoke, yet, but the mists swirled and coiled in their light beams. The fog made the woods on both sides of the road seem mysterious. Troy heard the furtive, rustling sounds of nocturnal animals. Marader had complained about raccoons and coyotes, he reminded himself. A paranoid person would think they were being stalked.

Rolling toward them, the fog seemed to thicken. Now Troy smelled gravel dust. The slight breeze carried it down and past them. He blinked, seeing a dark shape shambling toward them.

"Something is coming," Silke said. A gun in hand already, she was a quick draw.

"Don't go gunslinger on me," Troy said, then he realized he had a tight grip on the tire iron.

The shape became a figure, tall and thin, lurching along. It saw them, hands outstretched. Silke stepped back.

Troy was about to demand the figure identify himself when he finally recognized Walt Copper. Bloodied and battered, he staggered toward them. His eyes were dazed, and now likely night blind. Troy lowered the flash beam. "Is that you, Walt? What happened?"

"Hey, Troy. Yeah, it's me. I ran into something. A deer or a bear, maybe, up the drive. I'm not really sure," Walt said.

With another step, his knee buckled. Troy caught him before he fell far, and Silke took his left arm. Together, they supported Walt, walking slowly downhill toward the marina.

He looked back and forth between them, mostly staring at Silke. He was bleeding from multiple scratches across his face and neck, a smashed nose, and split lips. "Am I in the afterlife?" Walt mumbled.

Silke looked fabulous, a gift from heaven. She reminded Troy of his bedside angel. He wasn't surprised Walt thought the same.

"You are in God's Country, and Silke is dazzling, but we are at Maraders Marina, and we still need doctors here. Knives won't be thrilled about working, but he will take a look at you," Troy replied. He heard a loud snapping twig that made him turn toward the trees.

"I'll bet you've felt like this, but worse. Have you found Dillon or John, yet?"

Troy looked over at Silke. Should he tell him now? Or wait?

Troy found his throat constricting. He really didn't want to say the truth out loud again. John was dead. "We found John's body on the bottom of the lake."

"What? He drowned? He's a naval diver for Christ's sake," Walt snapped angrily. He sounded much like Troy's thoughts.

"We're not sure what happened. We found him inside a big house in the underwater town, Old Wreythville."

J-Man crossed the gangway, meeting them on shore. "I thought I heard something. Nobody else did, and they keep saying I'm losing my hearing. What do they know?" J-Man said.

Despite what he had said, one other blood brother had followed him. Jay and Jambo took Walt's elbows and guided him up the plank and into the store, taking a short cut to the bar. As the door closed, Troy heard. "Hey, I left my phone. And my laptop."

Troy and Silke headed back up the gravel road to recover Walt's electronics and luggage. They had briefly debated driving, but Silke wanted to stretch her legs. Along the way, Troy felt watched. The movements in the woods sounded like failed attempts to be stealthy.

About where they had met Walt, Troy thought he heard hissing. They agreed it sounded like a radiator with a leak.

"There, I think I see it," she said. At the edge of her light, through a thinning curtain of fog, metal glinted and gleamed. A few steps closer, and Troy could see more of the front of Walt's car, a badly damaged white Mustang. The middle of the front bumper was concaved and driven so far into the car that the headlights crisscrossed, and the engine poked up through the tented hood. Steam arose from the Mustang, like a long last gasp. Walt had hit something, no doubt. But what? There was nothing dead or injured in the drive.

"A bear would have survived," Troy said.

"Look at the damage. I see blood on the ground," Silke said. With her flashlight, she pointed to splatters of red on the brown stalks of grass and weeds.

A reminder of winter, a cool breeze blew through, stirring up the fog. It rankled his nose and caused him to shiver, calling to mind a wet dog or an old wool sweater drying out. He noticed something fuzzy in the grill. He pulled on it, finding bloodied, black fur. He showed it to Silke.

Troy felt scrutinized while they grabbed Walt's briefcase, laptop satchel, and an overnight hard-sided suitcase. He was weary of feeling under observation and not knowing why. Had he become that aware of ghosts, perhaps?

As he turned to leave, he thought he heard a growl. "Did you hear that?"

Silke smiled. "The frogs make some wild sounds, don't they?"

He peered into a stand of birch, among poplars and oaks. For a moment, he thought he saw glowing eyes, like those of a feline, but too large to be a house cat, even a bob cat. A blink later, the eyes were gone. He waited, watching. He didn't see them again and began to wonder if he had really seen them. The trip to the underwater mansion had left him sad about John's death, worried about Dillon, and paranoid about shadows.

"Are you all right?" Silke asked.

"I'm tired. It's been a full day."

"I think Walt's wreck confirms that we are not going diving tonight," Silke said. Her lip quivered, but she remained dry-eyed. Somewhere close by, it sounded like coyotes howled. It made the forest fall quiet for a while. Everything held still, holding its breath or song, trying to remain unnoticed. The coiling fog made it feel mysterious and dangerous.

"Those aren't frogs. I thought I saw eyes in the woods," Troy said.

Silke visually searched the woods. She kept her gun ready. Lower brush and bushes started to rustle as something pushed them aside. The creature suddenly bolted ahead, racing for the road. Silke cocked her gun, finger white on the trigger.

A dog bounded out of the woods, tongue waggling, ears flapping and tail waving. Troy recognized Jambo's hunting hound as it ran by. Right behind him, a chocolate Lab followed, both dogs caught up in the scent of a chase.

"Ace and Scout, Jambo and Jay's dogs. That got my heart pounding," Silke breathed.

"It did that," Troy said, though his heart beat already raced. "Let's get back."

Knives and the boys took good care of Walt. They

concluded he would live, be very sore tomorrow, and fed him NSAIDs with a rum and coke. J-Man used ice to pack Walt's neck, and Heidi stuck on small band aids, leaving Walt looking like he had nicked himself with a razor.

Silke excused herself to bed. Troy was weary, too, but he hadn't seen his blood brothers in a long time. Silke was giving him time to get lost with the boys.

For a time, they drank and shared stories, enjoying a good buddy vibe, and speculating on what had happened to Dillon and John. When everyone else went outside to see the damage to Walt's car, and Father Dennis to offer a blessing, Troy begged off. He felt so weighed down by sadness he could barely put one foot in front of the other. Even as beat as Troy was now, he feared he might not sleep. He could see John's face, alive one moment, waxy and dead the next.

Troy limped to the boat. Perhaps Silke could work her healing touch on him. Sure. Any excuse to have her put her hands on his body. He guessed those gym guys got hurt all the time.

He relished sleeping under the stars and planned to grab a front porch lounger cushion to carry to the roof. For too many months, he had slept in a hospital bed or a rehab bed. Sometimes ceilings and walls seemed to be closing in. Often, it was after dreams of his spirit soaring, free of the pain of his body. Pain. It was part of being alive as much as pleasure in shaping how people lived.

As Troy approached his temporary and buoyant home, the Rentzel houseboat, he felt a presence. He wasn't alone. His step faltered when he stepped onto the bow, and then through its short front gate to the covered porch. Was that perfume? He thought he recognized it, but his mind was too muddled to name it or who might wear it. With his luck, it would be the Dark Lady.

His eyes adjusted to the darkness of the shadow of the front porch, and he realized why he felt watched, perhaps even hungrily eyed. He could feel heat from her. Sitting in the lounger, Desiree's dark eyes glinted mischievously while she studied him as she might a future dessert. She stretched, displaying lean ribs and a flat stomach between her frilly white tank top, pulled tight to straining, and her sheer short shorts, little more than lingerie. He reminded himself to be careful what he wished for.

"It's been a strange, difficult day. Would you like to chat?" she asked with the lips of a siren.

At this time of night, talking isn't what she had in mind. "It has been that. I apologize, but I doubt I'd be much of a conversationalist. I'm almost dead on my feet."

"What an interesting phrase. I thought you might need . . . a release. Sometimes, when somebody dies, it's heartening and healthy to perform . . . a life affirming act," Desiree replied. She looked absolutely delectable, and he had been already impressed earlier. Her eyes were bright, her lovely, full lips playful. His body, stirred by her beauty and figure, was making promises it couldn't keep. John, who he was lamenting, would highly recommend laying with her.

Tomorrow was unknown. The present was a gift.

Her look grew speculative. She was far too charming and incredibly beautiful to refuse. Then again, he was diving in the morning. Dillon, Troy thought, was killing his love life.

"I thought you looked like you needed to embrace life. That you needed some adult playtime with a playmate. Someone like . . . Ava."

She stroked his arm, and he tingled all over, even as he broke out into a sweat. He felt like he was speeding down the hill with no brakes. So what else was new? Controlled sliding and skidding. That made him think of Ava, wanton, carefree and astounding.

"I asked Tommy about you. He said you'd only gushed about two women. Raquel and Ava. I like a man who is discerning."

"Then you know I look before I leap. That tempting stretch of powder with the awesome fall line might be an avalanche zone."

She laughed. "Says the man who nearly died in one."

"What's the saying? Live and learn. I prefer to think the earth moved to kill me, not the snow. So yeah, the earthquake laid me up for a long time, literally a wreck."

"Laid up, now that sounds interesting. I could be your Ava while you're here," Desiree said. Her voice had a massaging effect and struck his taste like smooth milk chocolate.

"Well, I've been told I'm a terrible liar, so I won't even try to contradict you," he said. Her smile became impish. He grabbed his imagination before it was too late. Oh hell, it was too late. "I haven't had the pleasure of female company in this life time, but I have to wonder about getting intimately involved with a woman who drew a knife on me just a couple of hours ago and almost stabbed me. So pardon me if I doubt your intentions."

Desiree chuckled, placing a hand over her mouth. "Oh, I did, didn't I. I never apologized, did I? You almost scared the life out of me. I didn't know I could jump in fins underwater. I was jittery. Something about that cold, creepy place."

Troy suppressed a shudder. When he blinked, he could see John starring accusingly at him. Troy had come back from the dead. How?

"Well, I could apologize now," she said, brushing up against him. By her eyes and body language, she told him she wanted him here and now.

His body reminded him he could be dead tomorrow. Seize the moment. The rational part of him knew he was getting up early in the morning. Fool. Surely, he could stay awake for an hour.

Desiree cocked her head, she snagged a long Silke hair from his shirt. With disdain, she tossed it aside. "At first when I saw you, I thought you were with Silke," Desiree said.

Silke? Her name caused him to reconsider this moment. He valued what she thought of him. How would it look if he got entangled with Desiree after knowing her less than a day?

These walls were thin. She could probably hear them or feel them from the heat radiating outward.

Distracting him, Desiree stroked his chest. "But I asked Tommy. He told me about her brother, how Dillon threatened all of you with a beating if you even thought about kissing his sister, the boss called her Legs, so I figure there's no chance of a romance there. Isn't Dillon a black belt or a ninja warrior?" she asked.

"Yes," Troy replied. And Dillon had a knack for finding him.

"So, is Dillon a bad ass?"

"Yeah. John got indignant one time, you can't tell me what to do kind of thing, after basic training, and faced off with Dillon. It wasn't even a contest. John said it was worse than anyone he tussled with, including his hand-to-hand training instructors," Troy said.

"Poor girl. Her loss. My gain," Desiree said with a pleased sigh. "I can't believe you're saying wait to me, but then again, I find it irresistible that you can hold off when you clearly want me right here and right now. And who said anything about making love? You can have me any way you want me," she whispered.

She tilted her face up, raised on her toes and slowly, passionately kissed him. He couldn't stop himself and kissed her back.

He drew her closer, tighter, having lost the battle, when he felt a burning in his chest. It broke the enchantment of the moment, leaving him reeling when she drew back.

"Good luck, as I doubt I'll be up early in the morning when you leave. It's my day off. I would ask to spend it with you, but I understand that you're looking for your friend. I find that kind of loyalty seductive." She brushed his lips again leaving a first-degree burn. "And, I hope that's good incentive to stay safe. That mansion is a dangerous place. Next time, I promise, I won't carry a knife. But, I must warn you, my fingernails can be sharp."

He told himself he was an idiot as he watched her sashay to the marina and disappear through a side door, heading upstairs to her room. He should get some sleep, except his body was now restless.

After a cold shower, he tried to sleep in front of a fan. In the small, tiny-windowed bedroom, Troy felt claustrophobic.

He finally got up, grabbed the lounge cushion from the front deck, and headed back inside, through the kitchen lounge dining room and down the hall to the back door. He could hear his noisy friends still up drinking and laughing, probably sharing John stories.

Outside and above, he heard a noise. A scooting and shuffling sound that tugged at his curiosity. After today, he couldn't help but wonder what he might find on the roof. He climbed the ladder, trying to be quiet.

Thirteen: Intruder

Peering over the rooftop in the moonlight, Troy spotted a long-haired beauty lying on a lounge cushion. Silke's hair shone as she sat up. She wore a white tank top and pink shorts, her tanned legs gleaming. His heart beat like it did when he was frightened before trying something dangerous and extreme. This was usually where he compartmentalized fear and spoke affirmations.

"Please, Troy, come sit with me. It's beautiful out tonight, and it would be a pleasure to share it with someone, especially after that dive today. Those skeletons! Like something out of a horror movie. Why were they like that? A Satanic ritual? When I close my eyes, I see those mocking skulls or John staring blankly at me. Sometimes," she caught her breath. "I . . . I see Dillon's face instead, eyes accusing."

He shouldn't be with her right now, but he knew exactly what she meant. It was one of the reasons he had to escape to the Great Outdoors and breathe. He couldn't just leave her alone to deal with this. That would be callous. When he closed his eyes, he saw John staring at him. You came back. Why can't I?

"Even if you don't feel like saying anything. The stars are bright, and I don't bite, nor do I keep my fingernails sharp. My clients wouldn't like it."

Well, she had heard him with Desiree. It was just as well he had resisted. Thank you, frontal lobe. "I have enough scars," he said. The words came out with an unexpected harsh edge. He climbed onto the roof and approached her.

"I saw. You know, you can safely rest your weary body here. There's no chance of romance," she said. Was that bitterness in her voice? Sarcasm? Sadness? Anger for certain.

A wise man would turn around and leave. He had been called foolish and insane more than once. This could be a nightmare, figuratively, anyway. He might as well face it. "You obviously heard . . . our conversation."

"I did, though I didn't intend to. Did she really pull a knife on you?" Silke asked, frowning at him. She was fuming, but he didn't think she was mad at him. But then, that could be wishful thinking.

"Yes, she did, when I went back and startled her while she was exploring the desk. That place made everybody nervous and jumpy. Who wouldn't be freaked out? Speaking of, how is your hand?" he asked.

"A painful reminder of that place. When I close my eyes, I find my mind drifting back to it, like a horrible accident on the side of the road that I can't look away from. I came out here, hoping to forget about it under the canopy of stars and the near full moon," she said and released a long sigh. "It's helped some, but my mind is trying to figure out why all this is happening."

"I won't figure anything out with a brain of mush. Sleep calls," Troy said. He dropped his cushion next to hers and collapsed on the pad with a thump and rolled onto his back to stare at the stars. He didn't plan on budging unless it was an emergency. His eyelids felt very heavy, wanting to close and stay that way.

"You're accustomed to more beautiful skies and places aren't you? With all your travels in the mountains and to remote places. It would be darker there," she said. Silke had a soothing voice.

"I've been to many beautiful places, it's true, but I'm not jaded. There's beauty everywhere, especially here," he said. Sleep beckoned, drawing him down like an anchor through water. Drifting . . .

"Troy, are you wishing you said yes to Desiree?"

He could pretend to be asleep, but he could feel Silke's stare. His mind struggled to say something calming or witty. His body sure wished it had been able to hijack his brain. Even now, it was trying to convince him to kiss Silke and see where that would lead.

"Honestly, I don't want to be shot by Mr. Fleenor and his gun club friends," he murmured. That was the truth.

"Seriously," she pressed.

"Honestly didn't count? Are you wearing your glasses?"

"Give me a moment," she said.

He was starting to wish he hadn't agreed to be her pretend boyfriend. But, he couldn't tell her that without offending her and explaining his reasoning wouldn't help matters. Mentioning her brother would only add fuel to the fire. "Silke, the way I see it, with my eyes closed right now I might add, is that I can enjoy the night with a drop-dead beautiful woman wielding a knife, and I've already seen too much knife work over the last two years . . . or with a to-die-for gorgeous woman who packs a gun. But I figure you'll keep me alive long enough to help you find Dillon."

She was quiet, but he could feel waves of anger and indignation. His attempt to be humorous and ease the situation had failed. Likely, she was crossing her arms and glaring daggers at him.

Dillon should be here to face his sister's wrath. "Tell me, is it true that Dillon threatened y'all?"

"You're taking advantage of a tired mind," he said. He started to climb to his feet, and she gently pushed him back down.

"The taking advantage of your tired body has already been tried," she said, sounding ticked about it. "Don't sidestep the question. Did Dillon really threaten y'all, warn y'all to stay away from me?"

She would only ask the others and learn the truth. Marader would tell her and laugh in her face about it, which would make her madder. Troy nodded. "Yes, your brother, who is very protective, strongly recommended that we stay away from you if we couldn't resist our base urges and sexual desires, then he carried through on the consequences as promised. He was really concerned about John and Marader making plays for you. Dillon knocked Tommy out with one punch. It's one of my favorite photos of Marader sprawled unconscious on his back."

She managed a terse chuckle. "For that, I thank him. But as far as warning everybody in the Tri Cities, well, I don't appreciate it, not at all. Err," she growled. She abruptly seized her pillow and repeatedly beat Troy with it, surprising him and making him role into a fetal position. "And you, y'all were in on it. I thought y'all were my friends!"

"I am," he said, but she was right. He protected himself and let her abuse the pillow against him. He figured her emotions were ragged after what they had seen today. She paused, crying and briefly hugging his back. Before he could turn, she walloped him some more.

If it had been goose down instead of foam, there would have been feathers everywhere. He figured it was good therapy. She had been holding it together wonderfully through a rough day with Dillon missing, her great aunt hallucinating, scuba-diving and exploring that awful house. Added to that, she had spent the day with Dillon's blood brothers, a boatload of testosterone.

"I'm sorry I was scared of your brother," Troy said.

"Oh, you're just like everyone else," she said.

"Ouch," Troy said. He was not like everyone else. He would take being beaten by pillows, but her comment was a low blow. He was not getting any sleep here. Another padded lounger waited on the front deck.

"I'm sorry. That isn't true," she said. Dropping her pillow, she started to mash and rub forcefully on his back. It felt good, and he rolled onto his belly. He felt her tears drop onto his back, the second time she'd cried on him tonight, but he remained quiet, letting her release. She gave him an aggressive back and neck massage, working out some of her anger on him. It seemed to be doing them both some good as his muscles loved the attention. Any excuse, he mused.

"You know. When I see Dillon next, I'm going to hug him, then slap him or wring his neck, I haven't decided which, all while I demand an apology."

Troy drifted off to sleep with her fingers digging into his flesh. She truly possessed magic hands. Did he really want to find Dillon since he would be upset right now? He had trouble working up the energy to worry. John's ghost seemed to rest, too, so Troy slept.

He seemed to awaken to a gentle but painful touch. It reminded him a bit of waking back up in his broken body after dying, feeling off kilter and out of whack. Was he drugged? If so, it wasn't helping.

All his nerves seemed afire, pain flaring. One finger became a caressing hand, and her touch was smoothing, trailing all over his body like frosty butterflies. Coolness gave way to an exciting heat, and the pain, while still there, was superseded by the overwhelming pleasure. Was she bringing life back into his dead body? Troy thought back to his guiding angel at his deathbed. She had been glorious.

He could think until he opened his bleary eyes, and then he could only focus on her sitting before him, finally, again, after all these years. His beloved had returned. She was a vision, as pale as lace, with ruby red lips and curly white-gold locks falling upon her shoulders. Despite the darkness, her sultry eyes lit up the room. Black pupils on red irises saw inside him, smiled, and stroked his thirst for life, his lust for adventure.

"Ah, beloved, you have survived the first day," she gushed. She kissed him, her eyes open, staring into his eyes. Their connection covered years, and he felt strangely young again. When she drew back, he felt incomplete.

"I died. You saved me," Troy replied. She was his world. "I owe you all, beloved."

"I am thrilled to see you on the mend. Methinks more kisses would speed up the process," she said.

The next kiss seemed to blind him for a while, and he realized he tasted blood where she had bitten him. Even so, his body hurt less than before. His heart rampaged out of control until she caressed him, calming him. The lessening of pain, the vigor of her touch, and vim of her lips allowed him to clearly see the worry in her eyes.

"What's wrong?" he asked.

"Your friends and family are a problem."

He chuckled, and his chest rattled. "What did they do?"

"They have been to the mansion twice, the fools! They took personal effects from it along with a dead body, the mortal Von Damme killed," she coolly told him. More than once she had delivered the news of death, even murder.

"Who?" Troy knew, but he still had asked the question.

Why? Who was he?

"The one from the military, I believe. More of your friends will die if we fail to act soon. Trouble will find them and your sister now. She has handled the crux. They all have. It will only end ill for them."

Troy didn't have a sister. Was he Dillon?

"But it will be far worse than death if we fail to stop Von Damme and the Damned. I am confined by day, even as the abominations are free to roam. If we do nothing, it could be the dawn of the vampire."

Shaking awakened him. "Troy. Troy! Get up. There's an intruder," she whispered. The gorgeous woman with a halo of red-gold hair shook his shoulder again. She didn't look so dark now, though darkness surrounded her, and stars, too. Now she reminded him of Silke. Her eyes were luminous, but instead of burning with passion, they pleaded, worried about something.

He struggled to make sense of it. The dream lingered, bringing along emotions. Silke looked bedraggled and sexy as if they had been grappling with each other.

"Troy, please, wake up," she said, her voice on edge.

"I'm half awake. What's wrong?" he asked.

"I saw a wolf. He trotted right into the store."

"You were awake and saw a wolf?"

"I heard him come down the dock. Don't look at me like that. I saw a wolf, big, brown-gray and furry with bright yellow eyes and the better to eat you with sized teeth. Seriously big teeth. He looked up at me, and I think he smiled."

And Troy thought his nightmares were wild. "There's already a wolf in there named Marader,"

She groaned. "That's funny and true, too, but I know what I saw. Even if I'm wrong about the wolf, it might be a feral or lost dog."

"I'll bet you want me to go chase it out," Troy groaned. He had a wry thought. This was similar to a husband or boyfriend moment. Aunt Jada was demented, all right.

"I'll go with you. I'm armed," she said.

"And dangerous. Is this where I run in after telling you to cover me?" he asked.

"Grumpy when awakened in the middle of the night are you?"

"It depends on the reason I'm being awakened, and I'm a saint compared to your brother."

"Amen to that. I'll e-mail a letter to the Pope recommending you for sainthood," Silke said.

"Sorry. I blame jet lag," he yawned. He rubbed his jaw, and

his eyes, trying to remove the grit, and fumbled for his phone. When he dialed Marader's cell, his call went directly to voice mail. No surprise there. Troy tried the bar phone, and after the initial ring, he heard breaking glass. The second ring was cut off and silenced.

Troy exchanged curious and concerned looks with Silke, and then they descended the ladder. On the way through the houseboat, Troy picked up a baseball bat and a flashlight. He carried them along, feeling outgunned by Silke who also was equipped with a taser. He was conscious of the noise each of their steps made on the dock boards, and the way the marina gently rocked and rolled. They weren't going to take the wolf by surprise, that was for sure.

All the outdoor lights were dark at the marina except for one at the gangway to land. More illumination played through the windows from displays in the store and beer signs in the bar area. The marina and store looked peaceful. The quiet seemed loud.

Silke sniffed. "Do you smell smoke?"

"Don't start," Troy said. An acrid waft breezed in from the southeast. "Now that you mention it. Yes, the winds must be shifting."

On the door, Troy noticed scratch marks freshly scored. Was that from whatever had pushed open the door? Bat ready, he entered the store first. Silke followed but left the door open and clear so the animal could flee. The Skoal clock's display read 4:05.

He stood quietly crouched, listening. All he heard was Silke's breathing, the soft lop-lop of small waves against the pilings, and the hum of the refrigerators. They searched the store, aisle by aisle. Troy started to feel silly, and yet, he sensed a presence behind the checkout counter. He could hear heavy breathing, but when he looked in the cashier's station, he saw nothing amiss.

Ghosts? His imagination running wild? Fatigued induced hallucinations?

He frowned at Silke but kept checking. Due to all the glowing liquor advertisement behind the bar—Cuervo 1800 tequila, South Holston Brewing Co, and Wild Turkey—along with emergency exit signs and the lights from the old-fashioned style juke box, the bar lounge and dining area were well lit. Nothing hid under the tables.

Troy heard a familiar repeating tone. He peered over the bar, finding the phone's receiver on the floor near a shattered tumbler and broken glass. Silke flipped on lights in the commercial kitchen. It was clean, packed with supplies for the upcoming grand opening, and unoccupied, except for Tawny.

The tan cat crouched wide-eyed atop a cabinet near the ceiling. "Poor kitty. Something spooked her," Silke said.

They heard the sound of paw nails clicking upstairs.

"Marader might be in for a surprise," Troy said.

While they carefully treaded up the flight of steps, he swore he could feel something breathing heavily, and yet, the second floor sounded quiet except for the low purr of box fans. Silke held her gun ready and worried her lower lip.

Troy reached the top of the steps. He turned on a flashlight, looking left and right, the beam slashing across the lounge, its furniture, the gun displays, and into the private kitchen of yellow. All three bedroom doors were closed, but the door to the balcony gaped wide open. He could see the moon's glow illuminating the planks, and then a shadow passed by.

He gestured with the flashlight toward the balcony and darted to the doorway. Outside, on the balcony's deck, claws scrabbled, changing direction. He wondered if the dog was running away or going to attack. He didn't want to corner it and stood aside to offer it a direction to escape.

"Ready?" he asked Silke. She nodded.

Troy stepped around the corner, expecting to see a big dog. He was shocked and taken aback, retreating a step and bumping into Silke, who uttered an oath at the sight of the creature. The wolf-like beast was larger than any dog he had seen, at least as large as a mastiff. It was black with a streak of gray down its back, starting from a pale muzzle and bandit mask. One eye was dark and glittered with an eerie amber light while the left was milky white.

When Bandit saw them, the beast barred its teeth, showing bloodied gums. Its sharp canines gleamed in the moonlight like metal blades snapped up from a butcher's block. Troy thought it seemed wounded and thereby more dangerous. The beast held itself at an odd angle, guarded and yet ready to spring. Bandit's snout and jaw appeared to have healed wrong, crooked from being broken too many times like a boxer, giving it a sneer.

"What is that thing?!" Troy said, barely managing a whisper.

He wished he was carrying a gun. Actions spoke louder than words. Silke fired her taser. Her aim on target, all three darts buried in Bandit's fur. Electricity danced through the filament into the beast.

It snarled, jerked several times, spasming as it staggered back. Bandit bumped into the railing, loudly cracking the wood, then the wolf recovered. Gathering itself, the beast charged forward.

Troy reacted instinctively, swinging the bat. Bandit backed away and then lunged. Its jaws snapped out, seized the bat and jerked it from his grasp. The wolf-like beast stared at him with disdain. It mouth-tossed the bat over the railing.

"Damn!" Troy said. This didn't seem to be a normal wolf. "I didn't know we had wolves in Tennessee. I wish I had one of Marader's shotguns."

The low growl started in its throat, turning into a snarl.

"The taser should have dropped it. It weighs less than a man," she said. Silke readied her gun, a Glock 43. Her actions didn't seem to bother the creature. It stalked toward them, forcing them to back away.

Troy bumped into a charcoal grill, almost knocking it over. That gave him an idea, and he seized it, rolling it into Bandit's way. The wolf leap back as the lid snapped open. The BBQ spat out the grill, sending the metal rack tumbling. The cooker was cold, but it had been full of ashes now roiling in a particulated gray cloud over Bandit. It coughed, glared at Troy with rheumy, angry eyes, then the beast sprang.

Troy braced himself for the blow, but Bandit surprised him by awkwardly scampering over the railing. The wolf disappeared over the edge and into the lake with a splash.

They kept watch for a few minutes, never seeing any sign of the animal. If it hadn't been for the cracked railing, the missing taser darts and snapped wires, they could have imagined the moment. Troy wished he had taken a photo as proof.

Fourteen: Search and Rescue Dive

Troy released the wheel of the Bass Buggy, letting the pontoon boat putter along by itself into the miasma of smoke and fog. He donned his windbreaker, warding against the damp humidity and Silke's cold shoulder. He missed her sunny smile which would have made the early gloom seem irrelevant.

Troy was trying to keep his mind off what had happened and what might be coming. Today was the first day of the rest of his life, he reminded himself. Most mornings he told himself that. His taste buds were replaced and renewed every ten days. Every seven years humans grew a new body, including brain tissue. Right now, he was on year two of living a second chance in a modern wonder of a body.

A new day. New chances. New adventures. Except John was dead. May he rest in peace. The world was a darker place. It was a reminder to Troy he could be dead any moment. Dead again.

Silke looked serious with her glasses on and her hair pulled back in a ponytail. Somehow, she looked like an unhappy ray of sunshine. Dressed in a white hoodie, leg warmers, socks and Crocs, she was clad for the early day's conditions.

Was she mad at him? Or at her brother? Or just bracing for the worst? Whatever, he had a feeling it was going to be a quiet ride.

When he considered it, he could understand. They were going diving again down to that horrible ruin where John had died and Dillon might have died. Her brother's best friends, who she had thought were her friends, had kept a secret from her.

Silke's foul mood added to the strangeness of the weather cocktail of thin fog and dense smoke. He might be able to see fifty feet. Everything now appeared a sickly yellow, a bile color, and unhealthy to breathe. Troy used a GPS Marader owned to help navigate. Keeping track of their location, he drove the pontoon boat at half speed.

The platform was surrounded by railings and driven by an 85 hp outboard motor. The Bass Buggy had benches, a captain's chair, wheel, and party table currently folded up. It all sat atop two long air-tight barrels. A partial hard roof canopy stretched over the back half. The deck needed sweeping and appeared to be used for maintenance duty around the marina, but it would do, eventually getting them to Cemetery Ridge.

Silke had arisen early, talking with Deputy Burt and convincing Marader to loan them a boat, this did qualify, and diving gear, so they could guide the SARS dive party. Marader's comment, when Silke was out of earshot, was that whatever Troy had done last night to piss off Legs, please keep it up. If Troy had been more awake he would have slugged him.

"Girls Just Want to Have Fun" played on Silke's phone, so she answered. "Hiya, girlfriend. What are you doing up this early? Thanks, but I'm fine. What do you mean I don't sound like it? There's a lot of reasons for that. Listen, Shania, let's not go into them now, okay? Dillon is still missing."

Troy slowed, hearing the bridge ahead.

"You're right, I didn't. One of Dillon's friend's, Denny, has a houseboat. I stayed because I knew I was getting up early to go diving again. Yes. I spoke with Deputy Glazier, and he's allowing us to lead the SARS crew back to a creepy mansion. No, it's not cool. It's a crime scene now. Troy found John Traylor dead. Yeah," she sighed. "I guess it hasn't made the news yet. No, I did not! What?! I'm not going to discuss this now. Later," Silke said and hung up.

A motorcycle roared by, sounding very close above. A car passed over, clacking as it crossed the 421 Bridge. Troy slowed the boat, remembering there was a launch ramp near here. He sounded his horn. The only reply was the heavy rumbling of a semi and its trailer shaking the metal of the bridge. It was all as it should be based on the map and GPS coordinates.

Troy heard another motor and slowed, pulling back on the throttle. A moment later, an aluminum john boat zoomed past his bow like a warning shot. The fisherman in his backwards, Atlanta Braves cap smiled and waved as he passed, and then he gave his boat more speed.

"Thank you, Lord, for that near miss of fools," Troy said.

"I should keep a better lookout instead of talking to my housemate. She was worried about me not coming home last night."

"With your history, that's understandable," Troy said.

"Speaking of history. Last night . . . did you talk to Tommy about the wolf visitor?"

"Yes and no. He was ranting about the broken glass and rail, so I told him about the break-in by a wolfhound." Marader's response had been that if he'd been busy with Silke he would never have heard it. "I didn't think he'd buy it if I told him there was a wolf that winked at you."

Silke blinked. It was the most reaction he'd seen all morning.

"That was unnerving."

"Thanks for letting me sleep, procuring our chariot and packing it," Troy said.

Her glance was cool and detached. "I knew you were beat

and desperate for sleep," she said icily. Troy thought the mansion might seem warmer today.

"So, Tommy thinks a big dog broke in," Silke said.

"He's not thinking straight. I don't know why, but Marader won't let that jewelry box leave his sight. I joked his new lover was called Silvia. He claims he's contacted somebody at *Antique Roadshow* to assess its worth. It could be worth 100 grand. Earlier, he was carrying it under his arm. Now it's in a backpack. You picked it up. You aren't obsessed with it."

"Marader has always been interested in superficial appearances. It's gorgeous, but it's an empty box. Besides, I have different . . . obsessions right now. Dillon has been missing for twenty-four hours. I can officially file a missing person. I thought I would drive into town to do that and see Aunt Jada. I called and spoke with her. I had hoped she knew about Dillon, but she has a headache. Sister Elva thinks it's the smoke. Do you know where we are?"

"The Laurel Yacht Club and Marina is coming up on our right in a bay. We won't be able to see it, but we might hear it. Soon after, if you remember, it's going to narrow and there's islands to avoid."

For a moment, he thought it was snowing, then he realized it was ash drifting down. It accumulated on the water's surface resembling a gray pollen, and it grew thicker and heavier the more they traveled south.

They reached the Rock Garden at the sight of a boulder barely underwater, the surface brown and muddy. It needs a warning buoy, he thought. He hadn't remembered that one. He trimmed the motor, trying to keep the prop near the surface. He steered to port and eased around another hunk of rock, this one marked with a buoy and light.

Raquel had hit this one, getting him in trouble. A sign warned of hazards, a little late in his opinion.

After clearing two more rocky areas, he guided them into the main basin of the lake. He swore he could sense Cemetery Ridge, or perhaps it was the house.

"Tommy complained of nightmares. I had them, too. I blame that house. How about you?" Silke asked. He nodded. "I thought so. Just before I woke you up, you were . . . thrashing a bit."

"Uh. Um. I was being . . . questioned by a woman," Troy said.

"Desiree?"

"No, the Dark Lady like Dillon describes her," he replied. He didn't see much point in mentioning his dreams had been sexual in nature. Not a surprise after his evening. He did tell her about the questioning, how the woman had been trying to persuade Dillon to help. "She had me confused for Dillon. Or I was Dillon. I don't know," Troy said.

"Your neck looked much better yesterday. Today it looks dark. I haven't seen anything quite like it."

"What do you mean?" he asked. He rubbed his neck, mindful of where he had been bitten in the nightmare.

"The aura of light around you, it's very dark there, four points, almost in a square" she replied.

He shuddered and touched the spot.

"That's it. Can I take a closer look?"

"Sure. I'm suffering a Marader," he said.

"What, oh, a pain in the neck," she chuckled. It was a little disconcerting to have her caressing his flesh. Why did he have to be attracted to her? "It's a cold spot, and you're tense. Your muscles are like iron, and not in a good way."

"I know. The plane ride, I assume. You are helping, thank you. Uh, in the nightmare, the Dark Lady mentioned that we were in danger. That we had taken something important from the house."

"Did she say what?" she asked. Her fingers dug deeper into the cords of his neck.

"A crux, whatever that is. She claimed that she was limited to the night while the others could go about by day, or something like that."

"Like Aunt Jada was talking about. She mentioned

nightwalkers out by day," Silke replied. He felt her shiver.

"Anyway, the woman was trying to impress upon him that we were in imminent danger. She promised to reward him for helping her," Troy replied. He found the wind blowing by him wasn't enough to cool his sweat.

"What did we take from the house?"

"Desiree took that letter opener and money clip. Of course, there's Marader's precious jewelry box. You found it. J-Man brought up the books Spider is reading."

"This is all too weird. And now this smoke. How can you see?" she asked.

"I can't see very far, that's why I'm puttering along."

"I never thought of you moving at slow speed."

"There are times when it's wise," he said. He could tell she disbelieved him.

"Such as?" she asked.

He was thoughtful. "School zones. Driving icy roads. Skiing cliff areas. Tricky ascent faces. Leaping out of a perfectly good plane. Dating women."

Her hands drew back. "Did you really just say dating women?" she asked aghast. He nodded. "So, you just associated romance with jumping off cliffs, driving icy roads and skydiving?"

He nodded but said no more. Likely, his explanation would leave her displeased. Once you're already in a hole, stop digging.

They arrived first, pulling ashore on the north side of Cemetery Ridge. With the smoke, Troy couldn't see if any other boats were coming, but he would hear their motors.

It was much warmer without the boating wind, so Troy pulled off his shirt. This time, he had come prepared with a wet suit, thanks to Knives, so he wouldn't freeze to death. Troy planned to wait for the authorities to arrive before wrestling it on. Until then, he stretched on a towel across the floor.

Silke kicked off her Crocs then slipped out of her leg

warmers and her hooded sweatshirt to reveal she was in her red and black lightning one piece. She immediately donned a dive skin, a blue lycra covering making her legs look like they should be starring in *Avatar*.

Next, she laid out a wet suit. "I want to be prepared, even if I'm not going inside."

Troy agreed. He had packed flares this time.

"Did you notice that outbuilding, a barn or something nearby? To the right of the mansion if you're standing in the front door looking out?" she asked.

He shook his head. She was up to something.

"We haven't been forbidden from going in there. It isn't a crime scene. We can't even be sure it's part of the same property, although likely it is."

"What do you think it might be?" he asked. What was she after?

"A barn? I don't know. A secret laboratory, maybe? Spider said they were moonshiners and tobacco growers. Something to do with that maybe? We'll have to wait and see."

"You think Dillon might have gone in there?"

"Honestly, Troy, I don't know what to think. My head's spinning."

"I hear you."

"But I'm all right not going back in that house. Let somebody else find Dillon if he's d-died in there," Silke stammered. "Troy, I'm sorry about last night. Did I leave any bruises?" she asked. He shook his head. "Thanks for being there and taking the hit when Dillon couldn't. Do you think we'll find him today?" Her voice had a bit of an edge to it.

"I don't feel him," Troy said.

The whine of a motor growing louder, then slower, a deeper moan, announced the county sheriff's boat arrival. It was the same one they had seen yesterday. Captain Morris and Deputy Burt waved a good morning to them.

Raquel stood with them. Her expression was difficult to read, her arms crossed, but she nodded and offered a wan smile of empathy. She had known, laughed, skied and swam with John, too. Troy was surprised to see Denny's sister, Mary Beth, all ready to dive. Taller than Troy, she was big and blond with a generously wide smile. Troy could see the sisterly resemblance with the shared smile, upturned nose, and prominent chin. He recalled that she worked for Sterling Sports.

He didn't recognize anybody else, but he disliked the appearance of two of the four male divers. The tall, bony one looked perpetually surprised, his face open, his eyes big, nostrils flared, and his brows wild compared to his flat top haircut. His partner possessed a pinched face with a tight mouth, narrow nose, and close-set eyes below wiry black brows. Troy wasn't surprised to soon find out that Johnson and Richards had been contracted by the TVA to investigate Von Damme's creepy underwater mansion of death.

The sketchy pair were the opposite of what looked to be a father and son team. Troy pegged the elder as retired military man and the younger for a lifer in law enforcement. Dillon had taught Troy the signs. Dillon loved to people watch.

Deputy Burt, donut in hand, introduced Troy and Silke to everybody. They were met with stony stares, except by Raquel and Mary Beth who offered heartfelt condolences. Homer Maxwell wasn't happy they were coming along. He considered them a liability. Silke was a second from exploding with anger when Deputy Burt forestalled her.

"Home, I asked them to consult. They were the ones just down there yesterday. They gave us the GPS coordinates, shared photos and video, and described the place, which is where our map came from. I've already spoken to Silke. She knows, and I suspect she told you, Troy, that y'all are prohibited from going inside the house. It's a crime scene now. You're only to lead the others there."

"Let's gear up. This is my son, Wyatt," Homer said, introducing his son. Troy and Silke shook Wyatt's hand. "I see you're already acquainted with the gals. We're going to split and go in through the two entrances you found, searching the ground and second floors."

They tied the boats together and anchored. Everyone diving donned wetsuits, fins, BC vests, scuba tanks, and dive masks.

Troy and Silke retold the story of their adventure inside. They warned about the inexplicable cold and gave examples of the dangers of instability, including the falling doors.

"Welcome to Search and Rescue, the recovery version. It's never nice. It's ugly work," Raquel said. Her smile was soft. "But it's important to people, and somebody has to do it. I'm capable."

There were many that thought Raquel was a spotlight or glory hog. He knew better. And now, he sensed she was less interested in the spotlight than ever.

Troy watched Raquel fall backwards into the water. Next to him, Silke forced a smile, stuck the regulator in her mouth, put her hand on her mask and stepped backwards off the pontoon boat into the water. He should feel like a lucky guy diving with two mermaids, but his purpose here took all the joy out of the moment. He waddled to the edge, sat, and fell off the side backward, letting his weights draw him down and under.

They had anchored above the mansion, so they should be able to dive straight down to the coordinates. He checked the underwater GPS, finding them on target then led them deeper. Troy hoped it worked better than the ones he had used while driving. Otherwise, they might get turned around and end up in Virginia. It might be better than where they were headed, though.

The light faded as they descended, reaching fifty feet. He adjusted his mask, pushing out a little water by blowing through his nose into it and filling it with air. Gurgling bubbles surrounded him, and he could see clearly. In the distance, he spotted the vague shadowy slope of Cemetery Ridge. Since they were right over the mansion, they missed much of the rocky descent. Below, there was a scattered layer of debris sitting on the thermocline. He was better geared and braced for the cold this time.

The divers continued to lose color along with the light, the red of Mary Beth's outfit and the yellow of Raquel's suit. The guys wore black and blue anyway, with some neon green. When the light hit it, the color stood out. Troy didn't think the clarity was as good as yesterday, likely due to the rainfall runoff from Saturday night. Or, he thought irrationally, the mansion was trying to hide from them.

No, he figured, it was lurking, and he was right.

At eighty-five feet, he caught the first dark shadow of the mansion. Its copper roof gave off faint glimmers, as if to offer false hope. With each stroke nearer, he could feel the temperature drop. He could tell by the reaction of others, as they shivered or shifted uncomfortably, that this seemed abnormal.

The darkness of one hundred feet encroached upon them. In this dimness, Troy thought he saw green lights splaying out the shutters from inside the house. When he blinked, they were gone. Wyatt took a flare, lit it and dropped it. It bounced off the roof and tumbled off like it had been batted aside. The flare landed top down in the mud, almost disappearing.

Troy had come prepared, thanks to J-Man, and lit up two. He set one in the corner of the gutter of the house near the open window. The glaring brightness threw harsh shadows that wavered with the current but seemed to be doing a seductive dance to tempt one to be reckless.

Raquel and Mary Beth directed their headlights on the hanging shutter and open window. The pair swam inside to begin the upstairs search. Troy mentally wished them luck.

Silke guided the others around the corner to the damaged front door. The opening felt like it was mocking Troy. A hazy glow seemed to float out the door like a bubble, then it stretched tall. Troy blinked.

It reminded him of a person. The details grew clearer, and he saw a ghost looking and scowling like John. As the others moved toward the door, John tried to wave them back. He gestured several times, then he grabbed his throat along the side. The apparition seemed to be choking or drowning. Troy's neck ached, and his lungs started to constrict, his chest cramping.

He pushed the fear aside, analyzing what he was seeing. Nobody else noticed or reacted to anything unusual.

When Homer tossed a flare inside, John's image vanished in the garish light. Troy blinked. Was he narked? Really seeing ghosts? Or both?

Homer and Wyatt swam inside. Troy knew they would be bracing against the bitter cold. Johnson and Richards followed, pausing at the entrance, shocked by the iciness.

Troy and Silke weren't supposed to go inside. His body didn't even want to go inside, but he hated the idea of Raquel being in there.

John had died there. Had Dillon died here? Troy didn't feel his presence, nothing like when John's body had still been inside. This time Troy thought he could feel loathing, gloominess, and spite.

He didn't realize he had still been headed inside until Silke grabbed him by the shoulder. He smiled wryly, shrugged and tried to apologize. Silke nodded, and she pointed to her wounded hand.

She gestured for him to follow her around to the side, looking for the outbuilding. A courtyard with a grilling area spread outside the kitchen door. Across the way sat another stone building, a much smaller one, more like a barn or workshop.

The structure might have been made of concrete, now thick with algae, green, furry and slimy. The corrugated roof had rusted over the decades. It looked more like one expected of underwater ruins. With its open space, the door missing, leaving an empty maw, the building looked like a good place for fish to hide. He recalled the nightmare with the gar. He hoped that had nothing to do with reality, but already it seemed too much from his nightmares echoed life.

In a blink, darkness fell like a hammer. It struck down all light, extinguishing it and pressing on Troy. He felt hot, nervous to nauseous, all cramped in a tight space. The biting aroma of alcohol, even mellowed with generous amounts of syrup, burned his nose and caused his eyes to water. He smelled oak and the stink of his own fear and sweat. How was he smelling this? He shifted and fluid around him moved, so he was mostly submerged, like he was being marinated all the way up to his chin.

Feeling around, he touched smoothness and slats. A lid pressed down on his skull. If possible, it seemed he was stuffed inside a barrel of moonshine. Sour mash whiskey? A distillery? How had this happened? He heard harsh, guttural voices and a growl, sounding like a wild animal. Maybe he would hear more clearly if he could calm his galloping heart.

Suddenly, with the squeal of broken wood, the barrel's lid was wrenched off and tossed aside. A furry-faced man with a long nose and yellow eyes stared down at him. Hairy snarled and snatched up the barrel as easily as if it were empty and tossed it off the wagon.

A moment of flight, brief weightlessness for Troy, led to a crash, the barrel smashing into the gravel. The booze splashed across the earth and rock, making the drive muddy. He rested there, stunned, trying to figure out what was going on. He had been scuba diving, underwater, moments ago, now he was sprawled in a muddy puddle of whiskey and pieces of shattered oak.

The hairy and heavily bearded man, his face almost lost underneath wild brows, stared down his snout at Troy, and then Hairy grabbed him. A clawed vice lifted Troy off his feet, and he suffocated, his weak hands tearing feebly at the hold on his throat. Through the spots of his vision, he could see the beast's eyes.

It was a wolf in man's clothing. The wolfhound on the balcony flashed through his memories, and he thought they shared the same eyes. The loping way they moved, their crooked gait, and especially their blurring speed indicated a kinship. Troy kicked and kneed, hearing Hairy grunt. Troy kept at it, desperate and near panic as he began to black out, dark spots blotting out his sight.

He found himself abruptly sitting on the ground, his throat free, able to inhale gulps of air. He could feel it bubbling around him. His sight returned and adjusted to the sticky and silvery night. The full moon's brilliance caught the pale of the wood, making it shine, and created shadows of the wagonload of barrels, his former hiding spot and a failed one. Had they smelled him? Or had they heard him?

The weasel-faced driver stood reins in hand, frantically looking all around at the barn with its wolf weathervane, the tall oak trees, and the brooding mansion of river stone. Its shutters had been thrown wide open to embrace the night air and let in the magical light of the moon.

The place looked freshly repainted, stately and menacing at the same time. The building he had thought was a church was instead, a barn. It looked like it stored barley and corn. Some of the grain leaked out gaps between boards and doors. Across the hill behind it, where he thought he had spotted a graveyard, tobacco was growing.

The mansion, the barn and the outbuilding stood on a hill outside the small cluster of structures of the town. He could see the lights from the dark collection of houses, cabins, and commercial buildings, perhaps a small bank, post office, hardware and grocery store. The winged Pegasus of Mobile meant a gasoline station. Nearby on the valley floor wound the south fork of the Holston River that would eventually flood, and then later be dammed to form a lake. Troy realized he was seeing Wreythville and Holston Valley as it had been. How could that happen?

A cloud passed over the moon. Darkness dropped like a black shroud. The temperature plunged. The air was charged, dancing across Troy's skin, itching madly like lightning gathering to strike.

"Mona, sugah, you should know better than to try and leave. Nobody ever escapes Von Damme. Well, let me correct that. Nobody alive. As you know, bodies leave here all the time!" Hairy chuckled harshly.

Mona? Troy wondered. Maybe he had misunderstood the southern accent.

Hairy seized Troy again, yanking him upright and forcing him to stand. Through a painful red haze, he saw the nameless driver jerked backwards, vanishing from sight without a sound. A white-haired man, strange looking with dead fish-pale skin and red eyes like an albino, peeked over the top of the wagon. The brute grinned, displaying bloodied teeth.

Troy could imagine the driver's throat being ripped out. Hairy was going to be next.

"Come with me, bitch," Hairy snarled. He hauled Troy to the side door of the mansion. The wolfman was reaching for the door knob when he abruptly whirled, releasing Troy to assume a defensive stance. With an animalistic instinct, Hairy sniffed and tasted the air, frowning afterwards.

Troy had never seen anyone move so fast. Claws out, Hairy circled warily, ready for an attack. Talons popped out of the leather from the front of his boots.

What was he?

Troy couldn't hear anything but Hairy's breathing. The night had grown eerily quiet. Even the mosquitoes and crickets were silent, waiting. Troy took advantage of being loose and crawled under a table. He knew it wouldn't do any good, but he might live a few seconds longer, gasp a few more breaths, offer a prayer up to the Lord before the nightwalkers drank his blood.

Hairy shuffled over to the table. He reached underneath, grasping for Troy as he scrambled away. He bumped into a stone wall.

The side door to the barn slammed open, banging loudly on the wall, and a gruff, heavily bearded man limped out. He grunted, took several steps then collapsed, his head falling to the side, barely attached by the spine, his neck almost severed. As if the body slapping the ground was a signal, night creatures appeared. They were clad in black with darkly painted faces, red lips and eyes. Like a horde of giant black widows, they scuttled about. The figures were silent and so fast they blurred, seeming to have more than two legs and arms.

In the blink of an eye, four of them seized Hairy, tearing him apart limb from limb. Blood splattered on the table top. One tossed the arms aside. They bounced off the center base of the table right before Troy's eyes and landed nearby, a gruesome view of his future. He tried to close his eyes, but even as his throat constricted in fear, his muscles cramped, his eyes remained locked wide in horror.

Troy knew he was next to die, but instead, the nightwalkers knocked down the front door and charged inside the mansion. He caught a glimpse of a silvery box carried by a shadowy figure. More silent, supernaturally swift creatures arrived, swarming over the building, slamming the shutters closed, and driving spikes into cross beams to secure the closure.

Some of the Rulers of Night scampered across the copper roof to stuff and cover the chimney, wrapping rope around sheets patterned with strange symbols that seemed to pulsate. A fog appeared, tendrils rising up along the house like ghostly rose vines.

More stealthy beasts, long-limbed, agile, and carrying stilettos in their taloned hands, scrambled over the mansion, converging like ants, scratching and clawing symbols into the wood, rock and even copper surfaces. Hieroglyphics were everywhere, even floating and wavering in the air. A dozen painters carrying buckets and brushes sealed the scratches and created more writhing symbols over the first. Witchcraft and deviltry in these modern times, Troy thought.

From inside, he heard inhuman screams and howls. One shutter shook, cracking, but it remained intact. He sensed a fight, a life and death struggle. Nightwalkers against nightwalkers? Troy wondered. The world thought vampires were a myth, but Mona knew better, though most called them nightwalkers. Many of the undead tried to escape, pounding and ripping into shutters, but they couldn't. Even blows that shook the walls did little more than loosen dust.

Amid the destruction, Troy saw her. Fair hair silver in the moonlight, a deadly-beautiful vampire strode toward the table. He couldn't tell much about her, except she was tall and gorgeous, because she wore black and a cape that blended seamlessly with the night. She knelt down, and he saw her eyes, unable to look away. They were black and yet reddish, like a blood moon, and compelling.

Troy was awe-struck by her beauty, that of a 50's pin up girl with curly locks, big eyes, high cheekbones, a pert nose, and ruby-red lips. She smiled. "Ah, honey, fate is unkind, isn't it? You are in the wrong place at the wrong time."

"I knew I was going to die tonight." he heard Mona say.

"I am sorry, Mona. There can be no living witnesses."

Troy recognized her now! The incredible blond from his sexy dreams last night. The Dark Lady. Dreams were strange, and yet, he was awake. He was underwater diving outside a haunted mansion. He wanted out, and yet, perhaps this would reveal something he wanted and needed to know.

"I'll make this quick and painless," the Dark Lady said. She held out a hand as if to help Mona rise. Compelled, Mona had no choice. She reached out and took it.

In two blinks, he was back underwater. Still under water?

For a moment, the girl was there, the ghost of her pale against the darkness, then he moved his head. Mona vanished in his headlight.

Silke? Where was she? Had she drifted off? He didn't think she had returned to the mansion. He found her inside the outbuilding, struggling with a metal coil. Somehow, it had wrapped around her neck and upper body, and she appeared to be wrestling with the old distilling machinery. He couldn't cut her free, and the unwieldy sculpture for making alcohol seemed on the verge of pinning her. Troy managed to get underneath the coil and catch it. It felt far heavier than it should, as if something unseen pushed down on it.

He found Silke's eyes, and he found the relief he felt. No, he wouldn't lose her to this place. Troy realized the foolishness of coming back here. Had they been mesmerized? Was this a trap? By what? The evil spirit of the mansion?

He held the coil up long enough for her to slither loose, sliding past him. Once she was free, he let go and shoved back as he kicked away. Somehow, the falling coil jerked a chain off the wall. It fiercely dislodged a set of ice hooks. The water slowed their flying, giving Troy time to turn. He tried to evade them, but they clanked off his tank. When he tried to swim on, he jerked to a stop. It nearly yanked the regulator out of his mouth. He seized his mouthpiece, pressing it against his face. He backstroked one-armed, moving toward the chains, then he tried swimming again, only to find himself restrained.

No luck. He was hooked. He needed help. That's why having a dive buddy was a must. Silke was there, thank God for her, and she freed him. She reached around his back and detached the hooks, one by one until he was loose of all four. What were the chances? Out of the corner of his mask, he saw the pitchfork dropping toward Silke's shoulder.

He kicked and thrashed with one arm, using the other to hold her while spinning, taking her with him. He heard the clack of the metal on his tank. He didn't bother to see if there were any more.

Taking Silke's hand, he steered her toward the door. He heard and sensed the roof fall, and they kicked furiously as Troy dragged her out. The falling weight and displaced water shoved them into the open water. The roof slowly crushed the still, covering it like a coffin lid.

Troy breathed a sigh of relief, watching the bubbles rise, ready to do the same. He and Silke hugged, awkwardly because of their gear, and then gripped each other's hands, sharing a moment glad to be alive.

Mud and debris surrounded the ruins in a growing cloud, forcing them to back away. Now he felt more concern about the mansion collapsing and Raquel's safety. While he and Silke were swimming toward the front entrance, he noticed lights in the door, the SARS crew, departing. Four divers, including Raquel, thank God, seemed to be waiting on the TVA divers. Troy was relieved that they hadn't found anything, no extra body among them.

The elder Maxwell waved them on, so Troy and Silke started their ascent. Slowly rising to the surface gave Troy too much time to think about what had happened below.

Had he hallucinated seeing the mansion in its past and the attack on it? Whoever closed it up had intentionally sealed those within. What about the outbuilding? He hadn't been there for the still falling on Silke, but that pitch fork appeared to have been thrown. Underwater poltergeist? It was well Troy had a regulator in his mouth, or he would laugh abruptly, crazily.

Silke was staring at him, studying him with those beautiful and caring eyes. Did he look dazed and confused? He noticed abrasions on her neck and one along her cheek. They would need some TLC. She smiled, now knowing that Dillon hadn't also died in that house. They could forget about it. Well, Troy doubted he could do that, as much as he would like to wipe it from his memory, but he could leave it alone.

At the surface, they celebrated, filling their vests to float and breathing in fresh air, even if he could see it and taste it. He removed his mask and turned his face to the sun, feeling the warmth on his flesh. "Ah! It's wonderful to know your brother isn't down there,"

They hadn't left Dillion there to rot overnight. The guilt slipped away. So where was he?

"What happened inside the barn?" he asked Silke.

"As soon as I entered, the current drew me in," she said, shivering. "Then the still fell on me. I didn't even touch it. I was looking at all the steins on the wall. Then you came and rescued me. My hero. Martin was right."

"He left out where I had to be rescued. It seemed like the place was trying to kill us," Troy said

"I saw some pale haunts, but they didn't seem to be paying any attention to me, making moonshine, bottling it, pouring it into kegs and loading it."

"Huh. I didn't see that. A ghost by the name of Mona touched me and shared the memory of her death. I'll tell you about it at the boat after the sunshine warms me up," Troy said. She wasn't shocked or even surprised. He found that comforting.

He waved to Deputy Burt, then they dog paddled the thirty feet to the sheriff's boat, where they shared what little they knew. Burt looked concerned each time he checked his watch. Troy figured the rest of the dive party should be surfacing by now. It had been more than ten minutes since Troy had seen the foursome waiting outside the mansion for the TVA divers. They were running out of bottom time.

Fifteen: The Beguiler

Where were they? Troy wondered. Face mask down in the water, Troy heard a ring tone.

Silke answered her phone. "Hey, Tommy what's up?" she asked. She waited, frowning, then she smiled. "That's good news. Sure we will. I'll tell him. 'Bye."

"Crank call?" Troy asked while treading water.

"Not this time. Lakeview found a Maraders Marina Sea-Doo, the one my brother used. There's dive gear stowed on it. I said we'd boat over and tow it back. This way we'll get the first look at it. I hope to find some clues. I'm relieved to know, though, thank God, that he didn't go diving."

"They're late. I wonder what's delaying them. Crap. I hope there isn't a problem," Deputy Burt said. He mopped his forehead with his handkerchief.

"Burt, I hear there's been numerous missing persons reports, coming from out here," Silke said.

"Yes, the department has been swamped. It's mostly here at the southern end of the lake, where the wildfire is. It worries me, like there might be a kidnapper or serial killer. Just too many people suddenly vanished, not even including Dillon or John, God rest his soul. This week is not a good time for this to be happening with the concert and the races, so many strangers and tourists. Dammit, where are you, Maxwell? I don't want to have to call another SARS crew. They won't get here in time, and divers aren't a dime a dozen around here."

"We're here," Troy said.

"How long do you need to wait before you dive? I know jackshit about this stuff."

"I don't know. I'd have to look at a dive table. Not long. Perhaps ten minutes. If we stop to equalize, more," Troy said, making an approximation. It was fortunate they hadn't spent the entire bottom time allowed.

Precious minutes dragged by. He wasn't sure what his options might be. Could the mansion have collapsed on them? Raquel, Mary Beth and the Maxwells had been outside, though.

Troy peered down one more time, hoping, prayed, and saw bubbles rising. He informed the others, and shortly, he let them know he saw shadows. As she swam nearer the light, Raquel's yellow dive suit gained color and brightness. His heart seemed ready to leap from his chest. Despite this, he breathed easier, thrilled she was well. She noticed, smiled and waved at him.

All six divers were there, but as they ascended nearer, Troy noticed something wrong—too few bubbles, too little movement. Two of the divers remained still, the TVA agents dragged along lifelessly by the Maxwells. Regulators floated alongside the dead. Had the mansion murdered them?

Troy clutched hands with Raquel as they rose the last ten feet to the surface. They swam to the boat. Troy climbed the ladder into the boat, where he helped everybody as they handed up their BC's and air tanks.

"About time! What the hell happened?" Deputy Burt demanded.

"God, that was a scary place. Haunted I think," Raquel said.

By John's ghost? Troy almost asked aloud.

"You think ghosts killed them?" Homer Maxwell asked. He swam one of the bodies around to the back. Troy saw no sign of blood or injury when he got a good look at Johnson's neck. He couldn't see his partner.

"Did you see anybody?" Raquel asked sharply. Troy helped her into the boat, and then he gave a hand to Mary Beth. Both shivered, and Silke offered towels, wrapping one around Troy. He thanked her with a smile.

"Were they murdered?" Deputy Burt asked. He climbed onto the back platform to examine the bodies. He noted nothing obvious.

"We have no idea, sir. To start, we went into the study, the crime scene, and Johnson and Richards went the other direction. After they failed to rendezvous, we found them dead in the kitchen. No sign of struggle. No wounds. No weapons. An accident, I guess," Homer said.

"The house scared them to death," Mary Beth grimly mused.

"No air," Troy questioned as he pressed Richards' regulator it remained silent when it should give a burst of air. He checked the TVA man's tank. The valve was closed, so he twisted the handle. Another tap on the regulator released a hiss of air. "That's odd."

"How did that happen?" Deputy Burt asked.

Johnson's tank was also closed off.

"Troy, I'm so sorry about what happened to John. That place. You were right," Raquel drawled in the way of apology. "Frightening, fascinating and frigid. It feels like a place of death. Strangest rescue dive I've ever done. Life is so fragile."

Troy had thought the same. He locked eyes with Raquel, and he knew she had the same thought. Life is short. They needed to talk.

"Damn! I've got calls to make," Deputy Burt said.

"As do I," the captain agreed.

Troy and Silke gave brief statements then were allowed to go.

Raquel kissed his cheek. "I'm very glad you still care. Call me, please, soon."

Troy made no promises. He liked to keep his word. He untied the pontoon from the sheriff's boat and shoved off. Silke fired up the engine, shifted into reverse, and the Bass Buggy ponderously backed up, curving to turn around.

"What do you think happened to the TVA agents?" Silke asked.

"Maybe they were attacked by another part of the house."

"So are you going to tell me about what you saw down there?" she asked.

He cleared his throat then recounted his vision. How he believed Mona touched him, the ghost showing him the past, how she had died the night Von Damme's mansion had been raided and sealed. His glimpse of the jewelry box. How the blond resembled the female in his dream with her brother.

"I'm starting to wonder if I'm going crazy," Troy said.

Silke nodded. "Well, you're considering seeing Raquel again. I heard once, that trying the same thing and expecting different results was the definition of insanity."

Troy laughed despite the sharpness of her words. "Well, I have been told I possess the crazy gene."

He used the GPS to guide him to the entrance to the marina. It gradually appeared from the smoke haze, gaining detail. Lakeview was set in a shallow cove in the hillside, most of which was lost in trees and the obscuring yellow haze. He idled in and finally spotted the gas pumps, steering there, figuring he would find somebody at the store. Signs for beer, bait, jerky, and pre-packed food, all the joys of civilization, greeted the eye. A poster for the music series graced the wall below the window. Surrounding it were posters for the upcoming NASCAR race.

A boy of ten or eleven trotted out to meet them before they reached the dock. It was generously lined with pads, but Troy hadn't lost his touch. He parked the Bass Buggy with only a slight bump. The nudge to the dock didn't disturb the gray-faced golden retriever who snoozed a few feet away in the shade.

"Fill 'er up?" the boy asked.

"No, thanks. I'm here to pick up a Sea-Doo lost from Maraders Marina. Are you the one that found it?"

The boy vehemently shook his head, as if he didn't want to be blamed for that. "Pa! There's people here looking for the lost PWC!" Done with them, he bolted.

An elderly gentleman strolled out of the store. Troy climbed onto the dock, and they exchanged greetings. "Sorry it took so long to call. You see, my boy, Gerald, well, he found it yesterday. It had floated near the entrance, so he towed it in. He had a hot date, so he forgot all about it. Had that look, you know, dazed, kind of like you two, come to think of it."

"Excuse me?" Silke asked.

She didn't look dazed. Hopeful and angry, yes. She was about to chirp at the old man when he shouted. "Gerald!"

A tall skinny teen, all elbows and knees in cutoffs and a tie die shirt wandered over. He had a hang dog look, keeping his eyes downcast.

"Hey there, Gerald. Thank you for finding the Sea-Doo," Troy said. He handed the kid a twenty dollar bill which made him grin and meet their eyes.

"Hey, you look familiar. Um, do you snow ski professionally?" Gerald asked. Troy nodded. "Any chance, were you in *Leap, Steep and Deep*?" Troy nodded again. "Dude, you're Troy Bane! You were rad plus mind-blowing awesome. But I heard you crashed and burned."

Silke put an arm around Troy. "Oh did he ever. He died, then he came back, just like most mythic heroes. I think he should change his last name to Phoenix," Silke said, tongue-in-cheek. Troy winced. He might never live down the moment at the gym with Martin.

"Troy Bane Phoenix. That's so cool. Unless, Troy Phoenix Bane. No, then you sound like you're bad for the capital of Arizona."

Troy was surprised when Gerald led him to the storage room. A Red Bull poster had him plunging down the side of a cliff. "Red Bull Gives You Wiiings." Troy signed it. He glanced over at Silke who was beaming. Likely she would give some lucky guy wings, though, he would never compare her to a red bull.

Gerald smiled. "Come on this way. The Sea-Doo is over here."

When Troy saw it, he paused. It was the same PWC from his nightmare. He recalled putting a camera away. "See if I . . . he left a camera in the dash," Troy told Silke.

In a central compartment, she found Dillon's waterproof camera right where Troy had dreamt it would be. Silke took it inside to look at the images while he tethered the PWC to the back of the pontoon boat.

He would let it play out about ten feet and trail behind. When he was all set, he went inside, seeking Silke. She was still looking at images. He peeked over her shoulder. The photos showed the island at night, the old clothing and articles, then images of predawn. Dillon shot an image of his hand holding an expensive looking pin, red gems set in silver in the shape of a crescent moon. It could also look like a smile, a frown, or sharp incisors depending on which way he held it. The next photo was a selfie. In the background there was a gleaming, classic wooden boat. Dillon's body blocked the stern, the motor and whoever was driving.

"Maybe we can get a registration number off it. What? Are you all right? You paled," Silke asked.

The boat also looked familiar, coming from his nightmare. He felt a little dizzied by the coincidences. "I told you about my nightmare about getting mugged by senior citizens. This was their boat," Troy replied.

"You're dreaming what happened to my brother," she said. Troy must have made a face. "That means you experienced what that woman had to offer?" He might have flushed. "I see. Well, you do have his blood in you. This is amazing."

"I won't share that with Deputy Glazier," Troy said. He phoned the deputy and left a message. Silke kissed Gerald on the cheek, stunning him, so Troy had to untie from the dock.

"Now you've done it," Troy said. He pushed off and headed out into open water. It must have been some kiss, because the boy was just touching his cheek now.

"Done what?"

Troy gave her a skeptical look. "Beautiful girls' kisses have magical powers, especially to boys that age. He'll never forget and try to find someone like you and likely be frustrated, as you're unique," Troy said. That might be an understatement. He wasn't sure how to gauge her expression, whether she felt complimented or slighted.

Shortly after they cleared the entrance, they were surrounded by water and smoke, again. The haze seemed thicker than before, a sickly brown added to the bile yellow color of the air. Ash fell heavily from the sky, so much so that Troy tasted it in the back of his throat. The breeze seemed restless and indecisive, shifting often. Troy could relate. The surface of the water had taken on a whitish tinge. So much for lake clarity.

He started feeling jittery, needing to move, stretch or even pace if possible. He almost suggested Silke drive. The uneasiness turned to a touch of nausea. At first, he wondered if the stench and unhealthiness of the smoke was making him ill.

Silke drew her ankh from under her shirt and caressed it. Her smile was tight, and he knew she sensed something wrong, too. He heard what sounded like the cough of a motor. It sputtered closer, or they cruised closer to it. Troy wasn't sure which direction it was coming from or its proximity. The low sound carried oddly in the smoky fog. Drawing back on the throttle, he slowed.

Finally, to the starboard bow, a seventeen-foot bass boat, a faded blue and silver Pro Craft, sputtered into sight, its outboard spewing black smoke. The driver hid behind huge sunglasses while he stood tall next to the wheel. Despite the heat, he wore a wide-brimmed field worker's hat, long pants and a gray, long-sleeved shirt, as well as gloves as if he were dressed to cover sensitive skin. Troy would have figured the thickness of the smoke would be protection enough, but he was aware some medications created the side effect of skin burning easily with exposure to sun. Even so, it seemed odd.

The Pro Craft's engine coughed, wheezed and died. The boat coasted forward. The man waved. "Pardon me, but do you know the way to the Lakeview Marina?"

Troy suffered an uneasy sense of deja vu. The way to where? Lakeview? Or the 421 ramp? He wondered what were the chances the dream was trying to tell him something. Before yesterday, he would have said nil. Now, he felt uneasy and disoriented.

Silke blinked, the ash getting to her, and pointed in the right direction. "It's that way. Off your port side," she purred, her voice throaty and sexy. It sounded like she was breathing in Troy's ear.

He started to turn to her, but he glanced back at the stranger when he replied. "You are as helpful as you are beautiful." He removed his sunglasses. His eyes were dark and yet bright like polished marbles dancing with red sparks. His broad, toothy smile was more unnerving than friendly. Those eyes reminded Troy of something. He couldn't quite recall what, as his thoughts seemed liquid, oozing through his mental grasp.

"I see in your eyes and faces that you have been below to visit Wreythville. A gloomy and oppressive, even suffocating place now. It was not always such. Yes, you know it, and its hopelessness. It dwells in your heart, eating you like Consumption."

Across the distance, his odd eyes seemed to grow, dominating his face, then larger, filling Troy's vision. He didn't know what the man was doing, but it was befuddling them, making them pliable.

Everything else seemed to fade away, meaningless. Hopelessness. Powerlessness. Weakness. Failure. The feelings swept over him like a rogue wave knocking him down at the beach. He had endured this crushing squeeze while inside the underwater mansion of Von Damme. Troy stubbornly refused to surrender. He trusted his body, and it perceived danger, the prey instinctively sensing the predator. He had hunted enough to know the feel. Now, he felt hunted and wanted to bolt, but, he had endured it before and dealt with it. He was not his emotions.

"I am Zane. I am your friend. I can give you hope and fulfillment. Come with me. Bring your boat closer so that Zane may help you."

"Have . . . have you seen my brother, Dillon?" Silke asked, then she gave a description.

"Dillon. Oh yes, I can take you to him."

"Oh, yes," Silke moaned.

Troy wanted to look at Silke, take his eyes off the strange man, but he couldn't. He glanced down in disappointment as his hands seemed to move of their own accord, turning the wheel, steering toward the stranger's boat. Troy's body seemed hijacked, his heart running tachycardic. He felt like he was vibrating in motion, like spinning tires waiting for the car to be put into gear. Troy tried to get his hands to do something different, but all he seemed to be able to do was breathe, stand, sweat, and shake in fear and frustration as would a held rabbit.

Silke was in danger, too.

He glanced over at her where he got an eyeful. Silke, aglow with passion, eyes hooded, and wet lips parted, longing to be kissed, slowly drew her shirt over her head and tossed it. It landed on Troy's shoulder. She tantalizingly stripped off her shorts, leaving her in her bikini. Her breathing grew heavier, then she stretched languidly and wantonly threw back her hair. He had seen her in a bikini, but never in this mood, in what must be heat because it made him sweat. She was not his best friend's little sister, that was for damn sure.

He had forgotten about the stranger, caught by Silke's aroused mood and body, until Zane spoke. "Throttle up. Bring your boat closer to Zane," the strange man crooned. "There is room for both of you. You will know no more fear. You will know peace and release."

Despite his desires, Troy kept steering them to danger, though more of his body was drawn to Silke. He tried to keep his gaze on her, hoping it would snap his body back on line. Her hands wandered along her breasts, stirring the nipples taunt against the fabric, then her right hand plunged between her legs.

"You're taking too long," she moaned, then suddenly, she placed a foot and her hands on the side of the boat, ready to leap.

Passion and worry for Silke burned away Troy's paralysis. He grabbed her by the arm and spun her around to face him. She snarled and elbow-slugged him, catching him by surprise on the jaw. He saw stars, not the kind his body was expecting. He reeled back against the wheel, turning it. Despite being stunned, he managed to hold onto Silke, preventing her from jumping ship.

"Silke, stop!" he shouted.

She didn't recognize him. She reached for the throttle, wanting to go faster, so he grabbed her arm. She threw herself against him, headbutting him and bloodying his lip. He twisted to catch her bludgeoning knee on his thigh.

"Silke, stop fighting me!" he roared. Damn it. He was going to have to hit her, and yet, he didn't want to hurt her.

Kiss her or lose her forever. He could hear crazy Aunt Jada's voice.

Troy doubted Silke knew him when he seized her face in his hands and kissed her fiercely in a way that he hadn't kissed anybody in a long, long time. She stopped fighting and melted into him, all along his body like a second skin, making his breathing sprint and his body tighten. His ears thundered so loudly the boat could be ablaze, and he wouldn't know it.

It took a feat of will to pull back when she wanted to keep chasing his tongue. He opened his eyes, waiting for her to realize what she was doing. Finally, her eyes opened. She blinked. A light dawned within those incredible eyes as she recognized him.

When she did, he pulled back, found Silke's baggy purse, and drew her gun. Thank God she hadn't thought about it a minute ago.

He was almost in control of himself now. He had only been thinking of Silke when he kissed her, shaking off most of Zane's influence. He flipped off the Glock's safety and aimed at the man. "Zane, stop whatever you're doing."

Zane gaped, astounded and then he laughed. His teeth were bony white and sharp like a shark's. "You are resisting me? This is a first, I must say. Your encounter with the manse should have weakened you. How interesting," he mused aloud, like Troy wasn't there.

The gun pointed at Zane didn't seem to be any cause for concern. Such fearlessness frightened Troy. Not Silke, though, as she continued to toy with him, her lips nibbling his neck and his ear, making it nearly impossible to stay focused but easier to ignore the cajoling of the stranger.

"I want you, Troy," she whispered.

"And . . . and you tried to give me a command. Perhaps Zane's hunger has made him weak. Put down the gun, now!" Zane ordered.

Troy's hand quivered. He fought lowering the weapon. Silke was no help, or so it seemed, until she stuck her tongue in his ear and breathed. "I have waited years for you to notice me and kiss me. Now take me. I want you inside me." Her fingers trailed down his chest, hips, and legs then up the top of his thighs.

"Silke," he said, starting to tell her to stop, but he didn't really want that. He wanted to kiss her, damn the consequences, and carry her to the bench seat and rut, reveling in her body and the connection between them. He was barely hanging onto a lucid thought because his body was confused, caught between lust and fear.

He was not his emotions. He wasn't his body. He was thought and more.

Damn. This Zane guy was interrupting something really, really important. This felt like life or death, sending his body into an uncommon panic.

"You resist. Amazing! The smoke and fog shield me, but . . . That's it! The master must be told!"

Troy's mind and body weren't all working together. And with Silke all over him, he was in danger of forgetting he was in a deadly situation. If he couldn't fight, then he was all for flight.

Silke pressed him back, and with a hip, he shoved the throttle full ahead. The engine roared to life, but the pontoon boat was sluggish, especially towing the Sea-Doo. Troy would have liked to run over Zane, but he feared the stranger might leap onto the party boat. The surge of the propellers churned water, and the sudden movement stirred up waves, sending the Pro Craft rocking and forcing the stranger to seize a hold or be thrown overboard.

Troy embraced Silke to keep her from falling. When she regained her balance, she laughed and breathed in his ear. "This is a rush and so are you."

The pontoon boat missed the Pro Craft, but the Sea-Doo, like a barb on the end of a whip, skipped across the wake then plowed into the water next to the stranger's boat. Zane finally appeared concerned as the small watercraft nosed and augured. Somehow, the rope held, and the Sea-Doo was yanked upward. The jet ski tumbled, cartwheeling over and over, dancing over the Pro Craft's bow, ripping off its windshield before splashing down again. It tightened the rope and then came plowing after them.

Troy kept the throttle full ahead and sped as far away as fast as the party boat would carry him. He felt more like himself, in more control, with every passing second. He became acutely aware of Silke's heat and curves pressed against him.

"How are you feeling?" he asked. She turned her face toward him. Her eyes were radiant, and the light in them danced. Her glistening lips were kissably close and drew him as though charged. How had he ever denied kissing her was magic?

"I am walking on air, and you, you smile a smile I've never seen before. Two kisses. I have waited years for that. Much better than kissing you in the hospital. You didn't even know, did you?" she asked.

While he recalled that moment, a very vivid and clear moment, her smile deepened. That's why she had seemed so familiar at the airport. "The hospital in Florida? You came to see me?" he asked. She was his angel? The reason he had been inspired to come back to his body? She was real? His angel was Silke?! She let him study her face and eyes, the way they glowed, and he closed his eyes to listen to her voice.

"Yes, I came to see you with Dillon. I thought you were dying. I asked you to come back, but I kissed you farewell. I'm glad you fared well instead of leaving. I am thrilled you came home. What a kiss this afternoon!"

"Just like New Year's Eve, some time ago," he said.

She cocked her head, thinking back. "Is that why you and Dillon fought?" she asked. "I must have been inebriated to be so bold and forget. Remind me, please. Don't worry. I'll take care of my brother when we find him," she whispered.

She leaned in, her lips seeking his. They had just touched, Troy feeling seared, skin to skin, her tongue seeking his, when she suddenly went limp. Silke's eyes rolled back, and her knees buckled.

Sixteen: Side Effects

What had just happened? Troy was thunderstruck. He gently carried Silke to a padded bench seat. He checked her pulse, which was bounding, and her breathing. At least it had slowed some. If only his would do the same. She was his angel? His best friend's off-limit sister?

Whatever the stranger had done to them had been a physical, emotional, and mental strain. Troy felt confused, used, stirred, and grateful having been near death and escaped it again. He couldn't believe he had just followed Zane's orders. With a few words, he had used some sort of Jedi mind trick to take control of them.

How was that possible? Zane had expected obedience and had been surprised when Troy resisted. A loaded gun aimed at him hadn't scared Zane. What was going on?

Silke's reaction had been even more extreme. He touched his lips, finding blood. Those had been unforgettable kisses, and he would never look at Silke the same way. How could he after what she'd said?

Had she been interested in him for a decade? A teenage crush? That would explain the drunken New Year's Eve kiss that he had assumed was part of a sampling of the male population. Instead, he had been targeted. What did that say about Squaw Valley where she seemed to be in his way at every turn?

Ten heart-pounding, mentally agonizing minutes later, Troy was doubting what happened as he piloted the pontoon boat into Maraders Marina. Like gray snow, the ash fell here now. He couldn't see Marader, but Troy could hear him cursing over the humming of the air conditioner. The doors and windows of the restaurant, bar, and store were closed, and Troy looked forward to cooler air. He prayed it revived Silke. His heart lurched as he worried about what might be wrong with her, since they had no idea what Zane had done to them.

Would the whammy remain?

He realized Silke meant much more to him than he had known. Troy didn't know what he would tell his friends. Kissing and rubbing bodies with Silke had saved him. He seemed to recall someone saying that it was impossible to be worried about dying when making love to a beautiful woman. A few seconds more and he might not have noticed even if the boat had been sinking. Should he tell anybody what happened?

He tied up the boat to a pile, but he didn't leave. He wanted to stay near Silke, so he reeled in the Sea-Doo and inspected it. The bottom was scratched where it had taken off the other boat's windshield, and there was a dent in the side and a side mirror had been sheared off. Otherwise, it looked fine, considering. He wondered if he should blame it on Dillon. Looking back, what he had done seemed ridiculous, like he had been drugged. Would he have shot Zane? He wondered what he had caught on video, if anything. He might get some audio.

"Ow! Shit!" Marader screamed.

He sounded hurt, so Troy rushed to investigate. He seemed to be hurrying from one emergency to another. Two men in suits walked in as Troy followed the tirade to the storage room, discovering his blood brother uninjured but buried under several boxes of Mrs. T's mixers and bulk Kirkland Pretzels and Peanuts. Troy lifted a box aside, finding Marader still clutching the jewelry box under one arm. His obsession wasn't natural. Did it have anything to do with the vapors Troy saw around Von Damme's jewelry box? He didn't see them now.

"Are you all right?" Troy asked. Marader nodded. "Are you one-handed today?"

"I was using both hands," Marader replied.

"You have customers," Troy said. No point in arguing.

"Excuse me, is there anybody here?" called a voice.

Troy and Marader exchanged glances as Troy helped him to his feet. Marader continued to grip the sharp jewelry box.

The two men dressed in dark, power suits and ties waited at the bar. One tall and middle-aged, one short and young, both had the look and air of government agents as they removed their sunglasses and stowed them in their chest pockets. He expected them to flash badges.

They didn't, instead, smiling.

Troy heard a boat start up. It took a moment for him to realize what might be wrong.

"Morning. I'm Tom Marader. How can I help you?"

"Hello, Mr. Marader. I'm Dickson, this is Harding. We're with the Tennessee Valley Authority. We would like to speak with you about your dive."

Outside, a boat engine roared. Through the window, Troy could see Silke at the wheel, shoving the throttle lever forward, cruising away in the pontoon boat. Troy was only in shock for a split second, then he raced from behind the bar. He tried to dodge the tall man from the TVA, but he kept dancing in Troy's way, so he bumped him aside and sprinted outside.

"Lover's spat," Marader joked.

Troy burst out the door. The boat was already farther away than he could jump, but there was hope. The Sea-Doo trailed behind, coming to the end of the dock. Troy raced across the planks and launched off the end in a skimming dive, seeking distance. He almost reached the jet ski as it trailed along, but the PWC was beyond his touch. He swam frantically, his hand slipping off the fiberglass. Oh God, he wasn't going to make it!

He surged again, grasping for anything, snagging a bungee cord dangling from the back. It stretched to snap, but he kicked mightily and finally seized a solid hold on an aft metal ring used for towing and dragged himself onto the jet ski. "Silke! Silke!" he yelled.

She never turned. She couldn't hear him over the motor. What was she thinking? What had Zane done to her?

He couldn't see beyond the pontoon boat. The watercraft bounced off a buoy, sending it spinning. He gauged where they were and figured he didn't have long before the bridge where they had almost been hit earlier, and right after that, the Rock Garden. In her current state, she might crash and ground them.

If she got thrown, she could be seriously hurt.

She gunned it, full throttling the engine. Zane's influence must still be affecting her.

The keys were in the ignition of the watercraft, but it wouldn't start for him. It would turn over and die or idle until he tried to give it gas. Calling to Silke was futile. She had ignored the No Wake sign, and the Bass Buggy sped along, straining toward top lumbering speed.

With the personal watercraft being buoyant, he decided to pull himself closer. He found gloves in the glove box and began hauling on the rope, dragging the Sea-Doo with him.

Seeing the bridge, he sucked it up, ignoring the pain and burn.

It reminded him he was alive. He relentlessly drew himself and the PWC on until the Sea-Doo's nose bumped into the stern, portside of the churning motor. He grabbed the rail and boarded the pontoon boat. He didn't want to scare Silke, so he dropped heavily onto the deck, shaking it and making noise.

Silke whirled, beautiful eyes wide, surprised to see him, then she beamed a smile. "Troy! There you are! I thought you had left me," she said. She didn't see the trouble coming. The rocks and warning buoys were dead ahead.

"Never," Troy said. He rushed to her and for the throttle. She glided into his arms and kissed him even as he tried to prevent grounding the boat. He threw back the throttle into reverse, but they wouldn't stop enough in time.

He gripped her tightly in his left arm while his right hand clutched the wheel. When the boat hit hard, stopping abruptly, he flexed his knees and held fast. Silke screamed as she lost her footing. He kept them upright. He turned off the motor. When he turned to Silke, she passionately kissed him.

"I wouldn't leave you. Together, we are going to find your brother. So were you going out looking for me?" he asked her.

Something was wrong with her eyes as they appeared dazed. She might be concussed. He would prefer smitten.

"I was . . . um. I was looking, like you said for . . . the man who knows where Dillon is."

Troy frowned. "Zane?"

Her confusion broke. "Yes, that's his name."

"Silke, Zane doesn't know."

Her reaction was incredulity and beyond reason, almost childlike. "But he said he did!" she replied.

Troy thought for a moment. "Of course, he said that. He's a stalker," Troy said. He knew that word held a very negative vibe right now. Her eyes widened even as her mouth rounded in an *o* of realization. "A predator telling you what you want to hear so you'd go with him. Candy little girl? Somehow, he's a monster that can gauge your heart to offer more compelling lies. You know I want to find Dillon, find him alive as much as you do."

"Troy, what's wrong with me? I should know better."

She let him guide her toward the bench, but her knees folded, forcing him to catch her again. She was a pleasant armful, but he was deeply concerned as he laid her to rest, unconscious again.

As they entered the no wake zone Troy heard Marader yelling, "Get out! Get out before I throw you out!"

A few seconds later, the two TVA agents beat a hasty retreat out the door. They glanced at Troy and the boat, pausing as if they were debating on whether to question him. The taller of the two kept going, but the other man moved too slowly. Marader barreled into him, giving him a shove. The TVA agent staggered back. Before Marader could follow up, Spider and J-Man grabbed him, restraining him.

"We'll see you in court!" the shorter agent shouted back. The door to the store slammed. The TVA agents stalked off, heading up the gangplank to the shore and their navy-blue Town Car.

Troy didn't make the same mistake as last time. He tied up the boat, and then he scooped up Silke and carried her into the bar. The place smelled of bacon, a needed distraction.

"That looked like it went well," Troy said.

Marader was still flushed and shaking with anger. "They claimed whatever we found in the house was theirs," he snarled.

"Troy, man, what happened? Is Silke all right?" J-Man asked.

Spider looked up and laughed harshly. "Ha! Usually they carry them out of here, not in. Do you need a hand?" he asked.

What happened almost burst out of Troy's mouth, then he thought better of it. He would sound mental. Was he mental? "She fainted. Is Knives here?" he asked.

"No. He's still at work. What do you mean she fainted? Tommy said she drove off alone, and you chased her."

Troy placed Silke on the couch with her head down and her feet up. If she had passed out, blood to the brain was good. She was breathing fine, and her pulse felt steady. He examined her head and neck, looking for issues. He had seen enough head-to-toe physicals conducted by paramedics that they were second nature to Troy.

"Well? What happened?" J-Man glared in a fatherly way.

What would they say if he told them Silke had stripped and seduced him before fainting? He almost burst out laughing, and that's when he realized he didn't have his emotions under control. "She fainted right after we had a near collision with a bass boat. I think she . . . was so worked up and worried that she wore herself out. We conked heads when I swerved to miss the other boat."

"You almost wrecked my boat?! Did you do any damage?" Marader asked.

"To the old, rickety, puttering pontoon boat, the Bass Buggy?" J-Man asked.

"I might have gotten a scratch on it. The Sea-Doo, though, sorry man," Troy said, playing it up. Marader tromped outside, cursing under his breath.

"You look like you've seen a ghost . . ." J-Man said.

Spider chuckled. "Oh, he's seeing ghosts all right. But

you're right, he didn't look this laurel mountain white before. You've been in the sun, but you look bleached."

"Anyway, you know what I mean. You don't look well. Oh, that's right. You saw Raquel this morning, didn't you?" J-Man said.

"And they went diving to Wreythville," Spider said.

"What did the TVA want?" Troy asked.

"To be thrown out on their ears," J-Man said.

"Everything. They still think they have the bully power of the government behind them," Spider said.

"They wanted the booty from our underwater adventures. They wanted . . . the jewelry box, of course, and Tommy Boy overreacted. He hit the roof and then the shouting started. I thought there might be shooting," J-Man said.

"Marader? Overreact? Never," Spider jested, his timing good.

Marader burst in through the dockside door, letting it slam. He glared about, face flushed, lips tight. "What the hell happened to my Sea-Doo?"

"Oh, I can't wait to hear this," Walt said. Rubbing his hands, he followed Marader in through the door to survey the bar and lounge. Walt still looked half-asleep and shuffled like an old man.

Dressed in fishing attire, Jambo lumbered in to join them. He carried congenial air. "Hi, everybody looks expectant, except Marader, he looks pissed," Jambo said, summing it up. Like any brothers, they liked to needle each other, fight, and watch each other argue and fight.

"Tommy, relax. You're just worked up from the TVA. Troy, what did they find on your dive?" J-Man asked.

Mentioning Mona's vision seemed foolhardy. He summarized finding nothing but old stills and death traps, while TVA agents had found death. Why had their air tanks been turned off?

"Creepy," J-Man said.

"I warned you," Spider said.

"Guys, can we get back to what happened to the Sea-Doo?" Marader asked.

Troy explained it without mentioning Silke's amorous advances. He mostly edited the truth, leaving it to a sudden, near miss collision as the bass boat roared in out of nowhere. Troy had himself steering the pontoon boat clear, but he blamed the stranger for getting in the way of the Sea-Doo. It was Zane's fault, though he didn't tell them his name. He downplayed the impact, making it a glancing blow instead of one that sheared off a windshield. He didn't consider himself a liar, but now that he thought about it, if he had told the truth about the encounter with Zane, he would sound delusional, or enduring post-traumatic stress disorder. Was he suffering from PTSD?

"Funny. You're damn lucky it's insured. Did you get the boat's number? Did it have an annual tag?" Marader fired off questions.

Troy's mouth worked soundlessly. His memory was only a little help. He tried to think back. He could remember the appearance of the dark stranger and Silke seducing him and not much other detail.

"Did you happen to record this?" J-Man asked.

Troy shook his head and hated lying again. "I did on the way to Lakeview, but I didn't bother on the way back because of all the smoke. Nothing to see here. Sorry. I should have just let it run."

"What did the boat look like?" Walt asked. After Troy described it, Walt pulled up an image from the Net onto his phone. "From the *Bristol Herald Courier*. Check it out. This boat, a Pro Craft, was stolen from Camp Sequoia."

"That's it," Troy said. There was no doubt in his mind.

"That would explain why he wouldn't want to stop," Marader said. He sounded a touch mollified. "With your friends around, it's good to have insurance."

"The ash was worse at Lakeview. Here, this was in the dash of the Sea-Doo. It's Dillon's," Troy said.

He handed the waterproof camera to J-Man, who, after finding a proper cord, connected it to his laptop. He downloaded the photos and clicked through the file of images, finding Sunday morning. Dillon had walked about the island, taking photos of the water-logged graves and a new discovery. The red crescent stick pin caught everyone's attention, as did the selfie with the boat in the background.

It was not the same boat that Zane had driven. The number on the fishing boat was clear. Walt and J-Man raced each other, searching for the Virginia boat registration number.

"I have something. The owner lives on the northern part of the lake, on Driftwood Lane. Let's see, that will be on our way to the funeral tomorrow," J-Man said.

"When we go, guys, I'm driving. Right now, I need to call my lawyer and my insurance agent. She might want to talk with you and Silke," Marader said. He tromped off to use the landline.

Troy eased down on the couch next to Silke and took her hand in his. Her flesh tone looked better, and he realized she might be awake. She took a deep breath and sighed. Troy was thrilled when her eyelids fluttered.

"Hmm. Hi, Troy, Oh. I'm on a couch and inside the bar. Last I recall, we were on a boat. What happened?" Silke asked. She sat up, stretched and yawned. "What's that look in your eyes?"

"Worry?" he replied then cleared his throat.

"Hey, Silke's awake!" Spider said. The word spread quickly enough through applause.

Troy asked her several questions, but she recalled little, mostly confused. "Now that you mention it, there was a guy in a big hat," she replied with a lazy smile. She stretched, and the way she moved increased his blood pressure. "The guy wore a ton of that zinc oxide, mostly white with red around his eyes. Are you talking about that guy?"

"Do you remember driving off by yourself to go back out on the lake?" he asked. Her blank expression required no other answer. "Do you remember hitting heads? I thought so. How do you feel now?"

"A little confused. But, actually, quite good. While y'all are here, I have a question," Silke said, perking up. She sounded entirely too sweet, setting off Troy's danger sense. She offered him a tight smile, then she turned to Denny and Spider. "Gentlemen, did my overprotective brother ever threaten y'all with bodily harm if you had thoughts of asking me out, stealing a kiss or checking me out?"

Troy winced. Jambo coughed. Spider laughed so hard he snorted and doubled over.

Silke glared, unamused. "I take that as two yeses. And you, Mr. Beck?" she asked J-Man.

Jay shifted uncomfortably and let out a deflating breath. "I was just one of many who received the public health warning."

"He hit me," Walt said, shrugging. "Sorry. I thought, uh, still think you're amazing."

"Thanks, I'll hit him back for you," she replied.

"Oh, and Pete. Likely there are other doomed Romeos unknown to us," J-Man added. Troy had frequently warned Dillon that it would backfire someday. That day was here. Dillon wasn't. Lucky Dillon.

Silke fumed. Troy could feel the heat emanating from her. She started to take on the appearance of a dark, avenging angel. Dillon, if he was alive, would not find safety at home with family. Silke had a determined look, ardent about finding him and passionate about enacting revenge by her own hand, or at least venting her displeasure for the next couple of decades, never letting him forget it. "Yep, when I see him, I'm going to hug him then strangle him. God, what an idiot! He . . . And I'm having to search for him! Strangling is too fast. This has gone on for years!" Looking much healthier, she stormed out of the room.

"She recovered fast," J-Man said.

Seventeen: Dam Employees

Saying she was light-headed, Silke asked Troy to drive her to an appointment with some old men, elderly friends of Aunt Jada's who had worked during the construction of the dam. It was less than ten miles, according to Google Maps, and Silke claimed to know landmarks. She worked as a navigator but said little else.

Instead of frazzled, she fumed, looking like the proverbial fiery redhead sveltely wrapped in green, a matching ensemble of a head scarf, tied up shirt, and capri pants. An angry faerie princess, the boy at the airport might have said. She simmered with resentment for her brother and his friends, perhaps any male in the Tri Cities and three counties. Cowards all.

Troy was upset with Dillon and himself. He now knew why Dillon had lied to Silke about all of those imaginary girlfriends. It was to keep them apart. No question what Dillon thought about them as a couple.

Troy suspected they were both influenced by what had happened with Zane. Trying not to think about an amorous Silke, Troy forced himself to pay attention to the curvy road snaking along the undulating terrain. Very little was green or growing when summer should still be rich with glorious flowers and foliage. The recent rains had added a tinge of green to the grass, but the fog of smoke gave it an Apocalyptic air.

"Here it is," Silke said looking at her phone's screen. "Turn left."

Troy glanced at the battered mailbox, like it was often hit, and the name J. Corning confirmed that they were at the right place. He eased the Land Rover through the gate, over the cattle guard, and headed up the bumpy gravel road.

Leaving a cloud of dust, they passed several signs. No trespassing. No soliciting. Trespassers will be shot. If you think you're lost, you are. Turn around before it's too late! Owners close friends with Smith and Wesson. Duck Crossing. Troy couldn't help but wonder if Silke was trying to get him shot.

"Aunt Jada said that Jeremiah Corning worked for the TVA for decades, off and on, starting in the forties," Silke said.

On each side, the forest grew densely, full of chestnuts, hickory trees, basswood, yellow poplars and red leaf oaks, like a wall against the civilization of the road, then the view opened into growing fields. Troy recognized tobacco plants. Several dilapidated barns and sheds, one looking ready to fall sideways and down, sat among the different crops, including collard greens and corn. Water sprayed from long tubes on cart-like wheels to irrigate the rows of green struggling with drought. It all appeared stunted, some brown tinged. Beyond the plane of faded leafy greens was a small house.

The sound of gun fire rang out, echoing. Troy glanced at Silke. She looked straight ahead, determined. Another shot rang out. Troy couldn't tell from where. Thankfully, nothing hit the car. Were they being shot at?

He drove to the front of the house, stopping near the walkway. The country home was one story, mostly composed of red stone on the bottom and wooden slats on the top. The stain had faded, and the boards seemed to be warped. Draped in shadow, a covered porch stretched along the front.

Both front windows were illuminated, spilling light on the stoop. A solitary figure sat in a rocker. A hint of red, like an ember being stoked, flashed then dimmed. An old hound dog with a gray muzzle slept at his feet. The dog barely lifted an ear as Troy climbed out of the Land Rover, but the hound stood and sniffed the air when Silke appeared.

"There are ghosts here," she said.

"Happy or unhappy?" Troy asked.

She glanced at him, amused. He hadn't doubted her. Troy marveled at how typical it all seemed for Appalachia. He breathed deeply, noticing the all-too-potent smell of natural fertilizer. A woodpecker pounded on a maple tree near the house. Troy smiled tightly. It was almost too tranquil, too normal. Good, because he was beginning to see danger everywhere. It's only paranoia if it isn't true. That is what John used to say.

Troy followed Silke up the walkway to the steps. "Good evening, sir. Are you Mr. Jeremiah Corning?" she asked.

The cigarette tip grew bright red then dimmed. A cloud of smoke drifted from the porch. Troy tried to see the man's face, but he wore a hat. Troy could tell that he was old, as Troy expected Jeremiah to be, and was dressed in overalls and boots. A shotgun lay across his lap.

"Depends on who's askin'," the man replied in a thick drawl. His eyes narrowed in suspicion.

"I'm Silke Urich. This is my friend, Troy Bane. Jada is my great aunt. She suggested I talk to you."

"Jada, eh? You a reporter?"

"No, sir. We're searching for my brother, Dillon. He's gone missing at the lake."

"Been known to happen. Alcohol usually involved."

"And a very good friend, John Traylor, died under strange circumstances in the Von Damme mansion in the underwater town of Wreythville," Troy added, hoping to get a reaction.

Corning paled, then he smiled uneasily. He didn't touch the shotgun, but he tipped his glass back. Troy could smell the bourbon.

"Aunt Jada thought you might be able to help, especially related to the Dark Lady and your time working on the dam."

"Ah, most folk don't take the Dark Lady seriously. Why should y'all?" he asked.

"My brother did, and since he's missing, I was hoping you might answer some questions about your time working on the South Holston Dam Project," she said, arms crossed.

Another blast of gunfire interrupted.

Corning didn't even react to the sound. He leaned forward and squinted as he adjusted his spectacles. Again, he took a long draw on his cigarette before speaking. "Ya know, ah was just talkin' about it to Luther and Basil. We were wonderin' when somebody was gonna visit, askin' all sorta questions since people are disappearin' again. A reporter named Kirkland called. You ain't her?"

Silke turned to Troy. They shared a look. Again?

Corning turned to the window and yelled, "Martha, we got comp'ny. Gonna need more mint juleps," Corning said as he stood. He wobbled for a moment as he gained his balance, by leaning on the shotgun which Troy hoped had the safety on, then the old man ventured across the porch.

Troy got his first good view of Jeremiah Corning while the senior citizen hobbled down the steps. His hat was made of straw and filthy. Stringy gray hair hung from under it, framing a badly sunburned and wrinkled face. His nose was flat over blackened lips. Corning's eyes were barely visible, deeply set, and surrounded by folds of skin, but they seemed to twinkle when he set his eyes on Silke. "Y'all's timin' is good. Got some fellow survivors here. Do them good to see such a purdy thing, it will."

The door banged open. "Hold ya horses, Jer," the elderly woman said. She wiped her hands on a towel. "Ah was cannin' 'n had to clean up a bit," Martha said. She had a gentle, round face with soft blue eyes. She patted her short, black hair, peppered with gray, into place. Her apple-round cheeks glowed when she smiled. Martha ushered them up onto the porch saying, "Welcome. Have a seat. Rest yourselves a while."

"That name Urich sounds familiar," Corning mused.

She looked at her husband and shook her head, "You're getting' old when ya cain't remember Lawrence Urich."

Silke's eyes widened.

Martha noticed. "Is that your grandpa, dah'lin'?"

"Yes, ma'am. Y'all knew my grandfather Lawrence?"

Martha laughed. "Mah sister dated him fer a while. We would go on picnics in Ginya, to Hungry Mother State Park, 'specially when the leaves was changin'. I'll be back with . . . Well, lookin' at y'all, yer eyes spinning, I think I'll bring some sweet tea with those juleps."

Troy felt like his head was spinning. Were his eyes following? If he had a mint julep, it would be worse.

"It's such a small world, ain't it?" Corning said.

Silke sat on the porch swing. Troy paced. Before going back inside, Martha eyed him and frowned like he had done something wrong, likely blaming him for Silke's fuming.

A stout, elderly man dressed in tennis wear exited the house to hold the door for her. He possessed a florid complexion, jowls, and broad, welcoming smile. "Jer, I finally got that squirrel. Well now, we got guests," he said.

He held the door for a tall but stooped man who leaned on a cane to shuffle out. In his other hand, the bald man held a bottle of Bud. He peered up with milky eyes from under his bushy brows.

"The tennis fanatic is Luther; the Bud drinker is Basil. This is Silke, granddaughter of Larry, niece of Jada, and her beau, Troy."

Troy started to speak up and stopped. Silke offered a wan frown and narrowed eyes, not quite a glare, but she didn't correct him.

"Well, I knew Jada the Matchmaker had a niece, but never a fine example of southern beauty. I am charmed," Luther said.

"Thank y'all, kindly. Did y'all work on the Holston Dam project, too?"

"One of my first jobs. I drove a truck. You didn't happen to bring any Circle burgers with you, did you?" Basil asked.

"Basil, I told ya that place closed decades ago. We'll have to go someplace else for sliders," Corning said.

Luther laughed. "Dam work, oh yeah. That kind of work inspired me to save money and go back to school at King College. Accounting is easier on the back than moving rock or digging ditches. Plus, I can afford to play tennis at the Country Club," Luther said.

"And shoot skeet," Corning said.

"You know, I really miss the Wooden Nickel," Basil continued.

"He's been a little off, ya understand, since he met the Dark Lady at a young age," Corning said.

"My brother thought he had seen the Dark Lady. It was a minor obsession," Silke said. Troy wasn't so sure about minor. Dillon had talked about her incessantly when younger. Only a woman on his arm kept him off the topic.

"I understand," Basil said.

"Why are you not surprised?" Silke asked.

"I expected a reporter or two, because the TVA and conspiracy theory go together like a glove in a hand," Luther said. Troy didn't correct him. Silke just listened. "So, just makes sense that the Tennessee Valley Authority failed to relocate some of the bodies of Cemetery Ridge, either to save money, due to bureaucracy, incompetence, or all three, likely. Expect a coverup."

"Please tell me more," Silke said.

"I applied when I was thirteen. I lied about my age, but I was tall and experienced operatin' a motor vehicle. Truck drivin's easier on your back, harder on your backside," Corning said.

"What did you haul?" Troy asked.

"Mostly rock. Sometimes men. Workers."

"Did any of you ever visit Wreythville? Maybe involved with the relocation of people and their possessions?"

"Yep. I still have nightmares about it," Luther said. He mopped his sweaty brow.

"Anything go wrong during it?" Silke asked.

"Thangs were goin' wrong all the time. What'd ya expect from government work?" Luther asked in a grumpy tone. His eyes had hardened into a glare. "Every day somethin' new and different went wrong, but it wuz worse for those doin' the relocatin'. I was lucky, very lucky. Many folk caught a disease, or ended up with boils, rashes, and dysentery. Not so many died, but they suffered, were slowed down or infirmed. Some claimed it was the curse of Von Damme."

"That name again. Why?" Silke asked.

"Why? He owned Wreythville and didn't want it flooded. Fought in court, the papers said, through duded up lawyers. Some said he undermined work on the dam in any way possible. Some claimed he paid to have people vanish. Just gone. Lots of superstitious folk and more than a few shiners, if you know what I mean," Luther said.

"Others claim, the vanishings were due to the Dark Lady," Basil said. He smiled, and his eyes shone feverishly. "Some were lucky enough to see her twice. Many of us waited, hoping, at dusk, after our shifts were done. I used to dream of having dinner with her at the Martha Washington. Ah, speaking of Martha's, food and drink are here!"

Martha pushed through the door with a tray. Luther moved to help. Corning smiled fondly at his wife. "Thank God for Martha, she talked me into quittin'. Second smartest thing I've ever done. First of course, askin' for Martha's hand."

"What do you mean by gone?" Troy asked. He avoided the mint julep and drank tea. It was cloyingly sweet. He had been gone too long.

"Missin'. Disappeared." Corning waved his hand abstractly. "Rumor wuz folks disappeared on nights like they nevah wuz. Walk behind a pile a rocks or dirt and nevah come back. That's what folks were sayin' anyhow. More accidents back then, too."

Troy thought back to Zane, and how the stranger had beguiled them. He could see someone walking off, especially if the Dark Lady could befuddle and compel.

"Nevah worked nights myself, ya see. But Ah remem-bah at sunset one day watchin' a friend of mine ease into the woods to piss, and he nevah returned. Ah waited and waited, an' Terence nevah showed. We nevah did find him."

Troy didn't remember reading about disappearances. There were accidents, of course, but missing persons? History said little about it. "Was that kept quiet?"

"Not really. Just sorta blended in with all the accidents and the shiftless, restless times, people always moving, more by train back then, less by auto," Luther replied.

"Accidents? You said there were a lot?"

"Oh yeah. Besides folks fallin' or tumblin' into pits 'n breakin' their fool neck, there wuz loads droppin' 'n cables snappin'. Rock slides 'n the like. Some blamed ghosts, of course."

Troy could imagine. There were ghosts at the mansion.

"The strangest, a truck accident, happened while they wuz movin' the coffins from the town cemetery. Driver had a heart attack and keeled ovah. Plowed into tree. Fella ridin' shotgun slipped into a coma. Just 'fore he did, he babbled on 'bout a dark lady, with dark eyes, purple-black hair and red lips to die for. Scared a bunch, by golly. As I said, the Dark Lady was credited with lurin' most of the missin' fellers away."

"Remember, poor Thomas Hillwood?" Basil asked.

"Yep. Got himself stinkin' drunk one night and claimed that the Dark Lady came from Wreythville. Convinced one of the night watchmen that bulldozin' the town was the right thang to do and set 'bout doin' it. He hit a powah line that was supposed to be dead. It made Thomas dead. Lit up like a Christmas tree, they say," Luther mused.

"So, were all the coffins moved?" Silke asked.

"Supposed to have been. I don't know many who would trust a TVA report, especially from that time," Luther said.

"Was there any place where more strange things happened than others during the project? Or more people disappeared"

"The Bent Branch Spillway where I helped pour cement. The area to the southeast has so many caves and several mines, most that never amounted to nuthin' like that magnesium dig where moonshine was stored. I used to have a minin' map of that area, probably still do. It's rugged terrain," Luther said. He looked at Jeremiah who shuddered. Basil wouldn't meet their eyes.

"Anyone ever attacked by wolves?" Silke asked.

"Wolves? Hmm. No, but there were many feral dog attacks, you know, wild hounds in a pack. Fellas that survived the wounds were kinda crazy aftah that, claimed the beasts came from hell, with red eyes burnin' like coals and breathin' fire," Corning said.

Troy felt his skin crawl. His mouth was dry.

"Do you know of anyone else who's still alive and lives near?"

"A few. Lemme see. It wuz a long time ago." He rubbed his squared jaw as he thought. "Thar's Lester Pickard that lives near the country club, and Joey Leonard who lives close to the State Street Methodist Church in a senior livin' center. Pop Homgreen lives east of Abingdon."

"Dear, don't ya remem-bah? Pop moved to Richmond to be near his grandkids."

"Oh yeah, bad 'nuff gettin' old, gettin' senile too," Corning said, but smiled as he said it. "Tom Smith still lives near the dam, I think."

"Did you know Zane Aldridge?" Silke asked.

"Jada's betrothed? Yep. He drove a truck, too. Nice guy. Too bad he vanished."

"What did he look like?" Silke asked. Corning's description disturbed her and Troy. It sounded like the same man, discounting the strange eyes.

"Yeah, he nevah liked the sun. He burned too easily. Wore a big, broad brimmed hat to shade his shoulders. I remember it blowin' away one day and him chasin' it. Each time he got close, gust of wind carried it off again. Ha! Yes, I do," Corning laughed.

Troy shuddered.

"Somebody walk over your grave?" Luther asked Troy.

"Would you like to see some old photos, black and white, in my album, of the area, the dam in progress? Plus, you can see what a fine, strappin' young man Jeremiah was," Martha said.

"And how you have only gotten more beautiful ovah time, dah'lin'," Corning crooned.

"See. No wonder he sweet-talked me into marryin' him.

Come on," Martha said as she rose to her feet. She drew Silke along, leaving Troy outside with the men.

They were staring at him with what looked to be a mixture of hunger, envy and curiosity. If the old men had been younger, Troy might have been concerned about being lynched. Then, a memory from a nightmare stole over him, the old man and woman in the boat. He could feel her grab his arm and yank him into the boat. Troy took a step back then glanced at the screen door. Should he be worried about Silke?

"Is the Train Station Grill still open?" Basil asked.

"I think that closed when I was young," Troy said.

"Iffn' you don't mind me askin', what do you do for livin'?" Corning asked.

Troy thought for a moment, then explained about past and present, outdoor sports films and photographer/cameraman. He kept an ear on Silke's voice, hearing her laugh inside.

"Troy Bane. They named a burger after you, the Golden Extreme Bane Burger. Had a wonderful golden bun, golden mustard, sweet and hot, caramelized onions, cheddar cheese, it's sort of golden colored, you know . . ." Basil yearned aloud.

"Stop, you're making me hungry," Luther bemoaned. "So, Troy, tell me why is your honey so ticked off at you?"

Troy blinked. Should he pretend here? They had spoken honestly with him, he should do the same for them. "We aren't together, aren't a romantic couple," he said. He tried not to notice that those words sounded wrong.

"I admire your fidelity. Whoever your lady is, she must be somethin' to ignore such a fine example of womanhood," Luther said.

"Unless ya ain't interested in women," Corning said.

"I am very interested in women. I don't live here. I travel a lot. She's my best friend's younger sister," he said lamely. If they were trying to distract him, it was working.

"Are you daft, boy?" Corning asked.

If Troy had a dollar for every time people had referred to him as crazy, in one word or another, he would be wealthy enough to retire to his own island.

"I don't understand. What young man in his right mind wouldn't be dating that honey?" Luther asked.

"He did mention extreme sports. A head injury?" Basil said.

"That explains a lot, uh huh, it does," Corning said.

Little did he know. Besides, when had his love life become so public? What would it be like with Raquel?

"You two look great together. Natural," Luther said.

"Ya might as well get to it and apologize for bein' daft. Done wonders for me. Ya might as well accept that there's no arguin' with a woman that beautiful. Plead temporary testosterone insanity. The beauty and charm of the women of this region will do that to a man," Corning said.

Troy sighed. "If we're going to talk about women, can I ask another question about the Dark Lady?" Troy asked.

Basil perked up. He shuffled closer. Troy asked him to describe her again. She didn't sound anything like the modern urban legend, the Marilyn Monroe lookalike. That bothered him. "Gents, why do you think the Dark Lady changed her look?"

Corning shrugged. "Women like to change their hair and such."

Basil waved him off. "No. No, that's not it. Not it at all."

"They're not the same Dark Lady?" Troy asked.

Basil nodded briskly, bald head bobbing. "Yay, yay. You got it. You might be ignorant of women, but you ain't stupid."

Troy was thoughtful. There was a special light in Basil's eye, the madness of a witness. Troy had seen such a look, one who had seen wanting to share the experience, to tell their story. Or, it could be obsessive behavior, like in a pathological biological relationship. He had no idea about one of those. "You've seen her more than once, haven't you?"

Basil barked a laugh. "You betcha. I used to go out wandering, hoping I would find her, you know. I saw her that one time. She kissed me, and nothing has been the same since. For that time, everything seemed crisper, sharper, more magnificent and alive. After that, I couldn't do anything but think about her, dark eyes swirling like a cup of espresso with a touch of cream, and lips as sweet as hot chocolate."

"Dammit, Basil, you make it hard to diet," Luther said.

"Anyway, I didn't see her for years. I thought, perhaps, she had left or disappeared. Then, one night, about a month after the lake started filling up, I encountered a woman looking like Norma Jean strolling along the shores, appearing like an ethereal vision made of full moonlight," he said in a hushed tone. "I could tell she was like the first Dark Lady."

"How?" Troy asked. Norma Jean. Marilyn Monroe.

"The woods and lake hushed, waiting to see what happened. The frogs quit bellowing. The crickets stopped moving. The fish no longer jumped. The mosquitoes even disappeared. An owl left the area, silent and scared, aware a deadly beauty was loose. The moonlight felt heavy, and the night air seemed ripe with opportunity, importance and sexuality, if you know what I mean. I was scared and excited all at once."

Troy nodded silently encouraging.

"She strolled up to me, stared at me for the longest time, and said that my obsession was gone. I was free. Except I wasn't."

Much of his story reminded Troy of Dillon's tale of encountering the Dark Lady, the pale goddess, a daughter of Venus.

"You had a new obsession?" Troy asked. A phone rang, "Your Mother Should Know".

"Oh, yes," he sighed. "Hair shimmering as moonlight. Eyes you could fall into. Lips and the voice of a seductive siren. Reminded me a little of a mermaid I once saw while in the Navy. I couldn't take my eyes off her. I asked her if she was the new Dark Lady. She laughed pleasantly then told me she was a nightmare and dream in one, cursed and blest at the same time."

Basil grew silent, giving Troy a lot to think about.

"Bah, dreams and visions. Sonny, special women like that Silke come around once, yes sir, once in a life time. Surrender and apologize," Corning said.

"Even if it ticks off the rest of your world, and you lose your friends?" Troy asked.

"Listen, you can regret doin'. And you can regret not doin'," Luther said.

Troy watched Silke push the door open, returning outside.

"Which regret is worse? Doing or not doing?"

"Doin'," Luther said.

"Not doin'. Keep wonderin' about what if," Corning said.

"Eating too little," Basil said.

Silke paused. "Sorry, gentlemen. We have to leave in a hurry. Aunt Jada isn't doing well. She's on her way to the hospital."

Eighteen: Angry Wolves

"Thanks. Did you learn anything new?" Silke asked Troy from the passenger seat of the Land Rover. Her golden-red mane swirled about her.

Troy nodded. "The Dark Lady of the forties looks different than the Dark Lady of the fifties, from tall dark and gorgeous to the pale, blond and busty, Monroe lookalike," he replied. He steered the vehicle into a Y and turned around, heading out the gravel road.

"I wonder what changed?" she asked.

He recounted Basil's story. "What if, the first Dark Lady was imprisoned in the mansion?" Troy said, thinking back to the ghost's memories. "Maybe the woman that killed Mona is the new Dark Lady. She certainly looked like her." He didn't add that she looked like the woman in his exhausting dreams of Dillon.

"So you think someone imprisoned Von Damme. Looking at the shutters I can see why. But now he might be free?" she asked.

Viktor Von Damme is free at last! Troy could still hear it ring in his memory. "Sounds insane."

"It does. Plus, you say we saw Zane Aldridge, who my aunt saw the day before, who was betrothed to her in the 1940s. Could he have been trapped as well?" she asked, going improv with his lunacy.

Her phone rang and sang "Don't Worry. Be Happy".

"Hi, no, I'm not coming home. Thanks for covering. No, thank God he wasn't there, but, well, two of the search team died. Now, I guess, they'll send somebody else. Thankfully, we don't need to go back," Silke said and shuddered. "Listen, I really rather not talk about it. What? I am not! No. I do not. We just finished interviewing three elderly, former TVA employees who worked on the Holston Dam project. How's that for exciting? Now, we're headed to the hospital because Aunt Jada went in. No. No. I am hanging up now, bye."

"Roommate again?" Troy asked.

"She thinks you and I are running away together," Silke said coolly. She sat petulantly with her arms crossed, making him believe it sounded like a bad idea. "Instead of brought together in the search for my idiotic brother!"

Thinking back, Troy would have fought Dillon years ago, but they had learned that Silke kissing him was a sampling of males on New Year's Eve during her wild child phase. Now, she had told him differently. Could he trust what she had said while under Zane's influence? He wasn't sure how to even approach the conversation, or if he should at this time.

"What's going on with your aunt?" he finally asked.

"She grew dizzy and fell," Silke replied.

"I'm sorry. I know she means a lot to you."

Her phone rang again, playing "Your Mother Should Know". After a short chat, Silke turned to him.

"Where are we going now?" Troy asked.

"If you don't mind, back to Bluff City to Aunt Jada's place. My mother asked me to pick up some of my aunt's things. Sister Elva left so quickly she forgot stuff my aunt finds comforting. They also left Ginger loose. They asked me to put her in the garage."

"As you wish."

Silke sat stiffly, still mad, simmering, now an extra worry added to her concerns. He really was her friend, even if her jerk of a brother was his best friend. "Oh, now who brings up *The Princess Bride?*"

At least it kept her distracted from asking him about this morning. He might wreck if he had to recount it while driving. Even so, he had an obligation to tell her about it. She needed to know that Zane had put a whammy on them.

He recalled the video. Earlier, while Silke had freshened up, he had watched the recording. The camera had sat in front of Troy, clipped to the top of the windshield. It had mostly recorded bow forward, picking up on the silver and blue Pro Craft and Zane. The man had looked odd, shadowy, indistinguishable features and bulky clothing, certainly not handsome. When Zane spoke, it sounded like wind rushing through the microphone, although conversation between Troy and Silke was clearly audible. The recording confirmed he hadn't imagined their fighting or their kissing.

His whole world had shifted from his encounter with Zane and Silke's revelations.

He hadn't told anyone about the recording. He had contemplated deleting it. But, what if he needed to show Silke for her to believe him?

"Troy, who is Ava Vaupel?" she asked. She seemed pleased by his reaction, having to shift gears. "Jay told me a little about her. I couldn't trust what I'd heard from Dillon, as you can understand. Jay said she was the only woman you've ever mentioned since going west. He said she was a French Dream. I looked her up online and found out he was right. Ah, I take by your silence that she is of some importance."

Troy didn't understand why his friends were discussing his lack of a love life. "Was. Past tense. We were together for several years, one of those on again off again romances that ended four years ago when she returned to Paris."

"I see. What did Desiree mean she wanted to be your Ava?" Silke asked.

"I don't know."

"Guess."

Ava had been a few years older, coming to the US to ski and attend college after barely missing the cut for the French National Team. She hadn't wanted to get emotionally involved long term. "I would guess, guess mind you, no commitments. Friends with benefits. Uh, somewhat secretive. She was also very passionate about extreme sports. She climbed, biked, and skated. I couldn't get her to base or bungee jump."

"Then she's smart, too. No wonder you associate dating with extreme activities."

"Why not? It's a rush and a risk. Thrilling. Barely on the edge of control, or not, a rush headlong. I've tried to develop a sense for what terrain is questionable and dangerous. Sometimes that incredible stretch of snow is an avalanche waiting to happen. Or that perfect looking rock hold will break off in your hand when you put weight on it."

"I guess I shouldn't be surprised. I've heard the debate, which is better, skiing or sex," she said.

"I don't go there," Troy said.

"Perhaps because Ava and Raquel were both skiers. You look at me differently this afternoon. Why?" Silke asked.

What a segue. In his eyes, she had only grown more gorgeous, or his brain had finally relented to the truth. "I look at everything differently since being down there and that grisly vision with Mona. I am even more grateful than before, and that's saying a lot," Troy said. That was true, if not the only reason. "And I didn't sleep through the night, somebody woke me up and interrupted my REM sleep."

"I apologize. What was I thinking? I should have just let the wolf stroll in. Maybe he and Tommy are friends. Or, in better times, he would eat him. Wait! I should have guessed. Marader is a werewolf! He could change the title of the bar and lounge to the Wolf's Den," Silke said.

Troy's phone rang. He glanced at it, seeing it was Deputy Burt. He suggested she answer it.

"Hi, Burt. This is Silke. Troy is driving. Yes, I still plan to file the report, unless he's shown up or somebody's seen him. Oh, Troy sent you an image. You're running it through the data base. I'll tell him." She hung up and looked at him. "Did you record the near collision?"

"Yes," he said, not wanting to lie to her. He didn't tell her he had lied to the guys.

"Will you tell me what happened? Or should I just watch the recording? Is it on here?" she asked.

He almost grabbed his phone, but he recalled he had password protected the video file. Dodging a cyclist brought his attention back to the road. Troy gave her a terse, dry and abridged version of their Zane encounter.

"How did he know about Dillon?"

"I have no idea. But you didn't care. You believed him and wanted to go, but I was scared of him. I can't explain why, but then, a moment later, it was like he had taken over my body, at least my hands. Then, he told me to boat over and I couldn't stop myself. I was helpless, really," Troy said. He didn't look at her, feeling her watching intently.

"Are you okay? You're sweating."

"What Zane did, taking over my body, is unnerving. When you mention it, I can feel it happening again. That, and I have a wheel in hand," he said, and Silke by his side.

"So you were following orders, commands, you didn't want to?" she prompted.

"Yeah. I fought, but I felt locked out of my own body. You didn't think I was driving fast enough, so you got ready to leap out of the boat. I snapped out of my haze in time to grab you. In appreciation, you elbowed me. You got a headbutt in, too. I have a bruise on my thigh where you tried to make sure I'd never father a child."

"Oh, my God. You're joking. You're not, are you? That's

how your lip got that way? It wasn't an accident?"

"We wrestled, bumped into the throttle and nearly ran over the other boat. The Sea-Doo struck it and broke its windshield. We just kept going, not looking back, until the Rock Garden where you collapsed," he finished.

"I . . . I don't remember any of this. How did he convince you to drive over?"

"That worries me. I have no earthly idea. The evil eye? The whammy? His voice was beguiling and frightening at the same time. It was like I was powerless, trapped inside watching my body but unable to affect it. I guess I was a puppet or run by remote control."

"And I was in a hurry to find Dillon, I'll bet. Can I pull up a photo of him?" she asked.

Troy told her how. She succeeded, looking at the image. It was a bit blurry, and Zane's face appeared to be covered in thick sunblock.

Silke shook her head. "He doesn't look familiar. I hate losing my memories."

"I wish I could forget being held captive in my own body. We were lucky to escape. You rescued me. If you hadn't cleared my head with an elbow, we might not have escaped."

"So, I saved us by punching you?" she asked, smiling wanly.

"Physical therapy," he said. She burst out laughing, a wonderful sound. He was hoping to change subjects. He didn't think it was a good time to show her the video.

"I would like to see the recording," she said.

Troy mentally flipped through excuses. He didn't need one, seeing the driveway ahead. "Ah, here we are," Troy said. He pulled into the driveway of the mini estate.

Silke returned his phone. "What aren't you telling me, Troy?" she asked. A patient stare of astoundingly beautiful eyes greeted him.

He needed air and exited the vehicle. He took a deep breath, and the air seemed oppressive with smoke and humidity. He noticed the quiet, the lack of bird songs. He shook himself, spooked as he recalled the old men's stories. Out of the corner of his eye, he saw movement at the edge of the house. The dog? Ginger?

Deja vu?

"Troy? Are you okay? You bolted."

A strange, cold breeze rustled through, ruffling his hair. He shivered. Silke threw her arms around herself.

"Sorry. This place gives me the creeps. I keep seeing things out of the corner of my eye," Troy said.

She glared at him, frowned, then spun on her heel. "You don't have to go inside with me," she said. She strode briskly ahead.

"I followed you into the underwater mansion of doom," he said.

"I know you love my brother," she said coolly. Calling for Ginger, Silke stalked toward the house. "You can look around the yard for her. I'll be right back."

"Okay, I followed you in the still building," he said.

She stopped.

A dust devil swirled through the driveway, picking up pebbles, and then it veered across the yard, kicking up dirt and dead grass. The miniature tornado spun in place, in their path, for a few seconds that seemed longer, then it faded away.

"Playful ghosts," Silke suggested.

Troy thought it seemed more like a warning. He couldn't explain why, but he strongly felt that he should stop her. Last time he had taken her arm, she had decked him.

Digging in her purse for a key, Silke approached the door. With the way things were going, Troy expected it to open on its own. The knob turned freely when Silke tried it, so she pushed open the door into the house.

Cold fingers danced down Troy's neck, spine-tingling and giving him the jitters. Spider might have called it bad voodoo vibes. The wafting of a faint breeze brought a foul odor. No corn bread this time. Rotten eggs?

Silke's phone played again, her mother calling. "Hi . . ."

"Dear, Aunt Jada is hysterical . . ."

"Silke, get out! Get away! Get away from the house now!" Aunt Jada yelled over Mrs. Urich.

Something in her voice galvanized Troy. That and the stench. He grabbed Silke, dragging her away from the house.

"What? Troy! What's wrong? What's gotten into you?!"

"Gas smell! Move!" he said as he scooped her up, ready to throw her over his shoulder. He would carry her to the car.

"Troy, I hate to be manhandled."

She was going to clobber him. That's how much she loved him. A loud and powerful force blasted him forward, lifting him off his feet. He had a brief feeling of flight and a limp, bone-jarring crash, then he lost time.

Painful feeling returned, along with a ringing in his ears. His body throbbed and vibrated like he'd taken a terrible fall. His back burned like a serious case of road rash. He could tell he no longer flew, no longer moved. He was grounded but surprisingly comfortable. Had he landed on something?

His vision slowly cleared, and he realized he rested atop Silke who had unintentionally cushioned his landing. What had struck them? He hoped he hadn't hurt her.

Far from injured, Silke looked alluring, those gorgeous and caring eyes staring up at him. They possessed a special sparkle, one he had seen before on the pontoon boat, a glimmer he thought might be supernaturally inspired, but then, here, he saw it again. And instead of glowering, she glowed. But, why did she have debris in her hair?

Fiery ash fell around him. She spoke, but he heard nothing even as her lips moved. Finally, she grinned fiercely, grabbed his head and resoundingly kissed him on the lips. The ringing in his ears changed tone, and his head spun from a different smiting. He forgot everything else, seized by her hands, her lips and her passion. The long slow kiss led to a second, longer, savory kiss.

"Ouch!" Silke said. He could hear again! "Your shirt is

smoldering! Off! Off!"

He tore off his shirt and tossed aside the smoking heap. "It was that kiss," Troy said, watching Silke blush, then she burst out laughing. Burning debris was scattered across the gravel driveway.

Pieces of paper and ash drifted downward. The house was all but gone. Little remained but the charred chimney and fragmented ruins of blackened walls leading to the yellow sky. By the devastation, it looked like the work of a tornado, except the trees were still standing. Slivers of roof and shards of furniture burned in the branches.

His brain seemed to lock for a minute, trying to figure out what happened. It worked, finally putting things together. The smell of gas. A gas leak. Somehow, it had ignited, blowing up the house.

Low growling, like that of a large canine beast, mingled with the crackling of flames. It was a strange and dangerous sound, and he had heard it before, recently. He hadn't expected to hear it at the marina, or here now.

"A wolf," Silke said, eyes wide.

Troy glanced over his shoulder. They weren't imaging things, though he wished they were deluded. A large, pale wolf, head low and snarling, left a copse of red oaks to stalk toward them. Except for its ghostly gray coloring, the creature reminded Troy of Bandit from the marina. The look in its albino-like eyes was similar, that of intelligence, and its snarl resembled a whiplash smile.

"Let's get out of here," Troy said. He drew Silke to her feet and herded her backwards toward the Land Rover. They kept their eyes on the ghostly wolf as it padded steadily toward them. If they moved swiftly, and Ghostly didn't break into a run, they would make their escape.

Climbing behind the wheel of the car, Silke fumbled the key into the ignition and fired up the engine. In a movie, it would have flooded or vapor-locked. Troy buckled up, but Silke didn't take time as Ghostly broke into a trot. She shifted into reverse and floored the accelerator, speed-backing away. The beast only followed them to the end of the driveway.

Troy checked his phone to dial 911. "No signal."

Silke shook her head, finding the same. "We'll have to drive to the nearest house. It's several miles," she said.

"That wolf sure acted oddly. Not to mention that there shouldn't be wolves! What's it doing here?" he asked. He didn't wonder aloud if it was somehow related to the house exploding, but they were both thinking it. Silke Y-turned the car around.

Troy spotted the wolf in the sideview mirror. Tongue hanging out, Ghostly sprinted toward them. Silke punched the gas pedal, leaving the beast behind. It dropped back as they turned a corner. Troy caught hold of his breathing and his wild thoughts, spooked by the wolf and the sudden destruction of the house.

Silke eased off the gas and let the Land Rover coast. They should be safe now. As he started to relax, his back burned, likely needing treatment, and he imagined he was still stunned by the explosion, the wolves, and those Silke kisses. He had avoided one death. Now he was flirting with another. Perhaps he did have a death wish.

"Aunt Jada knew! Poor Ginger. I wonder what happened to her. She was such a sweet dog. A couple more turns and we're there, perhaps a mile," Silke said. She didn't wait, leaning over to kiss him.

"Don't worry, I'll protect you from Dillon," she said, smiling fiercely like a woman warrior. When she glanced in the rearview mirror, her expression faltered. "Hey, unbelievable, that wolf's still after us."

"You're kidding me!" Troy groused. He turned around.

Ghostly loped along, its four legs seeming to have lengthened, devouring ground in a supernatural way. Silke quit dawdling and gave the metal tank some gas, expecting to outrun the beast of flesh and blood. Unless it wasn't. She had to accelerate past forty-five to increase their lead. How did wolves run that fast? He lost sight around a corner. Had it been smiling at him? Enjoying the chase?

"Oh my Lord! It's Ginger!" Silke cried.

The wounded red dog stumbled from the smoky woods to collapse in the middle of the road. Silke slammed on the brakes. The front of the jeep bore down. Tires squealed. Troy tried to will it to stop and prayed, too. The Land Rover slid, beginning to twist sideways. The dog didn't stir, just laying there, waiting to be hit.

Silke spun the wheel and released the brakes. The Land Rover seemed to leap forward, swerving to the right. It straightened for a moment, then skidded along the narrow shoulder of the road in the loose rock, gravel clanging in the wheel wells. He feared the back end would slip off pavement, but the tires skirted the drop-off. Better yet, the car missed the dog and finally came to an abrupt halt a foot away from a hulking service berry tree.

"Oh, God. Thank you, Lord," Troy uttered. He still must have purpose.

Silke threw him a wild smile, unbuckled and hopped out of the car to run to the wounded dog. Ginger appeared to have been mauled. Shreds of fur and hanging flesh bled profusely, reddening the road, quickening her death and drawing predators.

"Wolves," Troy suggested. There weren't supposed to be any. Despite most stories, from what he had learned from living out west, wolves didn't attack people. How could Ginger outrun the wolves if they had been like the beast chasing the Land Rover? He started to have a bad feeling about this.

"There's a carpet in back. Get it! Please hurry. My aunt cherishes this dog. With the house gone, she'll need Ginger."

"But the wolf. Wolves, they could be here any moment."

"This will only take a minute," she pleaded.

Troy didn't think they had time, but like a stupid male and yet sensitive soul, he helped anyway. He didn't want to leave Ginger to die, though the dog looked more than half dead. He prayed Ginger was hardy while he carried her to the Land Rover and laid her into the open air back on another carpet. Silke climbed in to join the wounded dog. "You drive! Go! There's a vet on the way into town."

The Land Rover's engine turned over, but it didn't start. Troy tried again with similar, lackluster results.

"Oh, God, here comes one!" Silke scrambled for her purse, fingers questing for her gun.

They weren't out of gas. The battery seemed to have died abruptly. Or the alternator or starter could have gone dead.

The lone wolf began to howl. The wailing carried throughout the woods and seemed like it hailed from all sides to surround them. The hungry cries sang of the chase, of blood, and feasting and death. The forest seemed to magnify the haunting sound, swelling with it, gaining strength and worse, increasing in numbers.

Troy realized there were many wolves, a dozen or more. Fortunately, Silke had stopped on a downhill slope. With the old Land Rover, he could try a manual start. He released the brake and shifted into neutral. The nearly prehistoric SUV picked up speed, gravity hauling on the heavy metal.

He turned the ignition key and hit the gas. The Land Rover lurched, but it failed to catch and start, grinding away. He let it roll, needing to try again. The end of this short hill was coming too soon.

Troy glanced back, seeing the wolf almost upon them. Silke took aim, ready to open fire. Seeing the hill about to dip, flatten and turn, Troy tried starting the car again. The SUV fired up with a roar. He shoved the stick shift into first, and the Land Rover leapt ahead with a herky-jerky surge of speed. "Hang on!"

The wolf lunged and fell short, slamming into the back of car. The impact shoved it forward. Using the bump up in speed, Troy shifted into second, accelerating into the turn. Silke fired a burst of three shots. The blasts rang in Troy's ears, once his hearing returned. That was the second such assault on them in the last ten minutes.

"I swear I hit it! Oh, God! What if I need silver bullets?!"

Silke had probably missed, Troy figured. Did they want us or the dog? No time for contemplation, he paid attention to the moment and drove. His sense of focus, taking in the field of vision and knowing where to go and what speed, kicked in.

Two wolves bounded down the hill, landed lithely on the road, and lunged. Troy noticed them in time to veer away. He wasn't about to let them land in the open back cab with Silke. One wolf smashed face first into Troy's window, cracking the glass and spitting blood.

The other thudded solidly against the side panel. Both fell away, howling all the time. A glance in the rearview showed they were undaunted, joining the chase, now briefly making a four pack. The spectral beasts darted up into the woods and out of sight.

"Where the hell do wolves come from?!" Silke shouted.

"Is there a local wildlife park I don't know about?" Troy whipped his head back around. He was coming too fast into a turn. The sign showed a sharp S. He downshifted, braked and skidded, trying not to roll the Land Rover. The old metal tank lumbered through the turn, the tree trunks waiting on the side of the road to make them pay if Troy made a steering mistake. Touch and go, with deft steering, braking and shifting, he righted the Land Rover and navigated through a series of curves like a giant slalom.

"Unbelievably fantastic. Do you think we're out of trouble?" Silke asked. She gave him a smooch, lightening the mood. "Never know how long you have. I've been wanting to do that."

Troy wondered if he really had a death wish. If so, Silke was the most pleasant reason yet.

Seeming out of nowhere, a wolf burst from the right, downslope side, leaping onto the Land Rover. Its upper body made it inside, its hindquarters hanging off. The beast tried to wiggle its way closer until Silke shot it in the maw three times.

As if the creature hated swallowing lead, it snarled and jerked back, leaving a trail of blood as it spun to land with supernatural grace on its paws, kicking up sparks with its claws.

Troy shook his head. He must be seeing things. This wasn't natural.

"I know I hit it that time! That wolf shouldn't be alive. I need silver bullets!"

"What are they?" Troy asked. Werewolves? Was he dreaming?

"Oh, God! More of them! I'll try the tire iron!" Silke yelled.

More than a half dozen wolves burst out of the woods and swarmed around the Land Rover. Their movements were astoundingly adroit and swift, a mix of western pronghorns and wolfhounds. The one running next to Troy was white around its muzzle, making its teeth seem larger when it grinned. When the wolf prepared to surge and leap, Troy swung open his door, whacking the creature pre-jump and knocking it back. A second wolf couldn't evade the first. The two beasts collided, entangled and rolled like a furry tumbleweed.

Troy started to weave some, running over a wolf on the passenger's side. The Land Rover bounced, the right side hopping up. The jarring threw off his vision, so he didn't see the next attack. Only luck and good reflexes kept him alive. A red-eyed wolf punched through the driver's window, snapping at his neck. He instinctively threw himself sideways, leaning into the middle, getting jabbed in the ribs by the stick. Inches away the wolf chomped in a frenzy, teeth gnashing, spraying spittle while Troy blindly reached under the seat for a weapon. He touched a fire extinguisher then a screwdriver.

From the back, he heard the thudding and banging of the tire iron hitting flesh and missing, striking metal. You go, girl.

Troy snagged the screwdriver. Using it like an ice pick, he jammed the screwdriver in the left eye of the wolf. It was a clean hit, driving the tool into its brain. Howling in agony, the beast pulled back and fell away.

Troy glanced back, seeing Silke wrestling with a wolf. She had lost her weapon and was losing at grappling, barely keeping Bandit away from her face and neck. Was it really the same wolf from Maraders? Troy didn't dwell on the ramifications. He stabbed the screwdriver into Bandit's back. Seeing it jerk upward, Troy yanked the wheel and swerved, throwing the wolf off balance. Silke used the momentum to kick it with both feet, sending the beast wildly scrabbling over the side onto blacktop.

"They're all over!" Troy yelled.

From the left, another wolf lunged, misjudged, and bounced off the front windshield, cracking the glass like it had sprouted a spider web. Troy couldn't see as well now, the windshield smeared with saliva and blood. The car rocked violently as it ran over more wolves. They were throwing themselves in front of the Land Rover to slow it!

From across the road, a dusty brown beast leapt and scrambled into the back. It snapped at Silke, snagging her hair. Troy seized the fire extinguisher, wresting it loose, nearly running off the road, before hitting the wolf over the head with the metal canister. Silke kicked the woozy beast until it slipped overboard. Troy dropped the extinguisher and drove.

"Silke, are you all right?"

"Yeah, considering. Where are they coming from?"

Suddenly, something pale, furred and clawed crushed Troy. As if it had dropped from a tree above, Ghostly had landed in his lap, biting and ripping. Troy lost a grip on the wheel, instinctively protecting himself from the attack.

"Troy!" Silke screamed. She bludgeoned the wolf with the fire extinguisher.

"Hang on!" Troy yelled. Unable to see, he slammed on the brakes.

The SUV skidded and sped off the blacktop. For a moment the Land Rover hurtled airborne toward the trees, then it crashed through bushes and small saplings, barreling into the woods. Troy heard a terrible screech of metal—then nothing.

Nineteen: Concussed

Next to Troy, close enough to touch, Raquel relaxed in the golden sunshine, her dark eyes sparkling delightfully as she listened to him. It only seemed like he unloaded nine years' worth of experiences as she kept prompting him with questions, some deeply personal. He had been intimate with Raquel a long time ago, and while he distrusted her, some irrational part of him felt he could still confide in her.

She was dressed as he often remembered her, in a plain white buttoned shirt, sleeves rolled up, blue jeans and white tennis shoes. She somehow made beautiful seem easy, simple, and normal, a young Julia Roberts meeting Wonder Woman. She laughed, and she cried, not always liking his honest answers. Somewhere along the way, Troy realized he must be dreaming. Likely it was Raquel crying that set off his reality alarms. The young woman he had known rarely wept, except perhaps in pain or frustration. They had both been egocentric, headstrong, and passionately attracted to each other.

It must be a dream, because he couldn't figure out how he had gotten here or even where here was. He certainly didn't feel in his right mind, and Raquel just offered her delicious smile when he asked her questions. Her fragrance was right, but she fiddled with a bracelet of pearls. While she might be into medals made of metal, she wasn't bedazzled by jewelry. Or hadn't been. What did he know? Over nearly a decade, she couldn't help but change.

"I'm not awake, am I?" Troy said.

"Oh, is that why you're being so frank with me?" she asked.

"I know how this ends. Either a doctor, or a European skiing stud or a handsome actor comes through, and poof, you're gone. Hey, it was fun. I warned you about getting serious. So long. I should have known it wouldn't work out. The first time I kissed you, you ran away."

"That's true. But I came back. So, you expect this to go the same way?"

He closed his eyes, trying to will himself awake. "I hate reoccurring dreams."

"Troy, you are awake, but you're not all here. Think, how did you get here? What happened?" Raquel asked.

Troy struggled to recall. Boats on a collision course. A wreck.

"A boat wreck? Silke and I were coming back from Lakeside . . ." he said, groping for memories, grasping at straws. He opened his eyes. Looking concerned, Raquel was still here.

She smiled. "A wreck, yes. Boat, no. And Silke was there," she said, frowning.

Again, Troy closed his eyes. A pale face with demanding red eyes swam into view. Big eyes and a big hat. Silke in his eyes? His target? His heart lurched at the thought. As Troy wondered about her, darkness collapsed on him like a falling stage curtain, threatening to engulf and drag him down. He thought he saw consciousness way above, a light atop dark water.

Raquel kissed him, fully on the lips, lingering there until his eyes opened, gazing soulfully at him. The kiss kick-started his heart and unleashed dopamine to bring him more alert. She was a sight for his bleary eyes and a sore body, giving it inspiration to live.

"Why did you do that?" Troy asked.

"That was the good-bye kiss I was never able to give you. When you died, the way we ended went from bothering me to haunting me. We argued and split, and when we did, you really split, leaving all you knew and going west." Tears welled in her eyes, and he was surprised to see tears of joy. "You're right. I took you for granted. I didn't know what I had lost until later. Anyway, I appreciate you being honest with me. Finally, after avoiding me all those years."

What had he told her? The truth? He had missed her. Life had been dull without her unless he was risking his life. That he had avoided her because whenever he had come back, she had been coupled. "Stalk compulsively or avoid. I went with the latter."

She kissed him, lightly, but lingering, reveling in it. "You can think of those, if you wish, as our first kisses in this life time. I have a captive audience. Per doctor's orders, you won't be running away until tomorrow morning at the earliest."

A hospital? He was in a hospital bed? Oh, Lord, he hated hospitals. He could get the shakes thinking about one, a kind of claustrophobia that he might never escape the bed. His body hurt, battered, bruised, and even torn. The flesh across his back felt strangely stiff and numb. He glanced down at himself and moved a little, feeling the tubes and stitches pull. He had been sewn up across his forearms and ribs. His body throbbed and complained, and yet, no screaming meant nothing felt broken.

"Have you been here long?"

"Half an hour, maybe," she said. She fiddled with the bracelet. The pearls seemed to flash in her eyes, and her cheeks flushed.

"If I'm not dreaming, how did I get here? Last I recall I was trying to find my best friend."

"Who you are mad at," she said.

Troy nodded. How did she know this?

"And who you dream vividly about. You told me a little about your nightmares of him and Marilyn. Freud would have a field day with you. I would enjoy a field day with you."

Troy's head was spinning. "I told you?"

"You don't think anyone will believe you, except Silke," she said, frost on the name. "I know how close you are or at least were, to Dillon. Do you remember when I had a concussion?" she asked. He nodded. "You made sure I drank enough water and took care of me."

That had been at the end of the ski season, early spring. He wondered now, as he did then, if the head trauma had affected her and their relationship. Besides, he needed something to blame it on.

"You are miles away."

"Years," he replied.

"Oh, I guess I brought that on. A while ago, you told me about your visit home. Sounds crazy. The strange, psychic aunt who thought you were married to Silke. Diving the mansion. Ghosts, I swear. Wolves? Faster than the car? Really?"

Troy gave her a blank look.

"You don't remember it. So, you weren't fully awake."

Troy didn't recall telling her any of this. What else had he said? Something about her bracelet bothered him. Vague mists arose from it. "Did you find that in the mansion, under water?"

"Nice change of topic. Yes, how did you know?"

"The stuff found there, like Marader's jewelry box and the letter opener, give off bad vibes. You should get rid of it, or better, destroy it," Troy suggested.

"That's not going to happen. I like it. It reminds me that even in a depressing place you can find pearls, figuratively and literally."

There, Troy had only found a murdered friend, and the jewelry box had made Silke bleed. Those things he recalled. He didn't have the will to fight with Raquel if she felt as possessive as Marader. Back when, Troy lost fights all the time, because he loved her. "Are you going to tell me what happened to me?"

She bristled. "You're lucky to be alive. You hit your head when you crashed the Urich's Land Rover into a tree. Knives said you seemed to have been attacked by big dogs, those wolves you told me about, huge ones that can run as fast as a car."

"Wrecked? A car crash?" Troy asked. He remembered nothing. Had he been driving? "Was anybody else hurt?" Who had he been with? Where had he been going? Last he recalled, he had been on a boat, Marader's pontoon boat, looking for Dillon. They had been leaving the Lakeside docks, towing Marader's once-missing Sea-Doo.

They? Silke? His heart skipped a beat and fluttered. Silke!

Raquel frowned, noticing his reaction. "Silke is fine. You took the worst of it. That old car doesn't have airbags. She leapt clear. I swear, Troy, she's trying to kill you."

"Women and skiing. Do you know where she is?"

"Did you seriously say women and skiing?" she asked, exasperated.

He nodded.

"Fine. Silke went to look in on her Aunt Jada when I came to check on you. You were out cold. You're sweet on her, aren't you?"

"Sweet on Aunt Jada? Oh, you meant, Silke, Dillon's off limit sister, don't you?" Troy asked. He recalled nothing of it. But, his physical, visceral reaction to Silke's name confused him. What had he forgotten?

"Troy, what have you gotten yourself into?" she asked, sounding worried.

"I don't know. I'm just trying to find Dillon. He was only here a day or two before me. He couldn't have gotten into much trouble, could he? He spent all his time at the lake. This must have something to do with the cemetery and that mansion. Another reason to get rid of that bracelet."

"Could whoever killed John be trying to kill you, too?"

"Who would they be? Treasure hunters? Someone hiding a secret? I don't know, but I don't think we were having any luck finding out what happened," Troy said. He hated concussions.

"Well, you were at a house explosion and attacked by dogs before crashing. That's suspicious. I only know you're here because I was visiting a girl injured in a skiing accident, while practicing tricks into the water. I saw Burt in the lobby. Fortunately, the Bristol hospital is much closer than Florida," she said. He thought she wanted to say more, but like usual, she said nothing, making him read her mind. She nervously toyed with the bracelet. "How are you handling this place?"

She knew. He loathed being in hospitals. It brought back

horrible, painful and lonely memories. Raquel was right. They needed to talk about what had happened to their bodies, careers and goals. Life, mileage, and years had happened. "I'm screaming inside."

"I can hear it. We speak the same, physical language," she said. She tenderly took his hand, and he let her. He thought about resisting, but he didn't have the strength of will. She leaned in and kissed him. The pleasure threatened to turn to passion, masking the pain of his flesh and bones.

The door opened, breaking the moment, and their kiss. Even so, Raquel held onto his hand while Knives ambled in. "Think of that next time Silke kisses you," Raquel whispered.

That confused him. He might have looked like his blood brother.

Knives' eyebrows remained arched in shock at seeing them together. "Well, look who's awake. You're back in town two days, and you end up in the hospital. Don't you think there's already enough funerals? At least in movies, they throw in something festive, say, a well, uh, let's not make it three funerals, okay? Enough, already," he said.

"Thanks for taking care of him, Stephen. He's bullheaded sponsored by Red Bull. I'll let you two jaw. I'll see you tomorrow," Raquel said and departed, leaving the room dull and lackluster.

"Are you suffering from amnesia?" Knives asked.

"Short term. I have a concussion, don't I?" Troy asked. The good doctor nodded. "That's not enough reason to keep me here. You know I loathe being in hospitals. I get flashbacks. And to sleep here, you either have to work here or be on drugs."

Knives sighed. "Listen, I already visited you once earlier, when you seemed to be awake. You talked and answered questions, but now you don't remember it. Plus, you burned your back, though not badly. It's likely you strained your neck from whiplash. We haven't X-rayed you, but I did stitch you up, and you're on antibiotics because those wild dogs tore into you in a few places along your arms and ribs. Bites and scratches. Those dogs must have had really long nails. The Department of Animal Control will see if they can catch them. Hope you don't have rabies, buddy boy. The shots are painful."

"Rabies. More good news. You are full of it," Troy bemoaned.

"See. You don't remember. That memory loss and the mechanism of injury are both serious enough to keep you here. That and I want to make sure your wounds don't get infected."

"And that I don't do anything you consider stupid."

"Oh, far too late for that based on what I just witnessed."

The door swung open, and like a ray of sunshine, Silke peeked in. She grinned, relieved at seeing him awake. She rushed in, sat on his bed and gently gave him a hug, then a long, slow sensuous kiss. When she withdrew, she had a questioning expression. "I'm so glad you're awake. How are you?"

Troy imagined he looked stunned or confused. If he hadn't been completely awake before, he was now. He had forgotten something. Raquel knew, though. "I thought I was okay, but I'm addled, according to Dr. Stephen Curran," he replied. He told her the last he recalled about being at the dock. Whatever he said disappointed Silke, bringing on a crestfallen look before she recovered. Why? What had he forgotten? "Can you tell me what happened?"

"Please help him see sense, Silke," Knives said.

"You're asking for a miracle, doc," she sighed. Her shoulders slumped, and he felt he had let her down somehow.

"I am being positive and hopeful despite history stacked against us. I'll be back after I've made some rounds. And, Troy, I know the nurses. They won't let you sign yourself out without me examining you again. They're loyal to me. I feed them chocolate as a sign of appreciation." He left in a huff.

"He's worried about you. We all are," Silke said. She went on to explain what happened earlier, that afternoon, including the house exploding into flaming bits, how he had smelled the gas leak and grabbed her, getting between her and the blast.

At least his back already looked a wreck. It would be a shame to mar Silke in any way. She went on, telling about Ginger and the wolves chasing the injured dog, how they had attacked them, leading to the wreck. The details were gripping. He was astonished that he could forget. "Nobody believes me about the wolves. I wish we had recorded them, but we were kinda busy. Everyone, doctors, authorities, Burt, pass them off as feral dogs that look like wolves and run forty miles an hour."

"I believe you."

"Thanks, that means the world to me," Silke said, touching his arm. "You know, those wolves, something about them, their disdain and intelligence, reminded me of the one at Maraders."

Troy remembered it well. It had grinned at them. Troy fought off a shiver.

He sensed there was something she wasn't telling him. She seemed anxious and disappointed that he couldn't recall anything of the afternoon, then she laughed it off, saying they had both forgotten important moments, though she sounded wistful.

"Your eyes don't look right. And your neck is completely out of whack. When the swelling goes down, I can realign you. I'm so sorry we crashed, so very sorry. Damn those wolves," she said.

"It's okay. I'll be all right. I'm a really fast healer. Besides, forgetting is a small price to pay to make sure you're all right. Dillon would kill me if I let something happen to you, and I'd be furious with myself, too."

She stared at him, saying nothing.

"So, what next?" he asked.

"Paperwork. Hospital and missing persons forms. Burt will bring it by. How did it go with the Silver Goddess?" she asked.

"She was acting oddly and wearing a pearl bracelet she

found in Von Damme's Wreythville mansion. She kept fiddling with it, like Tommy Boy does with the jewelry box. I suggested, because of where it came from, that she get rid of it, but it reminded her that pearls can be found during the darkness of times, in the darkest of places," he said, then told her about the mists surrounding it.

"I know you're not crazy. You're not seeing things," she said. She showed him where the jewelry box had bitten her. The wound was puffy and swollen. "Not infected, they say. Just, trauma, like a dog bite without germs. So yeah, don't trust that stuff. You're not thinking of wrestling it from her, are you?"

He frowned. "What makes you think that?"

"Oh, you're just the same guy who picked me up to protect me from the house exploding and wrestled with me to keep from jumping ship."

"I don't recall either of those."

"Believe me, you did. You're a great guy. I don't care what your blood brothers say. Listen, you're looking tired and sleepy. That's no good for your memory, and I have to go. I'll check on you later," she said and seemed to breeze out of the room. She left in a different mood than she entered, her step heavy, her upbeat mood a facade. He could tell something bothered her, something about him.

Restless and trying to recall what happened, why Silke was upset, Troy paced. What had he done? He hated not knowing. Usually, in the past, whatever events had led to his amnesia had been recorded. His activity drew attention.

Knives checked in on him. "The nurses can feel you pace, you know. I wouldn't be surprised if the patients sense it, too, like the call of the wild," Knives teased.

Troy growled.

"Are you claustrophobic now?" Knives asked. Troy turned, showing him a pinch that grew as his arms widened until he felt the stitches. "You're a big boy, you can leave when you want. But, you know that I know how you feel so I would only keep you here if I thought it was really important to your health. That said, it would be all right if you took a stroll with your doctor. Feel up to it?" Knives asked rhetorically.

They took the elevator to the first floor. An evening walk around the block was certainly what the doctor ordered and helped clear Troy's head a little. Streetlights and headlights had strange halos, a side effect of his brain swelling.

"And you're suffering twice the affect, the accident and the two women giving you their attention. You know kissing two different women from your hospital bed is a good way to stay in a hospital."

"Ah, this guided tour comes with a lecture."

"Just that you should be finding Dillon, and it seems you are gallivanting around and almost getting yourself killed in a near boat wreck, a house explosion, a car wreck caused by wild dogs, and diving in that horrible place," Knives shuddered. "You went there twice, and you've only been here two days."

"Am I out of my mind, you're asking?" Troy said.

"No, I'm telling you that you are not in your right mind. Dillon wouldn't approve of you playing kissy with Silke."

"Are you telling me to stay away from Silke?"

"I don't do love counseling, but I thought you'd have suffered PRSD."

"Post Raquel Sterling Disorder?"

"Ha! Close enough. I think Shakespeare said the path to self-destruction is assured of the man with two loves."

"Ah, this is a unique tour. Are we visiting post-natal next where you discuss the birds and the bees?"

"No, but there is a psychiatrist on staff. You might talk to him. Listen, I don't want to be attending your funeral any time soon. I already thought I was going to have to once already, okay? Perhaps a tour of the morgue should be next. Hmm? It's in the basement. Dark. Gloomy. Cramped. Great for those who enjoy claustrophobia."

"Speaking of morgues and death, have you learned anything about John's murder from the autopsy?" Troy asked.

"Unfortunately, no. We were surprised to find that he died of ex-sanguination. There was very little blood left in his body. He should have bled into the water but not that much. The lack of blood affected lividity and strangely, decomposition. We're running some more tissue and blood samples."

"Any strange findings, like poison or alcohol?"

"No, nothing like that, but yes to something strange. It seemed John was on some kind of blood thinner. That would explain the bleeding out. Except, John shouldn't have a condition where he needed a blood thinner. I'm checking with his Navy doctor."

"So he died from wounds to the neck and bled out quickly due to the blood thinner?" Troy asked. Knives nodded. "Did you check the wound site like I asked?"

"I found what could be puncture marks. There's no way a blade could make them. It doesn't make any sense. None of it does, especially the condition of the body," Knives said.

"What do you mean?"

"Well, I can't explain why, but his body isn't decaying at a normal rate. The coroner would have put the death at a different time, a more recent time, one which is impossible because you found him dead when by the numbers he should have still been alive. Stop. Don't scratch those stitches," Knives warned then continued.

"On a more mundane topic, Raquel told a young patient you would stop by to see her. Lisa was injured performing flips and spins while launching herself into the lake. Does that sound familiar? She was thrilled to hear Raquel knew you. You can share injury stories. Maybe Lisa will learn vicariously what not to do from you."

Outside Lisa's door, Knives stopped and reached into his pocket to check his phone. "It's the coroner. Maybe he has answers to your questions. Hi, good to . . . what? Uh, sure. I'm on the second floor. I'll be right down. Troy, introduce yourself. There's some kind of incident downstairs needing my immediate attention. I'll see you back in your room. All right?"

Knives asked.

Troy barely had time to nod, and then the good doctor was gone on his errand of mercy.

It turned out young Lisa was thrilled and shocked to see Troy. They mostly commiserated, sharing stories of injuries, surgeries, and stupid stunts he would never do again that had almost led to surgery. Laughter was the best medicine, and Troy hoped Lisa learned from his mistakes, even if she remembered laughing at them.

When a nurse hustled Troy out, he wished his new friend luck and fast healing then set out to find his old, practical friend. Troy had a sense of something amiss. He borrowed Lisa's mom's phone and called Knives who failed to answer.

The last call had been from someone downstairs, perhaps in the morgue since Knives worked there part time. After all, he had been headed there for an incident. Doctor code speak for emergency? What if, as Marader worried, a killer stalked the blood brothers?

Troy caught an elevator, riding it down to the basement level. On the way, his nose burned, and his eyes began to water. He coughed. He didn't smell anything, but his nasal passages were irritated, his eyes and ears itching. What was going on? He didn't suffer allergies, but something bothered him.

When the cabin reached the bottom, it stopped, but the doors didn't open. The lights flickered. The twin doors sluggishly parted, letting in garish, red light. Troy stepped out, coughing, surprised to find the hallway lit with emergency lighting, giving the basement a lurid air. It seemed to waver as if a current pushed through. The exit sign to his right called his name, telling him to leave.

He thought about it, but he spotted a body, its legs in black slacks like Knives had worn, the shoes looking familiar, lying partly in the hallway. The upper torso was out of sight through two ajar doors. Was that blood? With rheumy eyes, Troy thought he saw a dark pool.

Wiping away tears made little difference. His eyes watered profusely. The blurry-looking sign on the wall ahead pointed left to the morgue. He figured the person had passed out and needed help. Could it be Knives? No way to tell. It didn't matter. Troy couldn't help. He was close to collapsing.

He started to hit the first-floor button when from down the hall, somewhere beyond the double doors, came the sound of rummaging. The loud shattering of glass made Troy jump. What was going on?

Troy took a step and stopped, growing dizzy. Needing air, he felt like he was drowning. Broken glass? Some kind of chemical was in the air. He must get out of here and get help. He vaguely recalled ski patrollers at Mammoth Mountain Resort dying while trying to rescue each other from volcanic vents unleashing toxic gases.

He blindly slapped at the control board and hung onto the rail. As he started to pass out, he wondered if he had hit the button to keep the doors open. The lights continued to flicker, staying dark for long moments, making Troy believe he had lost it. He grew weak, or gravity increased, maybe both, on his way to falling unconscious.

With his throat afire, Troy awakened on the floor. The ding of the doors opening was jarringly loud, like a reminder he had reconnected to the world. It yanked him alert. He realized that he had passed out, overcome by fumes. His eyes still burned. He needed clean air and to notify someone. He used the railing to drag himself to his feet, then he staggered out into the hallway, keeping a hand on the wall to stay upright. His legs felt like gelatin, but he knew a great deal about his body, mind over matter, pushing it to the limit. Keep walking. Knives needed him.

It was a hospital. Help should be close.

He encountered Nurse Carol coming out of Lisa's room and told her in gasps what had happened. After a moment of disbelief, she rushed to a nurse's station to use a phone. Now

Troy needed a scuba tank.

Having an idea, Troy hurried into Lisa's room. He borrowed the oxygen bottle and its non-breather mask from behind his new friend's bed and hurried to the stairwell. He didn't trust the elevator, or want to have to wait for it, so he took the stairwell.

Dashing downstairs two and three at a time made his head spin and black spots, along with a crack of lightning, danced across his sight. That wasn't good. He checked the gauge, turned the flow to high, and donned the non-rebreather mask, taking in fresh oxygen. He immediately felt better, stronger. He hoped it was enough. With the tank under his left arm, he yanked the door open and ran into the hall.

The quiet bothered him, the only sound his hurried footsteps and breathing inside the mask which hissed with oxygen. He started feeling claustrophobic, the walls closing in. This place reminded him too much of being in the horrible underwater mansion of Von Damme's. Troy didn't see how he could blame this on it, though.

He knelt when he reached the body, finding Knives. Troy immediately picked him up and arranged him in a fireman's carry. He appreciated his friend staying lean, making him easier to shoulder. In his condition, Troy doubted he could carry anyone else, and fearing for his buddy, he started to leave.

He made the mistake of glancing into the room. Blood splatters led to a head staring at him, the dead man's eyes and mouth open wide. His decapitated body rested on a table, one arm dangling to the floor where blood pooled.

Troy blinked. The sight stayed with him. Something horrible had happened. Flight took hold, and he turned. The lights failed. Darkness fell like a sledgehammer. Troy stumbled. Fear tried to sink in. Thank God the emergency exit sign remained lit. He focused on it, one hurried step after another until he shoved his way through the door.

He stumbled up the steps, carrying Knives to the landing.

There, he knelt, laid his blood brother on the concrete and placed the mask over his face. He might need a bag valve mask.

Knives still had pulse, but he failed to breathe. Troy removed the mask and gave two rescue breaths, hoping his friend lived to complain. When Knives didn't spontaneously respirate, Troy repositioned his blood brother's jaw, neck and head, then Troy gave breaths again, seeing Knives' chest rise.

Coughing and sputtering, Knives began to gasp. Troy kept the mask near his face to provide extra oxygen. "Did you kiss me?"

"It was that, or let you die. I thought, what if God sent me back to save Dr. Killjoy?"

"Phah! Now I've kissed those women, too without the thrill of flesh to flesh contact. Yuck! And for the record, it's Dr. Kildare."

"Are you always so ungrateful when subjected to your own field? Now I've been infected by all you've inhaled recently. Ick. So, what happened?" Troy asked him.

Knives raised his head to look at him. "Murderous thieves!"

"What? What would they steal?" Troy asked. Then it dawned on him.

"John's body! It's gone," Knives groaned.

Twenty: Near the Brown Cemetery

Even without a concussion, Monday night would have been a blur. Troy couldn't remember the name of what chemical had been spilled, almost killing he and Knives. Three others in the basement had suffocated and died. Troy didn't know why, but there was secrecy surrounding how one of the staff had died, but he was foggy on details. He had flashbacks of a truncated head and a headless body.

Several reporters waited for him to be released. He had no difficulty pretending to suffer a memory loss. Even the usually patient reporter and friend, Rae Kirkland, left frustrated, feeling he was holding out, and claiming she would ask him again after Pat's funeral.

Troy had already filed reports about the incident and answered enough questions to make him dizzy. He had been ordered not to mention John's missing body. The hospital still hadn't found it. Why would somebody steal John's body? Troy would have filled out more reports and forms, except a night of poor sleep, dreams about Dillon and the Dark Lady of the Lake rutting like Scorpios, hadn't jarred his memory of the prior afternoon. All he sensed was that he had forgotten something important.

Dr. Sugar Green evaluated and cleared Troy to drive. Without a headache, he could stand light. His vision appeared as acute as ever. Jambo had loaned him an old car, part tank, leaving the dark green Wagoneer in the hospital parking lot. It all but had a sign saying, Go ahead, try and wreck me!

Troy drove himself out to Tommy Boy's marina. He needed some alone time, not in the hospital, to think. He missed Silke. She had left a message, calling from work, saying she would meet him at the marina for the boat ride to the cemetery. Oh, the places we go, Troy thought.

Once at Maraders, he couldn't focus, so he stumbled to the houseboat, set an alarm and slept in the sun on the rooftop. The hours of dreamless sleep helped, and for a time, he laid there, baking, half awake. When Aunt Jada's words began to repeat through his thoughts, those about finding Dillon and stopping the flood of blood, Troy dragged himself to the shower.

He dressed for the gloomy occasion in a dark gray suit with hopeful blue pinstripes over an ash shirt and blue tie. Troy didn't want to go to Pat's funeral, but it felt necessary, although it seemed more like a prelude.

Outside, the sun was shining overhead, and yet it still seemed overcast, the light wan and the yellow-brown of mustard. He heard people in the bar. According to Knives, the planned departure time for the boatacade came soon.

He joined his brothers in the bar. Other than wearing black, it looked as if J-Man, Spider, and Walt had never moved from Sunday night. Jambo appeared to be napping while sitting with his elbow on the counter, hand propping up his head.

"You are a solemn quartet," Troy said.

"Thanks. We're the Four Glummers. You can be number five. A Handful of Glummers? Nice to see you survived another brush with death," Spider said.

"This was more like a solid bump," Troy said.

"How's Silke?" J-Man asked.

"When I saw her last night, she was good. She said I protected her from the blast, called me her hero," Troy said.

"Whatever happened addled her brain," Jambo said, not asleep.

"Troy, have you read the *Bristol Herald Courier*?" Walt said, mercifully changing the subject. He adjusted his bow tie and handed Troy a tablet with a news story on it.

Troy glanced at it, recalling. He had read about it this morning. Two boys were missing form Camp Sequoia. A mother had vanished from Tom Horn Camp. Two dads went for a walk from Little Oak Camp and never returned. In town, a couple of female King College students had disappeared. A friend said they had met a hot guy earlier and were all vamped up and going back out to see him.

That made nine. He recalled Mrs. Fleenor and her missing employee, the man who resembled Troy. Brew, where are you?

Looking weary and recovering from an illness, Knives strolled in, heading directly for Troy, who he embraced. "Thanks, man. For once, I'm glad you were daring. I owe you."

"Just call me Major Kildare," Troy said.

"What's going on?" J-Man asked.

More company interrupted explanations. Denny arrived. Now they had too many mourners for one boat, unless it was the party boat, so consensus concluded they should take two crafts. One would go directly to the meeting spot for those boating in a parade to Pat Ackles' ceremony at Brown's Cemetery. Dr. Knives and crew would stop off on the way at the address on Driftwood and see what could be discovered.

J-Man had been patient. Finally, he demanded an explanation of the rescue. Troy let Knives explain, since neither of them really remembered it.

"Well done, Troy. But guy, you're pushing it," J-Man said.

Marader, black backpack matching his dapper, vested ensemble, captained the boat. Heidi looked like a ray of joy in a yellow sun dress surrounded by storm clouds. Desiree wore a short black outfit, dressed formally and yet looking ready for a cocktail party, a visual reminder of why life was worth living. He caught her staring at him, and she didn't mind, smiling and continuing to stare.

Conservatively dressed in black with a steel gray jacket, Knives commanded his own boat and gloomily clad crew. Spider wore a black t-shirt with a white cross on it and black jeans. Denny was dressed like a missionary in stern, formal black and white. For the moment, he kept his tie loose and jacket neatly folded and stacked with Troy's. It was too hot and humid to wear them all the time.

Where was Silke? She had encouraged them to stop along the way to investigate the boat's owners. Troy heard rushed footsteps.

"Ah, I almost missed the boat," Silke said. She modeled a gray green blouse, along with black gloves, a dark skirt and black hose. A jade cross dangled from her necklace. Her eyeshadow, thick lashes, and lipstick were black. Half of her appeared to mourn while the rest of her celebrated life. Her outfit, cosmetics, and black onyx earrings turned her eyes the color of coffee. Wasn't he to beware of girls with dark eyes?

"Good morning. This boat is headed to the Swearington house on Driftwood," Troy said as he helped her into Knives' boat.

"Good morning. You look much better than last night. Sleep well?" Silke asked. She stumbled on the way into the boat, so he had to catch her and support her, giving her time to study his eyes and face. "What look is that?"

"Confusion? Or bewilderment?" he asked.

"Ha. I would have said caged and restless, ready to break free," she said. "Your aura still looks out of whack. You need some work."

"I'll take care of you both," Knives said. "You're on my boat."

"Yipee. The Med Boat was waiting for me," she sang to the tune of *The Love Boat*.

"Heading to the asylum," Knives announced.

When they neared the GPS coordinates for the shoreline address, Knives slowed the boat. The wind shifted, ending the brief clearing, and the smoke returned, carrying ash, but they could make out the hazy outline of docks and sometimes the glint of windows from houses up the short hill, now taller with the low water. Silke managed to locate the wooden boat from the photo, finding it winched up high in a pair of white slings under a covered dock.

They left Knives guarding the boat and making phone calls. According to him, the news was out about John's missing body.

"I wish, this one time, you guys were just pulling a prank on me," he bemoaned.

The landing party soon discovered that the two nearest, shoreline mini-mansions weren't the right address for the boat owners, so Denny, Spider, Troy, and Silke hiked across the street. They couldn't see the house ahead, but a post with a lifesaver painted with the correct address and Swearington Lodge was sign enough. It stood ominously alone at the end of the court. Beyond seemed swallowed by thick woods of ash trees, basswoods, maples, and Virginia Creepers.

"This is an old part of the lake for buildings, especially early vacation homes," Denny said. He led the way, following the driveway of crushed red stone into a heavily forested and shady area.

Troy turned to Spider. "How is your reading coming? Anything interesting? Insightful? Helpful?"

"Interesting, oh yeah! Believable? I would doubt it if I hadn't been to the mansion myself. Helpful, though, not a whole lot. The first book started with Von Damme's arrival in the San Francisco Bay area during the very early days of the Gold Rush. He owned and ruthlessly operated Vons, a holding company for bars, casinos, brothels, bathhouses and opium emporiums. It's sort of the rise of an empire beginning, if you get my drift. That volume, that book, ended with him getting ready to attend a meeting of immortals, RON, Rulers of Night, who were thinking of offering him a chance to join their affiliation."

"You're pulling my leg."

"Type it in the Google translator."

"You aren't yanking my chain? Fine. I apologize for doubting your credibility. I should doubt the author, this Ruler of Night."

"Rulers of Night? Nightwalkers?" Silke asked.

"It made me think of voodoo and vampires," Spider said casually. "In the one that I just started, Von Damme has been in Wreythville, Virginia, for at least a decade running several profitable businesses, all of them best plied by night. Early on, he goes on rants about the building of the dam and how he must stop it. From what I can tell, he's bitter about being driven out of California. He moved east to influence those in DC, but he was unwanted there, too. The powers that be there chased him out of our nation's capital. He seems to be a bit of a rogue pain in the ass."

"What makes you say that?"

"Well, he was a revolutionary sort, and a bit of an herbalist, poisoner, alchemist, and schemer. He specializes, supposedly, in transformations, including political. He's also quite a moonshiner and wine connoisseur. It's two of his favorite subjects, and he'll go on infinitum about grapes and hops and barley, even corn mash, and such, fertile land that will be lost, buried under the water."

"What did he want from DC?" Silke asked.

"Funding. He has been concocting some formula to make he and his friends even more superior. Not too different from those who promoted Eugenics, come to think of it. History keeps repeating it. Blame the immortals," Spider said. Often Troy couldn't tell when Spider was serious and when he was joking.

Troy tried to remember his history. Better, he recalled a conversation with Knives. Eugenics was promoted as a science without there every being a shred of research conducted to prove the theory. The Nazis weren't the first to believe in Uber men or the superiority of one color, one kind over another.

"Von Damme felt he was a superior breed of being," Spider said. Seeing Troy's question about his wording, he continued. "You know, I think he believes he's a vampire. Rulers of Night. Foes of Light," Spider stated simply, staring at him, waiting for the challenge.

"Well, I take all this with a grain of salt, but there are documented cases of people who believe they are blood drinkers. Poor confused souls," Father Dennis said, shaking his head. Despite his words, the priest now palmed a crucifix.

Spider waved him off. "To Von Damme, being a vampire is a normal condition, so it isn't really mentioned, and I thought he referred to other mean-spirited people as vampires. Their very presence turns men into craven cowards and women into insatiable vixens? I thought, big egotist here. But I think he believes he's a vampire with a close community of other vampires and slaves. I say that because we've been to his house. The Von Dammes are wealthy tobacco and corn farmers by day, their places run by thralls and slavers, and moonshiners and vampires by night. It was while working with stills and distilling booze that he found his alchemical answer to their greatest challenge."

"Which is?" Troy asked.

"I don't know exactly. He hasn't mentioned it much up to now. I would guess sunlight. Then again, they avoid rushing water too, letting their slaves deal with it for distilling uses and irrigating."

"You're scaring me," Troy said.

"My great aunt scares him," Silke said. Spider raised an eyebrow at that.

"Ha. That's true," Troy said.

"Reading this has been enough to make me think of carrying silver bullets. Von Damme has thralls that are wolves," Spider said.

"Wolves?" Silke asked. She glanced at Troy. She silently mouthed, I have some.

"He uses wolves as body guards, scouts and hunters. I think of those statues outside the study when he mentions them."

Troy wondered if they would find similar decor here.

"Troy, I just wanted to say thanks for saving Knives. The world could use more Dr. Stephen Currans," Spider said.

Troy nodded. Silke stared at him. "What?" Troy asked.

Spider missed the clues, but he recognized Silke hadn't heard. Unfortunately, his blood brother took it upon himself to relay Troy's selfless and heroic actions.

Silke made an exasperated sound. "Out of sight for the night, and you almost kill yourself," she said. He was touched by the depth of her anger and frustration.

"I'm sorry, sort of. I couldn't leave him, any more than I could leave you behind in such a situation," Troy said. He couldn't tell if that helped or hindered his case, but she only harrumphed and strode off, forcing him to catch up.

Finally, he could see the Swearington house. The big, old oaks had gathered closely around a two-story lodge. The shadows held it tightly. Spider and Denny oohed and awed over the architecture and quality of the stone and wood building, but Troy found it unsettling, mildly reminding him of the underwater mansion. Spider and Denny started taking photos with their phones. Instead of closer, both seemed to drift away from the house.

"Did it occur to you that we're headed to not just a brown cemetery but the Brown Cemetery?" Silke said.

"I did. It's another reason I wanted to stop by here."

"Aunt Jada mentioned being underground. Lots of rock and earth."

"I have my Dillon diviner on highly sensitive," Troy told her.

"You seem uncomfortable," Silke said.

"Some things Spider said about what he's read in Von Damme's diary have weirded me out," he replied.

"Are you saying you believe in vampires?" she asked.

Troy blinked. He hesitated, struck by a flash of recall. Zane! The image of the big-hatted, painted-faced man sent chills through him. Worse, made him want to run, turning him into a craven coward.

"Troy?" Silke asked. She leaned in close. Her scent overwhelmed him. He had another flashback out of time, Silke as an insatiable vixen, wonderfully all over him. She reached out and plucked a long hair off his jacket and tossed it aside, letting the wind carry it.

"Why would somebody kidnap Dillon? And do you think it was anything like the dream you had, him getting dragged in a boat?" Silke asked.

"By an old lady?" Troy asked. He doubted it.

Suddenly, it was as if thinking about Dillon had summoned him. Troy turned toward the house, swearing his best friend was close.

"Come on. I feel Dillon nearby." He started after Denny who moseyed ahead with his camera phone taking photos of the river stone and timber Swearington Lodge.

The tugging sensation grew stronger. "About the dreams, I don't know what to say," Troy said.

"Repressed desires?" she suggested.

"Are you always this helpful?" he asked.

"I'm a professional PT, not a professional counselor, but I do have a brother."

"As to why somebody would grab him, perhaps he discovered something about them or the ridge that they don't want anybody else to know, but they don't want to kill him," Troy supposed.

"I doubt he was taken as a sex slave," Silke chuckled.

Troy coughed. "Your brother's ego would be devastated," he said. He doubted Dillon had been taken for sex, and yet, he kept dreaming of him grappling with a blond.

"Good. He always thought too highly of his own opinion."

The house reminded Troy of a hunting or perhaps fishing lodge, mostly made of dark hardwood with overhanging eaves, a wide balcony, and shuttered windows. A mosaic of stones composed the lower third of the house, its foundation and possible basement. A pair of big, brawny wolf statues flanked the stone steps to the front porch. They reminded Troy of sentries and Spider's comments. He captured images of them to compare later.

The place still seemed mothballed for the winter, not ready for summer yet, except he suffered the prickly sensation of being observed. Troy thought it might even be a vacation home where the folks showed up sporadically instead of a summer cottage. Whoever it was liked shade, shadows, creepers, and roses with long, wickedly sharp thorns. He didn't see any peep holes or partly opened shutters, but the place no longer seemed abandoned.

Troy stood on the porch, haunted by the sense that Dillon could be just around the corner or behind this door. Or it could be his imagination. And yet, it reminded him a bit of when he had approached the underwater mansion, a combination of hope and dread. He looked at a window. Did a curtain move?

Denny whistled and crossed himself. "This place looks and feels old. Check out the size of some of these oaks and hickory trees." That set him to wondering if this had been built predam or post dam. On his smart phone, Denny discovered via the Net that it was built in 1940.

"It has a strange ambiance, don't you think? Or am I imagining it?" Denny asked and shivered. He had taken a rosary from his pocket, his fingers saying prayers along with him.

"Darkly seductive," Silke said.

The walls of the house were covered in vines, including roses the color of sexy, tempting lips. As they neared, the smell of the decayed roses and heather was so pungent it mingled with the smoke and almost made Troy gag.

Denny walked closer. "An odd vibe. Very odd. When I was in Germany, I went to many old castles. This place reminds me of . . ." A sneezing fit struck Denny, one ah-choo right after another into a marathon. He kept his EpiPen handy in case an allergen attacked him, and he needed a shot of epinephrine to combat its affects.

There was no sneaking around now. Denny's shotgun sneezes carried through the woods and likely, down to Knives at the boat.

Finally, Denny stood up straight. He wiped his bleary eyes and nose then sat. "Hate. Those. I need a minute. Or two," he said. He put away the unneeded EpiPen.

"Spider, what do you think?" Troy asked. When he didn't get an immediate answer, he turned around. Pallid and sweaty, Spider slowly backed away from the house.

"Is it like the mansion?" Troy asked. He had sensed it, but that had made him come forward. It seemed likely that if Dillon was caught up in something it would mirror Cemetery Ridge or the Von Damme mansion.

"Yes and no. Not so bad. Not so much pain, but unhappy ghosts are here," he said and turned to leave.

"Dillon?" Troy asked. He goose-bumped, then he felt stabbed and jabbed by thousands of cold fingers. The heebie-jeebies riffled along his spine and spread out across his shoulders. A breeze swept through, rustling the leaves and cooling Troy. The shaking leaves sounded brittle, too, more autumnal. Silke shivered.

"I don't see or hear him. I can't stay any longer. Too painful," Spider said, and then he staggered away. Troy let him go.

The double front doors looked sturdy and windowless with bulky, antiquated brass knockers. Silke let one fall like a hammer, and the blow echoed throughout the house and out to the road until the woods swallowed it.

"Heavy duty. Old. Made of real metal. This door looks like oak. What do you think, Denny?" Troy asked to nobody.

No longer with them, Denny had wandered off. He waved and strolled around the corner to study the side of the building. With the smoke, they hadn't seen much along the side except for trees.

"Right now, I feel . . . reckless, impatient and . . . hungry," Silke said and flushed. Troy sensed she wasn't talking about food, especially when she stepped close to him. If desire was a scent, it overwhelmed him, pungent as honeysuckle.

"I think Denny has the right idea. Either nobody's coming or nobody's here. Let's search around a bit," Troy said, taking her hand.

They descended the front steps, all the while feeling watched by the stone wolves, and followed Denny around the right side. They found him studying a stone wall covered in blooming rose vines. The wall stretched about ten feet high. The thick growth from the wealth of sumac, maples and white-barked birch trees created a second story and taller wall of brush looming darkly above them.

"Nobody home, huh? This seemed strange to me as a developer and landscaper. Spider, before he went off the deep end, pointed it out," Denny said. He waved ahead.

The longer Troy looked at the wall, the more he felt something was wrong. It seemed oddly placed. He noticed that some of the deciduous trees were more like bushes. He stepped closer to look and pulled out his penlight, shining it on one. It had thorns.

"They walled in a mound?" Troy finally asked. Dillon beneath piles of earth next to water and Brown's Cemetery. Could it really be?

"Yes, and it seems that the building goes into it. I wish I could take a closer look. It could be a wine cellar, of sorts, or even be an earthen geodesic dome covered with soil and bushes. Spider would know better. He's built a couple in Haiti and elsewhere."

Troy pondered what to do next. He had been a risk taker by nature. He had mellowed a bit. Right now, he wanted to climb over the wall and go exploring on a hunch, but he knew he wasn't thinking straight since this morning. And yet, the draw was powerful. Dillon was close. It made little common sense, but Troy simply knew his blood brother's presence.

"You think he's here, don't you?!" Silke asked.

"Why do you ask when you can read my mind?"

"I can't read your mind," she replied. "Are you thinking of going in there? Going exploring?"

He frowned at her and raised an eyebrow.

"You are. You're thinking of going ahead and leaving me here. I'm the one with the gun and a black belt," she said. She was obviously unhappy about it. "Do you want to know what else you're thinking about?"

Troy had goosebumps. Something about the tone of her voice caressed him like verbal velvet. He tried to relax when his body wanted to freeze. Silke moved close to whisper in his ear.

The air hung still, then it buzzed as if a dangerous swarm of wasp was headed his way. The sun seemed to slip behind a cloud, although it remained sunny, and the shadows grew darker.

"That you must find Dillon no matter what. Isn't that sort of what Aunt Jada said?" she asked.

Troy breathed easier. Denny glanced over at them, curious at how close they were. Silke's arm was around Troy. Watch out for women with dark eyes. Silke's were black right now. Kiss her or lose her forever. Help Dillon no matter how odd, no matter what the odds. Stop the flood of blood. "Your aunt said a lot of things."

That earned him an unreadable look. "Don't endanger yourself anymore. Dillon would prefer you were around to make sure Mom and I are all right," Silke said.

From his right and the woods, one snarl became two ferocious growls. Like shadows taking on flesh, a pair of Doberman pincers, their dun faces angry, trotted to the borderline of the trees and barked ferociously.

Troy's hair stood on end. In terms of fight or flight, flight won out, even as Silke reached for her handgun. "Let's back out of here," Troy suggested, gently taking Silke by the arm.

Denny walked backwards faster than anyone Troy had ever seen, thanking all those hours on the tennis courts. Silke moved slower, arming herself but keeping her eyes on the fierce dogs. Troy was wishing for a shotgun, or at least a long stick.

Each one of the beast's barks drew them farther out of the woods. Troy hoped there weren't any more of them. With each backward step, they added to the distance between them and the fierce guard dogs. He was glad he hadn't jumped the wall. The thick smoke started to obscure their view. Troy figured they were in good shape, soon to be out of sight, then Silke stumbled. Troy caught her, but despite keeping her afoot, the damage was done.

The moment of vulnerability was too much for the Dobermans to resist. They bolted out of the woods. White teeth flashing, the four-legged beasts charged toward them.

Twenty-One: Funeral Spirits

"Run!" Troy yelled. He was surprised by Silke's agility and speed. She recovered her balance, whirled and sprinted like there were devil dogs on their heels, which there seemed to be. Any other time, he might have enjoyed watching her run, but the dogs ran as fast as the wind. In what seemed mere moments, he could hear the canines' excited gasps over his harsh breathing.

His knee started to ache. This wouldn't have been a problem before the injury. Denny was a good thirty feet ahead of him. Silke kept up with him, but Troy began to lag. The dogs had four legs, devouring ground.

A few seconds later, he felt them right behind him. He imagined them snapping at his heels, then he heard jaws clash together. One barked, causing Troy to jump. Two steps later, he tripped. His coordination saved him from falling on his face, or breaking his fool neck, as he tucked and rolled down the slight hill, tumbling faster than afoot. He expected to be torn to shreds. He rolled to his feet and whirled around to brace the charge.

To his amazement, he faced brown Doberman hindquarters and stubby tails. The dogs had turned, trotting back to the lodge. Had someone called them back? Was he simply out of range? Lucky? Another close call, all of them associated with looking for Dillon.

"Whew. I thought we might be attending our own funerals. Spider was right about it being haunted by evil spirits," Denny said.

"Let's go apologize for doubting him," Troy said.

They returned to the boat without proof of Dillon being there, but Troy trusted his intuition. Others would need evidence, though. How could he show them? He wondered repeatedly while Knives steered his Stingray northward.

The gathering of boats happened slowly, a few at first, then more, an armada cloaked by the smoke and waiting for a surprise approach. Fishing vessels of many kinds had lined up, from john to canoe to kayaks and bass, and more with ski, leisure, party and pontoon boats. Motored rafts mingled with skiffs, several mini yachts, and a trio of sailboats currently using their outboards for power. Pat Ackles was well known and beloved, bringing out friends, family and fishermen.

Troy felt a little uncomfortable. Perhaps it was simply the funeral, the fact that Pat and John had been his age. They had been killed, and some part of him wanted revenge, at least justice. The unknown killer could strike again. Could it be Zane? Why would he be after them? Those thoughts circled with futile attempts to remember yesterday.

Knives seemed a bit of a celebrity, renowned at least, as mourners waved and doffed their visors, hats, and baseball caps to him. They were kind and friendly with restrained smiles due to the occasion. Father Dennis enjoyed attention, too, the exchange of greetings with friends and God's children warm and life affirming. A few people were startled to see Troy alive, and after a moment, waved with a pleasant enthusiasm. He could only guess that most locals assumed he was still dead.

He glanced at Silke, finding her thoughtful, looking but not seeing. It pained him to see her sad. He wanted to comfort her, but he was unwilling to make a spectacle of it. Besides, Dillon was alive! Troy could feel it. Seeing her brother again would comfort Silke, after she finished ripping into him.

Knives cruised directly to Maverick and Marader and crew. They had left a spot in the port side of the double line of the procession planning to cruise northerly to the Denton Valley boat ramp. Troy and others helped Knives erect symbolic fishing poles off the stern in honor of the Bassmaster.

A fog horn sounded. The lines eased forward, plowing the green water and sending the smoky air swirling. Banners and flags flew, several with Psalms of comfort, many with fish symbols and art, and others with personal words or simply Pat Ackles image on them. One had his face, a Fathead, his smile broad like he had caught a big fish or made another good friend of a stranger.

At the public boat ramp, the Ackles family had arranged for shuttles to carry the masses to the Brown Cemetery. Troy let

Silke hold his hand, as he could see her thinking they might be doing this again for her brother. He didn't know what else was wrong, but when he glimpsed her looking at him when she thought he wouldn't notice, she seemed wounded.

At the Brown Cemetery entrance, Troy stopped upon seeing spirits. Silke paused, giving him a questioning glance. He squinted, noticing what looked like an ethereal figure in the shadow of the left gate. From underneath a hat, the phantom watched people enter. Nobody seemed aware, except for Troy. He locked eyes with the former caretaker or gravedigger who felt this was home. The ghost nodded to him, tipped his cap, and waved Troy inside.

"Uh, do you see any unusual characters?" he asked Silke.

She appeared amused, not getting his reference, likely not seeing the gravedigger. "The Paparazzi? I'm assuming that's not why you went a bit pale."

"Any urban legends about this place?" Troy asked.

"Ah, do you see the little girl who was struck by lightning while bringing flowers to her mother's tombstone? Some people have seen her ghost. Or do you see a different one?"

"Guy with a shovel. Smiling at me."

"We can leave," Silke said. He marveled at how easy she adapted.

The ghost watched him as if he were wondering what Troy would do. He couldn't help but recall the dream of falling into an open grave. The spirit seemed to say, come on in, there's room for one more. Troy looked for other ethereal beings and thought there might be another lurking in the shade of a mausoleum. Spider caught Troy's eye and gestured thumb up. He was glad Pat was being buried outdoors.

Troy took a deep breath. If this was a new reality, he would have to face it.

"I'm ready," he said.

Silke looked concerned, but she was with him every step of the way. He nodded as they strolled past the gravedigger's ghost. Troy let people distract him, but he always kept an eye for the spirit and any others that might be nearby. He hugged and chatted briefly with his high school tennis instructor. He claimed the ski club mentor was here, too, somewhere. Coach Rolen had sent letters of encouragement during Troy's rehab, so Troy hoped to find him and thank him.

The ghost and the yellowish-brown smoke made for a surreal ceremony, casting a literal pall on it. A few friends and Pat's father spoke graveside. Father Dennis gave a wonderful eulogy, being a fisherman after all. Pat's mother wept most of the time. Troy recalled his mother doing the same at his bedside.

Walking by the open casket, Troy was starkly reminded of how fragile and evanescent life could be. Once, he had taken it for granted. He had fought, struggled, sweated, and screamed his way back from the brink. Yes, these people could have been looking down at his body. What a pointless death. He had been falling off snowy cliffs with style for a challenge, a thrill, and entertainment. Fool. An idiot people always said.

Did Pat grin at him? For a split second, Troy thought a ghost sat up, and then he realized a thick wafting of smoke swirled, giving the illusion of life.

He managed to coherently offer condolences to Shelly and the rest of the Ackles family. At times like this, Troy wondered why he had survived.

For a moment, he flashed back, plunging downhill, the wind tearing at his goggles as the world began to collapse and fall away about him. Knowing he was dead, he vowed to enjoy every second and threw himself down another cliff. For an amazing string of seconds, he stayed alive, until he wasn't going fast enough, and the world fell on him.

"Troy, are you all right?" Silke asked.

"I am now, thanks. Flashback," he said, hoping that explained it. She already thought he was weak and broken. Troy looked around, praying that he might spot Dillon in disguise attending the funeral. It was an irrational hope during a nonsensical time in his life, rife with deaths, ghosts, murders, wolves, wild dogs and crazy accidents.

Until they had approached the Swearington Lodge, he figured he would be going to a third funeral—Dillon's. Now Troy thought Dillon was in that house somewhere. What was he going to do about it? What would Deputy Glazier do? Yes, judge, I need a warrant based on Dillon's blood brother's feelings. That would go over well.

Silke found the Fleenors and introduced him to Woodrow, owner of the downtown gym and spa and president of the gun club. The salt and pepper-haired man looked like a workout fanatic, barrel-chested with hams for biceps and tree trunks for thighs. It likely took two suits to clothe his physique. Carrying a big gun would be easy.

Woody doted on Silke and wagged a finger a Troy. "Be good to her. I would hate to have to hunt you down."

Silke fibbed and said they were getting along wonderfully. When the Fleenors moved on, Silke confided in Troy, "I really want him to shoot Dillon, not you."

They encountered Pete and Paul Ackles, Pat's younger twin brothers and good friends. Both had been very close to John. Pete ran a health food store, and Paul managed a coffee shop. John had invested in both businesses. They promised to heft a brew or two in both Pat's and John's honor tonight while sharing stories of whopper fish tales.

"I wish this was one of your pranks," Troy told them.

"Us, too. Hey, any of you seeing Digger? You know, the guy that worked here for forty years, then fell in a grave, broke his neck and hangs around the yard?" Paul asked.

"I don't. What's he look like?" Silke asked.

"Hat and shovel. Overalls. Beard, supposedly," Paul said.

"Friendly sort?" Troy asked.

"I guess. Nobody I ever heard of complained about anything besides being thrilled, scared, or both. Hey, we'll see you tonight, and I hope, a lot this week. There's tons to catch up on. Stay alive until then, okay? And be strong, guy."

"What did he mean by that?" Troy asked.

"That's because you're in Her bull's eye," Silke said, her voice hard-edged. She glanced over his shoulder. "Here comes the Silver Goddess. Diana is with her. I'll give y'all some time. Just remember the definition of insanity." She turned a chilly shoulder.

Doing the same thing and expecting different results. Well, they were different people.

Silke was already off, warmly greeting friends and exchanging hugs. He could tell she had Deputy Burt in her sites. Troy needed to talk with him, too, but he didn't want to sound like a lunatic in front of Raquel.

He had tried not to think of her since last night. Had he confessed he was a fool and never stopped loving her? Watching her, his heart caught, captivated, and coherent thoughts left him. She looked classy, foxy, and solemn in a black dress with a belt embroidered with white roses, dark stockings, and a broad-brimmed hat adorned with a rose. It reminded him of what Ms. Sterling had worn in a Chanel Number 5 commercial. Raquel strode over, her heeled, leather boots loud on the hard, parched earth. He had an odd moment of deja vu, and he recalled her dressing like this in a dream to say farewell and go super modeling or leave him for one of the men on *Dancing with the Stars*. She removed her sunglasses, revealing those competitive eyes, now softened by events.

"You look dashing for someone just out of the hospital," Raquel said.

"Have you thought of changing your name? Troy 'Crash' Bane?" her sister asked him. Diana strolled alongside, a lazy grace to her movements. She looked entirely too much like a young Raquel ready for a date to a Grunge and Goth Dance.

"Afternoon, ladies," Troy replied. When in doubt, be polite.

"So formal," Raquel said. Her hands were together, nervous. Really?

"With the way you two look, it would be disrespectful to be casual."

"You've lost weight," Raquel said, eyeing him. She had a

predatory look, one he had loved when they were a couple. The timing seemed odd, a bit out of place, but people reacted to death in a wide variety of ways.

"It's the hospital food and the schlepping. I've done more uphill last year than in all my years since college. You've gone *Vogue*. I bet I'd maximize my audience if I took a selfie," Troy joked, trying to ease the tension.

Diana laughed, sounding haughty. "Of course, you would. After all, she is the Silver Goddess. She should have her own fashion line, for heaven's sake. Swimsuits you can downhill race in, from slope to pool, just ski right in, make a splash!" she teased.

"I never expected to be hit over the head with my own success," Raquel said. She was toying again with the bracelet on her wrist.

Troy blinked. Had he seen dark sparks around it?

He glanced over at Digger. The spirit had wandered closer. He seemed intent on Raquel, glancing away, then back, staring at her. Or at the bracelet?

"I'm your sister. I don't want to kick you while you're down. I just want to puncture your big head every now and then. Hi, Troy, I guess I should introduce myself. You might not remember me. Diana Sterling." She coolly offered him a hand. She had been eleven or twelve when he had last seen her. Time and genes had been a boon to her, and she was a younger, slender version of her powerful and voluptuous sister.

"Of course, I remember you," Troy said. She had fallen asleep then fallen out of a tree while spying on them one summer night in the Sterling's back yard. He had joked about how wonderful it was that two Sterlings had fallen for him. He could see Raquel remembered as she shook her head. "Guys were talking about how they wished you were older."

"Be careful what you wish for," Raquel breathed.

"Sis was telling me about that awful house underwater. Do you see ghosts, too?" Diana asked.

Troy was caught off guard. "You mean in this cemetery right now?" he asked her. That brought her up short. "Or when my colleague died on the mountain? Oh, or in the underwater house of horrors?"

"Uh, there," Diana said. She glanced sideways at Raquel.

"Yes, I saw them. Others on the dive did, too. Different types, some ethereal, others shadowy. But ghosts follow us around all the time, or perhaps better said, we often carry ghosts around with us, that's why Hollywood uses them as a fundamental element of screenplays," he replied.

"That place was very disturbing, but Troy's right, you don't have to go to a creepy underwater mansion to feel ghosts," Raquel said as she fingered the bracelet, spinning it. Troy became certain it was the piece of jewelry that drew the spirits. In the distance, he noted two more drawing closer. He couldn't tell anything of their gender or nature, mostly misty figures floating through people and tombstones toward them. He wished he knew what to do about them. Should he do anything?

"The stuff of nightmares," Troy agreed. "John died there."

"And the men from the TVA," Raquel agreed.

"It sounds cool," Diana said.

"No, no. It was bitterly cold, deadly, like having only one arm out of the grave, hanging on for dear life," he snapped and shivered. That place had wanted a piece of every party.

"Whoa," Diana said.

"Don't even think about it," Raquel told her sister. "The local news is all over, and it's closed as a crime scene. Burt authorized buoy signs, ropes, and closing the area as dangerous to the public. I think it's ready to collapse." She still toyed with the bracelet. "Troy, what happened at the hospital? I spoke with Lisa; she was thrilled you stopped by. She said you came running in after your visit to get her oxygen bottle, then out, and there was some kind of emergency."

He briefly recounted the chemical spill and going in to rescue Knives using an oxygen bottle and non-breather mask.

"Are you being reckless again?" she asked.

"I was thoughtful and careful," Troy said. He had even told the truth, and Raquel didn't believe him. Why did everyone think he was reckless?

"I think you two need time to talk," Diana said.

"A cemetery is not the place to discuss ghosts," Troy said. The spirits crept closer, their eyes on Raquel. He knew it would do no good to step in front of her or try to protect her. The ladies obviously didn't act uncomfortable. Troy felt as if the vertebrae on his spine had risen like hackles. He mentally wrestled with flight or fight.

"But it's great to dig up old dirt. Raquel says that she can't find a good . . ." Diana started.

"Sis?" Raquel's voice held a dangerous edge.

". . . good pair of shoes! Her feet always hurt. Ha. Or an honest . . ."

"Sister?" Raquel suggested.

". . . Financial manager. Troy, you need to come to the local store. It's awesome, if I do say so myself. I'm the assistant manager. We have your photo of Blackcomb with the rainbow snowstorm enlarged on a twenty by forty wall. Magnifique!"

"I am humbled," Troy said.

"I spy Eduardo. Be good to each other. I'll see you two later," she said and departed.

"She's beautiful, and at that stage, likely a wild, heartbreaker," Troy said.

"She won't listen to me. She's going to get in some kind of trouble."

Troy literally bit his tongue. Diana came by it naturally.

"Troy, seeing Pat there makes me think it could have been you."

"Or any of us, tomorrow. I've had similar thoughts."

He recognized the yearning in her eyes. She had driven him wild, then driven him crazy, to desperation to go west looking for a way to forget her, and off mountain steeps, trying to show her. No, he hadn't ever been trying to kill himself. But, he had died since then, changing his outlook. What did that mean about how he felt about her?

"I know you distrust me, Troy. But, we aren't the same people. You said so yourself in the hospital," she began.

"Excuse me, sorry to interrupt," Deputy Burt said. Raquel glared, but he was a sheriff's deputy, accustomed to it and worse, and shrugged it away like water off a duck's back. He was unaware that he had walked through the ghosts, too.

The digger pointed the handle of his shovel at Raquel's hand. It had to be the bracelet. Was something going to happen? The circle of spirits appeared grim, glowering. Troy sensed the menace of blame.

"Silke tells me you believe Dillon is at the Swearington Lodge off Driftwood. That address came from the boat registration in the photo, right?" Deputy Burt asked. Troy nodded. "Why do you think he's there?"

Troy glanced at Raquel. "I can feel him there."

Deputy Burt chuckled softly. "I see. You think I can use that to get a warrant?"

Raquel's stare was piercing. He took a step back. "If Troy said he feels Dillon there, he's there. They could always find each other, anytime, anywhere, within the county. That was true in high school and college."

"So, did you find anything there besides guard dogs?" Deputy Burt asked.

"Nothing concrete."

"So, the dogs kept you from exploring? Climbing the wall?" Raquel chuckled softly.

Troy frowned. She knew him too well.

"I'll follow up. In the meantime, don't take the law into your own hands."

"You mean don't go taze the dogs and search the grounds?" Raquel asked.

Troy frowned. There she went again. He tensed as the spirits stepped forward, or it seemed so, before they suddenly reversed direction, hastily departing. He saw two make warding symbols. They were curious about the bracelet, but they wanted no part of it. What did that mean?

"You are funny. I'll contact the owners. Someone has to feed the dogs. Make sure, though, that it isn't you, Troy. Too many funerals and far too many missing people already. I'm afraid there's going to be more. I don't know why, but I do. I'll call soon."

"Hey Sis, the Pap are here," Diana said, returning to them.

"I hope they got my good side," Deputy Burt said.

"There are always one or two around. They took photos at the airport. Home girl, homebound. No big deal," Raquel said.

"Rumors have you and Troy are an item," Diana said

Troy closed his eyes. He should have known. Now they had been seen together twice. Troy handed Diana his smartphone. "Please take a shot or two of me mugging with your sister. I can claim it as shameless advertising to boost visits to my site."

"You should have taken one of her in her SARs diving gear. That would have boosted your traffic."

"I did. Very Dior. Would you like to see it before I post it?" Troy asked Raquel.

"Yes, please," she said. He knew how she felt about her stretch marks, those along the top of her thighs from a fast-growing stint a couple of months before her junior year. She had gone from awkward to pretty to beautiful to divine.

"Don't smile. We're at a funeral," Troy said. He wondered if any of the ghosts would show up.

"Call it Grim Goddess," Diana suggested.

The very air seemed to change, thickening, growing cooler with a fog rolling in. Despite that, he perspired, experiencing a heat flash. He tried to control his pulse, but it went wild, leaping and bounding. He cursed his lack of will power, and then, over Raquel's shoulder, he saw her.

A vision had become flesh was his first thought. Movie star gorgeous, a curly-haired blond wrapped in a crimson dress squeezed so tight it had turned near black to match her elbow gloves and stockings. She reminded him of Marilyn Monroe, if she had buffed up for a role as a modern day femme fatale. Surely his imagination ran wild. Especially since there seemed to be a haze around her. He lost all train of thought when she lifted her chin, peering from under her wide-brimmed hat. Her look was hooded, her dark eyes aglow, and when they connected, it was lust at first sight. Desire surged through Troy like the morphine drip had once burned through his veins.

She held his gaze, a touch curious, perhaps offended by his direct look, and he felt he knew her. Even before she had looked up, hands on hips, tip of her tongue between her front teeth, he had the sense of her hands, lips, and tongue running all over his body. Why did he feel this so strongly?

By her cool expression, she wasn't interested in finding out. When she spun away on a heel, the intense attention no longer on Troy, he realized who she was. How could this be?

His dreams and waking world had collided. She was the gorgeous creature seducing Dillon. He blinked. Surely not. She stepped away from the crowd and sashayed toward the entrance.

"Troy? Troy are you all right?" Raquel asked.

No. He must be dreaming. She was also the woman who had killed Mona.

"Troy?"

"Sorry. But I believe I spotted the last person to see Dillon. Likely, she's a secret girlfriend. I'm going to catch up with her. It was fabulous to see you, Raquel. We'll talk tonight, when it's more of a celebration of life," he said, then he hurried after the woman in red. Along the way, there were people he wanted to see and talk with, but Troy didn't want to lose the dream woman, thinking she might be a figment of imagination. His recent nightmares had too frequently mirrored or hinted at reality, whatever that might be.

He expected Raquel would be mad at his sudden exit. *Dillon, the things I do for you.*

The woman in crimson didn't seem to hurry, but she covered ground swiftly with a long, graceful sashay. He had enjoyed watching Raquel's athletic stride and Silke's saucy glide, but the mystery woman's walk seemed a seductive dance, the way some birds cavort to attract mates. She never slowed to talk with anyone and somehow, everyone stepped aside.

Even so, he thought he might catch her at the gate, where, despite the wildfires to the south of the lake, people had gathered to smoke cigarettes, mixing ash and ash.

She reached the gate first, though, and an elderly man with a cane toddled into Troy's way, making him slow. He evaded the senior only to run into a mobile brick wall dressed in a classy, black suit. Troy apologized and tried to slide around him, but the stranger cut him off, moving into his way. The big man had a square, protruding chin and wide forehead over menacing eyes. Wide seemed to be a theme along with thick.

"Miss Swearington doesn't want to talk to anybody right now."

Swearington. Excellent. Now he knew where to find her. "I was just at her address on Driftwood, asking about a friend who vanished at the lake. His name is Dillon. Would you take her a note?"

Mr. Thick frowned and made a shooing gesture. Troy caught a glimpse of a shoulder holster and gun butt under his jacket. "No. Go away."

"I'm just going to show up at the door again. I'll come prepared for dogs this time," Troy said.

The bodyguard's frown deepened to a grim determination. He reached inside his jacket as if he were drawing a weapon, then his hand flicked out, and Troy flinched, feeling embarrassed when he took the business card from Mr. Thick's meaty hand.

From behind Troy, someone grabbed his arm. He whirled on Silke, quite concerned by the look in her eye.

"Troy, is something wrong? Are you leaving?" she asked.

"I saw Miss Swearington."

"Where?" she asked. Silke looked around.

"I was trying to catch up with her when this big guy intervened," Troy said and jerked a thumb over his shoulder.

Silke shook her head. "Who?"

Troy turned. Mr. Thick was gone. How could someone so big move so quietly?

"What about the Swearingtons? You saw one of them leaving this way?" she asked. He nodded, and she grabbed his hand, dragging him along at a brisk pace, searching for the woman. "Describe her."

Troy described her as a fit Marilyn. He also described the square-faced defensive tackle of a bodyguard. He didn't see him either. Silke sounded frustrated, too. They looked everywhere, the shuttle lot, parking lot, and the boat dock and found nothing.

Troy showed Silke the business card. "It was worth the chase. You didn't believe me. What did you think was going on?"

"I figured Raquel had made you angry, or well, you'd had a panic attack."

"I guess I deserve that. The spirits, especially, Digger seemed fascinated by Raquel's bracelet, the one from the underwater house from Hell, then as if confirming it was trouble, they all hurried off," Troy said.

"You didn't tear it off her wrist? Or are you waiting until you get her alone?"

Troy gave her a look and said, "I don't know that I'm not imagining this stuff."

"Or, maybe you're highly intuitive and have a special sight, a gift for all you've suffered," Silke suggested.

A gift? Troy didn't see how. "Miss Swearington looks a lot like the woman in my nightmares with your brother. Coincidence?" he wondered. He didn't really believe in those. Science had disproved them as well. He shared a look with Silke, and the connection felt thrillingly deep.

"You think he's there. What are you going to do about it?" she asked, her voice fierce.

"I promised Burt I would wait until he spoke with them."

Silke's eyes searched his. "You wouldn't tell me that and then go searching on your own, would you?" she asked.

He was interrupted by her phone ringing, "Your Mother Should Know". Silke answered and listened. Her expression fell grim, then she hung up. Tears welled in her eyes as she looked to Troy. "Aunt Jada's had a heart attack," she said.

Troy's heart went out to her. They embraced, and she sniffled.

"Then you need to be at her side as soon as possible. I'll bet there's a boatload ready to leave. I know I am," Troy said.

Twenty-Two: Life Celebration

A dreamless, two-hour nap did wonders for Troy's mind, body and mood. He had locked and wedged the door, so Desiree couldn't sneak in. He had resisted enough temptation, and he expected to resist more tonight. Raquel would be at the wake.

Silke's call had awakened him, letting him know Dr. Curran was coming to chaperone him to tonight's life celebration. She had sounded on the verge of breaking down. She refused to leave Aunt Jada, sensing her final hours, but she wanted him to talk to people at the wake about Dillon, hoping somebody had seen him. When he complained he might forget, she suggested he record it on his phone, or the old-fashioned way with notes.

"Perhaps you'll bump into Elke Swearington. Who knows? She came to the funeral. Then, after you've spoken with everyone, you should spend time with Raquel, forgive her and move on, or forgive her and embrace her, either way will be better for you," Silke said.

Troy mulled her words alternately with the other mysteries swirling around them. Knives picked him up in his crazy expensive, screaming red Porsche 918 Spyder. Troy couldn't help but be impressed by its sleek design, its hybrid function, and the way it rode, smoothing out the road. He sat back as they sped along the highway toward town, letting the wind clear his thoughts. He was trying to remember yesterday afternoon or figure out what had happened to John's body. It remained missing, becoming major news, especially since conspiracy theorists and *News of the Weird* associated the disappearance with the supernatural legends around Cemetery Ridge and its current exposure.

Troy realized he would rather be at the hospital with Silke. He disliked leaving her alone, there or anywhere. When had he become so protective? Perhaps because a slightly raw throat was a painful reminder of last night's adventure in the basement with his good-intending friend, Dr. Stephen Killjoy.

According to Knives, hospital video surveillance was no help. They were hoping finger prints might give them a lead. Either that or the thief was invisible, or John was a zombie. The last possibility bothered Troy in light of current circumstances.

Troy's attending physician drove uphill to the lot for the third story of the library and parked the car where they overlooked downtown, the tracks, the historic train station, the Presbyterian Church, and the state line. The multi-story civic center and book repository had been built to help revitalize Main Street over a decade ago. Made of brick, concrete and walls of glass, the building was a masterpiece of art and functionality set on the slope of a hill. It appeared modern without seeming futuristic and out of place, more a shining example of learning and public service.

"Do you have a book due? *Mysteries of the Coroners' Crypts?*"

"That's so not funny. No talking about that, remember? And yes, I requested some books on the history of Holston Dam. Mind if we do that before we head to Cumberland Park?"

"Fine by me," Troy said. The hospital and police wanted to control the flow of information. Troy wasn't even sure what had happened, except there had been a chemical spill, and he had dragged his friend to fresh air, like any friend or good neighbor would do.

"You could have rested tonight. Deputy Burt and others will be asking questions. Why are you so stubborn?" Knives asked.

"I blame the kids I grew up with. What about you? Why are you intractably obstinate?" Troy asked. They walked inside, giving them a dry, cool reprieve, toward the third-floor elevators.

"I credit the kids I grew up with," Knives said, smiling. "Silke said you think Dillon's at the Swearingtons' place."

"I don't recall it, but I don't doubt I told her."

"Her memory is suspect, too. Remember, explosion, car wrecks? Hey, no you don't because your brain is swollen. Just take it easy, all right? Is that too much to ask?" Troy didn't think there was any need to answer such a question. The doctor kept rolling. "The wake is down the street where they hold the downtown concerts and fairs near the tracks. The full moon concert will be there Friday night."

"You're socially plugged in."

"We see patients who had too much fun there. I patch people up so they can go out and do it again, hopefully smarter next time," Knives said. He glared pointedly at Troy.

He wished Silke were here. Her bedside manner was more gracious than Knives. He was his highly degreed nanny.

Troy found it hard to celebrate when Pat and John had both been murdered and Dillon was still missing. And yet, John had embraced YOLO, the you only live once philosophy. Pat was a good old boy and would want to be remembered drinking a brew, talking fishing and catching the limit at max sizes.

"Simple things have gotten complicated, haven't they? Well, if we find Dillon, and he beats the crap out of you, I owe you, so I'll put you back together again the best I can. Not saying I would do as good a job as the surgeon before, mind you."

"Why would he do that?" Troy asked.

"See. You have been hit on the head," Knives said. He hit the down button on the elevator then plucked a golden-red hair off Troy's shirt. "You wear her favor."

The elevator opened and they took it, descending. Knives kept at it. "Troy, I know Silke is way beyond the age of consent, but just remember that she's furious with Dillon right now. She might not be making the best judgment call. She seemed in a . . . dallying mood."

"Are you saying Silke would have sex with me just to tick off her brother?" Troy whispered. Knives gave him a readable look: what do you think? Of course, she would. Troy loved talking to his friends.

Knives snorted. "You've always said some lucky guy would get her. You might be the lucky guy. How do you feel about that?"

"I think she's wonderful and incredible, like sunshine. I wish she were here, my nurse and companion in adventure instead of the curmudgeonly Dr. Saveslives Killjoy," Troy said.

"Hah, that's not saying much," Knives replied.

The elevator door opened at the second floor. Troy sensed an odd and yet familiar change in the air, as if he had plunged into freezing water. He perspired, and his pulse jumped as a kind of claustrophobia kicked in, even with the door open. Nothing looked off kilter.

A hall of doors led to the meeting rooms. A sign out front was old, yesterday's scheduled event, a visiting fiction author, a former local, who wrote about vampires in Bristol. Perhaps that guy knew something.

The meeting room door at the end of the hall opened. A pale-faced man stepped out, his smile large, his teeth blood red, matching the color of his irises. Troy blinked. He had seen that face before. Behind him, a dark-haired woman drew him back into the room, but not before Paleface pointed a threatening finger at Troy, saying I'm coming for you.

The doors closed. The elevator descended, again. Who was that guy?

"Troy are you with me?" Knives asked.

"Yeah, I was reading the sign about vampires in Bristol. Creepy. Sorry. I really don't like leaving Silke at the hospital after what happened there."

"I understand. Last I saw her; she was entrenched at her aunt's bedside. You'd have to carry her out, and in your condition, you would fail," Knives said.

Troy remained silent while Knives picked up the books he had requested online. A couple of them were mostly photographs, as Troy flipped through them during the return elevator ride.

Back atop the hill, they left the books in Knives' fancy sports car and strolled down Lee Street toward Cumberland Park. Troy felt fine walking, already perspiring due to the warm night. They could already hear the music. The band played a lazy tune fitting the occasion and the heat.

Locals were accustomed to it, Knives taking it in stride. Troy had mostly been in dry climes, as cold snowy areas were arid, and he continued to feel less at home. Perhaps that was good, since he was attending a post funeral party. He shouldn't feel at home at a wake.

While they approached the park, Troy looked over the event, lacking gloom and celebrating life. It was arranged like a street fair with a variety of booths from local baked goods and donated dishes, akin to a giant potluck picnic, to game booths with tossing rings, pitching bean bags or launching stuffed dolls that looked like ogres and witches. Pat had loved arcades. He also loved to drink, as did many of Irish bent, so there were two bars to mellow the mournful mood. A country and blue grass band played from a stage near several, large above ground swimming pools stocked with live fish. Cane poles were the accoutrement of the evening, as everyone carried one. The free-standing pools sat on imported sand sponsored by the Bass Angling Tour and Pat's charity, Fishing for Life. Two volleyball nets stood ready, and one was in use.

"No volleyball. Promise me. I don't want you getting hit in

the head. Canvas the spectators, okay? And drink only water. Hear me?" Knives asked.

While they waited to cross the street, the heat seemed to dissipate, and Troy felt chilled by a cold breeze where there had been none. The sensation of crawling spiders, after he checked to make sure he had no hitchhikers, made him think he was under observation, and not just by Knives. Troy turned around, glancing to see if they had been followed, but he saw nobody behind them unless they were hiding behind parked cars.

"Don't do anything you wouldn't want to see in the news, in print, broadcast, podcast, or online internationally. Write that on the back of your hand in short hand if you think that will help."

Ambling over to them, cap on backward, J-Man found them. "Well, hello there. Don't you two look happy. Glad you could make it, Troy. You look good, considering."

"He's medicated," Knives said.

"Not to mention chastised, lectured, and constrained."

"Restrained could be next," Knives suggested.

Troy told J-Man about his plans, asking around about Dillon, hoping fishermen and lake people would know.

"Good idea. Expect to hear some tall stories. Me, I've been helping with the lighting and the wiring for the tribute. We'll be putting up a big screen. It's giving me ideas for John's celebration. Tommy Boy says anything goes as long as we don't burn the place down. Troy, you should get with Jambo. If it's hunting, target shooting, fishing, boats or cars, he's your man for networking. Besides, he's part professional gadabout," J-Man mused.

"Fine by me. Any wildfire news?" Troy asked.

"It's getting worse. There is so much dry fuel, and the winds fan it, making it move faster and grounding aircraft, which is why I am here. Any missing body news?"

"No. We're checking paper trails. You know how I live for the paper chase," Knives replied.

J-Man glanced over Troy's shoulder. "Oh, Lord, be merciful with your humble servant, the one you sent back to earth. Did you send him back for more torture?"

Troy gave him a look, then he realized that his friend was teasing him. He sensed Raquel's approach. He could feel, taste and hear her coming. He almost laughed, recalling Knives often telling him he had an addictive personality, a junkie to rush sensations, a thrill seeker with a death wish.

He barely had a moment to register her white blouse and black jeans inside boots before she hugged him. Her aroma was simply clean and physically feminine. She finished by breathing his name in his ear, dumping dopamine into his system. She could be both a pain and a painkiller. He even knew what was happening and could do little to deal with it.

"Hey, Troy. Any more close calls since the hospital?" Raquel asked, then she drew back to study his face and eyes. She hadn't been this warm in public back in the day.

"No, but there's still tonight to come," Troy said. Thank God, Raquel stepped back and let him breathe. The scent of her and her silken black hair clinging to him gave him a sense of vertigo, like skiing in a white out. Humor might save him. "I'm attached to the hip to my personal, grumpy, and no-nonsense physician, Dr. Stephen Curran, MD. MD stands for morbidly depressing, or morosely downbeat, pick one."

She looked fabulous atop black boots, jeans that showed off her powerful and shapely legs, and let them breathe, too, with diamond cuts along the outside. Her dark hair was fanned across her blouse and broad shoulders. She was wearing pink lipstick and light eye shadow, knowing she would be photographed. He didn't see her bodyguard, but he knew Chase Carter was nearby. Right now, Troy really appreciated it. He hated to think it, but Bristol wasn't safe.

He noticed Raquel still wore the bracelet of darkly smoking pearls. The mists seemed to twist and writhe, reminding him of snakes. Perhaps he could slip them off her wrist, help her lose them. Did it have anything to do with her mood? He explained his purpose tonight, asking questions to find Dillon.

"I know most of these people. They shop at my stores for gear, and most have accounts. I may not fish, but I hire locals who love to. Let me help. May I, gentleman?" Raquel asked his friends.

"He's a big boy. I have work to do. No tequila shots this time, Troy, I'm warning you," J-Man said.

"Good advice by me. Remember to read your notes every hour or so, especially the drinking water one. Raquel, his brain has been rattled. Don't let him do anything . . . energetic," Knives said lamely.

"Sorry, Stephen, but, even with my nickname, I lack the powers of a goddess."

"You will," Knives said while poking Troy in the chest. "Sit some. Rest. Excuse me, I've got a call. I'll catch up with y'all."

"Catch up. That sounds like a good idea. Since when did you come with so many rules?" Raquel asked Troy.

"They're more like guidelines due to special circumstances."

"Is there a guide book to Troy 2.0?" Raquel asked.

"Cute, though I think I'm more 2.1 or 2.2," he laughed.

"Are you really ready to be seen on my arm? You know they'll dig up our past and want to interview you and your friends," she asked.

Did he want that? "You make a good point," he replied. It had obviously never been an issue back when. "You know, I might not be good for you, publicity wise. I'm already dizzy. If I stumble or fall down, people will think I'm drunk or something. That would be lousy PR. Plus, we're already getting some unwanted coverage since we're connected to finding John's body."

"I don't care about the gossips and rumor mongers. I've learned not to trust most news and reporters, so why give it any attention?" Raquel said, taking his arm and hugging it.

Troy could be walking on air, or skiing powder by the thrill rushing through him. Despite the problems, everything felt better with her at his side. It took him back, and yet, he knew they weren't the same as a decade ago. He couldn't fall into the trap of thinking they were the same people. If they were, it wouldn't work. Speaking of work . . .

He looked around, seeking familiar faces to start the questioning. He saw Marader with a scowling Heidi, likely unhappy that Tommy Boy's attention was elsewhere. They shared a big blue drink in a large bowl with an umbrella and pineapple. Marader seemed pleased at seeing Troy with Raquel.

Troy briefly recalled their conversation and the timetable.

Silke's smile and eyes came to his mental mind.

He heard Marader laugh, even over all the sounds, drawing Troy's attention. Behind Tommy Boy and Heidi, just for a moment, Troy saw a flash of a white face and riveting pinpoints of black eyes rimmed in red. With a mouthful of teeth, the man grinned at Troy, and then he turned his attention to Marader.

It was little more than a glimpse, and then Paleface vanished so swiftly he could either turn invisible, or he was a magician. An icy trickle of sweat slid lightly down Troy's spine like the tip of a blade. The man seemed to be missing something? A hat? Sunglasses? Troy couldn't remember his name. Dane, Insane, Paine . . . but he should be wearing a hat. Troy mentally groaned about his loss of memory.

He knew a fair number of the attendees from high school and from summer camp. Raquel was on a first name basis with more than half and more by association. Of course, just her smile started conversations. He stood back and listened, always ready to record, using his smart phone and a pad of paper. Some people had thought him dead until seeing his name in the local news.

They encountered reporters from the big three and cable networks. Many of the media folk had heard about him finding John's body and rumors swirling around the hospital, and even Troy's car accident. They asked about Silke, irritating Raquel, who flipped her hair back, so they could feel her flat stare, the one given to race opponents. In short order, with his 'convenient' loss of memory, Troy frustrated all of them, telling them they were crime scenes, and mostly, I don't remember yesterday. Entertainment reporters were left with speculation, much the same as before.

"They have as much luck getting answers from you as I do," Raquel said ruefully.

"I figured I spilled all my secrets to you last night at the hospital," Troy said.

She smiled pleasantly. "Not all. You told me you never stopped thinking about me, wondering what might have happened if we had been older and wiser. Hmm. What else? Oh, how you got those Olympic photos of me racing when you supposedly were injured and unable to attend. I can't believe you did that," she said then sighed. "I also know you don't trust me, I didn't need you to tell me that, but you did, and that you doubt your instincts around me. And yet, here you are. Only to help Dillon, I suppose." Raquel mock pouted.

"And you probably answered all my questions, and I don't remember."

"I am footloose and fancy free and have been since my injury. Troy, you were a hard act to follow. Who knew the most amazing guy I would meet would be the first? Ah, that reaction. Same as then. You don't believe me."

Troy mentally bit his lip. Actions spoke louder than words.

They mingled and commiserated with Pat's friends, family, neighbors and fishing worshippers. While they lazily fished in the tanks and drank from sweating beer cans and mugs, the locals shared stories about Pat, mostly fishing, catching an alligator, or a seagull, or a bear along with a fish. Jumping out of the boat when a copperhead slithered in. A marathon volleyball game played until exhaustion. And the many heart-tugging ways he loved his kids.

They all shared a loss, a senseless waste of a good man. Troy was impressed and emotionally moved by Raquel's depth of sympathy. Everyone there couldn't help but be stunned by Pat's death, followed by John's, and now worry over Dillon. They chatted about the disappearances mentioned in the paper. Many of them personally knew a missing person. People were that close. On his phone, Troy showed photos of Dillon and handed out his business cards. Everyone heartily agreed to keep an eye out for him while they fished.

And yet, nobody had seen him.

Nobody knew the Swearingtons except by reputation as an art dealer in Abingdon. Nor had anyone purchased any art.

A man wearing black brusquely bumped Troy aside, causing him to stagger. The guy apologized but kept going, only glancing over his shoulder. His eyes were black and hateful, his smile sarcastic and unapologetic. It was the pale-faced guy again. Paleface winked and seemed to disappear with two steps into the crowd. Crane? No, that wasn't his name. Troy started to wonder if he had met him yesterday.

"Are you all right? You look uncomfortable," Raquel asked.

He became keenly aware of the way she constantly touched him as if she were gentling a horse. Her smile was innocent, though her eyes brimmed with mysteries and desire. He quickly regathered his wits seeing Rae Kirkland approach with a reporter's persevering air.

"You two look so comfortable you'll start rumors," Rae said.

"Oh, please. He's faking it. His shoulders feel like concrete," Raquel said.

"It's hard to celebrate when Dillon is missing, maybe dead. I am enjoying time with Raquel, but I feel like I should be out looking for him. But I don' know what to do next."

"You're right. As a reporter, I've had to get adjusted to that kind of thing. There always seems to be bad news and good. I was hoping you would have good news about Dillon," she said wistfully. Once, she had been sweet on Dillon.

"I feel he's still alive." Troy said.

Rae breathed a sigh of relief. "Good. That's something. You

two were always so close. It seems like he just vanished on Cemetery Ridge. It's scary how many people have disappeared the last few days," Rae said. She chatted about the homeless that had vanished from downtown, and it wasn't because the city was trying to clean up for all the tourists. The missing wasn't major news because of the deaths and the wildfire threatening the upcoming race.

"I can't help but wonder if Dillon stumbled onto something, so he disappeared. Or he's involved in undercover work," Troy said.

"I hope he isn't hiding out with an old girlfriend," Rae said peevishly. "There's rumors swirling that he found something on Cemetery Ridge and vanished. Choose your method: cursed artifact turns him into a water zombie, a magical crystal transports him to a parallel universe, he ate something from old Wreythville that transformed him into a lake monster, or he was kidnapped by the Dark Lady, lucky SOB. It goes on and on," Rae continued.

"He did have a bit of an obsession with her," Raquel replied.

"Just a little. Do you know Elke Swearington?" Troy asked

"Of course. She's a masterpiece collecting masterpieces, a gorgeous work of nature gathering magnificent works of man, meaning she's a beautiful woman and an art broker. I know she travels extensively. Has a house in town, above her shop, and one on the lake, one of the oldest, passed down by the family since the 1950s. Her sister, who lives out of town, I forget where, is beautiful, too. They have the sexy blond genes. No offense, Raquel," Rae said and patted her curls. "Why do you ask?"

He told her about the photo of the boat. "It's the only lead we have," Troy said.

"You might have missed a clue in the Wreythville mansion. Somebody should double-check," Rae said.

"Don't wish that on anybody," Raquel said, shivering and cuddling up with Troy.

Rae promised to find Dillon and departed. Troy had a bad feeling about their chat.

Rae wasn't the only female looking for Dillon. Lovely ladies from Johnson City and Kingsport recognized Troy but came looking for Dillon, hoping he was here, too.

When Raquel hugged Troy's arm, he felt transported back in time, especially when they conversed with Mr. Thomas, or Mr. T, as they had called him when they had worked for his summer camp.

Troy had met Raquel there. It had seemed like kismet.

Mr. T was elderly and wizen, now in his seventies and walking with a cane. He still strolled along the shore, he told them.

"I don't know what it is, but something has changed at the lake. It feels, I don't know, unnatural. I guess I could just be spooked by the smoke and the low water levels. It's never been like this. Ever. You'd have to go back before the dam was finished, and they started filling the lake."

"It does feel very different," Troy agreed. Raquel nodded.

"When I was a boy, we lived in Blountsville, not far from the Sullivan County Sheriff's Department, post flood," he said and shook his head as if he couldn't believe his memories. "My, oh, my, life can be so unexpected and short and swift as I suspect Mr. Bane here now knows. Anyway, I digress. Do you remember the scary campfire story of when I was a boy out fishing at Riddle Creek?"

Troy nodded. "I sure do. There's a place you're not supposed to go, of course, up north into Holston Valley, into what . . . Moon town?"

"Yep. Where they fixed moonshine. It was a busy place at night. When the wind was right, sometimes, I could hear them while I was fishing Riddle Creek. One night, I was catching fish hand over fist so I stayed late when I should have gone home. I heard lots of interesting noises, so being young, dumb and curious, when the fish stopped biting, I crept closer."

"And you were attacked by a wolf," Raquel added.

Shivers rippled over Troy. A wolf? Why were wolves showing up? This wasn't *Dances with Wolves*. The animals lived out west, once endangered even. He had seen them at Yellowstone, come to think of it, and none had been as large as the one on Marader's deck.

"It was huge, wasn't it?" Troy asked.

"You both remember!"

"I think I remember it because a lovely raven-haired woman came to your rescue. She commanded it to stop and go away," Raquel said. She made a show of patting her wealth of dark-haired locks.

"And it did, right when it was about to tear out my throat. I could see in its eyes that it wanted blood, my blood, but it turned away. She was the most gorgeous woman I have ever set eyes upon, though you, my dear, have blossomed into an incredible beauty yourself. I still get a shiver thinking about her. She told me to go home, to stay away from there if I wanted to live, to find my first love, then she kissed me on the cheek and sent me on my way. Smitten for life," he said, and then he cleared his throat, gathering himself. "But I did find my first love shortly thereafter. I recognized true love since I'd already been bitten."

Moon town. Could that be Wreythville? Troy could do an Internet search. He took notes. And bitten? Did he mean literally?

"Were you wounded in any way?" Troy asked.

"Only a broken heart that my Daisy May healed," he replied.

A passerby bumped into Mr. T, causing him to stumble. He started to fall, but Troy caught him. The hit-and-run walker glared over his shoulder, and Troy recognized Paleface, again. Kane? Troy shivered. Why was he causing problems?

"Thank you, young man. I'm glad you're strong with good reflexes," Mr. T said, clapping Troy on the shoulder.

Where was Paleface? What did he want?

Over near the beer booth, Troy spotted the troublemaker.

It was the eyes that stopped Troy. Where had he seen those cold and commanding eyes before tonight? Had they been behind sunglasses before? He kept thinking Paleface should be wearing a hat. Like he was the world's most interesting man, a woman hung on each arm, a voluptuous brunette with cropped hair and a willowy blond with long straight hair. He pointed a finger at Troy, then he used that finger to slash across the women's throats. They laughed, but the look in Paleface's eyes was no joke.

Fragments of the memories tumbled over in his mind. Paleface under a hat and standing in a boat. Huge frightening eyes staring at Troy, his hands locked on the steering wheel of the pontoon boat. Silke elbowing then kissing him. A near collision of boats. A flipping Sea-Doo. Shattering glass. Silke collapsing.

Was that yesterday?

When Troy came back to his senses, he looked back over at the bar. Paleface and his women were gone. Why was he here? What did he want? Could he be the reason people were vanishing?

Troy needed to contact Deputy Burt. They needed to find Paleface before it was too late.

Twenty-Three: Nightwalkers Wake

Mr. T cleared his throat. "Sorry, I still get chills. Worse, I get 'em thinking the lake feels much like the valley felt that night, like the breath of death on the back of my neck. Now, I'm afraid to go out after dark, and yet, I wonder . . . if I would see her, again. That would be enough. Her kiss still lingers," he said and touched his cheek.

Raquel squeezed Mr. T's shoulder to bring him back. Her bracelet of pearls seemed to spark, catching his attention. She didn't notice, but Mr. T was keenly aware, his gaze locking on it.

"That bracelet. Amazing! It looks so much like the one the

Dark Lady wore!" he said. He gently stroked the ring of pearls. "This really takes me back. Where did you get it?" he asked.

Raquel shifted uncomfortably, and then she summarized the dive. "Ah, then it might be hers. I would ask if you have attracted more men than usual, but you're honey to the boy bears!" he chuckled. "Oh well, enough of an old man's rambling." He wished them well and hobbled off.

"He knew this bracelet," she stated flatly.

"Perhaps it is hers. The Dark Lady's. Do you still want to wear it?"

Raquel nodded. He held back his exasperation.

"You seem on edge," she said.

"A lot has gone wrong recently, and people keep asking me questions about dying," he said.

"I'm not surprised that everyone is curious. I am. You've had a peek at what's beyond. Are you telling me you don't remember it?"

"Oh, I remember it." Troy recalled it clearly. In a timeless moment, he had visited all his friends and loved ones. Many of them had been watching the broadcast when he died. He could see their faces, their shock, and even feel the stab of loss. Dillon stood stunned. Knives sat down, face in hands, saying he knew this day was coming. John had been diving but sensed it. Troy recalled finding Silke weeping on the floor. Raquel had been carnally busy, the Extreme Championships paused on the screen.

"Troy?" Raquel asked.

"Sorry. Flashback. Seeing life in a non-linear way. Viewing it all at once, and then understanding how your every word and action, sometimes thought, as that expression can flash across your face, changes someone, something, or the world around you. It's thought-provoking, empowering and yet paralyzing, too."

"Paralysis by analysis from someone who throws himself down snowy peaks. So, you've been traveling to out of the way places to adjust to this . . . enlightenment? I had wondered how you had changed since that experience. Just injuring my knee changed my perspective. You lose trust in it, just like you can lose trust in somebody when they give way. You've never forgiven me, and I understand how you feel, I'm sorry to say, I really do."

Troy simply listened to the sound of her voice. His blood brothers had never believed Troy about their long talks where they practiced visualizing their successes together. He heard the hard edge and bitterness in her last words.

Over a loud speaker, they announced Pat's tribute. Everyone gathered around the main screen, used for downtown summer movie nights, and watched an emotionally stirring production of Pat's triumphs, some humorous tribulations, and fun and memorable moments with friends, fans, and family. All around, tears flowed freely, and Troy could feel palpable love in the air.

"Deep in thought?" she asked.

"Better than six feet under," he replied. He was starting to feel the way Mr. T had described the air around Holston Lake, sensing the cold breath of death across the back of his neck. Was the feeling concussion related? Or caused by Paleface's taunting?

"Troy, this brooding, unless you're a completely different person, you need to talk before it eats you up. People can help you figure things out."

"I've talked to Spider about it."

"I'll bet that was interesting. I don't know about helpful. And?"

"We saw some similarities in how our perspectives have changed psychologically and spiritually," he said. He didn't want to get into telling her about seeing ghosts.

Afterward, there were numerous toasts. Troy just loved hoisting water. Old acquaintances, surprised and pleased to see him, tried to tempt him with booze, ready to celebrate his return, but Raquel firmly shooed them away. She had developed a laser-cutting glare.

They wandered over to the fountains near the Veterans Memorial, where Raquel's sister showed up long enough to cause trouble. "Troy, how delightful to see you on your feet," Diana began with a dazzling smile. She acted a touch inebriated. "Our mother sends her best wishes for your speedy recovery."

"This was not the kind of homecoming news I wanted to make," Troy said.

"I know the feeling. The first week I had my license I wrecked Dad's car and the whole world knew. Anyway, our mom said to get well. That you were the best thing that ever happened to Raquel."

Raquel froze. Diana tried to look sweetly innocent.

"Winning her first silver medal is the best thing that ever happened to her," Troy said, ending a long silence.

Raquel gave her sister a withering look. "She may have grown physically, but otherwise she's still twelve," she said.

Diana tried not to look petulant. "Was winning the World Extreme Championship gold the best thing that ever happened to you?" she asked Troy.

He shook his head. He made sure he didn't look at Raquel as he grew thoughtful. His pause seemed long, the air still between them. "Being born in Bristol, of course. Good folks. Loved ones. Kindly people. The lake and mountains. I made friends for a lifetime. I learned to ski here and more. It's part of my DNA. I didn't realize it until this trip, I guess because I've been dead and gone," he said.

Diana frowned. "God, you sound like you're doing an interview. Would you like to dance?" she asked Troy, confusing him with the sudden switch.

"I would love, too, but, according to Doctor Killjoy, sometimes known as Dr. No, I'm supposed to avoid physical activity, especially with hot young women in their wild phase," Troy said.

"Party pooper. Raquel said you were quite the dancer. I see

Eduardo. He will dance with me."

"Eduardo will do anything for you," Raquel said.

"Isn't that great! I love it!" Diana said. She waved farewell and danced over to her boyfriend, pulling the handsome Hispanic young man out to shag.

"Come dance with me," Raquel cajoled. When she saw him start to protest, she placed a finger on his lips. "There are people out there that we haven't talked to yet, and we can slow dance," she purred. He failed to resist that sound and feeling of her satisfaction. She took his left hand. "You can post it on your page. Boost traffic. You don't have to smile, but try not to look like you're in pain. They'll think I'm stepping on your feet."

He would be lying to himself if he hadn't wanted to hold her in his arms again. Silke was right. He needed to know, to deal with a ghost so to speak, so he took Raquel's left hand, leading her and making sure there was air space, a firewall, between them.

He tried to use mental competitive training, setting emotions aside, and relaxed into the music, letting it carry him along. They danced in silence. He was afraid to speak and ruin the moment, though he had lots of questions. He had grudgingly learned to enjoy the Now, even the slow moments.

Blackness descended. All light went dark as power failed. The music abruptly died. At first, there was a shocked silence.

Accident? Or intentional? He had grown wary and suspicious, especially with Paleface nearby.

"You may have to forgive me twice," Raquel said.

He thought that might not be enough, then he turned into a powerful, devouring, full-bodied kiss, like she wanted him here and now. He couldn't think of anything, as a long ache was soothed and a yearning met. He forgot about everything else and reveled in a kiss nine years in waiting.

"Deny that you never imagined this moment? Eye to eye. Face to face?" she asked. She reached up and gently caressed his lips. "Well?"

Already a poor liar, he said nothing. He had dreamt of it both pleasantly and nightmarishly.

His silence encouraged a smile. "Besides, if you forget, a photo will likely be posted on the web. I told you I don't care about the national news. Do you? Enough to stop from finding out about us? Once you were bold," she said.

Troy didn't think this was like Raquel, the one he had known disliked public affection, but what he knew was history, a long time ago, or from her web site. Did he care that the world knew they were dancing?

J-Man yelled an apology. He promised power soon. Somebody played slow dance music from their phone.

"We have never celebrated our medals together. We should do that. I'll cook."

"You can cook? You're pulling my leg, aren't you?"

"I am not. I used to employ a chef. I learned from her. I'm not so busy now, so I can take the time. I told you we had some catching up to do. A wake doesn't seem like the best of places to talk about us."

"Yes. This is about Pat and life. I have never considered having a wake, but I like the idea of my friends getting together and sharing anecdotes."

"Like what? The time you almost broke your face trying to ski on an oar?" she asked with a chuckle. She laid a head on his shoulder. He could feel her laughter carry through him, pleasantly infecting him.

"Ow. That still isn't funny," he said.

"The time you forgot to put the plug in? We stopped for lunch and started to sink off Cliff Island? You searched frantically while I bailed?"

"What about you running over the sunken island in the Rock Garden? I took the blame for bending the prop. I paid for a new one and was grounded for what seemed weeks," he said.

"I snuck into your house and showed my appreciation," she said with a devilish smile. The space between them vanished along with the years. "That reminds me of the cross-country cabin outside of Breckenridge, when we got turned around in the blizzard. We survived by combining body heat."

Growing too warm now, he had better change the subject. "Going back to boats. I told the guys to put me in a small wooden barge, set it afire, and send it afloat like the Vikings of old. John felt the same way," he said.

"Does coming back from . . . beyond, change the way you see things? Add purpose? Urgency?" she asked. She was close, her face aglow, kind, beautiful, and ready to be kissed, again.

A courageously foolish young man would have kissed her. If he had been drinking, he would have taken her in his arms by now and savored her lips. He obviously wasn't himself. And yet, he had thoroughly enjoyed her company and seeing her among normal people, being herself, a woman, not the Silver Goddess.

The night suddenly seemed muggier and tighter. He felt trapped. A premonition? He wasn't sure that it had to do with Raquel unless this was a nightmare. Could it have been her question? Did he remember how he got here? Yes, Knives had been kind enough to drive and lecture him. Oh yeah, he remembered it too well. Nothing strenuous.

This was real. Raquel in his arms was real. So he crashed again. So what? The feelings of flight were gone. He found himself willing to see where this led. He had to either get her out of his system or embrace her. Silke was right. He thought of her at the hospital. He had offered to stay with her, but she wanted him to learn something to help them find Dillon. Had he?

Something made him pause. He noticed the fog had thickened along with the smoke. It wafted in long, yellow streamers. The acrid odor grew stronger and heavier. He figured the wind had shifted, bringing wildfire smoke.

Already hot, many couples didn't even notice, lost in embracing life and kissing each other, public displays of affection rampant as if they were feeling grateful and passionate about being alive. He saw Denny and his wife,

Colleen, as well as Jambo and his lady, Jane. Troy realized that is how he felt: grateful to be alive. Along with it came a surge of sexual desire. Those kissing began to grope, hands as well as lips exploring bodies.

Even at half power, the glaring lights returned, brightening up the place and breaking the sexual tension and passionate mood. It caused everyone to blink and take a step back. Troy thought some seemed drugged, as if the drinks had been spiked.

A tendril of panic and thrill took root and caused him to turn. Something was coming. Suddenly, the urge rushed to fight or flee.

"Hey, Bane," a muscular man said while he tapped Troy on the shoulder.

Troy recognized him as the guy whose back Silke had adjusted. Did he want to cut in? Tell him something about Dillon? His brain still worked too slowly, but he knew it wasn't Paleface, so he relaxed.

"Where's your lady? Where's Silke?"

Troy recalled that he was supposed to be dating Silke. "She's at the hospital. Her aunt isn't doing well. Silke refused to leave and wouldn't let me stay either, because she wants me to ask everybody about Dillon."

"Well, you didn't ask me."

"You mean you know something and didn't tell Silke?"

"No. Listen, I don't like the way you're dancing with this chick while Silke's at the hospital," the muscle man growled. His fists were clenched. "I'm very fond of her. And so is he." He jerked a thumb over his shoulder as a second beefcake joined him.

Troy disliked where this was headed. This was a consequence of being untruthful.

"You and Silke are dating?" Raquel asked.

"Engaged in finding her brother, and to dissuade Ray Berry's," Troy said.

Raquel blinked, catching it. She had suffered through a

stalker of that name. Troy wasn't sure she believed, but she understood. "I can see why she might be concerned."

"Is this guy two-timing Silke?" the second guy growled.

This was about to get ugly very fast. Troy glanced around, wondering if he had any friends close by. He would hate making news this way.

"I don't understand what she sees in you. Heard she's been pining away for years, and you do this to her."

Pining away for years? At first, Troy thought that was absurd, but it struck a strange cord, though that had been part of their story. Why did it feel so sound? That also blew Knives' theory out of the water that she was trying to seduce him just to tick off Dillon. Deep down, he had known this, he realized.

"She deserves your respect, and I'm the one to teach you about it."

Troy stepped back, ready to evade. The best defense was not to be there, Sensei Cosmo always said.

"Hey, now this moment looks tense," Martin said, showing up like a heroic sidekick. "Are Joe and Sam Metalhead bothering you?"

"Martin . . ."

"You're not going to say you work alone, are you?"

"It's great to see you, Martin."

"What's up? Is this a hero slugfest?" Martin asked.

"Martin, I'm a thrill-seeker not a Kung Fu fighter. This is a misunderstanding."

"Sorry. Hear that guys? He's turning the other cheek. Giving you a chance."

Actually, Joe and Sam were right. It did appear he had stepped out on Silke, and he was no longer working, getting off track. He glanced around. There were still a few people left yet to interview.

"This is bullshit," the muscle-heads muttered as they grew angrier, ready to lash out. Troy glanced, seeing Raquel's bodyguard closing in, then she stopped and turned.

Troy spotted what riveted her attention: a devilishly divine woman stalked them. With her dark hair and eyes, she looked like Raquel. He looked away from her eyes, afraid he might get mesmerized. Her body was a distraction, too, so he focused on her hands with long, red fingernails, looking for danger. She held a camera phone and what looked like an autograph book with a pen. As she neared, Troy's ankh grew warmer.

"Hey, Bane, I'm talking to you. Are you mental?" Joe snarled.

"At ease, boys. Take a breath, relax, and give a lady some room," the dark beauty said. Her voice wasn't loud, but it was clear and commanding.

The two fighters stood star struck, then when she shooed them, they stepped aside to give her room.

"Hi, I'm sorry to bother you, Ms. Sterling," she said breathlessly. "I'm Lyla, a huge fan of yours. I model my look after you. Simple. Powerful. Stunning. Immortalizing." She struck a breathtaking pose, sheathed in a white shirt buttoned low, black slacks and boots. Troy had never imagined a woman looking better at being Raquel than Raquel. "Please sign my book."

At first, Troy had been certain Raquel would say no, but Lyla had crooned an undeniable demand. He felt the power of her words. Moving. Compelling. Time seemed to slow, thickening like molasses, holding him but moving Raquel.

"Of course. I'd be glad to," Raquel said, surprising him. She accepted the pen and pad.

Silke's protectors remained thunderstruck. Troy double-checked to make sure he wasn't agape and found his jaw clenched.

"You handsome gentlemen," Lyla said, stressing the last word. It made Sam and his bud straighten and preen. "Should go for a peaceful walk, vent some testosterone, and flex elsewhere. Shoo." She blew each a kiss. With smiles, the muscle-heads departed floating on air like they had brains full of helium.

Troy felt both relieved and disturbed.

Lyla glanced away from Raquel to Troy. They locked eyes for a moment, and he saw it, the predatory look, that of a hungry animal. Her eyes possessed a reddish hue as if her passions were stirring a bloodlust. She was surprised for a split second by his recognition, but it was replaced by supreme confidence. Her beauty would allow her any eccentricity. She winked and offered him a sly smile. "Freeze and seize, Troy. Lyla will deal with you later."

Troy could hardly move, even breathing was a chore. He felt punched in the chest, his heart thunderstruck, his lungs stunned and windless. What had she done to him?

Lyla beamed at Troy's dilemma while Raquel signed away. When she returned the book, Lyla slipped the bracelet off Raquel's wrist. Troy tried to say something and hesitated, grateful to see those pearls go far away.

"Selfie," the gorgeous creature commanded. Lyla stepped next to Raquel and snapped two quick photos, the flash blinding Raquel. She stumbled, and Troy could move again, steadying her.

Somebody slammed into Raquel, shoving Lyla aside. He jerked on Raquel's arm. Troy elbowed him, but the attacker bowled through him. The shaggy blond guy in black and blue jeans dashed off.

Lyla was nowhere to be seen. Still stunned a little by the events, Raquel clung to him.

"Are you all right?" Troy asked. He gently hugged her.

"I think so. I'll stretch and check my body parts," she said, coolly stepping back. The earlier passion had been knocked from her. During her self-inventory for injuries, she noticed her pearls were gone. She swore under her breath. "So much for my light in the darkness."

"I'm thrilled you're all right," Troy said. He still struggled to come to grips with the moment. What had happened? Hadn't Lyla stolen the pearls? Had she known what they were? What was she?

Of course, the photographers were all over it, pouncing

faster than the local authorities. They both gave witness statements, similar except for Troy seeing Lyla lift the bracelet before the impact.

"Really? That woman stole it? You were watching her hands?" Raquel asked. She made it sound like there was no way he could have ignored eyeballing her figure.

"I wanted to make sure she wasn't carrying a weapon," Troy replied.

"That was thoughtful of you. Thanks."

He didn't tell Raquel that Lyla had paralyzed him with a word. Even so, he kept thinking about Paleface. Troy hadn't seen him in a while, but Lyla's eyes reminded Troy of someone from a vague memory. He had yet to mention the stalker to any officers or Raquel, partly because Paleface seemed a hallucination.

What connection was his fuzzy brain missing?

"How are you doing?" Raquel asked, giving him some space.

Her usual professional public demeanor had returned. Had the pearls made her less aloof? What did Troy trust?

"I'm a little muddle-headed," he replied.

"Were you hit?" she asked.

He didn't think so. He didn't say what he thought. Lyla had befuddled him with her stare and voice. His frustration had a familiar echo. Had it happened before? Like a flash of light, he recalled Paleface, Zane, commanding a boat.

"One more dance? I wouldn't want that to be our last dance, and you might do something dangerous and die before I see you next time, unless you want to extend this evening?" she asked, an eyebrow coolly arched in invitation.

Yes! or the more suave, "sounds like a great idea", almost leapt out of his mouth. He studied her eyes as he guided her into the music. He felt the tension leave her, and she relaxed in his arms.

When the song ended, Raquel whispered in his ear, asking her question again. "And if you don't come home with me, what are your plans? Are you really going to sleep? Or will you be off hunting for Dillon? Do I need to protect you from yourself and the Urichs?"

"Probably," he said. His world tilted. For the strangest moment, he felt Dillon nearby. Troy glanced around.

That's when he saw her standing by the sculpture, *Take the Stage*, near the bronze guitarist. Just like in the cemetery, Troy couldn't believe Elke Swearington was real and a twin to the woman entangled with Dillon every night.

Rae Kirkland was right about the woman being a masterpiece, a prime example of a ravishingly gorgeous blond. Elke Swearington certainly took the stage. She commanded attention by wearing a curve-caressing black dress, slit at the thigh, showing peeks and flashes of flesh. Her cherry-red lips, long nails, silken belt, and fashionable high heels screamed seduction. Like Aphrodite, as she passed couples, they became more energetic and intimate. Her smile seemed to ooze satisfaction. Her eyes held confidence. At first, Troy thought she seemed to glow, standing out among the couples, but he decided she was more akin to a burning ember, giving off heat but little light, and yet still setting things around her on fire.

That made him briefly think of Silke, who always seemed aglow, and wondered how she was doing. She would have some questions about Dillon's whereabouts. That sobered Troy. He hit the record button. Getting his head on as straight as possible, he went back to work, trying to find Dillon.

Twenty-Four: Downtown Brawl

"Troy, do you know her?" Raquel asked, a touch of awe in her voice as if he might befriend somebody famous. It was out of character.

The night had grown warmer, and every movement Raquel and the blond made seemed erotic and highly suggestive. The evening atmosphere wafted heavily with sex, life decisions and deathly consequences. His pulse had already leapt to bounding, and he wasn't doing anything strenuous. He knew that if it raced too much, it hindered his ability to think clearly and led to poor choices.

The heart-stopping gorgeous woman paused, poised and posed like a runway model. All eyes were upon her. "Pardon me, Ms. Sterling, but my name's Elke Swearington."

"How can I help you, Ms. Swearington?" Raquel replied guardedly. She remained calm, despite already having been assaulted and robbed once tonight.

"Your dance partner, Mr. Bane, has been asking around about me, and I must be leaving soon, so I thought I would address his questions. I must say I'm a big fan, Ms. Sterling, seeing you as a female success story and . . ." She leaned close to Raquel and whispered something Troy couldn't hear over the music, but Raquel relaxed against him.

Elke looked and sounded exactly like the woman who had murdered Mona in the vision. Elke also matched the unquenchable flame clad in flesh that ravaged Dillon every night. How could he have dreamed of her if he had never met her? Was Dillon really with her? What hold did she have over his friend, besides the obvious one, the same that messed with his and all others' thoughts?

"Too much attention on us. Troy, stay with me. Everyone, now, hugs and kisses all the way around. Lots of kisses. I love kisses, as does everybody," Elke sang in an intoxicatingly sultry voice. It swept over the attendees like a stirring breeze.

Couples came together, crushing each other in passionate embraces and open-mouthed kisses. Friends with any interest in each other locked lips. No one was immune, even if it was lip to cheek, as young and old alike followed her wish to kiss.

Troy felt a burning in his chest, as if his heart were afire. He realized it was physical, the ankh hot on his sternum. He grabbed the symbol of life, and his mind cleared a little.

"Troy. I wish to speak with you," Elke said.

"Good. I am very pleased to finally meet you, Ms.

Swearington. I tried to talk to you earlier but your bodyguard, Mr. Thick, stopped me," Troy said.

Raquel seemed to step back and melt away as the supernatural beauty took Troy's hands. He had the thought Silke wouldn't let him go so easily. The music and atmosphere carried him away to walk on air. Elke led him into a shag. Wasn't he supposed to be leading? Her grip was firm and guiding, as if she had taught men how to dance a thousand times.

"I feel like we already know each other intimately, don't you?"

He nodded, studying her face and her eyes. She appeared different when not in heat, but he could see the passion in her strangely feral eyes, red and black, blood and darkness.

"Please call me, Elke. I am impressed by the way you throw yourself through the air and downhill like an immortal. Flying is invigorating, is it not?"

"I imagine you can do anything you put your mind to do," Troy said. He felt a strange dichotomy, relaxed with her, almost comfortable, and yet high strung and nervous.

"Relax, Troy, I'm not a stalking fan. Deputy Burt sent me your way, after he finished questioning me about the boat and the photo. I'm sorry we weren't home when you stopped by and even sorrier that the dogs chased you. I'm so embarrassed but, I'm more glad no one was hurt. I blame my sister. She must have left them out. Again, I apologize."

Troy waved it off. He suspected most men would forgive Elke just about anything. "It's all right. I'm sure we invaded their space."

"You are too kind," she replied.

"How did you know Pat?" Troy asked. He watched her face. Looking at beauty? Or looking for lies?

"Through his charity. We give to Fishing for Life every year. Troy, the deputy said this had something to do with Dillon Urich."

Troy nodded and told her about her friend and the photo.

"My parents' boat, yes. Handed down from their parents," she said. She stared into his eyes as if she could read his history by scrolling along his iris. "Troy, I have a message for you."

"You do? A message? Okay. From who?"

"Dillon."

He doubted her, of course, and yet, he could easily see her coupled with his best friend. "The one who is hiding out with a gorgeous blond, bedside nurse? That Dillion?" he asked.

For the flicker of an instant, her placid facade cracked, and she blinked. Her eyes narrowed before she smiled flirtatiously. There must have been some truth in his words.

"For your safety and others, please stop looking for Dillon." Her commanding words struck him with a hint of menace, like a velvet-sheathed hammer used to rap instead of smash.

"What?" he asked in a harsh, disbelieving whisper. Her words still hung in the air. She gave him a look as if to say don't make me repeat it. "Stop looking for Dillon?"

Troy struggled with himself. He was about to blow it off and walk away. He had better things to do than almost kill himself searching for Dillon, didn't he? He was just getting in the way.

He almost lost a grip. Troy stuffed the emotions aside, compartmentalizing, focusing away from the distractions. He looked away from the women and dancers, up to the sky, seeing the BRISTOL TN/VA A GOOD PLACE TO LIVE. Ha, that was better than PUSH BRISTOL, the original sign over the hardware store next to the tracks, when the train depot had been a crucial part of town. He shook his head, trying to focus. The people here were in danger. He was imperiled, too. He sensed it as well as standing on the precipice in a blinding snowstorm, feeling the long fall without seeing it, yet.

"Why on earth would I do that?" he asked.

"Oh, my, he said you were strong-willed. That y'all would often test your endurance and will power. Sitting under cold waterfalls. Swimming in bone-chilling water. Ice climbing. Brr.

Hiking the PCT from Mexico to Canada. Swimming in a river to avoid a wildfire."

Troy didn't dare look at her. "Who is this he, again?"

"Dillon, as I said. He's convalescing in hiding. You're right. He said you would know. He wants you to stop before you locate him," she said, then she paused, dropping her voice. "You're unintentionally putting everyone in danger. Look what has already happened to you by diving Von Damme's place. Almost dying in a car crash. You were chased by wolves, weren't you?"

Troy was stunned. He worked to process what she was saying. Now, he could see in his mind's eyes the size and ferociousness of the wolves chasing their car. "Yes, they . . . Wait a minute, you know where Dillon is?!" Troy susurrated. He couldn't manage much more than a whisper despite the eureka moment. Dillon hid out at Swearington Lodge. He couldn't wait to tell Silke!

Elke's eyes held him, suppressing his vocalization much as teacher with a steely stare in a library.

She smiled. "You two are very close. He was researching a story and was injured. He would have died if I hadn't acted quickly, so I took him home. We have a doctor at the house to help with both my grandparents. Dillon is recovering in fits and starts, but, he pushes himself, sometimes too hard, to be up soon."

Troy made the mistake of looking at her. He found himself nodding his head and agreeing. "Soon. Good. I don't believe you."

"Listen, I know you would be crazy to believe that I met your best friend when he was in trouble on the lake, and that we fell in love and now he's hiding from the world because he fears for his life."

"Aptly phrased. Why didn't he give you an image file?"

"He will tell you when he sees you."

"A voice file."

"Same reason."

"Fine. A password. Surely, he would give the love of his life our secret passwords," he said, doubting he would hear it.

She leaned close to whisper in his ear. "Franz Klammer. His is Bruce Lee."

Troy jerked back, unnerved by her nearness to his neck, where phantom pains nipped him. The ankh had grown unpleasantly hot. He stared at her. She was correct about the passwords.

"You're jumpy? Once bitten twice shy?" she asked. Her voice was brittle. "Look at me, please." His gaze moved to her eyes and held her attention. They stared into one another's souls like lovers or hated enemies. He couldn't find anything, lost in the darkness of her and the dance of their bodies. The rest of the world ceased to exist.

"Ah, you have been bitten . . . in your dreams. How interesting. Lucky you. Better that way, some might say. Not I, of course. You and Dillon, blood brothers, best friends, you are so very close, as close as twins, perhaps closer. I have heard of such, but no one I know has experienced such a thing. I never knew I was making love to two men."

"What?" Troy asked. To say he was off balance was an understatement. At least he was an expert in recovering.

She teased her tongue with her teeth and lips. "You have dreamed about me. Or thought you did. I think you . . . experienced me. That should make you surer about what I say."

"What makes you think this?"

"It's in your eyes. Just like you think, I can read your thoughts in your eyes, though less easily than most people, because you are a Heavensent and have recently suffered a head injury. It alters chemistry, electricity, and consciousness, the greatest change."

"A concussion and enlightenment. What a combo. Is that where I forget I'm consciously evolved?"

"Haven't we all?" she chuckled. "Both limit what I can do."

"What you can do?" he asked. It sounded frightening and

alluring.

"I am a seer. You really are smitten with Silke, aren't you?"

A denial almost sprung to his lips, but she drew the truth from him. "I don't think it takes a seer to know this," he said.

"And you're only holding off because of Dillon? That is wise. He has been very moody and prone to ferocious anger. Listen, I am not the kind to do favors, but my beloved cares for you immensely but cares for Silke even more. A word of advice if you wish to live: leave Silke alone before he kills you for stealing kisses from his sister." The way she said it, cold and logical, made it sound likely to happen.

Troy felt slapped. "I didn't steal. It was a pretend beau kiss."

"You don't believe that."

Troy's head hurt. "Is Silke in danger?"

"Not from us."

"But he is from her. She's furious with him."

Elke stared at him, reading his eyes even as they danced.

"How do you dance without looking?" Troy asked, feeling it an inane question and yet important.

"I can feel everybody? Can't you?" she asked.

He closed his eyes. He realized he was getting off the subject. All he sensed was Elke, his body thinking her nearness meant she wanted him. He kept trying to tell it that she wanted him gone. "No, you sort of overwhelm me."

"Ah, you are so sweet, but I can tell that you're angry with me for suggesting you avoid Silke."

There it was again. She was right. Troy grabbed on to that anger and pushed past and beyond her sexy presence. He could vaguely sense people as they neared. He nodded.

"Those of us who have been closest to death notice these things. Troy, it might be wisest if you left town. Your headache would pass," she said coolly.

Troy felt the push. It turned into a shove. He mentally stood against it and stubbornly took his smartphone from his pocket. He reached to one touch dial Silke.

"I won't leave Silke to this mess. Tell him no. Or hell no. In fact, I'm calling her now," Troy said through gritted teeth. He hated head games. He hated being a toy or a pawn. A headache began to creep over him.

"Stop." She glared at him. He felt slammed. His brain reeled as his thoughts scattered in panic. "Listen to me and obey."

Shocked, the word ignited lighting in his body. It leapt to pay attention then sank into obeisance.

"You will be distant to Silke. Stay away from Silke," Elke commanded.

"I will stay away," Troy said. His tongue obeyed, but his brain rebelled. Stay away from Silke. No way.

Elke patted him on the cheek. "That's a good boy. When you were diving, did y'all find anything of interest? Buried treasure?"

"Yes. Several things. A jewelry box, tie pin, diaries written on vellum, a letter opener, and a pearl bracelet. A woman calling herself Lyla stole it. She reminded me of you."

Elke stared into his eyes. Troy felt moments of dizziness. "Of course, she did. You and Raquel are lucky to be alive, meeting two dark ladies in the same evening," she hissed. Troy felt jabbed with an injection of panic until she fondly patted him. "But alive you are. The county deputy, Burt, mentioned the jewelry box."

Troy nodded. "Marader is obsessed with it."

"Interesting and dangerous. I should relieve him of it. Having it could lead to his untimely demise. Hear me. Dillon is not at the Swearingtons. You were confused. Tell Silke that my grandparents saw him. That he had been injured in a fall off the Sea-Doo but was all right and waiting for the detective. My parents spoke with Dillon about the days before the dam and during the days of it being built. They last saw him around six."

Troy used his anger to shove his animal nature aside and become humanly obstinate and mull-headed.

"For your own safety, no more intimate moments with Silke. Find yourself another playmate. Be distant to Silke. Stay away from Silke," Elke said. The harder she pushed, the more stubborn he grew. "I am deadly earnest. Desiree would be a better coupling. You could leave town with Desiree. She would go with you. Let this blow over." Just with her words, luscious Desiree leapt into his thoughts.

She had always been there along the periphery. No attachments. His mind and body would like that, wouldn't they? "That is so tempting, but I have been told I'm supposed to help Dillon no matter what to stop the flood of blood."

Elke paled, momentarily, and then she rallied. "What did you say?" she asked. He repeated it. "That came from the seer, Jada, didn't it? Do you believe her?"

Troy groped for a moment. "Some. Dillon is alive. He is near the Brown Cemetery at your place. Silke and I share a connection, though, we aren't married like she thought."

"The seer saw you married to Silke?"

"She warned me about dark-eyed women," Troy replied. "Oh, you just happen to have beautiful eyes, dark chocolate with red-hot cinnamon swirls. Though Mona didn't see them that way. They were black and silver, like the flashing of two knives in the dark."

"Fine. Do it your way. I know you and Dillon are friends. People change. You were warned."

"What did he learn?"

"Something about the Von Damme mansion in Wreythville, but you suspected that. He expects you to keep his secret for another two days. Do you have any more leads?"

"You're the best I have. Then there is Paleface. I can't remember his name, but he reminds me of Aunt Jada's old fiancée who vanished back in the 1940s. He seems to have resurfaced recently, as wild as that sounds. I keep seeing glimpses of him here, tonight," Troy said.

"What did you say?" Elke asked, staring. "Zane? Oh, darkness, no. You did see him on the lake. He beguiled you and Silke. Oh my, what a moment you two shared."

Troy blinked. He no longer saw anything around him. That

world faded as memories came to the fore. He was staring across the water at Paleface, into his red orbs glaring and demanding from the shadow of his big floppy hat. He seized control of Troy's body, and he felt helpless. Powerless. Frustrated. He wanted to flee, to fly, but his body wouldn't respond. It moved like it was on remote control, his brain unplugged from his machine. He steered the boat closer to death.

"I am profoundly shocked to see you alive. You must be a special person," she said.

Troy heard Elke's voice like a narrator as he relived some of that lost afternoon. Recall came flooding back, bringing a second, amazed emotion. Silke in heat and undressing caught his attention. She tried to jump ship, and he stopped her, and she slugged him. They went from grappling to kissing and entangled bodies hungry for more than pressing against each other.

The memory came as a pleasant shock. He now recalled that Silke didn't remember it, either from shock or from something Zane had done. "Seeing Silke . . . in danger saved my life."

As if Elke hadn't already done it to his mind, she began to dance in slow circles so she could visually search the crowd. "You may be Zane's target. I suspect he's upset you got away. Hmm. I am tempted to use you as bait, but I fear I might be unable to handle him alone. He is juiced, on PEDs, so to speak."

Troy had trouble shifting subjects, now having memories of Silke and Zane, a mixture of love and loathing. She made it sound like Zane was chemically enhanced. "Why is he here?"

"My first guess would be for vengeance. For Zane to display his power and feast, to create chaos and more. For half a century, they have been trapped below the waters and starved. And yet, you have already seen the Dark Lady Lyla and live, so more must be going on. You said she took the bracelet."

"Yes. Could they be repossessing Von Damme's jewelry?"

"Hmm. Possibly. The zealots of Von Damme's inner circle are lethal. We are in great danger with the two of them here. If there are more," she said, shuddering as her voice trailed off. "I have companions here to defend me, if necessary, but we don't want to turn downtown into a bloodbath." Her voice sounded practical, coolly ruthless.

Troy reeled. He recalled Mona's vision. This certainly seemed like the same woman.

Elke must have caught a glimpse of her in his eyes and thereby memories. "How can you have known Mona?"

"You killed her," Troy stated flatly.

She didn't deny it. "You say it with such certainty."

Troy had felt it. Could still feel it. She saw that in his eyes. "You were possessed by her ghost, weren't you? Dillon never told me about this."

"Why did you kill Mona?"

"She was also one step from becoming an enthralled vampire of Von Damme's. If she had escaped, she would have been a danger to others, finding herself hungry, desperate, confused and untrained. It was mercy."

"With that story, I'm expected to believe Dillon is safe? Who are you? What are you?" Troy asked.

"I am a watcher of sorts. A guardian, if you will, though certainly not a guardian angel. Von Damme, Zane, Lyla and their ilk are deadly to humanity, and a danger to the Rulers of Night. Von Damme and his disciples must be stopped. There isn't time to explain more. For the moment, you're in danger. You must leave. I will help Tom Marader. Now go!"

Troy felt the shove. He gathered his fear and stoked it, stirring him to depart. Troy seized those feelings, compartmentalizing them as he did with the fear that tried to keep him from doing crazy stuff.

Elke sighed heavily. "I give. I have no desire to hurt you when you're being stubborn and protective. Ah, there he is," Elke said, nodding. Tommy Boy and a voluptuous, blond with curls and wandering hands danced closely, bodies pressed against each other. He didn't recognize the woman, but it wasn't Lyla. Everyone around her seemed too relaxed. Could she turn her appeal and fear off and on?

He realized he had been away from Raquel for a while. He didn't see her, or her bodyguard, and that alarmed him.

"I suggested she powder her nose. I didn't think she should have to watch us dance, since she has strong emotions for you," Elke said. "Ah, your warning was fortuitous. Don't move."

Troy felt rooted. He loathed this powerless feeling, his body a puppet to someone else's whims and word. He struggled futilely while he watched his best, untrustworthy lead to Dillon stalk off toward Marader.

As if Troy's eyes were drawn to his pallor and darkness, he spotted Zane zeroing in on Marader. The nightwalker commandingly steered his dancing partner, Rae Kirkland, through the throng of attendees. The reporter wore a blissful smile, no idea she was in danger. She didn't even notice when Zane bumped Denny and his wife aside.

Colleen stumbled, and Zane apologized as he stopped her fall, grabbing her wrist and giving her a quick jerk, swinging her around into her husband. Her head awkwardly slammed into his chest. Denny caught her as she crumpled. Zane slipped away as the couple slowly slumped to the ground.

Troy wanted to scream. Damn, Elke. He was stuck when he wanted to tackle Zane, so he wouldn't get in Elke's way. She glided gracefully between couples on a route to intercept Zane.

The SOB hipped Rae. She staggered and fell into Marader who let go of his partner to catch Rae. Zane moved so swiftly he blurred. Troy blinked, almost missing Zane drawing a switchblade, popping the blade and slashing.

Troy tried to yell a warning when a chilling breeze struck him. The ankh on his chest flared painfully hot. Was Lyla near? Or was there a third zealot of Von Damme's in attendance? That pain freed Troy even as dread overwhelmed him. He foolishly tried to intervene and tackle the newcomer, a whip-like figure with swarthy skin.

"Elke, look out!" Troy shouted.

All Troy remembered were the vampire's eyes, livid and black. He didn't even see the creature move, but in less than a blink, Troy found himself flying backwards. During his airborne moment, time seemed to slow.

Elke whirled. She snatched the newcomer, Whip, by the shirt. Spinning in a blur and moving like a hammer thrower, she hurled him off the dance floor. Whip sailed over heads, a dark blur that must have landed somewhere near the street.

Nobody noticed. How could nobody see it?

The wake of love continued even as vampires fought. They moved faster than what seemed reasonable and real, so anyone seeing them would doubt their own eyes.

With a left-handed slash, Zane cut along the bottom of Marader's backpack. A flash of silver fell into his right hand.

Troy finally crash-landed into somebody. Time returned to normal, the speed of adrenaline, fight or flight.

"What do you know? It's raining Troy Bane. What else is up?" Spider asked.

"Zealots of Von Damme are here, after Marader and the jewelry box. I think Colleen was injured," Troy pointed.

Spider took a moment to process his words. "That sucks."

Marader must have sensed the loss of his precious jewelry box, the shift in weight or the absence of its presence. He whirled, swinging an elbow and connecting, stunning Zane. Marader grabbed the box, cutting his hands, but he hung on, caught in a tug of war with a dazed Zane. Paleface kicked out, taking out Marader's legs. As he fell down, he lost control of the jewelry box. It seemed to slip free in a spray of blood.

Elke arrived in time to blindside Zane, adding to his momentum. He lost a grip on the jewelry box as he tumbled across a table. It tilted then collapsed. Mugs and glasses fell, shattering and splashing.

"Not here, Zane!" Elke said.

"You!" Zane shook it off, uncoiling to his feet, seeming

taller and fiercer. He was gawky and lean, dressed in black and grays. His pale complexion was flushed, his dark eyes engorged, and his nostrils flared. He smiled, showing off a row of perfect and sharp-looking teeth. He stopped grinning when he took into account the number of smartphones being trained on the conflict and glared. He seemed to reach a decision. A mist gathered around his feet and swiftly rose to surround him.

"Fight! Have a ball with a brawl! Whack a neighbor!" he shouted. His movements blurred as he darted to shove a man, toss a chair, and knock over a nearby table, spilling its contents. He pushed Mr. Fleenor atop it all.

Zane's words and actions incited.

After a short pause, as if everyone had resisted for a moment, the group of mourners turned lovers changed moods. Caring people turned irrationally hostile and violent. Even the Bristol Virginia police officers working as security were affected. Fists cracking jaws, they joined the melee instead of stopping it.

How could he stop this when Troy wanted to fight? It had been coming for Marader for a long time. He started after Tommy Boy. Someone grabbed Troy, so he whirled.

"Easy, Rocky. It's me. Let's get out of here. Be a lover not a fighter. I promised your doctor I'd take care of you, and you don't dare take a hit," Raquel said. She kissed him, leaving him reeling. She was right.

Hand in hand, she dragged him through the fight. Not everyone was slugging it out. A few had suddenly seen reason or been less affected like Raquel. Some simply fled, ducking and dodging. Those emotionally caught up in it all duked it out like something from a cliché western flick. What was happening to Bristol?

He suspected Zane was long gone. Where was Elke?

The best strategy was to not be there. Still, Troy had no choice but to elbow punch a guy to protect Raquel.

The brawl intensified into a vicious street fight. Bestial

natures reared. Teeth were barred, leading to growls, snarls and biting. Women scratched and clawed each other. Fists already sore and knuckles broken, wild men picked up chairs and swung them.

Someone large jumped on Troy's back. He shifted and flipped him over his shoulder and onto the ground where Jambo landed with an explosive grunt, having the wind knocked out of him. With the impact, Jambo's eyes seemed to clear. Troy's friend had attacked him. Everyone was crazy.

"Sorry. I don't know what I was thinking," Jambo said.

"You'll be sorrier," Paul snapped. He attacked Troy. Pat's younger brother was almost a pacifist, so Zane's command must have been powerful.

Troy dodged and grabbed a mug of beer. He threw it in Paul's face. The splash worked, and Paul blinked, coming back to himself. "Yuck, I hate lite beer," he spat.

"Troy! Look out!" Raquel screamed.

He turned in time to partly deflect the blow from one of the muscle-heads from the State Street Gym and Spa. It still caught Troy on the chin enough to ring his bell. His knees slowly buckled, and he slipped to the ground, groping about and wondering what happened.

He knew the muscle-head was going to hit him again, but he couldn't stop him.

Raquel took him out with a chair over the head. "What's gotten into everybody?" she screamed, her face flushed.

Two great booms reverberated throughout downtown. A moment later, light and sparks exploded against the dark sky, the fireworks catching everyone's attention. The dazzling chrysanthemum of fire was followed by purple stars and golden weeping willows. As they descended, symphonic music blasted out of the speakers' system, forcing everyone to grab their ears. The fighting had stopped. The light show jarred everyone out of the grip of berserking rage.

"Everyone, relax. Get a grip. Help someone who needs it and start cleaning up!" J-Man announced.

Next out of the speakers was the Beatles', "All You Need Is Love". Good old Eagle Scout, Troy thought and smiled.

His head was full of fuzz. Time passed strangely while people regathered their wits, walked around dazed and apologized, wondering how this could happen.

"Troy, man, it's time to go. Knives sent me to get you. We're going to the East Hill Cemetery. He got a call from someone there who found John's body in a fresh grave," J-Man said.

"You're going to a graveyard?" Raquel asked, incredulous.

"It can't be much more dangerous than this wake," J-Man pointed out.

"I can't believe I hit somebody with a chair," Raquel groaned.

"And I thank you. I'll see you tomorrow," Troy said.

He turned to go, but Raquel stepped into his path and into his arms, ready to be kissed. "Just in case, well, the off chance something happens." She didn't wait for Troy, kissing him, then it didn't matter who started it. The kiss was long, sticky and sweet, and somehow all too short at the same time.

"Does she make you feel that way?" Raquel asked before slipping away. Her bodyguard met her, and they departed the scene. Paparazzi were still here, but they were also part of the news. Even so, more cameras followed Raquel.

"I'm a fool," Troy said.

"The first step to change is realization. But I'm afraid you're about to go up in flames, or is it down in flames?" J-Man asked.

Troy gave him a look. He gestured to a photographer. Troy immediately recognized Deng who noticed and slipped away.

"What will Silke say when she sees the photos of you two sucking face?" J-Man asked.

"She would ask me if I learned anything," Troy said. Elke's command to stay away from Silke hounded him. Had Elke really told him the truth? Troy wanted to tell J-Man about Dillon. He opened his mouth several times, but he couldn't find the final will to speak.

"And did you?"

"That I'm crazy about two women," he said. Between the influence of the bracelet and Zane, Troy wasn't sure about the emotions of either Silke or Raquel.

"Crazy is a good word for it."

"Enough. You said Knives left already."

"Yeah. The guy he was talking to was cut off. When Stephen hit redial, all he got was voice mail. He told me to get you, then he raced off. This guy works the night shift at the hospital. He also got reamed for losing the body."

On the way to his truck, J-Man tried calling Knives, getting his voice mail. They waited for two ambulances, lights flashing, to drive by and park at the wake. Troy couldn't help but wonder about Colleen Rentzel. What had Zane done to her?

"We'll be there in five," J-Man said.

Twenty-Five: Grave Concerns

The sound of the truck door closing jarred Troy awake. He mentally wrestled open his eyes, catching a glimpse of J-Man in the headlights as he ambled to the gothic metal gates of the EHC. Troy struggled to remember what that was.

J-Man slipped in through a person-sized door in the right gate and disappeared into the night. In J-Man's flashlight beam, Troy spotted tombstones and grave markers, angels, crosses, and monoliths. Off to his right, Knives' sports car, the red Spyder, gleamed in the truck's headlights. The brilliant color called to mind a stop sign.

How tired was he? Troy had fallen asleep on the way, still buckled in.

For a moment, Troy thought this might be a nightmare, sitting alone in a truck with its headlights on, illuminating black gates with scrollwork, EHC.

He was here because Knives had been called by someone

from East Hill who had found John's body. The cemetery sat on the edge of downtown, its acreage split between Tennessee and Virginia, and set close behind the Presbyterian Church. Both were National Historic Landmarks. The graveyard held civil war era history with specific areas commemorating black and confederate soldiers.

Why did he keep finding himself in graveyards? Three in less than twenty-four hours? He did not have a death wish. Really, he didn't. Oh sure, he was smitten with two amazing women, one who had broken his heart and trust but never lost his love, while the other would lead to broken bones and perhaps paralysis or death, not to mention the possible loss of friendship with his blood brothers. And, he was searching for a best friend who had been captured by a gorgeous creature able to read minds and command obedience. Not to mention, Troy had felt her kill somebody. Elke wanted him distracted, out of the way, and away from Silke, so he wouldn't be looking for Dillon.

Now, Troy wanted to confront Dillon. He wanted answers.

No. No death wish.

The haze had thickened. The limited visibility further unnerved him. The fog and smoke wafted heavily in the headlights, coiling around the bars of the gates. Rivulets of condensed fog ran down the windows. The Spyder sat beaded and dripping like it was hot and nervous. His friends had left the headlights on, blazing through the gate, casting long shadows on the road and illuminating the smoky fog.

Troy didn't want to wake Silke, but he knew she would be concerned when injured people from Pat's wake showed up at the hospital. He started to wish she were here, then he rethought it, recalling he was outside a cemetery. His phone only had fifteen percent charge left.

He quickly typed and sent Silke a text message. Met Elke Swear. Knows Aunt J. Zane here after TM's jewelry box. Brawl. IM ok. At East Hill C w K & J-M.

He wanted to type to her about Dillon and his new lady

love, but his fingers refused. How could he not tell her? Dillon knew he was a horrible liar. Did he want Troy to piss off his sister? Then it struck him. Maybe Dillon did. He had lied about Troy to Silke and vice versa.

The sports car's headlights went dark, likely timed out, but still eerie.

Troy unbuckled and looked around for a flashlight. Buried under flares and fireworks, he found one, a Mag-Lite. He took the LED flashlight, a flare, two roman candles, and a pocket-sized fountain called Happiness. He carried them mostly from a memory of the roman candle battle they had enjoyed in a graveyard on All Hallows Eve their junior year. It seemed like a good idea to take several light sources into a graveyard.

Could Lyla or Zane be here? Why hadn't he thought of that before? He hated having a concussion. People doubted him. He doubted himself.

He entered the graveyard through the classic-style metal black gate and paused, hearing movement. He lost sight of everything, as the truck's headlights turned off, leaving him in the dark and briefly blind. He paused, letting his eyes adjust. The fog and smoke distorted sounds and clung like a wet sheet. His attention was drawn to interesting headstones, cherubs, crucifixes, open Bibles, stone flames, and one shaped like a loyal dog.

Just ahead, J-Man stopped texting on his phone and continued uphill, passing by history and the marked passage of lives.

"Knives, buddy, where are you? Stephen?!" J-Man yelled. Troy was about to call out when he heard his friend's surprise. "Hey . . ."

Troy instinctively moved behind a tree. He thought he'd heard a thud. He would have assumed a prank, and yet, the last few days had been odd. He wished he remembered more of it. Knowledge was power, and he was standing in the dark about to whistle through the graveyard.

Something obstructed the light coming from the caretaker's shed next to a larger concrete bunker building, looking more like an office. Troy sensed the figure stood silently while malevolently studying the surroundings for life. Troy didn't know why he had stepped behind the tree, staying out of sight, but he felt protected and comforted. After a long minute of listening to his heart, controlling his breathing and feeling his sweat drip, Troy heard the shed door shut.

Ahead, he could see light thrown from the small structure, out the window and around the ill-fitting door. He imagined a hanging lamp swinging back and forth. The smoke gave the semblance of movement everywhere, but Troy didn't see any shadows at the shed or hear any sounds. Troy tried J-Man's phone. It sounded from inside, playing Troy's ringtone: "One Big Rush" by Joe Satriani.

Inside, shadows shifted, light playing through the fog. The number connected then disconnected. That wasn't good. Could they have stumbled onto a crime? Body snatchers and organ stealers? Could that be the reason behind all the problems?

With no idea what was going on, Troy tried calling Deputy Burt, only to get voice mail. He left a message, and then dialed 911, getting a fast-busy signal. Circuits were still jammed, likely from the brawl, and perhaps the aftermath. Who knew what effect Zane had on people?

Troy turned on his ever-ready camera, sparing his phone charge, and crept stealthily to the side of the shed. He moved quietly along the wall, and it was just as well when a figure stood in the window, blocking the light.

Troy sensed a warmth on his chest as the ankh grew unpleasantly hot. He wondered again, what had Aunt Jada given him? Did Silke's do this?

"I'm sorry J-Man, Stephen. I wish you hadn't gotten involved. I wish I hadn't ever come home. Ah, life is full of regrets. Except, I'm not even alive, and I will regret killing you. How is that possible? I truly wish it were otherwise, but there is no disobeying this supernatural hunger," the man whispered in a gravelly voice, as if he hadn't used it in a long time. Cold and flat, it lacked humanity.

Troy had to suppress a shudder. Who would want to kill his friends?

The shadow turned as the figure moved away from the window. Troy held his breath and peeked up through the window into the shed. He couldn't believe his eyes. That had to be a man who just looked like a dead-tired John holding a hatchet over his friends, J-Man and Knives. Behind them was a third body. The caretaker, Troy assumed. By the way the impostor John held the hand ax, there would be blood soon. Did Troy have time to go back for J-Man's rifle?

"It might be just as well you die this way, my blood brothers. Lots of people will die horribly in a coming act of vengeance. Even now, Von Damme rebuilds his strength. Then, soon, oh so soon, the water will rush and his legacy will be free, God help us. No. I can no longer say us, for I am no longer one of you," Impostor John said.

Troy blinked. The John-lookalike knew they were blood brothers. It couldn't be John. He was dead. Troy felt analysis paralysis. How could this be? John alive?! Troy had seen the body. Knives had checked it. What to do?

"I know, if you were conscious, you would find it hard to believe I don't want to do this. Where's the cavalry?"

Troy sensed he only had moments. Charging in seemed like a poor idea without a weapon. He clicked his Bic and lit up the Happiness fountain. As he fled the area, he kicked the wall under the window. He heard a huh of surprise and saw the shadow move, rising, getting larger. Impostor John peered out the window. "Who is that?"

The pyrotechnic fountain erupted, turning his question into a scream.

The silvery sparks and fiery red bees would have blinded Troy, but he briefly closed his eyes. When he cracked them open, he almost screamed, too. He still couldn't believe his eyes, so he took a video of Impostor John, his pale face bleached in the dazzling silver and red brilliance of the gushing firework fountain. In his raised right hand, he wielded the hatchet. The light flared off the sharp edge, and for the moment, it remained unsoiled and unbloodied.

The light revealed a shovel. Troy grabbed it and swung, disarming the impostor. He snarled as the hand ax went tumbling through the air. It stuck solidly in the wall behind him. Troy swung again, but Impostor John ducked and backed away with tremendous speed and agility, like a gymnast on amphetamines.

"Ah, who could this be? Who would be concerned about me? Looking for me? Is it you, Troy? I hope not," he said. Impostor John looked like his best bud, but his eyes were bloodshot and inky black. "I don't want to kill you, too. You would be better to run away. You know, brave, brave Sir Troy, he bravely ran away."

Troy couldn't believe his ears. When did lunatics spout Monty Python? In a panic, he bolted. He raced downhill, dodging headstones and jumping over graves. The smoke seemed to have shifted, and the gibbous moon, near full, shined with silvery light so he could almost see the ground under a thick layer of fog. It looked like he ran on the mists, but it felt hard underfoot. He still wasn't much better than a chicken with its head cut off.

What kind of nightmare was this? John back from the dead? Ready to kill his friends. John wouldn't kill them, now, not yet. He would chase Troy, knowing Troy would go for J-Man's truck first and the rifle.

He passed the statue of a black soldier and started to enter through a gateway. He knew he hadn't come this direction. Where was he? The rolling hills blocked his view of the road, but he finally heard a car driving by the entrance. He headed that direction.

Moments later, he heard footsteps close behind. Troy broke into a trot. Behind him, the footfalls ran after him. He glanced over his shoulder, not seeing anything.

Troy's knee buckled. He tripped and tumbled. He landed on his side and slid across the damp grass. It seemed slow enough that he should be able to stop, but Troy inexorably skimmed along, then over the edge into a freshly dug grave. He crashed to the bottom, enough to jar him. Earth sprinkled atop him in a shower of dirt.

He fought his instinct to jump up and out. To keep running. Why did he run? He had been armed with a shovel and had disarmed John. How was he alive? Had lookalike John compelled him, too? Troy had endured more than enough. He forced himself to be still and calm. During an emergency, making just one smart decision could save your life.

"It seems such a waste. You die on the mountain but come back, amazing everyone. You almost died in Von Damme's mansion, escaping, unlike me, and now, you're going to die here," John said. He sounded closer, then he grew silent.

Troy strained to listen. Could John hear Troy's breathing? He forced himself to relax, to calm his heart, and control his runaway emotions. He grabbed them and held fast, then he compartmentalized them. He would face this as Martin expected, heroically.

When John next spoke, he was so close, he could have been standing over the grave getting ready to toss down a heap of earth. "That makes you wonder if there's a god, doesn't it, Troy? You can't elude me for long. I am a creature of the night and feast on blood. I will smell yours again soon enough," he continued, his voice getting quieter as he walked on by and toward the gates.

Climbing out of the grave, Troy hid in the shadow of a large cross tombstone. Why hadn't he smelled Troy? For whatever reason, Troy was grateful. He shook off some dirt and removed his phone, finding its battery had died. He pulled the roman candles out of his pocket. He had broken them.

He could hear John talking to himself, calling out, "Do you hear me Troy?" It was like John wanted to be heard as he stalked closer to the entrance and parked vehicles. A motorcycle roared by, casting light. John's shadow stretched long with the bars of the gate, like he was leaving a cell and walking toward the gallows. Troy decided to double back. He hoped J-Man had his sidearm with him. Usually, that would work, but would it do any good against whatever John had become?

Troy's knee threatened to give out again but held as he darted from shadow to shadow. The lights of the caretaker's shack drew him much as a moth to a flame. He prayed the results were different.

He paused next to a tree near the small building. He saw and heard nothing. How long would John be gone? How could it even be John? Troy tried not to think about it. He could work it out after Knives and J-Man were safe. After another moment of hesitation, of listening, Troy slipped to the door. He could hardly hear anything over his heart drumming in his ears.

Pushing the door open, he entered the caretaker's shack. The building was larger than it looked, part garage and office, with tools hanging on and standing against the wall. His blood brothers were crumpled on the floor, along with another body. All three appeared to have been knocked unconscious.

Troy grabbed a shovel handle, its blade long gone. He set a bucket just outside the arc of the door swinging open, hoping to trip up anybody coming in.

Troy knelt next to J-Man and shook him gently, even as he kept his attention up, his head on a swivel. J-Man groaned, and Troy remained insistent, shaking a little harder. "Wake up but be quiet."

It sounded like the door opening and the bucket tumbling, but when Troy glanced up, it was closing. The bucket bounced into him. Trouble neared, as the ankh grew hot. He turned back to J-Man, and John loomed there. He seized Troy and lifted him in a death grip by the neck on the verge of choking Troy. He kicked out, landing a hard blow to John's chest. He felt ribs crunch and bone give way.

"If I were alive, that would have hurt, maybe even disabled me. But, I am Undead, dead damned by Von Damme. That makes me powerful. I am difficult to harm, and I heal quickly. I also have no control over my body. I would prefer to be saving you instead of killing you. But then, I can't be in my right my mind. Last night, I walked naked down State Street. Likely, it's against the law in both states!"

Troy twisted and landed a knee punch.

"I can't stop me. You can't stop me. Stab me. Shoot me. Those will slow me down, Undead John, a little, anyway. Staking me just puts me on pause. Only the water and sunlight will destroy me. Unless you brought holy water. Even if you had reached the rifle, it wouldn't have mattered. I don't know what decapitating would do. Hmm."

Troy clawed at the hands. He kept kicking, but he saw spots before his eyes. The ankh grew intensely hot. Undead John was going to kill him, Troy thought. He saw a strange mixture of determination and regret, even pity, when John's eyes changed, a touch of surprise, a hint of feeling. Troy smelled smoke and dimly wondered what burned. His own chest?

The sound of gunfire shook the shack. The shots thundered and echoed inside the place, deafening Troy. Undead John laughed, confidently, like the real John. Troy must be seeing things, because John's arms smoldered, smoke rising from his flesh up to his shoulders.

"Ah!" Undead John screamed. Troy heard a whooshing, flame flaring up. The vice suddenly released, letting go of his throat.

Thank God, Troy could breathe. He barely noticed being dropped, now gasping for air. His entire world swam. His chest felt afire over his heart. What had happened? His questing fingers found the ankh, nearly scalding hot.

"What are you?" J-Man asked. He held a gun on John.

Undead John stared at his burning hands. Flames flickered from his fingers. Looking confused, John rubbed them to extinguish them. His hands seemed thinner, more skeletal and resembling claws, but they were unburnt. He reached for J-Man. "I am your death."

The Smith & Wesson muzzle flashed like lightning when J-Man shot him, again.

Thunder seemed trapped inside the shack.

Undead John staggered back. The bullet wounds began to close. "I am more than human. I am a superior breed now. I am beyond the normal reach of death. I live by night. Feed on blood. Dole out lust, fear and finality."

"What are you saying? You're a vampire?" J-Man stammered.

"You know, I believe you're right. Yes, you must kill me. You can't, but please, I am rooting for you," Undead John said. He raised a hatchet and approached at a steady pace on J-Man who fired repeatedly. Four bullets found their target in Undead John's heart. He staggered back a step at the impacts.

"Where's Sherry?" J-Man asked.

Undead John looked ready to cry, but he could no longer offer tears. "Von Damme stole her body. He plans to rise, renew his cult and destroy Bristol, Blountsville, everything."

Troy grabbed a rake and jabbed. The handle slipped between Undead John's legs, snapping it and making him fall forward. He fell on the blade of his hatchet, stabbing himself. Laughing hysterically, he sat up and removed it. He was wounded but didn't bleed. "I can't even kill myself! Now, if I had landed on the handle that would stop me."

Troy and J-Man glanced at each other, each knowing they were about to die. Undead John shrugged off bullets and a stab to the lungs. Even if he wasn't a vampire, he was certainly a monster, about to be a murderer.

"I really like Silke. She's incredible, a lot like Sherry. I would have challenged Dillon, but Silke only had eyes for you, Troy. She was crushed when you died and thrilled when you lived. She'll hate me. I hate myself. Kill me! Come on! Stake a jab at it," Undead John said.

J-Man swung a shovel. John caught it, but J-Man let go, driving a shoulder into him. The blow staggered John.

Troy tripped him, adjusted the broken rake handle and prayed. John landed right on it, the makeshift stake exploding out through his chest. He died with a smile on his face.

"Thank you. Now . . . leave me . . . to cook in the sun," he said, then his body relaxed and lied still.

J-Man rolled off the body and jumped to his feet. "What the hell?! Was that thing really John?"

Twenty-Six: Body of Debate

Troy felt lucky and blest to position the broken handle just right. He was thrilled to be alive, but it grew bittersweet when he took in John's joyful smile. The expression tortured Troy as he reasoned with himself. It had been him or them.

John wasn't staring accusingly. Besides, it hadn't been John. He was dead. Undead John had wanted to die. Die again? Really die? This was insane.

The moment stretched long while he and J-Man stared at the body. Seeing J-Man alive eased some of Troy's guilt. He finally grabbed a small tarp and covered the corpse, as if doing so would erase what happened.

"What in the hell is going on? That . . . he looked like John . . . I know John is dead. I saw him dead. Knives confirmed it. And . . . I shot him. He . . . he healed. So fast. Almost up. Four shots to the heart," J-Man said until he slipped into an uncharacteristic profanity fit, showing how freaked out he felt. "I'm so confused. Troy, did we just kill somebody?"

"No, we didn't. We found John's body. He was already dead. He even said so," Troy said. He winced at his own words.

"You do realize how ridiculous that sounds?" J-Man asked.

"Yes but look at him. Those wounds almost healed. Look at his hands and arms. They're burned from touching me," Troy said. He checked the ankh. The skin around it was red and swollen. "It burned me, too, but nothing like him. It was warning me and protecting me."

"Warning you of what?"

"I'm not sure. Silke's aunt gave us each an ankh. She claimed there are night walkers, vampires, loose in the Tri Cities."

"You have headed down the crazy road."

"All I did was spend two days with Silke searching for Dillon. Maybe I am deranged," Troy sighed. "I've seen ghosts, an evil mansion, wolves and now John, who is supposed to be dead, trying to kill me and you and Knives. Yep, I'm certified, but you, you're not. Still, you shot a walking dead man who shrugged off bullets and healed the wounds. Jay, he knew stuff about us. Stuff only John would know. And he wanted to die. He wanted to fail. He wanted us to live. He told us how to stop him."

"Yeah, I guess he did, didn't he?" J-Man said. He thought a long moment, remaining stoic. "What now?"

"I don't know. Do you think anybody is going to believe what happened here?"

"Hell no! I don't believe what happened here until we look under the plastic. If he's a vampire, he could be gone. I can't believe I said that," J-Man said. He peeked under the tarp anyway. John's corpse remained smiling, reminding too much of a pale-painted clown, the Joker, silently telling them the truth.

"The jokes on us. Life and death aren't what we think," Troy said. He started to laugh but caught it. If he got started, he might not be able to stop. "John said sunlight would destroy him and free his spirit. I think we should do that."

"You mean leave his body in the sun? That isn't going to happen. As soon as we call the sheriff, they'll put him someplace cool and dark for an autopsy." J-Man said.

From nearby, somebody moaned. Troy startled, then he realized the caretaker stirred.

"What if Undead John rises again?" Troy asked.

"What are you suggesting? We take the body?" J-Man asked.

Down the crazy road.

"How about borrow? Relocate?" Troy asked.

"I was kidding!" J-Man said.

"What do you suggest?" Troy asked. He watched his friend struggle with the decision.

"God, I don't feel like we have any choice. We owe John that much," J-Man finally agreed.

"That and we don't want him to revive and kill people. I think that's what happened in the hospital morgue," Troy said.

"No way I want to live with that."

"Dillion and my old sensei would say it's honorable to kill one to save many."

"Like I said, no good choices. Let's do it," J-Man said.

J-Man located the gate keys on a ring hanging by the door. He walked down, unlocked the gate and returned with his truck.

"I can't believe I'm doing this," J-Man said.

All the while, Troy waited for somebody to move, and he couldn't help but think what John had said about Silke. It chimed with what one of the muscle-heads had said. Troy realized he remembered the code he had used to encrypt the video of their pontoon adventure. He jotted it down on his wrist.

They wrapped John's body in the tarp, put it in a pine box and loaded in the back of the truck. J-Man closed and locked the top, then he drove off for Marader's Marina.

Troy called 911 again, this time with Knives' phone and made it through to the Bristol dispatcher. He was told, that with all the activity, it would be a little while before anyone could be sent since it wasn't a life or death emergency. Any more, Troy wanted to add. He texted J-Man the news. To Silke, Troy's text only mentioned her need to contact him using Knives' number.

Knives' phone immediately rang, and the caller ID display said Silke. Troy answered. He wanted her to know he was all right. Was he, all right?

"Troy. Hi! They've been bringing in people from the brawl. How are you? Where are you?"

"I am okay. There was a fight over Marader's jewelry box. Now I'm with Knives and the caretaker of East Hill Cemetery. They were assaulted, but they're okay. We are waiting for the authorities."

"I wish Tommy would get rid of that box. Did you learn anything helpful from anybody?"

How to answer that? He had learned there was such a thing as nightwalkers, vampires, led by Von Damme and John was under his influence, now one of the undead. Oh, yeah, they had learned something. But could they prove it? "Sorry. My mind is spinning. It's a long story. I'd rather tell you in person with the sun shining."

"Did you find what you were looking for? Find John's body?"

"That's part of the long story."

"Aunt Jada is doing all right. I'll drive out to you."

He pictured her having a flat tire or pulling over to help someone that turned out to be a vampire. "No!" Troy said. He said it with enough emphasis that Knives stirred and started to snore. On the other end, Silke might have flinched.

Would it sound insane to tell her he believed more than one vampire was out hunting? How many coffins had there been? Five?

"Ah, I see. You could just tell me you're with Raquel instead of concocting this story," Silke said.

Fortunately, Knives was snoring. Troy held the phone next to him, and Knives rewarded him with a snort followed by a long, reverberating, chortling snore. "There, are you happy?"

"Wow. The Silver Goddess snores like a guy. I never read that in any of the articles or photo captions," Silke chuckled.

"He smells like one, too, but with a touch of antiseptic."

"Okay, why don't you want me to come out there?"

"Listen, it would sound ridiculous over the phone, and it might be dangerous to drive out. That said, Aunt Jada would believe what happened to us tonight, but I doubt anybody else would."

"Troy, are you all right? You don't sound like yourself."

Ha. No, he was definitely a long way from all right, he thought. His best friend was in hiding and wouldn't let him tell his sister, who he had been told to stay away from, and the other best friend was one of the undead who had just tried to kill them.

"I don't feel like myself. It's been sort of surreal. I want you to be safe, okay?" he asked. He was only abetting in the transporting of a friend's dead, or undead, corpse out to the lake to test whether it was a vampire, or not, by letting the morning sun wash over him. Why would Troy be nervous? "Promise me you won't come out until light."

"All right, if you promise me you won't go anywhere else tonight or do anything stupid, I'll be out to the marina before dawn."

"I can promise the first. I don't know about the second. Trouble seems to find me," Troy said.

He had wanted to tell her that he had missed her, but Elke's voice rebuked him, intervening and silencing him.

Knives and the caretaker awakened. Both remembered nothing, which was helpful, but they kept asking questions, repeating them after he had answered them.

J-Man returned long before the police arrived.

Tennessee law enforcement officers Deputies Steele and Green took statements. The questions were similar to those asked earlier by Knives. Like him, the deputies repeatedly asked their same questions in different ways. Troy was familiar with the technique by now, having dealt with the concussed as well as the nosy and curious.

J-Man, Knives and Antonio frustrated law enforcement

with their memory lapses. Troy's answers were too fantastic to believe. Deputy Green gave them all the evil eye, likely his cop sixth sense telling him there was more to the story than an assault and vanished, missing body. He reminded them to call when they remembered something.

Troy accepted Knives' keys for the Spyder when Dr. Killjoy complained of blurred vision. Troy climbed into the driver's seat. He buckled while Knives slid into the passenger seat.

"Well, I didn't see this coming. Who knew I would be chauffeuring you around?" Troy said.

Knives groaned. "The concussed driving the concussed."

"I sure appreciate you letting me drive your fancy car. Does this count as strenuous activity?" he asked.

"Don't try to be funny when my head hurts. Start her up," Knives said. He coached and cautioned Troy in starting, driving and handling the car. "Usually you need to take a special driving course, so be extremely careful. You step on the gas too hard, you'll be doing 120 in a few seconds."

Out on the road, Troy felt like he was trying to tame a wild animal, feeling lucky to make it to Maraders. The Spyder's steering, acceleration, and braking were hyper sensitive, responding at the speed of thought.

The fog appeared as they neared the lake, thickening as he eased onto the gravel road to Maraders Marina. Troy could barely see ten feet ahead, so he slowed down even more. Is this how Walt had run into the wolf? Troy wondered.

He had flashes of wolves attacking the Land Rover, bouncing off it and breaking the windshield. Jaws and teeth snapping at them. Silke bravely protected the wounded dog by shooting at the wolves. The beasts had shrugged it off. Whatever Elke had done to him had unlocked those memories.

J-Man's truck sat next to Dillon's near the gangway. In the diffused lamp light, the fog wafted in layers of white, gray, brown and yellow. Troy parked, checked Knives' vitals, and then left the sleeping doctor locked in his car.

J-Man and Troy went to work, sweating profusely while they unloaded the pine box onto a dolly with industrial-sized wheels. J-Man rolled it down to the dock where they could keep an eye on John's body. All the while, Troy felt watched. He hoped there weren't any Paparazzi lurking, though, werewolves would be worse.

"I feel weird about this," J-Man said.

"How odd. I feel perfectly normal," Troy replied sharply.

"Point made."

With the smoke swirling about them and to the serenade of desperate crickets and cicadas, they rolled the box up the gangway to the marina, around the side of the building, past the tanks, and set the pine box on the boards. Troy kept wiping the sweat out of his eyes. The air already felt muggy, and they had hours before sunrise.

"I think we should do a Viking funeral but keep the boat attached to shore with a couple of lanyards," J-Man suggested.

Troy nodded. He liked the idea.

"What are we going to tell Knives? After all, we expropriated a body," J-Man said.

"I know this goes against some of the things you believe, but we are investigating the truth."

"You're preaching to the choir. I hate breaking laws, but I shot him, in the heart, four times. Besides, we don't have to tell Knives the whole truth until the morning."

"The truth? What's that?" Spider asked from the shadows.

Troy jumped, nearly having a heart attack. J-Man cursed and drew his sidearm.

Their blood brother had been sitting perfectly still and quietly in the shadows. His head was down, and he seemed menacing, his head at an odd angle. "It's deceptive. Like the leaves really aren't green. We only see their true colors in the fall."

J-Man holstered his replacement gun. "Good, God. What are you doing hiding in shadows? You scared the piss out of me!"

"So that leaves only vinegar? I couldn't sleep so I came out here to meditate and pray. Did I hear mention of stealing a body? You said expropriating, but it amounts to the same thing."

Troy took a deep breath. "I misspoke. We're dealing with the supernatural and putting a friend to rest."

"I get it. Why don't you think Knives would accept this?"

"He would feel responsible for the body," Troy replied. He opened the pine box and showed Spider. His blood brother stood shocked, taking a few steps back. Finally, he gathered himself and studied the body.

After a moment, Spider settled and said. "He was animated. Walking and talking. Wasn't he?"

Troy didn't even ask how he knew. "Yeah. He tried to kill us."

"That counts as animated, all right, unless it was flatulence. John was known for his killer farts, after all. But, if he's a vampire, that stake is all that is keeping him from tearing out our throats. Pleasant thought that. What now?" Spider said. He appeared relaxed and calm, chatting about the undead.

Troy summarized events, including how John suggested they destroy him. Spider knew where there was a battered but buoyant canoe. It had washed up months ago. Marader stored it in the boneyard, a place for junk that might be useful in the future. Spider paddled it over to the dock near the pine box. Troy found a plank to use for a backboard. They arranged the board atop the canoe and tied it down. Two rope lines were set up as lanyards. Together, the blood brothers laid John on the board, hoping all the time he wasn't playing possum, waiting for them to get close. They loosely tied him on.

Troy heard Knives staggering down the gangway. J-Man intercepted him while Troy and Spider used towels to cover the body.

"Hi y'all. I almost hate to ask, but I have to know. How did I get here?" Knives asked.

"You already asked that," J-Man said.

"Really? I did? That's the sign of a concussion."

"That's what you said last time, too."

"Figures. Do you know what happened? Last I recall I was walking into the East Hill Cemetery to meet Antonio who had found John's body there in a fresh grave. That's it."

"You were assaulted by a muscular guy, reminded me of John," J-Man said.

Troy was afraid he would start laughing and coughed to cover it. Knives glanced at him. "You okay?" Dr. Killjoy asked. Troy nodded. "That explains my head, the bump, the pain, the memory loss, and dirt in my pockets. Did you report it?"

Troy droned on about giving reports to the police, repeating that they knew almost nothing. Nothing anyone would believe, Troy knew. He hoped Knives would go inside and sleep. He wasn't in any condition to drive home, and ignorance was bliss in this case, as the good doctor couldn't be held culpable if something went awry.

Knives cussed, unusual for him. "I hate concussions. I might be worthless for days." He slumped into a chair. "There's too many unanswered questions. Why would somebody attack us? Is he connected with John's missing body? Did you learn anything tonight about John or Dillon?"

Troy edited the conversation with Elke Swearington. He tried to tell them all the truth about Dillon, but her lie came easily to his lips. He hated it.

"What are we going to do about Dillon? He's bound to be dead. Drowned or hit his head. Do you think somebody murdered him and John? And if so, why? Why were we attacked? It makes no sense. It all started with those floating coffins, or even before maybe, with John diving Wreythville," Knives rambled on, so unlike him. He jumped afoot and paced. "What's under the towels?" His eyes narrowed and focused on the covered body.

Troy acted nonchalant. He wanted to drag his friend away, though, he knew eventually he would need to know the truth.

Was Troy that scared Undead John would rise again? "A surprise for John's wake."

"Ah. Surprise me in the morning," Knives yawned. He sat back and closed his eyes. "I may sleep after all. I'm couch bound."

Troy sighed with relief. He shared a long moment of silence with his blood brothers. J-Man wiped the sweat off his brow.

"That was close," Spider breathed.

"I thought he was going to unveil him," Troy said. He heard a car pulling into the lot. Its motor stopped.

"Here comes trouble," Spider said.

How were they going to hide the body? Troy wondered.

Perhaps J-Man was right. They should deal with this now.

Shortly, a car door slammed shut. They heard the infamous Marader laugh along with footfalls on the gangplank and dock. Moments later, Tommy Boy strolled languidly around the corner.

"Well, speak of the devil," J-Man said.

Marader smiled broadly, lighting up the night. His hands were bandaged, but he still held the jewelry box. He appeared weary and frustrated, both which showed in his eyes, not the usual blue but a strange reflective yellow.

"Ah, the Prodigal Son returns," Knives said as he pushed back outside through the screen door. It banged shut, sounding loud and echoing.

"Thanks, guy," Marader complained as he gingerly touched his ears.

"He has a concussion," Troy said. He sighed inwardly. This was going to come to a head. He prayed it didn't get ugly.

"Hey, is this the after-wake party? I thought that was tomorrow, but we can start tonight without the fights. The furniture is new, but boy, I could use a drink after talking to the cops for an hour and getting stitches," Marader said, grinning. He liked to scrap.

"From the brawl?" J-Man asked.

"Some shithead cut my pack and tried to take off with the box. We wrestled. I won, except for my paws. No biggie. They'll heal," Marader said, glancing at his bandaged hands.

Troy recalled the tug of war and spray of blood. He was surprised Marader still held the box. Troy remembered how the third assailant had tossed him.

"Man. What a night? What's Bristol coming to, huh?" Marader asked. He touched his nose gingerly. He was already getting double black eyes. "Let's break out a bottle of Tanqueray and crank some tunes. Troy, you look like you could use a belt from honeyed Jack, or just a honey."

"I would love one, but Dr. Killjoy's orders say no. It would mess up my mind," Troy said. That had already happened without the aid of alcohol. He wished Marader would call it a night and just go inside.

"Hey, Stephen, are you all right? Your eyes look kind of weird," Marader said.

"Knives took a hit on the head at East Hill," J-Man said.

"What? Come on, guys, what is it with you and graveyards?"

Knives explained why he had gone to the historical cemetery, how he had been called when John's body had been discovered. He had been pleased that sending out an alert to med schools, cemeteries and crematories had worked to find John.

Troy finished the story, mentioning how his arrival must have spooked the attacker. They had waited an hour for the authorities to show. Well, he hadn't lied.

"What's that?" Marader asked, nodding to the towel-draped canoe. Of course, Tommy Boy would notice. This was his dock, and Marader was right on target, strolling over to the body.

"A surprise for tomorrow," Troy said. He fought the urge to stop Marader. It was his dock.

With a toe, he flipped off a towel. Two slid off, revealing John's body, the rake handle sticking prominently out of his raw chest.

"What the . . .?" Marader gasped. He blanched and staggered a step. "Shit! Is that a dead body on my dock? John's! What were you thinking?" he asked as he whirled on J-Man.

Knives stared at the body then glared at Troy and J-Man. "Relax, Tommy, relax. It looks like John's corpse, if he had just died a little while ago, but now, after all this time, he would be bloated and discolored, plus he'd stink to high heaven, worse than he ever did after beer and pepperoni pizza. Good makeup, y'all. Nice try guys. Are you trying to piss us off? For a moment, I thought you'd found John's missing body. Not funny. Not at all," he said.

"Aw. I get it!" Marader laughed uneasily. "You guys made an effigy to burn. Hey, the likeness is amazing. Was this your work, Spider?" His smile faded to a puzzled expression, and he sniffed like he smelled something wrong. "Going with the horror angle, the stake in the chest, huh? Have you guys done mushrooms or something, tripping out? Peyote buttons? Mescal worms?"

Troy wondered if they should improv and roll with it, playing it up as an effigy.

Knives knelt by the body. He would know the truth in a moment. Troy was tired but gathered his courage for a fight. They were going to have it out right now. Why not? He didn't think Knives would drive the body back tonight. He might call the authorities. Or Marader might call, wanting the body off his precious marina. Troy couldn't really blame him, but it was one of them, a blood brother. They deserved to know the truth, and then they could deny if it they chose.

"Why does this waxy, or is it plastic, John lookalike have a stake in his chest?" Knives asked.

"You're certain that's not John?" J-Man asked

"Yes. If this were John, he would have bite wounds here, along his throat, and the body would be decomposed. There would be lividity, blood pooling, rigor mortis, and on and on. I see no sign of treatment or chemicals for viewing, and he is still flexible," Knives said. He lifted up a burnt arm, bending it at the elbow and wrist. "See. Feels like flesh when it's cool and clammy, but there's no sign of cell degeneration."

"What happened to his arms? And are those gunshot wounds? Is this what you think happened to John? If so, why the stake?" Marader muttered. His nostrils kept flaring, and his hands kept clenching like he was preparing to hit something.

"They're quite realistic, if you were going for partly healed," Knives yawned. "You guys should . . ." He paused and blinked at seeing John's tattoo of a water dragon on his left bicep. Curious, he checked the palm of John's hand, finding the slight scar from their blood brother rite. He looked inside John's mouth, seeing his bridge missing from when he had knocked out teeth while mountain biking. Knives opened his eyelids, checking the color. "You have the details down. What's the plan?"

"To send it off in the canoe and set it afire in the way of the Vikings. It's how John wanted to go," Troy said.

"True, and it would be against the law to use a real body, so this is a clever idea," Knives said.

Troy tried not to look at his blood brothers. Knives believed it was a fake, and he certainly sounded right, and Marader trusted the doctor. If Undead John had not tried to kill Troy, he would have believed Knives, too. Troy touched the bruises on his neck.

"How did you get those? Did those come from tonight's brawl? I should look at them under better light. No wonder you're addled. Let's go inside," Knives suggested.

Troy nodded. He thought they were off the hook, that the confrontation would wait until morning.

"Tommy, what's wrong?" J-Man asked.

Marader was sniffing around the body. He went from staring to gingerly poking the body. "Guys, this is not an effigy. It was alive once. Who or what is it?" Marader asked. He slowly turned and stepped away and aside from the body. "And where did you find it?"

"It's what the caretaker found when he called Knives, though nobody knows for sure because Antonio doesn't recall," J-Man said.

"No wonder he thought it might be John," Knives said.

"Stephen, check the wound will you, just for grins?" Marader asked. His frown told the story. For some reason, he was suspicious.

Knives sighed. At first, he reached right inside, expecting to find nothing but stuffing underneath the flesh, but he felt slimy viscera. "Is this really what Antonio found?" He started to remove the stake.

"Stop!" Troy said.

Spider was there ahead of J-Man and Troy, preventing Knives from removing the stake. "Leave it in. John wants it there."

Knives now looked worried. "Y'all concern me. Seriously."

Troy and J-Man nodded. "Is it or is it not John?" Troy asked.

"Of course not. I told you it couldn't be. A DNA test, or dental records would be conclusive."

"So is this even a real body?" Spider asked.

"Neither the blood or the body smell right. They don't have much of a scent at all, and as I mentioned, it isn't decaying, so is it plastic and rubber? The tattoo is perfect," Knives said.

"So this isn't a cadaver that looks like John? Like if he had a brother?" Spider asked.

Knives shook his head. "I'm sort of stumped. It looks real, feels sort of real, but it doesn't react like flesh and bone."

Marader sniffed. "Did you guys spray him with Axe after shave?" he asked. It was what John liked to use. The rest of them could barely stand the smell when he splashed it on himself. Knives swore it would become part of his skin.

"Of course not," Troy said.

In a blink, Marader shoved Troy, sending him flying back against the wall. Just as quick, Marader rushed in. Troy kicked out a foot, which slowed the attack. Tommy Boy slipped much of it to seize Troy by the shoulders. Angry eyes pinned him. Troy didn't flinch. "Tell the truth. What happened tonight?"

"Hey, take it easy. He already has a head injury," Knives said. He and J-Man tried to pull back Marader, but he stood his ground and pressed Troy.

"That will be the least of his worries. Now, the truth!" Marader demanded.

"Let him go! The guy who attacked Knives looked like John. Said he was John. That is his body right there. He fell on a rake while we were fighting," J-Man said.

"What kind of story is that? Have you been hit in the head, too?" Knives asked.

"Not buying it!" Marader slammed Troy into the wall again. J-Man tried to pull Marader away, but he slipped the grip and shoved his blood brother backwards. J-Man fell into the lake. Knives took a glancing blow, staggering back, holding his nose.

"You pinhead! I think you broke my nose!" Knives yelled.

Marader didn't seem to care, but Troy had endured enough. He violently kneed Marader in the gut, knocking the wind out of him, then with a shove, Troy sent him back, giving them breathing room. Despite being white-faced, Marader's eyes shone red with bloody murder in mind.

"Tommy, relax. They're jerking your chain," Knives said.

"We are not. John begged us to kill him. That he wasn't in control of his body," Troy began. "I took video, but the audio is messed up for some reason and John's face never appears."

"Why the bullet holes?" Marader gasped.

"John attacked Troy. I shot him. Yeah, multiple times. It didn't stop him. Hell, it didn't even slow him. He started to heal," J-Man said as he climbed out of the lake. "If you've ruined my phone, I'm going to kick the snot out of you."

"The police were at the wrong place," Spider said.

Knives cocked his head. "Really? That story is something else. But, look, there's no blood, like you shot and stabbed a corpse, and the bullet wounds, as I pointed out, look partly healed. Love the tall tale of undeadness, but was there really

John's body somewhere there? Tommy's right. We need the truth."

Troy gritted his teeth and spat out the next words. "Our attacker said his body was controlled by vampires, that only moving water, holy water or sun light would destroy him."

"I am going to schedule a CAT scan for you. You're seeing and hearing things," Knives said.

"Then make it two," J-Man said.

"They'll call it Dead Man's Cove, and you'll be more popular. Dead Man's Cove Beer. Dead Man's Cove Ghost Tours. Dead Man's Cove Band," Spider cackled, not helping.

"Screw you!" Marader snapped. Fists swinging, he lunged at Spider who stepped back. He evaded, even as Marader threw more punches. Spider wasn't a black belt, but he had been close, dodging and deflecting.

"Stand and fight."

"Why? So you can hit me?" Spider asked. He slipped a punch.

"My turn!" J-Man barreled into Marader, shoving him sideways. He tumbled, losing his balance, and teetered on the edge of the dock. J-Man waved. Arms flailing, Marader tossed his smart phone to Knives, and then he lost to gravity and splashed down.

By the time Marader climbed up the ladder to sit dripping on the dock, everyone had settled down. "Sorry, guys. I lost my temper. That thing scares me. How's the nose and the phone?"

"I don't think it's broken after all. I'm getting ice," Knives said. He glared at Marader then went inside.

"So, you guys think John was a vampire? That's what the stake is all about?" Marader asked. His question seemed quite direct.

"We don't know what this is, or why it looks like John, or why it attacked us, except it claims to be related to John and Von Damme," Troy said.

"Tommy, after the ceremony in the morning, we'll let

Knives take the body back to where it belongs, if it belongs anywhere," J-Man said.

"Actually, I think cremating it sounds like a good idea. Didn't John want to have his body burned?" Marader asked.

Troy wondered why he sounded a little like a believer.

"We should keep it refrigerated," J-Man said.

"You are NOT putting that in my walk-in," Marader growled.

"It doesn't matter. He's not decomposing. You don't smell anything like that, do you? He's not dead. Not alive," Troy said.

"Undead, huh?" Marader said. To Troy's questioning look, he said, "I've seen some odd stuff out here on quiet nights."

Knives returned, talking around an ice pack over his nose. "Let me see if I have this straight, as crazy as it sounds. Hatchet in hand, John attacked me, J-Man shot him, and Imposter John fell onto the rake handle, putting that stake through his chest. Is that correct?" he asked. Troy and J-Man nodded. "And you have none of this recorded?" Knives asked.

"It shows us, and you can hear us, but not John. He sounds like static, all distorted," Troy said. He got out his GoPro camera and played the recording. John was nowhere in sight, except for his shadow in the glare of the pyrotechnic fountain. They could hear Troy and J-Man clearly, but Undead John's voice was garbled. "I don't know why it's messed up."

"Sure," Knives said. He got out his phone and took a photo of John. He walked over and showed it to Troy. He blinked. There was an image of Undead John's corpse. "No problem. Perhaps it was your camera."

"He isn't dead, and they aren't going to want to bury him with a stake in his body. He'll rise again. That's what he says," Spider said. "John wants us to set him afloat in the sunshine and let it do its work. Sunlight will destroy his cursed body. Von Damme turned him into a monster. Into a vampire. He hates it. Tommy, quit your bitching, he says. You owe him big time for never telling Jambo about Loren."

Marader sneered. "Loren? How do you know about that?"

"I don't. Oh, and Tamara," Spider continued.

"Tamara? Really?"

"And her . . ."

"Fine. Whatever. Keep it off my dock," Marader muttered.

"Did you bring him here in my car?" Knives asked, his voice dangerous.

"Strapped him to the hood. We used the bungees in the trunk," J-Man said with a smile. Knives was ready to explode, until he noticed his blood brother's expression. J-Man relented and explained about the pine box in the back of his truck.

"God, you two are something. You should have just called 911. What happened to common sense?"

"I saw my best friend come back to life and try to kill us. Knives. Stephen, I know this is impossible to believe without proof. All I'm asking is that we set him in the sun in the morning."

"That's all you want, is last rites and letting the model of John's body bask in the morning sun, then you'll drop this foolishness? Because that's what it is," Knives said.

"I'll drop the whole matter if you check to make sure he hasn't been altered by chemicals, embalming fluids, paint or whatever, then in the morning, once the fog has burned off, we float him out into the water into full daylight and see what happens," Troy said.

J-Man nodded. Knives nodded. Marader gave a thumb up.

"I'll call Denny about last rites," J-Man said.

T w e n t y - S e v e n :   V i g i l

Knives and Marader went inside, leaving Troy, J-Man, Spider and the cat, Tawny, to stand sentry. At least that's what Troy felt he was doing. What if something tried to rescue John?

J-Man set up a trip wire attached to buckets to warn them. Spider provided the shirt and shorts, and he and Troy dressed

John's body. Troy couldn't help but be paranoid that John might suddenly grab him again.

Spider placed a crucifix on John's chest, where it smoldered, the smell of burnt flesh filling the air. He quickly moved it onto the shirt, where it no longer caused problems. "How traditional."

When he was done, J-Man sprawled on one of the two loungers.

Troy slumped into the other. Spider took first watch.

For a few minutes, Troy tried many different ways to tell him about Dillon being alive, but even attempting to start a conversation on the subject either left him tongue-tied or too cotton-mouthed to speak. He even tried writing, and his hand had cramped! Trying to send a text, the same debilitating pains returned. If he couldn't inform them, he doubted he could tell Silke. He hated lying to her, and he seemed to be avoiding the truth a lot.

"Get some sleep," Spider said. In his arms, Tawny's eyes were closed, and she purred.

Later, Spider awakened Troy from another nightmare. He took his turn as the knight on watch. Spider resumed the lotus position, head down and seemed to go to sleep.

During the wee hours, in the white noise peace of crickets and cicadas and the light of the pungent, citronella candles, Troy mulled everything that had happened.

The strange dream of John dying. It seemed to have started with that dive, going into the underwater mansion of death. Sherry was still missing. Didn't John say Von Damme had her? Troy could imagine a creature like Zane, telling Pat to excavate the graves then slitting his throat. Pat's boat had been left behind. Marader's boat had been sunk in Riddle Creek. Why? The ex-dam employees had named the Bent Branch Creek area as a hot bed of problems long ago. Now the spillway stood there. Coincidence or connection?

He wished he could remember more about the interviews.

At least he recorded them. He went back and listened to his discussion with Corning, Basil, and Luther, learning little new. He wondered if any of the rest of the footage would help his recall, then he thought of the encrypted file.

Troy watched and listened, disappointed that Zane's voice sounded garbled on the video. He could clearly hear himself and Silke. He peered at the image of Zane, able to tell little about the man because of the big hat and huge sunglasses, then almost forgot about the nightwalker, listening to Silke trying to leave the boat, their tussling, kissing, and escaping.

Shocked he could have forgotten, he played it again. Silke had forgotten, too, or acted like it.

Predawn, with the fog heavy and the sky a gloomy slate gray, Troy was awakened by the sound of a text message. Alarmed, he startled, fearing something had happened during his nap.

He looked around. John's body still remained, damp like he'd been sweating. Under a towel, J-Man snored nearby. Spider sat in the lotus position. The fog made everything damp and chilly, though the thermometer read 60.

Troy saw the text message from Silke. She was on her way.

Knives pushed open the door, ambling out onto the deck. He appeared half asleep, his eyes puffy. He rubbed his face. "Denny will be here in about twenty minutes. We will pray for John's soul this morning, plus yours and mine," Knives said.

He set down a backpack and proceeded to examine John's body, searching for any chemical residues. He shook his head frequently, the body looking unchanged from last night. Knives took samples of hair, skin, fingernail, and saliva.

"Despite the incredible detail, this can't be a body. It doesn't change, but I'll run tests when I get him back to the coroner's office. Y'all should apply for jobs in the movie industry, monster make-up or something. Wow," Knives said. He stood, dusting his hands of it.

His timing divine, Father Dennis arrived, each footfall

landing heavily on the planks. Clad in priestly robes, he straightened when he saw them and tightened his jaw. "I hope this isn't another stunt, y'all. I have a lot to do. There was a break-in at the facilities last night. The thieves stole a truckload of dynamite," he said, worrying his hands.

"OMG," J-Man said.

"How is Colleen?" Troy asked.

"Not well. It doesn't look good, but I know better than to rely on appearances. She dislocated several neck joints, and the swelling is a serious problem. The doctors have induced a coma, hoping it'll keep her still and help her heal, God willing. I would be by her side, but I keep being called elsewhere. Stolen dynamite! And Mary Beth hasn't been the same since the dive. She can't sleep at night and has grown claustrophobic," Denny said.

They gathered close together while Knives led a prayer for the Rentzels. Father Dennis added he hoped the authorities safely found the dynamite.

"All right now. Did you say you found John's body?" Denny said.

They showed him. Upon seeing the corpse, Denny removed his glasses, rubbed his eyes, and then glanced at them. "I expected it to have deteriorated."

"See. It's a detailed replica," Knives said.

Denny peeked under Undead John's shirt. "And a gruesome one at that," he murmured.

"Thank you for coming. This will give us some peace of mind," Troy said. J-Man and Spider echoed his sentiment.

While giving the last rite blessing, Father Dennis sprinkled holy water. Wherever it landed on the body, the flesh blackened and pitted, giving off smoke. John's body twitched. The stench made Troy gag. He feared he might vomit, but he stumbled away to breathe.

"Never seen that happen before," Denny said.

"Heard of it?" J-Man asked.

Denny hesitated, then he shook his head. He dropped

water on himself and J-Man when he stuck out a hand. After that, Father Dennis sprinkled Undead John again with the same burning, stinking result. Shaking his head, Father Dennis prayed aloud for John's soul and touched a crucifix to John's cheek. It charred during the few seconds of contact, leaving a scar.

"Explain that," J-Man said.

Knives glared. His lips moved, but he said nothing.

"That is quite disturbing," Denny said and licked his lips. His white hand clenched the crucifix.

At that moment, Walt showed up, blissfully ignorant, strolling over from the houseboat. The rest and sleep had done him a world of wonders as he looked younger and less brittle. He could walk and scroll along his smartphone screen at the same time.

"Hey, guys," he said, hardly looking up. He had yet to notice what they were doing. "What's for breakfast. Did somebody burn bacon?"

They said nothing. Walt was on a roll.

"There are some amazing photos of last night's wake and the brawl on several web pages, local papers, of course, but also TMZ and the Sterling Fan Page. Troy, that was some kiss. The photo of you and Raquel has gone . . . Uh, is that really John's body? Or an effigy?" he stammered, finally having seen it. Wide-eyed, he stalked closer. "You guys are jerking my chain."

"It's John. We're giving him a proper send off," Troy said.

"Oh. He . . . he looks really good for . . . you know, being in the water for so long. What's that mark on his neck? And what happened to his hands? So much for my appetite. Uh, do I smell burnt hair?"

"Flesh," Troy said. He thought it might only be the beginning.

He heard another car arrive and smiled, thinking it was likely Silke.

"Knives thinks it's an effigy," J-Man said.

"It is not John, nor is it a body," Knives maintained.

"Right. Neither of those burn when touched with holy water," Father Dennis said. He seemed to be leaning toward doubt.

In jeans and an emerald green, Squaw Valley Ski sweatshirt that brought back memories, Silke entered like sunshine beaming through the fog, even when she frowned. Troy vaguely recalled her complaining of how she looked in the morning. He thought women would pay good money to look that great in the evening. She glanced around, offering wan smiles until she saw Troy.

Her expression was guarded, her narrowed eyes throwing daggers. He figured she had seen the online photos. She noticed his unshaven and slightly battered, probably deranged look, frowned, and withheld whatever acerbic comment she had planned.

He stood his ground, the insistent voice nagging him to stay distant. He didn't have the strength to fight it, Silke's anger, and deal with the possibility of the impossible becoming real. This was about love, friendship, loyalty and the truth. The last seemed at odds with what he had been doing, and he felt sick about it.

"I'd say good morning y'all, but it's another funeral, isn't it?"

She stood distant and crossed her arms. Troy could feel the stiff chill from her cold gaze.

"We are saying good-bye to John," J-Man said. "Father Dennis just performed last rites. Now, we're just waiting for the fog to clear, and the sunshine to grace us."

"Uh, no flaming arrows or setting the boat afire?" Silke asked.

"We thought about it, but this is mostly symbolic. Although, considering the occasion, we can give him a twenty-one-rocket salute as loud as guns. I have rigged up a couple of rafts worth of fireworks. That's what I did during my watch last night," J-Man said.

"Watch? You watched over the body? Are y'all knights? First dancing, then brawling, fighting a thief in a cemetery and now rescuing a friend's body so you can watch over it before letting the sun carry its soul to a final resting place? Sounds armored knight-ish to me. I thought that courtly romance stuff was BS," Silke said.

Troy thought he should tell her the truth about what might happen when sunshine hit John. He couldn't be honest about Dillon, so he felt he should be honest about John. Even thinking about her brought back echoes of Elke's commanding voice.

Silke strolled along the dock, near the edge where John's body bobbed gently on the old canoe. She started to cry and sniffled back the tears. "I'm sorry, I thought I was prepared," Silke said.

"It's not really John's body," Knives said.

No surprise, Silke looked confused. She had joined the crowd.

"Would you like some coffee? It might still be a while before the sunshine breaks through. Please tell me about Aunt Jada," Troy said. Silke nodded and strode briskly inside to the bar where it smelled of cappuccinos. Someone had set the steamer on the counter. From the half full pot, he poured her a cup.

A long drink made her smile. It faded to solemnity when she returned her attention to him. Her temptress lips were gone, forming a white line. "You look like you had a night of adventure. Your eyes glint with secrets."

"Or the light of madness and glimmers of fatigue."

"Mad to some and insanely cool or amazing to others. It's a matter of perspective. So it is, or is it not John's body?"

Troy smiled. He could talk to her about this, unlike Raquel.

"What happened to your neck? Did Raquel play rough?"

Ouch. If looks could kill, he would be critically wounded. "No. Those are John's paw prints."

"What?" she asked, taken aback.

"I told you that after the brawl at the wake, we went to the cemetery."

"Were you dead on your feet? There are some great photos of you dancing with Raquel and a blond."

He let her be angry. It helped keep the distance while he told her what had happened and carefully watched for her reactions. He started with seeing Zane and the woman who he believed might be the Dark Lady, how she had stolen Raquel's bracelet. How he had just watched, powerless.

"Lots of pretty women," she replied.

"None trustworthy." He told her about Elke Swearington, what he could anyway. He tried to tell her about Dillon and his vocal cords locked up, making him frustrated. "I think she knows something."

"Thank you. You were thinking of my brother after all," Silke said.

"I was thinking of you. Now I'm thinking of hitting him. Elke knew about Wreythville and Von Damme and the first Dark Lady, the one who stole the bracelet. Elke said she's a watcher," Troy said. He could tell Silke about those things, at least.

"You mean she's sentry for the underwater mansion?"

He nodded, took a deep breath and plunged ahead. "Do you remember me telling you about Mona, and the woman that killed her?" he asked. Silke nodded, eyes wide, almost as if sensing what was coming. "Elke didn't deny it."

"That's hard to digest," she said. Troy had the sense that she didn't believe him.

"After we talked, she set her eyes on Tommy Boy and the jewelry box and gave a command to create confusion. I ignored it, followed her, and got thrown aside by a third party. The ankh warned me, but I moved too slowly." He told her of Zane's attempt to steal the jewelry box. "When confronted, he commanded everyone to fight. The wake went from a love-in to a brawl. He caused it."

"Zane is the name of Aunt Jada's love."

"And the name of the man who tried to get you into his boat. I'm starting to understand how she feels."

Silke gave him a strange look. "You're sympathizing with my aunt? She did say Zane Aldridge. His eyes were . . . big. Huge."

Even so, if he read her eyes and body language right, she thought he was lying. This is what keeping secrets had led to. It made him furious.

"What are you thinking about?" she asked.

"Punching your brother," he said. That made her smile.

In detail, he told her about what happened at East Hill, downplaying the danger until recounting John's mobile corpse and what he had said, their struggle and his death. "I can't believe I had to kill my friend, except he isn't dead. When Denny sprinkled holy water, John's skin burned."

"No wonder you think you're going crazy. Besides being bruised, I can see bubbles of dark light around your neck," Silke said. She sat unnaturally stoic. She didn't offer to help him heal. Likely, she thought he should suffer.

"That's where John's corpse grabbed me. The ankh grew hot to the point of burning me."

She brought her own into the light from under her shirt to examine it. "Yes, I noticed it growing very warm when I was near the effigy. Do you think it's a warning device? Aunt Jada is full of surprises. It sounds like you're coming around to her way of thinking."

"Yes, and it's starting to worry me," he said, and then he could see her misinterpret what he said, referring to being married to her. "The flood of blood. Help Dillon no matter what. The no matter what is going to kill me."

"You need to take better care of yourself," she said, sounding business like. She was right here, and he missed her. He could punch Dillon right now. Kick him, too. Why had Elke done this to him?

"Ah, I hear it's the company I keep," he said. He was accustomed to dangerous and extreme conditions but coming back home had been even more harrowing.

"Troy?" Her eyes large, Silke was concerned, a little less angry.

He flashed back to the pontoon boat and watching the video. "Sorry, I hardly slept. Silke, we're about to find out if my friend was murdered by a monster and returned as a vampire or zombie or whatever. J-Man saw him, too, so lunacy is contagious. John didn't have control of his body. Does that sound familiar?" he asked.

"I had an interesting nightmare about that. Do you remember the pontoon boat trip yet?"

"More of it. It's still a blur, like my emotions were really high," he said. This wasn't a good time to show her the recording, let her hear them. Besides, it was a challenge to stay near her. He had pushed Elke into the background like a teenager ignored a parent.

"Thank you for laying it out there for me."

"Thank you for listening. I needed to tell someone who might believe me. Knives certainly doesn't, and Denny has doubts."

"You didn't tell Raquel?" she asked. He shook his head. "You confide in me but not Raquel?"

He nodded. "I trust you, and you're open-minded."

Silke poured another cup of coffee. "What does it mean if the sun sets him afire?"

"That vampires exist. That they are here, and Aunt Jada was right. That for some reason, we have become involved with them through Cemetery Ridge and Wreythville and perhaps your brother," Troy said.

The door opened with a smack against the wall. J-Man peeked inside and said, "Hey, there's a ray of sunshine. Time to put up or shut up."

T w e n t y - E i g h t :   T h e   L i g h t   o f   D a y

Outside, the sun gradually burned away the fog. They were in luck, as the wind carried the smoke in another direction right now. Out at the end of the marina's cove, hazy beams of sunlight streaked down to set the surface of the lake alight. It glittered lively with sparkles.

Troy recognized Jambo's big feet on the gangplank. He arrived looking half asleep but smiling. "What's going on, Troy?" he yawned.

"Too much. It might be the death of me," Troy said

"Aw, you got phoenix blood in you," he replied.

Marader finally showed up, stretching, groaning and rubbing his face and its shadowy beard. It had finally grown in. His fuller hair line made Troy suspicious of Rogaine use. Under Marader's left arm waited the jewelry box. It had cut the bicep, and he bled.

"You guys know I don't like morning funerals as much as night parties," he said. Even so, he was present to see the fate of a blood brother.

Troy and J-Man said farewell, forgiving John for trying to kill them. Looking solemn, regardless of what she believed, Silke pulled out a bag and tossed rose petals. Spider wished him Godspeed while the rest said nothing, expecting to see the body again. Jambo nodded off. Shaking his head, Knives watched them curiously. Marader yawned. Walt tapped his tocs.

J-Man lined up the old canoe, then, after making sure the line was secure, he shoved it out into open water. It sliced swiftly at first, but after twenty feet, slowed down and drifted through the fog, heading for the marina's entrance and open water.

"Are you ready to look like a fool?" Marader asked Troy.

Troy nodded. "Thanks for letting me say good-bye to John this way," he said.

J-Man and Walt got out their guitars and started playing

Amazing Grace.

A glory hole opened up, casting dazzling sunlight on the houseboats across the way. With each passing moment, the area of light enlarged, almost reaching the dock. Another patch of light appeared on the port side of the canoe as it continued to lazily float on.

A cawing noise preceded the descent of a black bird. The raven landed on John's chest and pecked down into his body.

"Should I shoot it?" J-Man asked when he paused his playing.

"A crow is a carrier of souls. I'm not so sure about ravens," Silke said.

"Odin had them," Spider said.

"Pagans," Father Dennis murmured.

The sun continued to burn off the fog. It grew warmer, and the cove slowly brightened. The light touched the dock, and Marader put on his sunglasses. It suddenly felt much warmer, hot on the way to steamy.

The canoe seemed to come to a stop about forty feet out in a stubborn patch of fog. Troy had the sense it was protecting John, but it couldn't resist the sun. The obscuring mists shrank, and sunlight graced the stern of the canoe, flashing off the metal and glinting off the water. A vulture swooped in, passing by. The raven flew off.

"I told you nothing was going to happen," Knives said.

"Much ado about nothing. See, I'm literary," Marader chuckled.

Troy looked over at Silke. He found little solace there. She seemed less hostile and yet her arms were crossed. He hadn't convinced her.

"Are you boys in a hurry?" she asked.

A turkey vulture swung around to land on John.

"We've got to bring him in," Denny said.

"I'll take care of it," Marader said, but he went inside.

J-Man yanked on the rope, disturbing the buzzard. It flapped its wings and swung its tail to balance itself, holding on with its talons. "I can set off the firework barges, that will scare it away," he suggested.

The vulture pecked into John. Silke turned away. Troy thought this wasn't such a good idea. It wasn't turning out like he expected, either way, as the scavenger took out another chunk. A second, smaller vulture glided in and landed on John's leg, turning around to get situated.

Marader returned with a Remington rifle and took aim. "Dead birds coming up."

The canoe was drifting toward the dock from the yank, getting nearer. John's corpse left the patch of fog. A ray of sunshine fell on him. Troy thought John might have smiled, but nothing obvious happened.

"I guess I'm really crazy," Troy said to Silke. He could clearly remember what John had said.

"You did hit your head," Silke began.

Marader fired. The blast echoed, but the bullet missed. The vultures continued their meal. The sunshine didn't bother them, either. "Crap."

"How could you miss?" Knives asked.

"Let a real man try it," Jambo suggested. He held out his hand.

"One more try," Marader said. He took aim. His finger tightened. The bigger bird suddenly fell over and thrashed with convulsions.

"That's bizarre," Denny said.

"I must have winged it with my first shot," Marader suggested.

"You're so full of it," Jambo said.

"Look!" Silke said.

Atop the canoe, John's corpse smoldered. Tendrils of smoke twisted upward in the calm morning air.

"What did you guys do to him?" Walt asked.

"Nothing," J-Man replied.

With a resounding whoosh, flames erupted from John's body. Troy felt the explosion of heat all the way to the dock.

He stepped back along with his friends to watch in horrible fascination.

"Dear God," Father Dennis exclaimed. His eyes were saucer-sized wide above his spectacles. They had slipped down his nose, following his jaw drop. "What wonder now?"

"No way! I tested it! There was nothing combustible on that body. What did you guys do?" Knives demanded and glared.

"Thank you. Thank you! John says," Spider announced.

Troy looked for John's ghost. He didn't see it, but he waved anyway.

The fire raged and roared as if it were fanned by storm winds, though the morning remained calm. Surprised, the remaining vulture reacted too slowly. Its wings burst aflame as it tried to fly off, sending it plunging into the water.

Troy didn't say he told them so. He hadn't really known. Besides, who believed in literal vampires, real bloodsuckers that were nearly invulnerable, except to holy objects, moving water, and direct sunlight?

"That's somethin'. C'mon! What did you guys do?" Knives asked.

The vampire's body burned intensely, swiftly disintegrating clothes and flesh, down to the bones. They flared, burning white hot, creating a radiant skeleton. The flames seemed vengeful, setting the backboard alight. The conflagration continued to roar, licking at the canoe, turning it black and warping it. The torch-like body of his friend burned through the wooden backboard, dropping to the bottom of the canoe. Fire rippled along it before the craft was engulfed in flames.

Troy recorded and watched it all with a grim stoicism, while most of his blood brothers stood shocked, much as he had been seeing John the first time. He glanced over at J-Man, their eyes meeting in confirmation. They hadn't imagined it. Human bodies didn't react like this.

"What did you soak that body in?" Denny asked.

"Nothing," Troy said.

"I'm sorry I didn't believe you," Silke said. She moved

closer to Troy.

He ignored the naysaying voices and embraced her.

"And as far as a missing body, that couldn't have been John's body. John's body had throat wounds, had been fished out of the water, and wouldn't go up in flames like that. Isn't that what you told me, doctor?" Troy asked.

"Near enough," Knives replied.

"Better no body than one that rises at night to kill you," J-Man said.

Denny shook his head. "I don't understand."

"We don't either," Troy said.

"John's spirit expected this. He didn't want to be a nightwalker. Didn't want to be a vampire feasting on friends and family" Spider said.

"I don't believe in those," Father Dennis said. He crossed himself.

"But you believe in evil. And whatever Von Damme and his Damned are, they are evil. One of his cult touched your wife last night," Spider said.

"Zane is his name," Troy said. He had mixed emotions about this proof that vampires existed.

"Aunt Jada was right," Silke whispered in his ear. He heard it clearly over Elke's voice.

In denial, none of the other blood brothers wanted to mention vampires, but eventually they would have to discuss it. Troy finished pulling in the rope, what was left of it. Funeral debris covered the still water where their friend and canoe had burned to ashes in mere minutes.

J-Man, Knives and Marader climbed into a motorized dingy and set out to explore the floating ash. They returned shortly to report that if anything was left, it had sunk.

"Let the waters purify it," Father Dennis said.

Troy realized they were all in shock, going through the motions. "We need to talk about this," he suggested.

"What? That John spontaneously combusted?" Jambo asked.

Knives continued to stare out over the water, perplexed. "There are people who lose pigment and their skin burns badly, but nothing like this. Chemical reactions. I can't think of anything that burst into flames with sunlight."

"It was probably the raven or the buzzards. Perhaps they set off the sudden combustion," Troy suggested, tongue-in-cheek. Silke elbowed him.

"Yeah, bat guano is combustible. Perhaps bird do-do is, too," J-Man added. Spider laughed so hard he coughed

"I'm glad you find this funny. If I tell this to anyone, they'll think I've lost my mind. But guys, this wasn't humorous. It could get us in a lot of trouble," Knives said.

"We didn't kill anybody," J-Man said.

"By later today," Troy began. "You'll be in denial and think you imagined it. That's when I'll show you the recording."

"What are we going to tell the police and Deputy Burt?" Knives asked.

"Same as before. The truth. We were attacked. We don't know what happened to our attacker, do we? Or why he was there? I can't even explain what happened to the body that looks like John's body," Troy said.

"I know what happened, but not why," Knives said.

Troy sighed. "It's your reputation. You decide."

"Whatever we say or do, John's body, that corpse from the cemetery is gone," J-Man said.

Knives crossed his arms. "I won't know if you're messing with me until I retest the samples from the replica and compare to today's," he said and shook his head. He checked his watch. "As far as I'm concerned, John's body is still missing. You guys, always screwing around. We'll talk more tonight. Right now, I have a meeting at the hospital. Later," Knives said. Confused and justifiably upset, he departed.

Denny left to go to Colleen's side. J-Man split for wildfire duty. Troy didn't think he should be flying, but J-Man swore he could fly half asleep. "After what I've seen, I'm not sure I can sleep for a while, maybe days."

Jambo stayed around to fish. Walt joined him. Spider grabbed a rod and reel but seemed to fall asleep sitting before he ever cast.

Silke studied Troy, her expression unreadable. "I'm heading back to town. I've had some urgent calls from customers seeking relief."

He knew where Dillon was. His mouth worked but no words escaped.

"You look half dead on your feet, Troy. Go get some rest. Sleep well. Tonight doesn't sound like fun, though, it was fun before you became lost with the boys," she said sadly. "I won't be here tonight to hear y'all debate. I have a date." With that, she was gone.

Troy felt rocked and dismayed. His world had shifted again and not for the better. He feared it would get worse before it turned around. He would have to prepare the best he could.

Twenty-Nine: Supernatural Debate

While waiting for the others to show, Troy thought back over the day. He had napped, and then borrowed Spider's van to purchase and pick up supplies, which included a stop at a church to obtain blest water. He had something to deal with the dogs, a taser and a cattle prod from the Washington Co. Farm and Feed Store. In an army surplus warehouse, he had picked up flash bangs and more flares. He wished he had a tranquilizer gun.

He was still figuring out what exactly he should do about Dillon and Elke, but Troy planned to confront them at Swearington Lodge. He was certain Dillon was staying with Elke. Troy planned to wear a nicotine patch to stay focused, see if it kept him from being bewitched, beguiled, or befuddled. He didn't intend to sneak in, though. He had Elke's card, and he planned to call from her front porch.

The problem was he couldn't focus on the problems. Well, Silke going on the date would prevent her from tagging along tonight. He fought off a wave of jealousy. She had gone from a distraction to an addiction.

Marader stepped behind the bar and blended icy margaritas, one of John's favorite concoctions. It seemed appropriate to drink while discussing what was believed to be impossible. Troy accepted one and sipped it. Likely, Dr. Killjoy would disapprove.

Rumpled by the windy ride, Knives arrived, looking frustrated and agitated, especially compared to amiable Jambo who lumbered in, kicked back, relaxed, and took a nap while sitting at a table next to Walt. He was still working his tech skills to clean up, or find the voices, in the audios of the videos Troy had given him. They included his encounters with Undead John and later, Elke at the wake.

J-Man tromped in smelling of smoke and accepted a strawberry margarita. "Cheers. I almost got too close to the fire. Ten minutes later, one of the other choppers went down, killing old Ned. Damn it! He was a salt of the earth kind of guy, give you the shirt off his back, you know. Because of that, no surprise, they have temporarily suspended fly overs and water drops," he said.

"I'm sorry, Jay. I'm glad you're here," Troy said.

"Yeah, us lunatics need to stay together, right?" J-Man asked.

Spider seemed to just appear. Troy never saw him come in.

Denny showed up last, looking even more weary than before. His eyes possessed a haunted look, worried about what was happening and what they were about to discuss. He started off with a flat denial. "Y'all, the Church has no record of and gives no credence to the belief of vampires, and yet, I know something sinister happened to Colleen and to everyone in that brawl. My friends and neighbors are not brawlers."

"Ghosts, werewolves, and vampires, oh my," Spider said.

"This is serious. This could be our licenses and perhaps our lives on the line," J-Man said.

"Yes, it is serious, and I need the truth. After today's

meeting, I'm under medical board review and pending suspension," Knives snapped. He picked up a handful of darts and started viciously throwing them at the board. "They blame me for what happened in the basement, where I almost died, plus John's missing body. That doesn't even include last night's incident and this morning's fiasco. When they learn about it, oh boy, shit will hit the fan."

"What happened, happened. We didn't hide anything," Troy said.

"Really? You hid the body."

"We were trying to protect you, plausible deniability," J-Man said.

"Listen, Mr. Eagle Scout. We have to find John's body," Knives said.

"As far as we know, it went up in flames," J-Man said.

"How did you know it was John? Like I said, the wounds were wrong," Knives said.

"He told us," Troy said.

Knives crossed his arms. "Science tells us that we can't trust our eyes or our memories. Both can be fooled and trick us, so neither are totally reliable, less so when strong emotions are involved. The observed affects the observation and all that. I'm sure you don't want me to quote studies and statistics. Plus, there are significant questions about the witnesses' mental states."

"Then again, the tattoo was spot on. So was the dental work and old scar on his foot where he stepped on a nail," Spider said.

Knives glared at him. Marader chuckled. Knives stared daggers at him, too.

"You know, John wouldn't have tried to kill us if we hadn't been at the cemetery, and there would only be the mystery of what happened to the caretaker," Troy pointed out.

"Fine. Let's start there," Knives said. He waved as if to tell J-Man to tell his story. Troy's memory had been deemed suspect.

J-Man waxed eloquently, even riveting, about driving up and leaving Troy snoozing in the truck while the hero in the story boldly strode through the graveyard. He whistled a Grateful Dead tune while he walked by a field of tombs, headstones, plots, and gnarled, creepy trees. He explained how he had called out to Knives, only to hear a thud that sounded like a body hitting the ground. He vaguely remembered seeing Knives sprawled unconscious. J-Man vividly recalled awakening later to the sound and light of fireworks. He saw John with his hand around Troy's throat, intent on killing him.

When J-Man paused, it was quiet except for the hum of the refrigerators and coolers. Somewhere a clock ticked. That felt appropriate. Time was slipping away.

The door opened, bringing a flash of light and a breath of fresh air sweetened with honeysuckle, the scent of Silke. "Hey, guys, I'm going out," she said. Her sashaying into the room changed the mood and diverted most rational thought. Troy didn't need to see what he was missing.

She bedazzled in a green shirt with a deep V to make her eyes glow and guys' eyes roam, not that he paid much attention. A necklace of jade stones the size of fingernails drew even more attention to her cleavage. Her black skirt was just above the knee but slit, showing off fishnet stockings. She slowly spun. Much of her back was exposed, though her red gold curls veiled some of it, making it more sensual.

"Well?" she asked.

She wore less cosmetics which was more, but enough shadow and lash to bring attention to her gorgeous eyes, lively with humor, intelligence and the delight of revenge. Or so Troy imagined. Her lips needed no adornment, but she wore hot pink lipstick and an attractive smirk, as if she could read his mind.

"Lucky guy," J-Man said.

"Dillon wouldn't let you go out dressed like that," Denny said.

"You're perfectly dressed if you intend to cause accidents,"

Troy said. Silke narrowed her eyes, not sure if that was a compliment. He thought telling her she looked like dessert would be inappropriate even if true.

"You'll make girlfriends, wives and mere mortal females envious," Jambo waxed eloquently.

"I'd do you in a heartbeat, babe," Marader said, grinning.

"Are you wearing your glasses?" Troy asked.

"No," she replied and smiled flirtatiously.

"Dressed like that you should be armed," Spider said.

"That I am. Bye guys. Y'all have fun. Don't burn the place down," she said. She glanced at Troy, pausing, then she left.

The bar was quiet for a different reason.

"Troy, I think you were supposed to stop her," Jambo said.

"You think?" J-Man said.

"She'll be safe when something comes to kill us later tonight," Troy said, half joking, half serious.

"What makes you think that?" Spider asked.

"Nothing has tried to kill me yet today, but there's the night to come," Troy said.

Spider nodded sagely in response.

"Should we post a watch?" Walt joked.

"I brought Ace. He'll do the trick," Jambo said. "He likes Silke, too, so he won't bark at her, if she comes back. Troy, there's still time."

"I can see this must be discussed. Let's make it simple. Those opposed to me asking Silke if she would like to be my lady? I would like to know how many of my blood brothers I might have to fight or that I will piss off," Troy said.

He could have heard a pin drop. His friends just stared at him. Likely, they didn't want to get caught in the middle, except, they already were, thanks to Dillon having threatened them.

"Well, I know where I stand with Tommy. Marader gave me a week to decide. If I won't, he will," Troy said.

That earned Marader frowns and glares from all around. He laughed boisterously. "I'm just trying to give Troy a nudge."

"Knives said he would patch me up after Dillon kicks the crap out of me. I take that as approval," Troy said.

Knives nodded. He rolled his hands to silently say get on with it. He had places to be, lives to save, joys to kill.

"Go for it. I have a taser you can borrow," Walt said.

"I told you I have your back," Jambo said.

J-Man frowned. "I can't believe you let her go on a date. I'd prefer to see her go out with you than anybody else as long as that's what you truly want," he said.

"Ditto," Spider said.

"You're a brave guy. You know what you're getting into," Denny said.

This was better than Troy had thought, but as well as he had hoped. "Listen, I think Silke's amazing. But, being around us, especially me, is dangerous right now. So, I'm looking out for Silke, all right?" Troy said. Besides, Elke's voice inside his head grew loud and demanding when Silke was present.

"She doesn't think that. I'm just telling you," Jambo said. He raised his hands in a don't blame me gesture.

"Back to Undead John. Knives, I recorded it. Walt, any luck with the audio?" Troy asked.

"Nope. It still sounds like caterwauling. Unless there was a cat there, and you forgot to mention it?"

"None that I recall. What I do remember is that Undead John said Von Damme turned him into a monster. He said the sunlight would destroy him and it did. We all saw it. We didn't do anything to the body, and it went up in flames. Knives, did you find anything when you tested the skin?"

"Oh, did I ever," Knives rolled his angry eyes. He had been waiting for this. "You guys are great actors, but the tests don't lie. What kind of game are you two playing? It didn't even test as human flesh. Is this some kind of *Candid Camera* pranking?"

Troy and J-Man looked at each other. "We shouldn't be surprised that it didn't test as human. John said he was undead. Shooting barely phased him," Troy said.

"Y'all, I can't tell you how deadly serious it is."

"I think I understand more than you think," Troy said.

"Really? Y'all made me think you found John's body and keep acting like it now. Stop it!" Knives said.

"What? It wasn't real? It looked real," Marader said.

"It really was an effigy, wasn't it?" Knives asked.

"So, was it made of paper mache?" J-Man asked.

"Don't give me that! What did you use?" Knives retorted.

"What did you find?" Troy asked.

"We're still working on identifying it. What did y'all use?" Knives persisted. He began to pace, a sure sign of frustration.

J-Man guffawed. "Nothing. What went up in flames is what we brought back from East Hill. The only thing we did was add clothes, and the stake, of course," he said.

"Who else was in on this?" Knives demanded. He slowly spun to look each and every one of them in the eye. "And do any of you know where John's real body is? This situation could ruin me. And is Dillon really missing? Or is this some joke, too? Does Silke know he's safe?" Knives asked and snapped his fingers. "That's why she's off on a date, isn't it?"

"She's on a date because she's pissed at Troy," Marader cackled.

"Walt, can we play the video?"

"Sure thing," Walt replied. He pressed the control and function keys on his laptop, connecting to the big flat screen TV. The video was herky-jerky, as Troy was shocked by what he saw. In the glare of the Happiness fountain, Undead John's face was briefly illuminated and murderously twisted. To Troy, it clearly looked to be their blood brother.

"It could be John," Denny said.

"I thought that vampires couldn't be photographed," Jambo said.

"New vampires can, but only for about the first week, according to Von Damme's journals," Spider said.

Knives rolled his eyes. "I thought you said the video didn't show John," he asked.

"Walt worked on it," Troy said.

"I was able to enhance the images. They were faint."

"Listen to yourselves. Enhance the images?" Knives said.

"I set down the camera to wake up J-Man, so whatever comes next only shows part of the room and isn't helpful," Troy said.

They watched the rest of the video anyway. It showed J-Man, Knives, and the caretaker unconscious on the ground, then Troy set down the camera. Over the next few minutes, they caught glimpses of Troy and J-Man, but no picture of Undead John. Still, they only heard Troy and J-Man's side of the conversation.

Knives applauded. "Very well done. Better than the *Pumpkin Ranch* video. Now, seriously, who is in on this? Everybody?" he asked, looking around.

"Despite what you think, somebody murdered John," Troy said.

"Yes, likely his missing girlfriend, but she didn't turn him into a monster. There is no such thing, unless you're talking psychopaths," Knives said. "I think we should let the sheriff and deputies do their jobs. I like it when people let me do mine. So, out with it! The truth!"

Troy wrestled with his growing frustration. He could see why Knives wouldn't believe them. Troy tried to put himself in his shoes. He wouldn't have believed himself before he had died. "This all started with John diving that mansion. Whatever he freed or escaped is the reason people are missing," Troy said.

"The Lady of the Lake?" Jambo suggested.

"Troy, you are jumping to conclusions and making assumptions. That would be like saying the dynamite stolen from the Rentzel facilities has something to do with John's murder," Knives said. "Any news?"

"No. Missing people. Missing dynamite. Colleen in a coma. These are dark times. No time for jokes," Denny said. He pointedly caught each of their eyes with his glare.

They debated for thirty minutes, and then argued for another thirty without reaching any sort of agreement on what to do or what to tell the authorities. Most of them didn't believe their eyes, so there was no reason to call the police or sheriff departments, because it was just an effigy! Only J-Man and Spider truly understood. The others, Knives, Jambo, Denny, Marader and Walt had only seen John's body react oddly and go up in smoke. It wasn't enough, partly because they didn't believe it had been his corpse, or that it had once been animated.

"Guys, y'all, I'm done here. I'm sticking with what I said because it's the truth. We were attacked by someone who looked like John. We fought. We found what we thought was John's body and gave it last rites, when it burst aflame. I'm going to get some air," Troy said and left.

He really hadn't expected much to be accomplished. There was too much supernatural to be believed unless experienced. Knives had thrown doubt on everything because John had no longer been human, now a monster, so comparing his DNA wouldn't jive.

Piss on them. He was going straight to the source. He wished he could have told them about Dillon, but Elke still had her verbal hooks in Troy's mind, entangling it and tying his tongue.

On the houseboat, he ducked into his room to grab his gear and packed bag. He had already written a note containing his plans and whereabouts in case he didn't make it back. Now he left it in an obvious place.

He heard the houseboat's front door yanked open and an angry, frustrated scream. "Men!" He started to peek out and stopped as something dark whizzed by his door and struck the wall somewhere down the hallway. His first thought was to wonder if he were under attack. Had that been a dagger? A throwing star? Why would . . .

A black, high-heeled shoe rebounded to stop in front of his doorway.

He peeked out, seeing Silke angrily removing her other shoe.

Human brains are wired to react first to threats, emotions, and sex. All three were in play. This was a perfect exclamation point to his comment that beautiful women were dangerous, but now wasn't the time. Silke was crying, and he sensed her anguish. She didn't know Dillon was alive. Troy hated keeping that secret and felt she no longer trusted him.

He cared for Silke and cared what she thought. Compassion moved him forward, and he pushed aside Elke's commands. "Silke?"

She viciously flung the other shoe. Upon release, she saw him too late, her eyes wide.

The spiked heel of the shoe stuck in the wall about a foot to his left. The thrown shoe quivered for a moment as if it still carried some of her murderous rage.

"Troy, oh, I'm so sorry," she stammered. Now she appeared shaken and frustrated. Her eyes brimming with tears.

"Sorry you missed?" he asked, thinking of her men comment. He tried to say it with levity, hoping she might laugh. "I am male."

"You are that, thank God," she said, breathed deeply and sniffled. He wasn't helping, so he shut up and grabbed a box of Kleenex handed it to her. Instead, she threw her arms around him, crying on his shoulder. "I can't take it anymore."

"Wow, that must have been some first date," Troy said. She squeezed him tighter, and he enveloped her in his arms. He immediately noticed how wonderfully electric she felt in his hands. He tried to ignore her tawny bare back under his fingers. Her thigh slid between his legs as she burrowed in. His not paying attention to it seemed to set off Elke's nagging and proximity alerts.

"Ah, you feel good. Solid. I told Mom that you felt Dillon was still alive. That made her feel better. She's holding onto hope; kind of like I'm holding onto you."

"Did you tell her that you're mad at him, and that he might

be hiding from you while he's having a torrid, covert romance?" Troy asked. He believed the latter half to be true, but he wasn't credible.

"No, I didn't tell her that," she chuckled. "That would be too much info even if it were true. Troy, I should have listened to you. You were right. I'm an accident waiting to happen. Roy and I didn't even make it to the restaurant for the rehearsal dinner."

"I'm glad you're all right," Troy said. He thought back to what she said. An accident waiting to happen. Is that what he'd said?

"It was mostly a fender bender. He couldn't keep his eyes off my chest. Men! Do you do that?"

Troy blinked, a step behind. "Do what? Wreck cars? You know I do. You were with me."

She laughed. "I meant admire cleavage."

"Oh. Back up. Back to what I said earlier. Did you think I said you're an accident waiting to happen?" he asked. She nodded, her frown flattening gorgeous lips. His mind was not helping. "I think I said, I tried to say, that the way you look could cause accidents, you know, distract men. But then, take what I said with a shaker of salt. According to Knives, my brain isn't to be trusted, stress on the prefrontal cortex, therefore, neither am I." That sounded more bitter than he intended. "According to Stephen, I could be hallucinating that you're here. I mean, who looks beautiful when they've been crying and can fling high heels like an assassin, besides Angelina Jolie?"

Silke chuckled, and that resonated with him, making him feel comfortable. "I missed you. Troy, I'm very real."

He realized he should let her go, but his hands ignored him. His arms, too. "You know, I was throwing a perfectly good snit when you came and blew it away with your men-angst-ridden fit," he replied.

"Knives pushed your buttons?"

"Yep. You can't even beat the truth out of me. According to

him, I would just think it was the truth. And honestly, we have no proof. It went up in flames, literally. Oh, sorry, that wasn't a body. It was a well-crafted effigy."

"But you remember being chased by wolves," she said.

"I do now, though I didn't until last night," he said.

She looked around, seeing a bag packed on his bed. "Where are you going?"

"I told you I was having a snit prior to your fit."

"I believe that. But you usually go for a walk or a ride, even a swim. Oh, Lord, Troy. You're going over to the Swearington Lodge tonight, aren't you? I caught you on your way out. Tell me. Is it her?"

He shook his head.

"Not her. Dillon. You're that sure?"

"Yep. Though remember, I'm delusional, amnesic, and untrustworthy."

"And loyal and . . . you're going after my idiot brother by yourself. Foolish. Brave. I should have known. Seen it. You wanted me gone tonight so you could leave. Here, I thought you would head out to see Raquel, or I'd find you lip-wrestling with Desiree," Silke said. She leaned back against his arms. If he let her go, she would fall.

"So, do you remember what happened on the pontoon boat?" he asked.

She shook her head, still confusion in her eyes. That was part of the problem. He remembered. Despite Elke trying to bury it, the heated memory resurfaced.

"Tell me. Whatever happened affected us."

"Yeah, it did. I told you that Zane's words somehow affected your mental and emotional state. You were so eager to get to him that you were ready to jump and swim. When I stopped you, you showed your appreciation by slugging me."

"I'm sure you deserved it," she said, smiling.

"I didn't know how to stop you without hurting you," Troy said.

She waited. "So, what did you do? Aikido? Jujitsu?"

"Not quite. You were so fierce, so beautiful, I kissed you."

"I forgot kissing you?" she asked skeptically.

"I guess. While kissing, we bumped into the boat's throttle into high speed. It missed Zane's boat, but the Sea-Doo augured, went airborne and sheared off its windshield," he continued. She laughed, aghast. "We slowed down at the Rock Garden where you passed out."

With doubt, she stared at him. "I'm sure I would remember that."

His first reaction was anger. He let it go. He shifted so she could get her balance and let her go, too. "Well, yeah, I get a lot of that today," Troy said. He forced a smile.

"So, you're planning to go to the Swearington Lodge to rescue my brother from her grasp?" she said. She saw it in his face. He also wanted to confront her brother. "You're really that certain?"

He said nothing.

"You said Zane had a beguiling voice power. Does this mean Elke does too?" she asked. He nodded. "How do you know? What did she command you to do?"

He couldn't tell Silke about Dillon, or that Troy had been commanded to stay away from her and resist Silke's charms. This was a different kind of powerlessness.

"She commanded everyone to smooch. That started the lovefest that preceded the brawl when Zane simply said the word. It was sort of like Belushi in *Animal House* but violent."

"So, are you saying you kissed Raquel because of some ridiculous command? An order to kiss?" Silke asked.

How could he get out of this conversation? "No, I kissed her farewell. She thinks you're going to kill me," he replied. He would prefer to live in Silke's arms than die there.

"The thought has crossed my mind," she said and sighed. Then a sexy, secretive smile played across her lips. "Have you shaken that command?"

He hadn't as he yearned to kiss Silke. If he kissed her, it would be because he wanted to, and he had longed to taste her lips and tongue again, to breathe in her breath. He leaned closer.

The door burst open, jarring them both. They stepped back, surprised to see Denny. He looked flushed, rushed and slightly panicked. "Troy, there you are! I need your help. Mary Beth is in trouble!"

"You got it. What kind of trouble?" Troy asked.

"She and three friends went diving Wreythville looking for treasure. We're going to stop them, or look for them, fools! Are you coming?"

Troy didn't want to go back to Wreythville, but his friend needed him, and people were in danger. "Of course."

"Thanks. Now hurry, Godspeed, please," Denny said. He whirled around and left. The moment of silence felt heavy.

Troy started to follow. Silke grabbed his hand. "Don't go. You know that house is a deathtrap."

"Which is why we have to go. To stop her or help her," Troy said. He started to leave, but Silke squeezed his hand harder.

Silke pulled herself against him, and they kissed. They melted into each other, lost in the moment, savoring the taste, the feel, the sensation of being intimate. They lingered until the boat horn honked. Troy swooped her into a dip and kissed her lustily. He brought her back to her feet, enjoying her surprised and delighted expression.

"Our pontoon kisses were more like that. Gotta go," Troy said, then he ran for the boat, even if it was one he preferred to miss.

Thirty: Night Dive

J-Man had quickly rigged up and remounted the forward spotlights, so Maverick's high beams would blaze a path ahead for three hundred feet across the water.

John would have come along, if he had been alive. Dive to the rescue, he would be first in line. Dillon would have come along to help and chronicle the story. Troy deeply missed their presence, even as he habitually looked for them sitting somewhere in the boat. Providing ballast, Jambo, Walt, and Knives perched in the bow. Even Spider had come along. He was sucking it up, despite what they both knew about the terrible and deadly place. How could Troy do any less?

"No, you can't come," Marader told Desiree. She pouted.

"We're all here. Cast off," Denny said. He sat shotgun, in the co-pilot's chair. He began a blessing.

"Not without me!" Silke yelled. Partly changed into her suit and carrying clothes, she sprinted for the boat. Marader didn't wait, so she leapt the two feet onto the back sun platform. Troy caught her to keep her from falling over, and instead, she wrapped herself around him. She kept finding a way into his arms. "You, Mr. Bane, are accident prone. You need a guardian angel nearby."

Troy was pleased to have Silke at his side. He was also concerned about her safety.

Desiree also refused to be denied. She lithely made the long jump, sticking the landing on the stern platform. She scrambled inside the boat and grinned at Marader then Troy. "You aren't leaving me behind, boss. Adventure is my middle name."

"Whatever," Marader said. He pushed the throttle ahead, giving Maverick gas. By the time it passed the entrance buoys, the boat ran near top speed.

Denny leaned back to talk with Silke. She drew on a windbreaker and threw a towel over her legs and leaned into Troy, huddling for heat.

"Who called you?" Silke asked.

"Raquel Sterling," Denny replied.

Silke stiffened, as surprised as Troy. Annoyed, she crossed her arms then asked, "Why you?"

"Her younger sister and my sister are BFFs. Diana and Mary Beth heard about the dive from the rescue divers at Sterling Sports. They wanted to see it before the area is blocked off.

They agreed to take a reporter with them, surprise, Rae Kirkland. The four of them are overdue. Raquel knows better than to dive alone, so she called me, hoping I was at Maraders. Thanks for coming, y'all. I know how you feel about Raquel."

"Your sister needs help," Troy said.

"Does Raquel know the cavalry is on the way?" Marader asked.

"We're texting. She's taking a Sea-Doo out, since her sister took her boat. At least she's closer, leaving from the Yacht Club."

Maverick sped around the corner. With the heavy smoke, Troy could barely make out the silhouette of the metal framework of 421 Bridge against the sky where a gibbous moon blazed near full.

Past the bridge, where the sound of the motor echoed and their surroundings seemed hard and walled, Marader downshifted, slowing a little to maneuver through the scattered obstacles of the Rock Garden. Marader proclaimed he could do this with his eyes closed, not to worry; but thankfully, he kept his eyes open and ahead. Denny and J-Man provided extra eyes for scouting shallows and rocks, but Marader knew the route and steered decisively. Since every second might count, those planning to dive geared up on the way.

"Were you joking with me back there?" Silke asked.

"I was trying to get you to laugh instead of killing me with your footwear or whatever you might throw next. Extreme Athlete Killed by High Fashion Heels is not what I want as an epitaph," Troy said.

"I meant about Zane and the pontoon boat?"

"Yes. Likely, you forgot about it because it was stressful and traumatic," Troy thought, giving her an out. "Shows how powerful their mind games can be."

"Hang on. I'm cranking it!" Marader shouted. Shoving the gas lever forward, he turned the boat loose, gunning it. Troy prayed no boats were in their way. The surge put Silke in his arms again. Neither of them protested.

Denny looked down at his smartphone. "Raquel's there. She missed them. Whoever's left up top reported Mary Beth and the others started their dive ten minutes ago."

The water was calm, and the boat relatively steady, but putting on a BC with tanks was a bit of a struggle. Slipping into fins was possible as long as Troy stayed seated. J-Man passed out glow sticks, so each of them carried several. Troy attached one on each side of his weight belt. J-Man suggested dropping them onto the site, lighting up the underwater buildings. Troy loved that idea. That place could use as much light as possible.

"Whoever has been there should buddy up with somebody who hasn't been there. Silke, you're with Jambo," Knives began.

"I'll pair up with Denny," J-Man said.

Denny frowned. He sat on the edge of the boat, long past ready to drop off and dive.

"Spider, are you sure about this?" Knives asked.

"For Mary Beth. They don't have very long," Spider said through clenched teeth. "With eight of us, we'll be in and out."

"I'll go with you, Spider. I've survived it already," Desiree said.

Spider thanked her and got an okay nod from the doctor.

"You can deal with Raquel, right?" J-Man asked Troy.

He nodded. He could keep her from panicking, he hoped.

Up ahead through the smoke, Troy could see dim lights around Cemetery Ridge. Some bobbed, likely to be boats, while reflections glimmered murkily off the lake's surface. As Marader slowed and steered the Mastercraft closer, they could see a pontoon boat rigged with lights and anchored close to shore. Under the smoky ambiance of spotlights, a woman was speaking at a man with a camera. Reporters, Troy figured. A fishing boat was dragging the area with a net.

"Treasure hunters?" Father Dennis suggested. He grew less practical and more spiritual, speaking the Prayer of Protection.

Troy paid them little attention. The third boat, a

Mastercraft, had three people, a man in his late teens, a muscular blond in black, and Raquel, clad in a wetsuit and standing impatiently on the ski platform at the stern. A Sea-Doo PWC bobbed next to it. When she saw them, she waved, and then she finished getting ready, slipping into her BC and tank. She was a beautiful contrast of nature and technology, and his heart still skipped a beat. She wore the same swimsuit and gear as in his nightmare.

Marader steered slowly closer, keeping some twenty feet from her boat and the dive flag. Denny stood up and called out. "Any news?"

"No! I'm glad you're here. If they went to the mansion, they're either on their way back or running late. I was in the water a minute ago, looking for lights and bubbles. Nothing. With y'all here, I'm going in," Raquel said. With a meaningful glance at Troy, she brought down her mask and toppled over backwards into the water.

Carter said nothing, the bodyguard's face chiseled stone as she took them in. Unlike Raquel, she wasn't clad in dive gear. She glared at Troy and pointed after her boss.

"We're ready, too," Denny said. He pulled down his mask, stuck the regulator in his mouth and jumped in.

Troy took a deep, focusing breath and yawned three times to reset his mental state. He had a horrible awful, nauseous feeling about this, but he couldn't let it get in the way. Usually he followed his instincts not to do something stupid or dangerous, and yet, he couldn't say no. He called on his courage. He could be cautious, but he needed to be positive and upbeat to deal the underwater mansion's cold, gloomy oppressiveness. He hoped that's all it was and not a horrific evil spirit.

Desiree blew him a kiss. "Be safe," she said. She stepped off the back, using her fins to break the surface and holding her mask.

"Hey, Troy," Silke said. He turned right into her kiss, warm and succulent, changing his attitude and temperature. He responded with a full-bodied kiss. Despite his close reign on his emotions, her caress set off a tingle as if he had been jolted by an electrical shock. She pulled back too soon. Her eyes twinkled and seemed to laugh at him.

"For luck?" he asked.

"Definitely. It's dark down there. I wanted a good recent memory to help me fight my fear, so I can flood my brain with dopamine," she said, then kissed him lightly. Even so, he felt rocked, not counting J-Man jumping out and leaving the boat rising and falling. The cool splash brought Troy back to reality.

"Be smart. Be safe," Silke said before sticking the regulator in her mouth. She dropped into the water.

"Don't expect me to kiss you, playboy," Knives said. He fell backwards into the water.

"What he said, but that looked like more than a lucky kiss," Jambo said, the next to plunge into the water with a big splash.

"Troy, guy, I look forward to seeing you juggle Raquel and Silke. One broke your heart and is national news. The other is your best friend's off limit sister and carries a gun. Sweet!" Marader laughed wildly. He scooted out of striking range to the bow where he prepared the floating anchor. It was a water proof bag that slowed drift by drag and resistance.

"We're rescuing people here," Troy said.

"You're going to need rescuing," Marader laughed.

Troy followed everyone into the silvery-topped black water. He let himself sink, not worrying about buoyancy. He had put on extra weights to sink faster. He immediately equalized his ears and adjusted his mask, releasing its squeeze, on the way down.

Above, the surface parted and an illuminated floating anchor entered the water. The weighted bag dropped past them carrying a light to forty feet at the end of the rope. They briefly gathered at the anchor, nearly halfway to the bottom.

J-Man and Denny sparked flares, bringing glaring light to the dark, deliquescent world. Troy followed their lead and fired up another. They couldn't have too much light down there. Everyone but Raquel ignited the underwater torches and dropped them. Seven fiery lights drifted to the bottom. As they swam deeper, the flares looked like bio-luminescent fish returning to the depths of their abyssal lairs.

Troy and friends plunged after the fall of lights. Two of the flares landed and stayed on the copper roof of the mansion, one near the weathervane, casting a long skinny shadow knifing through the water. The metal roofing reflected the light, lessening the gloom. The third flare tumbled off, spinning as it sank farther, throwing a flickering light until it stopped to illuminate the roofless moonshine shack.

All the other flares had landed near the house, one in back, one on the right side, and two in front near where J-Man had broken the front door. It reminded Troy of a chipped tooth, and he had the absurd thought that the house was angry. Despite the lights, it seemed to gather the shadows and darkness of the deep as closely to it as would a murderer his cloak and daggers. Troy realized he was giving personality to the house, but John had been slain there. It was an accessory to murder, maybe murders.

At the broken door, they partnered up. Raquel and Troy exchanged glances. They remembered what it was like inside. Jambo, Knives, and Denny hadn't been here. J-Man paused to ignite another flare even as Denny pulled on the frame to draw himself inside. Raquel swam close behind him.

Troy kicked to follow, but then he stopped and blinked. The mansion looked to be smoking. But how could it be on fire? Or maybe it wasn't smoke? A fog? A haze? A cloud?

Suddenly, Troy felt jerked and spun around. He raced from the house, down the stairs, only to be harpooned. It buried into him with blinding agony that only grew worse as someone used the rope attached to the barbed metal spear-tip to reel him back to the house.

"No escaped slaves. You know the rules. I declare you fodder," proclaimed a flat voice. He jerked, and Troy knew

Henri LaConte was dead, spitting out a death curse. "I hope someone blows the Hell out of this place."

Troy snapped out of another vision. His hand held onto the ankh. It felt warm. Was the haze a miasma of spirits? He could feel them swirling around him, poking him.

Her eyes beseeching, Raquel had paused to look back at Troy. She frowned until he gave her the thumbs up. J-Man bumped Troy and handed him a flare and started another as Troy and Raquel floated into the main hall. In his opinion, this place needed flood lights.

The freezing cold was more bitter than he remembered, or it had grown worse. He felt like he was being pinpricked to death with frozen pins and needles. It made his ears hurt, giving him a headache, and his eyes watered, making his nose run. He kept moving and his breath steady to maintain circulation. He could see Denny and Raquel slowing, floating, wondering where to go next.

The grand foyer seemed vast and desolate. Their lights appeared muted, the water full of a black ink that absorbed their attempts to push away the darkness until they concentrated on the chandelier. When they hit it with their headlamps, the entire place brightened with an eerie greenish glow. Troy swam to the chandelier and zip-tied two flares among the gemstones. Red light blazed throughout the room, giving it a lurid ambiance of blood-lusting.

Now, he was standing on a ladder, cleaning the chandelier, polishing it to gleaming. Something hit the ladder, and it tumbled out from under him. He leapt, tie flapping, hands desperately grasping for something anything. One hand seized the metal framework and held, even as his tie caught. He hung there, one arm away from hanging by the throat and choking.

"Hey, I'll bet ya didn't see that happening," a woman chuckled.

"No, I expected him to break his neck," a gruff-voiced man

said. Troy thought it sounded familiar. Hairy? "How's it hangin', Jeremiah?"

Troy felt his grip slipping. He tried to hold on, but he was losing strength. He prayed. He cursed. His pinky slipped, followed by his third finger. His index and fore couldn't hold him, and he fell. The tie remained, jerking him to a sudden stop.

The water quaked, seeming to shift, bringing Troy back to the present. He thought a huge underwater current shoved him aside, but he held onto the chandelier. It pulled free and dragged him toward the floor. He released the lighting. When it hit, the impact kicked up a dark cloud of silt.

Troy grabbed the flares and stuck them in the mouths of the statues guarding the study door. They appeared unhappy about it, eyes squinted, jaws quivering, threatening to bite them in half. Despite his best efforts, the room remained obscured as sediment drifted up from the chandelier's crash and down from the ceiling.

Denny passed him, swimming into the study, the site of John's death, the murder room. J-Man followed him. Raquel headed straight ahead down a hallway. Silke studied Troy. She signed OK? He gave her a thumb up. She blew him a kiss, then she swam after Jambo to check the upstairs. Desiree followed Knives into a parlor they had yet to explore.

Down the hallway, Raquel searched her way deeper into the house. She already had a good lead on Troy. He kicked and swam to keep her in sight, but he let his eyes wander, looking for signs of recent visits or problems. The shadows taunted him and twitched. Whatever haze enveloped the house thickened in the kitchen.

The place was huge, built to be operated by slaves or servants, or both. To the left was a dining room with a fuzzy green table, complete with manacles, and chairs. Troy blinked and held onto his ankh, seeing a fleeting sense of being pinned to the table and being torn apart. Raquel swam into the feasting room.

To the right was a stovepipe oven, multiple sinks, and stone counters, along with rusted-metal ice boxes. Next to the brick oven, he found a long metal spatula for baking breads. He noticed a light beaming from another direction into a room beyond an archway at the end of a short hall. Silke and Knives swam and searched that way.

When Troy looked back left, Raquel wrestled with an attacker. Bubbles roared furiously from their regulators and lights splayed about as they fought and thrashed. She held onto his right wrist, keeping the long, kitchen knife away, even as her assailant tried to choke her.

Troy surged in and grabbed the guy's arm. He let go of Raquel and whirled on Troy. He stared into the white face of wide-eyed panic. Behind a fogged mask, the man's dark eyes were twice as large as normal, the pupils dilated by fear. He seized Troy's regulator and tried to yank it from his mouth. Troy let it go and grabbed the man's mask, pulled then released. It snapped back. The diver immediately clutched his face, but he still held the knife. It glinted sharply in the light.

Troy grabbed his regulator and stuffed it back into his mouth, glad to be back on air. The crazed diver put his fins against a wall and pushed off, chasing Raquel.

Damn! Troy grabbed the metal spatula and shoved off the wall, hearing it creak. He shot through the water and jabbed with the butt of the spatula, poking the metal end into the guy's ribs. Momentum gave him extra force. The spearing drove the attacker back, stopping the pursuit. He coughed bubbles and paddled backwards.

Raquel gave Troy an okay signal. It seemed she needed a bodyguard even here.

Troy wasn't sure what to do next. Tae Kwon Do had never said anything about fighting underwater. The swimmers might have a better idea, but they weren't here.

Raquel handed him the note pad. ITS ED FRM STORE. She erased and wrote in large letters: DIANA? She showed it with light shining on it so Ed could read it. Troy realized this must be Eduardo, the guy so crazy about Diana that he would do anything.

What could they do? Troy knew better than try to subdue him if it was a seizure or panic attack. That would only make matters worse, and somebody might get hurt. They could let him pass out and haul him to the top. There would be enough air in his tank as they ascended to keep him breathing, as long as they could secure the regulator in his mouth.

Knives and Desiree joined them, and they all exchanged glances. Seeing reinforcements, Ed backed away toward a dark doorway. Could that be where Mary Beth and Diana were? Thank God, so far, there was no blood in the water. But they were running out of bottom time. Ed should be running out of air.

He waved the knife at them and continued kicking. Suddenly, a net dropped over his head and yanked back. A meaty paw shot out and grabbed Ed's wrist, crushing it and forcing the release of the knife. Troy swam in and grabbed it while J-Man wrestled with Ed.

Knives swam into the fray. Troy was surprised to see a syringe as the doctor injected Ed. A few seconds later, Ed quit fighting and went limp. J-Man exchanged looks with Knives. He arranged the net to keep Ed's regulator pressed into his mouth.

Raquel bolted past. Troy followed her fins.

Ahead, Troy spotted Denny with others' lights outlining him. His headlamp was focused on a black metal grill gate over a doorway leading down to where three female divers, Mary Beth, Diana and Rae Kirkland, were trapped. They couldn't have much air left. Denny handed his regulator through the grill to Mary Beth who must have run out of oxygen. Diana waved at Raquel, and they clasped hands between the metal bars.

A rusty lock held the gate closed. Denny worked on the lock, prying with his knife. The old, rusted metal wasn't brittle.

In frustration, he yanked on it, but it held fast.

Desiree inverted to grab the bars and place her fins above the grill against the wall. Denny joined her, so Troy and Raquel moved in, side by side. They took hold of the metal, braced themselves, and then they all pulled, straining, attempting to yank the gate or its frame off the wall.

Troy felt like he burst several blood vessels, but the grill remained stubbornly attached. It seemed impossible considering how long it had been under water. Except for the stonework, the whole house should be rotted.

The lock might look rusted, but it was solid. The bars only had a fine layer of orange rust he could scrap away with his knife. They were going to rapidly run out of air at this depth.

Eyes burning with frustration and impatience, Denny showed them a stick of dynamite. He could spark it with a flare. The fuse would still burn underwater, but they didn't know how much damage it might do. It could bring down the ceiling, or worse, the entire building.

What could they do? Venting a little, Troy stabbed his knife into the wall. It bit deep, driven into the hilt. Everyone looked at him, then the knife, and they all seemed to have the same idea. Jambo and Denny drew knives and joined him, ripping into the wall. Raquel kept giving Mary Beth breaths of her oxygen. Jambo and Silke joined the rescue effort. She and Troy exchanged relieved smiles. Jambo reached in with his long arms, his fingers tearing away sections of wall.

After a long few minutes, they had created a hole large enough for the ladies to pass through. Denny dragged out Mary Beth. They shared air as they swam out. Raquel guided Diana down the hall, seeking escape. Rae was injured and unable to kick. One of her fins hung at an odd angle, her left ankle broken and bruised purple. Jambo and Silke took her by the arms and drew her along.

The black hole was empty. The darkness yawned, attempting to mesmerize Troy. He caught a glimpse of a figure, Dillon there, then gone. Troy knew better. Desiree took his arm and dragged him along.

Their headlamps and flashlights, all of them, abruptly died at the same time, leaving only the radiance from their glow sticks. The darkness's grasp grew colder and tighter. Troy tried his flashlight, and nothing happened. Pushing down his panic, Troy cracked another glow stick. The shadows seemed to leap away from them, their claws yanked back as they returned to normal.

As if a silent train rumbled past, the whole building shook. Mud drifted down from the walls, and then, in slow motion, the ceiling and walls collapsed. In unison, Troy and Desiree raced for the nearest window. Rotted wood and loosened rock tumbled down around him. Troy kicked and swam to escape, reaching the shutters, but he couldn't see anything in the muddy mess.

Debris struck and knocked him around. The shutter blew out, taking him with it. Troy thought he had escaped when something large and heavy landed across the back of his legs. He yanked his right leg out, but the left remained trapped, squished painfully into the mud. He reached down with his hands and found a beam pinning his leg.

Everything was dark, except his gauges. Even his glow stick had been torn free and buried. He considered himself lucky to only have one leg caught, and he hadn't been hit in the head or back.

How much of the house had fallen on him? On Silke, Desiree, and the others?! They might be trapped, too, and injured, perhaps dying.

His fearful thoughts fed him raw energy, but he forced himself to slow down. He closed his eyes and focused on slowing his heart rate and breathing. Panicking would simply kill him quicker by consuming his air faster. He tried to twist to see better. The sediment had created a dirt fog, so he couldn't see anything.

What had happened to Desiree? There were no bubbles nearby and no sign of her. He would have to free himself then worry about the others. He couldn't count on a rescue. They might all be dead.

Stonework rested under the muck, so digging failed. He could sure use that metal spatula now as a lever.

He unsheathed his knife and started hacking chunks out of the beam. It was slow work, but it could be worse. He began to pray, the only way to keep his mind off what might have happened to the others. Had he survived dying on the mountain and in the hospital and all that rehab to die like this?

Once, he had been buried in an avalanche in the back country while shredding with John, Dillon, Knives and a few crazy college buds. The oppression felt similar although Troy could move more now than then. In the snow, he had been held immobile. He had worried about his friends then, hoping they had escaped.

John had found him. Almost blacked out, Troy could easily remember his smile. But then, this place had killed John. Troy had an insane urge to give the mansion the finger, irrationally feeling it had done this intentionally to them. He found some satisfaction in cutting away chunks of beam, but it was happening too slowly. There was no reason to waste time checking his air. Either he cut through, someone showed up, or he died. Cutting off his leg was not an option. He would bleed to death.

In between the mantra of the prayer of protection, regrets tried to push in. He wished he had passionately savored kissing Silke earlier tonight. He longed to know if that spark was more than a passing fancy, more than comfort against the fear of how short life could be.

If nothing else, he wanted to live long enough to face Dillon and punch him.

Troy kept hacking into the beam, now more than halfway through. He realized he wasn't going to make it.

That's when he saw John's ghost. With a devil-may-care smile, he strolled out of the darkness, bright like a beacon of life and hope. He reached down and tried to lift the beam up, but it remained immobile. He pointed to Troy, then at the beam, making a lifting motion.

Troy shook his head, but he tried. Of course, even lifting together didn't work. John pointed at him again. Troy was about to get angry when he realized John pointed at his BC. Why? It wasn't trapped. Slipping out of it wouldn't free him. Inflating it wouldn't drag him free.

Then it hit him. John smiled, too. Troy unbuckled and unzipped his BC, also taking off his tank. He put it back on, removed his weight belt, and stuffed the flattened buoyancy compensator under the beam. With little choice, he used the last of his air to inflate the bladder in the vest. It swelled, rising, and lifting a little. He could barely move his leg, having to use his hands to drag it out as he pushed with his right, slowly, agonizingly scraping his limb loose.

The beam resettled, squishing the BC. Something failed, likely the valve, as air was forced out, bubbles floating up.

Free! He wanted to shoot up to the surface. The exhilaration made Troy dizzy. He drew in a breath and felt nothing left in the tank.

Empty.

He grabbed the valve on the BC just as the last of the air escaped. It was one hundred and ten feet to the surface. He began kicking and rising. He thought he might be able to make it if he traveled at the speed of the bubbles. Because of the lessening pressure of the water as he rose, the air in his lungs expanded. Scientifically, he should be able to reach the surface. Deep divers did this all the time.

But, he had been on the bottom too long. He might get the bends. Those could kill him. On the other hand, not reaching the surface would kill him in sixty seconds. He prayed that as he rose, there might be some air left in his tank.

He kept his strokes and kicks slow. The exhaled bubbles crawled across his face as they headed for the surface. This was sometimes what it felt like when he awakened from sleep, slogging his way to the surface of consciousness. In the distance, he could see a dim glow. It slowly brightened. He felt like each little bubble of air was only being exhaled because he was rising.

His tank seemed completely empty. Without fresh oxygen, his legs and arms grew heavier, turning into lead. The glow at the surface seemed to grow wider, then suddenly, it shrank. Blacking out, Troy thought. He couldn't swim any faster.

Something snagged his leg, dragging him down. He wasn't going to make it.

Darkness washed over him.

Thirty-One: Post Night Dive

Troy followed the crowd as they shuffled ahead, moving out from the overhanging shadow into the sunshine. He was disoriented, but he knew their solemn dress and gloomy mood meant another funeral. Who this time? He recognized most of the people, acquaintances and childhood friends from the Tri Cities.

Ahead, he heard weeping so powerful it made him hesitate to continue, but he found he couldn't resist and gravitated toward the sound. Below the heavy sighs and murmurs, the soft lapping of water tried to comfort the mourners. Cycles were natural. Life began and ended every day, all the time, all year, for centuries and millennia. Instead of ashes, water to water, he thought.

He grew concerned as he wove his way between people to the front, by his high school ski coach, past Mr. T, and Mrs. Fleenor from the gym and Martin, by Deputy Burt. Troy realized Silke was weeping, which meant Dillon was dead.

His blood brother stood on the dock, getting ready to lower a canoe into the water. Father Dennis said some kind words Troy never heard, so shocked at seeing Dillon alive and himself dead on the canoe. Silke laid over him, even as Dillon tried to guide her away. She refused until Jambo gently drew her aside. Raquel, tears running down her cheeks, kissed Troy goodbye, and then his friends lowered the canoe into the water.

With a foot-shove, Marader sent it gliding out, the rope trailing behind it. Troy watched as the Viking style funeral boat slid across the water, leaving the shade for the sun. His body began to smolder, much as John's had smoked during his last rites ceremony. Abruptly, flames burst around Troy's corpse with an echoing whoosh to swiftly consume his body.

No! This was a nightmare!

His body toppled and crashed through the burnt side of the canoe. The flames devouring his body were extinguished by the water. Sinking slowly, he headed for oblivion.

In the darkness, Troy vaguely realized he was swimming toward a circle of light on the surface of a placid lake. He wasn't as exhausted as last time, feeling stronger with the ascent. Something drew him upward, a current perhaps, making it easier to swim. The circle of light brightened to glaring. The water round him grew pale green, then turned blue before finally clearing. He was close enough to see the calm surface.

He reached up and broke into consciousness. He gasped, taking in sweet air and seeming to swell into himself. It took a moment, after a second painfully sweet, rattling breath, for his senses to return. He tingled all over, his lungs burning with life, even as he inhaled a third time, savoring it, and the taste of someone zesty. Raquel. She was well, or he was in heaven with forgiven, fallen angels.

"If she gave me mouth-to-mouth I would be revived, too," Walt said.

Troy opened his eyes and blearily stared up at Raquel. Her dazzling smile and dark eyes were a welcome sight. He coughed then said, "Ah, thank you."

"You're welcome," Raquel said, smiling as if all were right with the world. "I'm not ready to say farewell, evil house or no."

The mansion had collapsed! Troy recalled. Everyone had been inside. Silke?! J-Man! Knives. "How's Silke? Jay? . . ."

"I'm here, and we're better than you, daredevil," Silke breathed in his ear. Instant relief calmed his exhausted body. Troy finally realized he was resting on his back atop the ski platform with Raquel kneeling next to him. Silke floated in the water, her face almost level with his. Her smile beamed with sunshine in her eyes. She was safe and sound. Thank God. There were things to tell her. He could feel fatigue returning and the need to sleep. What if he slept and forgot more?

"You had everybody worried. You stopped breathing," Raquel said.

"Yeah, it was just getting exciting, like a scene from MASH. Knives was going to step in, cut open your chest and massage your heart," Marader joked.

"What about Desiree?"

"I'm here, alive with a headache. Sorry, I left you. I was dizzy and confused," Desiree said.

"I'm glad you made it," Troy replied.

It sounded as if everyone had reached the surface alive and well. Spider leaned in and put out an open palm. Troy weakly slapped it.

"You made it. I believe in miracles," Spider said.

"Thanks, Raquel," Silke said.

"Bless you for bringing him to me. I know how to bring him back to life," Raquel replied. Her teasing smile would revive a dead man.

"Well, you've come back from near dead again. You can stop testing your mortality. You're twenty-eight. By now, you should be over Young Man's Invulnerability Syndrome," Knives said.

Raquel stepped aside for the good doctor. He had a stethoscope with him, checking Troy's vitals. "How do you feel?"

"Grateful and weary."

"A good combination. Your lungs sound clear. Silke found

you in time. Good work, young lady," Knives said.

"God must still have plans for you," Father Dennis said.

"Amen to that," J-Man said. "Somehow Silke knew you were headed for the surface and found you. She dragged you the last ten feet."

"Hey, I saw him and jumped in to help," Spider said.

"Thank you, Spider. Y'all are Godsends, especially Silke," Troy said.

She beamed and kissed him on the forehead.

"Hey, I'm just glad I didn't have to kiss you," Spider replied.

From behind those close to him, Troy heard a scuffle.

"What? What's wrong?" Denny asked.

"I just need the lights on, that's all!" Mary Beth pleaded. She flipped switches, turning on all Maverick's lights. First, the cabin ones lit up the boat, then the external bulbs set alight the night.

"Isn't that overkill?" Marader asked.

"Not after being down there. I can write quite a story about fear and terror after that place," Rae coughed. She had her leg up, her ankle wrapped in a bag of ice.

"I will never look at the darkness the same way. Never. It's alive now. I can hear its heavy breathing when there's no wind to conceal it. The light. The brightness will keep it away," Mary Beth rambled.

Troy turned to Silke. "I know how she feels, except you're my light. I owe you my life," Troy said.

She smiled. "Then I must think of some recompense, but mostly, you owe John. Now rest. We will celebrate later," she said.

A scream ripped the night and startled everyone, as Eduardo attacked Denny. The impact pushed him back where Denny bumped into Knives. Spider grabbed him and kept the doctor on board and dry.

Snarling, Eduardo landed atop Denny, driving him on the sun deck. His head hit hard on the padded platform, and his eyes rolled. Diana tried to pull Eduardo away. His elbow caught her on the jaw, dropping her, sending Raquel to her side. Eduardo fought through Denny's hands to grab him by the throat, choking him, until Jambo put the crazy young man in a full Nelson and lifted him into the air. Knives grabbed another injection from his medicine bag and administered a sedative.

Sometime after dawn, Troy awakened groggily to multiple body pains. He felt like he'd been in a bad crash landing. He groaned, feeling like a house had fallen on him. Oh yeah, it had, although, it had been a mansion collapsing on them, he recalled, so it wasn't completely personal. Bless John's soul, his ghost had saved him. Had Troy really seen all those ghosts, hundreds, and relived some of their memories? Was he going insane and taking others with him, railing on the "Crazy Train"?

Unfortunately, Troy had the aches to prove it wasn't a nightmare.

The air was quiet with the soft lapping of water. A gentle rocking had helped him doze and stay asleep. Where was he? It felt like a couch.

He pried open his eyes and found himself in the lounge on the couch of Denny's houseboat, celebrating breathing on the Salibration. Sunshine splayed through the window blinds, creating rainbows and telling him he had survived another night to reach the day, thank God and John's ghost and Silke.

He wondered about everyone else and vaguely recalled Marader dropping off Eduardo, Diana, Rae, Mary Beth, Raquel and Denny with the paramedics and ambulances at a boat ramp. He thought there might have been news crews swarming all over, of course, because of Raquel and Rae. The paramedics had assessed Troy's condition and turned him loose to the care of Dr. Curran and preferably, Silke.

Troy Bane had almost died again, he mused. Now he was dying to tell Silke the truth: that her brother was alive, and that Troy loved her, thinking she was incredible, his reason for living. He didn't want to live without her. He wanted to be that lucky guy, and they could tell Dillon to get over it.

Earlier this morning, before Silke had departed, he had meant to tell her all that and more. He had been so wiped out that he couldn't remember much, except for her kiss before she departed to visit her mother and Aunt Jada at the hospital. Sex, drama and danger are what the brain remembered, he recalled. He should have begged Silke to stay and use her magic hands on him.

He struggled to sit up on the couch. Honestly, he felt better than expected, considering what happened to them. He took the ankh and held it in the sunlight to watch it glint and sparkle. Might this have healing properties? The power of life created new and renewed, healing. If he believed it, would it make it placebo so? Even if it did, he was going to use modern medicine in a pill and likely, it would be a day of icing his body.

Missing Silke, he picked up his phone to call her and found a message from her: Good morning. IM @ hospital. Jada with us. How RU?

How was he feeling? Exhausted and yet hopeful. His thoughts spun from recent events and experiences. They had saved four people from the mansion of death. Feeling lousy was better than incapacitated or dead. Sitting on the table was a tall glass of water, a bowl of fruit, and a bottle of ibuprofen. Silke looked after him. He took four IBs with a banana and drained the glass.

He checked other messages, including a text from J-Man. Spoke with D Burt. Upset about effigy.

Great. Well, Troy knew this had been coming. Standing to pace, Troy stretched and wondered how long he had until the deputy showed up. Troy didn't think he had done nothing wrong, or had he? He and J-Man had taken John's body from the East Hill Cemetery, even if it hadn't belonged there. Why didn't that seem wrong? Because they didn't want him to kill again. There was no way to explain it. Who would believe that

John had returned to the world of the living as a vampire, killed those in the morgue, escaped the hospital, and walked across Bristol to the East Hill Cemetery, where he was ready to kill some more?

Troy could still hear John's voice, telling them what wouldn't hurt him and how to kill him. Troy couldn't forget watching the light leave John's eyes, but then, that had been supernatural shine, not really John. Even in his ghostly form, he had come to Troy's aid, just like one would expect of a naval diver.

He sent off a message to Silke: Crazy about U. He limped and staggered into the shower and tried to wake up.

Troy dressed, including socks and shoes, just in case he ended up in jail.

The boat rocked with footsteps. Troy looked up, seeing a shadow approach the door. The figure knocked on the door. Troy felt an uncomfortable chill, despite the sunshine and the warmth of the houseboat. Touching the ankh to check its temperature, he limped to the door. The ankh remained cool, so he opened the door to sunlight and a grizzled, rheumy-eyed Deputy Burt.

"Troy Bane. It's about damn time we had a heart to heart. May I come in? I have some questions about what happened last night," he grumped in a gravelly voice. He rubbed his eyes.

Instead of inviting him in, Troy stepped outside. He noticed the deputy didn't sit, so Troy stayed afoot.

Damn. Troy had to keep his wits alive. Sounding crazy and getting thrown into jail wouldn't help anyone.

"Are you all right?"

"No, I feel one step from going to ER. Sorry, the pain relievers will kick in sometime soon."

"Tell me what happened last night," Deputy Burt prompted. He crossed his arms.

Troy recounted being called to help Raquel and Father Dennis rescue friends and family. He hadn't wanted to go, and yet, he couldn't say no. He had never done well at telling Raquel no, and how could he let down Denny, too?

In need of caffeine, Troy limped over to the restaurant. The deputy shadowed him and accepted a Cup of Joe from Sandy before she went to work in the back room.

"You have just been in the middle of numerous strange happenings. Give me some reasons for not arresting you," Deputy Burt said.

"For what?"

"Entering a crime scene to mention one."

"To perform a rescue."

"Obstructing an investigation for two. Three, for removing evidence from a crime scene. If you go to jail, you'll miss Silke and Raquel and the lovely ladies who work here."

What had he removed from the crime scene? Troy wondered. A cufflink? Or was Deputy Burt talking about the effigy?

"Why did you come back to town?"

"I came back to help search for John, and I wound up hunting for Dillon."

"And failing. So much for you vaunted sense of where Dillon is."

"Oh, I felt where he is. I told you: he's at the Swearingtons. I just haven't figured out a way to contact him or prove it to anyone," Troy replied.

"Yeah, well, like I said, we don't have anything else to go on. Frankly, I'm concerned because Dillon was looking for why Pat was murdered. Investigative reporters have a tendency to rub people the wrong way. I figure you and your buds have pissed off somebody. First, there was the discovery of Pat's body and the realization there is a murderer out there. Then, there was a suspicious house explosion followed by a car wreck. Dillon's great aunt's house, right? I spoke with the deputies involved. They see no reason to charge you in either case, especially after both Silke and Sister Elva mentioned Jada seeing a strange man outside."

"She said his name was Zane."

"True. Then, you just happened to be in the hospital when the basement was flooded with toxic chemicals, and you saved Dr. Curran. That's the same night John Traylor's body went missing. Bizarre, don't you think? Coincidence, I think not. What are you not telling me?"

"Do you believe someone is trying to kill John's friends?"

"I guess that could be. John is dead. Dillon is missing. Walt had a car wreck. Dr. Curran was poisoned. You've had your close calls. You could make a case. What about the others?"

"Jay's been having issues with his helicopter. And Father Dennis' wife was injured in the brawl where Marader was attacked during a robbery attempt," Troy said.

"He and almost everybody at the wake," Deputy Burt said.

Troy could feel the caffeine working. He would still have to wait on the pain relievers. Sandy returned with a bag of ice for Troy. Along with a towel, he used it to chill his injured leg.

"After the downtown brawl, you went to graveyard where John's body had supposedly been found. You, Dr. Curran, Jay Beck, and the keeper were assaulted. Tell me about the assailant."

"He looked like John's brother, except he doesn't have one," Troy said.

"And he just stopped attacking you?"

"Hell no. I hit him hard with a rake, knocked the wind out of him" Troy said. He was telling the truth. "That's when I noticed what I thought was John's body but wasn't. As Knives said, it couldn't be for lots of reasons. For one, it didn't look waterlogged. Two it wasn't decomposing. Anyway, I saw what I thought was John. I don't know what happened to his doppelganger, our attacker."

"Uh-huh. Did you remove anything from the East Hill Cemetery?"

"Yes, that strange effigy of John. It had been damaged during the fight."

"Did you report this to Bristol PD?"

"No," Troy replied.

"Why?" Deputy Burt asked and leaned closer. "You realize the police can press charges. You're smart. You knew this. And yet, you did it anyway, and so did the Eagle Scout Jay Beck. That's not like him. He is not a law breaker. So why? Why did you take it?"

"I thought it might help us find John's body or even Dillon," Troy said. He hadn't wanted John to kill anyone else, or attempt to kill them, again. Telling the deputy that might open Pandora's box.

"You made a mistake. We might have used it to help us find John's killer, but I hear it spontaneously combusted. How God damned convenient," Deputy Burt snapped.

"It was startling. Beforehand, Knives performed tests on it to confirm it wasn't a body. We don't understand why it went up in flames. There was nothing combustible in the canoe or on the effigy," Troy said. "Knives doesn't believe that, but he has his own test results."

"You are a poor liar."

"That's true, but I am telling you the truth."

"J-Man confessed that he fired numerous shots into the attacker."

"Hit or miss, the assailant who I think of as Imposter John kept attacking us."

"There were no slugs in the walls. There was no blood, either."

"I don't understand why shooting didn't stop him," Troy said.

"You are so full of it, Bane. I can't do anything about that event except forward the report to Bristol PD. What I can do is arrest your ass for entering a crime scene. You knew better than to dive inside the mansion. Maybe a little time in county will jog your memory about what you've forgotten to tell me, and I'll get the whole truth. Stand up. Troy Bane, you are under arrest," Deputy Burt said.

"Will I be seeing, J-Man?"

"Once he gets off fire duty, I'll arrest his ass, too."

"Then arrest me as well," Raquel said. She and Rae Kirkland entered the restaurant. Raquel glared daggers at the deputy as she strolled to Troy's side and kissed him on the cheek. "Thank you for helping me save Diana. She's with Eduardo in the hospital. He isn't doing well."

Rae approached Troy from the other side. She pecked his other cheek. "I am grateful y'all came to my aid. I wonder if this will improve my street cred, reporting from behind bars." She and Raquel smiled sweetly at the deputy who scowled at the new arrivals.

"Don't tempt me," he groused.

"I'm sorry you got hurt. I'll try never to do something so stupid like this again," Rae told Troy.

"Don't make promises you can't keep. I'm glad everyone made it out. That doesn't always happen," Troy said.

"We went in to save lives. Too cold to go there for any other reason. Anyway, I guess what I am saying is, you should arrest my ass, too," Marader added. He still carried a beer.

"Now that is music to my ears. Unfortunately, county lockup is already overcrowded."

"Oh, I love race time. How about you?" Marader laughed.

Deputy Burt glared at Troy and Marader. "You burned what could have been an important part of investigation. I could and should arrest y'all, the whole lot of blood brothers."

"That would clear you two," Marader said to Raquel and Rae. Looking determined, they stood their ground next to Troy.

From somewhere, Spider appeared. He took a selfie with them in the background. "My last photo bomb before going to jail. I'm at least an accessory to the accidental destruction of evidence," he said. He hit a button on his phone. "There, posted to my account. Possibly the last sighting of Spider Adder."

Walt limped in. He noticed the group and sauntered over.

"Walt was there. You'll have to arrest him, too, officer. I

swear he said some heated words," Marader said. Deputy Burt scowled at him.

"What? Where? I swear, Marader made me do it," Walt stammered.

"He's upset about the effigy," Marader said.

"Oh, well, who wouldn't be? It was disturbing," Walt replied, calming down.

"You'll see me again, soon," Deputy Burt groused and left.

Troy watched the deputy leave. He was sorry he couldn't confide in him about the supernatural. Taking the body now seemed irrational, but at the time it seemed like nothing was more urgent. Could Undead John have influenced them like Zane?

"Hey, everyone, thank you for the love and supporting me," Troy said.

"Ah, it's nothing," Walt said.

"I love jerkin' Burt's chain," Marader said.

"I want you to be treated fairly," Rae said.

Raquel smiled warmly. "You were there for us. All of you were. Because of that, I'm having lobster and filet and champagne and other spirits delivered for tonight's life celebration," she told them.

"I would rather be celebrating the living tonight, instead of the abrupt end of a life," Troy said, trying to keep the bitterness out of his voice.

"Oh, baby. This wake is going to be a blow out," Marader said. He celebrated with fist pumps.

A truck horn honked on the shore side.

"That might be them. Thanks, Raquel. Cheers!" Marader said and rushed off. He was ready to unload and get loaded. Some things never did change.

"Troy, what was the deputy talking about? Taking a body from East Hill?" Rae asked.

"Rae, do a want to conduct that interview now, about last night's dive?" Spider asked.

"Sure, my camerawoman, Jeri, is over here," Rae said,

leaving Troy and Raquel alone.

Raquel touched his face and held his eyes with her intense gaze. "I won't be here tonight. I'll be in Knoxville. There's a benefit for Para Olympics. I'm supposed to speak, which I hate, but I promised. It's for a great cause. So, because of that, I won't be here tonight. I wanted to personally thank y'all. I'll have to catch up with the others later, hopefully at something more festive."

"I'm glad you were here, or I might be in jail," he replied.

"Ah, this was minor compared what you did for me, for us, considering how you've felt all these years," Raquel said.

"I let that burden go. It's in the past. I am reborn. Heavensent, I've been told. It's a new life with a different attitude and choices," Troy said, taking a breath. He had finally reached that place while almost dying on the bottom of the lake. He knew who and what was important to him.

"You forgive yourself. What about me?"

"I forgave you a long time ago," Troy said.

Raquel beamed, her smile transformed, no longer hesitant but full. He felt her relax and a tension between them melted away. "I'm glad we can talk with each other again. So, are you going to tell me about this John effigy?" Raquel asked.

"It is better that you don't know," Troy said.

"Does this have anything to do with the downtown brawl?" Raquel asked.

"I think so. I think John or Dillon stirred up some kind of hornet's nest. It might be best if you stayed out of town for a while."

"Really? Why?" she asked.

"I have a feeling it's going to get wild, like the downtown brawl or worse," Troy said. He hadn't told her about Undead John. Her genuine smile came easily. "You care for me. That's wonderful. But, I see that you're staying."

"I can't leave my blood brothers and their families. My friends might be targets."

"I can't leave either. I have friends, family plus a business here, and this is a special place. You know that. Is Silke a target?" Raquel asked. That question sounded like two queries.

"Yes, because of Dillon, and she's been to that evil place, too, twice now."

Raquel held up her arm. She had bruises where the bracelet had encircled her wrist. "I believe you were right. I was different while wearing the black pearls. I think that place stained us all," she said and shuddered.

"Just another reminder of how fragile life is. I'll do what I can to protect my friends and Silke. I think she's special."

"I can tell," Raquel replied. She drew a long Silke's hair off his shirt.

Did he want Raquel back? If so, this would be the time to tell her. There might not be a tomorrow. How could he turn down his heart's yearning? Because of Silke. They were special together.

"We aren't a couple, yet, but I am going to ask Silke to be my lady," Troy said.

Raquel nodded calmly as if she had expected this news. He couldn't tell how she felt about it. Unlike Silke, Raquel kept her feelings to herself. It had been one of the challenges of the relationship with him guessing about what was going on with her.

"I am envious," she finally replied.

"Thank you for that," Troy said.

The moment grew awkward.

For years, he had yearned to be near her and have this kind of rapport. Every part of his DNA and his soul had screamed for it, prayed for it, and now that he had it, he was going to let her walk away. Raquel still made his heart race, perhaps she always would, but Troy was smitten with Silke and ready for a new adventure.

"Farewell," she said and kissed him on the cheek.

"Travel safely and Godspeed," Troy said.

Carter waited for Raquel at the corner. Together, they departed.

And with that, Raquel was gone, perhaps out of his life for good. He hoped she would be safe and well. For once, he didn't have a sinking feeling. He felt lighter for having let her go.

His phone rang with an incoming call from Denny. "Hello, Mr. Bane. How are you feeling, brother?"

"Grateful to be alive, thanks. How are you and Colleen?" Troy asked. He caressed the ankh, watching it catch the light.

"No changes. I pray no news is good news. Unfortunately, Mary Beth is getting worse. She has developed paranoia since last night's trauma."

"I'm sorry to hear that, but I understand," Troy said.

"I got your message. I would be honored to bless Marader's place. It could use it, I'm sure. We will keep away the evil spirits and drink and toast the good ones. Hmm. I've got another call. See you tonight. God bless," Father Dennis said.

When Troy looked up, Rae stood there. "Got a moment for an interview?" she asked.

"Really? Now? I'm half awake, and I look ill. Can't it wait?"

"You helped rescued me, so no, it can't wait. Don't worry. You look rugged. Just a few questions about the dive, and nothing else, unless you'll say something about coming back to life and returning to Bristol. You could put out a public plea to help you find Dillon," Rae said.

"That's a good idea," Troy lied. Not really, since he knew where Dillon hid. Even so, he must play the game when he would have preferred to tell the truth. "What questions?"

"What was it like dying and coming back? How long did it take you to get back to walking and skiing? Do you now have a different perspective on life?" she said. He nodded. "And about last night. Why did you go back in there? What happened? How did you escape the place's collapse? No more than ten minutes, I promise. Don't make me beg," Rae said.

She had also stood by his side. The interview took almost an hour. By that time, Troy was exhausted. "Later, when not on camera, I'm going to ask you what Deputy Burt was haranguing you about," Rae said with a wink, and then she and her video camera-toting sidekick departed.

Back in the houseboat, Troy took off his shoes, put down his phone and readied to nap on the couch. Tawny jumped on the counter, landing on his phone, and then Marader's cat sprang into his lap. Troy petted Tawny and started telling her about Elke and Dillon. He actually found his voice and fell asleep talking to the cat about the selfish lovers and what they had compelled him to do.

Not dead to the world, Troy slept until late afternoon. He was surprised Silke hadn't called. He checked his phone, finding one message: IM @ spa. He also discovered his smart phone had been on, recording while he slept. He played the video from the beginning, where it started with a bounce and a flash of a departing Tawny cat. Continuing to listen, Troy realized that it had recorded his soliloquy about Dillon. Troy couldn't tell Silke, but he could play the recording. What luck!

He tried calling her but she didn't answer. Worried about her, he tried the land line to the main desk of the spa and reached Mrs. Fleenor. "Oh, boy, Sonny. You are in trouble."

Thirty-Two: Confrontations

Frustrated and concerned, Troy found Dillon's keys in his truck and drove twenty-five minutes into town to the State Street Gym and Spa. Mrs. Fleenor had promised she wouldn't let Silke leave early. According to her, Silke was furious with him after catching snippets from his interview, seeing him with That Woman.

Troy was angry enough, a simmering fury toward her brother and his lover, that he felt he could tell her about Dillon's new antics and Elke, though, that seemed less important than telling Silke that he didn't want to be a pretend beau. He wanted to be more, whatever that was and wherever it headed. He would tell Dillon to live with them being a couple. Troy noticed his clenched fists and relaxed them. All these secrets were hurting his relationships.

Well, he was going to shine a light on them.

In the parking lot, he sat for a minute, going over what he was going to say. Once he told her about Dillon, she might quit listening, or demand to go there now. Take tear gas, a shot gun, and kick down the front door of the Swearington Lodge. Troy mentally shook himself, trying to release his anger. He wasn't mad at Silke but frustrated by events and furious at her brother's manipulations.

Troy walked into the gym's lobby and heard Mrs. Fleenor talking. She stood in Silke's doorway. He was headed that way when he was intercepted.

A huge young man, as wide as he was tall, a mini hulk wearing a green jersey and purple shorts stepped in his way. Mini Hulk shook a meaty fist under his nose. "She doesn't want to see you."

"I would like the opportunity to apologize," Troy said. Mini Hulk grunted and stalked on by.

Troy approached Mrs. Fleenor and tapped her on the shoulder. She turned while Silke kept saying she couldn't stay for another customer, regardless of the problem.

"Well, I need plenty of work and urgently. I have a death wish along with numerous physical challenges."

Silke's head jerked up, hearing and now seeing him. "Mr. Bane. You are a piece of work. And I can see you have a death wish, so get out. I don't want to see you today. I'm tired," she growled.

"I told you," Mini Hulk said, putting his hand on Troy's shoulder.

"Take your hand off me before you regret it," Troy said, his anger slipping out. He was furious with Dillon and Elke, not this guy. Mini Hulk's grip tightened. Long ago, Dillon had shown Troy how to deal with big dudes.

Troy performed a judo move, swiftly shifting to lock Mini

Hulk's arm and pressure it, threatening to pop it from a socket. The muscle-head dropped to a knee, yelping in pain. "I asked you to take your hand off me. You're lucky I don't make it useless," Troy snarled.

Silke grabbed him, shaking him. "Troy, stop! Stop! Let him go."

Troy regained hold of his turbulent emotions. He released the Mini Hulk who staggered back.

"Are you messing with my hero, man?" Martin asked. He showed up to defend Troy.

Troy only had eyes for Silke. Livid, heat radiated from her. "You aren't acting like yourself. I wonder if I know you anymore," Silke snapped.

He realized she spoke the truth. He didn't usually get this angry. It was all the people manipulating him. At the moment, in her gorgeous, blazing eyes, all he could find was her fury. He could relate to her disappointment. It splashed him like cold water.

"You're right. I'm not. I'm sorry, I'm not mad at you," he said to Mini Hulk then spun on his heel and left. Troy felt like he could kick down a door. It sounded like an excellent idea right now.

In a flash, he made the decision. To hell with Deputy Burt. Troy Bane would not idly wait for Dillon to show up, especially since Elke could be lying to him.

Silke might have called his name, but he kept going. He didn't want her to see him confront Dillon.

Troy found himself outside, where it was hotter and humid, like a storm was brewing. He didn't break too many traffic laws leaving town.

On the drive to the north end of Holston, Troy had plenty of time to think and several phone calls to ignore. Dillon had known he would come looking for him. Why hadn't he contacted him sooner? Elke said he had been recovering. Why didn't he contact Troy directly? Why had he lied about Troy to

Silke? Did Dillon think Troy was unworthy of his sister?

He checked his watch. He still had plenty of time before the wake started, if he lived to see it.

Thankfully, it was summer, so despite the hour, the daylight stretched on, now along with the shadows. There were two hours left until dark, though the heavy woods provided an abundance of shade and cover for the Swearington Estate and its denizens. They had kept everything well-watered, so it remained protected from the sun. The gates stood closed and locked, but there was no surrounding wall out here, only closer to the house. He recalled the ditch, almost like an empty moat around the place, and wondered if Dillon's truck could navigate it.

Walking in would be foolish because of the guard dogs.

He parked outside the gates to look around before doing something rash. He opened the backpack that he had loaded. The phone rang again, but it wasn't Dillon. Knives was calling. No, he wasn't all right; he was furious and not fit to be around people.

He visually searched the area, seeing neither man nor ghosts. Should he? While Troy explored the ditch, finding spikes that would shred the truck's tires, his phone rang again. He wasn't going to answer it, but it was Silke. What kind of place had guard dogs, a mini moat, spikes, and a walled lodge? Elke also had a bodyguard, Mr. Thick.

Troy answered the phone. "Hi, Silke. I'm sorry to have barged in on you."

"Troy, how are you?"

He looked at the spikes then off toward the house. "Aggrieved and angry with your brother."

"Join the club. You want to talk now? Where are you?"

"I'm blowing off steam, so I'll be tolerable tonight at the wake," he said. He cocked his head, hearing a distance howl. Dogs?

"Do you plan to stand up and share about John tonight?" Silke asked. Troy felt a cool breeze, an oddity. It smelled heavily of espresso, reminding him of John who had dearly loved strong coffee. "Troy?"

"I smelled coffee, so I thought of John," Troy said.

"Where are you?"

"Trying to get to your brother," Troy said.

"You know where he is?"

Troy startled, seeing a patch of fog gather into a shape. He almost dropped his phone. A bug flew in his open mouth, and he gagged. An impish smile, so like John, flickered across his face as an apparition floated before him. When he saw he had Troy's attention, he waved in a warning gesture.

"Can you talk to me?" Troy asked. John glared, made a shooing gesture, and pointed behind Troy. The foggy figure wanted him to leave. There was no doubt of that communication. The ghost walked with John's rolling gait.

"You're obviously not the ghost of Christmas present," Troy rambled. He began backing up.

"Troy, can you hear me?" Silke asked.

"Now, I can, you cut out for a second," he replied. In the distance, he thought he heard hounds baying. They had loosed the dogs on him. Good, he had someone's attention. He hurried back toward the front gate, thinking the truck would protect him. He hoped the beasts couldn't rip off the doors. Well, if not, he had a few surprises in hand.

"Where are you?" she asked.

"On my way to Marader's," he said. The dogs were incredibly fast, getting louder.

"Are those dogs I hear?"

"I don't think they're wolves," Troy said.

Materializing silently from the shade, the dark shadows became hounds. The beasts surrounded the truck. He cursed before realizing he had human company, the surprising keeper of the dogs.

"Troy, are you all right?" Silke asked.

Moving with a feline grace, Desiree sashayed toward him. As usual, her appearance lived up to her name, looking quest worthy, almost too good to be true. Her leopard-print tank top was drawn tight into a black, slit skirt. What was she doing here? She patted two dogs on the head as she passed them to stalk toward Troy.

"If I don't show tonight, swear and lodge a complaint for me," Troy told Silke.

"Troy?!"

Whatever he would tell her would only lead to problems. He hoped desire didn't kill him. "See you soon. I have a lot to tell you," Troy said and hung up. "What are you doing here?"

Desiree stopped inches away, kissed him on the cheek, and then stepped back, studying him. "Saving your life. The dogs think you taste succulent and so do I. Take your pick? Give me a ride to the party, or let the hounds eat you?" Desiree replied.

"I think you deserve a classier ride than a truck."

"I'm more interested in your driving skills, and the way you're going," she laughed wickedly.

Troy thought this should be fun. Walking into the wake with Desiree seemed like an unwise move, unless he wanted to anger Silke more. He sighed inwardly. Giving the sexy Latina a ride might be a mistake, but he had little choice since he wanted to know about her connection to Elke and the Swearingtons.

Once in the truck, Desiree snuggled up next to him. "I didn't know John, but it's always interesting to hear what people have to say about the deceased. Or if nobody speaks at all."

"You go to a lot of wakes?" Troy asked, joking.

"More than I want. Comes from having a large, extended family. Do you ever wonder what people will say about you?"

Troy cleared his throat. "I certainly do now, but I hope I'm closer to people than Facebook friends. What were you doing at the Swearington Lodge tonight?"

"Waiting for you to do something passionately reckless," she replied. Her lips parted, and she breathed in his ear.

"And you knew I'd be there because we're one heart beating in two bodies?" he asked, playing along. Or was he playing? "Or is it just lust?"

She peeled with laughter. "It's more than just lust. We have a lot in common. You probably didn't know I almost drowned in Holston Lake. In fact, I did drown. I died and had to be revived. I hit my head doing flips off the dock. Stupid, right?"

Troy could relate. "Elke?"

Desiree nodded. "Her bodyguard, Bryson, you call him Mr. Thick, dragged me out of the water. Elke brought me back from the dead. She's the reason I can attend wakes, and why I think of what others might say. We are a large family and yet still close, but distant to most others. I clearly remember dying. The moment of peace. Leaving my body. Speeding around like a thought splintering in different directions as I said my last good-byes. For those few moments, I saw the world differently. A veil had been drawn back. When I returned to my body, thanks to my aunt, I perceived the world differently, and that has affected my mind and body."

"I can understand that."

"Yes, and you had to fight your way back to a healthy body. I found I had more time by taking time less for granted, and I honed my body. You like, I can tell. I can do more than water ski and dive. I am quite adventuresome and surprisingly rugged, if I do say so myself. I am a very skilled knuckledragger, sky rider, base jumper, and wingsuit pilot, as well as a Kama Sutraist. See, I told you we had many things in common. I know you've been looking for someone like me, charming, smart, sexy . . ."

"You're trying to distract me," Troy said. He focused on driving to see Silke.

"And failing. Strange how thought can override physical sensations, will over emotions. That's the way it works. Thought. Will. Emotion then the physical. Am I right?"

"Yes."

"We do think alike, too." She sighed when he said nothing.

"Well, it must be true love you have for Silke. I must say I haven't encountered it before. Heard about it, though, mostly in stories and songs. What were you doing at the gates to the estate?"

"I think my missing blood brother, Dillon, is a guest there. He might be a reluctant guest of Elke's, but I doubt it."

"She might have saved his life, too, as she saved mine."

"Are you related to your aunt?"

"Adopted but without paperwork. I reside there during the summer and holidays and take care of the dogs when I can to repay them, plus the dogs are so loving."

"I'm sure, if you're into things that sink their teeth into you," he said.

"I am, as I've mentioned."

He let it drop. "I was hoping to confront Dillon."

"He might be there. I know Elke has a new beau that I've yet to meet. I've never seen her so happy, especially with all the stress," she said and continued when she saw Troy's questioning look. "There's a big event coming up soon. Believe it or not, art collecting, mostly making connections with eccentric people, is demanding. I chose not to follow that path as I am a sun lover as you can tell. That's why I'm studying biology and chemistry."

"Your Aunt Elke doesn't have you spying, does she?"

"Working undercover? At Maraders? Give me a break. I would work undercover on you, or is that for you or with you? They all sound good."

"John would have liked you," he said.

"You almost said, too."

"What are you doing, Desiree?"

"Trying to keep you alive for when my night comes," she said with a confident smile.

Troy didn't smile back. Aunt Jada's warning about dark eyes returned to him. He felt very much in danger, his life fragile at the moment. "What did you do with the letter opener and stick pen you found in the mansion on the bottom of the lake?" Troy asked.

"Gave them to Elke."

"Do you believe in nightwalkers?"

"I am a night prowler. Does that count?"

"How about vampires?" he asked.

"I already told you about things that bite. Those dogs are right. Your ears do look tasty and your neck yearns to be nibbled. And if you're unwilling, there will be boys in uniform to tease tonight."

Troy breathed an inward sigh of relief. "You will make them fall over themselves. Still, I hope this is more mellow than Pat's wake. It should be, unless you plan to make waves."

"They are Coast Guard boys. No promises. Don't worry. I won't mess with you and Silke. You two face enough challenges, Romeo. Like I said, I'll be trying to keep you alive."

"You're protecting me? From what?" he asked astonished.

"If nothing else, yourself. I haven't given up on you. There will come a time when you need me. According to Jada, it will be necessary to take you through the shadow back into the light."

"You visited Aunt Jada?" Troy asked.

"Yes. She conducted readings for Elke and others, like myself. She knows, or knew, as she has lost much of her memory, about Von Damme and Moontown, a.k.a. Wreythville. Von Damme and his ilk stole her Zane, who tried to steal your Silke. Nightwalkers, as she liked to call them, enjoy stealing passionate people. Nightwalkers is such an innocuous term for such a deadly creature, don't you think?"

"Are you talking vampires?"

"Yes, you know they exist. You have encountered at least three in John, the Dark Lady Lyla, and Zane. I am not one, though I do enjoy vamping. And I am a patient lady. Well, maybe not a lady, but I can fake it, though it's less fun than vamping," she chuckled. "Life is fragile and short. The present is now, and all we have. Right?"

"I am not kissing you, even if I agree with you," Troy said.

What she had said echoed with what he had been thinking. The importance of now had inundated him since he had drowned. Life was short and fragile. Now he had his theme for his memorializing John, who had embraced a similar philosophy, you only live once.

"Elke mentioned you were watchers? Are you watching over Von Damme's mansion?" he asked, recalling the conversation.

"She told you that? Interesting. They were looking for any sign of the cult's return to sound the alarm."

"Alarm to who? Are there vampire hunters?" Troy asked.

"Yes. She will alert those who buried him."

Troy shivered. He recalled seeing Mona's last few minutes of life. "Will you share this knowledge with Silke and my blood brothers?" Troy asked.

"Hmm. I could trade favors," Desiree purred. He frowned. "Fine, but you will owe me. Besides, you figured out much of it. What does Nike say? Just do it? Weren't you in a commercial of theirs? Just do it? Kiss me."

"If I kissed you, I would probably end up a wreck. And here I thought you were protecting me from nightwalkers and myself," Troy said.

"You make fun of me now, but you'll be glad to have me around when all Hell breaks loose. I should have been with you at Pat's wake and the East Hill cemetery. I won't make that mistake again."

"I feel stalked."

"Cherished and protected," Desiree laughed. "After all, we have made it here without incident. Twenty minutes ago, you were about to be dog meat. So, I should get one mark in the to be trusted column."

Troy turned onto the marina road. Dust still hung in the late summer day air from recent traffic. A sign read: CLOSED except 4 boat owners. Gas available. Another displayed: AWAKE 4 JOHN. With the window down, Troy could hear a live band playing Pink Floyd's "Time".

The Rentzel Construction trucks were gone. Now, cars, trucks and SUVs lined and crowded the wide gravel road. It had been made for trailers and RVs, but Troy still had to carefully maneuver the truck to squeeze between the parallel rows of automobiles. He doubted there was any place to park, but his blood brothers had surprised him, reserving a spot for him.

HANDICAPPED. Below was a photo of Troy on crutches when he was a teen. Reserved for Troy Bane. A second sign read: Violators will be denied booze. He figured that was the only reason it was open and pulled into the spot. A flashing light started spinning and a horn sounded twice. "I guess they want to know if you're here, or if someone is in your spot."

"I can feel the love," Troy said.

"Hmm, this place feels different. I believe it's been blessed. That might give us some peace tonight. Might," she emphasized.

"Good. We can thank Father Dennis. How can you tell?" he replied.

"Oh, I'm a sinner, so I can tell. But it won't keep me out, unlike others," Desiree said. She blew him a kiss, opened the door, and whistled as she sashayed saucily toward the short bridge to the dock. It had been installed and decorated with LED's that slowly changed colors.

Troy waited a moment, going over what he would say if he saw Silke. He smelled BBQ and citronella, and the band started into "Bad to the Bone" by George Thorogood.

He noticed all the statuary of angels and cherubs, as well as different crosses and crucifixes staked around the parking lot. Father Dennis had sanctified the place. It should be safe. Shouldn't it?

Getting out of the car, Troy felt something jarringly wrong. He peered into the woods, looking for wolves and broke out in a sweat. He caught movement out of the corner of his eye. Had it been a dog? Or a trick of light?

Thirty-Three: Dead John's Wake

Troy steeled himself for tonight. It was more than saying good-bye. He feared some of Von Damme's dark agents might be here, so he stayed attuned to the ankh and its temperature. He hoped Father Dennis' blessing kept trouble away.

The pavement to the floating dock was lined with small American flags strung with red holiday lights. Visitors were greeted by a memorial collection of photos and objects important to John, all illuminated by flickering battery-powered candles. A Bristol High swim kickboard stood next to his Connelly slalom ski and over a baseball mitt. A Pirates' baseball cap hung from a tennis racket with a pair of trunks that looked like primary colored paint had been splashed over them. Troy's eyes roamed over the photographs of John enjoying life in Bristol, at the lake, at Viking Stadium, on the baseball field, in the pool, and at the Naval Academy. Another photo reminded Troy of the day they had ascended the slick face of Laurel Falls. A large picture of the blood brothers, sixteen years young, had them assuming silly poses under the Bristol sign.

John's Coast Guard buddies stood there to greet everyone who came in. They challenged Troy to a game of darts later, one of John's favorite drinking games.

"There you are! Where have you been? I could have used help rigging up the twenty-one-shell pyrotechnic salute," J-Man said. He was carrying a crate around to the lakeside of the store as Troy strolled up.

"Sorry. I was looking for Dillon and venting," Troy said.

"God, Troy. We were concerned. Silke called. She's upset and worried about you. What did you do to tick off Ms. Silke?" J-Man asked.

"Nothing. I think it's a misunderstanding," Troy replied.

"Knives saw her. Her great aunt is failing. He doubts she'll be here tonight."

Troy's heart sank. This day just kept getting better.

"Any news or clues on Dillon?" J-Man asked.

"Yes, he's not dead."

"You heard from the SOB? Know where he is and what the Hell's going on?"

"I really should tell Silke first," Troy said.

"Getting back to her, I'm serious about you treating her right. What do you think Dillon will do?"

"Ask me if I'm insane then shake my hand?" Troy asked wistfully.

J-Man laughed so loudly Troy left him to head for the food and drink. The wide-open restaurant doors let in the night air. With the band on break it was quiet except for conversation. He recognized almost everyone in the crowd of sixty. Raquel's sister, Diana, worked on a laptop next to Denny who was touching and dragging images to create what Troy assumed was the presentation. Troy marveled at him, here despite his wife's health.

J-Man cursed Marader, hopped into a skiff and trolled over to a floating island of mortar tubes, wires, and fuses.

John's parents found Troy, and they commiserated over the lost body. They also thanked him for finding it. Troy expressed relief that John's soul was not lost. He couldn't find the heart to tell them the truth about John's body, that he had let it burn in the sunlight. They wouldn't believe him anyway. John's ghost waved and hung around, but his parents never noticed, though they seemed to brighten and relax as if they subconsciously sensed him.

After Troy promised he would keep in touch, and John's parents moved on, Spider introduced him to several spirits: Beatrice had drowned, Ernie had hit his head, and Gordy, a spirit who simply loved the lake. Justin claimed to have been killed by the Dark Lady, swearing to Spider he had followed her back to Wreythville. They mingled among the guests, and Beatrice danced with John.

The pavilion over the stage and bandstand had been removed, and a large projection screen had been erected. J-

Man keyed the music, and Denny clicked to start the presentation. The digital projector show paged through John's short, adventurous life.

There were many action photographs of John at Warrior's Path and Steel Creek State Parks, the high school pool and baseball field, and of course, Holston Lake. Running, diving, swimming, catching Frisbees, skiing on snow and water, hiking the AT, swinging a bat and pitching a baseball. Flying off an inner tube. Skipping across water. Standing over his buck, an arrow sticking out of its chest. Sleeping fishing. Sleeping studying. A group arrangement of the blood brothers, sober, drunk, and wearing glasses, mustaches, and smoking cigars after the high school ceremony. His graduation from the Naval Academy. John in his dress uniform. John and Sherry at the dock, the last image taken by Marader. The couple looked in love, but what did Troy know?

When Denny called for anyone who wanted to share something about John, Troy stepped up.

"John was one of my best friends, and a blood brother. He literally gave me his blood when I needed a kidney. Who would have thought Dillon, John and I would be a compatible match? Our moms maybe when they watched us together. I guess in some ways, not only did I have extra brothers; I had extra moms, too. I should call my mom, thanks for reminding me.

"I have hit my head a few times over the years. John saved my life once when I did just that. A ski hit me in the head and knocked me out. John dove in and dragged me out of the water. He said that was the day he decided he liked rescuing people, becoming interested in paramedics and Search and Rescue, and then later, he went into the Coast Guard. Though we all know he would have rather played professional baseball."

John's ghost seemed clearer than before, his arms crossed though he was smiling. His legs appeared to come and go, so Troy tried not to look at him, especially since he was making goofy faces now, like he had done during the sports award ceremony their senior year. Troy had given a speech on motivation and will. He should have added spirit.

"We loved to waterski at this time of day, right on the edge of twilight through the changing sky and water colors. My mom hated it. Be back before dark. I thought she meant the boat ramp. She meant home. That night I got grounded, John claimed it was only because he got hurt, but it wasn't. He saved me a couple of weeks, made me sound like a hero. Mom seemed really proud, and I felt sheepish about that.

"So I wouldn't be here without John, and from what he told me, when he was bragging on his mates, some of you I see here, that thousands of people would be dead at sea without him and you guys. I know I'm speaking for all of us when I say I wish I had been able to return the favor. I feel like he was stolen away."

John's mates were nodding. Troy didn't dare look at John's spirit. He drew some strength from the expressions of J-Man, Jambo, and Knives. Even Marader's typical mocking cock of an eyebrow had smoothed out, and he appeared more humane.

"I hope we can enjoy the night and memories of John without a brawl breaking out," Troy said. Someone sighed loudly. One of the Coast Guarders made a disappointed aww sound. "Really? Well, if you need to vent, John believed in making plans but also seizing the moment. I think Marader has stocked some of those inflatable boxing gloves in the back if you feel the need to punch something," Troy said. That brought a cheer. It would be louder after more drinking.

"John and I have talked about never knowing if there will be another tomorrow," Troy began.

Silke stepped into view. He paused, dramatically, wondering where she had been hiding. She looked sad and yet stunning, but he couldn't tell what she might be thinking while her beautiful eyes guardedly watched him.

"Living knowing life happens. It's fragile. It's short, and what you do with your life and who enjoys the ride with you is what makes life worth living. There could be an accident at work," he said, winking at Knives then looking at Marader. "Or a jealous beau, or a hunting accident with friends and loved ones. More common, a car accident around the corner," he mused, sharing a small smile. "Even a mountain might fall on us one lucky day."

"Amen," Father Dennis said.

"I was fortunate there were people there to drag me back to life. John told me if I could survive this and come back stronger, I could survive anything. But it was those around me that lifted me up, and I've certainly had some timely angelic intervention, on the mountain, in Florida, and here," Troy said, keeping eye contact with Silke. "It has been difficult to survive John's death, barely able to face my second mom feeling like I should have done something. With y'all's help, I hope I can withstand this breaking of my heart and find a way to heal.

"John, though, wouldn't want to be wholly remembered for his good deeds or for us to be maudlin. He believed in bringing joy and laughter which also meant playing pranks, like putting kill switches on friends' cars and then claiming only he had the magic to start them. Or the fake Holston monster production which brought out the local news crew," Troy said.

After a few minutes, he had them laughing and left them that way. Except Silke, Marader had touched her, whispered something in her ear, then they turned and left out of sight, not out of mind. What Troy said must not have touched her.

Elke's command to stay away harassed him, but Troy ignored it, living in the now, and went after Silke. John's ghost intercepted him, hugged him, and for a moment he heard John's laughter, then he was surrounded by Coast Guard buddies. He answered a few questions while Jambo stepped up to the microphone. When it squealed on him a couple of times, breaking the emotional moment, Troy escaped and went hunting Silke.

What was she doing with Marader? Had Marader made his pitch, and she had accepted? It made Troy ill thinking of them together. No way, he kept telling himself. But, he would have thought the same about Raquel.

He followed the sound of weeping and found Silke crying in Marader's business office. Before he knew what he was doing, Troy had crossed the distance and taken her in his arms.

"Silke, what's wrong? How can I help? Was it Tommy Boy?"

She started to struggle, and he let her go. "You've done enough, thank you," she said, gasping. "Aunt Jada transitioned. Marader just let me know. My mother called here. I couldn't hear my cell."

"I'm sorry for your loss," he said.

She hugged herself. "Watching you up there, I kept thinking you could say those words about Dillon. About how he had given you a kidney. Saved your life. Then, while saving it again, in the snow, he discovered writing about you was news, so he wrote more. He became an investigative reporter, who is now missing. He's probably hiding because I would like to kick his butt."

"Silke," he started.

"Don't worry. If I throw a fit, I'll keep my heels on. You know, they could have been eulogizing you, or even me, if you hadn't been there to rescue me from drowning," she said.

Troy thought of almost dying in the collapsed house. "Listen, you saved me, too."

"Really? That's nice of you to say, but I won't be there all the time, will I?" she asked, her question sharp. "What got into you earlier today? You reminded me of Dillon."

"Ouch. I'm frustrated, mostly with your brother. His secrets are causing me problems, especially between us," Troy began. He wanted to tell her about Elke, but his tongue tied again.

"Listen, I would love to chat, but I've got to go to the hospital," Silke said curtly.

Troy thought about Aunt Jada's advice. "Wait, please. There's something you need to see," he said. He held out his phone, the video cued.

"Troy, really, I don't have . . ." Silke said.

He was going to lose her. Kissing her right now seemed like asking to be slapped. He tried psychology based on what he knew about her past and present. "Fine, Dillon doesn't want you to see this anyway," he said and started to put away his phone.

"Wait. What doesn't he want me to see?" she asked.

That did it. "Are you sure? It will change your life."

She put her hands on her hips. "What are you hiding from me now?"

He winced and hit play and handed his phone to her.

She had questions in her eyes, on those kissable lips, but she waited and watched. "Hey, Tawny. I'm not supposed to tell anybody this, but I would really like Silke to know. I would tell her, but I'm hexed so I can't tell anybody."

"Hexed?" Silke asked.

He had chosen that over bewitched. "Compelled."

The video recording played on. "It seems cats can't talk, so it's okay to tell them. So here goes. Elke Swearington gave me a message to keep secret. I'm supposed to stop looking for Dillon. Seriously. Yeah, I know, it's hard to believe, too. He sent it to me with our code words."

Now he had Silke's full attention.

"Elke says he's safe and convalescing with her at the lodge. I guess my senses are still keen. She says, if I keep looking, I'll put him in danger and likely, Silke, too. After being chased by wolves and the brawl at the wake, it seems there's danger whether I keep looking or stop."

She hit the pause button. "Dillon's there?! Why didn't you tell me?! I figured you went to the Swearington's this afternoon. I was worried you might kick down the door, if you didn't end up as dog food. Oh, God. Elke. She looks like the Dark Lady, doesn't she, as Dillon has always described her? Dammit. I should have seen it. That's why you were interested in her."

"It's not romantic, but she can compel and influence us like Zane," Troy said.

Silke blanched and held her head, briefly closing her eyes. "That man who tried to lure me into his boat? You think she did something like that to my brother?"

"I doubt she needed to. She's powerfully attractive and enchanting, but that's because she's more than human."

"Why should I believe this?" Silke asked.

"You're not celebrating the news in the way I expected."

"I'm stunned and a bit overwhelmed."

"Silke, listen, I don't care what your brother thinks. I believe you would be a wonderful daily habit."

"What are you saying, Mr. Bane?"

"Silke, I don't want to be your pretend beau. And I don't care whether my blood brothers think we should be together or not. I feel we should be together. We are better together than apart."

She smiled broadly, and her eyes sparkled, "What makes you think I'm looking for a beau?" she asked, starting to tease, then the rest of what he said registered. "Hey, did you say your friends, your best friends, your blood brothers, don't want us to date, but you don't care?"

He nodded. "My ears ring from their protests. They'll kill me if I mistreat you, though Knives promised to patch me up when Dillon beats me to a pulp."

"You're serious?" she asked, hands on hips.

"Elke said he was combative and volatile. I know he has a temper. He obviously doesn't want us together. He lied to you about all the women I was allegedly dating, and he tried to keep us apart at Squaw Valley, and elsewhere."

"You've thought about this a lot. Your brothers really don't like us?"

"J-Man and Knives, not really. Denny, I don't know. Spider, yes with warnings he'd kick my butt if I don't treat you right. Jambo is pro us. For Marader, it's personal. He still wants you. I'll be glad to tell him that you are my lady and to bug off."

"What about Raquel?"

"I told her farewell. That I wanted you to be my lady. Silke, I care deeply for you, I'm smitten, and I trust you," he said.

Silke grew thoughtful. "What makes you think I want to be with a crazy man who is nearly killing himself daily?"

"The way we kissed after Aunt Jada's house exploded."

"Oh, you remember, do you? Since when?"

"Elke tried to steal that memory when she discovered it. She's like Dillon and thinks it's best we're not together."

"You honestly want me to believe you remembered kissing me while you were slow dancing with a gorgeous blond?" she asked.

"That blond is your brother's new lover. If you remember, I asked you to accompany me to the wake, and you wouldn't, not that your presence would have stopped Elke, but she might have told you to stop, too. Silke, that . . . woman could see into my thoughts through my eyes, but instead of taking away the memory, she reawakened it. Right after that, she commanded me to leave you alone."

"What?"

"I'm supposed to stay away from you."

"Is that so?" she asked, her voice taking on a dangerous edge. He stayed alert for shoe throwing.

"Wanting to be by your side is more powerful. And, I'm not the only one who has forgotten a kiss. And that doesn't include that New Year's Eve. You were eighteen and drunk. Dillon slugged me." He opened another file, still remembering the password.

"That's why he slugged you? My girlfriends told me we kissed, but I was painfully hung over the next day. I didn't believe them because I didn't remember it, and you didn't mention it."

"I'm sure that apology will work well for me one day. Sorry Silke, I was just really drunk."

"That's not funny. You should have said something."

"I was having trouble talking around the fat lip your

brother gave me. That seems to happen when I kiss you."

"Are you referring to the pontoon boat ride?"

"Yes, I am. I thought you should hear Zane mucking with our minds and playing with our emotions," Troy said. He hit the play button and let the pontoon recording run.

Silke watched and listened intently. Zane's clothing was normal, the definition good on the video, but his face was blurred. His sunglasses and hat appeared to float above his shirt collar. She flinched when he spoke and covered her ears.

"What's happened to his voice?" Silke asked. She looked at him, her eyes hinting at a once hidden fear.

"I don't know. Nobody can clean it up. Walt has even sent it to some of his buddies. Should I turn it off?" he asked.

"No, please. I want to know," she said, so he let it play out.

"It's that way," Recorded Silke purred, her voice throaty and sexy on the audio file.

Troy watched her tilt her head as she listened and mentally focused. He had no trouble remembering, even now breaking out in a sweat. Troy spoke Zane's words.

"That I know." His voice had been cool and oily. Troy remembered when Zane removed his sunglasses. His eyes had been dark and yet bright like hard marbles alight with fiery-red sparks. His broad, toothy smile was more unnerving than friendly. "I see that you have been below to visit Wreythville. A gloomy and oppressive, even suffocating place now. It was not always such. Yes, you know it, and its hopelessness. It has stayed with you. It is in your heart, slowly eating you like consumption."

Across the distance, Zane's odd eyes had engorged, dominating his face and commanding attention. Troy still didn't understand how he had been befuddled and manipulated. He tasted the bitter sense of hopelessness and powerlessness. Abject failure. Such depressing emotions had washed over him like a tsunami wave, flattening him and burying him in the sand. His body had sensed the predator. Fight or flight. He was not his emotions.

"I am Zane. I am your friend. I can give you hope and fulfillment. Come with me. Bring your boat closer so that Zane may help you," Troy continued.

"Troy, that's creepy," Silke said.

"I'll stop," he said. Zane's words seemed etched in Troy's head now, like the song that kept playing in your brain. Better though, he recalled what Silke had said.

"Have . . . have you seen my brother, Dillon?" Recorded Silke asked.

Zane's response was garbled.

"Oh, yes," Recorded Silke sighed.

Silke gasped. Her hands went to her face. "Is that me?"

Troy's heart had raced, but his body had been sluggish to respond. He shifted, stirred by the memory of what came next, Silke disrobing down to her bikini. Seeing her, he worried about her reaction.

On the recording, Silke moaned. She had readied herself to leap over to the other boat. Passion and worry for Silke had vaporized Troy's paralysis. He had seized her, pulling her to him.

There was the sound of scuffling. She snarled, and he grunted from getting punched. "Silke, stop! Ow! I don't want to hurt you," Recorded Troy said just before she had head-butted him.

"That's how I busted my lip. Fortunately, I got my leg in the way when you tried to knee me in the crotch," Troy told her.

Silke glanced at him, caught between believing what she heard and what she remembered.

"Silke, stop fighting me!" Troy roared. The recording grew quiet, followed by moaning and heavy breathing.

"We kissed, didn't we?" Silke asked.

"I think I pleasantly burnt my lips," Troy said.

The recording continued. "Zane, stop whatever you're doing," Recorded Troy said along with the cocking of a gun's hammer.

Troy said, "Zane went on, shocked. 'You are resisting Zane.

This is a first. Your encounter with the manse should have weakened you. How interesting.' Zane was surprised that I didn't do as he said."

Troy reached over and stopped the recording.

"Was that the cocking of a hammer on a gun? My Glock?" Silke asked.

"Yes, I picked it up. I was so thankful you hit, kneed and elbowed me instead of shooting me," Troy said.

"Oh, my . . . So, what happened? You can't stop the recording now. Why didn't you let me hear this earlier?"

"At first, I thought you might not be in control of your emotions. I certainly wasn't. I didn't know what Zane had done. Then when I wanted to show you this, we had wrecked, and I couldn't recall the password."

"Were you really going to shoot Zane?" she asked.

"You bet. He wasn't even the slightest bit concerned," Troy said. Her jaw dropped. "Besides, I wouldn't have been able to hit the broad side of the barn at that moment."

"Why?"

"Uh, your tongue was in my ear," Troy replied. Silke hit play and listened.

"I have waited a decade for you to notice me and kiss me. Now take me. I want you inside me," Recorded Silke gushed.

"Wow, how could I forget being that subtle?" Silke asked.

"Notice no gun fire. Zane babbled on, something like, the smoke and fog shield me! The master must be told!"

"That sounds right," she said.

The engine roared. The surge of the propellers churned water.

"We bumped the throttle to full power. We nearly ran into Zane and the Procraft. Marader's Sea-Doo, the one Dillon used, buried in a wave then went airborne. It shattered and tore off the windshield. Zane looked worried, like we might sink him."

On audio, the pontoon boat's engine continued to moan and surge, powering up to an urgent whine.

"I am walking on air, and you, you smile a smile I've never

seen before. Two kisses. I have waited years for that," Recorded Silke said.

"Silke!" Recorded Troy cried. He could be heard shuffling around, whispering and praying for her.

"You passed out and forgot all about it. I brought you back to the marina. When you woke up, you tried to drive off in the pontoon boat to go after Zane. I don't have that recorded," Troy said, shortening the story.

Silke uncovered her face, "What now?"

"Since we're being honest, is it true?" Troy asked.

"What?" she asked coyly.

"That you have wanted to be kissed for years? Or was that the vampire beguiling you?" he asked. He stood and took her hand.

"Yes, since I was thirteen. You were a senior and head over heels in love with Raquel."

"That was then. She's never around when I need her. You are. You are my angel," he said. They kissed, and this time her lips warmed, and she melted against him like she'd been basking in the sun. For wonderful moments, there was only the two of them. Now, he could breathe and relax, the sun shining amidst the gloom.

Breathless, Silke finally stepped back.

"Aunt Jada said to kiss you or lose you forever. I did, but you forgot."

"Oh, really? She did? And you remember me coming to Florida? Are you trying to tell me something? If so, I'm confused, because you came here with Desiree draped all over you, and you held an interview with your ex," she said, acerbically.

"She left before the interview. Desiree is a spy beholden to Elke Swearington, who I believe is being disingenuous about her interactions with your brother. Desiree claims she's my bodyguard."

"You do need one."

"I've resisted hotter than Desiree."

"Oh, have you?"

"Well, until a few moments ago, anyway, now I can't make that claim, can I? You know, that time I was supposed to pretend to be your beau, that kissed rocked my world," he said.

"Good, now let's rock the boat," she suggested.

They kissed and stayed together for a long moment, savoring each other's lips, breath, taste and warmth. Any longer, they would need a room. "This could become habit forming. I will fight Dillon to date you, if you want," he said.

"Those words are music to my ears, but it sounds rather medieval. What changed your mind? My throwing myself at you?"

"It was a highly intuitive move," he smiled. "Silke, I think we're great for each other. Let's find out. If we're bad, well, we can part as friends, not that it will matter. I will be dead. You are worth the risk."

She worried her lip. "What do you mean?"

"It's sort of all or nothing. If it doesn't work, your mom would hate me, and my blood brothers will come after me. Then there's Mr. Fleenor."

"An apology. Honesty and an offer to be a couple. Kisses to make my head spin. How could I resist?" she said and gently kissed him. "I still want to go to the Swearington Lodge and scream at the top of my lungs, maybe tomorrow. It's not preferable to spending the evening with you. Do you think Dillon might show up tonight?"

"Might. You know, it's possible that whoever murdered John might be trying to kill us. It's one of the many reasons I came to see you at work," Troy said.

"What do you think is going on?"

"That's what I hope to discuss tonight after the wake. But, at this moment I figured we should go see your mom."

Silke shook her head. "She knows why I'm here, and she'll love the news we're a couple. She adores you. Besides, there's nothing I could do to comfort her but cry to sleep with her, and once I tell her about us she'll want me to stay here. Besides, I'm not sure I could sleep. Afraid I would wake up and discover what you've said is a dream. Or, I would worry and wonder what you and the boys were plotting."

"Us, plot? I feel like I'm running around like a chicken with my head cut off."

"Ah, you do love me. Troy, I want to spend our first hour as a couple hugging on you, kissing you whenever I want, and seeing how your brothers react to us. I have my 9mm if they protest too much," she said.

Outside, Denny continued, "I want to finish by saying that horrible, horrible Wreythville house below Holston Lake killed John. It almost killed a dozen others. It might have killed John's gal, Sherry. She's missing. My friends and I had to rescue Mary Beth from there, and she hasn't been the same since. Today, I promise that I'm going to look into getting a permit to remove the safety hazard by demolishing it."

Troy turned to Silke. "Here, here. He has my vote and support."

"There are some who think it should be preserved, a landmark of sorts. They haven't been there. It's the type of place that makes you long desperately for life, love and sunshine. If John were here, I think he would heartily agree. What better way to pay tribute than to prevent such a tragedy from ever happening again? We're sorry it led to this, John, but your sacrifice will not be in vain. May you rest in peace," Denny finished.

The people of the wake were abuzz. They appeared expectant as well, wondering who would step up next and what would be said. J-Man was headed there when he saw Troy and Silke arm-in-arm. Silke made a show of kissing Troy.

J-Man barely raised an eyebrow. "Well, a better choice would be me. I'm handsome, daring and flying with the greatest of ease, unlike Mr. Crash N. Burn," he said.

"Says you. I've flown with you, Mr. Mid Airstall. Or would

you prefer Mr. Cloudsuck?"

J-Man raised his hands in surrender. "Point made. I give. Anyway, what I was trying to say, is that Troy is a good second choice. I promise to trip Dillon so you two can run. If you're lucky, I might fall on him. Buy you a few extra seconds. Oh, that's right. Silke's armed. No worries. She can wing him."

"Jay, you are so not funny," Silke said.

"What's your point? I was serious. Speaking of, Deputy Burt is here. I think he's worried you are skipping town."

"Not without Silke," Troy replied. She hugged his arm and nuzzled him.

"Are you two going to go all googly-eyed?" J-Man groaned.

"Yes," they said.

"On that note, I think I'll go glorify John. Wish me fortitude so I don't end up blubbering in front of everybody. Lordy, I miss the fish boy."

"Just say it's ash or cinder in your eye," Troy suggested.

"How did you manage it?" J-Man asked Troy.

"John's ghost was standing next to Spider and making faces."

"I never know when to take you seriously," J-Man said and left.

Silke and Troy hugged on each other and listened to J-Man regale them with stories of yore, from the days of Boy Scouts with John. During that time, she noticed the ghosts. After J-Man had said his piece, John's spirit came to stand by them. Flabbergasted, Silke recognized him.

"Is this really John?"

"His spirit, yes it is," Spider said.

"The first time you saw ghosts was in Haiti, right?" Troy asked. He tried to give Silke time to recover.

"I saw signs of them there. Odd things happened. Lights. Objects floating. Voices. After I died, I could see the cause of those strange occurrences. It was the spirits."

"But not just there, right?" Troy asked.

"They can be found anywhere. In Haiti, they often appear

ragged and gaunt, having starved to death or passed due to disease. Ghosts in battlefields are bloodied and wounded. Other ones seem normal, surprised to be dead."

"And the ones in the mansion?" Silke asked.

"They seem drained, little more than shadows seeking to suck the life from light," Spider said, sounding poetic. "Except for John. He was there to help us. He had not given up hope, even from the other side of the veil."

"He seems to be peering through," Troy said.

"He has a foot in both worlds. You know what that's like. Say, you two make a cute couple. Silke, I told Troy if he didn't treat you right I'd make some suggestions with the heel of my foot."

"Thanks, but I use sweets instead of the stick," Silke replied.

"Hey, you finally made a move?" Marader said. He strolled up, grinning.

"If you mean, did I tell her she's my angel, and I'd love her in my life every day, I don't think I used those words, but I meant to," Troy said. Silke kissed him.

"Ah, well, you win some, and you lose some," Marader said. "I can't wait to see how Dillon deals with this. Cannonball? Or intercontinental ballistic missile?"

"Guys, Dillon will be fine with it, just like us, right?" Jambo asked. He loomed over everybody. Silke left to hug on him.

Jambo finally slipped away to step up to the mic and chat about John. Spider joined him, and they did a skit covering some of John's less than stellar moments.

Deputy Burt chose that time to approach Troy. "There you are. For a while, I thought you might not make it. You've been having an awful lot of accidents. Cars. Houses. Boats. Next thing you know you'll have insurance investigators after you, too."

"Burt. How wonderful to see you off duty," Silke said.

"I wouldn't miss this. John was a great guy. He helped me with some bullies when I was in third grade. And he really did like helping little old ladies across the street, even if they didn't have pretty granddaughters with them. Damn, but I want whoever killed him. This is all so twisted and bizarre. I'll bet, though, the simplest explanation is the answer."

"The butler did it?" Troy asked.

"Ha. It's his bitch. Sherry. No sign of her. Boyfriend dead. She's the prime suspect, all right. Hey, are you two together? You wouldn't happen to be the inheritor on that property that exploded, would you? Worth a lot. Y'all could run off together," Burt said.

"You're off duty, right?" Silke asked. Burt nodded. Silke slapped him, flesh on flesh loud despite the music. "Don't even joke about my great aunt's house like that!" She stormed off.

"Thanks, Burt, for making our first date memorable. Do you think if I throw you in the water it will win me boyfriend points?" Troy asked.

Burt scuttled off. Something seemed to have changed about the Sullivan County deputy. All the troubles had given him a harder edge. Troy guessed that was to be expected. How could they not be affected by this? He went looking for Silke.

Walt intercepted him. "I found something odd in the audio of your video taken at East Hill," Walt said, excited.

Thirty-Four: Harried After Hours

Troy couldn't believe the hour. Time had flown by, despite waiting to hear more from Walt and J-Man about their breakthrough. They had huddled together about an hour ago to work on the video's audio, trying to clear up Undead John's voice. Troy believed it would help him convince the others that he and J-Man spoke the truth.

Even after midnight, none of the guests wanted to leave the wake when there was so much of John's life still in the air. Little did they know. Troy's hands grew sore from clasping so many to say farewell.

He and Silke were wished well often, bolstering their new

relationship. Silke donned a long sleeve and huddled closer. Her gray-green eyes shone radiantly like emeralds catching the light of a hearth fire. Since they had agreed to be a couple, she had glowed.

He and his girl, his blood brothers, and Walt, along with Pete who had an obvious crush on Desiree, stayed to clean up and unwind.

Heidi yawned first. She remained near Marader who still fondled the precious jewelry box like a cold-hearted lover. In Troy's opinion, it looked sullen. Nobody had tried to steal it yet tonight.

Troy and Silke helped Marader and Heidi roll, close and lock the wall panels into place, giving the bar four walls and shutting out the Great Outdoors. The fans' roaring sounded loud in the absence of a crowd, so Jambo turned them to low. The evening had cooled from sweltering to muggy with a fog drifting in.

Jambo's dog, Ace, watched them from his guard spot while Troy and Denny lifted the bridge. Now they were surrounded by water, tethered but floating.

Troy paused, thinking he heard footfalls in the gravel.

Ace's ears perked up, then the hunting basset hound stood, ears nearly dragging. They flicked, and Troy wondered about bugs, about the time he squished a mosquito on the back of his hand. After half a minute, Ace dropped comfortably back onto the deck.

In the distance, a coyote howled. A disjointed chorus joined in.

Gunshots sundered the peace. They roared from the other side of the building. The blasts echoed back and forth inside the cove.

"What the hell?" Troy asked.

Denny touched him. "Easy there. It's target practice. You probably didn't notice Tommy setting them up." He caught Troy's look. "Hey, some people ski, walk or hike to blow off steam. Other people shoot things, not people or living creatures, just things."

"Some people fish," Pete said. John's ghost followed Denny as he and Pete carried the memorial inside. From over his blood brother's shoulder, the life-sized cardboard cutout of John smiled at him. Creepy.

On the lakeside of the marina, Marader, Heidi, Jambo, Knives and Desiree were all armed with rifles. Jambo had brought his own. Troy assumed the rest came from the gun cabinet upstairs. He joined Silke who stood watching. The five had their backs to Troy while they studied the floating, illuminated targets bobbing on the surface. Desiree briefly aimed then her slugs obliterated the target.

"Why aren't you shooting?" Troy asked Silke

"I didn't want to scare you off," she said.

Walt burst out the door. "Hey, Troy. Listen to this," he said and handed him his smart phone. On the screen, he could see the fireworks lighting up Undead John's face.

Troy hit the play button. He could clearly hear Undead John's voice. "That's it! What did you do?"

"I found parts of the voice in three separate ranges: a low and high pitch out of our range, and a middle range we hear as garbled. Put them all together, plus remove some static that sounds like clicking, and you can understand what's being said."

"That's great, Walt!" Silke said and kissed him on the check.

"I couldn't have done it without Jay. We're working on your Elke recording now."

"That's not as important. Run this over the speaker system," Troy said.

"Give me a minute," Walt said. He headed inside. Troy and Silke tailed him. Troy stood in the doorway, wanting to watch his blood brothers' reactions.

Spider and Denny started a game of eight ball. Spider paused, cocking his head, like he had heard a strange noise coming from the shore through the open door.

John's voice sounded over the music system. Everyone

instantly stopped what they were doing to listen. In this version, there was only John's eerie voice, not even static in reply. His soliloquy certainly sounded like he was talking to Knives, J-Man, and Troy. He could see J-Man reliving the moments as John discussed killing them and how he wished he could stop himself.

Denny dropped his pool cue on the floor where it landed with a loud clattering. "Oh, dear Lord. Bullets don't hurt him. That sounds exactly like John, senior year, when we recorded that skit, "The Living Shadow", along with "The Pumpkin Ranch Prison"."

Knives cocked his head. "Is this a recording trick?"

"No," Troy said.

"This audio only contains John's separated voice. Here's the mixed version," Walt said. He played the recording, and now they could hear J-Man and Troy trying to stop their undead friend from killing them, including the gun shots.

Silke clutched Troy. He suspected the voice reminded her of Zane, callous, cool, cajoling and compelling. Troy realized, suddenly, for the first time, John had used it to urge them to kill him. They had been empowered to end him, perhaps even help convince them to let the sun burn his body.

Was he doing anything of his own volition? Troy wondered.

Knives eyes had narrowed. He was still suspicious. It was too bad his voice wasn't on the recording, since he had been unconscious. Denny acted spooked and speculative, far from convinced. Marader hardly paid attention.

"John apologizes, again. Denny, Father Dennis, now you know why holy water caused his flesh to burn," Spider said.

"This is freaky," Jambo said.

"I see him. He stuck his tongue out and flipped you the bird," Pete said. John's spirit followed the lead and did, whether the Ackles' twin saw him or not.

"I think he's jerking your chain," Marader chuckled.

J-Man lightly slapped the top of his friend's head. "You

weren't there," J-Man said.

"I'm glad I wasn't. I don't think I would have been able to do what y'all did," Jambo said.

Desiree stood and said, "Yes, you would have. John used the power of his voice to get his friends to kill him. He knew he must. Otherwise, you would have hesitated or used rational thought, and would now be dead. John would be roaming as a rogue vampire, feasting on innocent people."

"That's insane. What makes you say that?" Knives asked.

Desiree smiled, unfazed by this scientific doubt.

"Y'all, for the record, the Church doesn't believe in vampires. The priesthood has no records of such evil. If it did, we would be out fighting it," Father Dennis said.

"How do you know about the power of John's voice? Have you heard it before?" J-Man asked Desiree.

"Y'all are dealing with dangerous creatures that your friend John accidentally unleashed. They turned him into one of their own then abandoned him," she replied.

That stopped everyone cold, whether in mid breath, mid blink, or mid thought.

"Enlighten us, please," Spider said.

Desiree took a deep breath, making sure she had their attention. "The Swearington family has been tasked with observing and keeping track of the lake and anything to do with the underwater mansion and its prisoners . . ."

"Prisoners?!" Denny exclaimed. Knives echoed him.

"Yes, its owner and occupants from the thirties and forties, now going on seven decades of habitation until Saturday. Thanks to John and Sherry, Viktor Von Damme and his cult are free. Now this entire area is in great danger," Desiree said confidently. Denny's incredulous expression merely made her smile, as if she had seen doubters become believers many times over.

"Who and what did you do with Desiree?" Marader asked.

At that moment, Troy's phone vibrated. Hoping it might be Dillon, he checked it, finding Rae Kirkland's name. What could she be calling about? Perhaps she had left something behind. Desiree pinned him with her stare as he slipped outside. He could hear her detail what happened to John: terminal vampire combustion.

"Hey, Rae, this isn't a good time," Troy said.

Over in the parking lot, a car alarm sounded. Lights began to flash.

"Sorry to bother you, I really am. This will just take a second, and I thought you would want to know firsthand," Rae said, holding him on the line.

"Not it. Too new. Sounds expensive," Jambo said as he ambled out the door. Knives and Denny followed, drawn to the sound.

"Probably mine," the doctor said.

"I'm sorry, Rae. I can't hear you over the car alarm. What did you say?"

"I'm at the scene of a car accident not far away. Raquel's car is totaled, Chase Carter is dead and . . ."

Troy heart skipped two beats. "What about Raquel?"

Ace began to bark, howl and growl. The hound kept getting in Knives way, preventing him from reaching the bridge. Ace didn't want anyone going ashore. Troy sensed a change in the air. He couldn't explain it, but something was wrong.

"Ace, what's up, buddy? Calm down," Jambo said. He ambled up to his agitated hound. Ace stood protectively, keeping Knives from the portable bridge.

"Troy, Raquel's missing. I'm sorry. The car's torn up. The tires are blown out, the bulletproof glass broken, and there are strange scratches in the door, not just the paint, but into the metal."

"Oh, God, no," Troy said. He thought back to his last drive in the Land Rover. "Like it had been attacked by wolves."

Gun in hand, Desiree rushed outside. "Stop! It's a trap!"

Silke joined Troy. "Is something wrong?" she asked.

Troy looked at her, processed the phone call, then he took in what was going on around him. Had Desiree said trap? Troy stared into the woods near the parking lot. Feeling watched, the hair on the back of his neck bristled. Did he hear breathing?

"Yeah, wolves, how did you . . ." Rae asked. The phone sounded like it had been dropped.

"Rae? Rae?! Damn! Raquel is missing, and her bodyguard is dead. Wolves attacked her car," Troy told Silke. He felt sick about Raquel, but he had to deal with the danger now and save his newfound love. He was afraid he knew why Ace was agitated and afraid.

"What's wrong with your dog?" Knives asked Jambo.

"There are wolves out there waiting for you," Desiree said.

"Ha! There aren't wolves in east Tennessee, at least not the four-legged kind. Are you talking about men who act like animals?" Knives replied.

"No," Desiree said. Like a pro, she deftly removed the clip from the rifle and stuffed it into her large shoulder bag, from where she removed another clip. She slid it into place, locked and loaded, as if she had been shooting all her life.

"Desiree, babe, you're scaring me, though, I got to admit, it's hot and sexy, too," Marader said. He glanced at Heidi who crossed her arms.

"You should be scared," Desiree said. She peered down the gunsight.

"Des, what's gotten into you?" Heidi asked.

Desiree fired. The flash and thunderous sound made them all jump. There was no ricochet, nor any metallic sound similar to a slug hitting a car, rock, or sign. Troy distinctively heard a grunt.

"What the hell?" Marader asked.

"Who are you shooting?" Heidi asked.

"Stop shooting!" Knives demanded. "If there's somebody out there, you could have hit them, or one of our cars." Knives pointed his fob at his car to shut off the alarm and blinking lights.

"I always hit my target. Now about werewolves, I must

admit that I'm very prejudice in the negative since one tried to rape me. I shoot first and don't worry about the questions," Desiree said.

Marader blanched.

"And you thought I was dangerous," Silke told Troy.

"There are no wolves in this part of the country. You must have seen wolfhounds. I don't see anything," Denny said.

Knives' expensive car began to flash and sound its alarm again. The Spyder looked like it was dancing.

"Malfunction?" Denny suggested.

"It's a brand, new car," Knives replied.

"You let Troy drive it, right?" Marader asked.

"Who knew it could do multiple three sixties and stay perfectly centered down the middle of the road?" Troy asked. He couldn't resist jerking his buddy's chain.

"What?!" Knives asked.

J-Man walked up, steak in his hand. Marader did a double take, starting to speak up, too late. J-Man heaved the beef as far as he could onto shore.

It seemed to tumble through the air in slow motion as Marader screamed. "That's filet! Is everyone out of their mind? Damn!"

Desiree reached into her shoulder bag. From it, she removed a black wand to hand to Silke. "Shock stick. Human cattle prod. Appropriate for use in the coming situation."

"Why are you giving me this?" Silke asked.

"Troy would die for you. Use this to stay alive and keep him alive. Oh, here they come. Now get inside!" Desiree said.

A huge, gray wolf dashed out and gobbled up the meat. It looked around guiltily, caught in the act, unable to resist. A second beast was tempted. It possessed a crooked snout, a dark fur mask, and deranged, mismatched-colored eyes. Bandit stepped back and disappeared.

"No wolves, eh, Dr. Curran?" Desiree said.

Troy recognized that beast. Silke gasped. She also knew it from when the wolves had attacked the Land Rover. The memory came back so strongly Troy missed a step.

Desiree fired two shots. The gray wolf staggered a step then collapsed, motionless. Most of the guys stood in stunned and shocked silence.

Troy had learned not to leap to conclusions or judge. The rest of the blood brothers immediately jumped on her case.

"You just shot it? It is one of God's creatures," Father Dennis said.

"You are so wrong, Father D," Desiree said.

"Aren't wolves an endangered species?" Jambo asked.

"No, it's y'all tonight," Desiree said. Troy could imagine her dark eyes sparkling. By her voice and smirk, she seemed to be loving the danger and adventure. She had made it clear she disliked werewolves.

None could believe their eyes as the dead wolf's hair receded, leaving it almost bare-naked. It seemed to reshape, less body, more long-limbed, with its back legs getting thicker and longer, then it transformed into a human corpse.

"Holy shit," Walt exclaimed.

"Well, isn't that somethin'," Knives said.

Spider spun and strode inside. Nobody had to tell him twice. Walt edged toward the door. Pete moved protectively closer to Desiree.

"What the hell?" Pete exclaimed.

"Exactly! Werewolves. I can smell 'em," Desiree said.

"Really?" Marader asked. He wrinkled his nose, then he kissed Heidi and nudged her back toward the building. "Get inside, babe. Lock the doors and bar the windows. I'll get my silver slugs from upstairs. Hurry!"

Heidi rushed off, taking Denny with her. Marader followed swiftly. The rest of them were slower learners.

"There's more of them. A lot more of them," J-Man said.

Over a dozen huge wolves, including Ghostly, stalked out from behind the cars in the lot. They sniffed the air and snarled. Their eyes and bloodied teeth glowed ruddily in the dim pink light of the parking lot lamps. Where had Bandit gone? Troy wondered.

"They were waiting for you to go to your cars. Follow Tommy, go inside!" Desiree told them. She readied herself to fire and backed toward the entrance to the store.

Troy took Silke by the elbow. She willingly headed for the door.

Everything was happening quickly, and they moved in slow motion.

Seeing their prey leaving, the wolves broke into sprints, surging toward the marina. Ghostly stood back and watched. The other werewolves were undaunted by the distance from land to dock, gaining speed and gathering themselves to leap.

Desiree opened fire. The muzzle flashed in the night, and the rifle bellowed, its roar echoing. The slugs ripped into the wolves, sending them darting for cover.

"My, they are brazen. The charge doesn't make much sense," she said.

"Don't hit my car!" Jambo and Knives yelled. They had stepped back to look.

Troy kept going, hurrying Silke ahead. She followed J-Man, who grabbed Knives and tailed a fast limping Walt. Father Dennis prayed aloud and thankfully as he assisted Walt inside. Knives and J-Man stumbled after him, almost falling. Spider nimbly danced aside. He and Heidi worked on lowering the bars that deterred burglars, letting the grate drop. It struck the wall with a whack and shudder that shook the building.

Troy spotted wolves scrambling out of the water, up over the sides. The beasts must have been swimming closer while their prey was distracted. One he recognized, Bandit, sprang with such blinding speed at Desiree that Troy couldn't spit out a warning.

Even so, Desiree stepped aside. The hurtling beast slammed into Pete and knocked him off his feet. His head hit with a sickening sound.

In a flash, Bandit was splashed in red as he ripped open Pete's throat. Ace barreled into Bandit, and they snapped and lunged at each other. Jambo brained the werewolf with the butt of his rifle. The blow caused Bandit's eyes to roll and stunned it. A second wolf, a gray streak, barreled into them all, sending man, dog and wolves into the lake. The dropped rifle clattered onto the wooden planks.

"Jambo!" Troy yelled. He started to go after his friend, but Silke tackled him.

Still shooting, Desiree backed up into the building. J-Man slammed the door, catching the charging wolf on the snout. It yelped and pulled back, giving him the moment he needed to shut and lock the grated door. Two wolves barreled into the bars, their snouts sticking through.

Troy realized the lakeside remained unsecured, the doors and windows vulnerable. Through the window, he could see that a grill had been knocked over. Burning charcoal glowed with each puff of breeze as chunks lay scattered across the dock planks. Near the LPG tanks, the deck was afire, its hot glow illuminating the danger.

"Guys, the dock is on fire!" Troy yelled.

He couldn't do anything about it with the wolves in the way. He had to make a choice and shoved the lakeside door shut, keeping his weight behind it. He didn't get it closed, trapping a beast between the door and jamb. Troy leaned in, holding the door tight as the wolf wiggled to get inside. A beast behind it pushed, adding its weight and strength. The wolf gnashed its teeth and red spittle dripped on the floor as it began to force its way in.

"Help!" Troy yelled. The beast was too strong.

Silke used a waterski from the wall to repeatedly smash the werewolf over the head, breaking the ski, then she zapped the beast with her cattle prod. It withdrew. Troy slammed the door and locked it. Silke threw the bar across it. The door was solid and windowless.

Denny and J-Man lowered the lakeside protective bars, but they were unable to close them as a ball of savage fury, a mottled, peppery black and gray wolf, hurtled through the window. It knocked the bars loose from their hands, allowing a second, black-faced wolf inside.

Blackface lunged at Silke, who hit it with the cattle prod. The shock slowed the beast, giving Troy time to side kick it. Blackface stumbled, hit the floor and bounced back up to its paws, where Desiree shot it.

Or tried. Her gun jammed.

It leapt at her. Desiree backhanded it with a silver truncheon, stunning it, and giving them a moment to breathe. "Lock down those damn bars!" she yelled.

Troy and J-Man latched them. None too soon, as first one wolf, then two and three beasts, crashed into the thick metal grate. In frustration, the werewolves repeatedly threw themselves against the bars, frantically trying to get in and join the pair already inside.

"Done!" Troy yelled. They had locked themselves in with two killing machines, but what choice did they have?

"Tommy! Hurry!" Heidi yelled.

Where was Marader? The two beasts, Blackface and Pepper, fought like four-legged whirlwinds. Pepper struck Denny a glancing blow, knocking him aside. Knives broke a pool cue over the mottled wolf's back, but Pepper shrugged it off and turned on the doctor. The beast snarled a chilling sound before it leapt.

Walt stumbled and shouldered Knives aside. Instead of eluding the blow, Walt took the full impact.

Pepper drove him backwards. Walt crashed into the bar. Snapping jaws aimed for his throat caught his arm as he protected himself. Walt screamed as blood spurted. The beast's paws seemed to grow larger into claws, shredding his clothing and flesh to maul him.

J-Man tackled Pepper with a blanket and wrapped it around the werewolf. Tossed about, he wrestled the beast to the floor, trying to contain the frenzied creature while Knives hammered at it with a baseball bat. The doctor's eyes were wide, and his face was contorted with desperation, effort and fear. Sharp claws and fangs began to tear through the blanket. Unaffected by the blows, the beast writhed its way free.

Blackface lunged at Spider. From somewhere, he had found a walking stick. He jammed the wood into its maw to keep its teeth away and unable to snap shut. Spider kicked it in the throat, and it spat out the stick and stumbled back.

Heidi grabbed a shotgun and blasted the werewolf, blowing away hair and enraging it. As Blackface turned on Heidi, Spider gave her a reprieve. He tripped the beast when it leapt. The werewolf crashed short of Heidi, where Denny smashed a stool over its head, causing it to pause and shake it off. Leering, it stalked Denny who drew a knife. The beast scoffed and spat in a very human gesture.

Under the blanket and J-Man's weight, Pepper ignored Knives hammering and ripped its way to freedom. Grinning as it escaped, Pepper lunged, open-mouthed into a cattle prod. Silke then poked the werewolf in the chest.

Desiree handed Troy the silver truncheon. "Keep it busy."

Before Pepper recovered, Troy brained it. He watched the werewolf's eyes roll back, but he didn't assume it was done and struck it again, breaking teeth. Despite all the punishment, it sprang loose of J-Man, by Silke and into Troy. He rammed the silver rod into its crotch, slowing its charge. He felt its fetid breath on his face as it coughed and bowled him over.

He used a Judo move to roll with the impact and throw it. Pepper crashed into the steps, only to rebound. It lustily eyed Silke and charged.

Troy shoved a table in Pepper's way. When the werewolf leapt, Troy hit it with a chair. The blow diverted it, and Silke evaded the beast. Pepper slid and recovered, sniffing at the door. It nosed the bar out of the way, working to let the others in.

Troy couldn't let that happen, but he didn't think he could get there in time. Unable to help, most of the others had their hands full.

Denny struggled with Blackface. The savage beast stood

atop his chest, trying to claw and maul, but it couldn't bite or tear effectively while Spider held the walking stick against its neck and yanked backward. He had wrapped his long legs around its body. His face scarlet, Spider rode the bucking wolf, putting all his weight against the stick and its spine. The wolf's eyes bulged with furious determination. Denny stabbed it, futilely driving the knife into its chest. It angrily snapped the walking stick in half. Spider flew off as Blackface lunged at Denny.

Knives seized the fire extinguisher. He directed the foam into Blackface's open, snarling jaws, making it gag. The doctor slammed the tank over the vomiting beast's head, dropping Blackface to the ground where it twitched.

"Oh, my God. Lord, please deliver us from evil," Father Dennis said. He crawled onto his knees. "Walt needs help."

They all did. Nobody could reach the door in time to stop the werewolf from opening it.

Marader unloaded both shotgun barrels at Pepper, splattering the beast across the inside of the door, keeping it closed. "Sorry, everyone. I had my gun securely locked up."

"I think mine's working now," Desiree said. She fired two bullets, execution style in the other werewolf's head. Blackface twitched once, then it began to transform, returning to human form.

"Unbelievable," Knives said.

"No worries. They are just detailed replicas," J-Man said.

Troy heard the crackling of flames and saw the glint of firelight in the windows. Things were bad, but Troy feared they were about to get worse. "What about the fire? Is there a way to put it out from inside?"

Thirty-Five: Up in Flames

"Hey, what do you know? Troy's right, again. The dock is on fire. The bastards overturned one of the charcoal grills. Nothing to worry about, yet. Marader has sprinklers, a fire suppression system we put in," J-Man said proudly.

Marader gave Heidi a reassuring kiss, and then he left the room. He cursed a blue streak on his way to turn on the pumps.

Troy glanced out over the docks on fire, but there were more immediate issues. Walt was dying, his life bleeding away. Knives rushed to his side. Their friend's eyes rolled back as his hand feebly tried to slow his blood loss. Troy used bar towels to staunch the flow. The white cotton swiftly turned red. Panic widened Walt's eyes. Troy sensed it would be over in moments. Spider must have felt the same, as he joined them.

"Walt, buddy, you crazy guy, saved my life," Knives said.

"Being a hero is dangerous," Walt moaned.

"Thanks, Walt. You allowed me to show them that I'm not crazy and prove something dangerous exists. You saved a lot of people," Troy said.

"Yeah, if you get out of here. I don't think you'll be taking me with you," Walt said. Troy clasped Walt's hand, and the grip was firm for a moment, then it relaxed to limp. Troy thought he saw a mist rising, but when he blinked, it had vanished. Walt's eyes glazed over.

"He's gone. Rest in peace, buddy," Knives said. He checked for vitals, looked at the wound, then, grim-faced, he closed Walt's eyes and moved on to examine Denny.

"Sorry. My gun jammed," Desiree said.

Troy kissed her on the forehead. "You were awesome. Without you and Tommy, we would be dead," he said.

Outside, the werewolves howled and raked the walls and doors. He shivered at the sound, then at the sight of two dead naked and hairy men, no longer wolves. He wondered if they had caused the explosion at Aunt Jada's home. Camera in hand, Troy now recorded what happened around him. This needed to be documented.

Knives examined and bandaged Heidi, bleeding from the hands, arms and an ear. Spider and J-Man hurried around double checking on the bars and doors, making sure they were secured. The supernatural creatures snapped at the bars, surprised and frustrated that they couldn't easily bite through them, so they hurtled themselves against the building. The walls shook and rattled as though a storm bludgeoned them, and the howling sounded like a gale-force wind.

The lights flickered. A motor sounded in the back room. Marader had the pump going.

"That should do it. Give it a minute to fill," Marader said, returning to the room. He picked up his silver-plated shotgun. He cocked it and took aim through a nearby broken window at one of the werewolves trying to chew through the storefront door. He unleashed one barrel.

The explosive sound and concussion stunned Troy and everyone else with its intensity and volume. The beast's head exploded, brains, fur and flesh spraying the dock.

"Hot damn, we're gonna have to remodel again," Marader said.

"If we survive this, we'll fix it," Denny promised.

For a moment, the werewolves backed away, as if they were wary or maybe letting the fire work. Troy realized the sprinklers had yet to spray the dock. He could hear the pump.

"Werewolves and silver bullets?! Tommy, why do you have silver shot and slugs?" Knives asked. His voice had a strained edge.

Marader grinned. "I encountered something strange late one night here on a full moon last October. Guy beat me up. I shot him, he laughed, beat me up some more then left. All I could think of was Wolverine, the mutant character but no metal claws," he said as he caressed the scar under his lower lip. With a grunt, he picked up the phone. A second later, he slammed it down. "Dead."

Silke checked her cell phone. "Speaking of dead."

They all checked. Nobody had a signal.

"If you ask me, this seems suspicious to lose the landline and cell service," J-Man said.

"It sounds like a trap to me," Desiree said.

"Tommy, why aren't the sprinklers coming on?" J-Man asked.

Marader looked outside then ran into the back room. Shortly, he returned. "Everything seems to be working fine. Just no water."

"They clogged the intake," Desiree said. Knives guffawed.

"Whatever. She's right, though, that it must be clogged."

"Thomas, isn't there a trap door we can use to leave? A sneaky way out, besides your second story zip-line, to elude angry boyfriends and fathers?" J-Man asked.

"Of course, it's in the store room," Marader said.

"They might see us wade ashore," J-Man said.

"You want to stay here?" Marader asked.

"A car isn't enough protection, and we couldn't drive fast enough when we were attacked last time. We'd be better off taking a boat," Silke said.

"Amen to that," Troy agreed.

"Will they go away come dawn?" Heidi groaned.

"Not likely, babe. I have a CB radio I can hook up. It's in the closet upstairs," Marader said.

"Great idea! Get it," J-Man said. "Meanwhile, we can reinforce the doors with furniture. Put the chairs, couch, dresser, pool table, and the rest against the openings to make sure the wolves can't break in."

Past the metal bars, Troy looked out the window. He could see the dock was burning steadily. One of the outside tables and a bench danced with blackening flames. It wasn't anywhere near the gas tanks, but it was near a white propane tank.

"Can't we spray water on the fire from the upstairs balcony?"

"Sure, unless there are wolves up there, too. They might have jumped the gate and headed up the outside stairs," Marader said.

"The windows!" Heidi cried.

"Relax, babe. I was so weirded out after Troy said I had that wolfhound visitor that I barred them," Marader said. He led Troy upstairs. Unfortunately, the supernatural wolves were there, too, on the balcony.

Troy pointed out the nearness of the flames to the propane tanks. They might go boom sooner rather than later.

"That might get people's attention," Marader said, understating the danger. "The hose and sprayer nozzle are in a closet behind the bar. We can use them."

Troy rushed downstairs while Marader went for the CB radio. Troy arranged the fire brigade. He ran the hose to the window while Spider hooked it up to the yellow kitchen's faucet. Silke attached the sprayer then called for water pressure. While waiting, she watched the wolves nudge one of the rolling propane grills toward a wall. She pointed it out to Troy.

"J-Man, Knives, look outside! They're trying to blow up the wall," Troy said.

The wolves were nose-pushing a second grill toward the downstairs wall. Troy turned the hose on them, the spray surprising them and delaying them a moment. He swore one smirked, as they bodied the grill into the fire. The tanks rolled loose. The flames slowly heated the volatile gas under pressure.

"You're giving them intelligence. What are they trying to do, blow their way in?" Knives snapped.

Troy sprayed the area, but it must have been a chemical or gasoline fire, because the flames would lessen, then flare back up. He grew concerned about the tank. Changing tactics, he kept the water focused on it, keeping it cool.

The wolves intervened. They sprang and stood in front to deflect the stream. Silke couldn't believe it, and they were both surprised when a wolf lunged at the bars, trying to bite the sprayer. A second joined, and Troy couldn't keep the water on the tanks.

"Y'all, they're blocking the water!" Silke yelled down.

Desiree rushed up and shot the two wolves in the window.

They fell back, giving Troy some room to work. The wolves below scattered as Marader fired off his shotgun.

"Stop!" Desiree yelled.

The blast ripped apart the wall in a churning, fiery cloud of debris and burning fuel. The concussion threw Desiree and Troy back toward the stairwell.

He couldn't hear anything, and his vision was blurry. Silke knelt next to him. He read her lips, asking if he was all right. What had happened? She and Spider helped him stand.

Troy's hearing rang then returned, bringing the sound of desperate footsteps, hungry wolves howling, and the devouring roar of flames.

He turned to watch his blood brothers rush in, Denny and Marader carrying Heidi who appeared unconscious. Knives was right behind them, immediately tending to her. J-Man and Spider dashed through last, and Desiree slammed shut the door to downstairs. They pushed a gun cabinet to block the way.

Next, they moved a dresser and a couch. The windows in this room were broken but barred. Wolves stuck their snouts in and sniffed then barked and howled.

"I think we're about set. Unless they can walk through the walls, that is," J-Man said. He wiped his brow.

"They don't need to get us. The place is on fire. Maybe they like their meat cooked," Spider bemoaned.

"Screw it! We either get eaten or blown up!" Marader waved his arms. "If the fuel tanks go, we'll ride the crest to Kingdom Come."

"I think now's a good time to pray," Father Dennis suggested. He gingerly folded his hands and led them in a prayer. Afterward, he looked around. "We human beings are divine ideas. Any inspirations?"

Outside, the beasts began to howl in concert as if they were singing to a blood moon. The noise was deafening, making it hard to think and cutting deeply into the soul. The loft seemed to quake under the vocal onslaught.

Troy glanced at Spider. Neither wanted to die again. Troy looked to Silke. They had just realized they should be together. Now he must figure a way to escape a burning, floating building, surrounded by water and werewolves.

"Shut up, goddammit!" Marader yelled as he banged the butt of the shotgun into one wolf snout after another like a dangerous, twisted game of Whack-a-Mole.

"I don't think that's what he meant," Spider said.

"In case you haven't been paying attention. There are wolves in the stairwell. We can't zip line out past them, or swim underwater to get out. How's the CB coming along?" Marader snapped back.

J-Man was fiddling with it. He seemed to be getting a signal. He turned the dial, listening for trucker chatter. "Breaker, breaker. Anyone out there? I have a 911 and fire emergency," he said. Nobody responded, but he kept trying.

"Do you have any more of that silver shot if they break in, or we need to shoot our way out?" Troy asked.

Marader pulled open the drawer of the shaking gun cabinet. He found the box, loaded the clip, then he handed a shotgun to Troy. He stuffed his pockets with silver shot. He didn't have a good feeling about this, but he couldn't think of any alternatives.

"What do you guys plan to do?" Desiree asked.

"We can protect people while you jump off the balcony to swim to the boat," Troy said.

"Hmm. Swim for your life! I like it!" Marader said.

"Well, we almost made it to thirty," Spider bemoaned.

"Too bad we can't cut a hole in the roof and jump out from there. Wave at the wolves as we go by," Knives said.

"I can swim over to Maverick, fire her up, swing back by and pick up everybody. You'll just need to clear me a gap in the wolves, so I can get past them," Marader said.

"A gap. A hole," Troy said, pondering.

"It sounds better than trying to blow our way clear down the steps and into the storeroom," Denny said.

"I'm faster than you are," Knives told Marader.

"By half a second. Besides, Heidi needs you," Marader said.

"You've been drinking," Knives said.

"So? I've been swimming for all my life. Only drinking for half of it."

"I'm faster than both of you," Spider said.

"Y'all, the whole place is going to burn down around us, killing us, and y'all are arguing over who is the fastest swimmer? Would it kill you to . . . poor choice of words, there, sorry, to make a decision and just go?" Silke said.

"Until the wolves notice, everybody should go who's a fast swimmer," Troy said. He looked at Silke. "And all these guys swim faster than I do, especially with my left leg the way it is," Troy said. He watched her worry her lip. "We are going to get out of here."

"I smell smoke all the way over here," Knives said.

"It's getting worse," Spider said.

Troy touched the floor. "It's hot."

A crack and pop sounded like dry logs in a fireplace. "Let's go splatter some wolves," Marader said.

Silke nearly clung to Troy as he tried to move away. "Be careful," she said with wide eyes.

He gave her a tight smile and joined Marader. "Extreme skeet shooting," Troy said.

"Like I said. Blast me a hole and I'll run through them. Damn, I could use a jigger shot first," Marader said.

"Wait, doesn't your kitchen pantry face the boats, but it doesn't have a balcony on the other side?" J-Man said.

"Yeah, so?" Marader asked.

"We could blow a hole in the wall with shotguns without worrying about wolves on the balcony. Jump from there," J-Man said, finishing with a cough.

Another series of loud, crackling pops assaulted their ears and diverted their attention. The walls had started to blacken and smoke poured around the door and windows. It coalesced ghostly then stretched across the ceiling, growing thicker.

Soon, it would be too difficult to breathe. Black, smoldering streaks climbed up the walls. Suddenly, the lights flickered. Hissing preceded an electrified pop, and the lights went out, plunging them into darkness. The acrid smell of burnt wiring filled the room.

It was as if death's dark shroud had dropped over them. Darkness added to their desperate plight as the wolves howled, and the fire roared, edging its way toward the gasoline tanks.

Troy felt a wave of heat swell through the room. The east wall burst aflame. Blue and yellow tendrils of fire streamed up the surface while smoke billowed along the ceiling.

He, J-Man and Marader loaded their guns with normal shot, then they aimed at the pantry's outer wall, intent on creating an opening to the outside. Marader fired, the concussion pushing him back. Immediately, J-Man let loose with both barrels. Troy's ears rang, nearly drowning out the howling of the wolves. The sound of guns excited the beasts.

Troy would always remember Marader's leering face while flame and sound exploded from both barrels and slugs tore into the wall. Troy pulled both triggers. The blast rocked him, then he cocked to fill the chambers and fired again. Wood and dry wall scattered and flew, a cloud of debris thickening with the smoke. Troy felt like he was trapped in a sulfur mine. He could barely see in front of him.

They paused. The shot had created holes in a four-foot diameter but not yet large enough to escape through, so they reloaded. He could see outside and thought he felt a small breeze, a breath of fresh air desperately needed.

"Guys, hurry, please!" Knives called. Then no one could speak, and no one could breathe. Twisted shadows danced through the smoke-filled room as the fire spread across the ceiling. It crawled as it ate its way toward them.

Troy, J-Man and Marader fired and reloaded, fired and reloaded. Now the group was deaf as well as nearly blinded. The explosions went on for what seemed hours instead of two minutes.

Finally, humid fresh air was sucked into the hole, rushing across their faces, drawing away the smoke and leaving tears to clear their eyes.

Spider staggered forward and fell to his knees next to the gap in the wall. It was a jagged tear nearly five feet wide and tall. Fragments still hung in the way, cluttering the opening. With a few swipes of a broken chair, Spider easily cleared them.

"Go Marader! Go Spider!" Troy shouted.

Marader launched and dove out through the gap. With a little slap and barely a leg splash, he carved into the lake. Spider followed. He landed awkwardly in the water then swam furiously. Denny was next, joined by J-Man. His splash soaked the wolves that had just noticed and seemed to hesitate, debating what to do as a pack.

Troy watched the four swim-sprinting for salvation in the form of Maverick, the Master Craft. He wanted Silke to leave.

"I am not the swimmer those boys are," she told him. "And I'm not leaving you."

The werewolves decided to give chase. Troy unleashed both barrels as two beasts jumped off the dock. They spun in the air and dropped like stones.

"This is not how I imagined dying again," Troy said. He kissed Silke.

"Let's prove your imagination right," she said.

"Tommy is going to bring us a boat," Heidi groaned.

"Ah, just in time to go swimming," Knives said.

Troy watched the swimming wolves. Paddling with all four, they were closing too quickly on his blood brothers.

Desiree readied a rifle, aimed and fired. Every one of the dark-haired beauty's shots made the werewolves roll over in pain or dive under the surface, swimming under water.

Fastest, Marader reached the boat. Spider was right behind him with Denny and J-Man closing.

"It's getting hot," Silke said. Her eyes were out of focus, and Troy pushed her closer to the gap. Like all of them, she was soaked in sweat. Black clouds rolled past them and out into the night. The five huddled around the only source of clean air and coolness.

Feeling the heat scorch his back, Troy hunkered lower. Time was running out. The place could blow any minute. Only minutes ago they could see the fire clawing its way along the ceiling, floors, and walls. Now the oily black cloud only allowed them to see each other.

He wasn't surprised to hear the crash. He expected the place to collapse or blow. The scratching of claws on wood and the growling was unexpected, unwelcome and likely to be deadly. If these flames didn't kill the wolves, there was nothing he could do. Wolves in front and wolves in back. They were going to have to go and take their chances in the water, hoping the boat would reach them first.

He thought he heard the roar of Maverick starting up. Hopeful imagining, or for real?

Then he heard another noise. Or felt paws and claws scrabbling on the floor. He turned, ready with the shotgun.

Out of the fire and smoke, the wolves leapt and bounded swiftly, like rushing flames. Troy knew they would never make it out alive. He shoved Silke out the gap, sending her flying. He turned to Knives, who tossed a blade, catching one of the beasts in the eye. It stumbled, tripping the one next to it and the nearest one behind, entangling and rolling like a burning tumbleweed.

"Jump! Now!" Desiree yelled. She shot one beast and kicked a second aside, acting as a professional bodyguard, but the surging pack swarmed over her.

Knives held onto Heidi and leapt out, jumping for the lake. She screamed on her way to splash down.

Too many, too fast, the wolves overwhelmed Desiree. One knocked Troy down mid leap. He landed on the edge, his legs dangling. Troy pushed off, but his clothing caught. He tried to tear loose. Above, Bandit sneered at him. Below, another jumped up and tried to bite him.

Troy pulled up his legs. He needed a miracle or luck.

Running out of the flames, Dillon finally appeared, materializing like the God of Fire. His red hair flowed with the flames, and his eyes were bright with the light of the inferno. Troy couldn't believe it as his best friend, smiling grimly, grabbed Bandit and another wolf by the scruffs of their necks. He slammed their heads together, leaving Troy hanging but left alone.

"Yeah! Go buddy, about damned time!" Troy screamed

"You go!" Dillon shouted. He grabbed Troy by the arms, pulling him up, then his savior tossed him out the gap. He tumbled over dizzily when his world exploded.

In a fiery blast of splintering debris and shattering glass, the marina erupted. Troy was dimly aware of falling, then he plunged into the lake. The water's coolness soothed him as he recovered from the impact. He struggled to stay alert, knowing there were wolves everywhere. He clawed his way to the surface.

Troy smelled gasoline. The fumes stung his eyes,

A crunch and crash sounded like a car had been dropped. Troy glanced over, seeing the gasoline pumps take a hit from what he thought must be space junk, before he recognized the mangled water heater. Only a miracle kept the pumps from exploding. He would need a second miracle to escape as four wolves dog-paddled to surround him.

Silke and his brothers couldn't reach him with so many wolves in the way. Better to die by burning or torn apart by wolves? Could he opt for drowning to death? Any chance that he could swim underneath them? But to where? Maverick was leaving. He was missing the boat as his friends fled.

No, he didn't believe it.

Something hit one of the wolves atop the head, bounced and tumbled toward Troy. It struck him in the shoulder, and then a rope slapped him in the face. He had been pegged by a thrown ski handle and rope many times before. It was a good reason to keep one's mouth closed. Great, they planned to pull him loose. Could he still barefoot? It had been years.

Ski or die. If you can't ski with the big dogs, in this case supernatural wolves, stay on the dock. Except it had exploded and burned like a funeral pyre. Ghosts haunted the waters. Was any place safe anymore?

Troy heard the motor, growing in pitch. The rope uncoiled, straightening, and started to slither away. He seized it with one hand then both.

The wolves closed in. Their eyes and teeth reflected the firelight.

The marina and water's surface erupted into flames. The gasoline ignited with a whoosh and spread out like a rolling wave across the cove.

The rope grew taut then jerked. Troy hung on for life as his arms were nearly pulled from their sockets, but he had known this was coming. He had done this, in a previous life. He remembered how. His arms, shoulders and hands screamed for him to let go, but he knew better. This was his miracle lift. This wouldn't even be possible without Dillon. What about Desiree?

Water hammered at Troy, trying to dislodge him. It surged, churned, thrashed, and choked him. He hung onto his life line. He rebounded off a wolf, even as it futilely snapped at him, and rolled onto his back to skim across the surface. He was dragged by and out of the reach of snapping jaws. Clear, he tried to spin around and stand.

Amazed at himself, he stood up, crouched and wobbling, trying to find his balance. He leaned back and straightened his knees, and the water felt almost firm beneath the soles of his feet, trying to catch his toes. He managed to stay upright for several long seconds, enough to be hauled away from the beasts and way past the No Wake buoy.

Troy suddenly lost his balance and face-planted.

Thirty-Six: No Longer Missing

When they lifted Troy into the boat, the intense pain awakened him then led to a near blackout. He heard himself screaming, asking them to stop. Through tears, he saw a black-faced and weary, Knives examine him.

"His shoulder is dislocated. Relax, my friend. I can maneuver it back in. This will hurt then feel much better."

The doctor took Troy's left arm, almost numb with pain. He adjusted it gingerly until Troy felt relief as the humeral head slid into the AC joint. His body calmed, and his head cleared. While he hurt less physically, knowing Pete, Jambo and Walt had died left a deep wound. Had anyone else died? He almost panicked. Silke! "Silke?! J-Man . . ."

"I am here with you, my love," Silke said. She leaned in and kissed him, making him breathe deeply to inhale her scent. Another reason to be glad to be alive. "Jambo is alive, too. He was already on the boat, getting it started to help us."

"Where's Desiree?" Troy asked.

"I haven't seen her. But, she's full of surprises, right? I imagine she'll show up. You know, there's another tank . . ." Marader began.

A second eruption rocked the night. Troy could feel the wave of heat. The inferno suddenly expanded, the flames growing with the spewing fuel. Fiery gasoline rained down around them, forcing Marader to pull farther away. A glow surrounded Silke. The force of the blast pushed her closer.

Tired and aching, Troy awakened in Silke's arms. "We're here, my man," she said. She was tousled, windblown and smelled of fire, but she felt wonderful and looked gorgeous right now.

"Where is here?"

"Virginia Shores at Jay's place. He and Tommy ran inside to use the phone and call 911."

Troy looked around. So, J-Man and Marader were all right.

Spider was tethering the boat. Heidi and Denny looked asleep. Jambo was watching Troy with a big grin. It seemed to remain, like the Cheshire Cat, as Troy slipped unconscious again.

He dreamt of driving Dillon's truck. He bumped along a vaguely familiar road, the drought-stricken, low-lying lake and shadowy houses to the right. When he passed by the entrance to the Swearington Lodge, he turned off the headlights. Most of the building was dark, but a few first story windows radiated a dim glow.

One of the many garage doors opened, rising slowly to reveal a place darker than night. He drove in, parked and exited, feeling comfortable. This was home now.

A figure sprang out of the darkness. The blond wrapped her legs around his waist and smothered his face with kisses.

A siren sounded. Red, white and blue lights flashed around, making the world seem like it was moving. Troy awakened to the swirl of colorful, EMS lights from the ambulance dancing across the trees.

After the paramedics examined him, agreeing with Knives' conclusions, Silke led Troy limping along the sidewalk to the back of the J-Man's house. Lights shone through the first story windows and over a balcony, pushing away the darkness. When they neared the back porch, automatic landscape lights flickered on creating a guided path to the downstairs porch and stairs up to the back balcony. Many of the house's walls were wood-framed panes of glass to take advantage of the lake view. Troy wished he was in the mood to appreciate it.

"So, what term of endearment would you like me to use, Troy? Honey? Sweetheart? Dear? Babe? Lover?" Silke asked.

"I like hearing you say my name, though the others are wonderful, too," he replied.

Silke opened the door, leading into a downstairs lounge and game room. Several doors, opened and closed, led to a bathroom, bedrooms, a wine cellar and storage area. It looked like a perfect place to recuperate and convalesce. He would just like to lie with Silke in his arms.

That's when Dillon would show up. Did he feel Dillon? Driving?

Silke closed the door behind them. He waited, leaning against the wall and leaving a big black smudge, while she set the house alarm. Nearby stood a shotgun against the wall.

"Lights and sirens set. Worry not. Jay's dog, Scout and I will guard you. Knives went along with Heidi in the ambulance. The others went back to the marina to talk with the authorities. We can do that tomorrow. Tonight, I'll guard you."

Would they find Dillon? No, they would find Walt's and Pete's body.

Troy tried to take heart, it could have been far, far worse. "Silke, I saw your brother."

"What was he doing this time?" she asked, assuming he meant a dream.

"Back at the marina, when Knives, Desiree and I were waiting, the wolves rushed us. She tried to stop them, but she was overrun, then, out of nowhere, Dillon jumped into the fire, pushed the wolves aside right as they tried to eat us and shoved me out the gap before the water heater or whatever blew."

Silke starred. "Dillon. You really saw him. In the fire?"

Troy nodded. "The fire didn't seem to be bothering him, a lot like the werewolves."

"Did you tell him I'm mad at him?" she asked, an eyebrow arched.

"I was too surprised. You don't believe me."

"Oh, I wouldn't say that. I'm really open-minded right now. One dream has come true," she said and kissed him. "Alone at last. I'm fine if Dillon doesn't show up until tomorrow."

"Hmm. Little did I know perfume de gasoline and marina fire were aphrodisiacs. I would have had a bonfire a long time ago. You must be the action hero loving kind of gal. Martin had us pegged."

"Ha. Don't forget the acrid smell of gunpowder," she joked. She guided him to the nearest bathroom and to the shower. She turned on the water, leaving it cool.

Silke carefully drew off his borrowed shirt. "I've wanted to do that for a long, long time," she said, her voice husky. "Dirty and sexy, lover. Well, while that sounds good." She wrinkled her nose. "I would prefer kissing your body, mapping it with my lips, when you're clean. And since I'm memorizing, it will take more than one go round."

"Well, if I wasn't in shock before, I am now," Troy said.

"Scout should warn us if anything comes close. If you fall asleep, I'll come in there after you. I really need to forget what happened," Silke said.

For once, Troy didn't have nightmares nor dream of Dillon and his sexual escapades. Troy had slept deeply, comfortably and healing, thanks to Silke. He pulled her close, enjoying the smooth, warm electricity of her nakedness. He wondered if he might be dreaming. If so, this dream smelled wonderful, her hair fragrant and her body clean with a passionate tang. They had finished showering together. He opened his eyes to be sure that he had really experienced sharing body and soul with her.

She wore a smile while she beauty slumbered. No, he wasn't dreaming. Why had he resisted for so long? It didn't matter. They were entangled now, flesh and soul.

He heard a noise, but he couldn't quite define it. It wasn't regular, as he listened carefully. Had it been a bell? Is that why he was awake?

He didn't hear it again, but he was more awake when he recognized footfalls upstairs. They were soft and furtive steps. None of the guys walked with that light of a tread, not even when sneaking or stalking. They hadn't grown any lighter, and none of them could be called dainty or light-footed. Did the door close quietly? He wondered why the alarm hadn't sounded. What about Scout?

Troy kissed Silke on the neck, nuzzling her, then he gently shook her shoulder as he whispered in her ear. "Silke, love, I hear footsteps, and none sound like the boys coming back. We might have visitors. So far, the ankh is cool."

Silke cracked open an eye. "Is it still dark?"

"Yes," he said. He sat on the side of the bed and pulled on a pair of shorts with Marvin the Martian on them. He slipped out into the lounge and to the fireplace. The silver moonlight illuminated the floor and wood furniture, throwing shadows and darkening corners. Troy grabbed a fire poker, just in case. It seemed rather pitiful considering. He touched the ankh from Aunt Jada and waited, hearing the dog and someone descend the stairway.

"Scout?"

"Troy, it's me, Dillon, with Scout," the figure said.

Troy flipped the switch, turning on the tract lighting overhead. He was surprised but not shocked.

The glaring beams caught Dillon slinking through the darkness. He stood startled, hands up to shield his face, eyes closed to the light. His hair had turned silver and his skin was ashen, still looking ill. He seemed slimmer and yet broader of shoulder, maybe even taller. "Did you have to do that?"

"Yes, to be sure it's you. I have experienced unwanted, late night visitors," Troy replied. Of course, Dillon's timing could have been only a little worse. Troy could have still been entangled with Silke when Dillon sauntered in. "How do I know it's you and not some shapeshifter?"

"Getting suspicious and cautious, good," Dillon said. Troy glared. "Okay, in the hospital, when I first woke up and saw you after giving you my left kidney, I said, welcome to the family."

"I thought you weren't going to get involved in someone who is high maintenance," Troy said tongue-in-cheek.

Dillon blinked. "Yeah, I know. Elke's incredible, and she saved my life. If I survive this, I doubt the future will be boring. I may go where no investigative journalist has gone before."

"It's about time. You had me worked up and worried that more werewolves were trying to kill us, or the Dark Lady, the first, not the second. You are a sight for tired, searching eyes," Troy rambled. He felt unsettled by the ankh growing warmer.

"You have no idea how good it is to see you well. I've had the strangest nightmares. Sorry I had to shove and run, but when the explosions started happening, I knew the authorities would be there soon," Dillon said.

"You've always liked to push me in the water," Troy said. Dillon chuckled. When they shook hands, the ankh started to sear Troy's skin. He let go before he started to cook. Dillon didn't seem to notice. Troy grew worried. "Why didn't you meet Burt?"

"I'll talk to Burt later. How are you?" Dillon asked.

Troy started to say he'd been better, but considering, he felt terrific. Silke was crazy about him, and his best friend had reappeared. "I'm alive, mobile, and in love. Is Elke with you?"

"No. She's . . . busy. She said you knew, know about us. How?"

"Interesting dreams. I don't usually dream about fair-haired, alabaster skinned and dark-eyed beauties, but I have since you disappeared."

"Did you say in love?" Dillon asked.

Troy nodded. "You have a ton of questions to answer first, before I tell you anything. How did you manage to escape the fire unburnt? You don't look touched," Troy asked.

"I changed clothes before coming here," Dillon said. He wore ash gray clothes—a shirt, faded black jeans, socks and shoes that looked more like slippers.

"Not your clothes! You!"

"I died and came back, like you, but in a different way. I returned a changed man, too," Dillon replied with a shrug.

Troy didn't think he looked, sounded or felt right. Not only was the ankh warning Troy, but he felt Dillon's vibe was off. Troy had known him long enough to sense something was amiss. He might look like Dillon but not be Dillon. At least he hadn't attacked him like John's body.

"I smell a story. Should we compare notes about pulling a phoenix?" Troy asked.

"Sure. Is my sister here? I saw her in the boat leaving with y'all," Dillon said. Troy nodded. "How is she? Have you taken good care of her? I'm sure she was worried sick," Dillon said. His brows knitted together, he studied Troy. "What? What's that look for?"

"I am crazy about your sister."

"What? My sister is crazy? I already know that. But how is she?"

"Oh, Brother, so kind of you to ask about me. To care about me." Silke strolled in wearing only a long shirt that had a miniskirt affect. She was smiling a comeuppance time grin. Her brother noted that she was wearing a crucifix and carrying a grudge in one hand and her gun in the other. Troy hoped the safety was on.

"Silke. You're all right!" Dillon said. His eyes brightened, and his smile was genuine. He took several quick steps forward. Silke meet him in a brief hug. "Sister, I was so frightened they would come for you. You look great. You glow."

"I'm better than well. I'm in love," Silke with a broad smile and whimsical air. She threw Troy a kiss.

"And you smell of sex," Dillon said. With furious, betrayed eyes he glared at Troy. "You're sleeping with Silke?"

"Sleeping and loving. I waited a long time for this night," Silke said, not helping.

"I love your sister. She's wonderful. Awesome. My angel. The best . . ." Troy began.

Moving with blurring speed, Dillon set Silke aside. He yelped and there was flash of light around his hands. He released her hard enough that when she hit the couch, it tipped over, sending her rolling. In a blink, Dillon jumped Troy. Even ready for him, Troy reacted too slowly.

Troy ducked an elbow and punched his best friend in the gut. He lost his breath but not momentum. He body-slammed Troy into the wall, shaking it, knocking photos off the wall, and causing Troy's world to blink in and out. His shoulder screamed its protest. More body parts joined the chorus.

"You betrayed me. I warned you!" Dillon hissed. Spittle flew. His teeth were barred and reminded Troy of Zane's, longer and sharper, like those of a feline.

Troy kicked and repeatedly kneed Dillon, but his best friend held him like a child. Unable to breathe, Troy felt helpless. The ankh grew from hot to scorching. He smelled burning skin, his flesh.

He would die speaking the truth. "I love your sister. She's worth fighting for," Troy wheezed.

Dillon didn't even blink. He squeezed harder.

Dillon was in a killing rage, so Troy brought both hands down upon Dillon's inner elbow. It bent, forcing Dillon to release him. His hands were smoldering, wisps of smoke surrounding them.

Dillon was undead or supernatural. For the worse, he was a changed man, perhaps no longer human.

Troy kicked out in a leg sweep, taking Dillon out at the ankles. When Dillon leapt, Troy hit him with the fireplace poker across his right elbow. Troy winced as he heard the bone break. Dillon didn't slow, body-bludgeoning into him again.

Troy thought he blacked out for a moment. He couldn't breathe. His best friend, after days of searching for him, had been found, ready to kill him.

Silke shoved the Glock against her brother's temple and cocked it. "Let go now! Gently, of the love of my life. The safety is off, as you might notice, my finger is flexed, the hammer cocked, and I am thoroughly, completely, and royally pissed off at you, in a killing rage, you might say, like off with his head, or modern colloquial, blow off his head!" she snapped, spittle landing on Dillon's shocked face.

"You're being unreasonable."

When he didn't let go, Silke backed up and shot a teddy bear on the love seat, blowing stuffing everywhere. "And he was an innocent bystander!" she raged. She took aim at Dillon again. "I don't know what Elke did to you, but I won't let you hurt my man. I keep having to help him recuperate just because he's been looking for your ass while you've been out screwing around with some blond . . ." she paused long enough to let another b word pass. "Keeping your whereabouts and health secret. I'll bet Mom would like to belt you, too."

Dillon finally released his grip on Troy, stepping back. Flames flickered along his hands then slowly died. "Silke, it wouldn't matter if you shot me. I'm different now," Dillon said. A dagger appeared in his hand, and, in one smooth motion, he stabbed himself in the palm of his left hand.

Silke stepped back, shocked.

"I died and came back, different. Some better. Some not. Still not perfect. As you can tell, it hurts, but I heal really fast," he said, then, he wiped the blood off his hands. The flesh around the blade wound knitted together, soon a fading pink scar.

Silke still looked beautifully furious. "That's good to know," she said and pulled the trigger, shooting her brother in the foot. Troy saw the leather ripped apart by the slug and blood splattered across the tiles.

Dillon screamed. "OW! What the hell?! What did you do that for!" He hopped around, holding his left foot. It would have been funny to Troy if it had been on TV or a cartoon, but his best friend and the woman he loved were fighting. That seemed a ludicrous understatement.

"You sure you'll mend all right?" Silke asked sweetly. Troy recognized the tone from her younger, tantrum years. It did help to have a shared past and history.

Dillon nodded and swore as he limped around. "A minute, or less," he said through gritted teeth. "What did I do to tick you off?"

"A minute. That's all? That's too fast. The sting of a slap lasts longer. Not enough suffering in my opinion to make up for eight years."

"Eight years? Silke . . ."

"I don't know what happened to you, but I don't feel bad about this, you vampire," Silke snapped. She shot him in the right knee.

Dillon screamed and crumpled. "Stop that! Why?"

"Because you just showed me that slapping you wouldn't have made my point, and I can't kill you either!" she raged.

"You shot me instead of slapping me? I always knew you were a few cards short. Explain yourself, please."

"Because you hurt my lover, your best friend in the world who almost died trying to find you, perhaps rescue you. Oh, what the hell," she said, and elbow punched him.

Dillon staggered and blinked. "I'm sorry, but . . ."

"You prevented us from getting together years earlier. You and your idiotic edict."

"Edict? What edict?" Dillon said, on the defensive.

"Okay, how about strong-arm coercion? Don't look at my sister or even think about kissing her, or I will break your arm?" Silke asked sweetly. Her face was bright red. Her eyes were touched with madness. "Do those words sound familiar?"

Dillon glared at Troy. He spread his arms. He had only confirmed it.

"Don't blame him. Marader spilled the beans. Thank you for hitting him, but not Troy on New Year's Day," Silke said.

"Oh, is that all you're mad about. It was for your own good," Dillon said, shrugging it off. "Hey, we really have something more important to talk about."

Based on those words alone, Troy thought Silke would shoot him again. Instead, she kicked him between the legs. Despite Dillon's transformation, it still caused him to double over.

"Stop telling me what to do, or what's good for me! You're lucky I didn't make you regrow your balls!"

"Really, I was afraid . . ."

"Stop, don't make me take up a shotgun. Just shut up! God, we've been searching for you, killing ourselves, and you're like this. Pete, John, and Walt are dead! Did you hear me? They are D E A D. Dead. We almost died, too, and you're like this, you shithead!"

Troy wondered a little about this wild woman. But then, many of them had seen this coming. Not the shooting, but the fury of a wronged young lady. He took note so he could avoid being the target of her wrath.

"Silke, can you take it out of him a little every day for the rest of your life instead of all today?" Troy generously suggested.

"Don't defend him! See, he loves you, too! You choke him, and he still loves you. Dillon, you're acting like an idiot and a moron, and you're neither," she said, stomping toward the door. She paused before going outside. "And just so you know, I have another three thousand days of reminding you of this," Silke said. She stormed outside, slamming the door. It shut and cracked the glass. A painting fell off the wall. The frame clipped a lamp, which also fell, onto the floor where it tumbled and rolled to stop at Dillon's feet.

"Wow. I guess this is why Desiree didn't come. She knew," Dillon said.

Troy was relieved. "I'm glad she's all right. She's got the hots for me, but I love your sister. Can you see the light, brother?" Troy asked, gesturing to the lamp. Still smoldering, Dillon glared at him. "I think your sister is a wow. I couldn't resist her. Whether you like it or not, we're a couple."

"I can't believe you'd do this to me."

"Listen, bro, I'm not doing anything to you. And when you think about this, you brought us together."

"What me? How?" Dillon asked. He seemed shocked, like he couldn't imagine that happening.

"If you had picked me up at the airport, this probably wouldn't have happened. So I don't blame you, I give you credit. Your sister loves me. I love that and her. I want to see how we are as couple. Besides, she comes from good stock, though I'm starting to wonder about her brother. He seems to have gone off the deep end."

Dillon waved it off. "You got that right. But you said, it's not about me. What about Raquel?"

"Been there. Done that. Healed the wound. Carry the burn scar. We've been out on a date, sort of. She's changed. I've changed. We didn't grow together. I am certain your sister is far better for me. I feel blest, and I will be good to her and great for her," Troy promised.

Dillon was sullen, still angry from being shot. Troy gingerly rubbed his neck and watched his best friend process all this. "Well, based on that mother of all hissy fits, Silke loves you. She only gets that incensed about things she's passionate about. I mean, she shot me. Are you sure you want to date her? Are you insane?"

"Yes and you know I'm different," Troy said.

"Are you on drugs?"

Troy nodded. "Pain killers. I dislocated my shoulder. I'm lucky it didn't go out again when you one hand pressed me. But you might have piled on my concussion by slamming me into the wall."

Dillon stared into his eyes. "That explains it."

"What?" Troy asked.

He chuckled, sounding more like his old self. "Why you want to date my sister. Your brain's been addled."

"I thought you might be able to see it in my eyes."

"What? Oh, not yet. As you can tell, I'm having trouble with my temper. It's one of the many reasons I haven't come to see you until tonight. I'm irrational. Elke knew. That's why she kept me to herself. Hey, Troy, buddy, I'm sorry. Silke is right, I'm being an asshole. You risked your life for me. I am grateful for your friendship and your help. I'm trying not to be a jerk, although I feel like one, sorry. I'll make it up to you somehow."

They managed a shoulder hug. Something still remained between them. Troy could feel it, including the heat of the ankh. He could see it in Dillon's eyes.

"What are you and Silke wearing? It makes my skin burn," Dillon said.

"A gift from your Aunt Jada. She passed away last night. Silke's upset about that, too."

"Oh. So, tell me what's been going on before tonight's party burned down the house."

Troy felt the compelling but rolled with it. He watched while his friend processed his visit to Aunt Jada, finding John's sunken boat, the first dive to the underwater house of doom and death and discovering John's body.

Dillon peppered him with questions about the haunted mansion, especially about the objects they had found and brought to the surface. Troy told him what he had learned from Spider reading Von Damme's diaries. He could see his blood brother mentally taking notes. Troy told him about the wolf at Marader's, now what he thought was a scout, and the dive with SARs, the moonshine shed still where he experienced past events, the entombing of Von Damme, and Mona's death.

"That's incredible. You saw a woman she killed?" Dillon asked. He only sounded surprised that Troy had witnessed it. Did he know Elke was a killer, way beyond drop dead gorgeous?

"Like the ghost had passed on a memory. Elke didn't deny it. She said she could see the truth in my eyes. I kept thinking any minute she would kill me or kiss me and make me a slave. I wanted to run, and I wanted to pledge myself to her, except I am smitten with your sister."

"You know that means divinely struck, right? Elke told me you refused to listen to sense. And here I thought she was just talking about you stopping your search for me."

"She told me to stay away from Silke."

Dillon whistled. "I told her you were stubborn, but, well,

from what I know, you must really be in love to shake a compelling. I was already crazy about Elke, so I had no chance. How did you find me?" Dillon said.

Troy backtracked in his story. He mentioned the images on this camera found on the Sea-Doo, encountering Zane and his compelling by daylight, and his relationship to Aunt Jada. How his worry for Silke had allowed him to fight obeying Zane's order.

"By day. Sweet Lord, it's worse than I thought. I knew he followed Von Damme. I learned Aunt Jada worked with Elke. I didn't know the connection. You've done some digging."

Troy told him about the former TVA employees and their stories, then he backed up, covering the wolves chasing he and Silke and wrecking the Land Rover. Troy now blamed them for blowing up the house.

"Too bad. That was a beautiful place, though I thought it was unnerving and bizarre. Ah, the Land Rover. It had a good life. It survived a lot. I guess they can't say werewolf tough in a commercial, huh?"

"You're casual about this," Troy said.

"When you almost die, it can transform you," Dillon said. Troy laughed and couldn't stop for a while. Dillon didn't see the humor in it. "I know you don't think dying is funny."

Finally, Troy caught his breath, able to speak. "No, no. Not that. It's just, now, you understand what I was trying to tell you. Spider and I see ghosts. So does your sister," Troy said. He played the recordings of Undead John at the cemetery and a little with Zane in the boat.

"That's horrible. I think I still have purpose. We can stop whatever disaster Von Damme has planned. From what I understand, he is a hundred times more dangerous than Zane. You had the parking lot and marina sanctified and protected against his followers, so he sent werewolf minions. Only back among the living for a few days, and Von Damme is assembling a cult to wreak vengeance. That's one of the reasons people are missing," Dillon bemoaned.

"That sounds frightening," Silke said. She returned to slip under Troy's arm, hip to hip. He talked about the funeral, coming out to the lodge where the dogs chased them away.

Dillon laughed. "Chewy, Muffy, Ginger, and Adonis are so lovable and cuddly, you would not believe it, like big lap dogs."

"No, I wouldn't," Troy agreed. He summarized Pat's wake, seeing Zane and dancing and chatting with Elke, and then Zane attempting to steal Marader's backpack with the jewelry box. "To cover his escape, he started a brawl."

"I watched the recordings on YouTube. I didn't see what started it, as the instigator couldn't be recorded. Now I know why. Von Damme and his group of vampire zealots."

"Vampires? Is that what we're truly dealing with?" Troy asked.

Dillon nodded. "Vampires, damn them. Damn us, as I am now one," he laughed bitterly.

Silke gave Troy a look and squeezed him. "Seriously? A blood sucker?" Silke asked.

Dillon nodded sadly. "From what I understand, I'm on my way. It was either death or this," he replied. He gestured and shrugged as if to say, this is how it is. Accept it.

"Have you killed anyone?" Silke asked, aghast.

"No, but I have considered it," Dillon said.

"Me, too," Silke said.

"So, you're in love and feed on people, but you can't stand the sunlight?" Troy asked.

"I don't have to feed on people," Dillon said.

"I've seen a lot, but I have trouble swallowing this. I guess I don't want you to be a vampire," Troy said.

Silke looked at Troy. Both had been in the hypnotic grip of a vampire. "You're under her control?" she asked Dillon.

"Yes and no. Not exactly. I am her consort," Dillon said.

"She saved you to make you part of her household?" Silke asked.

"She told me that she saved me so that I could help her save the people of the Tri Cities and Tri State area," he said, sounding noble. "That's what she says. The Cult of Von Damme will exact its revenge for flooding his lair and keeping him submerged for all those decades."

"Do you plan to tell the others?"

"Nobody else can know. I told you because you're family. As for our blood brothers, how much luck have you had getting them to believe in the supernatural? Hmm?" Dillon wondered.

"I suspect they'll be more open-minded now," Troy replied.

"And Mom?" Silke asked.

"I can say I developed a skin issue where I can't be out by day. Now, what else has happened? It may not seem important, and yet, it might be," Dillon said.

Silke told him about the Viking funeral of John's body, how it had burst aflame.

"That proved to J-Man and me that something was amiss. Before we had time to do anything about it, there was another emergency," Troy said. He recounted the rescue of Denny's sister and the others, and the underwater mansion's subsequent collapse. How John's ghost had inspired him.

"Is there any treasure left from the dive?" Dillon asked.

"Spider has the diaries. Marader has the jewelry box. They stole a bracelet from Raquel, and Desiree said she passed on what she had to Elke."

"The way Elke explains it; the box still contains some of Von Damme's power. He wants it back, like he's missing part of himself," Dillon said.

"How do you know this?" Silke asked.

"I'm coming to that," Dillon said.

Dillon checked his watch then strolled to the window and studied the sky. He frowned and sighed before coming back to them. "I'm getting short on time, so I'll give you the condensed version." He took a deep breath and let it out slowly, repeating the process twice more before continuing.

"I went looking for evidence and ready to dive around Cemetery Ridge. While I was waiting for Burt, I was walking around, searching for clues and any sign as to why there were open caskets, Pat was dead, and John was missing. We had found his torn-up dive flag, so I was concerned. Frankly, I thought I had felt him die," Dillon said.

"Me, too," Troy agreed.

"Anyway I stepped on a coffin nail, and it pierced my shoe and foot," Dillon continued.

"That was the pain I felt. I thought it was sharp rock," Troy said.

"It had some sort of dark magic on it, a curse, and it was killing me. Elke noticed it while she was talking with me. I was dying right before her eyes," Dillon said. Troy wondered why he had dreamt her as an old woman, but dreams were odd, even those attempting to mirror the 'real' world. "She could have let me die. Her family is unhappy about her decision."

"I can sympathize," Silke said, light on sarcasm. She reached out to touch her brother's face. "I am sorry I shot you. I have been angry and frightened. But this Elke, she might just be using you. I have been in a vampire's verbal grip, confused, my mind in a fog, my heart lusty . . ." she said and glanced over at Troy. That had worked out all right.

"I have thought of that. It is difficult to think of anything but her, but I can because she wants to make sure you two are well. She knows how much I love you and am loved by you. Ah, Elke. She is the air I breathe."

"Silke is the twinkle in my eye and the reason my heart beats faster," Troy said. Silke hugged and kissed him.

"Uh, this will take some getting used to, seeing you together like this. If we're lucky, we'll have enough time, and I'll adjust," Dillon said, then he continued on in a serious, journalistic tone. "As you know, there were vampires living in Wreythville. Von Damme was a mad scientist of sorts, called himself an alchemist. He wanted to make his kind not only immortal, but invulnerable. His experiments called attention upon those who live by night. Several Rulers of Night trapped Von Damme and his cult under the waters of the reservoir to keep the danger buried, so to speak. Vampires don't deal well with moving water. As you might imagine, the lake wasn't supposed to get this low. Blame the drought.

"Elke believes that, now that the vampires are free, they will rebuild their cult. First they will regain their power by feeding. That's why people are disappearing. Lucky for them, it's race time, or it would be more noticeable. Elke also thinks they broke into the pharmaceutical plant to steal the chemicals Von Damme needs to make the vampires resistant to light. Elke believes he's going to build an army from the people coming to the race and then turn them loose on their loved ones."

"Sounds like a zombie apocalypse," Troy said.

"They didn't know about such things back in the forties," Dillon said. "When a vampire is newly reborn, if isn't trained, it runs wild. Rogues typically go on killing sprees. Generally, the vampires try to police their own and keep killing from getting out of hand. Von Damme doesn't care." He paused and blinked, then he checked his watch and glanced outside. "I have to go."

"What are we going to do?" Troy asked.

"You have already done enough. It would be better if you just stay out of it. Leave."

Troy and Silke exchanged glances. Could they convince others? Would the blood brothers go away for a while?

"Let the vampires deal with their own. Chances are, though, they will come after you. If you won't leave town, you will need to prepare this place. I promise that I will ask for suggestions on how best I can protect you. Like I said, it would be wisest if you left the area," Dillon reiterated.

"Aunt Jada told me I must help you, no matter how odd, to stop the flood of blood," Troy said.

Silke stared at Troy then said, "Then we can't leave."

"That's too bad. Yeah, I know. Mom is here, too. I'll try to convince her when I call her later this morning," Dillon said.

"With Aunt Jada's passing, I don't see it happening," Silke

said.

"And you?" Troy asked.

"I have no choice. I'm involved. I . . . can't leave Elke. I need to see what she and the others want to do. They feared Von Damme might get free one day. Now he has. Love you, sis," Dillon said, kissing her on the cheek.

"I love you, but I am still angry with you," Silke said.

"Well, look at it this way. If you had hooked up earlier, it might not have panned out," Dillon said.

"What can I do to protect us?" Troy asked.

"Nothing really. Those ankhs work decently well. When dealing with thralls, you have to do a lot more damage. For werewolves, use silver bullets, especially hollow points. Those would work on thralls, too."

"Holy objects?" Silke asked.

"Unless blest, minor deterrents. Someone powerful blest those ankhs."

"How about installing sun lamps, you know, bulbs that give off the same light wave lengths as sunlight?"

"Ha. I don't know. Give it a try. Stock up on some holy water. Keep Father Dennis close. I love you two. Be great to each other. I'll talk to you soon, I promise. I have to go," Dillon said.

"Are you walking? Or turning into a bat and flying?" Silke asked acidly.

"No, I walk the shadows. There are corridors between the light. I guess night walkers could be called shadow walkers, too."

Silke shivered. "Sounds frightening."

"You have no idea. I would love to do a story, but well, that's not going to happen. Be careful. Be safe. I'll see you tonight," Dillon said, waved, and then he left by the back-porch door.

"That went well. I'm still alive," Troy said.

Thirty-Seven: Betrayed

Shortly before sunset, Silke noticed the elderly woman standing next to the old, pink Cadillac with its steaming front end and executed a U-turn. Unlike the Land Rover, her mom's white VW Bug made the 180 without using the road's shoulders.

While Silke parked the car behind the Caddy, Troy studied the senior. The tall and yet stooped, silver-haired woman smiled thankfully. With big sunglasses and a large rounded nose to sit upon, most of the woman's face was hidden.

Silke climbed out without a second thought. "Hi, can I help you?" Silke asked.

"Yes, dear, it's so sweet of you to stop. My car overheated, and my phone died."

"Would you like me to call a towing service? Or give you a ride?" Silke asked.

"Call a shop, please, sweetie. My car has been in and out of Earl's. I have his card somewhere," she said, digging into her pocketbook. With an "ah ha", she produced a piece of paper and handed it to Silke.

She took it and began dialing.

Seemingly out of nowhere, the woman produced a taser. Troy shouted and swiped at her arm and missed. No, his hand had passed through her. It took him a moment to realize that he was disembodied, a ghost, or spirit! How could he be here?

The taser touched and zapped Silke with electricity. She collapsed unconscious and spasming. The old woman popped the trunk lid then easily hefted Silke into the compartment. The senior shut it and washed her hands.

Troy frantically tried to stop her, but he was a phantom. His hands passed right through Silke's attacker, even the trunk lid.

"Von Damme will be pleased," the woman said in a different voice, a deeper one. She hurried around and jumped into the car. The steaming engine had no issues, turning over and starting normally. She pulled off her wig and sunglasses, revealing she was a he. Deng put on lean shades. He drove off, wiping away his lipstick as he headed down the road.

Troy jolted awake. Yuk. Another nightmare. Or was he seeing what was happening? He fervently prayed he was not some kind of dreamwalker.

He grabbed his phone and dialed Silke's number. It rang, and he waited impatiently, willing her to pick up. Her voicemail responded, and his nagging worries grew. He redialed and roamed around the house. Tail wagging, Scout kept an eye of him. Troy petted him, thinking that happy tail was a good sign.

The golden sunshine still poured through the west facing windows of J-Man's lake house. The weak light meant it was less than twenty minutes to sunset. Clouds and shadows gathered. He could see the sun slowly sink.

Silke should already be back by now. She had returned to town to see her mother. They hadn't hugged and cried together since Aunt Jada's death. Troy understood why Silke felt she must tell her mother something about Dillon.

Where are you, Silke? His beloved had kissed him and raced off to town, vowing to return an hour before sunset or earlier. He hadn't wanted her to leave, but she had taken two clips of silver bullets from the munitions that Desiree had stored in the garage. To stop Silke from leaving, he would have had to fight her, and, in his condition, he would have lost.

Having no luck, Troy left a message, then he tried Dillon's cell number. He didn't answer either. Another voicemail recording, Troy cursed to himself.

Troy continued to pace J-Man's house. The place had been protected by various means. Earlier, he and Silke had walked in on a colleague of Father Dennis' while Father Ryan was blessing the abode. Troy could see several crucifixes and two statuettes of the Virgin Mary. Would that also keep out Dillon and Elke?

Father Ryan wasn't the only visitor. A friend of Jay's, a house fixit guy named Ray, replaced all the inside bulbs with those that shone with a radiance similar to sunlight. Outside, he mounted grow lights. Troy could see what J-Man had in mind. Could you fry a vampire with grow lights? With only a raised eyebrow, the priest also left Troy with bottles of blessed holy water.

Troy loaded two guns and set the alarm. He told the chocolate lab that he was on sentry duty, to bark whenever anybody, anything, came near the house. Scout happily followed him around, except when he paced, then the dog sprawled on the floor and watched him.

Silke, where are you? Dillon, answer your phone!

Troy's phone rang, and his heart leapt. His euphoria didn't last. It was J-Man.

"Hey, Troy, I'm running late for tonight's gathering. Has Ray been there?" J-Man asked. He was piloting his copter so he had to speak up.

"Yes. The lights are upgraded to high intensity and sunlight. And Father Ryan blest the area. And, Desiree came through. She loaded us with silver ammo," Troy replied.

"Then what's wrong?"

"I'm afraid Silke is missing or kidnapped," Troy said. He told J-Man about the dream and only reaching her voicemail.

For a few seconds, Troy only heard the noise of the chopper blades, then J-Man sighed. "Tell you what, my friend, I'll fly over that stretch of road on my way there."

"I'm going to drive out there."

"No! You stay put! You don't want her to show up after you leave and run around in circles. Call Burt."

"And tell him what? He has no time for speculation. He's made that perfectly clear."

"He has resources. Speaking of, a tall guy named Nick, a friend of Jambo's, is bringing over some ordinance, flash bangs and such to use when we get attacked again. I don't think my hunting rifle and bow will be enough," J-Man said.

"I haven't seen him."

"Strange, he should have been there by now."

"You know, we could have left town," Troy suggested.

"Not with it on fire and my friends being murdered. No way!"

Scout barked. Troy peeked out the window, seeing a Rentzel van. With God as his co-pilot, Denny must have been driving fast because Spider seemed to bound out of the passenger's side so quickly that he might have been spring loaded. He staggered and leaned on the van. His shirt read Lost Boys.

"Denny and Spider are here," Troy told J-Man.

"See if they saw Silke. Call me back."

Troy hurried outside to greet his arriving blood brothers. "Hi. Denny. Any news about Mary Beth?" Troy asked.

"Nothing. How can this happen?" Denny asked. He looked drawn and worn out.

Curse of Von Damme, Troy thought. He didn't want the love of his life to end up missing like Mary Beth or Raquel. "I'm worried about Silke. She's running late. Did you see her car on the road?" Troy asked.

Denny shook his head. "I've been preoccupied. Sorry. Nice bruises on your neck by the way. It doesn't take a medical degree to notice them. Dillon?"

"He was displeased when he first realized his sister and I were a couple. Silke straightened him out. Denny, I dreamt she was kidnapped, and now she's not answering her phone."

"It is a time of nightmares. Keep the faith. You know the truth," Father Dennis said.

"Trust your intuition. You are Heavensent," Spider said.

Troy looked at the sky. The sun waned while the full moon rose and appeared to sit atop the mountains. Shadows stretched long, looking gaunt. It was now the time of darkwalkers.

"You two stay here. I'm going searching for her. And so you know, J-Man's running late and will be later. He's searching for her car," Troy said.

When he headed for the Wagoneer, Spider grabbed him. "No, don't go. Von Damme's forces are everywhere. We are safe here. I can feel the power of the blessing. It will protect us."

They all paused, hearing it. A loud truck sounded like it took a corner too fast, tires squealing, then the roar of a gunned engine. Troy watched as a Maraders Marina truck careened into the driveway. The Ford clipped a fence, breaking a post. It snapped off and went flying, breaking two props on the statue of a helicopter in the front gardens. At the wheel, Marader swerved to miss Denny's van.

In a drunken, Jedi move, Marader managed to miss everybody, only grazing the Wagoneer. Flashing a beaming smile, Tommy Boy flung the door open and hopped out energetically. "Cheers, everybody. We're safe now," he announced.

"Safe now that you're no longer driving," Spider said.

"What's wrong with you? Why are you drunk?" Denny asked.

"Celebrating. Heidi is doing well. We are all alive, and we'll stay that way because, because, you want to know why?" Marader slurred.

"We're safe? How do you know this?" Denny asked.

"I know because we no longer have the jewelry box! That's what they wanted, and I sold it for a bundle to an antique dealer. Good riddance. My hands are healing, and I feel like I have my pep back, you know," he said, showing them his empty and only slightly scarred palms.

"What makes you think that's all they want? They've taken others who went diving. Maybe last night, the attack, was a kidnapping gone bad," Troy suggested. "I don't have time for this. Silke's missing."

"She's not here?" Marader asked.

"No, and she's not answering her phone."

"Well, I saw her mom's Beetle. It was parked on the side of

the road, facing me. Of course, I stopped. Nobody was there. I figured you picked her up. That's bad, isn't it, dude?" Marader said.

"Did you pass a pink Cadillac?" Troy asked.

"I sure did. How did you know? It looked like some guy in drag was driving it," Marader said.

Troy really didn't have time for this. The sun, their supposed protector, would set any minute. Silke was in danger. The Cadillac couldn't be too far ahead. He might get lucky. He could call Deputy Burt along the way. He hopped inside the Wagoneer and turned the ignition. Nothing happened. He tried again. The battery seemed to be dead. It needed a jump. He didn't have time for this.

"I need a car," Troy told everybody. He dialed J-Man. "Hey . . . Look for a pink Cadillac. I think it has Silke. She's been taken," Troy said.

"Shit! All right. I'm on the hunt. I'll call, hey, I see her car now," J-Man said.

"I'm on my way. Marader, your truck's in my way. Give me your keys," Troy said. He hung up and stuck out his hand, palm up.

Troy's phone rang, once again briefly raising his hopes, except the phone read Knives. Troy took the ring off mute and answered. "What's up? I'm about to leave J-Man's. I think Silke's been kidnapped."

"Then hang up. I'm just calling to say I'm going to be late. There's an accident. A doctor's duty calls," Knives said.

"Is it a pink Cadillac?" Troy asked.

"No, a motorcycle. I've got to wait for an ambulance. Godspeed. Let me know!" Knives said. He hung up.

Marader tossed Troy the keys, grinned, and said, "It's about time you got serious about chasing that woman."

Troy climbed in and started the truck. Before he could put it in gear, a classic hot-rod, a smokin' red '65 Mustang, pulled into the driveway. It seemed like everyone and everything was getting in Troy's way.

Desiree sat behind the wheel of the classic muscle car. She waved and danced out of the Mustang, coming to Troy's window. "You can't leave now. Dillon is here, and Elke is on her way."

"You're blocking the way. Move!"

"You can't leave! They are coming to see y'all. I don't think you understand. This is highly unusual," Desiree said.

"I think Deng kidnapped Silke. I dreamt it, and Marader saw her abandoned car. Get out of the way," Troy said.

"No worries. Dillon put a GPS on her," Desiree said and smiled.

"She might not have her phone. Now move."

"Just get in. You're not leaving without me, and I know this car better than you do," Desiree said.

That was true. Troy climbed in the passenger's seat of the Mustang. Once buckled, he took his phone and one-touched dialed his beloved's brother, calling Dillon's phone.

"What's up, Troy?" Dillon asked.

"Silke's been kidnapped. Where are you?"

"What's this about Silke?" he asked.

Troy summarized the situation for Dillon. He immediately pulled up the app on his phone. Troy waited impatiently. Again, Dillon kept getting in the way of Troy reaching Silke.

"Yes, I'm tailing my sister. She's had a stalker, you know," Dillon said. Finally, his phone pinpointed her location. "She isn't moving." A closer look placed her where Marader had seen her car. "I can't leave. I have to anchor this end for Elke," Dillon said.

"Anchor the end of what?" Troy asked. "This is your sister who's in trouble!"

"A shadow gate. Elke will arrive swiftly, then, after whatever discussion is necessary, we will be about our business, including finding my troublesome sister. Desiree will help you. I'll be there in a minute," Dillon said and hung up.

Troy cursed Dillon and answered another call. "Cadillac, Cadillac, long and pink, shiny and bright. If you can't tell, I see it now. I'm following from a distance you could say. What do you want me to do? Fire photon torpedoes or phasers? Seriously, though, I wish I had a tractor beam. What do you suggest?" J-Man asked.

"Just follow. We'll catch up. Desiree is driving."

"Wear a seatbelt and hang onto your hat," Desiree said.

As Desiree backed up, a county sheriff's car pulled into the drive. The light bar flashed once along with a short burst of siren, then Deputy Burt climbed out of the passenger side. He looked upset and ready to pop a few buttons on his uniform.

"Jeez. It's the cops. Spider, you drove my truck over," Marader said.

Hitching up his belt, Deputy Burt now joined them. "Hey, what's going on? You leaving already, Troy? Why? This looks like a party. Got a permit for a special event?"

"Burt, Silke, was kidnapped by a guy named Deng in a pink Cadillac," Troy said.

Deputy Burt blinked. "Seriously. How long ago?" he asked.

"Fifteen minutes maybe. J-Man is flying over a pink Caddy. We don't know if it's the one," Troy said.

"I'll put out a call," Deputy Burt said. He returned to his car, leaning in the open door and pulling out a mic. "Do you have a license plate?" he asked before keying.

Troy relayed the question to J-Man. Shortly, the J-copter pilot rattled off letters and numbers to a North Carolina plate and its current location. The Caddy seemed to be headed for the South Holston Dam. Troy relayed the number and watched anxiously as Burt called in the troops.

"Down, Boy. We're on it. Whoever has her won't get away. Now, let's go inside and have a chat while my fellow officers take care of business."

"You can talk with Dillon. He can explain. I'm going after Silke," Troy said.

"Dillon is here? I don't believe it. You'll have to show me," Deputy Burt said. His expression grew stern to no nonsense.

"Hey, I think someone is shooting at me," J-Man said.

"Jay, get out of there," Troy said.

"May Day! May Day!" J-Man called out. "I guess I took a hit. My engine has stalled and won't restart. Doesn't look like there's any good place to land. I'm heading in for a rough . . ."

All of them looked stunned, starring dumfounded at each other.

"Lord help us. We have to go to Jay," Denny said.

"Listen to me, y'all. I want this to be loud and clear. You're not going anywhere, except inside, where I can talk to Dillon and y'all about what's been happening to our fine town. Rest easy, I'll make more calls and the professionals will find Jay Beck and Silke Urich."

Troy and Denny hesitated.

"Inside! That's an order or I'll arrest y'all's asses for obstructing an investigation," Deputy Burt snarled. "I'm tired of being lied to and led around by the nose. I'm going to get to the bottom of this."

Two county sheriff trucks drove up. A deputy exited each vehicle. Troy didn't recognize either of them. The two deputies, broad-chested and beefy like bouncers, nodded at Burt and began a foot patrol. The two county trucks cruised in a slow sweep. Their headlights seemed brighter, everything now in evening's shadow.

Silke, where are you, my love?

"I have everything well in hand. Gentlemen, if you will," Deputy Burt said as he gestured toward the house.

"Do you really need me for this?" Troy asked.

"You're a witness, and you sent me video of the wolves. They are double-checking to ensure they haven't been altered or enhanced. All we found in the watery ruins of the marina were Pete's and Walt's bodies. No wolf or any other human corpses," Deputy Burt said. He eyed Troy. "Don't get any ideas. We will find Silke. If you had been up front with me about what's happening, none of this would have gone down."

"I didn't know what was going on, and what I think sounds crazy."

"And what the hell is going on?"

"I told you once, and you didn't believe me. I'll let Dillon tell you."

Exasperated, Deputy Burt hounded him, staying on Troy's heels like he expected him to make a break for it. The two deputies on foot and two patrolling trucks should make Troy feel safer, but instead, he felt under house arrest.

Denny held the front door for Troy, so he could stalk right in.

He didn't see Dillon, just Spider looking around nervously. Marader knew where J-Man's bar was located and parked there, helping himself.

"Nice place. Where's Dillon?" Deputy Burt asked. His eyes searched the room. "Or did he slip out by the back door?"

Troy heard a Jeep. He peered out the window. Jambo had pulled up. The tallest of the two deputies questioned him then waved him on.

"Dillon's down there," Spider said. He pointed to the door to the basement. It stood closed, bright light and deep shadows splayed out from under it. Troy recalled that Dillon had been babbling on about a shadow gate and the need to anchor it.

Suddenly dizzy, Troy felt the world turn inside out. Light and shadow seemed to flip. Was he standing on the ceiling? Couldn't be. It just felt like it. The world blinked, and a wave of nausea swept over Troy as if the earth shifted and his guts with it. He returned to the floor.

"Troy, are you sandbagging on me?" Deputy Burt asked. He hadn't noticed anything amiss. How could you miss the vertigo?

None of the others seemed to notice anything strange, except for Spider who acted agitated and shaken. He kept looking to the basement door.

"Just some aches and pains from yesterday and the day before, and the day before that," Troy said. He realized that Elke was here. Whatever they had done had successfully brought her in unseen.

He glanced outside. Twilight rays still stretched across the sky, turning the clouds a deep red and purple. Soon, dusk would rule until dawn. An attack could come any minute. That would make Deputy Burt a believer.

Silke, my love, I will find you, Troy promised.

Deputy Burt answered his phone, listened, smiled and said, "Good news, boys. They have eyes on the pink Cadillac. Unfortunately, nobody has found J-Man, yet."

"Maybe he pulled it out at the last second. Don't tell him I said this, because I would deny it, but that Eagle Scout is amazing. Jay likely MacGyvered the engine by using radio parts," Marader said.

"Tommy, you are a piece of work," Deputy Burt said.

"It takes one to know one," Marader grinned.

Troy paced the kitchen and breakfast area with the others. Spider sat at the table with Denny who drummed his fingers. The air reeked of tension, and Marader acted like a caged animal that just happened to be rattling ice in a glass. A drink wouldn't help Troy.

"Something has changed," Father Dennis said. He took a rosary in hand and started praying. Troy wondered if he sensed Elke, too.

"Hey, everybody. Why all the deputies?" Jambo asked. He let himself in by the front door. He had a bandage wrapped around his forehead. Troy hadn't noticed his wounds last night, but Jambo winced when he smiled.

"Ask Burt," Troy said.

"Have a seat, Mr. McGillis. So where's Dillon?" Deputy Burt asked.

The door from the basement opened. Dillon strolled out.

"About Goddamned time you showed up," Deputy Burt greeted him.

Dillon seemed to ignore him. "Everyone, my lady, Elke," the blood brother announced and stepped aside. With a hand, he guided Elke into the light.

A pale, golden-tressed beauty sheathed in black velvet, the

lady vampire slipped from the shadow with the ease of a panther. Every movement was sensual, enhancing her supernatural beauty. She seemed built for sex, the perfect figure, poise and voice. Would it be different for each guy?

Having been enamored of her before and knowing better then to get lost staring, Troy watched his friends' reactions. The others noticed their missing blood brother, their eyes lighting up with joy, no longer worried about him, and ready to celebrate with hugs and back-slapping. Then one by one they noticed Elke. If you were breathing, it was impossible to ignore her. Human beings were wired to pay attention to sex, drama, and dangerous situations. Elke evoked all three emotions.

Marader grinned. Father Dennis managed a double take. He touched his crucifix, likely sensing her unusual nature. Spider stared but appeared to want to run. His legs might take him, but his eyes wouldn't leave her.

"Relax everyone. It's good to see y'all, though I wish Knives and J-Man were here for this big moment, and of course, John, too, since I often go on about the lady I met at the lake," Dillon said. He took a moment to introduce each of them by name.

Father Dennis's frown deepened with every passing moment. Spider backed away. Jambo genially shook her hand. Marader, obviously inebriated, offered a flourishing bow. Deputy Burt tried to look nonplussed as he wrote down her name, but he perspired and took his time with the notations. She studied him with more attention than simple curiosity.

Was Elke trying to control the deputy? Troy wondered. He breathed deeply and slowly to calm his pulse. He called to mind Silke, focusing on her, and of course what they had been through together, but mostly her smile and her laugh.

"Troy feels Silke's in trouble," Dillon said.

That snapped Elke to attention, pulling her away from Burt to Troy. It felt like a million eyes on him. "Show me what you saw. Think on it. Recall it," the Dark Lady commanded as she turned her mesmerizing eyes on Troy. He felt pinned and as if something rooted around in his thoughts, flipping through memories like they were pages of the book of his life. Troy closed his eyes and pushed back. He felt her breath on his face. When he opened his eyes, she was close enough to kiss. She darted forward and bit his lip. Troy yelped and drew back, complaining along with Dillon.

"Never doubt me, my love. Troy knows. I don't know how, but part of him is with her. Your sister has been kidnapped," Elke said.

"We must help her," Troy said.

"We will, soon. I believe I know where she will be taken. Others have been kidnapped. Others, like you, who have been to Von Damme's waterlogged mansion."

"I'm listening," Deputy Burt said.

"The Cult of Von Damme is our dire problem. It was a grave issue long ago, in the first half of the twentieth century, and it is becoming increasingly dangerous with each passing hour." She had everyone's attention, so arresting that it was nearly impossible to do anything but look and listen.

"Do tell," Deputy Burt said. His phone interrupted, and he answered. "Good. Good news. Finally." He looked to Troy. "They stopped the pink Cadillac. We have Silke. She's okay but unconscious."

Dillon smiled. Troy tried to breathe a sigh of relief. It didn't happen.

Silke still felt imperiled. He wouldn't relax until she was in his arms.

Elke scrutinized Deputy Burt.

"Will they bring her here?" Troy asked.

"You will see her soon," Deputy Burt smiled.

"She doesn't feel safe," Troy murmured. It just didn't feel right.

Elke studied Troy before her attention returned to the deputy. She turned to Dillon. "He's lying. We must leave now."

The door burst open. Desiree rushed in. "Milady, werewolves are about," she said. Her clothing was torn and shredded from wrestling with the beasts.

Scout barked wildly until the chocolate Lab saw Elke, then he quieted. "We have been betrayed. We must leave," Elke said. She took Dillon's hand as she pivoted on her heel and headed for the lower floor.

Desiree let out a surprised grunt. She pulled what looked like a tranquilizer dart from her shoulder. Her eyes rolled, but she steadied them long enough to attack Deputy Burt. Even as he tried to draw his weapon, she grabbed him and threw him out the window.

"Traitor! He works for Von Damme!" Desiree said. She looked coldly furious and fierce as she wiped the blood from her cheek.

"Burt is working with the enemy. Oh, God! Silke!" Troy said.

"Werewolves. Where there is one, there is usually more. I feared this might happen. Von Damme's zealots are coming for y'all," Elke said.

Windows broke and alarms sounded as canisters spewing gas bounced inside the house. Scout barked then coughed. The toxic cloud caused eyes to water.

"Tear gas!" Dillon shouted. Troy was surprised and shocked. They had prepared for a supernatural attack. Nobody had expected a conventional assault. More gas canisters crashed through windows and bounced around. They were trying to smoke them out.

Howling sounded from all around the house. Troy flashed back to Maraders Marina. They had barely survived there.

Elke turned to Dillon. "We must be gone."

"Gone?! Where are you going? We have to rescue Silke," Troy asked.

"Someone will need to rescue you," Elke said.

"Beloved, they are my friends. My blood brothers," Dillon said.

"There is no time, and we mustn't get caught. This is bigger than all of us. Out through the Shadowlands. We can lose them there," Elke said.

The front window shattered, spewing glass. A body crashed through and landed heavily on the floor, taking out a table and lamp. Troy recognized Mr. Thick from the Swearington Lodge.

A deputy stepped in. He pointed his taser and fired at Spider, hitting him with a dart. His arms and legs jerked out straight, and he started to thrash.

Marader dodged behind a chair as a second deputy stepped in and fired. Trailing hot wires, the barbs shot out. They struck and stuck in the wood trim and padding of the armchair.

Troy could barely see. He staggered back and looked for a way out, following Desiree. They must know a secret way out. Elke had managed to get inside unseen.

A werewolf, foaming at the mouth, landed in Troy's path. The beast's eyes shone with bloodlust, and Troy saw his death here and now.

Daggers seemed to appear out of nowhere like a magician's trick into Desiree's hands, and she gutted the werewolf. It staggered into Dillon who seized it and broke its neck. That gave everyone a moment to blink, think and react.

Jambo grabbed a shotgun from somewhere hidden, just in time to greet the next leaping werewolf. The silver shot shredded its fur and stopped it, giving Desiree an opening. She stabbed on target, sinking her knife in its eye. The beast spasmed, crumpled and thrashed into death throes.

The tear gas wasn't affecting Elke, Dillon or Desiree, but Troy could hardly see or breathe, his eyes and lungs burning. Denny collapsed in a coughing fit.

"Out. Now, beloved!" Elke commanded. "Desiree, cover and close."

"But . . ." Desiree and Dillon started.

"Now!" Elke ordered.

Everything happened too fast to follow, and Troy wasn't sure he trusted his eyes. A horde of wolves swept into the house, knocking down doors, leaping through windows, and even plunging down from upstairs. A black beast slammed into Jambo's back, knocking him into a wall.

A blur of fur slammed into Troy, and he staggered back.

What had happened to Dillon, Elke and Desiree? Elke was gone, but Dillon stood with Desiree poised on the edge of a shadow. Dillon mouthed a brief apology, and then Desiree shoved Troy's blood brother into the darkness where he vanished.

"See you soon, Sugah," Desiree said as she slipped into the shadows. There was no room for her where Dillon should be, but neither of them were there. Troy no longer sensed them. Desiree's heat and Dillon's presence were gone, now distant.

Troy knew he was powerless against the werewolf attack. He tried to dodge, hopelessly trying to escape. To where? To what? Just survive. Find Silke! He stumbled over a hairy beast, as a second struck him, driving him back.

He fell, expecting to hit the floor, but darkness swept over him.

Thirty-Eight: Shadowlands

Troy awakened, if you could call it that, in cavernous darkness. The oppressiveness reminded him of being held helpless under the ruins of Von Damme's underwater house of horrors. It had all started there, that cursed, embittered place of cold, dark terror.

The mansion felt like evil personified. This darkness seemed impersonal, more a force of nature.

Was he breathing? He wasn't sure. He couldn't feel his chest move or the air flowing in and out of his nose or mouth. He counted.

After two hundred, he knew he didn't need to breathe. Why didn't he need to breathe? Why couldn't he move?

Or could he? He couldn't tell if he blinked. He didn't seem connected to his body, as if it had gone wholly numb. The crushing on his chest had nothing to do with his lungs bursting. They weren't straining. He couldn't feel any sensation other than the pressure trying to break all his will.

Hopelessness assailed him. He waited for a connection, for pain to remind him that he was alive.

Because he wasn't dead.

He had been dead and near dead. Almost dead? Where was Billy Crystal when you needed a comedian for humor at a dark time? Troy couldn't even laugh, and yet he found it morbidly funny. The humor bolstered him.

What was this darkness? It was something different than death.

Biting cold. Hollow. Forbidding. The opposite of everything he loved about life. Even in death, he had revisited places of sunshine and seen his friends in glorious light.

Then he had been sent back. Given a second chance.

For what? Sent back for what? To die again? To fall in love with Silke and die on her? What a horrible thought.

Silke had been there to save him from Von Damme's mansion. Now she was in trouble and needed saving.

Troy had been thinking of desolation. Could he muster sunshine? He thought of Silke, of her smile and the sun sparkling in her eyes and gleaming off her hair. Her smile was special, a conspiratorial, we are in this together expression.

He remembered when she was thirteen pulling her out of the water, cold, blue and unresponsive, and carrying her to the beach. He breathed for her and shared a breath for the first time. Forwarding in time, he recalled their surprise, strawberry margarita New Year's Eve kiss.

Then there was the revelation, finding her crying next to his hospital bed, and thinking she was an angel.

Was she crying now? Yes, he thought so. He sensed it and surrendered to the feeling, letting her sadness draw him as a current would drag him to drown.

Moments with her flashed by. Being wowed at the airport and thinking she was someone else. Had she seen it in his eyes and that led to the downtown kiss? Her hair had been all over him, reminding him constantly of her. So what if it had taken a vampire's threat to bring them together? He could feel her presence firmly against his soul while he soared into the great unknown of darkness.

He finally heard Silke's voice. "What am I doing here?" she demanded, followed by a sharp intake of breath. "Zane!"

"I am glad you remember me," he said.

Troy had yet to see anyone or anything, but he heard them. He hoped he was suffering a nightmare.

"I almost forgot, but you are unforgettable."

"It is my nature, thanks to Lord Von Damme, to be irresistible. Soon, you will see."

Troy burst from the darkness, back into the world of light. A grimy old lantern sitting on a bench managed a faint glow that barely touched Silke, but her eyes shone with courage. She stood up to Paleface, and he seemed a little smaller, though he still loomed large, fists clenched, disdainfully over her. The vampire appeared to emit a pale bioluminescence as if to make himself more appealing instead of a black pit of despair.

Swooping down, Troy tried to intervene and realized he was little more than a ghost. And yet, this didn't feel like death, as somewhere he vaguely sensed his body.

"My aunt never forgot you. Jada never forgot you."

Paleface paused. "Jada? You knew her?"

"She is my aunt. Was my aunt. She died yesterday," Silke said

"Died?" Zane repeated roughly. It sounded foreign coming from the vampire's undead lips, as though he were testing them, perhaps having heard of death long ago. "Then her presence and soul are gone."

"No, some of her remains with me. And you, because I can see you remembering her kissing you on the cheek when you left to go to work that morning," Silke said.

Troy smiled. Silke had Zane relating to her. She was trying to touch his human side. Would it matter?

"My mom said Jada blew you a last kiss. I wonder if you felt it? So, her last thoughts were of you, wishing you well," Silke said.

Zane touched his cheek. His red-black eyes faded inward and intense, his thoughts cast back in time. "Ah, Jada," he said, verbally caressing her name. "I am too far beyond well. Now she is beyond pain. I didn't want her to be hurt. That's why I warned her. I wouldn't have hurt her none."

"She kept hoping you would come back."

"Maybe if I had, right after it had happened, but after a few days . . . How odd, still, I never imagined she would shake hands with the Rulers of Night."

"That should tell you something about the dangerous company you keep. Zane, why am I here?" she asked.

"You have something Von Damme wants," Zane said.

Agonized cries echoed off the walls. The very air vibrated with them, and Troy felt the pain and despair scrape across his spirit. He spotted a silvery glint, the hint of a faint cord stringing through the air and disappearing into the shadow of Silke cast by the lantern.

"What was that?" Silke said and shuddered.

"The Master is taking it from Mr. Adder right now."

"What? What's he taking? Spider sounds like he's dying!"

"That's likely," Zane said simply.

"What does Von Damme want from me? Blood?"

"Naw, there's plenty of that to go around. But you are special. You've been inside the mansion."

"I don't understand," Silke said.

Zane shrugged. "That place radiates power. Anyone who was there absorbed some of it. He wants it back to feel whole again."

If Troy had a body, he would have shivered. The mansion had tainted them, some of Von Damme's essence polluting their souls. Is that why some of the things that he had seen and experienced had happened? Blame it on Von Damme.

Spider unleashed a gut-wrenching scream. It lasted long, a wailing lament to being painfully alive.

The door opened, and Marader stepped inside. Like the cat that just ate the coal mine canary, he grinned at Silke, then he glared like an alpha male at Paleface.

"What are you doing here?" Zane asked.

"The Master gave her to me. She is mine until he sends for her," Marader said. His bullshit-eating grin returned. "Silke, I am going to do you every which way but loose."

Troy had never hated anyone so much. He found himself in Marader's face, choking him. The action was futile. Marader laughed right through it. Troy was immaterial, so he had no hands. He couldn't affect him. He hated this state. Hated being powerless.

"No, she is mine. I have first compel rights," Zane sneered. He glared as his jaw stuck out, and he leaned forward. He had seemed taller than Tommy Boy, but now they stood nose-to-nose. Fists clenching and unclenching, Zane stood ready to fight.

For a time, they stared down each other. To Troy, it appeared a staring contest of wills.

Troy tried to get Silke's attention, but she never saw him. He tried nudging her. Caressing her. Kissing her. Whispering in her ear. Nothing worked. Or did it? She started to whisper his name among her prayers.

Zane moved swiftly, driving a knee at Marader who danced nimbly aside. He slapped Paleface across the back of the head.

"Ha! Von Damme knew you were soft on her. That's why he sent me," Marader laughed.

"You lie!" Zane roared. The vampire swung, kicked, elbowed and kneed as he tried to steamroll over Marader. He dodged and evaded like a ninja on PEDs, then he shoved Zane in the back. The vampire stumbled ahead, using his hands to prevent smashing in the wall. How was Marader so fast and strong? Was he a thrall now?

Marader didn't follow up. "Can you read, Zany?" he asked.

"Of course! I finished ninth grade!" Paleface snarled.

"That is amazing," Marader said. With swift fingers, he

folded the sheet of paper into a paper plane and tossed it. Zane caught the paper dart before it struck him in the left eye.

"Read it and weep," Marader said.

Zane unfolded the note, tearing it but still leaving it readable. He frowned then balled up the paper and threw it at Marader's feet. He laughed while Paleface left, slamming the door. That seemed to silence Spider's screams.

"Ah, I do have a special way with people. Just like I will have my way with you."

"Troy will find me," Silke said.

"If he's ever found. He disappeared into a shadow, lost in darkness, babe. Nobody ever survives that unless they are a vampire or a thrall. Sorry, just staying. So, nobody will come for you. Or protect you. Except for me. And that's only if you do as I say."

"I hate you."

"Hey, I am here for you. If not for me, you would be next instead of Jambo, though if asked, he's man enough he would volunteer to go ahead of you. Better him than us," Marader said. He grinned. "Come on, work with me, will ya?"

Spider unleashed another long peel of agony. The force of it nearly made Troy sick.

"What happened to you? That's your blood brother dying. What about blood's thicker than water?" Silke asked.

"I couldn't save him, or you, or me, so I joined the winning side, sweetheart. This way, somebody gets saved. The fact is, Von Damme's blood is more powerful than our blood. You should throw in, too, or you'll be screaming like that instead of in ecstasy."

"Hate isn't a powerful enough word to describe how I feel about you," Silke snarled.

"Hey, you know love is stronger than hate, stronger than blood, too, I think."

"What would you know about love?"

"You'll see. You'll love me once I'm done with you," Marader barked a laugh. He took a step toward her, then he turned and strolled to the door. "But, hey, you know me. I prefer the two to one odds, and since Raquel is here somewhere in 3M, that's McKinney Magnesium Mine for you slow learners, I think she'll find this waiting room much more pleasant than where she is!" He cackled all the way out the door. The sound lingered like a curse.

Oh, God, no. NO! Raquel was here, too? Troy roiled in anguish.

This was worse than any of his nightmares.

Silke stared forlornly at the closed door. Troy called out to her. The second time, her brow wrinkled, and she appeared to look at him, then right through him. He waved to her but by her actions he knew she perceived him as wishful thinking, perhaps as hope.

Her eyes opening, she suddenly rolled to face him. "Troy? No! No. No, Troy you can't be dead. No, please, God. Just strike me dead right here if it's true."

"Don't say that," Troy told her. "I will find you!"

She started weeping.

Spider's final scream savaged the air. It battered Troy, bringing back painful memories of dying in the avalanche. Spider's voice was abruptly cut off. The death shriek died, and Troy's blood brother, too. He sensed it, and a moment later, Spider's ghost manifested nearby.

In Troy's peripheral vision, he first saw a luminescence. It beckoned him.

"Troy, my blood brother, you're not supposed to be here. You still live," Spider said. He made a sweeping bow, gesturing to the silver cord that led into Silke's shadow. The bright tendril extended from Troy's ankh.

"What are you doing here?" Troy said dumbly. Even knowing he wasn't thinking straight didn't help clear his confusion.

"I died. This time, I don't think I'm coming back," Spider said.

He touched Troy. In a blink, he seemed to have been

transported, now looking into what appeared to be an opulent chamber of velvet-sheathed furniture, curtained walls, and thick rugs around a large wooden table. There, Spider's wizen corpse lie contorted, not even bound, long, skinny arms wound around his torso in a futile attempt to protect himself. He had aged as he died, eyes open, his mouth spread wide, the jaw broken from the intensity of ripping the life from him.

While Troy's blood brother looked a hundred years old, the man from the mansion's painting glowed with malicious vitality. The ruddy light of a furnace being stoked by madness flashed in Von Damme's eyes. Their color matched the jewels on the opulent silver necklace draped around the vampire's neck. The six fire opals seemed to give off heat as the air writhed around them and crackled.

Charged up, the vampire prowled like a ravenous beast eager to be turned loose upon sheep. An aura of malevolence writhed across his undead body. Its misty tendrils reached out to ensnare everybody, coiling around Zane and Lyla, the Dark Lady, and now withdrawing from Spider.

"There was something odd about the skinny one. He should not have died," Von Damme said.

"He was Heavensent. Bad juju," Lyla said, sounding like Spider. "Ah, mortals are so fragile. Play with one, it breaks."

Troy had never hated so completely. This monster would do the same to Silke and Raquel and more. He would feast on loved ones, friends, neighbors, innocents and strangers. Fury threatened to consume Troy. He tried to choke the vampire, but he couldn't touch the monster. If he had been flesh, Von Damme might have burst aflame.

"I feel watched," Zane said. He shifted uncomfortably.

"I share your perception, so it may well be true. Make sure the generators are secure, the LEDs are working, and shadow dimmers are active in all areas," Von Damme said.

Shadow dimmers? Troy wondered. What were those? Lime lights were old-fashioned stage lighting.

"Do you miss the days of walking the Shadowlands?" Von

Damme asked. His restless fingers caressed the fire opals, creating a whining sound.

It reminded Troy of a vibrating and discordantly ringing champagne flute. It hurt his senses.

"A little but not much. I can still fly, now day or night, and that more than makes up for the loss. Zane! This one is done! We're ready for another to give up its ghost," Lyla chuckled. She was a cruelly gorgeous figure, a snarl in her eyes above her whiplash smile.

Like a huge sack of potatoes, Zane tossed Spider over his shoulder and carried off Troy's blood brother's body. He mournfully watched as Paleface tossed the skinny corpse atop two other bodies. It took a moment for Troy to recognize the elder Maxwell, but he recognized Eduardo immediately. Lightless eyes open and their jaws slack, the two men who had gone diving in the Von Damme's mansion were dead by the claws of the master of that domain. Troy didn't see their ghosts anywhere, but then, they might have died some time ago from the looks of their corpses, blood settling to lividity.

Who was next? Troy didn't want to know. Why was he here?

"Come here," the female voice commanded.

Troy felt the order ripple over him, but it couldn't take hold. He had no flesh. It rested elsewhere. Where was his body? Troy wondered.

Jambo, sweating and yet appearing composed, lumbered over to stand before Von Damme. The master vampire critically inspected him, staring into his eyes, into his soul, and poking at the big guy's flesh. Had Jambo been standing there the whole time, watching this happen? Troy felt sick to his soul. He knew what Jambo dealt with as his body was no longer his own, no longer responding to his will. Jambo was trapped inside his own flesh and bone cage. Troy screamed in frustration for both of them.

A look of disappointment crossed Von Damme face. He sneered and slapped Jambo. "Take him away. He has nothing of me, nothing for me. He slept on the boat while others visited my mansion. Next!"

Zane took Jambo's arm and led him away like an invalid. It was far better than being dead and tossed over the shoulder.

If Troy had been breathing, he would have exhaled a sigh of relief for Jambo. So sleeping all the time had been a saving grace. But who was next? Troy wondered. He looked around and saw Denny led from the shadow by the Dark Lady. She had donned gloves to handle the priest. It seemed to Troy that his blood brother was smiling.

"Has he been stripped of his holy symbols?" Von Damme asked.

"Yes. Fortunately, he has no tattoos. He has obeyed me, but there's something odd about him," Lyla crooned.

Von Damme chuckled harshly. "All Men of the Cloth seem that way, wrapped in faith. I'll have to strip it from him as I take back what is mine. I have broken many men of many faiths. Lie down on the table and surrender to me," the master vampire commanded.

Troy felt the power of his voice, but it was Denny who could amble to sit on the table. His priestly eyes were calm with the peace that passeth understanding, and his lips moved slightly with prayer. Troy realized his blood brother could still move, at least a little, of his own volition. Had Denny come of his own free will?

Yes, Troy could see it. Father Dennis would come to stare into the face and eyes of the monster that had critically wounded his wife and left his sister paranoid, fearful and housebound.

"I see you seek righteous vengeance. Many have tried. All have surrendered, as you will also put up a noble fight then succumb, pitifully defeated, too," Von Damme said. He peered into Denny's eyes then seized his face in both hands. The master vampire's claws extended, burying their tips in flesh, burrowing to meet skull. He seemed ready to rip Denny's head in half. "Give up what is mine!" he commanded.

Troy blinked. Dark, oily energies oozed from Denny's pores to bead upon his skin. Troy recoiled and wondered about himself. Was that inside him?

The evil taint bubbled like it boiled, creating a hazy cloud that Von Damme inhaled and sighed. The cult leader removed his nails to drive them into Denny's ribs and neck, causing the vampire's smile to widen, threatening to split his face. His eyes grew larger as his body was engorged, growing stouter and taller, lording over and looking down on the world of puny mortals. Wisps of smoke, like steam but darker, arose from the vampire's head, creating a dark, polluted halo.

Von Damme's satisfied smile slowly changed as his hands and arms began to smolder. Troy thought he saw bright sparks but anything looked light compared to the darkness of the master vampire's presence. Whatever was happening, it distressed the vampire. Good.

"No more! There is something more!" Von Damme yelled. He yanked his claws back, removing the red-dripping talons from Denny's body. The effort left the master vampire staggered. He slumped against a shelf of bottles, chemicals stolen from Bristol-Meyers.

"Viktor?" Lyla asked.

"I endure growing back into myself. I didn't know that I had lost so much power. I was, still am, a shade of myself, but that will change each time I take back my strength. But, for now, that is enough. I have indulged myself and need respite," Von Damme said. He took two steps and stumbled. Lyla rushed to his side to assist him.

Troy hoped whatever Von Damme had eaten would kill him. Would feasting on a priest hurt him? What happened when the master vampire extracted his power? What else did he take with him?

Spider's ghost turned to Troy. "Go! He is stronger and yet vulnerable now. You have purpose. A reason to live. Go back! Find Dillon. Destroy Von Damme. Save Silke and the others," Spider said. He shoved Troy.

The tremendous push sent him flying, or falling, he couldn't tell, through the vast darkness. Troy must find his body. He had many reasons to live again.

Thirty-Nine: Dark Transformation

Troy fell out of the darkness through a doorway from hell to purgatory, from shadows to a wan light, from numbness to damp and cold. He hovered over his very own motionless body. Now this was dying. He had done this before, he thought dispassionately. He realized his disinterest meant he had been gone too long.

Dillon, Elke and Desiree stood around Troy's pale flesh suit. Spider had said he wasn't dead, but Troy thought his friend was wrong. Troy looked like a carcass just starting to cool.

He followed the silver cord to its origin and laid down within his body, even as Desiree attempted to revive him with a passionate kiss that should have sent his pulse racing and his blood pressure skyrocketing. He felt nothing except frustration that he couldn't reconnect to his flesh and bone. He could see and hear but nothing else, and now that he thought about it, this seeing was different, almost colorless, more defined by light and shadow like a world brought to life by charcoal on paper.

"What did you do?" Dillon demanded. He grabbed Desiree by the shoulders. Before he could shake her, she slipped his hold. He growled, but she held up a hand.

"Von Damme would kill him, so I brought him here," Desiree replied.

"You brought him through the Shadowlands! That's insane! You certainly killed him now! Nobody alive survives it!" Dillon snarled. His face was flushed, and he breathed loudly, venting fury. His hands clenched and relaxed, only to make fists again.

"There has been precedent of Heavensent surviving. I have read the journals," Desiree said coolly.

Why couldn't Troy be attended by J-Man, Knives and Jambo? Instead, Troy was surrounded by two vampires, even if one was his best friend, and Desiree, who he had never seen crying, now wept. Since learning she spied for Elke, Troy had assumed her interest in him an act. Somewhere, Silke cried for him, too.

Silke! If he could, he would cry for her. What he needed was to live for her then find her!

"Jada said Von Damme would kill him if I didn't do this," Desiree said.

"You're crazy. She's crazy. Troy's going to die here, instead," Dillon said.

Desiree seized Troy's face and kissed him. She caressed him and urged him to return. Troy couldn't feel the difference, whether he touched his body or Desiree's.

"So much for my belief I could raise a dead man with a kiss," Desiree said, despairing. She collapsed and laid across his chest. She suddenly started beating on his chest. "If you won't live for me, live for Silke!"

"What am I going to tell her? I can't lose my best friend and sister," Dillon bemoaned.

"We have the necessary equipment here to revive him. Get the AED," Elke said.

In two blinks, Dillon rushed off and back with a padded, red medical device, an automated electronic defibrillator. Sister Elva, Aunt Jada's stern companion, worked alongside Dillon, helping him. Did she work for Elke, too?

Sister Elva and Desiree placed the contact pads for the AED on Troy's chest. She ran her hands over the pads to smooth them flush against his skin. Next, Desiree removed the ankh necklace from around Troy's neck.

He felt its loss. What had happened to the silver cord?

"I don't want it sparking," Desiree said.

"Analyzing," the machine said. They waited. "Shock advised."

"Come on Troy," Dillon urged.

He had a feeling this was going to hurt. Or worse, it wouldn't.

"Clear!" Dillon said. He looked around to check then hit the flashing button.

The electrical charge surged through Troy. His body lurched upward. He felt nothing, but he must, because he loved Silke and his friends. They needed him alive, even if just for a day or so.

"Analyzing," the AED announced. Troy knew his body wasn't alive. "Shock advised," the AED said.

"No shit. Come on, Troy. Come on!" Dillon yelled, then he hit the button again.

Electricity arced through Troy's body. It lunged and spasmed, but he remained where he was, lying in his flesh suit, disconnected.

"Damn you! Don't die on me!" Dillon screamed. He moved to start chest compressions.

"Stop," Elke said.

Desiree stepped back.

Dillon froze. "No," he gasped.

"You know what must be done. You sense it," the Dark Lady said.

"There must be another way," Dillon said. He cringed at whatever she planned.

"You have tried to revive him. Do you want your friend to leave this mortal coil?" Elke asked.

"You know I don't."

"Then let me be about my business. He will not be like us. He isn't that far gone if I move with due alacrity."

"And yet, he'll be enthralled," Dillon protested.

"He will be alive, though. He's likely to die trying to help us."

"My sister will despise me either way, but you're right, at least she might live if we can get to her in time. First, we have to find her. I can't believe all those tracking beacons, pingers, and homing apps failed," Dillon bemoaned.

"Von Damme is no fool, or he would have passed on long ago," Elke said.

Troy didn't understand what was going on. Thinking grew more and more difficult. He felt a light from above, a spotlight shining on him.

"I will be as gentle and loving as I can be. Don't worry, Dillon dearest. Nobody can replace you, my love," Elke said as she leaned over Troy's body. She kissed him, and then she tenderly nibbled along his neck before her teeth easily parted flesh, a hot knife into butter, and opened his carotid artery. Her fingernails dug into his wrist, just as her teeth found his jugular and set his blood afire. Supernatural chemistry burned through him, and transformed him, seizing his spirit, dragging him back into the world of the living as a changed man.

Was he still a man?

Yanked into his body, Troy spasmed and thrashed. Every nerve raged its anger at the sudden and severe changes. The agony blinded him, and he could neither see nor hear. Troy gasped in a raw breath, sucking it down deep. He coughed, his chest feeling as if a lung flapped and was ready to rip free. One more cough might do it. He dry heaved a few times before successfully calming his gorge.

"He will live, and he is mine," Elke said.

What did she mean?

Then Troy knew.

Whatever Elke said, it was true. If need be, he would make it true. He would will himself back alive or even steal a way to whatever her wishes might be, for then, she would smile upon him. He adored Elke Swearington from her blond tresses to her cute little toes, which could sprout claws and rip out his throat. He vaguely realized he was not all there, or perhaps, there was more of him, so much more feedback and input than he could process.

He felt too big to be inside his body, now trapped and needing to run, and yet unable to tear himself away from Elke and the sparkle in her eyes, and her laugh, oh, her chuckle, the sign he had delighted her.

If he hadn't been lying down, he would have dropped to his knees to worship her. She was the air to him, the sun and moon by which he enjoyed the day and night.

"How do you feel?" Desiree asked.

Troy glanced over at Dillon. His blood brother warily watched him. Did he fear competition? No, why would he? He thought Troy unworthy. His fury surged.

This was all Dillon's fault!

In a blur, Troy's no longer dead hands seized and clamped around Dillon's throat. He drove his surprised blood brother into the wall, making sure to stab a knee into his gut. Troy repeatedly smashed Dillon's head, keeping him stunned, so he could bring up knee to deliver the coup de grace. He felt Dillon go slack, likely a trick. Getting a grip, Troy readied to snap his old buddy's neck.

"Stop. Take your hands away," Elke said.

Troy fought through the compelling, finding his passion for Elke pushed him on. Dillon was competition. Dillon was in his way. Dillon had been in his way for a long time. Troy just hadn't known it.

"We must save Silke, our love," Elke said. Troy heard the love in her honeyed voice. She nearly wrapped him around her finger with a few words. "Tell us about Silke. Did you see her? Visit her?"

Troy blinked. Silke. He remembered her. She would want to beat the crap out of her brother, too. And yet, she couldn't.

"We think Silke's in danger, kidnapped by Von Damme," Elke continued, sounding very concerned. It struck a chord with Troy who felt the cold knot of worry in his gut and lower back. "Do you know where she is? Can you find her?"

Fear for what would happen to Silke overwhelmed Troy's anger. He used that strong, stubborn will to subdue his supernatural rage.

"Spider is dead," Troy said harshly. He wished he were, but he couldn't leave Silke in the hands of Von Damme. She still had her whole soul. Troy let go of Dillon, stopped fighting and backed away. "Von Damme sucked the life out of him. He would do the same to Silke."

"Silke. Tell us about her?" Elke asked.

Her wish became his fervent desire. Troy searched the darkness of his memory. Had he been alive then? Could he recall what had happened when he was out of his brain? Of course, he had done it before. Had he seen Silke? Yes. Marader had her, taken her for his own, from Zane, who held her for Von Damme. Caverns surrounded them. They were underground. He remembered seeing railroad ties. Mining supports. Where? He even mentally closed his eyes. He replayed their conversation. He heard a strange name twice. "It was an old mine, uh, McKinney, Marader said. Yes, McKinney."

Elke cursed. "I have never heard of it."

Troy felt he had disappointed her. He had been so angry he hadn't absorbed everything, thereby letting her down when she needed him to know crucial information. He tried to recall more of Marader's blathering. He mentally sent himself back and found frustration and fury waiting there, and a little information. "It is or was a manganese mine. 3Ms."

"That should help," Elke purred. Troy reveled in her appreciation.

"There are maps of old mines," Dillon said.

Desiree whipped out her phone, starting an Internet search. She finger flipped and groaned. She kept looking.

Troy felt time, life, slipping away. He had a feeling he should know this. Or perhaps, he knew someone who knew?

"Y'all, I can't believe I can't find anything. There's a Mc Arthur mine and a Murray but no McKinney," Desiree said.

"Perhaps it was exploratory," Dillon said.

Troy snapped his finger. "That's it. Corning. And if he doesn't know, then Basil might. He has been wanting to see the Dark Lady again. I completely understand that. Who wouldn't want to be awed by my lady again?" Troy asked. He recounted his visit to the old East Tennessee farmer and his trigger happy and hungry buddies.

"Would you pay him a visit, Elke, if I may be so bold?"

"I think it is a worthy idea," Elke said.

"I will take you there," he said.

Elke gestured for him to be patient. "No need. I have seen it in your eyes. And, to tell you a secret, I can find anyone whose eyes have met mine," she said, and he believed her. "Stay away from Dillon. No fighting between you two while I am gone. Save your strength to rescue Silke. She and I will be asking for all you have, body and soul. Desiree, show Troy his new skills. Troy listen and learn. I'll be back, soon," Elke commanded. With a reassuring smile she vanished into a shadow.

Troy glared at Desiree which always made her bolder. She grinned, showing teeth in a feral response.

"No doubt, you're upset with me. Do you want to go to the gym, see how strong and fast you are now? Then, if there's time, I can show you some wrestling moves," she said. Her tongue peeked out to taunt.

Troy disliked the innuendo, but he needed to know his limitations. He had been able to hold Dillon after being helpless just the day before. How strong was strong? Was he quick or fast or both?

"You were in the Shadowlands a long time. I think that caused the difficulties in reviving you. I am deeply remorseful. I tried to get you out faster, but you fought me, desperate to get to Silke. You kept repeating her name. Anyway, I feel like I failed you."

"I have a chance to do Elke's bidding and save Silke. What more could I ask?" he said. Likely he would die doing it. That would be a better way to go than his death in the past.

"I might be able to make it up to you. I have read the journals. There might be a way for you and Silke to have a happy ever after. But you have to survive, first. Are you willing to fight? Do you want to be with Silke again? Or was Dillon doing the right thing, keeping you two apart?" Desiree said.

She was trying to push his buttons. It worked. Troy felt like he could crush rocks in his fist and bite nails in half.

"Show me," he snarled.

Desiree led Troy to an old gym with free weights, a medicine ball, wooden katanas, and boxing gloves, all surrounded by floor to high-ceilinged mirrors. Sister Elva followed and watched. How many spies did Elke have?

Each moment without her nearby seemed stretched to the point of breaking, but after her sexy thrall stunned him, and then kissed him, a second time, Troy forced himself to stay in the moment. He must learn his limitations to please Elke and rescue Silke.

Desiree backed away and smirked even as she shook her head and said, "Listen, to a vampire, as humans and thralls, we're either meat, bait, a servant, or a toy."

"The Dark Lady has my soul," Troy whispered. It hurt to simply say it when he should be shouting it out.

"Now, you are stronger and faster than before, but no match for a vampire, even if you had black belts in several disciplines. Let me show you some tricks I've learned from years of dealing with men with roaming hands. The moves will help with werewolves," Desiree said.

She kept pushing Troy to fight harder, faster, and find his limits. She was incredible, better than Dillon ever was. She didn't have enough time for him to hone anything, just rediscover and remember throws, blocks and punches from his youthful days, before he had left martial arts for skiing.

"Not, bad," Desiree said as she used another judo move to throw him.

Elke returned.

Once Troy saw her, he could think of little else. Elke commanded him to listen to her words. If he could become all ears, he would have transformed right then and there.

"You were right, Troy, the one named Basil knew. Now, I

have directions and a plan. Would you like to save Silke?"

Troy felt the need, both to rescue his beloved and please his goddess. Such a task would thrill Troy. Elke outlined her scheme to the three of them then commanded them into action.

"Are you sure you're willing to sacrifice yourself, if needed?" Elke asked Troy.

"For you and Silke, anything."

"Good. I believe Heaven sent you back to do this. Now, get yourself ready, then I have a few private words of encouragement to share before you depart," Elke said.

"J-Man should be here any minute. He agreed to fly you into the fire," Dillon said.

Flying was easy. Landing was difficult. Sneaking into Von Damme's lair sounded like a suicide mission.

Forty: Flying to the Rescue

Waiting for his lift, Troy stood slightly dazed on the Swearington dock while he stared up at the stars. He wiped away sweat, noting that thralls still perspired in muggy humidity. It bothered him more to be away from Elke than getting ready to skydive into a wildfire. No doubt, madness was upon him.

J-Man was coming to take him away, ha, ha, or so Troy had been told. He thought over Elke's plans and her commands. He would be flown in, drop a satchel with equipment, then he would glide into enemy territory, pick up the satchel, locate the lair, send out a signal, then breach the lair, rescue any captives, and blow up the cavern. Locate. Rescue. Distract. It sounded like a job for Special Forces or Marines.

His mistress didn't expect him to live, but it was certainly possible. She commanded that he only sacrifice himself in dire circumstances. Her orders mentally repeated like a loop of audio.

Most of her words, her movements, gestures and even

breaths, he remembered clearly. Other words hovered on the periphery, waiting for the right moment or clue to enable him to apprehend them. Those words had been given as a gift to him in private. She had sealed them with a kiss to his forehead, his third eye. He would hear them when the time was right, she assured him.

Tonight was life or death for so many, though those terms were less final than Troy had originally thought. Stop the flood of blood. Aunt Jada's words resurfaced, washing away other ponderings. Troy shook his head. Why flood? Was that literal? Or metaphoric? A flood meaning massacre? Or something to do with the water in the lake? The dam had stopped the flooding.

Dillon hung up from his call with their mistress, Elke, and strolled onto the dock. "I would say don't do anything foolish, but it's too late for that, isn't it?"

"Way," Troy agreed.

"Why are you so angry at me?" Dillon asked.

"Why did you tell Silke I was dating all your girlfriends?"

"Because I knew Silke liked you, and in her wild phase, she would have come looking for you, and one of you would have gotten badly hurt after you slammed into each other. I didn't want either one of you hating the other. I thought it was going to happen when we were at Squaw Valley, the way you two looked at each other when you thought nobody would notice."

"And I should be grateful for that?" Troy asked.

Dillon shook his head. "Troy, you know Elke is sending you in to die," Dillon said.

"She is sending me in to save your sister, someone I care very deeply about, and it's likely I'll die in the process. Yes, I know this."

"I saw the vest of explosives in her eyes," Dillon said.

Troy snorted. "If I make it that far I will consider this adventure a success. Silke and I could have been together a long time ago."

"You still can be. You have to think that way."

"I live, think and breathe Elke," Troy said with a sigh. "We all want Silke safe, but we will act dangerously reckless to please the Dark Lady. At least, I know I will, and she knows it, which is why she cautioned me. I suspect she warned you as well."

They glared at each other until they heard the sound of a helicopter.

"I hope Desiree reminded you how to fight. Everyone will be trying to kill you or take control of you. I should be going. I'm the better fighter," Dillon said.

Troy thought of the intense workout with Desiree. The self-proclaimed expert in hand-to-hand combat with men with four arms had helped him test his newfound strength, speed, and coordination. She had also injected him with a blood pressure medicine to keep him calm and less likely to be compelled. He had learned, not surprisingly, that vampires raised human's blood pressure and heart rate, but he hadn't imagined it could lead to control, though he knew racing hearts often led to poor judgment.

"You swore you would never fly in a wingsuit again," Dillon said.

"That was a different life. I've died since then," Troy said. Some people would consider gliding in a wingsuit full on crazy, especially considering the takeoff platform had spinning blades. One updraft, and he would be splattered like Meat Boy into red rain. "Besides, I wondered what to do after racing an earthquake down a mountain side. Now, I am going to fly into a wildfire and land in the lair of the undead. Good thing the helmet is rigged with Go Pros."

"Go super squirrel," Dillon said, attempting to get Troy to smile.

"I prefer calling it a bat suit. More heroic. And I am working alone."

"We'll be following your progress. Just stick to the plan, set up the surprises and stay alive. I'll come as soon as I can. Stay breathing, my friend. Silke will be pissed if I let you die,"

Dillon said.

"Then likely she's going to be furious, again," Troy said flatly. He had died. The previous time had changed his perspective and perception. This time, he had been changed physically, stronger, faster, and bound by enthralling, his choices altered. That had left him with a cold rage solely focused on the success of this insane rescue stunt.

"You know, Elke did what she did to save you, so you can be with Silke, and she knows I love you both," Dillon said.

"Your timing needs work," Troy replied. It was a challenge not to think of Elke. His heart beat in time with her name. El-key! El-key! His entire being seemed to pulse with her flame. There was nobody else for him, but he would help Silke because his mistress commanded it, and he had given Silke his love before his soul had been stolen and bound. "Why the change of heart?"

"I told you. I saw how Silke was with you. She's never been that passionate about anybody. I mean, she shot me! And I spoke to Mom about it. She says it's been going on for almost a decade."

"So, that's why your ears look singed."

"Yeah, she smacked me with a huge piece of her mind."

"Good. Somebody should. Too bad Sensei Cosmo isn't with us anymore. He would straighten you out. Listen, Dillon. I'm a pawn. We get sacrificed for the greater good of the game," Troy said.

"And brought back to the board even more powerful than before, as mighty as the queen," Dillon said. Troy must have donned his stone face. "I hate that look. You're not a God-damned pawn. You're a phoenix who arises from the ashes better than before."

"Well written, but that's bull shit. You don't believe that. You can't even fake it with conviction because you know better."

"So you don't care what I think any longer, but Silke, she believes. I know you value her opinion," Dillon said.

"She was in love with who I was."

"Listen to me, you are more powerful than ever, and you're nothing like what happened to John, or even to me. Believe it or not, you are your own man. More than that, you are the mentally toughest dude I have ever known, stubborn, even if you complain like Daffy Duck sometimes, but you make a mule look meek, and I love you, man. You can survive what's to come and save my sister. You must."

"If you say so," Troy said. Emotions would only hinder him.

"Damn. You shouldn't be doing this right now. The stress . . . God. I guess I can still use His Holy Name without being stuck by a blue bolt from Heaven. Troy, it's too soon. You're still adjusting."

"There is no time for me to adjust. I'll have to do it on the fly and see if I can do it before I have a crash that I can't crawl way from," Troy said.

"You've gotten morose."

"Yeah, well, Marader and Von Damme have Silke, Raquel and our friends. Why else was I sent back but to make this right? Fools go where angels fear to tread, so Heaven sent me, a fool. Sounds so much better than idiot or moron, doesn't it? That makes a warped kind of sense, if you ask me," Troy replied.

Dillon grabbed and shook him. Troy simply stared. He thought he might hate his friend, except he couldn't because Dillon was the consort of Elke. Besides, if Troy beat the crap out of his blood brother now, he might not have the energy needed for what was to come.

His former best friend got in his face, nose-to-nose. "You will not survive unless you know what's important to you. My sister and Raquel are import to you."

With disgust, Troy brushed away Dillon's hands, getting a pigheaded expression in return. Troy looked to the dark sky, finding a large red helicopter, its lights flashing, coming in low. He guessed the J-copter wasn't flight worthy. That didn't matter since J-Man lived. It bothered Troy that he hadn't given

J-Man's crash more thought.

"Go. This will be a reunion between old friends who thought each other might be dead," Troy said.

Dillon glanced at the helicopter. "I'm coming for you, too."

"I sure as hell won't hold my breath. You were supposed to pick me up at the airport," Troy reminded him.

"Yeah and look how that worked out. You fell in love with my sister who loves you as much as breathing. My friend, you are stronger than this, I know it. A long time ago, Aunt Jada told me I would have a friend who would die and live again and die and live again, but only if I helped him."

"You are so full of it. You never believed Jada. Thanks for all the help. By the way, good buddy, I'm an organ donor, so you'll need to reclaim your kidney quick if you want it back."

Dillon snarled. They were a split from attacking each other when Desiree sashayed onto the dock. Bags in hand, she walked between them, breaking the stare down soon to be a smack down.

"Troy, you have a way with people," Desiree said.

"Perhaps it's all the dying that makes it difficult to relate," Troy said.

"See you made a joke," Desiree said, spinning his words.

"Gallows humor. Not much different than paramedic humor. Come on, J-Man, let's get this show on the road. I've got a thrill-seeking date with werewolves, thralls and vampires camped out in a wildfire. Ha, if people thought my hair was on fire when I was skiing, they should get a load of me soon," Troy said.

"In a hurry to die?" Desiree asked.

"Naw. Been there, done that, thinking about writing the guidebook," he replied.

"I can't say I like this you," Desiree said.

"You don't like your handiwork? Lucky you won't have to deal with me much longer," Troy said. What was he ready for? The thrill of flying? Diving into a wildfire? Seeing Silke and seeing her safe? Coming back to see Elke again, see her smile, pleased with his efforts.

"Remember what Sensei Cosmo taught us," Dillon said.

"I leave the Kung Fu to you," Troy replied.

J-Man brought the whirly bird in low. The helicopter was a much larger, rotor-propelled aircraft. It looked military grade, one used to move troops in war or carry smoke jumpers into wildfires. Once J-Man maneuvered the aircraft over the dock, he lowered it until it hovered inches above the boards.

Troy climbed up and in, immediately meeting a greeting hand and shaking it. "I didn't expect to see you again," Troy said as J-Man said the same. They chuckled.

"Glad I was wrong," Troy said.

"Me, too. I can't believe somebody shot me down. Drones yes. Helicopters, no. Luckily I set her down atop a haystack."

While Troy listened, he took three bags from Desiree, who surprised him by sliding along his body and into the chopper. She sat next to him in the roomy aircraft.

"Elke changed her mind, thus, a change of plans. I personally oversee this and drop the satchel," Desiree said.

"As she wishes. A new ride?" Troy asked J-Man.

"Yep. This one's a troop carrier. I heard you might have a dozen people to evacuate. Plus, it doesn't have any bullet holes in the fuel tank. Really good to see you, Troy, except you look like death warmed over," J-Man said. Underneath night-vision goggles, he had dark circles around his eyes.

"Not that warm. Jay, you are very astute. I don't care what people say about you."

J-Man blinked. "I think your humor is getting darker."

"It matches the rest of me," Troy said. He slipped into the bat suit and gave directions and coordinates. He also explained about the kidnapping of their friends and others.

J-Man guided the helicopter over the water and southerly, heading across South Holston Lake. Swearington Lodge sat at the north end, while the fire raged on the opposite side, southeast of the dam. The fire's glow could be seen low on the horizon.

"What's in the bags?" J-Man asked.

"My superhero suit and weapons," Troy replied. One contained explosives, various grenades, and side arms with silver bullets to go along with silver weapons when he encountered werewolves. He didn't know about the others Desiree kept close to her.

"Jay, stay up high until we are close to the drop point. You're going to need to be extra alert and careful," Desiree began.

"I will be. After all, I am flying into a wildfire."

"Where thralls will be shooting at you. That is why those two other helicopters crashed. It wasn't the wildfire, it was gun fire," Desiree said. "Von Damme's followers also set the fire, built a lair inside it, and have been kidnapping people, including your friends."

"Why?"

"Why were your friends taken? Von Damme is leeching the power that he believes y'all stole from the underwater mansion, just by being there and swimming in those unholy waters. He will never stop until he captures Dr. Curran and you." Desiree replied.

"I have some vampire in me?!" J-Man asked, sounding strangled.

"Von Damme believes so," Desiree said.

"Yes, I have seen him take it back from Spider, in a nightmare that seemed real," Troy said.

"I don't know what to say to all of that," J-Man replied.

Troy tried to explain shadow walking while Desiree helped him finish detailing his bat suit, surely named after the mental condition of anyone willing to fly it. The suit added a synthetic flesh to his body, giving him under arm wings, like those of a flying squirrel but hairless, to turn him into a gliding man. It was the closest Man had come to flying without a powered device or craft.

"You know this is like flying into a living, breathing hell on earth," J-Man said. He kept glancing at Troy to see if he were serious.

"Your point? Fools go, you know," Troy said.

"Yeah, yeah. We're about two minutes from flying over the east coast's largest bonfire, violating current flight rules. I hate breaking laws! Why can't we take this shadow trail to get to them?" J-Man said.

"Undead travel through the shadows since most of their bodies are a manifestation of thought and force of will. Thralls can also do it but less effectively," Desiree replied.

"Fine then. It sounds like you couldn't take anybody out that way to escape, since our friends don't have any darkness in them, any shadow or thrall or whatever you call it, but couldn't you use the Shadowlands to sneak inside? Or are there guards?" J-Man persisted.

Troy shrugged. Desiree spoke up. "A short time there will drive anyone crazy, so no, we don't have to worry about guards there, just those in or outside the mines. Also, much of Von Damme's cult lost the ability when they accepted the alchemical transformation enabling them to walk by day. Instead of guards, it's much easier to simply eliminate shadows in an area by using multiple lights, for the shadow must be sharp and stark."

"Surreal doesn't even begin to describe this," J-Man sighed.

"Traveling is not done lightly, no pun intended. Troy should never do it again, for each time a thrall goes there, we lose a part of ourselves that loves the sunshine and light. Can't you tell?" she asked.

Troy nodded. He seemed to have lost a lot of himself. He wished he had the ankh and prayed for guidance. He would need providence to survive diving into a wildfire.

The distant forest fire backlit the shoreline, leaving the trees silhouetted and dark, while the lake's surface reflected the reddish glow in the sky. It was peaceful here, but just a couple of miles in, fires raged, and flames devoured their way, leaving charred woods. Heated winds carried waves of sparks and debris skyward to form fiery clouds. Flaming whirlwinds, taller than the hundred-foot trees, spun and erratically cavorted along the rolling hills.

The helicopter left the water behind, now flying over a dense swath of green, brown and dead-gray trees. It all looked ready to blow up into a huge fireball. The winds began to batter the copter, pushing it around.

"Are we really back to vampires and werewolves, oh, my, and if so, how do we fight them?" J-Man asked.

"Well, Jay, I'm sure you have heard the term, fight fire with fire," Desiree purred. "Sometimes a fire needs water, other times, a back burn or firebreak. In this case, vampires and thralls like us have to deal with Von Damme. We are the firebreak. In his anger, Von Damme plans to kills thousands. Humans, though, are too frail to fight directly, unless we want to involve the clergy. That would be a long term, big picture mistake. You, though, can be a big help in influencing the outcome of this intra-species conflict."

Troy glanced at her.

"What? I've been through college three times, three different degrees, including psychology and a nursing degree. I even specialized in the master studies of human sexuality. I have mastered Judo, Jujitsu, Aikido, Tae Kwan Do, and the sword. What did you think I did with all my time, chase hunks?" she asked. Troy said nothing. "So, I like to learn new things while I browse. I'm glad you aren't turned off by smart and powerful women."

The helicopter hit an air pocket and dropped fifty feet. Wild winds yanked them starboard toward the flames. The tallest of trees were less than a hundred feet below. Too many were crowned by fire, their blaze leaping to other trees. Some were completely engulfed, creating giant-sized torches. The flames coming off those swirled and curled into fiery funnels. It immediately grew warmer in the cabin. With a deft touch, Troy's blood brother steered them higher, riding a thermal out of the gorge afire.

"You are talented," Troy said.

"Careful, praise goes to my head. And I don't need to be distracted right now. I guess I shouldn't worry about the future and the night of the undead when I'm presently dealing with a living, breathing wildfire trying to roast my helicopter, a loaner that flies like a pregnant goose," J-Man said while he wrestled with the joystick. It wasn't the best of times to digest all of this. "Wait. You said us. I'm not a thrall, I don't think. I'm more likely a pawn. Are you a thrall?"

Troy nodded. "I'm both." Visions of Elke challenged him to think of anything else. She hovered around every thought, inspiration behind every breath. He could liken the wildfire to the passion he saw in her eyes, or the zeal that ignited his body. "No worries. I don't expect to be one for long."

"I see you're wearing a wingsuit. Black is appropriate for funerals, plus the blood stains don't show."

"Good point. They are also good for insanely dangerous and sneaky rescues," Troy retorted.

J-Man laughed. "Now you sound like yourself. So, you are seriously flying into that fire? Wait, don't answer. I know you are. The suit is not for show, nor do you dress to impress. You love Silke and Raquel that much? Wait, don't answer. Are you crazy? Hold on, that's just an exclamation. Now, no need to reply. You do know the forest is on fire, smoky and the winds gust with gale force unpredictably?"

Troy stared.

"We've talked about this death wish of yours," J-Man said.

"I think it's irresistible," Desiree cooed. She laughed when Troy glared. "I just got a rise out of him. He isn't dead yet."

"What do you want from me?" J-Man asked.

"To not get shot down or crash for any reason and evacuate whoever gets free and carry them away safely," Troy said.

"I can do that. Now let me focus. Things are about to get hot and spicy, not to mention dicey, but then, we're all risk takers here, aren't we?" J-Man said.

"Of course. How else can you fall in love?" Desiree asked. She smiled and removed a necklace, taking Troy's ankh off over her head. He watched with trepidation as she looped it over his head. Would it burn him? Her cool fingers slid the round-topped cross under his suit and ensured it laid flat, pressing against his skin. The ankh remained cool. He took that as a good sign.

"Uh, Troy?" J-Man asked.

"Oh, Jay, don't worry, he still loves Silke. He's just forgotten. I'm reminding him there's reasons to live so he doesn't kill himself doing something tragically heroic to please Elke. Silke, Martin, Dillon, not to mention Troy's parents, would never forgive me. Nor would I forgive myself."

J-Man didn't know what to make of Desiree. Troy could relate, but his friend didn't have time to deal with her either. J-Man focused on guiding the copter while it bounced and swayed through the turbulent air. Wildfires created their own weather systems and winds, especially in mountainous areas. A wild swing of the helicopter threw Troy into the sidewall and Desiree into him.

Normal people would have been puking. Troy patted the ankh and double-checked the zippers on his suit. All the lines and wing additions looked good. He attached two Go-Pros to his helmet, one facing forward and one back. He stretched, feeling the moment was near.

"You've done this before, right?" J-Man yelled back at Troy.

Troy thought about it. "Not from a helicopter. A hot air balloon would be the closest." He hoped his chute worked, if not, he would have to try a landing. Those usually went poorly. He had practiced trying to land like a bird on a platform above a lake. He had always ended up going splash. There was no big body of water here, but there might be a pond near the mine opening.

Dizziness briefly confused Troy, and then he realized cloudsuck had seized the helicopter. It soared like a leaf caught in a whirlwind. The bulky aircraft spun around a couple times before J-Man used his deft touch to ride it up and away as if it were some kind of fire driven tide of air. Troy peered down some five hundred feet, looking to the south where the flames topped the doomed trees.

"You're sure about this?" J-Man asked.

Troy nodded. "I'll be sending. You'll be able to watch on her phone. Am I transmitting?"

"Yes. You know, I find a man who is willing to throw his body out of a perfectly good aircraft to fly into a wildfire to save his loved ones an aphrodisiac," Desiree said. She seized and kissed Troy.

No emotion touched him. Nothing could compare to Elke, except perhaps jumping out of an aircraft into a wildfire.

"You know, I think I liked your idea of waterskiing behind the helicopter better. Godspeed, my friend. Farewell," J-Man said.

He and Troy fist bumped. He patted his blood brother on the shoulder then opened the door. The wind tasted acrid, of burning death and destruction, of Nature's full-forced fury. He had never tried anything like this, with such violently turbulent winds. To start, he must avoid the chopper blade winds and hope the updrafts left him alone. He would ball up for a moment, hopefully let the helicopter leave to clear his air space.

A sharp, pinging sound filled the copter.

"Is something wrong?" Troy asked. A second metallic ricochet punctuated his question.

"Hells bells! Somebody is shooting at us. I'll roll away," J-Man said. He subtly tweaked the joystick, bringing the helicopter into the proper alignment to the valley.

"Gunfire! We must be close! Go!" Desiree shouted.

Trees along both sides burned with flames spinning off their peaks, creating small firenados whirling uphill. Troy scrutinized the terrain. If he hit the middle, he would find a stream and green. A little to the left or right, he would catch fire. More left or right, he would smash into the shale and limestone. It might be for the best that his emotions were locked away.

"You can do this, Troy," Desiree encouraged him. She pushed the satchel to the door and shoved it out. He watched it fall briefly, then black parachutes deployed. The phone he carried would track it. The ankh, the phone, his courage and luck were all he was taking with him.

He waited for the right moment. He hung on the frame of the open door and looked down into the inferno, trying to judge the winds by the flow of the smoke. He also prayed, asking to be guided at the right time.

A bullet ricocheting and sparking off the aluminum next to him told him the time was now. "Over there! Go higher up, Jay!" Troy said and pointed to where a series of muddy ponds sat low along a sluggish stream. Green vegetation was more fire resistant, and some had avoided being scorched. He would try to follow its path downhill.

A bullet whizzed by Troy's ear, blessedly missing everything. He had learned, when you ignored the first sign, the second grew more urgent. The third broke the side window.

"Troy!" J-Man yelled, saying in one word that he must go so Jay could pilot the copter out of danger. Even now, he guided them higher up, away from the fire.

Troy had jumped out of planes, at least those had doors, to sky surf. He deployed the same skills. When it seemed calm for a moment, inwardly and outwardly, Troy launched out and down, like a dive to start a swim race, and then he tucked into a roll.

The winds shifted, a blast of hot air carrying him upward. His heart leapt into his throat. He didn't have time to think, only feel, as the air was sliced. A spinning blade clipped the top Go Pro on his helmet and destroyed the camera. The impact jerked Troy's neck and spun him around. Another blade swished past his left heel before the copter turned away.

Thank God. With the blades gone, Troy spread his legs and arms to catch the thermal like a bird. He rose higher.

The super-heated air elevated turbulently, giving him

violent thermals to ride as sparks cavorted around him. He tilted his head, held back his arms, and shot through the sky like a human missile. Air peeled and whistled across his helmet, sounding like a thrilling scream toward delight or death.

The fire bellowed around him, the inferno reshaping the air. The choppy currents battered and buffeted him while he body-surfed the searing winds. When he inhaled, he sucked in ash, trying not to cough, but he smelled burning synthetics.

Cinders landed on his bat suit.

Small holes were starting to appear. His hands wanted to pat at them to snuff them, but he fought his emotions and maintained a proper flying form. To try to save the suit would be madness, sending him into a spin. He would die quickly instead of slowly, falling like a glider afire.

The valley zigged, so he tilted, slicing close to a rocky outcropping. Thankfully the wind remained steady. Perhaps the Lord was on the side of the dark angels. Or maybe he had presumed too much, as he felt flames burning along his arms and back. He imagined he looked like a miniature fighter jet on its way to a spectacular crash-landing.

He blew passed a copse of burning trees, one exploding and throwing him aside to the right. He barely managed to compensate, flying between two spindly pine trees, brushing the nettles on the surviving evergreens. A wave of heat carried him up. It seemed a perfect time to pull his chute.

He yanked the ripcord. The parachute unfurled, opening and billowing to spread wide. Flames raced up some of the cords, burning them away. The chute began to spin. That was bad news.

Troy released his parachute, seeing it flying away as a ball of flame. His back felt afire, and he feared his backup was burning. When he pulled it, he almost immediately ejected the fiery canopy.

So much for a soft gentle landing. He spread his arms and legs to control his descent. He was surrounded by smoke and fire and hemmed in by the oaks, willows, firs and pines. This low, he couldn't see the forest for the burning trees, but he didn't have any choice. Without a chute, he was committed. Somewhere ahead should be the area that had looked like a pond.

Out of the smoke a burning tree fell into his path. He couldn't slow enough, so he flattened out and prayed.

He crashed through branches, slowing him and tearing his suit. Patches along his ribs peeled away. He began to spin and swerve, so he couldn't wait any longer. He pulled up, trying to stall like a bird and land on the limb of a big old tree. He fell short, somehow, but managed to reach out and grab a branch. It slowed his fall before it broke free. He struck another branch, a larger one, stunning him. Smaller branches raked him while he crashed to the earth.

Forty-One: Brewing

Troy awakened blearily, on his back, stuck in the cool mud. The little lake that had kept these trees alive must have been spring fed. Drought had left it much smaller, but it had a ring of mud around it. All of him ached and hurt, though the slight chill of the mud eased his scratches. He tried to rise and found his body still stunned.

"I swear to ya, I heard somethin'."

A patrol had found him! Troy's body slowly awakened, tingling painfully. He silently cursed while he struggled to escape the wet earth's clingy grip. If he hadn't crashed like a meteorite, nobody would have come hunting. He finally managed to wrest his right arm loose from the sticky mire.

The footsteps and voices drew closer. "I think you're hearing things, Brew."

"Up yours, Vern."

Troy worked his other arm free. He couldn't push to sit up nor roll onto his side. The mud still gripped his torso. Moving his legs pushed him deeper. He needed a hand up or a tree limb or something to grab to drag himself free of the bog. Only, there was no time left. Close by, Troy heard rock grind and crunch under boots.

"Well, would you look at that," Vern exclaimed.

"Boy howdy, it looks like an intruder."

"You were right. Always a first time. Sorry, Brew. I'll mark it on the calendar," Vern replied.

"Screw you. Do you think he's alive?" Brew asked.

Troy kept his lids slitted so he could see. Vern stood big and bony with a thick brow, square jaw, and large fists. In one, he gripped an axe. On a belt, a M9 hung in a holster. He and Brew both wore goggles and damp masks over the lower half of their faces like bandits. Some of their hair had burned away. Brew carried a scoped, Remington hunting rifle and used the tip of the barrel to poke Troy in the ribs.

He didn't react, but he sensed Brew would poke him harder. Could he grab the gun and do something with it to prevent being beheaded by the axe? Troy made a judgment as he relaxed and let himself be prodded a second time.

"His coloring looks good. Poke at his eye. That's a reflex," Vern said.

Though sensations of fight or flight besieged Troy, he only had two choices. Flight was out of the question, plus he had flown in to be here. It was either surrender or fight from his back with only two arms free. What would Dillon have done? Wait to get out of the mud.

"What's he wearing?" Brew asked. He started to poke Troy, and he was ready to grab the barrel, but the guy stepped back. He cocked his head. "Did you hear something?"

"No, are you hearing things?" Vern asked.

"I wasn't hearing things last time, was I? Do you hear that whistling sound?"

"Probably a tree. They make weird, sizzling and whistling sounds just before they explode from the sap boiling."

"No shit?" Brew said.

"Hey, I think I saw him twitch," Vern said. He jumped back.

"Jab him in the balls. If he's not awake, he will be," Brew said.

That wasn't a much better option than sticking him in the eye, Troy thought. He heard the whistling. It grew louder.

Vern moved in and poked at Troy. He seized the head of the axe. A blink later, Troy was the only one holding it. He saw a blur as something slammed into Vern. Bones broke upon impact, sending him flying into a stout, burnt basswood. His neck snapped, and Vern was dead before he crumpled to the ground.

Desiree rolled to her feet.

"I'll be damned," Brew said. He reached for his radio.

Troy swung the axe handle, striking Brew's knee, dislocating the cap. The thrall crumpled, dropping his radio. As the guard fell, Troy brought up his knee, hitting him in the chest and breaking the sternum. Brew's heart was squished and spasmed. Gurgling, he collapsed.

Troy should feel sad, even guilty about killing another human being. Were they all still human? That should scare him, he realized, but he felt so . . . alien.

"Hey, sexy. How are you?" Desiree asked. She slipped out of her burnt and damaged wingsuit. She wore a snug shirt and tights.

"Pleased to see you," he replied.

"Think of me as your dark angel," Desiree said, and she offered him a hand to pull him out of the muck. The thick mud resisted, before he popped free like a cork into her arms.

He chastely kissed her on the cheek. "Thank you," Troy said. He could hear her heart pounding. Nobody else was nearby. "Why did you come to die with me?"

"Hells bells, what a hopeless attitude. I'm here to improve your odds, honey. This world's challenges were designed to be taken on in pairs. You may be Elke's thrall, but you're my inspiration. You know, this guy's face reminds me of yours, except for the eyes. They lack your intensity and depth, especially when you're scowling, like now."

"Brew? I've heard that before," he said. Her comment gave him an idea. The staff at the Main Street Gym and Spa thought the two, Brew and Troy, could be related. That coincidence might work in his favor. God was working on his side. Troy removed Brew's shirt and donned it. "How do I look?" he asked.

"A little like Brew baby," she admitted. Her eyes flashed, and she smiled slyly. "Why? Do you have something devious in mind?"

"Devious, perhaps. Clever, no. But it still might work."

"What?" she asked.

"Throwing you over my shoulder and walking into Von Damme's lair like I am Brew and belong there."

"It sounds bold. I like it! Am I your captive?" she asked.

"I would be pretending to be Brew and bring you in."

"Good, that was my idea, too, but without knowing we would find somebody who looks like you," Desiree said. She ripped her shirt down the front, revealing finely lace-covered breasts. She tore off a length of her tights, showing off a sexy expanse of leg. "See, you can't help but look. Come on, honey, let's find the satchel, then I'm all yours so you can play caveman."

Troy checked the tracker. It reminded him a little of the equipment used to electronically ping and find avalanche-buried skiers and boarders.

"You smiled. Why?" Desiree asked.

"At the absurdity of my memory, comparing my life, my time in the mountains and the snow to here, a dark forest afire, crawling with vampires, werewolves and zealots who only want to shoot me, instead of eat me. And to get here, I fell from the sky," Troy replied.

"If you want to be a dark avenging angel, you can be, too. God knows, the unsuspecting people of this area need angels on their side with what's to come."

Old smoke mixed with new to create an unhealthy miasma that obscured anything beyond thirty feet. It didn't help much to see clearly in the dark when the haze created veils.

Troy figured there would be other patrols and sentinels. During their short, intense combat training session, Desiree had explained how to expand his perceptions, as his senses were more powerful than before, especially in smelling flesh and blood and hearing heartbeats. If there was a vampire, though, he would have to depend on the ankh to warn him.

He found wolf scat everywhere, so much so that he expected to encounter one of the beasts. If any eyes were upon him, they would belong to the dead or undead, lacking a pulse.

Along the road, they hiked through a burned zone, blackened trees smoldering like victims in the aftermath of a bombing. He hated seeing the charred hickory, maple, chestnuts and no longer white birch trees. Tire tracks were the only thing that looked fresh.

The signal led them uphill to the east. The package's parachutes had caught fire, so the satchel had landed hard, tumbling downhill. The outer container was battered, as it looked to have bounced off tree trunks and rocks, but the weapons and gear packed inside looked unharmed. Along with Glock-made sidearms loaded with silver bullets, the bag held tasers, and all kinds of non-lethal grenades: flash bangs, tear and sleeping gas. He didn't see any holy water. He imagined it was difficult for vampires to procure.

He slipped on the explosive vest, finding it lightweight and flexible. The charge was supposed to bring down the cave and bury the vampires. If possible, he would take it off on the way out. Once the prisoners made it to the entrance, he would detonate it. He prayed it all went smoothly.

He slipped the Glock and a silver truncheon into his vest. He carried several grenades, putting them in various places on his body and in pockets. He would carry Brew's Remington rifle as part of the charade.

"What's that?" Troy asked. Desiree had picked up and pocketed an odd device about the size of a phone. It had a dial, a timer on it. He wondered if it was an explosive.

"Insurance," she said.

"I thought I was wearing that," Troy said. He tapped the vest.

"No, that's a kill switch. I don't want it to come to that. It's why I disobeyed our mistress," she said.

"You disobeyed Elke?" he asked. The thought boggled his mind.

"Yes, I want this to work. Any idea where to go?" Desiree asked.

Troy looked around. With all the smoke, he couldn't see any landmarks. His senses might be heightened, but the smell and haze left by the wildfire overwhelmed them. He turned to an internal compass. He had been able to find Dillon. Could he sense Silke?

Each minute wasted meant Von Damme might drain one of his friends or loves. Troy tried to quiet the noise of his mind and worry of his emotions.

He remained still, waiting for a pull or a perception. He felt drawn to the southwest. With confidence, he pointed in that direction. It didn't look any different than the rest of the blackened and charred woods, but Desiree trusted his senses.

"I am ready," Desiree said. She threw herself into his arms and kissed him passionately, and then smiling, she stepped back and roundly slapped him, surprising and rocking his world.

He blinked after the flash, and his ears rang. His knees threatened to buckle. His lips hurt, and he tasted blood. "That seemed a little too harsh and heartfelt."

"Well, that's the cost for pretending that you bested me, and it explains the blood on your shirt," Desiree said impishly.

Troy used Brew's shirt to wipe away the blood. What was it about the women in love with him wanting to hit him? Silke. Find Silke. She would likely kiss and hit him, too. After he beat Marader to death, he would lead her out to the helicopter.

If he could walk. Desiree's wallop had left him a bit dizzy.

She leapt into his arms, hopping to lay over his shoulder and staggering him. She was supposed to be playing dead, but instead she was fondling his backside. "Stop that."

"You need to be aroused when you get there. It's a thrall's natural state. You know this. Feel it. Let it radiate out from you," she whispered.

Their timing had been good. A couple of minutes later, he heard a heartbeat. He spotted the werewolf before it leapt to block his way.

Troy acted surprised and spooked, which was easy, and leveled his rifle at the beast. It rose from all fours to stand. The furry beast, its yellow eyes bright and lips peeled back in a feral grin, ran his claws through his hair. "Brew, you're late and where's Vern? I could use a cigarette," the beast said.

"Shit, man! I almost shot you," Troy shouted.

"Wouldn't have hurt. What you got, Brew?"

"A hellcat. She killed Vern. I tackled her, and she clobbered me. Broke my radio. Better than dead, though."

He sniffed Desiree. "This one's in heat." The werewolf stared at him. "Brew, you smell like blood and burnt plastic, and you're packing silver."

Troy showed off the truncheon. "I found this on her. Interesting, wouldn't you say?"

"And the bullets?"

"From Vern. We heard one of the boys got eaten alive. That ain't happening to me. I ain't no snack," Troy said and spat blood.

"Get your sorry ass in gear and take her to Winona," the werewolf snarled.

Troy nodded and stumbled on past. He could feel the sentry's eyes on his back.

At the next split in the road, Troy took the well-worn and driven fork. He trudged like he belonged here. He turned off at a wide trail leading to a wall of unburnt and thorny underbrush with sickly red berries. Two old and leafy Virginia Creepers stood as natural sentinels. From behind them, Troy heard a pair of accelerated heartbeats.

He reached to draw the false wall aside, but it slid open without him touching it. Standing before him were two guards, their eyes bright, their faces flushed. Baldly and Slim both carried hunting rifles with scopes, a Winchester and Remington, which were lowered when they saw Troy, taking him for Brew. Behind them yawned a cave opening, the McKinney Mine, and the source of the cooler, moist air here in the midst of a wildfire.

"Look at what I found," Troy said, his voice rough.

"Trouble, Brew. Or is that Trouble brewing? Ha," Baldy asked.

"Brewed. Vern is dead. Let me pass before I pass out."

"Vern kicked the bucket, eh? Did he trip over a rock or a stump?" Baldy asked.

"Brew, buddy, you should report that," Slim said.

"You think? That's where I'm going. My radio's busted," Troy replied.

"What's the password?" Baldy asked.

"Cuss word? What cuss word? Man, my ears are ringing. Is that what you said?" Troy asked.

Baldy laughed. "Nice bloody nose. Found a feisty one, eh?"

Troy nodded and grunted. "Like I said, she killed Vern and rang my bell."

"Password?" Baldy asked.

"Hell if I remember. I don't remember your name, either," Troy said.

Slim laughed so hard he grabbed his stomach. "You look like you barely know your own name."

Baldly lifted Desiree's head by her hair to examine her face. "Yowza. She's a looker. I'm surprised you brought her back. Did you play with her first?"

"No. I'm having trouble breathing," Troy said. He spat blood.

"We can't let you in without the password," Baldy said.

Troy turned around. "Then I'll come back when I

remember it," he snapped.

"Wait, Brew, we can't let you leave," Slim said.

"What are you going to do, listen to me guess the password? Okay, I'll start with Von Damme is our lord and master. How about Zane is a pain."

They chuckled at that.

"Wait, I know, today was mountain laurel, white mountain laurel."

Slim snickered. "That was yesterday's."

"Then today is Appalachian lily?" Troy guessed.

"No, no flowers today," Baldy replied.

Desiree shifted and groaned.

"I either have to hit her again or get her to a cell. Hairy told me to take her to Winona."

"I think we should make him guess the password," Baldy said.

Troy trudged back the way he came.

"Where are you going?" Slim asked.

"To Vern's body. I just remembered that he writes the password down and sticks it in his wallet. Hell, it could be red moonshine or . . ."

"Eureka! He got it."

"I guessed."

"I'll go with remembered," Slim said. He ushered Troy ahead to the cave mouth and the mine entrance. "Remember to duck! I don't think you can take another rap to the noggin."

Troy flipped him off and headed underground, descending into the tunnel. Just a few feet in, a portcullis hung raised and locked. Desiree tapped him, so he paused to cough, pretend sneeze, wipe his eyes, blow his nose and spit. By the time he was done, Desiree tapped him again, letting him know to go on. He continued his descent, eager to rescue his loved ones and complete Elke's mission. She would be so pleased.

Troy was surprised by the amount of light. While the lanterns were spaced far apart to signal intersections, two lengths of red, LED lighting strips ran along both the floor and ceiling, dimly outlining the tunnel and leaving the shadows murky. He thought he recalled the way to the cells and headed for them, hoping not to meet anyone else. The side tunnels were few and far between, leaving large stretches of the main shaft where there was no place to hide. He heard a heartbeat at the first intersection but kept plodding along like his back hurt and Desiree weighed a ton.

"Hey, Brew!"

Troy stopped and looked around. The Latino covered his mouth to stifle some of his laughter and let Troy stagger by. He wondered how hard Desiree had hit him. It had seemed too forceful at the time, but so far, it had worked wonders for helping him look like Brew and sound stupid.

Too soon, Troy discovered his memory wasn't as great as he expected, either that or his recall had been rattled. He had taken a wrong turn, about to enter the vampires' sleeping lair, when a hard-looking female thrall stopped him. Short-haired, dark-eyed, and tatted along her arms, she carried a long staff, a machete, and a sidearm.

"What are you doing here?" she demanded. She poked him with the staff, and he staggered back, almost falling down.

Was this Winona? Dare he ask?

"Sorry, I took a wrong turn. My head hurts. I can't see well either. I was going to the cells," Troy said.

"Dave, you're an idiot. Who do you have there?"

"Hell if I know. Vern and I found her walking in the road. She killed Vern and whacked me before I got her under control," he replied.

"A reporter, maybe. Von Damme will want to see her. I'll see if he's available," she said curtly, turned and departed.

Troy nodded, though he silently cursed. This isn't what he wanted. He had no choice but to wait. He gently set Desiree on a couch.

He paced, worried that Zane might come by. The ankh remained cool, so Troy tried to do the same. He started to tap his toes and forced them to be still when he ached to go find

Silke. The wind current shifted in the tunnels, and he swore he could smell honeysuckle mixed with old Chanel Number 5.

Shaking her head, Winona returned. "Take her to the cells. And do nothing to her until Von Damme has made his will known," she said and pointed the way out.

The minute of down time had helped Troy's head clear. Now, he recognized the turns leading to the cells. He kept his head low, as if he were doing a job and didn't want to be delayed. Ahead, there was a mass of heartbeats, some of them beating irregularly. At the entrance to the cell block, a muscular man wearing a Skoal baseball cap stood guard. Biceps glared at Troy.

"Here," Troy said. He tossed Desiree to the dumbfounded guard.

Biceps realized what he had and smiled. "My lucky night."

Troy spat blood. "Be careful. She's starting to stir."

"No worries. I can handle her," Biceps grinned.

The guard stopped smiling when Desiree kicked him between the legs. Biceps couldn't breathe nor scream as he doubled over. She landed an elbow to his jaw, and he fell unconscious.

While she dragged him inside, Troy put on the guard's Skoal baseball cap and took up his position. He could hear Desiree unlock the cells and her whispering. He thought he heard her passing out weapons. He figured this place had once been a storage or supply room. That led him to wonder if the Kentzel TNT might be here. He could use it to blow the place to Kingdom Come.

Wyatt Maxwell, looking battered and angry, stepped out of the cells. Troy handed him the guard's weapon but kept Brew's rifle. "I am sorry about your father."

The man nodded. "We get these people free, then I'll deal justice," he replied.

"Troy, is that you?" Denny asked.

"Yes, I have to find Silke," he said.

"Spider didn't make it," Denny continued as he stepped out and embraced Troy. Denny had wounds along his face and neck, having experienced Von Damme's questioning and lived. "Great to see you, my friend."

Jambo staggered up to join the group hug and almost knocked them over. "Did you bring any guns with silver and holy bullets?" he asked.

Troy handed him one of his two handguns, a spare clip, and a flash grenade, in case he didn't make it back.

"You know how to rescue party," Jambo said.

"Troy, you have five minutes to find Silke and Raquel and get back here, then we leave," Desiree said. She looked to Maxwell who nodded in agreement. She waved at Troy, then she slipped away in the opposite direction on a mysterious mission.

Forty-Two: Inside Von Damme's Lair

Inwardly rushed, outwardly calm, Troy returned to the main shaft. He ducked back, waiting. A foursome rolled a heavy cart loaded with crates labeled Rentzel and explosives. So it had been Von Damme who had stolen the TNT.

"This is going to be the biggest explosion Bristol has ever seen," Marader said.

Troy immediately knew who it was. His temper flared, and his blood could have boiled. Heat seethed out of him, and his clenched fists could have crushed rocks. He barely kept himself from running out and attacking his traitorous blood brother. Troy squatted and held himself tightly. His breath came raggedly, slowly releasing the fury within. He hoped the squeaking and rumbling of the cart covered his racing heartbeat and breathing.

"And I'll have it on video, recordings of the terrorists," said another. Troy thought it was Deng.

Well, it seemed Von Damme was really going to blow up the dam. Could that be the flood of blood? Maybe there was flooding and a blood bath? Troy debated going after them, but he smelled a hint of old Chanel Number Five and a strong wafting of honeysuckle. Silke and Raquel needed him. They might survive if he stuck with the plan. He wanted to see his loves safely away before setting off any charges of his own.

After the quartet was out of sight, Troy entered the main passage. It took all his willpower to keep from running. Following his nose, he turned left, and then left again, heading down the tunnels he recalled to Marader's room. He had no trouble locating the sturdy oak door.

He remembered flying disembodied along this hall back and forth to Von Damme's torture chamber. Troy prayed that in the time he had been gone, Von Damme had been too busy to drain Raquel or Silke.

Troy forced himself to slow down and pause, so he wouldn't just burst in. The door was locked from this side, the tunnel side. He listened for heartbeats, finding two familiar ones. They stood across the room from the door.

"Silke! Raquel! It's Troy," he said as he unlocked and pushed open the door. "We must leave now!"

He heard the sharp intake of breaths, as if the ladies had steeled themselves for the worst. Silke's scent wafted past him, and he paused, overwhelmed by it and Raquel's fragrance. Then, a moment later, he realized Silke charged him. He evaded her, then he caught her, swinging beautiful Silke around into his arms.

He hadn't intended to, but he breathed her name. What would Elke think? Well, he couldn't have Silke run out into the hall where her laughter would draw attention, could he?

"Troy? Troy! I knew you would come! Thank God!" Silke laughed. The joy sounded completely alien here. She and her eyes danced as she kissed him with gratitude and a lust for life. He didn't kiss her back as he heard Elke's voice demanding that he hurry. Every second counted. The memory of her commands compelled him. She owned him. She knew that Silke might change his mind and shake his will, especially if he got lost in a kiss. Some part of him wanted to crush Silke to his body and never let go. Wasn't that person dead? Just the walking soon-to-be-dead.

Silke stepped back, confusion in her eyes and body language.

"I am thrilled to find you both healthy. We must leave now," Troy said, looking over to Raquel. Mixed emotions played across her face. No doubt, she was relieved to see a friendly face.

"You look like you've been through the wringer," Raquel said.

"No. I'm trying to avoid that. So far, I have flown in a wingsuit and on a prayer into a fire and bluffed my way by werewolves and zealots who might walk in here at any moment, so there's no time for chit chat."

His blunt words quieted them.

"Come with me. We are leaving with Denny, Diana, and the rest who still live," Troy said. He found he couldn't let go of Silke. He removed his necklace and placed the ankh over her head. "Here, you should wear this."

She grabbed him by the hair and fiercely kissed him. For a moment, he was lost with her, breathing in her breath. He had to call on Elke's image and compelling to pull away. Still, he took her hand. "Come, Silke. Let me know if the ankh warms." He scooped up his love and put her over his shoulder. He looked to Raquel, nodding for her to follow.

He listened, hearing distant voices but nothing near.

Waiting was not an option. He took off, hurrying through the red lit tunnels toward the next lamp light. It would be the opening to the mine spur to the cells. Raquel kept stumbling. Silke held out a hand, helping guide Raquel along.

Troy's balance had improved so he vaguely noted the uneven ground. Even in good light it would be challenging to follow him. The dimness and his speed added to the difficulty.

In the distance, he heard heartbeats. They were coming this way. Raquel was not moving fast enough.

He whirled, leaning close to her to whisper in her ear. "No questions. Hop on my back and hang on." He turned around, and she immediately mounted him. He ran up the tunnel, heading for the light.

If they saw him, he should look like he carried packages or prisoners. The cluster of heartbeats would seem less menacing, at least he hoped. He took long, ground-devouring strides without trying to look like he hurried.

As he neared the lamp and the side tunnel, Troy recognized the pair by their build and smell. Slim led the way. Troy didn't acknowledge the sentries from the front entrance and slipped swiftly into and down the spur leading off to the cells.

"Hey, Brew. What's up? You're not still carrying that babe, are you?" Baldy yelled.

Troy kept his mouth shut and listened. They were following him to the cells.

Ahead, he sensed heartbeats and the familiar, seductive scent of Desiree and the no nonsense air of Deputy Maxwell. He waited, alert and on guard at the doorway.

"Two prisoners and two followers," Troy said as he walked past the deputy. Raquel dropped off and hurried aside. Desiree rushed to stand out of sight beside the door. Troy kept walking, so when the guards entered, they saw him. They never noticed Desiree. With a punch and kick, she knocked them unconscious.

"Impressive. I wanted to hit someone, too," Maxwell said.

"Unfortunately, there's likely to be more. We must go," Desiree said.

"What happened to you, my love?" Silke asked. She slid off Troy's shoulders and down his chest, staying pressed against him.

"I died again. I'm stained this time and transformed even more. I am lost to the light," he said.

Silke didn't understand, but she could care less. "Get us out of here, and I'll be your stain remover and a light-bringer. What are you wearing? It's bulky," she asked.

"A flack vest of sorts, armor," he said, a half-truth with an omission. "I am sorry. I am not myself. My will is not my own."

"Elke? Bitch. You love me still, right?" she asked.

He managed to smile. "Yes, you and Elke, my sun and moon. Nothing is more important than seeing you safe, so let's get our butts in gear," Troy said. He looked around, counting their number.

After a long hug with Raquel, Diana leaned on Jambo. Denny carried Mary Beth over his shoulder. They would be leaving without Maxwell's father, Eduardo, and Spider.

"What about Marader? He was captured with us, and I haven't seen him," Denny said.

"He's a traitor, gone to the other side for longer life and more sex appeal," Troy replied.

"Tell me you're joking," Denny replied.

"I wish I could. I overheard him and others transporting explosives. They plan to use them to blow up the dam," Troy said.

"Oh, dear Lord, give us strength. It's Rentzel TNT, right?" Denny asked. Troy nodded. "We have to do something! Call somebody!"

"Like Deputy Burt? We don't know who else Von Damme controls," Troy said. He had always wondered about the lack of an investigation by the authorities, but then he had assumed they were busy. Burt being a turncoat explained it.

"Troy. I don't understand this," Raquel asked.

"I don't either, but I'll try to explain," he took a pausing breath then summarized. "A powerful, undead creature escaped imprisonment from the underwater mansion of death. He claims we absorbed some of him by being in his mansion and wants to take it back and enact vengeance on everyone in area."

"That's insane," Raquel whispered.

Troy took her hand. "Once we get out of here, Jay's waiting with a helicopter," he said. As long as it hadn't been shot down, he thought. He saw genuine hope in all their eyes now. They had an evacuation plan.

Still, just in case, Troy handed Silke a phone and a flare gun. "Are you telling me to evac to the chopper?" she asked, making it sound like a movie. Troy only wished it were a make-believe adventure. She smiled, and that gave him hope. He held back, waiting to embrace it. There was still too much to go wrong.

Desiree led them out of the cells while Troy took up the rear guard. So far, so good. This might work yet, brazenly walking in with one prisoner and out with eight. Perhaps he wouldn't have to resort to the plan. He realized the vest was lighter. Where had some of the explosives gone?

Desiree must have taken them. Why?

He listened for telltale heartbeats, straining to listen. For a short time, he believed they would make it. He could sense the fresh air and the door ahead. Nobody was behind him, but they weren't alone. Heartbeats came from the right, rapidly growing louder, and racing up a tunnel. Too late, he started to call a warning. Even so, Desiree would know.

"I knew I smelled something wrong," a werewolf snarled.

It howled as it sprang from a niche and attacked Desiree.

She evaded its strike, only to encounter a second werebeast, this one black as night. She spun her silver truncheon and deflected its claws. While they struggled, Desiree drew her knife.

The first werewolf ripped open Maxwell's throat. Jambo shot the beast in the head, the blast killing it and certainly sounding the alarm. He tried to shoot the dark werewolf, but it tore the Glock from his bloodied fingers. In doing so, the beast exposed itself. Desiree buried a knife in its ribs. It backhanded her, staggering her. It bounded for Jambo.

Troy shot at the beast, hitting its left leg. It stumbled. Braining it from behind with her truncheon, Desiree crushed the dark werewolf's skull.

They had slain the lycanthropes, but the attack had slowed them and alerted others. Troy heard a stampede behind them.

The enemy shouted a warning to those coming from ahead. Denny had taken up Maxwell's weapons. He and Jambo started shooting ahead.

Troy tossed a flash grenade over his shoulder. This should be a surprise. The explosion of brightness brought screams of dismay. He heard collisions, perhaps broken bones.

The bullets seemed to have cleared the path ahead, or so Troy had hoped. The portcullis slowly descended, until it caught on something and stopped. Thanks, Desiree. When he had paused earlier, she had jammed it.

"Faster!" Troy screamed. He rushed ahead, seizing Silke with one arm and Raquel with the other. Sprinting madly, he raced on. He had no idea how long the portcullis would remain stuck. Even now, it began shaking.

When it looked like they would make it, Troy heard a heartbeat. He saw nothing ahead, so he tried to prepare himself for a surprise left or right. He guessed left.

The attack came from above. Two werewolves dropped from a ventilation shaft. One tackled Troy. He used his momentum to throw Silke and Raquel ahead. They tumbled underneath the gate. Denny ducked under with Mary Beth and kept going, but Jambo turned to shoot the werewolf holding Troy.

Deep inside the mine, an explosion sounded. The walls shuddered. Rock pelted them. The floor swayed sideways, knocking everyone off their feet. Desiree tackled the second beast, and it fell on its back, kicking her toward the portcullis. Denny dragged her under and out, even as the werewolf charged. Troy grabbed its fur so it couldn't pursue.

Jambo shot it. "Come on, Troy!" he yelled.

A second explosion rocked the limestone caverns. Everything swayed and shifted. The portcullis slipped loose and closed with a clanging thud, leaving Troy trapped inside.

Just as Elke had planned. It was why he wore an explosive vest.

Troy's hand found Desiree's dropped knife. He slashed

open the beast's throat. He glanced back at the portcullis. He wasn't going anywhere, even if he could hear Silke screaming his name. He did love her. That is why he was doing this. He readied himself by putting plugs in his ears. They wouldn't help with the explosion, of course, but they would help with the vampires. He would be unable to hear their commands to stop.

"It is hopeless. You should surrender," Zane said as he strolled up and crossed his arms. "Oh, it's you. What a surprise? Well, this way we didn't have to chase you anymore."

Troy read his lips, so he thought that was what Zane had said. The Dark Lady strolled forward to strike a tempting pose.

Lyla called out to him. He didn't have to hear her to feel the smoldering siren's passion reach out to him. He couldn't look away from her beauty, her eyes full of bloodlust and her hips and lips making promises. "How about you come with me, and I will surrender to you?"

Troy felt the weight of their commands. He mentally conjured images of Silke and Elke, hearing their voices while he waited for the thralls to close in, two steps from leaping to overwhelm him. He blew a kiss to Silke and mentally kissed the world farewell. He would bury these vampires.

"He isn't obeying. Get him!" Zane yelled.

The mob of werewolves and guards charged. He pressed the detonation button.

Nothing happened. No explosion. It didn't work. He tried again. This was going to be bad, very bad.

The onrushing thralls dragged Troy down. They held him fast, while they beat him until he almost lost consciousness. With each hit, he prayed this was worth it, that Silke, his friends, everyone, had escaped safely.

"Take him to Von Damme," Zane ordered.

It was the last words Troy heard before a final blow sent him spinning into blackness.

Forty-Three: Tortured by Von Damme

A slap started Troy's rude awakening. So, he had been dreaming and not dead. That was good and bad for a variety of reasons. He shivered from the dankness of the cavern and the blood-chilling presence of a vampire.

"I know you are awake. Open your eyes!"

Troy fought the command. He had followed his mistress' orders. She would be pleased. They had rescued captives and distracted Von Damme. It could have gone much worse.

"Look at me," Von Damme commanded.

Troy slowly opened his eyes and stared into large, blood red orbs and so many they couldn't be real or human. It took him a moment to realize they were gems, fire opals, and not twelve eyes. As his double vision left, he realized there were only six fine gemstones sparking in the ruddy lantern light. He recalled them from the nightmare of John dying.

"Look at me," Von Damme said, taking control of Troy's eyes. They darted from the fire opals inset on the silver necklace to the emotionless dark eyes of the vampire. "You are healing. That is good, Toy Troy, because I want you to suffer as I slowly peel your life from you."

That sounded like dying again. Or Shadowlands traveling. Troy could hardly think straight. Breathing deeply hurt. He forced his eyelids apart.

"Thank you for coming to me. It saves my forces from hunting you, so they may capture Jay Beck, Dr. Curran and Ms. Kirkland. I am so glad that your explosive vest malfunctioned. Or did it? Hmm? Perhaps you are a pawn. I am quite interested to see why you have been such a pain in my neck," Von Damme said. The master vampire possessed cruel, black eyes, an arrogant tilt of the head, a condescending lift of the chin, and a disdainful smile. His features revealed his character and the evil superiority he saw no reason to hide.

"You know me from my diary, thanks to Frank 'Spider' Adder, your blood brother who died quite suddenly. I barely drew what I needed before he expired. And, you know me from being in my mansion, my paradise, and ultimately my prison. It will be a paradise again. Not that you will live to see it. Pain is part of the extraction process and will further empower me."

Troy knew what drove Von Damme. He wanted to be whole again. Somehow, the divers' very presence inside the mansion of doom had unintentionally stolen some of the master vampire's energy.

"You want that time from me. What if I freely give it?" Troy asked, although he knew better.

"So kind of you to offer what is mine to take. There is so much of the mansion's energy within you. You were there many times, almost killed, I see. I will take it from you. This will be the last time you will be coherent, as I must take memories, feelings, tastes, sounds, sights, even scents, along with the energy from you."

Troy forced a laugh. "I would be thrilled to forget being in your house. John died there. You murdered him. There are ghosts there. I almost died there. What happened to Sherry?"

"Who? Oh, yes, Sherry and John. Sherry was the first. When she donned my amulet, I took her whole body as I was without flesh and filled her, after shoving her soul aside, of course. I hear it weep pitifully every now and then. But I needed more to survive the water's corrosive force, so I devoured John, who provided sustenance, enough to shatter the foul imprisoning enchantments and allow me to ascend to the surface."

"You don't look like a Sherry to me."

"Ah, you still have a sense of humor. How surprising. That will change soon. But to your point, I am a master vampire, a rare breed indeed, and therefore a master shapeshifter," Von Damme said. His features, even his clothing, morphed swiftly, turning from male to a sexy female with long red-golden locks. In the time it took for Troy's eyes to blink, his heart to stop and his jaw to drop, Silke appeared to stand before him, except for her eyes. They were still Von Damme's brutal eyes. They mocked him when he caressed Troy's face.

Von Damme returned to his namesake form. "That hate in your eyes tells me you care for her a great deal, as well as wishing revenge on me for the deaths of your friends, though in truth, you no longer have friends, or even a chance with this woman because you are a thrall. Of who? You hide your mistress from me. Why? She was a fool to send you. Did you know she sent you here to die?" he asked.

Troy shrugged. His friends and loved ones were safe.

"Know you are simply a tool now. The explosions were supposed to bury us all and kill you, so I wouldn't eventually discover your mistress' identity. Sadly, for you, most of the explosives didn't go off, much like your vest. Unfortunately, what worked took out our generators. We have returned to the days of lanterns and are ready for an attack from the Shadowlands, though it will be too late. You have failed because the boat of explosives has sailed. It won't be long before a big boom is followed by a wall of rushing water. Good-bye Blountville, Bluff City and Bristol. Too bad the lake is so low we may not reach Johnson City.

"No one is going to rescue you. Even if you survive the extraction, you will be fed to my thralls. They will be hungry since so many of their meals escaped, and it is your fault."

Darkness seemed to spread from Von Damme's eyes. It grayed his face but caused the gems in the amulet to flare, matching the bloodlust now dancing in the vampire's eyes.

"I will take what you and others have stolen, then return to my mansion where I will be completely empowered. In the wake of disaster, I shall wreak havoc," he proclaimed.

Darkness turned Von Damme's fingernails black. He drove them into Troy's throat, left claw, then right, burying them. Troy would have screamed but the pressure cut off his air.

Agony. He was powerless to stop it.

"Take me there! Give me the memory! Give me my power!" Von Damme demanded. His features changed to

Troy's friend, his dead blood brother, John. The mocking smile and madness-lit eyes were Von Damme's.

The pressure and helplessness took Troy back to the underwater mansion. Frightened and confused, baffled at where he was and why, he floated outside the deadly mansion. The shutters seeming to zigzag before his eyes. He adjusted his mask and caught a glimpse of Raquel going inside.

When Troy moved to follow her, the giant gar floated out. Feeling like shark bait, Troy thrashed backwards, having to escape and stay outside to let the monster pass. The light in the window went out, and he knew he was losing his lady love. Worry pushed him forward.

Once he darted inside, the cold invaded him and numbed his extremities. He saw a glimmer of light at the door and swam there, trying to catch up with Raquel. He was spooked in the hall, backing into the wall and getting his tank stuck. Now he could see the mansion wall had leaned into him, trying to make contact. He struggled to get loose, and he sensed a distant maniacal laughter. It continued even after he pulled free.

The mansion? Or Von Damme? Which laughed at Troy's futility and helplessness?

Searching for Raquel, he swam through the slimy tentacles of wall paper, then on and into the grand entryway. He was vaguely aware something seemed amiss with this memory. He experienced a moment of duality. Hadn't he found a skeleton in the bed? His dive buddy had been Silke. This was Raquel. He had only been her buddy on the last dive. Were these false memories?

Troy sensed confusion, too, making him further baffled. He spotted himself in the mirror, looking like John. Down below on the first floor, an unfamiliar woman, Sherry, searched through the pockets of a hanging body. Troy knew his name, Morris the valet. Sherry seemed to find what she was seeking and fin-kicked over to the study doors where she inserted a key in the right one. Troy tried to catch her to stop her. Like in a movie, he sensed certain doom if she cracked the seal.

His world changed in slow motion as she swung the door open. The house shuddered to shake. The water quaked, throwing Troy about. He bounced off a wall. Stunned for a moment, he floated in the darkness, trying to recover.

Time seemed interrupted. When he regained his senses, he had entered the study. The cold attacked him with invisible spines. The darkness solidified to thwart the intrusion of light.

A candle of light in the gloom, Sherry, appearing confused, held a jewelry box. Blood swirled around it and her hands. She raised a crescent amulet of dull, orange-red gems above her head, then donned the necklace, turning the bloodstones into dazzling rubies. Lances of its light cavorted throughout the underwater chamber and stabbed at Troy.

I remember this. How did you see this? Von Damme wondered. This is truth, but it lacks substance. Hollow. Where is the power?

Troy checked his dive watch. Time was short. He wanted out of here. He motioned to Sherry. She nodded, adjusted the crescent amulet and necklace about her bosom, then she left the jewelry box and swam for the open door.

Oh, God, I am John just prior to his death. Troy realized.

Suddenly, he sipped water. His regulator failed him. He tried the backup hose and regulator. It bled water, too. He made the choking signal to Sherry, who smiled sympathetically, but it didn't touch her eyes. Troy realized it wasn't her. It was Von Damme!

She was gone, but John didn't recognize it yet. He swam for her, and she slowly drifted back. Now under Von Damme's control, Sherry always stayed just out of reach. Finally, Troy blacked out as John drowned, ending with sharp pains in his neck.

"I remember this. It was just after I reawakened. How do you know this?" Von Damme asked. For the longest time, the master vampire sought answers but found none because Troy had none. The memory seemed to replay over and over again.

Finally, Von Damme slapped Troy. His head rocked back and almost felt like it was torn loose as he nearly blacked out. He didn't fight it.

"Enough. This is a waste of my time. There is so little energy there. It is more like an echo, or perhaps, yes, now I see. It's a nightmare. Interesting. You were blood brothers. I believe I might have underestimated the connection despite knowing the true power of blood."

Von Damme left John's visage behind, transforming back into Silke. Just seeing her like this hurt Troy, her scornful stare and mocking smile. Troy tried to remind himself this wasn't Silke, even as she drove black and red fingernails into his flesh. The vampire leaned in and bit Troy's lip.

Flipping through memories like he was a channel surfer, Von Damme found Troy's first physical visit to the mansion of death and sucked the life from it, from Troy, his memory, thoughts, and feelings. He started with Troy floating outside with Silke, especially his admiration of how she looked in a swimsuit. Von Damme's attention was drawn to her, but he cursed when he noticed the strange runes and symbols scratched and painted into the shutters. His condemnations increased at seeing the attempted escape scars on the inside of the shuttering boards.

Von Damme recognized the dead skeleton on the bed. Hazel. Troy had a moment of seeing her using her talons in an attempt to claw through the boards. A stern looking woman, she reminded Troy of Sister Elva.

Marader had tried to enter the cold ruin and left, leaving Troy and Silke on their own. Von Damme seemed to relish not only picking apart Troy's memory of the visit but of Silke, too. Troy watched the memory of her fade away, disappearing out the door, along with thought of her. It vanished, too, leaving an empty ache.

The master vampire knew everything about the house. This door squeaked and was difficult to close when it rained, or the fog was as thick as pea soup. The floor was made of cherry wood. This section of wall had been repaired when a werewolf had been thrown through it during a drunken brawl.

All this washed over Troy then disappeared, leaving him empty. Every door he passed, a name was uttered, including Mona's. It was voiced with regret, and then the memory and emotions vanished. What had he been thinking of?

As Troy swam along the hall, he was caressed by the tendrils of rotting fabric and wallpaper. That slimy image and its sensations slipped away. He and Silke reached the grand entryway. The chandelier was Swarovski, shipped over in the 1920s. White hot blinding rage surged through Troy at the sight of the hanged valet's skeleton. Morris had taken his own life after decades of service.

At the study, Von Damme's rebirth flashed through Troy's thoughts. The master vampire's body had been destroyed, leaving his angry, powerfully evil life force trapped within the crescent amulet's gems until Sherry had unwittingly freed him. She had opened the jewelry box then donned the necklace and amulet. Those six skeletons surrounding the master vampire had given their existences to imprison him, and now, he was free again. They didn't know he could live as long as the mansion stood.

Von Damme savored murdering her boyfriend, John. Troy felt hate, then he forgot about the incident. His life reeled forward, sometimes without context. J-Man picked through the books. Desiree searched through the massive desk's drawers. Silke cut her hand, the blood feeding the house. The water shook as the mansion spasmed, loving blood as much as its master.

Where was the cufflink? Von Damme had yet to recover it. Where was it? Troy barely recalled slipping it into the pocket of the BC vest. Where had it gone after that?

Von Damme lingered, drawing painfully long every moment in the mansion, savoring the seconds and dissecting them. Troy and J-Man moved John's body, and the tussle between Spider and Marader flared up. Von Damme laughed when Desiree drew a knife on Troy then hissed, recognizing her as a thrall.

Troy felt empty upon leaving the mansion. What had happened? He knew why he had gone inside to look for Dillon. Had they accomplished it? The powerlessness, hopelessness and gloominess inundated him.

When Troy nearly hit bottom, Von Damme soared, still looking like Silke and laughing crazily. "No, no. You can't die yet. I feel better, but there is more. So much more. Somehow, as a returnee, you are observing and absorbing a far greater amount of sensation and energy. You are amazing. And this wonderful woman, this Silke, I want to know more about her."

"No," Troy croaked. He tried to compartmentalize Silke. It had worked before, though, that was before . . .

The fingernails, the pain, and the digging went deeper. Von Damme forced him to relive pleasure and pain, making love to Silke after the fire and the following morning, when they had decided to go beyond entangling their tongues and legs to their whole lives.

The God-damned bastard, Von Damme, leeched all color and emotion from the memories, eventually leaving Troy nothing, not a shadow or echo of his time with Silke after it winked out like a bubble bursting.

Further back, the master vampire stripped Troy of the time with Silke at Aunt Jada's. Von Damme devoured it, cursing the house and Aunt Jada, promising to get revenge on Silke for whatever her aunt had done. What had her aunt done? Jada had allied and worked with the Rulers of Night. It made sense that Sister Elva was an emissary

Threading back through Troy's life more, Von Damme found them after the dive, after meeting Zane. Silke had been living heat in Troy's arms before she had collapsed. Von Damme kept robbing Troy, taking away the memory of meeting Zane, his influence, their reactions, and the aftermath.

The emptiness left Troy numb.

"So that is what he meant. Lust triumphed over his

compelling. Well, more than that, love, too, but you won't remember that," Von Damme said. "Wait. What is this? A surprise!"

The master vampire dove into Troy's memories one more time, tearing and picking him apart. He found Raquel and morphed his form into the Silver Goddess, so she could torture him. Now it seemed like a nightmare he had suffered before. Von Damme couldn't understand that Troy could deal with this pain, as he had shouldered and stomached it for a long time.

This time, Troy and Silke watched four of the SARs rescue team swim in through the front door. Von Damme reveled in another angle. He laughed as the quartet disappeared within.

"It already killed the two fools who went in before. It has been so long, the house must be fed. What? Ah, you visited the still house where moonshine was . . ." Von Damme stopped speaking abruptly.

Mona's ghost swept over Troy, delivering a memory from the past. The beginning, inside the barrel, confused the vampire. He bombarded Troy with questions until the barrel crashed open, revealing mud, blood, moonshine, and the mansion behind the werewolf carriage driver. Von Damme, of course, recognized Hairy immediately.

"Jackson? Ah, Mona tried to escape. When did this happen? And why does this thrall remember it? He wasn't there. This was long before Troy Bane was born."

The master vampire was transfixed by the past, absorbing every aspect, the smells, fear, alcohol, sugar, wet werewolf, Mona's perfume, and the clean scent of the woods, as well as the sounds of the night and her heart romping in panic, discovered, soon to be feasted upon. Hairy Jackson dragged her along the paving stones toward the mansion, stopping suddenly to whirl in a complete circle, wary of the night.

"I know this night. It was the last thing I remembered for over half a century," Von Damme growled.

The darkness spat out nightwalkers—vampires, thralls,

werewolves, and the spidery etchers and a horde of painters. Like a plague of locust, they swept through the still operations, killing Jackson and blanketing the house. They worked furiously carving and painting symbols, while those inside, Von Damme knew, worked to entrap him at the cost of their souls. Fools!

Troy opened his eyes. Still looking like Raquel, the master vampire stood stunned. He forced Troy to replay the memory, attempting to absorb it. He grumbled and groaned, yanking and tugging at a haunting recollection that Troy would eagerly release.

When Elke slew Mona, the ghost memory shattered. "No more," Von Damme gasped as he staggered back. Their connection snapped.

The backlash whipped into Troy and carried him into unconsciousness, after he realized he had learned what he had been sent to learn. He held fast to knowing how to destroy Von Damme.

Troy awakened, surprised to be alive and painfully dawning to needling pains and breath-stealing twinges. Fogginess wafted through his memory and thinking. He was disoriented and confused as to where he was and why he was. Now what was he?

All but dead. Mostly dead? He heard Miracle Max's lines being imitated by Denny. It brought a smile to his face despite the pain.

What was it he recalled just before he died? A reason to survive.

He had to tell Elke something? Or was it Silke?

Suddenly, the present crashed back on Troy like a falling house. For the longest time, there was only pain, loss and a sense of longing. He was aware Von Damme was stripping him of his memories of Silke. He agonized over what to do.

Troy was powerless. He could do nothing. But, he didn't want to forget Silke. He compartmentalized their downtown kiss, where he was a pretend boyfriend, when he had felt magic.

Voices? Von Damme talked to a familiar voice. Two familiar voices. Marader!

"Yes, sir. We've loaded the boat. The explosives will be on their way to the dam soon, then kaboom!" Marader said over the speaker phone.

"And I've made sure the patrols will be diverted," said someone with the air of authority. Troy thought he knew the voice. Deputy Burt?

"You have done well, Deputy. You shall be part of the new breed and the new order, I guarantee it. Now, see it done," Von Damme said.

How long had Deputy Burt been under the vampire's influence? Von Damme knew everything they had ever reported.

"Yes, you see the depths of your futility. And how could Marader betray you?" Von Damme asked, even as his appearance morphed. Moments later, he looked and sounded like Tommy Boy. "Troy, hey, buddy, you're still alive. I hear you let my girls loose. If they didn't kill themselves on the way out, I can attend to them later. And, how could I? Easy. I'll name just a few choice reasons.

"Endless women. Vitality. Irresistibility. Immortality. There's some good vocabulary words there. What can I say? I like the idea of being young, handsome and magnetically charming forever. How could I not? Come on! We're twenty-eight. Next thing you know, we'll be forty and bald with a house mortgage, a wife-mom, three kids, a dog and two cats all supported by a boring job. I used to think that it was better to burn out than fade away. Now I don't have to! I know you'd switch places with me in a heartbeat, wouldn't you?"

"Go to Hell."

"As a vampire, Marader will never have to go anywhere," Von Damme said, returning to his 1940s form, cruel, dark, and arrogant. God only knew his original human appearance.

Von Damme took over, dominating Troy's vision. "Before I drain you of your final visit, I wish to find out more about your investigations. Ah, you went to see one who saw me, did you?"

Agony rooted Troy, blinding pain brought him to a clearing vision. He walked with Silke to visit the men who had worked on building the dam. He seemed to know two of the men. Von Damme picked at the memory, pulling threads of it, taking all the color away, leaving it like an old sepia-toned photo. The master vampire delighted in removing Silke from his memories, taking her light from Troy.

He found Troy and Silke outside Swearington Lodge.

"That's it! Swearington Lodge! Elke Swearington, she is your mistress, and Dillon Urich. They are the ones watching me for the Rulers of Night," Von Damme exulted. "I know where to find her! You, Toy Troy, have forgotten your love and failed your mistress. You are pitiful. Once I pull this last memory from you, you might as well die."

Von Damme's eyes bored into him again, prodding through his brain with a dental pick. The master vampire found the second dive into the house, the rescue dive to save Diana Sterling, Eduardo, Rae Kirkland, and Mary Beth Rentzel. While Troy floated, hesitating to enter the place once again, Von Damme was eager.

They had pushed in through the front door and spread out. With Von Damme's perspective, Troy could feel the house swell like an engorged beast. And yet, it could swallow and feed on more, many more.

And it will!

The burning light of the flares pained the house and Von Damme who shared it with Troy. He wished he was numb, but with his loss of memories and weakness, everything hurt more, like he was aging and going senile.

Was this why he had been sent back to the material world?

Von Damme pressed on the memory, forcing Troy to focus on it. He found Eduardo in the study. Von Damme reveled and rejoiced at returning, even in memory, to his place of power.

He seemed to ooze into Troy's memory, slipping by Eduardo and into the great black, throne chair. From there, he watched what unfolded, the discovery of the girls trapped in the basement laboratory.

"Say that again," Von Damme said. He removed his claws from Troy, lessening the agony.

Thankfully, he was jerked out of the memory. Gasping, sweaty and feeling slimy and abused from the stomping through his head,

Troy wished someone would take away the memory of this. He doubted there was any way to compartmentalize the violation and loss. It was too bad he couldn't die, yet. His mistress still required what he knew.

It took Troy a while to realize Von Damme was listening to Zane report. "I'm telling you, it is an emergency. Many are feeling sick and suffering severe stomach cramping. Puking werewolves is a pitiful sight. If we were to be attacked now, we would be vulnerable," Paleface said.

Von Damme grabbed Troy's jaw. He leaned in close and searched Troy's eyes for any knowledge of why this might be happening. He had no idea. "Bah, he knows nothing of this. Likely, it is a bug, and they will feel better shortly, but this is a world I haven't known for over half a century. Gather the whiners. I will examine them presently, then finish my work here."

"There is also a tornado warning in effect."

"Good, that will keep everyone else off the lake," Von Damme said. He removed his silver necklace and crescent amulet of fire opals to set it in a large lock box, a metal one with two dials and two keyholes. His departing words riveted Troy. "Stay there."

As commanded, Troy helplessly lied there. He shifted, trying to ease his pains. He felt pinched in his crotch and then something snapped. His feeble hand found a long Silke hair. He wore her favor? He smiled. Silke. And Elke.

Like a door opening, he realized that was part of Elke's

plan. It would only reveal itself after an event seemed to trigger that part of the memory.

Moving was a challenge, but Troy heard his mistress' commands. Elke had hoped it would come to this. All Troy had to do was defy the compelling, haul his near dead body to the nearest shadow, bleed, which he was already doing, breath, and spit, which was almost impossible now, to anchor a Shadowlands gate. That would bring his mistress!

The emotion excited and agitated him. Like a little kid, he couldn't sit still, no matter what Von Damme had ordered. Troy called on those youthful memories to his hyperactive days. He rolled back and forth until he had enough momentum to tumble off the table. He tried to land on his feet and stand, but his knees buckled, and he hit hard, almost knocking himself out. That seemed to clear Von Damme's last command from Troy's mind.

Now, he could move. He was exhausted, but he forced himself to focus. He knew Von Damme would go after Silke. Troy must stop him.

Earlier, when they had been alone, Elke had shown Troy how to anchor a gate to the Shadowlands. He needed a crisp shadow. Currently, there were too many lights on in the chamber. The shadows cast were fuzzy with multiple gradations. It wouldn't do. He would have to turn off all but one light, meaning he would have to stand and walk. If only he had landed on his feet, that would have lessened his challenges.

He would have to rise. His and other lives depended on it. Nothing was broken, he was simply running on fumes.

He reached up with leaden arms to grab the edge of the table. He planned to haul and push himself to his feet. His arms and legs shook weakly, leaving him to lean on his determination to stand. This reminded him of physical therapy days. He stubbornly refused to fail and pushed through near blacking out to get his knees off the hard dirt floor. The world pitched and spun as he clawed and crawled his way up like he was hanging on the edge of a cliff, and he was fighting to keep from blacking out and plunging into unconsciousness. Von Damme would return, and all would be lost. Troy must let Elke know how to destroy the master vampire.

Troy continued to slip. His fingers slid, scrabbling for a hold on the blood-slick surface. They found a knot hole in the tabletop, managing to grasp it. He felt stuck. He wouldn't let loose, and he didn't have the strength to pull himself up. His fingers began to grow numb and tremble. Clinging on was pointless. He had to stand. He tried to surge afoot, but felt like there was nothing to fuel him.

Even so, suddenly, he felt a boost, like someone had grabbed each arm and lifted. In a rush, he found himself sprawled on the table top. After a rest, he managed to push up until he stood. Again, he thought he sensed a helping hand. His vision steadied enough he noticed the two apparitions standing next to him. He immediately recognized Spider who smiled and gave him a thumb up. The second ghost patted him on the back, and Troy felt a tingling. He glanced over at the dead bodies, seeing Spider and Maxwell.

"Thanks, Home," Troy whispered.

He noted the light sources, three lanterns along with two rusty candelabra full of burning tapers. He must snuff those and leave only one source of illumination.

When Troy tried to walk, the world whirled around him. He pretended he was on a wild ride that was gradually slowing down. He didn't know if he had the strength, but he had the Dark Lady's orders to fulfill and women he loved to protect. He baby-walk-cruised, using the furniture to help keep him upright. He prayed Von Damme would stay gone long enough, that he had many followers to check, because Troy felt he moved at a glacial pace, while time raced.

He finally reached the nearest light, a Coleman gas-powered lantern and turned it off, dimming the chamber. Next, he clicked off the Eddie Bauer battery light. He left the lantern hanging from the ceiling and staggered over to the candles. He didn't have the strength to blow them out, so he snuffed them with his fingers.

Now the room only had one light source. Spider and Homer's ghosts were clearer now. They silently exhorted him to hurry. The shadows waited, stark and sharp, ready to be walked. Did Troy sense them waiting to come through? Or Von Damme striding nearer, about to walk through the door and crush his hopes?

No more thinking. Just do. Troy said a prayer, as well as giving thanks for ghostly aid, then he touched his forehead, finding fresh blood. He used it to outline the edge of the shadow, putting his entire focus into it. This would save many lives, many of those he loved. He had to work to get saliva, finally coughing up phlegm, then he spat on the blood. Next, the final step, he breathed on it, adding air to the other elements.

According to instructions, this should open the Shadowlands gate. He would anchor it, if he could stay awake long enough. Either he was losing consciousness, or the cave was collapsing on him.

Forty-Four: Dam Explosives

Troy had another strange dream, this one hopeful. Dillon and Elke's bodyguard thrall, Mr. Thick, slid out of the shadows. Dillon joined him and knelt next to Troy. Thick stopped before the lockbox where Von Damme had left his fire opal amulet and necklace. Thick pushed a gum into the locks, then he turned his attention to the dial.

"Troy, man, we're here. Things are about to get really hectic and chaotic, so you need to rise like a phoenix and fly," Dillon said.

"Did Silke make it out?" Troy asked.

"Yes, Desiree brought everyone out but you. Silke is so angry she could spit nails while going crazy worrying about you, so she holds me personally responsible for your safe return."

Dillon handed Troy a water bottle. "Drink this. It's not blood, but an energy drink specifically designed to rejuvenate people like you."

Troy sat up, taking the bottle. "I know how to kill Von Damme," he moaned.

"Fantastic! Elke will want to hear this," Dillon said. He checked the room for guards, pausing for a moment at the corpses to close Spider's eyes. After a brief farewell prayer, Dillon stuck a chair in front of the door to the tunnels before returning to Troy. "I expected guards."

"I hear a bunch of them are ill," Troy said. He guzzled the energy drink. His headache vanished along with his double vision and the shakes. Dillon offered Troy a hand and pulled him afoot.

"Desiree helped by dumping poisons into their food and water."

"I thought she just set explosives."

"As you were supposed to think. You weren't supposed to know in case Von Damme caught you. Elke, my love, it is clear."

Troy didn't see his reason for living anywhere. Where was she?!

Moments later, Elke sashayed into the room, exiting a shadow. Nothing else mattered. His senses were full of her scent, the sound of her lithe movement, and the uplifting sight of her beauty. She was dressed in all black, like a sexy burglar with her gorgeous blond hair tied in a ponytail and covered by a dark net. Cosmetics had darkened her skin to the color of chocolate. He noticed she carried a satchel under her arm.

Troy beamed. Just having her near energized him. He knew what she longed to know. How to destroy Von Damme!

"How excellent to see you, Troy. This is going well so far. I am sorry for your pain and losses. I am thrilled to see that you live despite Von Damme," she told him.

Like a pet hound, Troy basked in her praise. "As you

thought, mistress, the dream memories confused him, and Mona's ghost further disoriented him. I gather she was a favorite. I believe I know how to destroy him. It will take bringing everything together at the mansion; the necklace, the jewelry box, and Von Damme, and then blowing it all to Hell."

"Then the ploy worked. I have the jewelry box with me," she said, patting the hard leather bag then Troy, making him want to lean against her for further rubbing. "And, Bryson, wonderful, you have done it!"

"Yes, Mistress," Thick replied. He stepped aside and gestured inside the safe to the necklace. The opals flashed and gleamed sullenly in the firelight. Troy had a feeling they didn't want to leave.

Troy's mistress strolled over, took out a small wand to lift the necklace and placed it inside the jewelry box in the satchel held by Dillon. The opals joined the letter opener and stick pen. Elke added the black pearl bracelet to the box. Somewhere, the master vampire screamed.

"Von Damme will be coming," Elke said.

"He already is," Troy said.

"Wonderful. You two are connected. That will work to our advantage," Elke said. She entrusted Troy with the hard leather satchel holding the jewelry box. "You're right. This must be taken back to the mansion. It contains all that was removed from there, except his diaries and a cufflink. We never found it. It could still be on Marader's boat for all we know."

Troy had no idea. His recollection was muddled. "I believe Denny weakened Von Damme when he took back his black essence," Troy said.

Elke stared into his eyes and saw what he had experienced. "You are correct. Von Damme is finally vulnerable, as that little spark of good will work against him, but he remains powerful."

"I know," Troy said.

"Mistress, I am sorry to interrupt, but I also found this," Thick said.

He held up one of Aunt Jada's ankh necklaces. It had been Silke's.

"Excellent, give it to Mr. Bane," she commanded.

Thick ambled over and handed the ankh to Troy. He scrutinized it, finding one of Silke's hairs tangled in it. It felt comfortable around his neck, the ankh snug on his chest. "Thanks, Bryson," Troy said.

Elke patted the bodyguard's cheek. "Well done," she praised. He beamed, lucky dog.

Elke turned her attention back to Troy.

He straightened up, pretending he wasn't beat.

"Von Damme will chase you, Troy. You must stay ahead of him and do what we cannot. We will slow him here. J-Man is waiting with a helicopter to lift you out of here and take you to the lake. There, you must find Marader's boat. It carries the explosives you need. Stop them from blowing up the dam and commandeer the boat, which is already loaded with dive gear, and take the jewelry box to the mansion. Von Damme will follow you. When he does, set off the explosives. Escape if you can but fulfill the mission first. Farewell," Elke said and kissed him good-bye on the forehead, as if to bestow knowledge or a blessing.

At first, Troy thought it was the kiss that rocked him, but tremors caused dust and stones to fall and tumble from the ceiling and walls. He heard a second explosion, creating an earthquake. To stay on his feet, he leaned against the table as it scooted across the floor.

Elke slapped him lightly on the cheek. "Hear me. Stay focused. This is a war. The attack has started. You know my wishes. We will delay Von Damme. Now, go!" she commanded him. She guided Troy to an open door once hidden by a bookshelf lined with ingredient bottles. Dillon stood next to it.

"I'm going to take him to the exit," Dillon said.

Elke seized him. They engaged in a sizzling kiss that sent Troy into Von Damme's personal escape tunnel. Troy needed to get out of here. No time for kisses. On the other hand, if you were soon to die, taking time for kisses made sense. He shoved aside envy. No time for emotions. This was do and die.

He could smell a slight breeze, fresh smoky air, among the earthy confines. He definitely preferred the outdoors to the underground world. He would have made a pathetic vampire.

The satchel felt extremely heavy. He wondered if Von Damme could sense it moving, like a part of him leaving. Without the necklace, Von Damme would be unable to regain his full strength, so he would chase it and Troy. Back in the day, the Rulers of Night had no idea how to destroy Von Damme, so they had imprisoned him. The mansion had absorbed some of his evil undead essence and prolonged his existence. Now, the prison was part of the master vampire.

Dillon caught up with Troy. "I want to say I'm sorry about this. It's taken a horrible toll, but we must stop and destroy Von Damme. I wish I could go with you but the water. . ."

"Save Silke and Elke and a whole lot of people. I get it. It's a more productive way to go than having a mountain fall on you," Troy said.

"This mountain can still fall on us. We aren't out of here yet," Dillon said when another explosion shook the ground. Dirt fell from the ceiling, making it difficult to see and breathe.

That didn't stop Dillon from talking.

"Our original plan was to take you out the tunnels while the guards were busy throwing up. It gives us a window while they're weak. Von Damme and his five will cause the most problems."

Troy noticed a growing dimness. Moonlight peeked in somewhere ahead. He smelled fresh smoke and figured the exit was nearby. He had been listening for heartbeats, but so far, so good. Unless it was a vampire who had no heartbeat. Troy could hear Dillon breathe and talk and move, but his heart had stopped beating. Perhaps vampires needed to feed to keep their blood moving.

"I don't know how Von Damme knew Aunt Jada, but he hated her, so he plans to punish Silke, and likely most of my friends, too, those he hasn't killed already," Troy said, thinking of Spider, John, Pete, Pat, and Walt. Sadly, Troy knew they were a drop in the bucket of blood, and it would get worse. Due to Deputy Burt Glazier, traitor, it was unlikely law enforcement would thwart Von Damme or the boatload of explosives.

"Unbelievable about Marader," Dillon said.

Troy grunted. "And Deputy Burt. I never suspected. Why would I?"

"Vampires are literal control freaks," Dillon said.

"You'll be a great one."

"What does that mean?" Dillon snapped.

Ahead, splinters of nighttime dimness pierced the cavernous darkness. Troy was amazed to see the difference, and yet, both were brighter than the Shadowlands. With another few steps, Troy could see it was an old wooden door barred from this side. It had been reinforced with metal framing and grating. Troy listened. He heard nothing but the wind through brittle branches, causing a clatter like bones rattling.

"When you get away from here," Dillon began.

The exit door was yanked open so fast it seemed to suck the air out of the small tunnel. A white hand seized Troy. He wasn't surprised to see Zane, so Troy's reactions were swift. He countered, head-butting Paleface before he could speak to use his compelling power. That staggered the undead monster, clearing the exit for Dillon. Troy landed atop Zane and unleashed his rage, furiously pummeling Paleface.

The vampire ignored the blows and shoved Troy in the chest. The force sent him flying and tumbling until he slammed into a tree, numbing his right arm. Stupid. He wasn't the Incredible Hulk, getting stronger when angry. Emotions would get him killed. He must use his brain and will power. He laughed insanely. He would need a shit load, no, a heaven load of luck to survive this day.

Where was the satchel? He had lost his grip on it. He

visually searched, starting to panic when he didn't see it on the ground. It was difficult to find anything with the winds swirling, carrying debris. Troy noticed sparks. This area had yet to burn, but it seemed that was about to change.

"Run!" Dillon shouted.

"There is nowhere to run! A storm is coming!" Zane yelled. Through the loud winds, Troy thought he heard a freight train.

Locomotives thundered through in the area, but they weren't close enough to be this loud. Branches broke from tree tops, falling as window makers. Troy saw one coming and dodged. He couldn't leave without the satchel and jewelry box.

Dillon tackled Zane. The two vampires fought like cats, claws out, swift attacks blurring, slashing, swiping, darting, dodging and colliding, tearing pieces out of each other.

Where was the damned jewelry box? Troy wondered. He couldn't lose it. He should be able to feel the cursed thing. Black in a burnt forest at night didn't make it any easier to spot. Out of the corner of his eye, he saw movement, a swinging, thinking something might be attacking him, and discovered the satchel hanging by its strap in the branches of a nearby tree.

He leapt up, three times as high as he should be able, and snapped the branch from the tree as he grabbed the strap. He landed with the jewelry box and a small club.

Troy looked for Dillon, wondering if he needed help. Dillon had the advantage, sitting atop Zane and battering him. Dillon seemed unaware that a werewolf stalked him. A yell would warn his friend, causing him to turn, but then Zane would retaliate. Even now, Troy couldn't run fast enough to intercept.

Troy slung the satchel around like a throwing hammer, and then he let the whole thing go. It sailed trailing a leather tail. Troy thought he had missed, but the werewolf paused, as if he sensed something amiss. The monster got his claws up too late. The silver box caved in his head and nearly tore it from his neck.

Dillon glanced over as Troy retrieved the satchel. "Thanks. Holy Mother of God," Dillon gasped, gaping up at the sky. Wide-eyed, he took in the storm. "Go! Go!"

Troy turned, not wanting to believe his eyes. The black, ash and cinder choked clouds roiled low across the forest. A spinning funnel dropped down, whirling with flames to create mother nature's most angry beast, a fire tornado. All at once, it uprooted and burned trees, flinging them and hurling rocks.

Caught between vampires and a firenado, it just kept getting better, Troy thought. He couldn't go back inside, so he would have to outrun a tornado teaming up with a wildfire. It would play hell with J-Man trying to pilot the helicopter to evacuate him.

Troy fled. Off to his left, he heard gunfire. It was the guns he couldn't hear that concerned him. He darted ahead, slowing some, keeping his movement erratic as he fled through the charred desolation, keeping the roaring tornado to his back. The undead hiding among the smoking disaster seemed appropriate. Several small fires remained, casting a flickering and feeble light. Long, hopeless shadows seemed to wander the smoldering landscape.

He felt like this inside. Even so, there were patches of green, so it wasn't completely hopeless, it just seemed impossible. And yet, he believed in miracles. God, he couldn't let this happen to his home town.

Troy glanced up at the sky. Not all of it was cloud covered, and this wooded area had been cleared by a spot fire. He found the Big Dipper then the north star, calculating the direction to the lake, northerly and about three miles. The tornado would be on his right, to the east, moving who knew which way. Knowing his luck, it spun its way into his path.

A victorious bellow shredded the air.

"Troy! Come back here!" Zane compelled.

Troy felt the tug but ignored it. What had happened to Dillon? Had Zane killed him? Troy started to slow, thinking of turning around. He didn't trust Zane, the storm came from that direction, and yet . . .

"Run!" Dillon gasped. It wasn't loud, but the word carried on the smoky breeze, even as Dillon sounded stabbed.

Troy turned his run into a sprint. Unleashing his supernatural power, he bounded in long, leaping strides, passing over large stretches of ground, springing over fire-shriveled bushes and by dead and smoldering trees. The wind increased, whipping up ash devils to scurry about, and the hungry moan of the tornado grew louder. It either grew bigger or bounded closer. He couldn't see, squeezing his way through a thick copse of birches.

How could he leave Dillon, even if he had betrayed Troy?

Dillon was Silke's brother. Yes, I left him to die.

Elke's words powered through it all, driving Troy on. Somewhere, J-Man, if he hadn't been shot down or set afire, would swoop down like an angel of mercy and pluck him from this hell hole. Troy had to make himself accessible by getting far away from the fire.

He saw stars across his vision and stumbled, ready to black out, so he paused to slow his racing breath and leaned against a half-burnt oak. He rested his heart, feeling too close to collapse. He couldn't rest long. He could feel Zane getting closer.

Troy downed the last of the water bottle, feeling its power kick in, energizing him. Even invigorated, he doubted he could stay ahead of Zane for very long. Troy knew he had to try. So many were depending on him. Elke should have recruited a track star, Troy grumbled and broke into a sprint, evading trees and falling branches.

"Jay, I could really use a lift, now."

Their howls finding him first, werewolves now chased Troy. He slowed to unstrap Dillon's knife, checking to ensure the silver blade would clear the sheath when he needed it to cut.

Which would catch him first? Werewolves? Zane? Or the tornado?

None of the above. Exhaustion would catch him first. The others would finish him.

No! He ran faster. He would not fail Elke. He had already put her in danger by letting Von Damme learn her name.

Troy heard Zane high speed bulldoze through the charred forest. He raced closer with each passing second.

"Jay, the man who can fix anything, I am in a fix that needs fixing!" Troy breathed.

Closer, though, he heard a fast and powerful heartbeat. A sentry found him and sprang. Troy drew the knife and whirled, using a judo move to let go of the satchel, grab the wolf by the hair, and use its momentum to slam it into the tree trunk. He killed the stunned beast by driving the silver blade into the back of its neck.

Troy stared at the beast reverting into a long-haired and gray-bearded man. What was happening to him? Killing something should have severely upset Troy, but it didn't. He was desperate, he told himself, this was life and death, or perhaps more, immortal souls and love at stake. Either that, or his soul was broken. Would his sensei have been proud?

From too close and all around, a pack of wolves howled, lamenting a downed brother. When they found Troy, he would be the target of their fury.

Zane would catch him first. With each passing moment, Paleface drew closer, using some vampire mojo to move faster.

A large branch smashed into the trunk of the tree above Troy. Chunks rained down upon him. The tornado's train roar began to make it difficult to think, and he felt the heat rise.

Keep running. Each step might bring salvation. Thank heavens he had run often during his rehab, trying to regain his stamina.

The winds screamed through the forest, tearing away more leaves and branches. To his right, a tree fell, stopping against two others. The crown of another tree broke off and crashed to the earth ahead of Troy. He avoided it and redoubled his efforts. He had a feeling he was too close to the fire for J-Man to reach him, but the flaming whirlwind seemed to be chasing Troy, along with everything else.

Time lost meaning as Troy grew weary, his legs leaden. He stumbled, sensing the pack of werewolves and Zane closing in. The first manwolf bounded toward him, a leap away when a bullet dropped him. The second shot missed, off target, whining off a rock, before two more accurate slugs struck the nearest beasts. The last set of gunfire had sounded different, like there were a pair of snipers. The remaining werewolf paused, looking around, seeking the shooter. It sounded to Troy like the gunfire hailed from the treetops.

J-Man must be near!

Grateful for cover fire, Troy kept stumbling. He had to put some distance between he and Zane. Otherwise, Troy would never make it inside the helicopter.

Finally, during lulls between the howling wind and roar of the flames, Troy heard rotary blades whup-whupping, sounding like hope. Somebody from up there continued to unload their ammo clip, now targeting Zane as he closed in on Troy. Paleface paused to toy with his prey, now fifty feet, a mere leap away from Troy.

A bullet struck Zane. He smiled as the gaping wound quickly healed. "I don't know who your friends are, but the fools are wasting their time. Soon, they're going to find out the hard way. Oh, by the way, Dillon is dead. I shoved a tree branch through his heart, so there is no hope of rescue for you."

Troy hadn't felt Dillon die. Vampires lied with each breath, defying truth and life. But, Troy felt Silke above. His heart beat fast, fluttering and panicking like a trapped bird.

"Your friends in the flying machine above, the whirly bird, they cannot hurt me," he said. When two more bullets hit him, he looked up and flipped them the bird. "You know that old saying about words never hurting you, but sticks and stones can?" Zane knelt to pick up a large rock. He hefted it, ready to throw. "I will enjoy watching it crash and burn and hearing you scream."

Troy tackled Zane. With a snarl, the vampire whirled and pounced on him. Troy used the jewelry box to block the rain of blows, then he rammed it forward, slamming it into the vampire's jaw. Zane's head rocked back, but he recovered with supernatural speed. He spat on Troy even as he ripped the satchel out of Troy's hand and tossed it aside.

"Von Damme needs you alive, but only barely breathing. This is for the trouble you have caused. Be glad I don't toss you like a stone," Zane said.

Troy tried to buck him off and block the blows. Even when he did, Troy thought the bones in his arms might break. Zane spat in Troy's eye as he reached through his guard to choke him. Troy impotently kneed him and thrashed, trying to slip free and breathe. The ankh grew hot.

"What makes you so stubborn? Is it because you have already died? I see it, though you may not. It is love, futile, impotent love for your family, lovers, and friends. It will avail you nothing. When you awaken, it will be to the glorious sight of Von Damme and blinding pain."

How could he see if he was blind? Troy stupidly wondered. His mind played tricks on him. Zane's head appeared to be smoking. The vampire winced.

"Your religious trinket will not stop me," Zane snarled. Paleface spat again. Or did he?

Was that rain? More likely, condensation from the copter. Or melted hail coming out of the fire tornado, Troy thought absurdly. His chest was afire. He felt ready to combust.

A water drop landed on his cheek. Another splattered on his forehead. Crazily, he thought of being baptized.

"I think they got wise and stopped shooting, but not so wise as to fly away. The tornado will take care of them, or I will. I can jump that high once you turn into a limp sack of meat. Huh, I do believe it's raining," Zane said. He ignored his smoldering hands and arms.

Suddenly, the vampire arched back in pain. Zane howled

and tried to jump away.

Troy felt the rain. For some reason, it hurt Zane. Then he must not escape, Troy thought. He desperately hung on, dragging the vampire back to the ground.

A splash of water struck.

It was the first drop from a bucket. A temporal waterfall poured over them, tons of gallons of water usually dumped to fight forest fires cascaded over them. Troy felt pinned by the liquid onslaught.

Through the deluge, he watched Zane wash away. The water drops must have been blest, because the vampire dissolved as though he had been made of salt. Troy smiled as he watched the holy downpour strip Zane down to bones. Those shrank like he had been a sand sculpture, then there was nothing left but smoke and an acrid, wet stench.

Troy thanked God and his friends, at the least J-Man and whoever was shooting. Jambo? He was a crack shot. He would need to be as more werewolves closed in. How many did Von Damme have in his service?

A pack of four charged Troy. They never saw the attack from above.

This time, J-Man didn't use bullets. He dropped the bucket on the werebeasts. It slammed them into the ground and draped over them, entrapping them.

The helicopter lowered Troy a rope ladder. It thrashed back and forth in the whirling winds. He grabbed the satchel and agilely scrambled up and dragged himself into the helicopter, only to be immediately assaulted.

He reeled back. How had Von Damme gotten here?

"It's not every day you see a fire tornado, plus, water erode away somebody to nothing. We are so out of here. We should be playing the lotto," J-Man announced, even as the wind pushed the helicopter sideways. "Hang onto your hats!"

"Troy, my love, thank heavens!" Silke cried. She threw her arms around him, kissing him.

Troy rebelled, throwing Silke off and almost leaping out the door. He stared at her, trying to tell himself she wasn't Von Damme, though he could still feel the fingernails in his throat. "I'm sorry, Silke. I thought you were . . . Von Damme," he replied. Wait. Had she said love? When had that happened? What had he forgotten? It didn't matter. If he was successful, he was dead. Worse, if he failed he was dead and many he loved would die, too.

He glanced outside, watching a tree flying by. He thanked God it missed them. Now, from above the forest, he could see the tornado, wrapped in fire, lay waste to the woods. It left a black scar behind to mark the devastation.

Even as J-Man put distance between them and the storm, the winds continued to shake the copter. It whistled through the bullet holes in the windshield. Sticks and stones swirled and pelted the cabin like hail. J-Man was humming REO's "Riding the Storm Out".

"It's horrible, all of it, except you're here now. Thank you, love, for saving me. What's wrong?" Silke asked. She had started to embrace him, until she noticed him recoiling. "What has Von Damme done to you?"

Left me empty, Troy almost said. Not empty. Poisoned. He didn't have time to be maudlin, and yet, with the sorrow he carried, Troy was amazed they could be airborne. He felt leaden.

"A moment. J-Man take us toward the dam. Look for a boat. It might even be Marader's Maverick. We have to stop it. It's full of explosives meant to blow a hole in the dam, flood everything and empty the lake so Von Damme and his zealots can return home and enact vengeance upon the locals whose relatives approved the dam and strangers who had nothing to do with it," Troy called up to his friend.

"Well, hello to you, too. I guess we shake a leg, huh? I'll have to swing wide, take a little more time and give the tornado some space. Twisters are erratic and while I like harnessing the power of spinning, that's just way too much," J-Man said. He steered them higher, above the tree tops to speed northwesterly before turning east.

"Hey, thank you for the shower and saving my butt," Troy said.

"Saving your sorry ass is what I'm here for. Thank Father Dennis next time you see him. He blessed the water. He's with Knives on a boat in Riddle Creek Cove," J-Man said. "Besides, I believe we owe you a debt for getting everyone out of the gulag."

"Spider didn't make it, but he helped me out."

"I knew you would come. How can we help, my love? I would like some payback," Silke said. She patted a scoped Remington hunting rifle. For a woman who had recently endured capture, she looked beautiful. A mischievous glint shone in her eyes above a fierce smile. He felt a confusing mixture of joy and sadness.

Again, she had said my love. What had he forgotten? Were they dating? "That's a good look for you and Jambo."

From the front passenger seat, Jambo grinned and adjusted his infrared goggles. He replaced the clip in the rifle, silver flashing from the shells' heads. "Thanks, I'm glad I've been keeping up the target shooting even if I'm not getting in enough huntin'. Silke, though, she's a mean sniper. She said you died again, and I can believe it. You look as pale as a Canadian."

"I'd say death microwaved over," J-Man said.

"Not very warm," Troy said.

"I think you're hot," Silke said.

The helicopter swayed dangerously. For a moment, Troy thought they were sideways. He hung onto a strap, trying not to fall on Silke.

He had to look away from her and glanced out the window. He couldn't see the fire tornado any longer, but the winds were still powerful, bending trees, breaking a few, and turning branches into missiles.

Troy looked back to Silke. By the way she watched him, he knew something was wrong, but he didn't know what, except she had called him love. He had no memory of her saying it before. "I'm sorry if I hurt you, Silke. I'm a mental mess. Von Damme tortured me and stole memories, but I know what I have to do."

"Stole memories? God damn Von Damme! I knew something was wrong. Why do you flinch when you look at me?" she asked, hurt in her beautiful eyes. They were full of radiant love that touched something inside him, even if forgotten. Troy turned away again. His heart ached and panicked at the same time.

"Why do I scare you? Besides I carry a gun and my brother once tried to kill you," Silke said.

"Von Damme took, uh, your form while he extracted what he wanted from me. He used John and others, too."

"So, when you see me, you see . . . him?" Silke asked.

"Silke, I don't have time to feel, just do. Our first priority is to save the dam. Von Damme's thralls plan to remove it so he can restore his mansion, the seat of his power and revive the glory days. Some of his vigor and life force are connected to it. That place needs to die, too. You know, I really sound insane."

"You do," Jambo agreed.

"This is insane," J-Man muttered.

"I'll throw out open-minded," Silke said. She scooted closer. He felt like a young boy, trapped between incredible fear and irresistible beauty. He also realized too much would die if Von Damme succeeded.

"And you plan to do this how?" Jambo asked.

"Stop those with the dynamite stolen from Rentzel construction. They're on a boat heading for the dam. Marader is leading the party."

"You're shittin' me," J-Man snapped.

"He accepted thralldom on the way to being a vampire."

"Huh?"

"He's a servant of the vampires," Silke said. She watched Troy carefully.

"Like I said, he's on the boat with the explosives," Troy

said.

"Oh, of course he is," Silke said. She wiped away a tear. "Troy, look at me."

He did, but he couldn't hold her gaze. He could see falling in love with her. Or could have.

"Are you a thrall, too?" she asked.

Troy nodded. "And a pawn."

"Can we just blow up the boat?" Jambo asked.

"Anyone have any explosives? No? Hey, I see our boys," J-Man said. He made a brief radio call. "Knives, this is J-Man. Package has been picked up. Heading for boat with explosives near dam."

"Say again, please?" Knives asked. When J-Man repeated himself, Knives coughed. "You're pulling my leg."

"No, I'm dead serious. Be on the lookout for a boat, possibly Marader's, near the dam. Considered armed and dangerous. Over."

Troy peered down. "So, whatever they're using, I need some of it to blow up Von Damme's underwater mansion of doom."

"You're not going back there," Silke said incredulously. She grabbed his arm. He managed to resist yanking free.

"It's necessary. The boat has diving gear. I need a tank and regulator, too," Troy said, ignoring her pleas. "Silke, I would like to leave this all behind, but Van Damme knew Aunt Jada, hated Aunt Jada, so you're near the top of his torture list. He said she had allied with the Rulers of Night."

"Really?" Silke blurted, sitting stunned.

"Please, let me do what I think I can do to stop him. Don't make it any harder."

Silke grew quiet and crossed her arms. She was ready to cry, and he struggled to compartmentalize his feelings. "I wish it were otherwise. Jay, I'm going to use the ladder to drop down on Marader's boat."

"Well, that sounds downright action hero like. Do I get to lay down cover fire?" Jambo asked.

"You're having too much fun."

"Jambo rhymes with Rambo."

"Get ready to shoot anybody that isn't me," Troy said.

"I see three, check that, make that four, heat readings ahead. One is really hot," Jambo said. He adjusted his goggles. "We're coming up fast."

"You're really going back there?! Why you?!" Silke asked.

"Von Damme will be after me. He didn't tear all of what he wanted from me. He was too busy messing around. I'm still tainted," Troy said.

"Oh, God. No. No!" Silke screamed. She threw her arms around Troy.

"Hey, calm down back there!" J-Man yelled.

"You're going to bait Von Damme down there and blow yourself up!" Silke cried.

Troy sensed Von Damme in the distance, frustrated by something. Maybe the fire tornado slowed him. They could use as much good luck as possible.

"Blow up the mansion. I'll try to get out," Troy said. He would try. There wasn't any way, but he would try.

"You can't do this!"

"Silke, I'm doing this for you and my friends. I . . . don't recall what we had, but I assume it was amazing, as you are, as it has inspired me to go to desperate lengths," he said. Elke was keeping him alive long enough to destroy Von Damme. He hoped that Martin was right and that being a hero worked out. He started to give Silke his ankh, but she stopped him.

"I have one, and you need its protection more than I do. I am glad it doesn't burn you," Silke said.

J-Man steered them lower. The thick, coiling smoke made seeing difficult, worse than acrid fog, but Troy thought he spotted heat, too. He could make out four figures.

"Cover me and wish me luck," he told Silke. He looked down, took the rope ladder in hand, and prepared to leap. It wasn't more than forty feet, Troy judged. J-Man would swing him around.

"I love you more than life," Silke told him as she forced herself into his arms. She kissed him like it was her right.

It felt as natural as inhaling, as if he had just rediscovered breathing, so he savored her. Silke was reason enough. Von Damme would never leave her alone. Troy wished he didn't have to leave her. "Aunt Jada said if I survive this week, I will live a long interesting life. You would be very interesting."

"I am and will be," she corrected him.

The helicopter flew nearer, and Troy could see more clearly. Two figures were at the helm and bow, while two more stood on the stern deck, handing down containers to a fifth in the water. A sixth already had his load and dove. He would be swimming explosives to the dam. Troy was already running a little late.

"See y'all," Troy said. In this life or the next, he thought and launched himself out of the helicopter.

Forty-Five: Explosive Surprises

Troy had leapt out of helicopters before to parachute, ski, and bungee jump. The rope ladder wasn't made of the same flexible material. He hoped it didn't snap. He wanted to laugh crazily during the plummet, but he remained quiet. He hoped to stay unnoticed while the zealots of Von Damme focused on the loudly approaching red helicopter and its blinking lights.

His leap carried him out and away. Here it comes, Troy thought, the end jerk. It should pull his shoulders out of their sockets, except he was tougher now, a thrall, stronger than human. At least he hoped it worked that way. If it didn't, he would go splat and sink like a stone.

When he reached the end of his rope, which seemed symbolic, it snapped taut. It tried to flick him off as if he were at the end of a whip, but he kept a death grip. Through clenched teeth he screamed at the pain in all his joints, from his fingers, wrists, elbows, shoulders, and neck, along his spine. His legs lashed out, and then he was swinging around and taking aim.

Troy couldn't hear anything with the wind howling past his ears and the whupping of the helicopter until one of the men in the bow of the boat started shooting. Troy saw the flashes then heard the gun blasts. He thanked the Lord for small blessings. The guns weren't automatic nor aimed at him. They fired at the helicopter and his friends. He had to stop that.

It looked like the zealots had already unloaded about half the TNT, but there seemed to be enough remaining to demolish a haunted house. Four thralls stood in his way, two on the back ski deck and two near the wheel.

He set his feet to take the impact and deliver the blow. The man next to the gunman noticed Troy first. Number One thrall yelled, redirecting his weapon to unload at Troy. Number Two joined in, blasting away.

Troy recognized Number One. Deng! It was the bastard who had kidnapped Silke!

Troy wished he could correct his swing by a foot, but he didn't dare. It might throw him completely off. Missing would be disastrous. He twisted to aim for Deng. This was for Silke!

A hot needle ripped across Troy's right ear. A second bullet whistled past his left shoulder. A searing pain, like that of a knife, grazed his ribs. It was the last thing he felt before impact.

Heels first, Troy drove his feet into Deng, hearing bones crunch. The bastard tumbled backwards, arms flailing, trigger finger twitching. His gun sprayed bullets before going overboard. Slugs hit the muscular Number Three standing aft on the ski platform. He jerked twice and collapsed onto the smaller man next to him.

Marader? Marader!

"Troy? What are you . . ." Marader asked as he lost his balance.

He and Number Three fell off Maverick into the lake.

The traitor was here. Well, Troy didn't have time for petty revenge. But, he was willing to run Tommy Boy over if he got in the way.

Number One was kneeling and cradling his face, blood pouring through his fingers. Troy grabbed Deng, the supposed Paparazzi, in a judo hold and enjoyed tossing him overboard.

Now Troy felt a burning atop his chest. Oh, no, Lord no. The ankh had grown very hot, meaning a vampire must be near. He hadn't seen a vampire from above, but it must be here.

Up in the helicopter, they must have seen a figure moving. Silke and Jambo fired several shots. They found their target, eliciting grunts of acknowledgment from the vampire.

Even if the bullets didn't hurt the undead monster, it bought Troy a few seconds. He lunged into the driver's seat, gassed the throttle, turned the key, and gunned the motor to start. Maverick roared to life.

"Stop the boat," Lyla commanded. The Dark Lady rode with him.

Elke commands helped Troy resist Lyla's compelling. He threw the boat into gear. Maverick's bow rose, sending gear bounding and rolling along the floor.

"Stop the boat, now!" the vampire demanded.

Troy glanced in the rearview mirror. Despite the Maverick's wild movements, the original Dark Lady stood balanced and steady. Black eyes glaring, Lyla began to order Troy again. He kicked out at a life vest. The wind caught it and smacked her in the face, stifling the command. It gave Troy another chance to spin the wheel.

Maverick veered and swerved, like it was trying to lose a rider on an inner tube. Uncannily in balance, Lyla took two steps, reaching for Troy. She ignored two more bullets striking her and smiled.

Troy spun the wheel. This time, a dive tank broke loose and dangerously bounded into her, buckling her knee. That gave Troy a moment to take the ankh in hand.

Lyla recovered quickly. She body-slammed Troy and shoved his head into the windshield, breaking the Plexiglas and stunning him. She shifted her grip to choke him and bore down.

Troy struggled to hold back her strength. How could she feel like she weighed a ton? His throat burned. His lungs ached as he couldn't breathe.

The slight bouncing of the boat seemed to add pressure to the choking. Troy failed in every attempt to wiggle or slip free. Lyla threw him to the floor and stomped on his head. The world jiggled, his vision scrambled along with all thoughts, except he knew that he was failing Elke.

"You will lie there and watch me blow up this unnatural wall, setting us free once more to roam through the fog and the mountains," Lyla announced.

Troy thought he was hypoxic and delusional when he saw Marader, the traitorous bastard, somehow still alive, crawl hand over hand onto the back sun platform. His fingers seemed unnaturally long, their nails even longer. He kept low, crouching to sneak up on Lyla.

Troy could see clearly now, so he was confused when Marader reached down and grabbed the remote detonator. He grinned and winked while he raised a finger to his lips.

Be quiet? Troy couldn't breathe. Or spit. Or curse!

With mock casualness, Marader pressed and activated the remote. Troy prayed it wasn't connected to the TNT in the boat.

Lyla steered Maverick back around in time to face the underwater explosion. Her white face lit up with the flash of light then surprise, as a geyser of water erupted from the lake. The sound waves struck the boat, then the surface rollers hit as the lake bucked. Maverick thrashed, its hull bouncing, the boat bounding.

"What the Nine Hells?!" Lyla cursed.

Troy rolled into her legs and pressed his hands holding the ankh into her left thigh. Flesh seared then melted, even as Lyla screamed and arched in pain.

Marader seized Lyla and put her in a full nelson as he

hauled her out of the driver's seat.

"You are fools, especially you, turncoat. I am vampire. I have been gifted by Von Damme. I no longer fear the sunlight, nor even the waters. As long as I keep my wits and head about me, I shall live forever," Lyla declared.

While the two struggled, Marader's hands transformed into nailed claws that dug into her undead flesh. Extra hair sprouted along his arms, and he gained a beard, mustache and bushy brows. Troy was briefly shocked.

Marader was a werewolf?

Well, it would explain a lot. What else didn't Troy know about the world? His mind raced. What had Desiree said? What killed a vampire? Sunlight? Not tonight. Holy water? Not handy. Lyla claimed the water wouldn't injure her.

That left decapitating her. Or, just throwing her overboard. He preferred to destroy her, but right now, they needed to stay ahead of Von Damme and get the TNT to the underwater mansion.

"And you, werewolf, are a lesser species," Lyla said. Her arms bent unnaturally, allowing her to slip free of Marader's hold. The vampire's joints popped into place, then she backhanded him, sending him staggering back into the padded bench. He clung there to keep from tumbling out.

Troy climbed into the pilot's chair. If he drove crazily now, he would throw his blood brother over the side. It was tempting, but in this case, he preferred the werewolf's company to the vampire's.

Lyla glanced at Troy, thinking of retaking control of the boat. Marader threw a scuba tank at her. Lyla took a glancing blow as she knocked it away, crumpling the side of the tank. Somehow, it didn't explode.

Troy jerked the wheel and swerved starboard, trying to throw Lyla overboard. Instead, she lunged into Marader, claws slashing and ripping, cloth, fur and flesh flying. Troy tried to help, but the two were throwing each other around, both struggling to evict each other.

Von Damme was coming! Troy sensed him. Lyla was slowing them down! Troy knew they didn't have time for this. He must do something. Troy snatched up the ski rope and attached it to the anchor, getting prepared to pitch it over the side.

Marader attempted to kick Lyla off the boat. The vampire held on, and they crashed into the port wall. Lyla ripped off the copilot seat and beat Marader with the post. A crucial blow caught him on the chin, stunning him.

Troy rammed the ankh into her lower back before she could kill Marader. When Lyla snarled and twisted in pain, Troy looped the ski rope around her neck and tightened it.

Lyla slugged Troy, knocking him back. He bounced off the starboard windshield then slumped to the floor. He dizzily felt around, looking for the anchor. Any moment, Lyla would free herself of the noose. She tried to kick Troy, but Marader shot the vampire three times to distract her.

It was enough for Troy to roll and evade a blow to keep his head. Her kick sent a life vest flying up into the wind, and it was snatched away. Something hard dug into Troy's back, and he felt around, finding the anchor. He rolled, grabbed a metal fin, and hurled the weight overboard, watching its rope uncoil.

Lyla had both hands around Marader's throat, choking him. Tommy Boy's eyes bugged out, then he head-butted Lyla twice, the second flattening her bloodied nose.

The noose loop around her neck yanked her back, almost tearing her head off as the sinking anchor jerked Lyla out of the boat. She tumbled like a rag doll before slowly sinking into the lake. They couldn't waste time checking on her. Any time lost was Von Damme's gain.

Laughing wildly, Marader, still looking hairy, fierce and wolfish, turned to Troy. "I hope that killed the bitch. I would be more confident if it completely took off her head. Then the water would separate them and that might do it. Except for sunlight, vampires are as hard to kill as sexually charged rumors."

Troy blinked. He would never look at his blood brother the same again. "Who the hell are you, and what did you do with Tom Marader?"

"You shouldn't be surprised. I told you I joined a werewolf club to get hairy and get chicks. It happened while you were in the hospital in Florida, oh, about a year and a half back. Ha, you didn't take me seriously, did you? I knew you wouldn't," Marader crowed.

"Yeah, I thought you were kidding. Silke mentioned it, though. So that's why you had silver bullets."

Marader barked a laugh. "She could sense it. How is she?"

"Only slightly traumatized, angrier and sitting up in the helicopter with a rifle. I'm surprised she hasn't shot you."

"Ah she loves me, nothing like you, but well, I am charming."

"A huggable werewolf," Troy mused. There, Marader had confirmed that Silke loved him. Troy felt a lot missing and sensed a huge hole. "And is this werewolf transformation the secret that might get us killed?"

"One of them," Marader grinned. His eyes were the same, and the grin was the same, but the rest looked like a man wolf. "One detonator down, and a dam saved from Von Damme, meaning lots of lives and property saved. We should get a medal! A key to the city! But, we won't get jack. What now?"

"Von Damme is coming," Troy said. He could feel the master vampire. He tried to press the throttle forward, but they were already at top speed, faster than fifty according to the speedometer. They better not hit any floating debris. "We must take the TNT and the jewelry box down to Wreythville and blow up the mansion before he stops us."

"What good will that do?"

"End him," Troy said.

"You want me to drive? I can see fine, and you can get ready."

Troy moved and waved Marader to switch places with him, letting him drive his own boat.

"You know, going back there is absolutely crazy and death-defying daring do. I love it! Who cares if you died, what, twice? Three times? Four? My point is, you keep coming back! You fall down and die. Shake it off! Get back up!"

"I'm not counting, thanks. So you're quoting Captain America now, are you?" Troy asked.

"Is that where that came from? Listen, my brother, I work for Elke. Double agent. Super, supernatural spy. Even so, I'm not diving back down there. You shouldn't either. It's death wrapped in doom and gloom. Hey, I could be a poet! Almost dying brings out the best in me, doesn't it?" Marader grinned.

"It seems so. Tom, Elke is the air I breathe."

"Oh, man. You are so screwed. My number one rule is never kill yourself over a woman."

"She is a vampire and has commanded me to dive, taking your precious jewelry box home, along with some explosives," Troy said.

A pitying look crossed Marader's unusually hairy face. "That sucks for you."

"I thought you might want to save the box."

"Naw. I don't give a rat's ass about it. In fact, as many times as it cut me, I'll be glad to know it was blown to itty bitty bits."

"Do you know how to rig the TNT with a detonator?" Troy asked.

Marader grinned and nodded. "Oh, yeah. I rigged up the last one. It worked, didn't it? No worries. I've seen Denny do it a bunch of times!"

"Thankfully, that last load never reached its destination."

"Oh yeah it did. Took out two thralls. It's okay, they were Georgia Dawgs!" Marader chuckled. His hair began to recede, and he started to look human, like Tommy Boy again.

Troy prepared for the dive, putting a regulator on a tank and checking the gauge. 1500 PSI. That was more than enough. He wouldn't need that much air because he wouldn't be alive that long. He sought flippers that fit and a huge, old-fashioned anchor, one to drag him to the bottom. That and a heavy-duty weight belt should haul him down fast. Marader kept a specially built anchor for boat beaching, and it folded out to become three times larger to augur in sand and mud.

For a moment, Troy thought he could see through the master vampire's eyes as he extended his wings and took flight, leaving the mining caves. Did that mean Elke was dead, too? Troy couldn't stomach the thought. No, he would have felt it. Just as he assumed Dillon lived, too. "Von Damme's airborne."

"Is he? We have company. Knives is coming up on the starboard. He is taking an intercept course. Wait, there's another boat. A sheriff's boat. Damn, I'll bet it's Burt. That's all we need. Any ideas, Troy?"

As Maverick drew closer, Troy could feel the mansion below. It seemed to be calling to him. Or maybe it was calling to the Von Damme in him. It made Troy as nauseous as diesel exhaust on the roiling high seas.

"Troy? They're converging on the dive point," Marader said. Troy dug into one of the boxes of TNT. He pulled out two sticks. He found a lighter in the glove box.

"Now, the sheriff's boat is heading for us," Marader said.

Troy glanced up. The patrol boat's lights were flashing.

"Let's try a little radio," Marader said. When he turned it on, there was a blast of profanity.

"What do you think you're doing?" Deputy Burt finished.

Troy judged the distance. He recalled the deputies. Were they thralls? Compelled? On the take? Or innocent? Did he care?

Bullets sparked and pinged off the aluminum frame of the broken windshield. Guns boomed in the night, the sound loud over the water. Marader cursed and ducked. "Time for a big fire cracker. I love waterproof fuses."

"It makes my decision easier," Troy replied. He glanced over the port side. His peek was greeted by a barrage of bullets. A ricochet bit Troy in the left shoulder. At least it wasn't his throwing arm. He lit and tossed the first stick of

TNT, followed, after a wait, by a second.

The water erupted. The blast showered the front of the sheriff's boat.

Troy's second toss was accurate, landing in the bow. A second later, the front of the boat flashed, then the sound followed the explosion. Pieces spread out like a giant shotgun blast. The bow seemed to just vanish in a cloud. The canopy and windshield sailed high into the air where the wind caught them like kites. The rest of the broken boat hit waves. The back half augured, pitched and flipped, tumbling across the surface and disintegrating into a spinning cloud of debris.

"I would say there's some no longer repressed hostility there," Marader said. "First Silke. Now this. Good to see you letting your true self free."

Troy glared and returned to gearing up. Once his ears quit ringing, he heard another boat. It sounded like Knives' Stingray. Troy thought he caught a familiar, tempting scent on the wind. Silke?

"Ahoy, there!" Knives yelled. He cruised closer then put the Stingray's engine in reverse and neutral. The boat's momentum stalled, leaving about a yard between boats. Denny sat in the navigator's seat.

Hair streaming, Silke stood behind them. How had she gotten there? She must have climbed down a rope from the helicopter. She blew Troy a kiss then opened her arms.

The lake ruffled around them as J-Man guided the helicopter to hover above. Before the boats could drift apart, Denny tossed a rope. Marader caught it but didn't tie it off.

"Did you just blow up a sheriff's boat?" Knives asked.

"Yes, but they were friends of Von Damme's. Burt was his pal. If you noticed, they were shooting at us," Troy replied.

"Now, get out of here! Von Damme is coming!" Marader yelled. He tossed the rope back over. He started working on the TNT pack of Rentzel dynamite, a homecoming gift for the mansion. He bungee-cord wrapped the twelve pack of sticks to the metal anchor, giving it more weight.

"Troy, grab the rope," Silke yelled.

There was no time. Troy made sure the satchel with the jewelry box was secure. He grabbed a knife for when he wanted sudden access to it, cutting straps instead of detangling it. The box's sharp edges clung to the insides of the satchel, which looked a lot worse for wear, now sporting spikes.

"Troy, I love you!"

"What are you doing?" Denny yelled. He wore night-vision goggles. "What the blue blazes! That's company dynamite!" He encouraged Knives to drive nearer, threatening to push him aside and drive if he didn't, and then Father Dennis crazily leapt across the distance, five feet, sending both boats rocking. He landed on the rear sun platform, took two steps and started to fall overboard.

Marader grabbed him by the arm and pulled him back. "Are you deaf and dumb, Father Dennis?"

"Just full of faith. You know, I'm responsible for that TNT. I'm not letting you set off any more."

"Not me. It's Troy this time," Marader said. Denny looked dumbfounded.

"I'm going to blow up the underwater mansion," Troy said.

"I've changed my mind. That's a perfect use for it. Divinely inspired. I'm in," Father Dennis said.

"Denny, Father Dennis, this is likely a one-way trip," Troy said. Was this what he had been sent back to the living to do? Destroy Von Damme.

"This has become my mission. That place is evil. Von Damme is evil and a blight on the world. My wife and sister, dear God, after what he's done, they are hollow, now. Perhaps the vampire's demise will free them. Besides, do you know how it all works?"

"Press the button?" Troy asked.

Denny chuckled grimly. "You got a dive buddy who knows how to deal with explosives in case something doesn't go as planned. Think of me as your guardian angel on this trip, there to see the job done and get you back safely. Plus, I have a surprise for Von Damme. Time for God to make a holy stand," Father Dennis said. He showed off two of his EpiPens.

"Then hurry up. Von Damme's chasing me and the jewelry box and what's in it. I expect him at any moment. He's done something so the water won't harm him."

"Gearing up," Denny said. He shucked his shirt.

Troy made a final check of his gear. When Maverick started bucking and rocking, he almost overbalanced, thanks to his tank, and pitched over the side. Silke crashed into Troy, a full body hug, and he caught her.

"You aren't leaving without kissing me and promising you'll be back," Silke said. She had made the leap, too.

Troy didn't have time for this, but then, he might never have time for it. "Tommy, add some weight belts to the anchor."

"You might drop too fast," Marader said. Holding the homecoming gift, the jewelry box now bungee-corded on, he and Denny stood on the ski deck. Denny performed a brief blessing, then they lowered the anchor onto the ski deck.

"We'll trail bubbles," Troy said then his lips were busy. Silke kissed him, taking up all his attention. El-ke turned to Sil-ke, and he felt tenderness, longing and regret.

Silke fiercely kissed Troy. "Promise me you'll come back," she said.

"I promise I'll do whatever I can to get back," Troy said.

"Even come back from death, again, promise," she demanded.

"I promise I'll come back for you from anywhere, even death," he said. They kissed again. If he had time, he might be able to trade Elke for Silke, but he didn't have time.

"I love you," she breathed in his ear. "Let that bring you back."

Suddenly, it seemed Von Damme stood behind him. Troy felt the master vampire closing fast. The only thing that mattered was destroying the master vampire. "Denny, time to go. I love you, Silke."

Marader took out his phone and dialed J-Man. "Von Damme is flying in. I assume from the south."

"I've got a surprise for him," J-Man said.

Above them, J-Man turned the helicopter around and headed south. Screaming firework missiles shot from the underneath racks. The pyrotechnic barrage exploded with echoing booms and lit up the sky with clutching palms, sprawling chrysanthemums, angry bees, blazing peonies and a wall of white crossettes that looked like holy lattice work.

The fiery garden erupted around Von Damme. The flashes of light revealed his transformation into an avian, a werebat or bat monster. The blasts seemed to pain and infuriate him, slowing his flight. He arrested, dropping down low near the water.

Gun blasts sounded over the boat motor as Jambo fired his rifle. The slugs ripped into Von Damme's wings, making it harder for him to fly, but the wounds healed themselves too quickly, fashioning supernatural flesh anew. He seemed unstoppable.

The helicopter unleashed another fusillade. Comets streaked out to Von Damme. One exploding blast struck him, knocking him from the sky.

Troy felt the master vampire's rage churning. First, his most prized possession had been stolen, then the fire tornado had delayed him, and now, he had been affronted with mere fireworks. Troy knew they could blow off a hand or worse, but pyrotechnics would only slow Von Damme.

Having delayed too long already, Troy fell back into the lake, joining Denny. Marader lifted the anchor off the deck, letting each of them get a grip, then he dropped it into the lake, sending Troy and Denny on their one-way trip into the night time abyss of South Holston.

They plunged toward the bottom, hanging onto more than sixty pounds of weight. Troy glanced up, bubbles streaming past his face mask. The water above grew brighter.

A second later, the helicopter crashed into the lake.

Burning fuel scattered across the surface to create a fiery carpet that surrounded the craft as it slowly sank.

While Troy was dragged down, he could do nothing but pray that J-Man and Jambo would survive, and that Silke was safe. With every other breath, Troy prayed that he and Father Dennis would reach the mansion before Von Damme.

It was time for reckoning and to prove love was more powerful than hate.

Forty-Six: Death Blows

While the anchor dragged them down faster than they could dive, Troy made adjustments. The power of the plunge forced him to hold on with both hands, and the rush of the descent tried to dislodge his mask. He tucked his chin, relaxed and mentally worked to breathe normally. This wasn't exactly like a plane, or a helicopter ride, even a hike to a snowy summit, but he needed to keep the same frame of mind. Calm.

They plowed through the trashy thermocline to plummet into colder water. Without a wet suit, he keenly felt the change. The chill, especially that of the mansion of doom and death, would sap his strength, but he didn't plan on being in there for more than a minute or two.

Denny had braced himself, wrapping his legs around the package, and was programming the detonator. Troy was glad and sorry to have him along.

His headlamp shone past the anchor and into the green darkness of the lake. A startled catfish darted off. Beyond that, there seemed to be nothing, but Troy knew better.

He sensed them nearing Von Damme's mansion. He didn't need to see it. The old building felt like a mass grave area and as cold as an iceberg. Already, it tried to sap their vim and vigor. He could see determination in Father Dennis' clenched teeth and square jaw. His eyes glinted with holy fervor on a mission from Heaven.

Troy could accept that this was why he had been sent back

to earth.

Why he had survived dying.

He felt Von Damme brace himself to dive into the lake. The master vampire loathed the moving water and hated having to chase them below. He had been willing to destroy the largest earthen dam in the eastern U.S. just so he could avoid getting wet to reclaim his property.

Denny poked Troy, letting him know he was letting go. Troy also released the anchor.

It crashed down the last fifteen feet into the mud. Their aim had been true. The homecoming gift landed less than ten feet away from the front steps of the evil structure. Malevolent cold emanated from the walls and chilled Troy to the bone, slowing his breathing and heart rate. All movement seemed more difficult.

With sharp knives, they hurriedly detached the TNT and satchel from the anchor then swam for the front door. Von Damme's lair seemed less welcoming than before, the back half of the place collapsed like it was exhausted, a wounded but dangerous beast. The water looked darker and muddier, this atmosphere's version of gloomy fog. Troy could feel the building's predatory nature.

One stroke closer, one kick closer, and Troy could see them, the spirits of those killed here. The mass of ghosts showcased the evil place's trophies, numbering in the hundreds. Crowds of them wandered back and forth, passing in and out of the mansion through its walls while some paced and others sat, weeping and lamenting their fate. Many of the apparitions radiated a hazy, sullen glow, while a few glowered and flared angrily. All appeared roughly dressed from the first half of the previous century, many in misty hats from berets to Panamas to accompany long, translucent coats. No t-shirts and no outward labels, Troy noted.

He experienced the strange sensation of coming home. Perhaps it was the jewelry box returning to its owner's manse. Troy's ears rang, and he felt a thrumming through his vest on his left side. He reached into the pocket, bringing out a cufflink. There it was! Van Damme's cufflink! This must be the same vest he had used on his initial dive here.

The ghostly horde moved aside for Troy and Denny. A few spirits seemed curious, but most tried to shoo them away, gesturing for them to leave before it was too late. In some ways it was already too late.

One, perhaps a prospector, noted their package. The apparition spread the word, and Troy thought he saw looks of excitement on the spirits' previously glum faces. In some, he spotted the thirst for vengeance.

Thank God the ghosts left them alone. The last thing Troy needed were angry spirits trying to stop them. He didn't know if they could touch the real world, but Spider had done it. Troy didn't want to know what else might be possible.

He motioned to a window. Elke preferred he use the study as the blast site, since it had once been the master vampire's center of power, making it the best place to destroy the box. Who knew they would have to level the prison to destroy its last prisoner?

The shutters gently swayed in the current, but the pull was stronger, drawing them forward to the opening until Father Dennis held up his crucifix. The current lessened, and the water seemed to warm as well. Both Troy and Denny paused at the window, intuiting a trap. Or was it just the evil aura of the place causing them to balk?

Troy was cautious, and yet, he knew they must move swiftly. Even the ghosts looked eager.

He stopped, coming to a realization. It was Von Damme's evil that powered the mansion. His imprisonment had brought it to life. Somehow, Von Damme's supernatural malevolence was so strong that it poisoned everything that came into contact with the vampire.

Had it influenced Troy? He hated to admit it was likely. His life had spiraled into a mess. Had the mansion somehow drawn he and Denny back here to kill them?

True to expectations, as they passed through the window frame, one of the shutters fell. It caught Denny by surprise, but Troy deflected it, so the hunk of deadwood clanked off his tank. Together, they hauled the bundle of TNT into the front hall. The water swirled and ripped with a sudden fury as startled schools of crappie, trout, and catfish panicked and darted every direction. That stirred up the warp atop the carpet. The worn weave heaved and snapped, lashing out with tendrils that coiled around Troy's legs and fins. He mentally cursed the place, whipped out his knife to slash.

Then, like a switch had been flipped, the fish turned aggressive, attacking and slamming into them. Troy felt like he was being pecked and battered. He swiped futilely. A big carp knocked Troy's mask sideways. Another impact nearly knocked it off. Troy exhaled a burst of bubbles to scatter the fish, then he reset his mask. Now, he c-clamped a hand on it and his regulator. He would simply have to let himself be pelted while he used a knife to cut his legs free.

The threadbare carpet started to dig into his skin. Worse, as he began cutting the strands they seemed to contract, drawing him down to the floor, trying to grab his wrist and hog tie him. The carpet fibers even swayed to evade his blade, and he almost cut himself. His hand holding the knife began to go numb.

Von Damme felt moments away. The master vampire could see his mansion, a welcome sight. Revenge came soon. It would be tangy and bloody.

Troy severed a swath of carpet threads. It still wasn't enough. He prayed Denny was having better luck.

A barrage of attacking trout knocked the knife from Troy's hand. Carpet pile snagged it and hid it. He carried a second blade, but time was running out. The mansion seemed to sigh as its master neared.

Suddenly, it was bright. Water bubbled around the searing torch. Denny grinned, one hand spread in a claw grip to keep on his mask and regulator while the other hand held a flare. He reached to burn away the carpet's tendrils and free Troy.

Where was the TNT? Troy checked the floor where it should be. It was nearly impossible to see with the stirred-up sediment

Behind Denny, Troy spotted a school of fish hauling away the explosive bundle. It was tethered to Denny's leg, so they began drag him along, too.

Troy grabbed him, holding Denny close until he completely burned the tendrils holding Troy's leg. Once free, Troy seized the tether, reeling in fish and the bomb. Denny righted himself and grabbed the rope. Together they kicked and surged ahead toward the study.

They swam against the streams of frenzied fish, battering and nipping. Near the door to the study, Denny seemed to slow, then he fiddled with his mask and regulator. Troy could relate as the constant jostling and pelting caused pain, numbness and confusion. A group attack knocked Troy off balance, and he started to spin.

Through the swarm, he saw a school of crappie at work, bumping the handle that tightened the connection between the regulator and tank. Bubbles readily escaped upward. Denny had no idea he was rapidly losing life-giving air.

Troy batted away fighting fish to find the knob and tighten his own connection. They had been trying the same trick on him. Is this how the TVA divers died? He dove into the thick of the swarm around Denny and to seize the knob on his blood brother's regulator and turn it until it was tight. The oxygen stopped leaking.

Denny looked curiously at Troy's tattered gloves and bloodied fingers as he signaled thumbs up and OK.

They swam by the statues of stone wolves. After all that had happened, Troy expected the inanimate to jump up and bite them. They were blessedly left alone as they shouldered their way into the study and Von Damme's seat of power.

Denny held the detonator. They warily watched the entrances, the doors and shuttered windows for signs of Von

Damme.

The ghosts began to gather. With his arm around a female spirit, John appeared, watching them. Next to them and taller, Spider enacted a fist pump. Slowly fading in, Walt and Pete's apparitions strolled around the room, studying and poking the six skeletons in their chairs. While alive, they had heard about this place. There were others Troy recognized, including Homer Maxwell and Mona. The rest of the ghosts phasing ethereally through the walls and doors were spirits that had died long ago.

Why had they gathered en masse? Troy wondered.

The house grew quiet. A bitter current washed through, bringing an icy chill, and the house creaked and squeaked.

Von Damme was here!

The ceiling collapsed as the master vampire dropped down through it. He moved with the speed of a shark, having transformed his flesh into a manta ray with his face and talons. The ray's tail swiftly swatted the remote detonator from Denny's hands.

He didn't try to grab it back. Father Dennis flipped up a panel on the TNT, showing a countdown ticking from 19 seconds to 18.

How long had that been running? Troy wondered. He approved.

For the lust of Elke and the love of Silke, Troy took the ankh into hand and grabbed Von Damme's tail. He wasn't leaving. Caught between flesh and supernatural substance, the ankh seared his palm, fingers and the vampire's manta ray tail. Von Damme thrashed like he had been speared. Despite the pain, Troy held on, or perhaps the ankh welded to his flesh, so he couldn't let go, even as he was whipped about. Von Damme smashed Troy into the bookcases and the huge desk. Still, he held on.

The master vampire changed tactics, surging back and wrapping around Troy, knocking off his mask. He barely kept his regulator in his mouth. Von Damme squeezed, trapping one arm and the hand with the ankh. The aquatic vampire still jerked about in pain, even as he tried to kill Troy. A fin knocked the regulator from Troy's mouth. He couldn't get a hand free to retrieve it. Not that it would matter in 14 seconds.

Still, Troy struggled, recalling his promises.

The pressure on his ribs increased, trying to squeeze the air and life out of him. He thought his head might pop off.

Then, Father Dennis was there, crucifix in one hand and syringe in the other. He poked Von Damme with the holy symbol, but before Denny could jab with the needle and inject him, the monster swatted the EpiPen away.

In his painful convulsions, Von Damme released Troy.

The tail darted out, breaking Denny's mask. His head snapped back, even as Von Damme's appendage went limp as though the impact had broken it, along with killing Denny. The regulator fell from his dead lips.

His ghost, smiling sadly, left his corpse.

Troy had no time to mourn. He grabbed the fallen syringe from the floor. Von Damme seemed to be injured, having trouble swimming with his tail hanging uselessly. The master vampire saw him coming and started to change shape again, sprouting tentacles like an octopus. Troy stabbed one with the needle, injecting the monster with holy water. Von Damme lunged engulfing Troy.

This was working. Time had to be about up. They would die together.

Farewell, Silke. Troy would have loved to see where they would go together. Good-bye, my blood brothers. Sorry, Mom and Dad.

Suddenly the cufflink squirted up to spin in the water. The gold glinted seductively. The master vampire sensed it, releasing Troy to eagerly grab the piece of jewelry. Von Damme grinned triumphantly. He now had all of the mansion's relics together. He could restore more of his power.

The seconds ticked away.

The master vampire swam sluggishly for the TNT. Agony

from killing a holy man and pain from holy water flowing through his system hindered him, but Von Damme still reached the bundle of TNT, ready to snap off the timer with 9 seconds left. Troy was powerless to stop him.

The fish were long gone, but the skeletons and ghosts stayed to the end. The bony remains had sat for decades, their duty in the past, until today. Father Dennis hugged a skeleton and drew the bones within his ethereal form. He motioned to Spider who followed his lead, covering one of the skeletons, then they both moved.

Their bony hands sought vengeance and seized Von Damme's tentacles. He struggled, but in his weakened form, he couldn't fight them all. Troy thought it was Sherry, along with Walt's ghost, who empowered another set of bones.

Von Damme tried to change directions, to leave, but the skeletons dragged him down. Mona's ghost-powered frame piled on. Spider's skeleton slipped away to grab the flare and carry it behind the desk, creating a giant shadow.

What could be done in 5 seconds? Troy whirled and kicked. There was no way that he could escape before the explosion ripped apart the mansion.

A skeletal hand caught Troy's leg. He desperately kept kicking furiously, even though he knew it was futile. The skeleton shifted its grip to around his waist.

The flash of light flared first. The explosion seemed muted, but the force remained powerful. It crushed the tank against Troy's spine as it hurled him into darkness.

He prayed it destroyed Von Damme and the mansion. Lastly, Troy hoped Silke forgave him.

Forty-Seven: After Another Funeral

Dressed in a three piece suit the color of ash and a shirt of crimson to match his mood, Dillon paced across the damp grass. It had rained yesterday, upping the humidity, although it was clear for tonight's funeral.

He disliked going to burials and memorials, but as a journalist and reporter, he had attended many. He understood that last rites and public good-byes were necessary for closure. This one was held by night to beat the daytime's muggy heat, plus it allowed vampires like he and Elke to attend.

Fog wandered into the cemetery and sat among the tents and chairs, mingling with the crowd of mourners reluctant to leave after the graveside service.

Dillon groaned. And there were more funerals to come. Was this what immortality was like? Attending funerals? The 'terrorists' had killed more than fifty locals and more tourists. People had ample to mourn, as did Dillon. Would he eventually grow numb to it? He was sorry to have missed Pat's wake considering the stories that he had heard from Elke and Tommy Boy. Well, no longer boy. Tommy Wolf. Still, a brawl in downtown Bristol. Vampires browsing and snacking along State Street.

Elke promised they would round up any stragglers from the mad alchemist's zealots. Silke had told him about Zane getting a bucket of holy water dumped on him. Dillon couldn't help but smile. Silke hoped he was with Jada in the After Life. He sure wouldn't be in Heaven.

Tommy Wolf had recounted the near beheading of Lyla. That Dark Lady would not be missed. But, Marader, a werewolf? No wonder he had hair, not a weave or plugs, but werewolf hair. How was that going to work out? The blood brothers knew the truth now, about Marader and Dillon. Sadly, there were less brothers.

Dillon had also missed being there for John's impromptu Viking funeral, the canoe bursting afire when his vampire body had been exposed to sunlight. Those in attendance might not consider it so, but it had been a blessed event, though bedeviling to the authorities and John's parents.

Of course, John's body still hadn't been found. It never would be unless urban legends brought it back wandering State Street. And it might. The night before Troy, J-Man and Knives had encountered John in his confused, angry, fledgling vampire state, there had been three reported sightings of a naked man walking down State Street. Von Damme had simply turned Undead John loose to cause trouble. He had been walking toward home, only to reach East Hill before needing to hide from the dawn's light.

Dillon wished he could blame this all on John. His girlfriend had released Von Damme, but it could have been any of them. They had planned on diving Wreythville and exploring it as a group. They undoubtedly would have gone inside. Someone would have picked up the jewelry box and been devoured by the evil within. They might have all died right then.

He glanced back at the graveside crowd covering the gentle hills, battery-powered candles and LED lights held in reverence to remind them there was light everywhere, even in dark times. The hills looked covered in stars. He was afraid he was going to have to remind himself of that often. There were hundreds, perhaps a thousand people here to see his blood brother buried. Few would know about his heroism, how he had sacrificed to save them from an evil force incarnate. Dillon and the others couldn't tell anyone, even the family, the truth of it all.

John's parents were still here. Dillon was glad that he hadn't been there to kill John. At least in that case, Dillon wasn't culpable. It had changed J-Man, though. His laughs and joviality seemed forced. Dillon could see it in his eyes, the tipping point of altering the way he viewed the world, no longer white and black, life and death but with shades of both.

Mr. Jay Beck noticed the attention and nodded. J-Man was less mobile nowadays, his right leg set in a walking boot cast. That allowed him to wear a suit with shorts like some British rocker. Jambo and his lovely wife seemed to be teasing him about it.

It was great to see Mary Beth out and about, no longer suffering nightmares. Denny's sister and Diana knelt, signing J-

Man's cast while he regaled them with stories of Denny's courage. Good. Father Dennis had done what Dillon couldn't do, what none of the powerful vampires could do. Simply put, he had fought evil with good and sacrifice. That's why they had prevailed.

Wearing a deep purple sun dress with dangling silver stars, Rae Kirkland casually limped over to him. It was an effort because he was away from the maddening crowd. Dillon still had issues with large gatherings of people. In some sense, it was like walking through an organic restaurant with great smells and sustenance everywhere. He had needed some air, so he had put some space between himself and his friends and neighbors. Besides, Mrs. Fleenor from Silke's work place had been constantly glaring at him. He had been tempted to use his compelling powers to make her stop.

The reporter looked sleep-deprived and weary of tragic news and deaths. Rae didn't know the whole truth, so she wasn't avoiding him. "Hey, there, handsome. Long time no see. In fact, I almost didn't see you sulking among the trees," Rae said. She offered a wan, dimpled smile.

"I am darkened by sadness, but seeing you well lifts my heart," Dillon said. He was glad she hadn't been captured and scarred by Von Damme.

"Oh, you always were a smooth flirt. It lifts my heart to see you well, too. I wish I was seeing all the blood brothers together. It's been a sad, tragic series of events. You seemed to be there at the start and here at the end. What do you think about what happened at the lake?"

"I think it could have been a whole Hell of a lot worse. I'm glad J-Man, Knives and Jambo survived almost unscathed. I ache over the loss of Denny," Dillon said then braced himself to lie. "It was a good thing Deputy Burt and the other deputies were there to save the dam and the day or many more, perhaps thousands might have died, along with untold property damage."

Recently, Elke had been busy visiting the authorities and

nudging them here and there, though truth be told, very little influence was needed. Deputy Burt and the other deputies had been credited with stopping terrorists from blowing up the dam. He and three deputies had made the ultimate sacrifice. That explained the dead scuba divers, deputies, and the destroyed boat, even the mining hideout with the corpses from all over the east coast. Terrorists gave a reason why the helicopter had been shot down. J-Man had contacted Deputy Burt just prior to his crash. All in all, a nice neat story that only made Dillon mildly nauseous. He hated handing Burt a hero's tribute, but it was necessary. Otherwise, the rest of them might end up in prison or institutionalized.

Rae critically eyed him. "That sounded bitter and sarcastic."

"Sorry, I'm not myself right now. I'm disturbed by the loss of life," he said. Elke had told him it was minor compared to the potential disaster that his friends had averted.

"Oh, I've heard you that way before. Did you and Burt have issues?"

"I prefer not to speak ill of the dead," Dillon said. Though, you could curse the undead all you wanted.

"I understand. Everyone is sharing all the wonderful things Denny did for us, for the community. For Father Dennis to become unhinged and take it upon himself to blow up that awful place has rocked people to the core and yet helped them more than they know."

If they knew the truth, it would be worse, Elke had said.

"I wish I didn't understand, but I really, really do," Rae continued "Knowing that awful place has been destroyed gives me some relief. I had been having trouble sleeping. I kept telling myself it was just the story of what was happening here in Bristol that kept me tossing and turning, but at least part of it was knowing that a place like that existed in my own backyard. Though people don't know why, I believe everyone's soul exhaled with grateful relief when the Wreythville mansion was demolished."

"I believe you're right," Dillon agreed.

"So, are you going to tell me where you've been hiding and why?" Rae persisted. He could relate to her determination to see a story through.

"I was working on a story, which turns out to be about terrorists, when I injured myself. Then, I fell in love with the woman who aided me, Elke Swearington," he said. A week ago, Dillon wouldn't have believed his own story. He had been on the verge of dying when the Dark Lady of the Lake had come to his rescue. They had fallen head over heels in love. Below the lake was a cursed tomb of vampires, a haunted house submerged after World War II by the Rulers of Night to protect everyone from a mad alchemist and master vampire, Viktor Von Damme.

"Elke Swearington? Wow! So Troy was right!"

"Yes, yes, he was," Dillon replied. He ached thinking about what had happened to Troy.

"And what makes her so special?"

"I feel like I'm walking on air," Dillon said. He almost told Rae that Elke reminded him of the Dark Lady. Rae was familiar with his keen interest in the legend.

"Wow, you just smiled. She has a favorable effect on you. It reminds me of Troy and Silke together. They shine. Are you all right with that?" she asked. Dillon nodded and forced a smile. "I'm surprised Troy's not here. I was hoping to set up another interview. It's crazy how many accidents he's been involved in. He's lucky to be alive. Do you know where he is? I asked Jambo and J-Man and they said they haven't seen him in days, and the last time he was asleep in Silke's arms."

So that's how they referred to Troy being half dead, or half alive. Comatose. At least he wasn't brain dead. He didn't know where Silke had taken him within the massive confines of the Swearington Lodge, as she was avoiding him.

"I don't know where he is," Dillon said. He knew where the body was laying. He had no idea what happened to Troy's soul. They feared it was lost in the Shadowlands. "And Silke isn't talking to me."

"Is that because you threatened all the eligible guys in the county? Yes, I know about that. You're lucky she hasn't shot you. Seriously, it must have been traumatic for her to see Denny that way, difficult for all of them," Rae said.

From what he had been told, Knives, Silke, and Tommy had just finished hauling J-Man and Jambo out of the lake when the underwater explosion occurred. Shortly thereafter, Denny's body had floated to the top. His spirit was somewhere watching over them.

How many ghosts were in the fog? Dillon wondered. Thankfully, he didn't feel Troy near, though it bothered Dillon to feel nothing about him.

Knives spotted them, begged his pardon to leave a group of people, and then he strolled over to join them. Dillon hadn't seen him since the Saturday they had found the floating coffins, a little over a week ago. They shook hands.

"Wow, you have cold hands," Knives said.

"It's part of who I am now. I don't think I'm 98.6 degrees anymore."

"Any change?" the doctor asked. Dillon shook his head. "Well, I am not giving up hope. He's stubborn and surprising." Knives hugged Rae. "Hello, Ms. Kirkland."

"Ah, good to see you Stephen. Are you two hiding something?"

"HIPPA," Knives said and shrugged, referring to the confidential patient law.

"Of course, though not that secret, Rae. I have developed a blood condition. Among other things, it makes me sensitive to daylight, so I will be staying out of it for a while unless I want to blister and burn. I appreciate this memorial being held at night."

"That's sad. You love the sun and outdoors. I've read about diseases that can cause such a reaction. Will you be staying around for treatment?" Rae asked. They had once been close to being more than friends. But then, Dillon had never been able to let go of the Dark Lady. It was one of the reasons he had kept Silke away from Troy, because it didn't seem he would ever release Raquel.

Dillon nodded. "I'm thinking of staying here for some time, I don't know how long. I'll have to call my editor. Let her know."

"I'm sure Silke will be glad to have you around. Stephen, I hear things are going better," Rae said. Knives cocked his head, not sure he agreed with her. "I heard the hospital cleared you, and that you're back to work. I hated that you were suspended."

He nodded. "I'm surprised the investigation wrapped up so quickly but very pleased by their findings. I'm not sure we'll ever know the truth, except my colleagues will be missed, as will my blood brothers," Knives said.

Dillon inwardly grinned. Elke had paid a visit to those who had suspended Dr. Stephen Curran and convinced them that he was an innocent victim, a bystander at the wrong place at the wrong time, but not too horribly wrong, or he would be dead, too. Dillon would have lost another blood brother if not for Troy. He had been doing Dillon's job.

"What?" Rae asked.

"I wasn't worried. Dr. Stephen Curran does great work, and he's a stand-up kind of guy," Dillon said.

"Thanks," Knives said. He didn't sound like he felt he deserved the praise. Dillon knew what was dragging him down, what he believed was his most recent failure, being unable to revive Troy.

The memory washed over Dillon. In disbelief, he had watched a dripping Desiree slide out from the shadow gate. Darkness peeled back to reveal a dead fish-looking Troy thrown over her shoulder. His mask was missing, along with his weight belt, and he had lost a fin, his tank and regulator, either back in the lake or in the Shadowlands.

How was this possible? He looked over to Elke. Her eyes shining, she smiled hopefully. The Dark Lady, the beating of his heart, had arranged it. Perhaps love could conquer all, including the supernatural.

"A gift to you, my love. An attempt to save the life of your best friend," Elke said.

"How?" Dillon stammered. Could it bring back the dead?

"All the ingredients were there. A sharp shadow. His blood, breath, and spit floated in the water. Just as important, Desiree had been there before. She thought it might work. So far, we have been right. Did you think I would really sacrifice your friends?" Elke said.

He had. He knew how important this was.

"I thought you said he couldn't survive another trip."

"It is unlikely, but your friend is unlike anyone else, isn't he?"

"That's an understatement," Dillon said. Right now, his blood brother could be casting for a part in the *Walking Dead*. Troy's face was pale with blue lips and black circles around his sunken eyes. Despite his vacant look, there was hope, even if it was a sliver. Troy had eluded the Grim Reaper before and returned. How many lives did he have? Was this the last?

Troy looked and felt dead, his chest still, no breathing and no heartbeat.

Dillon sensed no connection with his blood brother.

"Troy, rise!" Elke commanded.

Troy's body shuddered and spasmed. He started to sit up, and Dillon felt hope, only to suffer despair when Troy collapsed. Elke tried several more commands, but Troy remained unresponsive. Dillon wanted to grab him and order him to come back, but he knew Troy wouldn't listen to him. Only his body listened to Elke. His spirit had left along with his soul.

No. Troy looked lifeless. Gone. Dillon wrestled with a growing angst, making it difficult to breathe. Silke was going to loathe him forever, whether she killed him or let him suffer by surviving the death of his best friend, being part of the cause of it, and taking him away from his sister, especially after preventing them from getting together.

Dillon would have preferred to have died than live with this.

He lost control and seized Troy by the shoulders. "You must live! You came back before! Come back again!" he shouted, shaking Troy.

"My love, you're not helping. Keep trying, Desiree," Elke said, dragging him away. She took out her cell phone and dialed a number. "I'm calling Marader. He has the doctor with him."

Dillon shook himself. Most wouldn't understand, but he felt blest to be with Elke.

He had his emotions managed by the time the Maverick and Stingray tied up to the Swearington dock. Pre-dawn had arrived, the start of a new day still an hour away.

Denny was lifeless, so Dillon was thrilled to see every one of his blood brothers who had survived, and of course, his sister. She looked sad, abandoned, barely able to walk, leaning on Jambo. When she noticed Dillon, she targeted him like a missile.

Her face twisted with rage and despair, she slapped him, and he let her. "Damn you to hell! You ruined my life and ended Troy's. I'll see you regret all you've done so that whatever long life you have will be as miserable as mine!" she screamed, then she stalked off where she collapsed to her knees and wept. Dillon didn't dare try and console her.

"Well, that went well. I brought the doc," Marader said.

"Who's hurt?" Knives asked.

"Nobody."

"Then why do you need me?" Knives asked.

"To revive the dead," Dillon said.

"Really? You have Troy?" Marader asked.

When they entered the room, Knives was shocked to find Troy packed in ice. The doctor touched him. "How did he get here?"

"Does it matter?" Dillon asked.

"Not really, unless his condition has something to do with his travels instead of his time under water and all that went before. Has he been warmed?" Knives asked.

Dillon and Desiree shook their heads. "He came directly from the mansion through the Shadowlands. It is very cold there."

"Uh, um, good, then. No such thing as cold and dead," Knives said.

"We used the AED on him last night," Dillon said.

"What?" Knives asked.

"Can he be shocked too much?" Dillon asked.

"Show me what you have and tell me what you've done," Knives said.

Thralls aided Dillon, bringing in the needed equipment, oxygen and an AED. Knives planned to electronically jolt Troy back to life. This would be at least the third time. Dillon had seen this done to Troy at the hospital in Florida.

Dillon wished it could be like it was then. Troy had survived.

Even before they shocked Troy, Dillon received a bolt of an idea. He rushed off, looking for his sister.

Silke saw him coming. Loathing radiated from her eyes. He pushed past it.

"We found Troy. He's inside."

"What? Is this some kind of way to confuse me so I won't rip . . ."

"Desiree pulled him through the shadow dimension, a horrible place, but we have him, at least his body. He's on the wrong side of the edge."

"Truthfully?"

"He's cold and pulseless, but, there's hope. They're going to shock him with an AED. Try bringing him back again. I think you need to be there."

"Take me to him," Silke agreed.

She wouldn't let her brother touch her, so he guided her to

his best friend. She burst into tears when she saw Troy and rushed to his side. They already had the electrodes set up. Elke gently detached her so Knives could hit the button on the AED and deliver a shock to Troy's body. Silke winced, watching him jerk and spasm.

Knives waited, letting the machine work. "Analyzing."

They all waited. "How?" Silke asked.

"He's been dead. Those who are or have been, apparently, can survive traveling through the Shadowlands. He survived once before, though I made him a thrall to save him. If he survives, he will be changed," Elke said.

"I'll help him heal and live," Silke said.

"No pulse. A second shock advised," the AED intoned.

"Okay, everybody clear," Knives said.

"One moment. Silke, anything you want to say or do?" Dillon asked.

"Here comes the sun," she sang the Beatles while she hugged Troy. Dillon watched her pour her love in words, feelings, and kisses into Troy. After a good minute, Knives eased her away, cleared the body, and let the device shock Troy again.

His heart lurched, his body jerked, and then he gasped loudly.

Dillon remembered smiling. He thought everything would be all right now.

But it wasn't. They had Troy's body. His spirit was elsewhere, leaving him comatose. Desiree claimed Troy was limbo. She claimed to have read historics where someone had awakened later, the basis for the Rip Van Winkle story.

Dillon wondered if it was all right to pray. He decided to go ahead, to pray for his best friend and his beloved sister. If he was struck by lightning and slain, it would save his sister the trouble.

The invigorating presence of Elke's arrival drew Dillon back to the present. With a touch and wan smile, his lover soothed his mood as she sidled up next to him. He introduced her to Rae and re-introduced her to Knives.

Tommy Wolf, grinning despite the occasion, joined them. He was clad in a tasteful and respectful black suit. He and Denny had been close. Now Dillon wondered if Denny had known the truth. The blood brothers had worked closely on the remodeling of the marina over the last year.

"Y'all, we've got to stop meeting at a place like this. Seriously," Marader said.

"I concur, except Spider's funeral is Wednesday," Dillon replied. They stood quietly, thoughtful and reflective.

"You know," Marader said, breaking the silence. "I used to think I wanted to be cremated but not after the dock fire. I think our luck started to run out then. Any change?"

Rae looked between them, wondering.

Elke shook her head. "No, I am making him wait. We haven't known each other long enough to get married, but he asks me every day."

Dillon rolled with it. He hadn't said it, but it was true. "And I will keep asking silently with my eyes," he told her.

Marader blinked. "Hey, it's your fune . . . fun party." He turned to Knives. "How's J-Man?"

"Obstinate. Why don't you ask him yourself?"

In a walking cast and leaning on a cane, J-Man trundled over. Small cuts healed all over his face, and his eyes were sunken. "Howdy, y'all. Is this the guilt trip section?"

"How are you, Jay?" Dillon asked.

"Inadequately medicated. You don't by chance, have anything that will help me forget this, do you?" J-Man asked Knives.

"You would still want to know where our friends were or how they died," Knives said.

"Jay Beck, you are a lucky man. You survived fighting a wildfire, getting shot down and crash landing, twice," Rae declared.

"I get your point. I don't feel lucky, but when you put it that way, it makes it obvious that I am. That we all are, because we are standing here."

They enjoyed a moment of silent gratitude. Dillon held Elke close, reveling in her presence.

That's why he didn't notice Raquel Sterling until she and her sister Diana were standing next to him. Tonight, Raquel looked like a weary goddess and the sorrow added years to her face and stance. He didn't know how close she was to her bodyguard, but to have her killed before your eyes and then get dragged from your car by wolves might alter one's grip on reality, even if Raquel hadn't been physically injured. She and Diana mirrored one another, their dark eyes haunted and unsure by what they had seen and experienced.

"Hello everyone. It's good to see y'all together after all we've lost," Raquel said. Her eyes scanned the area again, no doubt, searching for Troy. "Thank y'all for all you have done for Diana and me. It's incredible. Unbelievable."

"Mind blowing," Diana added.

"The terrorists took a lot from us," Dillon said.

And in truth, the vampires were terrorists, a small group of local radical zealots wanting to enforce their way upon everyone else. Did it matter that people had flooded their home?

"Have you seen Troy? I'm leaving for a while. I wanted to thank him and tell him farewell."

"I don't think we'd be standing here tonight without him," Diana said. Raquel nodded, the sisters agreeing on something.

"And last time I saw him; he didn't look like himself. I'm worried," Raquel said.

"When was that?" Rae asked.

"Inside the mine, that horrible night we escaped the terrorists," Raquel said.

Dillon kept from looking at his blood brothers. Tommy had slipped away at some time, probably seeing Raquel coming. None of them knew what to say either, glancing at Dillon, because he always knew where Troy was. "I don't know where he is," he replied.

Raquel raised an eyebrow in surprise and looked stricken. "I thought you two always knew where the other one was."

"We aren't as close as we were," Dillon said. He looked around, hoping Troy would make a miraculous appearance and give them a reason to cheer on this solemn evening. Big fail.

"But he is well?" she asked, tearing up.

Seeing her cry over Troy was a first. She must have really been rocked. Who was he kidding? Dillon mused. They had all been changed, only some hadn't realized it yet. "I don't know. I am sorry."

His lack of knowledge distressed Raquel. Diana tried to calm her.

"Are you ready to tell me that story?" Rae asked. Raquel shook her head, but the reporter pressed her.

"Ms. Kirkland. Now is not the time and this is not the place. People are still reeling and in shock. Please, give us some peace and space," Elke compelled.

Rae nodded agreeably. "Later, y'all. Sorry I got excited and a little pushy. Stay well."

Raquel turned to Elke. "Thank you. Do you know anything about Troy?"

"He's comatose. He may be that way a while, or he might wake up tomorrow. Silke is with him."

"But will he wake up?" Diana asked.

"With comas, it can go either way," Knives said.

"It depends on if you're hopeful, or hopeless. I believe this place has become hopeful," Elke said.

Hand in hand with his wife, Jambo ambled over to join them. His lady had a tight hold on him, as if she were concerned he might go off on some crazy adventure with them right now. And who could blame her?

"Hi, y'all. What's the good word? Is there any?" Jambo asked.

Dillon shook his head. "Same old."

"Well, if Father Dennis were here. He'd say a prayer. In

this case, I'll stand in for him," Jambo said.

The blood brothers and their loved ones gathered close. Marader reappeared, beer in hand, and joined them.

Dillon hoped Troy was having one of those experiences where he sensed what was happening to his blood brothers, then he would know they loved him and wanted him back.

Forty-Eight: The Afterdeath

Floating in darkness, Troy waited. This was different than the last time he had died. Did that mean he hadn't really died? Or was the moment between life and death stretched long?

In this timeless place, which he prayed wasn't the Shadowlands, he wished Silke would find love again one day. At least he had been able to say farewell. She had reminded him to come back alive, to return to her. She had made him promise. He believed in keeping his word. A man was his word. It was said God was the Word, Logos, as well.

Troy had known Silke for a long, long time. How had he missed it? He figured it was just hero worship when he saved her life, pulling her out of the water and giving her breaths. He recalled catching her watching him kissing Raquel. Curse Von Damme, Troy barely remembered if he and Silke had a relationship. Now, looking back, he recalled near misses.

It made him furious. He now recalled the reasons he had been angry with Dillon. He had tried to keep them apart. He had tried to kill Troy after the most incredible night of his life because he had made love to Silke.

He didn't remember those moments. How could he forget them coupling? Could he get those memories back? Rebuild them by what he recalled through other interactions with people?

Then he rediscovered a buried memory. Silke had introduced him as her boyfriend at the State Street Gym and Spa. To be convincing, she had kissed him. She had been convincingly passionate and knocked his world further off balance in a lovely way as a wonderful distraction, despite the fact she beat him with pillows and threw high heels at him. She had healing hands that compensated.

In the distance, he heard something.

Was that singing? Sunshine in my eyes makes me cry? John Denver, he recalled. That meant likely he was in heaven. The song changed, the singer going with the Beatles, "Good Day Sunshine". After a little while, the lovely female changed her tune again, now faster and upbeat.

"I'm walking on sunshine. Oh yeah! And don't it feel good?!" That sounded like Silke singing a hit by Katrina and the Waves.

Silke stopped and breathed his name. "And when we kiss, fire," she sang better than Springsteen. Fire was right. Had she kissed him? He felt something and saw a glimmer. Did he see sunshine?

"Hey, come on, Mr. Bane. Time to be a phoenix. Live up to Martin's idol and expectations and your promises. I dragged you out into the sunshine, despite Bryson's objection. Can you feel it? The sun feels glorious, like hope and life.

"Come back to me. I am your home. If nothing else, prove Dillon wrong by proving us right, okay? Show him he doesn't know us as well as he thinks. We have a future together. Here. You have lost your ankh, so you can wear mine. It is the symbol of the power of life. Let the sun shine on it and show you the way back to me."

Troy felt a warmth in his middle. Did he have a chest or stomach? Arms or legs? He must, for he started swimming. Was he still underwater and just disoriented? No, otherwise he wouldn't hear singing. Though, he vaguely recalled something like this happening before.

His surroundings lightened, as if it were dawn, or he had awakened in sun and kept his eye lids closed. He could feel the golden warmth seeping into him, reviving him. He finally sensed he had a body. He tried to open his eyes. He tried to sing with Silke.

Suddenly, he felt grabbed, shaken . . . and licked.

"Wake up and kiss me!" Silke commanded, then she sighed. "Because this kissing you like sleeping beauty isn't working, Handsome. Von Damme is destroyed. Everyone's nightmares have stopped. There's nothing to fear. Now, wake up and kiss me!"

How could Troy resist such an offer? A word could be a bond, especially when anchored by love. It was stronger than hate, thicker than blood and more invigorating than water.

Ginger barked and nose-nudged Troy.

The gasp of air was a painful breath. Troy felt like he was being stabbed in the lungs, but it hurt, so he must be alive again. He fought down nausea, savoring the scent of Silke so close, her grateful tears and joyful kisses falling on him.

"You're back! About time, Beloved! You scared me!" she told him, then she showered him with more kisses. "No more of this. I'll go gray at twenty-four!"

He smiled, the pleasure masking the pain. "I will stay with you as long as you'll have me, my love," Troy said. He weakly drew her into a closer embrace. "I survived the week. If you believe Aunt Jada, I'll be around a long time."

"Honey, dear heart, I love the sound of that. Oh, I think my brother just avoided eternal damnation, and I won't have to turn into Buffy the Vampire Slayer."

They both laughed and kissed again. Ginger sprawled across his legs.

Silke hugged Troy tightly. "Let me call my brother, let him know he has been spared endless days of fire and brimstone, and then we'll call the others. Let the world know Troy Phoenix Bane lives again."

"Sounds good. It's time to celebrate," he said then kissed her. He hoped Aunt Jada was right about a long wonderful life ahead. If this was the first day of the rest of his life, it had not dawned with vampires but with joy.

ABOUT THE AUTHOR

After almost thirty years, William Hill is a naturalized northern Nevadan. Bill is a native of Indiana, attended high school in Prairie Village, KS, and college in Nashville, thrived in Bristol, TN, toiled and sweltered in Denton and Dallas, TX, and played and lived in south and north Lake Tahoe, NV.

Bill learned to read reluctantly then fell in love with superhero comic books. He added spy-thrillers, Sci-Fi, and fantasy novels to his reading list, tucked in among the required classics. Bill earned a serious degree from Vanderbilt University and a MBA from the University of North Texas. After a house fire and an epiphany, Bill escaped the restrictive drudgery of the corporate world to craft his tales. Along with working in human resources field, Bill has been employed as a bartender, sports official, and a ski patroller. He and his wife, Kat, love to snow ski and visit/hike National Park sites. They live at the foot of the Sierra Mountains in the windy, high desert of the Carson Valley.

<u>Dawn of the Vampire</u> was Bill's first novel back in 1991. It was followed by eleven more novels, including <u>The Magic Bicycle</u>, <u>California Ghosting</u> and <u>Vegas Vampires</u>. Bill's comic, SnowJob, can be found on his facebook site and snowjobcomic.blogspot.com. Samples of his novels can be found on the website: otterpress.com. Bill intends to write and draw imaginative fiction and fantasy until dirt is shoveled upon his grave, and beyond if possible.